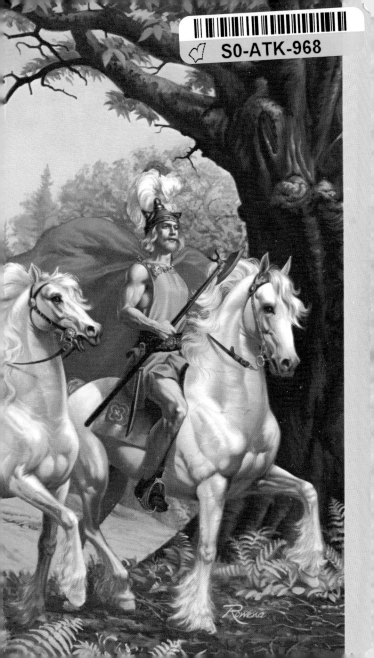

S0-ATK-968

1—
Sci Fri

THE
CRIMSON
CHALICE

THE
CRIMSON
CHALICE

VICTOR CANNING

CHARTER
NEW YORK

A DIVISION OF CHARTER COMMUNICATIONS INC.
A GROSSET & DUNLAP COMPANY

THE CRIMSON CHALICE

Copyright © 1976, 1977, 1978 by Victor Canning
All rights reserved
Published by arrangement with
William Morrow & Company, Inc.

Charter Books
A Division of Charter Communications Inc.
A Grosset & Dunlap Company
360 Park Avenue South
New York, New York 10010

Cover art by Rowena Morrill

2 4 6 8 0 9 7 5 3 1
Manufactured in the United States of America

For the One Who Wept
When the Dream Ended

Foreword

THIS BOOK DEALS WITH the life and times of King Arthur from his birth—roughly 450 A.D.—during the period when the last Roman legions had long been withdrawn from Britain, leaving it a prize to be fought over by rival British warlords and the Saxon invaders in the east. It follows him through unruly youth to a manhood fired by his tremendous mission to restore his country's greatness.

I have made no attempt to conform strictly to the lines of the accepted Arthurian legend, largely because I do not think it bears much relation to truth. What the truth was, nobody knows. That there was a truth—although there are no incontrovertible facts recorded in history about Arthur—is beyond dispute; otherwise, his legend would not have survived to become known worldwide and to be recognized as an imperishable part of Britian's heritage.

The renown of his life and deeds in the Dark Ages was lodged for over six hundred years solely in folk memory. Folk, being what they are, invariably alter and embroider a good story. William of Malmesbury, Geoffrey of

Monmouth and then Sir Thomas Malory were landed with the result. Lesser as well as better writers have followed them. Acknowledging that I come in the first of these two categories, I feel no shame in entering the lists poorly armed but securely mounted on a horse I have ridden for years called Imagination.

Contents

FOREWORD   vii

PART I / THE CRIMSON CHALICE   1

1 ● Forest Meeting
2 ● The Black Raven
3 ● Hunter's Dream
4 ● The Keeper Of The Shrine
5 ● The Centurion's Cup
6 ● The Circle Of The Gods
7 ● The Villa Etruria
8 ● The Flood Riders
9 ● The Fortress Of Birds
10 ● The Island Parting

PART II / THE CIRCLE OF THE GODS   177

1 ● The Brooch Of Epona
2 ● The Moorland Meeting
3 ● A Chaplet Of Purple Vetch
4 ● Between Sword And Sea
5 ● The Road To Corinium
6 ● The Villa Of The Three Nymphs
7 ● Horses and Men

8 ● Comrades Of The White Horse
9 ● A Gift From The Gods
10 ● Under The Banner Of The White
       Horse
11 ● Dawn Meeting

PART III / THE IMMORTAL WOUND   361

1 ● The Coin Of Hadrian
2 ● The Camp Above The Cam
3 ● The Return To Isca
4 ● The Taunting Of The Boar
5 ● Girl With A Harp
6 ● The Woman Of The High Rocks
7 ● Elegy For A Warrior
8 ● The Horses Of The Gods
9 ● The Holly On The Hillside
10 ● The Immortal Wound
11 ● The Breaking Of The Saxons
12 ● The Dream And The Dreamer

MAP   547
LIST OF PLACE AND TRIBAL NAMES   548

PART
I

THE
CRIMSON
CHALICE

CHAPTER ONE

Forest Meeting

As THE SUN TIPPED the eastern reaches of the forest and fired the pewter sea to silver at the far end of the valley, the May morning was full of song. Through the belling of tits, the monotonous sawing of the chiffchaffs and the melodious pealing of thrushes and blackbirds, Lerg, the big grey wolfhound, caught the clatter of a distantly falling stone on the valleyside path. Except for a slight lift of his muzzle from his crouched forepaws, he made no move; but his grey-flecked green eyes watched the turn of the path where it entered the wide glade. To his right Aesc, the water dog, with the long drooping red-furred ears, had heard the stone fall some few moments after she had caught the human scent coming up on the morning breeze from the sea. On the left of Lerg, Cuna, small, short-legged and wirehaired, neither heard, nor saw, nor smelled anything. Not long out of puppyhood, he was curled into a ball and, empty-bellied now for twenty-four hours, dreamt of vole and rat and hare and the dark tunnels of fox earths and badger sets.

Above them the body hung. The hide thongs about the ankles still bit tight, but those about the wrists, which held the body suspended from the stout horizontal branch of an oak, had stretched so that the balls of the tied feet just touched the ground. But it had been twelve hours since there had been any power in legs and feet to take advantage of earth's touch to ease the weight of the body on shoulder muscles. Bluebottles, and a small cloud of midges and early gnats, clustered over the crisp-curled head of hair and the brown, sweat-dried face. An hour before sunset a pair of red kites

had spiralled down, forked tails splayed, to roost on the
upper branches of the oak. Bran, the raven, had given an
angry *carp, carp* and had flown at them, chasing them away
inland over the rolling green sea of forest.

Bran sat now on the oak top and watched the newcomer
moving up the path toward the glade. Twice during the night
a lone wolf, ancient and pack-exiled, had come to the glade's
edge and Lerg had driven him away. Now, five miles away to
the east, the wolf fed on a calf among the slaughtered cattle in
a stockyard close to the fireblack ruins of a homestead. In the
dust of the forecourt an old woman sat holding her long grey
hair over her face to keep the day away, keening and moaning
softly to herself, numbed by the memory of the horror
which had filled the last two days.

The newcomer came to the edge of the glade. It was a girl
grown close to young womanhood. The hood of her short
brown woollen mantle was pushed back onto her shoulders,
leaving her fair hair free. Around her waist, over a white,
dust-streaked linen tunic, she wore an embroidered belt with
a bronze clasp in the shape of two dolphins. On her feet were
leather sandals held by a cross-gartering of doeskin thongs
which ran up her bare legs and were tied beneath her knees.
Over her right shoulder she carried a bulky sack made by the
knotting of four corners of a bedcover of green-and-yellow
striped silk.

Standing at the edge of the glade she saw the three dogs,
saw the rapid mouse-movement of a tree creeper work up the
rough trunk of the oak, saw the raven at the top of the tree,
and breathed with a slow, anguished tightening of her face as
she saw the body. For a moment she closed her blue eyes
against memory. A low rumble from Lerg frightened her. To
turn away, she knew, for she was no stranger to animals,
might bring the dogs after her. To go forward, too, she
reasoned, could start the trio of guarding beasts into a violent, rushing attack. She stood where she was and waited, her
eyes on the bowed head of the body that hung from the tree,
ringed with a moving halo of flies and gnats.

Lerg growled low again and Cuna, awake now, slowly sat

up but knew better than to move past Lerg. Lerg was the leader.

The girl waited, her body trembling under the swift assault of her fears. The strengthening sun burned against the skin of her right cheek. Across it ran a dark smudge of black ash, and above her right eye, dark against the fair skin, was a bruise as large as a crab apple. Lerg growled again and then slowly rose to his feet. The other dogs made no move. Long-legged, lean-bodied, the grey coat shaggy as lichen, he stood as high as a month-old calf. She knew his kind for they were highly prized now far beyond Britain for their speed and courage in the killing of wolf and deer. And the other dog, too, she knew, with its red coat and long ears—a kind that loved water as much as the otters and wildfowl it hunted. Then she remembered that her father had often said, "There is no dog that cannot read the cast of any mortal. Harbour villainy and they will return it. Offer friendship and they will accept it—but at their own gait." She forced herself to stand where she was and watch the slow movement of the hound toward her. He came, not directly, but on an arc which took him away to her right where she lost sight of him. Without words, the cry locked silently in her mind, she pleaded with the hound . . . *Your master suffers . . . there is suffering with me, too . . . leave me free to help him. . . .* She stared ahead at the hanging body. Its top half was covered with an undershirt, its front open, stirring slightly in the morning breeze. The lower part of the body was sheathed in tight-fitting leather breeches reaching just below the knees. On the feet were heavy, metal-studded, thick-soled sandals fastened by thongs at the ankles.

The hound paced back into her view and circled to her left, but this time halted within her sight. He raised his head, looked back at the oak tree and the other dogs, then swung his head slowly round and eyed her. Her instinct was to make some move, some show of friendliness, but she held still. Fear ran steadily in her, but it was a fear now that she fought to control. Slowly swamping her own misery and recent griefs there rose in her a warm compassion for the being who hung from the tree, who might still live and need her help.

The hound lowered his head and moved toward her, stiff-legged, hackles partly risen. He stopped close to her and, reaching out his muzzle, sniffed at her left hand, which hung against her side. She felt the warm breath on her fingers. Suddenly the hound licked her hand, gave a low, easy growl and turned from her. Lerg walked back to the other dogs and sat on his haunches, his eyes on the girl.

Then, as though possessed by some strange power never known to her before, the girl felt her trembling ease, the quick beating of her heart die down. Without hesitation she walked forward. There was no fear in her now. She eased her bundle to the earth and unknotted the covering. Reaching inside, she fumbled around for a while and brought out a small sharp-edged dagger. She put the haft in her mouth, then crouched and jumped for the overhanging branch. She got two handholds, then swung her legs up and worked herself to a prone position on top of the branch. She eased herself along and began to saw at the thongs of the left wrist. As she cut the last one the body lurched sideways, spun slowly on the stretched thongs of the right hand, and the bound feet dragged across the earth.

The dogs watched but made no sound.

She wormed herself farther along the branch and with a few quick slashes cut the thongs of the remaining hand. The body fell in a heap to the ground. As it hit the earth there was the sound of a long-drawn moan. On the oak top Bran called sharply *carp carp*, and launched himself into the air in a clumsy spiral.

The girl dropped to the ground. She cut the ankle thongs and rolled the body over onto its back. For the first time she saw the face clearly. It was the face of a youth of about eighteen, a lean, strong, tanned face, streaked with sweat and dirt, a young tawny-red beard growth fuzzing the square chin. Across the right side of his face was a jagged cut over which the blood had dried in a hard crust.

Oblivious now of the dogs, she went back to her bundle and brought out a small bronze cooking cauldron. She ran across the glade and along the path by which she had arrived.

A little way down it a small spring sprang from the hillside. She filled the cauldron and went back to the youth. Pulling a small earthenware beaker from her bundle, she squatted on the ground and lifted the youth's head and shoulders up onto her knees. She forced his mouth open and poured water into it. He moaned a little and choked, the water spilling over his face and neck. She tried again and this time eased only a little water into his mouth, her hand shaking, chiding herself, "Gently, Tia, gently."

Slowly she fed him water and when she judged he had had enough, she lowered his head to the ground, cushioning it on a woollen blanket from her bundle. She tore a long strip from the edge of her linen tunic and bathed his face, keeping the water away from the hard crust on his wound as much as she could since it was a better protection than any she could devise. His wrists were raw and bloody with the thong marks so she tore her linen facecloth into two strips and bound them around the wounds.

The sun was climbing higher in the sky. In a little while, she knew, the glade would be in full, hard sunlight. She would have to find shade for the youth and—since the times were what they were—some kind of concealment. There were men about who would murder for a worn pair of leather breeches and a pair of old legionary sandals.

She hurried away to the edge of the glade. As she went Lerg moved to the youth and lay down at his side, but the water dog, Aesc, followed her and, after a moment's hesitation, so did Cuna.

Not far from the edge of the glade she found a stunted yew with a tangle of wild clematis in fresh leaf trailing over its lower branches to form a narrow bower. She went back to the youth, took off her cloak belt and, looping it under his arms, began to drag him into the forest. Within the hour she had him in the bower, resting on a couch of old bracken growth and fresh branches, his head and shoulders propped up on her travelling bundle. She refilled the cauldron, fed more water to him, drank herself and ate part of a wheat cake she carried. She undid his wrist bandages, laid dock leaves around the wounds and replaced the bandages. Then she covered him with her mantle and sat by him, looking down at him. He was young, strong and hardened, and tight-muscled, and there were no wounds on him except for his wrists and the cut cheek. She sat patiently watching him, knowing that time and the water she had given him would do their work. A spear's length away from her Lerg lay couched under a bush. Of the other two dogs there was no sign.

And Tia, elbows resting on her knees, chin cupped in her hands, remembered the night that had passed and the days before it, and knew that there could be nothing in the future that could replace all that had been lost—her brother and his wife dead, the villa and the homestead huts plundered and burned, cattle slaughtered, and most of their own work-people turned against her and the family. Only the devotion of her maid's husband, Tullio, had saved her from the savagery of the estate steward, who had laid a drunken claim to her from which she had been saved by the dagger thrust of Tullio's old service *pugio*. In a few short hours the peace and ease of her life had been shattered, her loved ones killed and the security of her sheltered, rich life destroyed. She covered her face with her hands. Her body shook with quick spasms which she could not control.

Lerg gave a low whine and Tia straightened up, the spasms passing. As she did so the youth stirred and opened his eyes. He stared without moving at the roof of yew branches over-head, and she saw that his eyes were a dark, shining brown, reminding her of the colour of the closed sea anemones that studded the low water rocks of the beach that marked the estate's southern boundary. She reached to her side and dunked part of the hard wheat cake in the water of the cauldron. Cradling his head on her arm, she tried to feed him, but he closed his eyes and turned his head away. She filled the beaker and offered him water. With his eyes still closed he drank, and this time he swallowed the water avidly. When she lowered his head and shoulders back onto the bundle, he sighed. She sensed the slow ease taking his body as its strained muscles relaxed. He slept and his breathing, which at first had been heavy and troubled, took on a regular, slow rhythm.

The sun climbed higher. Aesc and Cuna returned and settled a few paces away. Cuna slept, curled into a ball, but Aesc lay couched, her eyes wide open, watching the youth. Somewhere, Tia guessed, the two dogs had discovered food. There was plenty to be found in the ruined huts and the yards and fields with their slaughtered cattle and poultry. Stirred by the tongues of the rabble-rousers, the country people had proved themselves as ruthless as any of the Saxon seafolk on their sudden summer raids. Soon they, too, would be back. Each year they came earlier, and each year more and more of them stayed to swell the ranks of their kinsmen who had made the Saxon shores and the rich corn lands and settlements east of Anderida their own.

The youth beside her began to talk in his sleep. At the sound of the voice Lerg's ears half cocked and Aesc raised her head. It was difficult for Tia to understand anything of what he said. He spoke sometimes in her own tongue, but it was the rough, slang-filled language of the army auxiliaries, the old language of the barrack blocks and camps, and sometimes he spoke in the true language of the country, of which she knew only a few words and phrases. In his voice there was, too, an accent and burr which was strange to her. After a while he slept without talking. Tia lay back on the grass, aware suddenly of her own fatigue and despair. She had travelled all night blindly across country, fighting always the panic in her thoughts. Within a few moments she, too, was asleep.

When Baradoc woke, the sun was halfway down the western sky. He lay for a while watching the dapple of sunlight through the yew branches, aware of the wrack and soreness in arm and shoulder muscles. He raised his hands and looked at the bandages on his wrist. A confusion in his head cleared slowly. Above him appeared the head and shoulders of Lerg. The hound gave a low whine. Baradoc fondled the grey muzzle and then, gripping the dog's neck,

eased himself to a sitting position. For a moment his head
swam and he shook it to clear his vision, seeing through a
blur Aesc and Cuna standing beyond Lerg. Then, as his head
swung slowly round, he saw the girl. She was sleeping on the
grass, her mantle flung open, the torn edge of her white tunic
rumpled above her knees and sun-tanned legs. Her short, fair
hair was breeze-fanned across her temples. He looked from
her to the dogs and then half turned, wincing with the pull on
his strained muscles, and saw the cloth-wrapped bundle on
which his head had been resting. Looking again at the girl, he
saw now that close to her side a small dagger lay on the
ground ready to her free hand. He smiled to himself, guess-
ing much of what must have happened, and knowing
gratitude, knowing, too, from one look at her face that she
was not one of his people. Her red-thonged sandals would
have cost more sesterces than any working country girl could
have afforded. Unexpectedly his head began to swim violently. He leaned forward, holding it with his hands, fighting
off the vertigo. The attack passed and, as he straightened up,
he realized that he must have groaned aloud. The girl was
awake and, half risen, was resting on her knees and facing
him, dagger in shaking hand.

They faced one another without words, and Baradoc knew
that, even though she must have cut him down and looked
after him, she could have no surety that such an act of charity
would be met with thanks. There were plenty of men in the
country today who merited being left to hang for the crows
and ravens to pick clean. He looked down at the small dagger
which she held in her unsteady right hand, and said, "You
won't need that." He spoke her tongue. "The gods were
good to send you, and the dogs marking your goodness let
you pass. I owe you a life. On my people's sign I swear it."
He pulled the edge of his loose shirt aside and touched his left
shoulder.

Tia, fear dying, saw that tattooed on the brown skin was a
small, black, crowlike bird with red beak and red legs. She
guessed then that he must come from the far west or north, for
there lived the only tribes who marked their skins so.

She said, "Who are you?"

"My name is Baradoc. I am from the far west where the land falls into the sea in the heart of which the father of all the oceans sleeps. Who are you?"

"I am Gratia. But mostly I am called Tia. My father was Marcus Pupius Corbulo. He and my mother are long dead. I live with my brother, Priscus, and his wife . . ." She broke off for a moment or two and then went on, "That is, I lived with them until yesterday. They are both now dead—killed by our own farm workers."

Baradoc let his eyes rest on the bruise on her forehead and then they moved to the bundle, to the water-filled cauldron and the beaker by its side and on to the half portion of the flat wheat cake and the broken piece of cheese that lay on a large leaf alongside it. He said gently, "These are bad times. Men easily turn against their masters. Some do it because there has been a fear in them ever since it was known from General Aetius that there will be no Roman help for us from Gaul. And others because a new fear is growing with every long boat that brings fresh crewmen to join their brothers along the Saxon shore. They fear the new masters and turn against the old."

Listening to him, Tia was surprised at the masterly manner of his speaking, as though his knowledge and authority admitted no questioning. Before she could stop herself, she said, "When you lay there sleeping you talked in the speech of the camps and the barracks. Now you talk as I do."

Baradoc smiled. "I have known many old legionaries, and I talk as they did. But also I was for years a servant of a retired Chief Centurion. If I did not speak correctly I felt the weight of his vine staff. I am the son of a tribal chief, taken as slave when I was twelve years old. My master took my education seriously." He grinned suddenly, deep creases bracketing the sides of his mouth, and added in soldiers' speech, "My belly grumbles for a taste of that cheese."

Tia laughed at the sudden transition and, in the midst of her laughter, considering all the darkness which still clouded her life, wondered that she could. She handed the cheese across to him. As he stretched out his hand and arm for it she saw him wince at the flex of his stretched muscles. She said,

"When you have eaten I will massage your shoulders and arms. This was something I did often for Priscus in our bathhouse."

Baradoc nodded, his mouth full of cheese. Tia, watching him, was sure now that she had nothing to fear from him. There was, too, she sensed, a strength and self-confidence about him which he could readily muster against trouble.

She asked, "This master of yours, is he alive still?"

"No." Baradoc scowled and his face suddenly turned grim. "The Saxons killed him a month ago. But long before that he had given me my freedom."

"You are going back to your people?"

"Yes." Baradoc reached for the water beaker and drank.

"You could have gone before. Since you were free."

Baradoc smiled. "I could have done easily. But my master was good to me, and there were many things he taught me. To read and write and speak his language. About farming and fighting, and how to read the stars, and to understand about building and mathematics and geometry and history and about the rest of the world out there." He waved the empty beaker vaguely southward. "So I stayed. One day I shall be the leader of my people. It is right that I should teach these things to them."

Tia smiled. "You will be a very important man, I see."

Baradoc chuckled. "Thanks to you, yes—since you came along and cut me down."

"Who hung you up like that?"

Baradoc frowned and said stiffly, "Two—that called themselves friends. One day I shall kill them both. But that is no business of yours."

Tia stood up, suddenly angry at his words and his abruptness. She said sharply, "True. Perhaps, then, I should have passed the tree and left you hanging there since that, too, was no business of mine!"

Baradoc reached out quickly and caught the edge of her mantle and said, "Hold now! Don't fly off like a hen disturbed from her night roost. I meant no rudeness. It was just the thought of those two that stirred me up." He let go of her mantle and grinned, his tanned face creasing. "You are full of Roman fire, aren't you? But that's good—especially in these days. But not good enough to take you safely through this country alone the way things are. So calm down and tell me where you want to go and I will see you safely there.''

''Even though you go west and I should say Eburacum?''

Baradoc laughed. ''Why not? Even though you should say Vindolandia on the North Wall—though that might give us a little trouble. I owe you a life. The longest journey would only be a little paid off the score.''

Tia slowly sat down. She said, ''My brother and sister are dead. All that I have in this country now is an old uncle who lives near Aquae Sulis. It is in my mind to go to him.''

''Then let it rest there. I will take you. And I won't pretend that I'm not glad it's on my westward road. Give me your hand.''

''What on earth for?''

Baradoc sighed. ''I shall have trouble with you, I can see, for you are not easily led. Give me your hand.''

Slowly Tia held out her right hand and Baradoc, smiling, took it by the fingertips. Then he turned and said two words in his own language to Lerg. The hound rose from the ground and came slowly forward and stood at Baradoc's side. Baradoc raised Tia's hand and placed it over the eyes of the hound, palm down, and he spoke again to Lerg in his own tongue. This done, he called Aesc forward and repeated the ritual. Then, ignoring Cuna, he gave an order to the three dogs and they turned and disappeared quickly into the forest.

Tia said, ''What does all that mean?''

Baradoc answered, ''You will see. Now remember always this word.'' He paused and then said softly to her, ''*Saheer*. You have it? *Saheer*.''

Tia nodded. ''*Saheer*. But what is it?''

''It is my word, and now, for Lerg and Aesc, it is also yours. Whenever you are in trouble, call it as loudly as you can.'' He grinned. ''Go on—shout it now. As loud as you can.''

Tia hesitated for a moment and then, taking a deep breath, shouted, ''*Saheer!*''

Almost immediately there was a crashing in the low forest thickets, and Lerg and Aesc came rushing to her and settled one on either side, alert and on their legs ready for action, growling and barking. A few seconds later Cuna arrived and began to imitate the action and growls of the other two.

Baradoc gave the dogs an order and they relaxed into sitting positions around Tia.

Tia said, "They will come—always—like that?"

"At any time, anywhere—if they can. And the gods help any man who is near you."

"Why didn't you give my hand to the other, the little one?"

"Cuna? Because he's young and still a little stupid. But the others will teach him. Sometime as we travel I will teach you the other words they know."

"These are words of your language?"

"*Na,* these are our words. There is a magic in them because only the dogs, I and soon you will know them. Can you whistle?"

"No, of course I can't."

"Then you must learn because there could be times when you might need Bran." Baradoc put his forefingers to his mouth and let out a sudden blasting whistle that made Tia jump.

Within a few moments a shadow swept across the sunlit patch beyond the bower. Then with a noisy beating of his great wings and a raucous calling of *carp carp* Barn, the raven, swept under the spreading branches of the yew. He circled twice around Baradoc and then settled on his shoulder, eyes alert, the great ebony beak weaving from side to side.

Drawing back a little, Tia said, "That's Bran?"

"Yes. And when he attacks he goes for a man's eyes." Baradoc reached up his right hand and Bran jumped to his wrist. "Take a piece of cheese and throw it into the air for him."

Tia broke off a piece of cheese and tossed it high into the air.

Bran made no move to take it and the cheese fell to the ground.

"He's not hungry."

Baradoc laughed. "Oh, yes, he is. Bran is always hungry. But he will take food from no one unless he, too, is given the word. Throw it up again."

Tia took the cheese and tossed it into the air once more and, as she did so, Baradoc called gently, *"Aka, Aka!"*

Bran swooped from Baradoc's wrist and took the cheese low to the ground as it fell and then flew off to the top of a nearby ash tree.

Tia said, "So now he knows I am allowed to feed him?"

"Yes. Though he fends for himself even better than the dogs. When you can whistle he will always come to you."

Baradoc stripped off his undershirt and rolled over onto his stomach, couching his head on his arms.

Tia asked, "What now?"

Baradoc grinned sideways at her. "You promised to massage me. My muscles are as stiff as salt-dry ropes."

After a moment's hesitation Tia went to his side and knelt by him. For an ex-slave he had an abrupt way of treating her at times, but she guessed that this came from his self-confidence and his pride in the fact that he was a chief's son. The women of the remoter tribes, she knew, were of little importance except to do the bidding of their men. Leaning over him, she began to massage and work his shoulder muscles in the way she had often done for Priscus. As she worked she pushed from her mind as much as she could the thought of her brother and his wife. In a handful of savage hours her whole life had changed. The gods had been good to them all for a long time, and now the gods had turned away from them. When she got to Aquae Sulis she and her uncle would make their devotions to the gods of the Shades and set up a stone for Priscus and his wife. And then? What would she do then? Her uncle was old and would not last much longer. This country—her country, for she had known no other, but not hers in the way it was Baradoc's— was falling apart. There was a darkness falling over the land. She could feel the coldness of its shadow touching her heart.

Easing and working the stiff arm and back muscles of the youth, she said, "How long will it take to get to Aquae Sulis?"

"Who knows? There is no marching these days along the west road like a century of legionaries, quickly knocking off the miles. We've got to take the old tracks and steer clear of towns and villages. It's taken me three weeks to come down from Durobrivae and there's not been a day without smoke in the sky from some villa or homestead going up in flames. Tell me, Tia—what have you got in your bundle? My two good friends, whose throats I'll cut one day, took all my stuff and the packhorse as well."

"There's not much. Some food. Some clothes. A few cooking things. A little money, the dagger, and a brooch that belonged to my mother."

"I see. Well, we'll need to acquire a few more things."

"Acquire?"

"Yes. Steal if need be." He rolled over and away suddenly and, looking up at her, said firmly, "But one thing you've got to remember—if I tell you to do something, you do it—fast! Any bush or thicket can hold a cutthroat. Understood?"

After a moment's hesitation Tia said, "Yes."

"And we must cut your hair even shorter. You've got to look like a boy, even if a pretty one. So don't pull a long face about it."

Although she hid it, there was a flare of anger in Tia at the way he spoke. Sarcasm edging her voice, she said with a little shrug, "If that's what the great Baradoc, son of a chief, orders—then yes." On her knees she made a mock bow.

Baradoc grinned and said, "Don't give me any of your sauce." He stood up and began to flex his arms and shoulders and then bent over and touched his toes, loosening up his body. As he did so, he went on, "You must know this part of the country well."

"Yes."

He jerked his head toward the glade. "Where does the path lead?"

"To the sea. It's not far."

"Is there a village down there?"

"There was until last year. A long boat raided it and it was burned. But there are still a few old huts the fishermen use when the shoals come along the coast."

Baradoc bent and threw open her bundle. He took out a thin woollen blanket, slung it over his shoulders and tied it about his neck. He smiled at her. "I'm going scavenging. You stay here." He turned and said something in his own language to the dogs and then walked off. Lerg and the other dogs watched him go. Cuna whined for a moment and then was silent. As Baradoc disappeared through the trees Tia saw Bran lift himself from the ash treetop and slide away on the sea breeze, slanting low over the forest toward the coast.

Tia moved to the open bundle and began to tidy the things that Baradoc had left in disarray. She arranged them neatly in the silk cover but left out the small cauldron and the beaker and her dagger. Before tying the ends of the coverlet together again she unwrapped from a piece of linen her mother's brooch. It was a small gold oval set on a strong pin. On its face, worked in relief, were clasped hands. Around them ran the inscription "To Januaria Hermia, my dearest. Marcus." The brooch had been given to her mother on her betrothal by her father.

Holding it, Tia was struck by a sense of desolation. Alone now, with no need to cosset her pride or hide her feelings from anyone, she felt the strange dark knowledge of utter loss possess her. Resting back on her heels, she put her hands to her eyes and wept silently, her shoulders shaking, her head bowed.

After a while she felt the warm lap of a tongue caress the back of her hands. Looking up, she saw that Aesc had come to her and licked her hands. Behind her Lerg sat upright on his haunches, his great tongue lolling from his mouth as he watched her. She fondled Aesc's silky head and, as she did so, Cuna gave a little whimper, came to her and flopped his head into her lap.

She fondled Cuna's head, setting his stubby, docked tail wagging. The gods took, she thought, and the gods gave. There was no questioning their ways. Yesterday was one life; today another—and one for which she was utterly unprepared or fitted. Well, so what? She thought with a moment's heartening defiance. She must learn to live a new life. And then, almost as though she could hear his voice, a favourite saying of her brother's came back to her. *The blackest night must die under the fiery wheels of Apollo's golden chariot.*

It was close on sunset when Baradoc returned. He came with the blanket slung over his shoulder, bulky with his findings. He carried in his right hand a long, wooden-shafted fishing spear, its socketed three-pronged iron head missing a tang and the two others badly rusted. He dumped the bundle on the ground and, squatting by her, laid out his pickings from the fishing huts. There were some rusty hooks of different sizes; a length of worn hempen rope; part of a circular throwing net with some small stone weights still attached to its skirts; a tangle of old catgut lengths; a sailmaker's needle with a broken point; a small wicker-woven birdcage with the bottom missing, into which he had stuffed odd lengths of cloth; two wooden platters, both badly cracked; a large lump of beeswax; a raggedly shaped piece of goat's hide as stiff as a board; a thick woollen fisherman's shirt, with a slit down the side, half a sleeve missing and the front coated with tiny, dried opaline fish scales; a well-worn piece of striking flint; and a small length of tallow candle with a rush wick.

As he laid all these out, Tia watched in silence. He took no notice of her until he had pulled out the last of his finds, a pair of long coarsely woven leggings that reached down to the ankles, stained with rust and pitch marks and with a great hole in their seat. He dropped them on the pile and looked at Tia with a grin of satisfaction.

"What do we want with all that rubbish?" she asked.

He shook his head and said, "I know the kind of place you come from. Like my old master's. You had servants and maids, fine clothes, and fine table furnishings. Aye, even glass in your windows and worked mosaics on the great-

room floor. Baths and hot rooms and everything you wanted
for the table. You've lived soft, wench—but now the world is
upside down.''

Tia jumped up and said furiously, ''Son of a chief you may
be, but call me 'wench' again and I walk from here and find
my own way to Aquae Sulis. My name is Gratia. As a mark
of friendship, Tia to you. Name me so and not as a herd or
kitchen girl.''

''Whooah! Rein back! I meant no rudeness. Tia it shall
be.'' He reached up, took her hand and pulled her down.
''Should we fight now, whose side would the dogs and Bran
take since they have been given the word for you?''

''I'm sorry. I have a quick temper.''

''No, 'tis pride and that is a good thing. I shall not offend it
again—except by mischance, for which I ask forgiveness
now to save further trouble. So, let's get back to our rubbish
which is no rubbish. What one man throws away another can
use. A fish spear with two prongs is better than no fish spear.
Fish can be eaten but first they must be caught. So I brought
the spear, the hooks, the gut and the piece of net. I can
sharpen a new point to the needle and with threads pulled
from the cloth and waxed you can repair the shirt and the long
hose.''

''Who are they for?''

''The shirt is for me. The hose for you.''

''I wouldn't wear those filthy things!''

Baradoc was silent. For all that she had recently suffered
Tia was far from realizing what change had come over her
life. Never before had she ever had to think of a black
tomorrow, of a tomorrow which would be as full of want as
all the yesterdays. In this wilderness of place and evil times
she was no more able to survive alone than a fledgling,
unfeathered, pushed from its warm nest. He could have
wished that it had been some simple herd girl who had saved
him and who would have needed no teaching. Still . . . she
was not. He said with good humour, ''The clothes can be
washed first and mended after. In long hose and the legs
gartered you will be a handsome young fellow. And don't
frown at me—it must be so for your own safety. Now, do I

have to explain the rest as though you were a raw recruit, goggle-eyed in barracks for the first time?'' He took the flint and, holding the spearhead jabbed into the ground, struck the stone against one of the iron prongs and brought brief, blue sparks spurting to life. ''Raw fish or fowl cheer no belly. Fire we must have to cook. And have I not brought two cracked platters to go with your cooking cauldron and that wicked little dagger you keep always close to your side?''

''And this—this stinking piece of hide?''

''It's a long way to Aquae Sulis. Those fancy sandles of yours could need new soles in a week. Now—let's get packed up and moving. And, Lady Tia, leave the rest of the cake and cheese near the top of your bundle. We shall need them before the night is out.''

Marching, Baradoc watched the moon and the stars in their slow swings, and shaped his course, but even in pitch darkness the magic compass in his mind would have served him, though less finely. Once or twice he heard an owl call, and now and again came the harsh screech of a hunting nightjar. The forest was alive with Nature's hunters, whose skills were more precise than any man's. Now and again either Lerg or Aesc would come from the darkness to his side for a few seconds and then disappear to their posts once more. Toward morning, with daylight like a grey wash of cobwebs through the eastern trees, he sent Cuna out to the right flank. Of all the dogs he and his old master had bred for export abroad, there had been none to touch Lerg or Aesc. They had been kept jealously for the household. Cuna would learn the wordless signs in time. Of all animals, the gods had gifted dogs with a magical kinship with man, but only to some men the gift of the words and signs that held them coupled in understanding and loyalty.

CHAPTER TWO

The Black Raven

IT WAS ALMOST midmorning before Tia woke. There was a fresh westerly wind blowing and the sky was full of low, rolling grey clouds. She sat up and looked around her. She had only the vaguest memory of the last stretches of their march and the moment when Baradoc had halted and said they would make camp. She had been conscious of his stirring around in the moonlight and shadows, unloading their bundles and spreading covers on the ground, of herself dropping on them and finally of his throwing the blanket across her.

She stretched her arms, yawned and rubbed the last of sleep from her eyes. The camp had been made on a high bluff which rose clear of the forest, in a small ravine whose sides were a jumble of broken stones. Behind her the rock face rose sheer and smooth like a fortress wall. The sound of running water reached her ears. Away to the left a thin stream dripped down a moss-covered cleft of the rocks and was gathered into a small gravelly pool, from which it seeped away down the hillside in a marshy slope bordered by primroses and blue-starred periwinkle growths. There was no sign of Baradoc or the dogs, but Bran sat on a spur of rock above her, beak-combing his flight feathers and scratching himself about the head as he made his morning toilet. Tia smiled to herself and decided to follow his example. Her tiredness was gone but she felt dirty and tousled.

She went to the pool, stripped off her tunic and took off her sandals. Wearing only her short woollen drawers, she splashed and washed her face, the top half of her body and then her legs. There was a blister on her right foot where the sandal had rubbed her during the march. She wiped herself with a corner of her bundle cover and dressed, and shivered a little until her clothes began to bring back warmth to her body.

Then, seeing close up against the rock face the contents of the bundles that Baradoc had opened up, she picked up the dirty old seaman's shirt and the filthy pair of long hose. There was no sign of the fishing spear. Baradoc, she guessed, was away with the dogs hunting for the pot. At the thought of food, she felt her belly empty and hunger bring saliva to her mouth, and she knew that she had never been so hungry before.

She took the shirt and the hose to the shallow scoop of pool, threw them in and then began to tramp and knead them underneath her bare feet. The water flowed away muddy.

Above her Bran turned his head away. He had seen many women pounding and beating away like this before. His eyes followed the dark-crested, rolling spread of the forest top away to the south. Distantly there was a glimpse of a thin arc of the sea, iron grey and still, and away to the west a sudden fall in the trees to a narrow edging of marsh- and grasslands biting up into the forest. Through this valley coiled and looped a wide, slow-moving river.

Moving slowly up the river, a good five miles away, was something else which Bran had seen before, a long ship, the oar blades dipping and flashing rhythmically. The saffron-coloured sail had been half struck and loosely furled. Bran watched the swing of the rowers' backs and arms, saw three men standing in the raised stern and a solitary man perched high in the prow who now and again swung a weighted sounding line overboard to read the depth of the river. As the long ship moved into a broader reach of the river, the stern steering oar was put hard over and the ship swung slowly round in a half-circle to the left bank. Oars flashed with waterruns as they were lifted and shipped, and from stern and bow men jumped ashore with mooring ropes. As the ship was made fast a party of men moved out from the forest that

fringed the river meadow and made for the ship. There were
ten or twelve of them, helmeted and armed with swords and
spears, and with them came four pack horses laden down
with loads slung across their backs. That, too, Bran had seen
before. Had he been free he might have launched himself on
his broad wings and swung down valley, quartering against
the crosswind, and taken a closer look, for anything that
moved excited his curiosity. But the freedom was denied him
because he had been given the word to mark his place by
Baradoc before he had left with the dogs and the fishing
spear.

Below him Tia wrung out the shirt and the hose and spread
them over the steep rock face, weighing them down with
stones. Looking at the roughly woven hose, she made a wry
face. Before she got used to them they would probably chafe
and rub her legs raw. Still, Baradoc was right. For her own
safety she had to turn from a well-bred young lady to a ragged
country youth—but, thank the gods, only until they got to
Aquae Sulis. She stood for a moment, thinking of her uncle's
beautifully furnished and decorated villa, and the soft silk-
and-cotton-covered beds with their mattresses of swan and
duck down. Then she put the thought from her and, taking
her dagger, went back to the pool, which had now cleared.
Leaning over it, she began to saw and hack at her fair hair.
The wind took strands of it away like floating cobwebs and
some fell into the water, drifting away on the slow current.
Once as she worked, the dagger slipped and the sharp edge
nicked the side of her thumb. Without thinking she used her
father's favourite curse word and sucked at the wound. Then
she grinned to herself. Why should she not curse and condemn the bloody knife and the bloody times to the darkness
of bloody Hades? They were a man's words and she was now
a man—albeit a very good-looking one.

Tia was sitting with her back to the rocks, pulling threads
loose from a piece of cloth and drawing them through the
lump of beeswax which she had warmed in her hands. One
moment she was alone, frowning over her work—and then
there was Cuna at her feet, Lerg by the pool and Aesc on a

rock ledge above him, with Baradoc at his side. The suddenness and silence of their appearance startled her, making her
heart thump quickly. But almost immediately she realized
how glad she was to see them all.

Baradoc said something softly to Bran, and then jumped
down to the poolside and came across to Tia. Bran lifted
himself from his perch, beat upward in a slow spiral toward
the grey sky, which was now showing an occasional break in
the clouds, and then drifted away southward. He was free
now to do his own foraging. There would be something to be
picked up down by the river where the crewmen of the long
ship were now busy setting up a shore camp. Such men ate
until they were full and then tossed their leavings over their
shoulders to make easy prizes for any ready scavenger.

From his shoulder Baradoc dropped the hind leg of a
young deer to the short grass. Then, from the inside of his
shirt, he pulled out a handful of different fungi.

Squatting on his hunkers, he took out his dagger and began
to skin the leg, looking at Tia for a moment with a smile and
saying. "Fill the cauldron with water, Lady Tia, and then
search around for dry grass, dry twigs and some of that
crumbly dry moss from the rocks." He paused and nooded at
the clothes she had washed. "I see you have been busy. Turn
your head."

Tia slowly turned her head so that he could see her cropped
hair. She said with a note of sarcasm in her voice, "I hope it
meets with the great Baradoc's approval."

"*Aie!* but 'tis a pity to see such a fine flow of golden locks
go. Still, a few weeks in Aquae Sulis will see them back and
you'll be able to look in your mirror and admire yourself
again."

Rising to get the cauldron, Tia said, "You are in a good
and teasing humour."

"Why not? The hunt was quick and easy. The dogs have
already eaten and I brought only what we might need for a
while."

"How did you catch it?"

"One day soon when your wind and legs are stronger I might show you. Now fill the cauldron and tip the toadstools into it."

"Are they good to eat?"

Baradoc sighed. "Would I have brought them else?"

Tia filled the cauldron and did as she was bid, by which time Baradoc had skinned the meat and cut off four fair-sized portions. Then he gathered the little heap of kindling and tinder moss together that Tia had gathered and carried them to a dry flat stone at the foot of the rock face. As he arranged them he said, without looking at her, "Bring me the spear and the flint and your mantle."

It was no order. He just said it as though it were the most natural thing in the world to order her around without thought of resentment from her. So, she told herself, if she wanted to get to Aquae Sulis it must be.

He took the spear and jammed the two prongs into the ground at the edge of the stone, easing the dry grass and moss close to it. Then taking up the flint, he said, "Drape the mantle over me and hold the edges so that no wind comes in." At last when her arms were aching from holding the tented mantle around Baradoc she heard him blowing gently without stopping. Then a thin trickle of fine blue smoke seeped through the edges of the mantle. Baradoc lifted away his covering and put aside the spear. On the flat stone little tongues of flame were working through the dried grass and twigs.

Baradoc, face covered in sweat, said, "Now build it. But remember only dry wood. We want no heavy smoke from damp stuff. What little there is this wind will whip away from the top of the bluff. The fire and the cooking is all yours."

"All mine?"

"Why not?" Baradoc was genuinely surprised. "Did you think you would ride the whole way to Aquae Sulis lolling on a litter and not a hand to lift for any comfort or food?"

"But I've never cooked in the open. In fact I—" She broke off.

Baradoc grunted. "In fact, you've never cooked at all.

Well, a late start is better than none. I've brought you the meat and the flavouring and made the fire. Would you sit by and see me do woman's work?''

"And what are *you* going to do?"

He held out his blood-stained and dirt-streaked hands, and said brusquely, "Take a bath, of course. It's a habit my master beat into me. When that's done, I'll grind a new point to the needle, and wax some more threads—so that you won't be left idle after we've eaten."

Tia looked at him in silence for a moment or two, and then said evenly, "What you say is fair, though not gently said. But"—her voice began to rise—"don't think, Son-of-a-Chief Baradoc, that I can't do as well as any tribewoman with greasy hair and dirty face. I will do all you ask of me, but speak me fair—or I will set Lerg at your throat."

Baradoc stared at her round-eyed with surprise. Then he burst out laughing and said, "I am sorry. I was wrong to give you offense. Now, *please*, do as I ask. And also"—a twinkle came into his dark eyes—"since I don't want to offend you again keep your eyes from the bathhouse. I haven't washed for three days and I'm going to strip."

He strode away toward the pool, and Tia turned back to the fire and her duties. As she worked she heard the splashing of the pool water and his cheerful low whistling as he washed himself. There were times when she liked him, and times when she could kick him for his cocksureness. Still, whatever he was, she needed him to get to Aquae Sulis.

Two hours later they ate. When they had finished, Baradoc cut the rest of the raw deer flesh into flat strips. He laid them on the hot cooking stone, put another flat stone on top of them and then raked the hot embers over the stones and covered these with slabs of turf cut with his dagger. By the time they were ready to move off at night the meat would be cooked dry and easily carried as emergency rations. Then Tia began to mend the shirt and hose with the waxed threads while Baradoc with a piece of grit stone—on which he had re-pointed the needle—burnished and honed the tangs of the spear to put an edge and point on them.

As they worked, in answer to a question from Tia, he explained that in normal times they could have walked the distance to Aquae Sulis easily in four or five days. But now that journey would take longer because they must pick their route to avoid large towns and settlements and the old Roman-built main roads. He said, "The only people on these high roads will be armed parties, able to look after themselves, and not always to be trusted to give a true greeting to a couple of strangers." As she sewed, his spearhead finished, he drew in the loose gravel for her a map of the southern and western parts of Britain, marking in roughly the towns, rivers and forests and the areas of bare downs. He showed her where they were now—to the west of Anderida, a quarter of the way toward the next coastal town of Noviomagus. He stabbed the gravel with a stick, reciting the names of the towns like a litany . . . Portus Adurni, Clausentium, Venta, Sorviodunum and Lindinis. Tia smiled to herself for, though she recognized most of the names, she knew that quietly Baradoc was showing off his knowledge.

She asked, "And where is your country?"

Baradoc's stick swung far to the west, and he said, "Down here, beyond Isca, beyond the Tamarus River, on the north coast two days' march from the Point of Hercules, in the valley of the great rocks. Away farther, right at the end of the land, is Antivestaeum, where the sea stretches away to the edge of the world." As he finished speaking Baradoc reached for the unwashed cauldron and ran two fingers round the inner rim to collect the grease gathered there. Without looking at her, he reached for Tia's blistered foot and spread some of the grease over the red, chafed skin. Then he tore a piece from one of their collection of rags, bound it around her foot and tied it in place with a couple of waxed threads. This done, he looked up at her and smiled, saying, "In the days of the legions a man would get a beating and lose a week's pay for neglecting his feet." He stood up, holding the cauldron, and began to move away.

Tia asked, "Where are you going?"

"To scour the cauldron for you."

"Woman's work?" Tia grinned, pulled a thread tight and bit off the end.

"I see no woman around here—only a crop-headed Roman lad, sewing up a rip in the backside of his long hose."

Tia watched him kneel at the pool and begin to scour the cauldron with sand and pebbles. There were two Baradocs. She preferred the gentle, thoughtful one. But she knew that at this moment it was the other Baradoc she needed more, for he was the only one who could take her safely to Aquae Sulis.

Baradoc brought back the pot and said, "I leave Aesc and Cuna with you. There is something I saw early this morning which interests me."

He turned away and began to climb up to the top of the bluff and was soon lost to view. Although he spoke no word nor seemed to make any sign, Lerg went with him. The other dogs remained, stretched out beyond the fire. A dark shadow swept across the ground and Tia looked up to see Bran come to roost on one of the high rock points.

At the side of the river stood a lone alder tree, its lower branches still festooned with the jetsam and flotsam of the past winter's floods. Baradoc was wedged in the fork of the trunk close to the top, where he commanded a clear view of the river downstream. Below him the banks were broadly fringed with reeds that gradually gave way to the new growth of this year's meadow grasses. Lerg sat at the foot of the tree. The air was full of birdsong. Out of the corner of his eye Baradoc caught the high crescent-shaped silhouette of a falcon poised for the stoop and kill. But his real interest lay downstream, a quarter of a mile away.

There, moored against the same bank as the alder tree, was a long boat. The saffron sail had been lowered and was now stretched the length of the middeck over its own boom to make a tented canopy. There was some large black design painted on the sail, but because of its folds Baradoc could not make out what it was. He had seen long boats before and he knew it would be some device to give recognition of its sea-warrior master to others of his kind.

It was no Saxon ship. It was the long keel of a far-North sea raider, of a race that sought no foreign soil to hold, no land to conquer. These men looked only to plunder and slaves and to the easing of the deep salt itch in their blood, which was only stilled as the seas rolled under their keels and the winds of all seasons filled their great emblazoned sails of finely dressed skin.

On the bank two hide shelters had been set up and the smoke of cooking fires rose into the air. Men were carrying supplies and loot aboard and other men worked around the fires. When the work was done the feasting would begin. Somewhere along the coast or in the leagues of forest that rose beyond the water meadows, he knew, there would be ruined huts and homesteads, burning barns and byres, and the fly-clouded corpses of men, women and children.

That morning, returning from his hunting, he had seen one of their raiding parties moving down the river path, and with them they had been leading four sturdy ponies carrying their bundled loot. The loot meant nothing to him. But the ponies had made his eyes glisten with desire. With one or, better still, two of them, he and Tia could make faster time to Aquae Sulis and—when he had delivered her to her uncle—a pony would bring him home that much quicker. Home he longed for now with a longing which was a great thirst in him.

The ponies were in his sight now. The four of them had been loosely hobbled and were grazing in the meadow grass not more than a spear's throw from the first slopes of the forest. Within an hour all the crewmen, he guessed, would be drinking and feasting and soon would have no thought in their minds for the animals, which they probably planned to slaughter for meat to ship aboard with them the next day.

Baradoc watched as the sun began to slide down the sky. The shipmen had stowed their gains aboard and were now gathered ashore around the cooking fires and the rough tables set up outside their skin tents. Their voices, as they ate and drank, became louder and were broken by great gusts of laughter and now and then the lusty roaring of a song. Baradoc marked a spot on the westward crest of the forest and, when the sun touched it and the alder threw a long shadow across the rushes and the meadow, he slid down from the tree. He picked up the fishing spear which he had left at the bottom with the length of salvaged rope. He looped the rope about his waist and, keeping to the rushes, went back up the riverside with Lerg following him. When he was safely out of sight of the ship he swung away across the meadow grasses and into the skirts of the forest at the bottom of the hill. He worked his way through the trees until he was almost opposite the place where the ponies grazed.

He wet a finger and tested the wind. It was quartering upstream and toward him. He made a half-circling hunting sign to Lerg, and the hound moved off into the tall grass. Marking the slight crest movements of the long grasses, he watched Lerg's progress until the hound was between the ponies and the long ship and upwind of the animals.

Baradoc slipped to the edge of the forest and crouched behind the dark cover of a holly bush. For a moment or two the ponies grazed peacefully. Then Baradoc saw first the farthest pony and then the others lift their heads and cease grazing. Coming downwind to them was the scent of Lerg. It made them restless and puzzled them so that they moved slowly away from it, awkward in their gait from the hobbles they wore. Then they settled to graze again. But after a while their heads went up as Lerg, belly to the ground, slid nearer to them through the grasses. They moved closer to the trees.

Three times Lerg moved the ponies forward, and the third time the leading pony, a sturdy, rusty-red mare with a pale-golden mane, was almost within spitting distance of the holly bush. Gently Baradoc began to talk softly to it in his own tongue, calming it with words whose magic lay not in their sense but in their sound. "*Aie!* you red and gold beauty . . . *Aie!* who is it with the eyes like dark crag pools and the soft mouth, softer than the dove's breast? 'Tis you, my handsome, my proud, with the taste of sweet grass like honey on your breath. Come away then, come away . . .''

As he spoke the mare came to the side of the holly bush and Baradoc rose with an unbroken, slow movement, stepped smoothly forward and put his hand on the pony's muzzle and then ran it up the long cheek and caressed one of its ears. Talking to it still, he unslung the rope from his waist and looped it over the mare's head, making a rough halter. He drew his dagger, crouched, and cut the hobble between the forelegs.

He led the pony slowly into the shelter of the trees, took his spear from where it rested against a tree, and turned to lead the pony up the forest track. As he did so, a man stepped from the cover of an oak trunk less than six paces ahead. Baradoc checked the movement of the pony with his hand on the halter. He cursed himself that he should have been caught with the fishing spear in his left hand.

The man standing slightly above him on the slope of the narrow track smiled, swayed a little and then said gently in the Roman tongue, "'Twas well done, lad. And bravely done with my crew only a few cables' lengths away and you, risking your guts to garter their trews if they'd spotted you—and all for the sake of a pony! You understand my talk?"

Baradoc shook his head.

The man gave a low, tipsy laugh. "Your ballast has shifted, lad. Your brains must be lopsided or you would not shake your head to say no if you did not understand my talk. O brave lad who can talk strange love talk to a part-broken forest pony, a lad who wears a soldier's castoff sandals, and a lad who has not turned tail in fright like a startled hare, and even now stares me boldly in the eye when one sight of me would make most Britons void their bellies with fear. Speak me fair, for you understand me. Why do you steal my pony?" He hiccoughed.

From his manner and speech it was clear to Baradoc that he was someone of authority, used to command and to be obeyed. The odds were that he was the master of the long boat. He was bareheaded, a tall, powerfully built man, wearing a flared tunic with a wide whale-skin belt, from the left side of which hung a broadsword in a decorated scabbard. His thighs were bare to his knees and his legs were wrapped

in saffron-coloured cloth and bound with black thongs down
to his black sandals. Across the front of his tunic was embroidered a spread-winged black raven. But the most unexpected thing about him was that his skin was black, as black
as the Aethiop auxiliaries who had been with many of the
legions. In his right hand he held a short-hafted throwing
axe. The whites of his eyes rolled now, as he hefted the axe in
his hand and said impatiently, "Answer me!" and hiccoughed again.

Baradoc said, "How can I steal from you that which is not
yours?"

For an instant the man's face tightened with sudden anger.
Then, unexpectedly, he smiled, and said, "By Odin, you've
a bold tongue to speak so saucily when in the blink of an eye I
could split your skull." He tossed the throwing axe lightly in
the air and caught it deftly.

Baradoc answered, "*Aie!* You could throw your axe and
kill me. It is a skill I know your kind have. But you would not
live long. There is one who stands behind you who would
tear your life out by your throat before you could shout for
your men."

The man's smile broadened and he shook his head, swaying a little. "Oh, no, my gamecock. You think that I, Corvo,
master of the Black Raven, am to be fooled into turning by
such an old trick, and give you time to use your spear? Now,
turn the mare shipward. We've lost two men. We can use a
good pair of slave shoulders and hands on the rowing
benches. The rope's end and leg- and neck-irons will soon
take the fire out of you. Around with you, and thank your
country's good mead that you still live."

Baradoc, who, under his courage, knew fear and was not
fool enough to fancy yet that any advantage was his, said,
"No, Captain Corvo, my way lies past you. And I do not try
to fool you." He threw his spear to the ground. "Now, look
behind you."

Corvo blinked at Baradoc for a moment or two and then
slowly turned. Five paces behind him stood Lerg, the great,
grey shaggy body tensed, the powerful long head lowered,
jaws parted, showing his long fangs, the breath easing from

him in a sudden low growl. Slowly Corvo turned back to
Baradoc. Anger and admiration fought a battle across his
face. Baradoc guessed that the temper of this man was not to
be trusted. Anger and drink might spur his recklessness and
he might risk all. The thrown axe could take Lerg first and the
sword himself afterward. Few along Britain's coast had not
heard of Corvo and his reckless courage.

Suddenly Corvo gave a loud laugh, spun the axe again into
the air, caught it and said, "Bacchus is on your side, lad. The
drink runs smoothly in me and your daring teases my
humour. Take your pony. That marks the two of us as
thieves. But since you must know who I am, it is just that I
should know who you are."

"I am Baradoc, son of a chief of the Dumnonii. I travel far
westward beyond the Tamarus River and for this need the
pony."

"Which you now have got. Aye, I know your country and
have sailed beyond it, pass the Blessed Isles, where the
natives eat only fish and seabirds and their women have scaly
tails and from the rocks sing songs of love to tempt wife-
and-sweetheart-hungry crews. So, what think you of the
great Corvo now you have spoken face to face with him?"

Baradoc said, "First, that it is well that you were no Saxon
for I would have put the hound at your throat long since. I
hate them all."

Corvo laughed. "Aye, and so do I for they are land-
grabbing coast-crawlers that risk the sea only on summer
waters. Now, answer—what think you of black-skinned
Corvo?"

For a moment Baradoc hesitated, then with a frank grin
said, "That he is a man with a dark skin and a darker
reputation, but that there is a goodness in him which comes
not from drinking mead."

Corvo shook his head. "Two horns less of mead or two
more and I would have chopped you and the horse for
dogmeat and forced your great hound to eat it. Now go, lad,
before my gentle humour leaves me." He stepped back off
the path and made way for Baradoc to pass.

Baradoc, knowing there was no certainty that the man

would not send a party after him, led the pony quickly up the rough track through the woods to return to Tia. But when he got back to her he knew that he would say nothing of his meeting with Corvo. What she did not know of the dangers around them could not upset her. As he marched, he recalled the many tales that were told in the country about the man. It was said that his mother had been an Aethiop slave of a wealthy British family near Lemanis who had been captured while a young girl by the sea raiders and taken to their country, where she had conceived Corvo by her master. As a youth Corvo had saved the life of his master and father, had been given his freedom and had thrown in his lot with the long-boat men. He called no man chief but, while he still lived, had grown into a legend.

Well . . . either from drink or some lingering goodness the man had attempted him no harm.

CHAPTER THREE

Hunter's Dream

THAT EVENING THEY MADE a start long before darkness came.
Baradoc gave Tia as reason for this that it was a bad part of
the country and the sooner they crossed it the better. It was on
the tip of Tia's tongue to point out that if this were so, surely
it would be better not to move until night came. Something in
Baradoc's manner made her hold back the words. She was no
fool. Not for a moment did she believe that he had found the
pony wandering loose in the river meadows. He had stolen it.
It was a sturdy pony with a mild nature and gentle manners,
placidly standing to be loaded with their two bundles slung as
saddle packs across its back by the hempen rope.

"When it gets dark," said Baradoc, "you can ride and we
shall journey faster."

Meaning, Tia knew, faster than if she were stumbling and
tripping along at the pony's heels in the dark. Well, why
should she grumble? The pony was strong and would take her
weight easily.

She said, "The pony should have a name now that it has
joined the party."

Baradoc, standing at the animal's head, ready to lead it
off, smiled and said, "Then, as you're going to ride it, you
name it."

"Well, she's red and gold, so it is no hard thing. She shall
be Sunset."

Baradoc nodded. "It's a good name. Come on, Sunset!"
He gave the halter he had made for the pony a jerk and began
to move off.

Without any sign or sound from Baradoc, Tia marked, Lerg and Cuna moved ahead of them swiftly and disappeared over the rocky bluff top that sheltered their camping place. Aesc dropped back at her heels, and Bran flapped lazily away out onto their left flank and was soon lost to sight.

They travelled for two hours and in all that time few words passed between them. Baradoc stayed at the head of the pony and Tia brought up the rear with Aesc. Their path lay through high woodlands which every few miles dropped into steep little valleys cut by narrow streams and rivers. Tia noticed that Baradoc kept their course as much as he could into the eye of the westering sun. North by west, away from the coast, that was the way to Aquae Sulis. At least, Tia—her memory now of Baradoc's map a confused one—hoped it was.

She walked behind Sunset, letting her thoughts roam idly, banishing them only when they turned to the cruel things that had happened to her brother and his wife and the villa and farm. The air grew chilly as the sun dropped and she pulled a fold of her mantle over her head because the breeze cut coldly around the nape of her neck where her hair had been shorn. Her rough hose, cross-gartered up her legs, were still slightly damp and the harsh material made her itch.

Ahead of her Baradoc halted the pony. She saw that he was looking at the loose sandy soil of the track they had been following through the trees. On his knees he examined the ground for a moment or two. Then he rose and led Sunset on. As she came to the spot Tia stopped and looked at the ground. Clear in an untouched part of the track was the imprint of a sandal. It was a man's heavy sandal from the depth of the print, the outer edges of the sole showing a rim of deep stud marks. In the center of the sole, studs which had been hammered into the leather made a pattern of five-pointed star in the sand. Well, that was not unusual; many sandals, for men and women, were often soled with fanciful stud patterns. But somehow she had the feeling that Baradoc's attention had quickened as he had examined the print. When he had risen he had glanced back at her and his tanned face had gone wooden, signalling emotion even as he sought to show no trace of it. Why did he have to be like that? she thought crossly. So self-important and secretive. If she let herself forget some of the nice things about him, she could easily bring herself to dislike him completely. Well, she supposed, some people were like that. They tried to make themselves impressive by keeping things to themselves. Something, she was sure, *had* happened when he had found Sunset. He had come back grim-faced and had just started packing up, hardly throwing her a word until they were ready to go. Well . . . if he thought she cared a fig he could go to Hades. She pushed all thought of him from her mind and began to think about Aquae Sulis and her uncle's villa . . . a lovely villa, full of treasures acquired by her uncle in his many campaigns all over the empire. Part of the covered walk beyond her room was an enclosed aviary, where he kept his collection of exotic birds. Having no children, he treated them as such so that they came to his hands to eat and their colours flashed through all the hues of the rainbow as they flighted free about the great courtyard when the weather was fine. . . . And the food at the villa! By the gods, it made her belly feel empty to think of it! And the soft, soft bed with the alabaster-carved lamp at its side!

Her left groin began to itch and she scratched at it, Aquae Sulis going from her mind. Fleas or lice for certain, no rough scrubbing with cold water killed them. Or maybe they had come from one of the dogs. Aesc was always scratching. Well, it was no good complaining. Baradoc would probably tell her that a flea had every right to take its living where it could.

Baradoc halted Sunset suddenly. Tia, engrossed with her thoughts, walked straight into the pony's hindquarters and was brought to the present by the sharp switch of its long tail against her face.

Without thought, she shouted, "Pluto take you! Why don't you give warning when you're going to stop?"

Baradoc turned, eyed her and said mildly, "Why don't you keep your eyes on where you're going instead of daydreaming along? And shout a little louder, then if there's anyone around they'll get a real chance of knowing we're here."

Cross with herself for her show of anger, Tia mumbled, "I'm sorry."

"That's all right." He chuckled. "Nobody likes walking into the backside of a horse." He patted Sunset's neck. "Luckily, she's good-tempered or she might have kicked out."

He began to rearrange the bundles on Sunset's back into a saddle pack.

Tia asked, "What now?"

"It's getting dark. It's better that you ride. Up you get."

He bent down and made a cup of his clasped hands for her to mount. Tia climbed onto Sunset and made herself as comfortable as she could with her legs dangling behind the bundles, her hands taking a loose loop of the halter. She looked down at Baradoc through the darkening gloom and said, "There was a print on the path some while ago. Does that mean someone is close ahead of us?"

"No," said Baradoc. "The print was not made today."

"I had a feeling the star pattern meant something to you."

"You're right. You have quick eyes. But for now, stop trying to read my thoughts and hang on tight." He moved forward and Sunset followed with Tia swaying on her back.

The next few hours were mild agony for Tia. Baradoc set a good pace. The going was rough, up and down the forest and valley tracks, with the occasional switch of a loose branch flicking across Tia's face so that she had to pull the cloak close about her head to protect herself. Within a mile the inner skin of her thighs was chafed, all feeling had been bumped out of her bottom, and her arms ached from hanging on to the halter.

When the moon rose, long past midnight, they stopped in a small clearing where years before the trees had been chopped down and the ruins of a woodman's hazel-latticed shelter still stood.

Baradoc helped Tia down from the pony. As she stood

bowlegged he smiled at her and said, "The stiffness will soon go. In a couple of days you will think nothing of it."

He took the cold deer tack from one of the bundles and the last of their cheese and wheat cake, and they ate, lying on the ground with their backs propped against a moss-covered fallen tree trunk.

He said, "There's no water nearby. But we'll drink at the next stream we cross." Then, as though she had asked him a direct question, he went on, "The star pattern comes from the sandal of one of the two who strung me up to the oak. He is of my tribe—my cousin—and journeys westward as I do. The other was a wanderer who had joined us. They could have killed me but that, because of the laws of our tribe, is forbidden to the wearer of the star sandals. So they strung me up to let death come without any dagger thrust."

"Why is it forbidden?"

"Because I am the seventh son of my father. The last son, too. None of my brothers is living. The gods will give no gifts, nor long years to any who kills, except in fair fight, the seventh son of a family. But to leave me to die was different." He grinned. "It's a nice point of morality. But when I reach home there will be a fair fight and a killing of my cousin—thanks to you."

"So, I save one life in order that another shall die."

"The gods have thrown their dice. They fell that way. The two ahead will soon take a different path from ours. I'll take you to your uncle and then my debt will be paid." He smiled and rubbed his hand over his beard-fuzzed chin. "Maybe your uncle will give me the use of his bathhouse and the loan of a razor to smooth my chin. With my people no man may grow a beard or long moustache until he is married."

"Is there a chosen girl in your tribe that you will marry?"

"No. My cousin and I were only twelve and gathering shellfish along the shore when we were taken by sea raiders and sold together as house slaves, first to a Phoenician trader and then to my master in Londinium, where he then lived."

"Your people must think you are dead."

"No—the word was passed many years ago. Nor did

either of us miss our freedom, for we are much alike in many ways and knew there was much to learn and a sheaf of years ahead.''

"But this cousin—"

"No more of him." Baradoc sat forward and tossed a piece of deer meat to Aesc.

Tia, not wishing to break their talk, said, "What are the girls of your tribe like?"

Baradoc laughed. "Like all other girls. Some fat, some thin. Some beautiful, some plain. At your age many of them are long married and having children. Sometimes I see in my mind's eye the girl I will marry."

"Tell me."

"How can I since the picture changes so often? Sometimes her hair is a dark flame, richer than the stag's coat when he stands in the full light of the morning sun. Sometimes it is blacker than the raven's wing spread against the year's first snows. And sometimes her skin is warm and polished, brown like a harvested hazelnut, or creamier than the finest goat's milk and blushing with the glow of a bright ember."

Tia teased him. "Spare me. I've had enough poetry."

"*Aie*, that is true. But there's always room in each day for a little—otherwise living is as flat as stale wine. We're not barbarians, my people. We have our songs and our stories, and there's not one of our kind who doesn't learn them from first talk and pass them on. So, even with death, they are not lost. Their magic cannot die so long as men have ears." He stood up, sucked noisily at a fragment of deer meat lodged in his teeth, and said, "It's time to move."

He turned away from her abruptly and went across to the woodman's shelter. He came back after a while, carrying an armful of bracken which he had found there, the remains of a rough bed. He bound it into a soft roll within their piece of fish netting and then wrapped it in her mantle to make a large, soft saddle. Without a word he helped her to mount.

Riding after him, Tia was touched by his rough, silent courtesy. Then, thinking of his dream of some girl waiting for him, she was amused that he had given no place in his

thoughts for a fair-haired girl like herself. Maybe there were
no fair-haired women in his tribe, but she doubted it.
Amongst the Britons of the south and east there were plenty.
Strange Baradoc, rough and kind, withdrawn one moment,
then easy with talk the next.

Early the next morning they made camp beyond the fringe
of the forest in a small willow grove on the edge of a clear
stream that flowed down from the distant line of the almost
treeless uplands which rose away to the north. They ate and
then slept while the dogs kept watch. When they woke,
Baradoc went down to one of the streams pools and with
willow stakes fixed their piece of net across the narrow gullet
through which the stream fed into the pool. Then he called to
her to help him, telling her to take off her long hose and
sandals, and roll up the skirt of her tunic and pin it tight with
her mother's brooch. Tia noticed that although he was concerned she should keep her leg hose dry, he seemed heedless
of wet or discomfort. He just walked into the water wearing
his leather short trews and his shirt. Rain or shine, wet or dry
seemed to make no difference to him. A few paces abreast
they waded up the pool, beating the surface with branches.
The trout and grayling in it went upstream to escape through
the gullet and some of them were entangled in the stretched
netting. Baradoc pulled them out, killed them and tossed
them onto the bank.

When they waded out together, Baradoc picked up the
fish, strung them on a slip of branch through their gills and
handed them to her, saying, "If you have not done it before,
you cut their heads off, slit them down the belly and shake or
scrape their innards out. The ones with the big fin on the back
are grayling and smell of dried thyme. The others are trout.
We'll eat them before we move off."

"Women's work, my lord." Tia said it with a straight
face.

Baradoc nodded, unsmiling. As Tia took her dagger and
started work, Baradoc went to one of their bundles and
ferreted about in the pile of old rags he had found in the

fishermen's hut. He sat down and laid out a long narrow piece of cloth before him.

Tia, her hands slimy and scale-covered as she gutted the fish, asked, "What are you doing?"

"Making a throwing sling. There are duck farther downstream which I can kill and Aesc will retrieve. The fish will serve us for today. The duck we can cook and carry for tomorrow."

He rolled the long ends of the cloth into thin grips, binding them with pieces of catgut. The center of the cloth he thickened into a pad by sewing one on top of another three squares of extra cloth. Then he gathered a handful of smooth small stones from the stream verge.

Coming back to Tia, he dropped a stone into the padded loop of the sling and said, "Watch. The top of the far stake I set up for the net." He swung the sling gently in a circle at his side to get the feel of the weight of the stone. "It was with such as this that the first of my coutrymen over four hundred years ago gave a welcome to the Great Caesar." He whipped the sling around and let the stone fly.

"You missed," said Tia.

"I expected to. With a new sling one must get the feel and the balance."

He slung another stone and this time only narrowly missed the stake. With the third stone he hit it a hand's span from the top.

Tia clapped her slippery, fish-slimed hands and said mockingly, "O mighty Baradoc!"

Baradoc shook his head at her, smiling. "You should not be too pleased. When I come back you will have a duck to pluck and gut." He tucked the sling into his belt, thrust a handful of stones into the front of his shirt and walked off downstream with Aesc following him. Sunset, tethered by a long headrope to a willow, cropped at the young grass. Bran flew down from a willow perch and took one of the trout heads. Cuna lay sleeping in the sun, and Lerg lay on the ground, head raised, watching the direction in which Baradoc had disappeared.

When Tia had finished the fish, she covered them with leaves against the sun and then washed her hands in the stream. She took off her tunic and spread it in the sun to dry. Wrapping their woollen blanket about her, she wandered around the willow grove collecting dried wood for the fire, and gathered a small pile of dried leaves and grasses so that Baradoc should have tinder for starting a flame.

Half a mile downstream Baradoc crouched, hidden in the rushes with Aesc lying at his side. The river was broader here and ran in two channels around a long island fringed with mace reeds and low alder growths. Coming downstream, he had put up several pairs of mallard and teal, but with no chance of hitting them. This was the courting and mating season and he guessed that the island would be a favourite nesting place, for the weed-thick shallows around it made good feeding grounds. He and Aesc crouched, still and watchful, hidden in the rushes. A dog otter came upstream, rolled like a porpoise, sun and water silvering its flanks, and dived to appear in a few moments with a large trout in its forepaws. It lay on its back and let the current drift it downstream while it ate the trout. Beyond the river and the far grassland, the forest trees rose in long swelling waves of changing greens. Distantly, above the farther tree crests, Baradoc marked a thin plume of blue smoke coming from some solitary fire. He guessed it to be some hours' march away. Now and again the smoke thickened to a dark, breeze-ragged plume. Whoever tended it, he thought, was well armed or foolish. These days men and women held close to their homesteads or villages for safety. The forest held only the spoiled or the spoilers. The dark face of Corvo came back to him and with it a quick stir of concern about Tia. He decided that if no flighting duck came in soon, or mating pair appeared from the island reeds, he would go back. Not even Lerg could protect her against some odds.

He smiled to himself as he thought of the way she teased him now about "women's work" and the flashes of angry spirit she showed from time to time. He guessed that she must long for the security and comfort of her uncle's villa at Aquae

Sulis. That was her kind of life. She had lived sheltered and lived soft, her family wealthy and with servants to come to her call for all her needs. In his time with his master he had known many such families and households. These Romans, most of whom had never seen Rome, lived in the dying radiance of the empire's glory and called this country their own. And so many of them, even now, did not understand that it had never truly been their country and that even now the strong hand of another race was closing on it. Back in the east, now far beyond Tanatus and Rutupiae, spreading north and south of the Tamesis River, encircling Londinium, their eyes looking ever westward to the rich lands of the Atrebates, to Pontes, Calleva and Venta, were the Saxons, driving forward slowly, making serfs of common folk and culls of British chiefs, Romano-British merchants and town dignitaries, all those of power and wealth who had lived soft too long. Only among the men of the north and west on mountain and moor and wild clifftop and deep riverfronts the dream still lived of dominion over all the land. It lived with him, too, like a slow peatburn waiting only the right wind and the right season to start the hidden embers to flame.

Two heavy splashes brought his attention back to the river. A pair of mallards, duck and drake, had planed in, furrowing the water as they landed. Baradoc watched as the drake began to display to the duck. Beside him he felt the faint tremble of Aesc's body as the dog watched, too. Under the sun the drake shone as though it were a jewelled bird, yellow bill and glossy green head flashing as it bobbed and dipped, the great white and purple wing patches opening like a fan as it preened its wings and rattled its quills while the duck, head lowered, slid away pretending lack of interest, but never going far. Baradoc fingered the set of his stone in the sling and slowly stretched the length of cloth even, held in both hands at his side ready to throw when he rose. *Aie!* it was a pity to kill when the day was so bright and the birds moved to the dance of love. But an empty belly drove all thought of beauty and poetry from the mind. Taking a deep breath and holding it, Baradoc tensed himself for the move which would bring him upright with the long sling already circling to take the drake, his left hand already holding the second stone for the duck.

He stood swiftly, smoothly, and the slingstone hummed like a hornet as it sped across the water and took the drake with a vicious blow on the right shoulder, breaking the wing joint. Baradoc whirled the sling again and aimed at the duck, which with a beating of wings and strong thrusts of its webbed feet had jumped into the air for flight. The stone narrowly missed the duck, which disappeared up the river calling with alarm. By the island the drake circled helplessly on the water, thrusting uselessly with one wing to find flight. Aesc, knowing her moment, slid into the stream and swam to retrieve the bird. She brought it back to Baradoc, who killed it quickly with a twist of the head which broke its neck. He pushed it into the front of his undershirt, looped the sling over his belt and turned to leave his cover.

As he reached out his hand to take the fish spear which he had thrust into the mud of the bank a voice said, "Touch it—and you get this through your head."

Standing full in the center of the break in the reeds through which Baradoc had made his way to the river was a tall youth, dark-haired, his skin brown from dirt and sun, a straggling growth of beard covering his chin. He wore old, tattered woollen breeks to the knees, the rest of his legs bare. From his shoulders hung a brown cloak held tight about his waist with a broad leather belt from which hung a deep fringe of rusty, finely linked ring-mail to form a short skirt. On one side of the belt was looped an unscabbarded short broadsword, rusty and blunt-edged. Hanging from the other side was a leather quiver full of short arrows. His arms raised, he held a charged bow, the arrow aimed at Baradoc. He was flanked on one side by a lank-haired young woman with a long, ill-humoured face, an old scar deeply marking her right cheek. She wore strings of coloured beads around her thin neck, the long loops falling across a dirty, ragged, long-sleeved white stole striped with red and green diagonal bands. At his other side stood another youth, who, small and sturdy, dressed in a belted tunic of furs, heavy sandals on his feet, carried a light throwing spear.

Baradoc, making no attempt to touch the fish spear, said calmly, "You need not hold the arrow on me. I mean harm to no one. I hunt and kill for the pot alone."

"You live around here?"

"No. I make my way west to join my people. I have been working up-country."

"You had a master there?"

"Aye. But he is now dead. He gave me my freedom."

The youth spat suddenly. "No masters are good. So you were a slave?"

"I was."

The young woman said impatiently, "Leave him, Atro. Take his spear and sling if you will." She laughed. "His clothes, too. And those good sandals and trews and the dagger at his belt. But leave him. We have better work at hand."

"Shut your mouth, Colta." Atro spoke roughly without looking at her. Then to Baradoc he said, "Come here."

Baradoc moved through the reeds onto the grass and Atro stood back from him, the arrow still levelled.

Colta said, "Now what is in your mind, Atro?"

"That we have to live. That he means nothing to us. That there is no tie between us except poverty. These days that tie is a cobweb broken by a breath. So"—his mouth twisted angrily—"he is a freed slave. But who should take his word for it? There are those in Clausentium and Venta who will buy without questions—and crop his ears to mark their property. Enghus, tie him."

But for the arrow tip a few feet from his head Baradoc would have made an attempt to escape. The iron-tipped arrow could not be denied. It would split his skull like an eggshell. Then the thought of Tia left alone stirred him to make a plea which came hard to his lips.

Baradoc said firmly, "Shared poverty holds no value these days. But we are of the same country and we have the same enemy. If you sell your own kind to slavery what can you expect for yourself when the new masters come? And come they will unless we hold together in a kinship bigger than this country has ever known since the old queen put Verulamium and Londinium to the sword and flame.''

Atro shook his head. ''Now you talk big and fancy. Such talk means nothing. Old kings and queens or new ones mean nothing. Today it is each for himself. Bind him, Enghus.''

Enghus, giggling, danced around behind Baradoc while Colta knelt to a travelling bundle that lay on the grass at her feet and brought out rope lengths. She handed these to Enghus. Then, taking his light spear, she pressed the point against Baradoc's neck, saying, ''Now, Big Talker of the good times to come, put your hands behind your back and stand calm.'' She scratched the tip of the spear lightly across the skin of his neck and laughed.

Baradoc put his hands behind him. Enghus bound them tight and with another cord roped his arms to his body, grunting as he jerked at the knots.

Atro lowered his bow and withdrew the arrow. He reached forward and jerked the dead mallard from the inside of Baradoc's shirt and tossed it to Colta.

''Take it. Tonight you shall roast it at the shrine keeper's fire. Eh, Enghus?''

Enghus gave a giggle of pleasure and, jerking his head to the west, said, ''But not until we have roasted him first to make him sing. The old fool, he burns his garden weeds, filling the sky with smoke as though the whole world moved at peace.'' Then he shook his spear and pleaded, ''But first, Brother Atro, promise, let me tease him a little with this to put him in the way of true speaking before the fire touches him.''

Atro laughed. ''Maybe, Enghus, maybe. Just to make you happy, my little bloodthirsty brother.'' Then, to Baradoc, he went on calmly as though there could be no hard feelings between them, ''Enghus is my brother. When he was born the gods touched him with a happy madness. Even when he feels like weeping he laughs. He laughs at his own pain and the pain of all others. Now, since you know us all, tell us your name.''

"My name is Baradoc."

Colta, now holding the fish spear, came up to him and touched his cheek and gave a sudden sharp tug to the beard growth on his chin. "If you were my slave I would beat you daily to take that proud look from your face."

"Enough of that," said Atro. "We move." Then looking around, he asked, "Where is the dog?"

Enghus said, "It moved off a while ago. And such a pretty colour. I could have made myself a hood from its skin and a belt pouch from its ears." He laughed to himself, jerking his head up and down.

Atro said to Baradoc, "Call the dog."

Baradoc shook his head. "It would not come. It is a stray that joined me only this morning. But someone has trained it well."

"So I saw when it took the duck. A dog like that could have been useful."

Baradoc shrugged his shoulders and made no answer. Atro turned abruptly away and began to walk down the riverbank. Before Baradoc could move he was pricked none too lightly from behind with the point of Enghus's spear. He began to follow Atro with Enghus giggling behind him.

Baradoc knew that Aesc would return to Tia. What she would do now that she was alone he could not guess. But one thing was certain. If he did not manage to escape from this ragged, broken-down band soon and return to find her, the dogs would leave her after a few days and come seeking him. Beyond that point he shut his mind to her fate.

Ahead of him Atro marched now with his bow slung over his shoulder, the ring-mail skirt swinging about his thighs, the rusty links making a soft whispering music, the battered old broadsword bumping at his side. The sword was Roman and uncared for, and the bow, an old one, but serviceable still, was of the kind which in the old days the Parthian auxiliaries had used, cunningly made of alternate strips of wood and bone. To have been taken by these wanderers touched his pride sharply, but he could understand how it had happened. When a man hunted all his mind was on his quarry. Lost in a hunter's dream, he had crouched in the reeds, all his senses concentrating toward the moment of the kill, and had allowed Atro to move up behind him.

When Aesc returned, still damp from the river, Tia expected Baradoc soon to follow. But time passed and he did not appear. She got up, walked out of the willows and found a rise in the ground where she could look down the river. There was no sign of Baradoc. She went back and carried on with the work she had taken in hand, which was to repair a large slit in one of the bundle cloths made by a broken branch or thorns during the previous night's march. But when Baradoc still did not appear, she began to grow uneasy and troubled. For the first time the black thought touched her that something might have happened to him.

Almost as though this fear, newborn in her, had been some mysteriously understood signal for which the dogs were waiting, she heard Aesc whine. She looked up from her sewing.

Lerg had risen and stood near her, his head low, the grey-brown eyes full on her. Aesc moved restlessly to and fro behind Lerg, whining gently, while Cuna lay still on the ground, his eyes watching the other dogs as though he were trying to read the meaning of their change of mood. Only Sunset seemed untouched. Tethered to a slim willow trunk on a lengthened headrope, she cropped the sweet green grass, flicking her golden tail occasionally against the flies. Tia saw that Bran had flown down to the ground and sat now on an old molehill, plumage fluffed out raggedly, head and beak drawn down between his shoulders, a picture—so her imagination prompted—of unhappiness.

Resolutely, pushing her fears from her, she went on with her work. Almost as though in protest Aesc gave a sharp bark and moved to the edge of the willow glade and back.

Tia went out of the willows and began to walk down the river. Aesc ran ahead of her, nose to the ground, and she turned to see that Lerg and Cuna were following her. She walked a couple of bowshots but could find no sign of Baradoc. When she turned back the dogs came with her reluctantly.

In the willows, she stood undecided for a while. The afternoon was wearing away. The conviction came strongly to her that something *had* happened to Baradoc. Without him she would never get safely to Aquae Sulis. The selfish thought made her immediately angry. Baradoc might be in real trouble . . . even dead—and she thought only of herself. She had to find him. Suddenly she decided that there was no sense in just staying in the glade while fears mounted in her.

She began to pack up the camp. It took her some time to stow all their possessions and lash the bundles across Sunset. As she did so Aesc and Cuna fretted around her, but she threw them a sharp word and quieted them. When, finally, she led the pony out of the willows Lerg ranged himself at her side and Aesc, followed by Cuna, ran ahead. Tia followed the line which Aesc took.

Half an hour later Aesc stopped at the break in the river reeds where Baradoc had taken the mallard drake. Tia saw at once in the muddy soil the marks of footprints.

As Aesc sat whining in front of her she waved the dog on. Aesc, head low, began to move down the riverbank. There was no doubt in Tia's mind that the bitch was following Baradoc's scent. A little later she found proof that she was following Baradoc.

She stood on a sandy beach where the stream shallowed to a ford. In the damp sand at the edge of the water were the clear marks of the studded sandals that Baradoc wore. With them, some confused and some clear, were the marks of other prints, though she could not decide by how many people they had been made.

Across the river was a narrow strip of wild meadow and sedge land from which rose great terraces of dark forest.

Leading the pony, Tia forded the river, which nowhere came more than knee-high. Cuna alone had to swim in places. On the far bank were more confused prints.

Aesc, head lowered, was already moving across the marshy meadow toward the woods. As Tia followed, Bran came flying up from behind her and with a sharp *cark-cark* beat his way over the trees and disappeared.

The climb through the forest was hard and slow going. Aesc was clearly following a trail which was fresh. Looking up at the sun, Tia realized that the afternoon was fast wearing away. The thought of the coming darkness frightened her. And the thought that she might never see Baradoc again, perhaps never get to Aquae Sulis, put a dryness in her throat and a weakness in her body that made her despise herself. Silently she cursed herself for her weakness and her selfishness, for she knew that the strongest desire in her was to get safely to Aquae Sulis. If she could have been magically spirited there now, leaving Baradoc to whatever was to be, what would she have decided? she wondered. She escaped answer by cursing, stringing together all the old army oaths she could remember—and finding a strong comfort in them.

She stopped twice to drink at small streams and to rest herself. Her arm ached from tugging and leading Sunset, who faced some of the thickets reluctantly, and there was now a persistent nagging pain in her right thigh where she had slipped and twisted her leg.

The sun was treetop low in the sky when Aesc, who had disappeared ahead, came back and lay down on the track before her, panting, her long tongue lolling over the side of her jaws. She waved the dog on, but Aesc refused to move.

Puzzled, Tia looked ahead along the narrow trail they were following. The trees had begun to thin a little. Twenty or thirty paces ahead the track disappeared over a thicket-crested outcrop of stony ground. Looking up, Tia realized that the tall plume of smoke which now and again she had glimpsed in her march was very close. As her eyes came back from the smoke, Lerg, who had never gone more than a couple of paces ahead of her so far, slowly began to walk away on his own. When he reached the bottom of the rocky rise, he stopped and sat back on his haunches.

Tia hitched Sunset's halter around a branch and walked forward. Neither Aesc nor Cuna made any move to follow her. The behaviour of the dogs puzzled her, yet at the same time there was a strange comfort in it. She had a feeling that they knew—even Cuna—what lay ahead and, by their actions, obeyed some sure instinct. When she was with Lerg she stopped and looked back. Aesc and Cuna lay on the ground close to Sunset, who was cropping at the low leafy branches of a tree. Bran, who had shown himself only now and again during the march, dropped through the trees and settled on the ground near the dogs and began to peck at the grit of the narrow track.

Tia had an uncanny feeling that the dogs and Bran now waited on her, that in some way they were all linked in an understanding into which she could and must enter. Between them and Baradoc, she knew, there was always a silent flow of knowledge and command which linked them magically even when they were not in sight of one another.

At this moment from beyond the outcrop there came a high half groan, half scream of pain that was followed by a burst of almost demoniac, giggling laughter. Lerg's hackles stiffened and the long ridge of his back was furrowed with the slow rise of his pelt.

As fresh laughter and a cackling of voices came from beyond the ridge, Tia, full of fear, but refusing to let it hold her, began to move forward.

CHAPTER FOUR

The Keeper Of The Shrine

BARADOC LAY on the ground on his side. A few feet behind
him were the nearest trees. His hands were still tied
behind him but now, too, his legs were bound at the ankles.
Before him, sloping in a shallow bowl, was a clearing which
rose on the far side to a crescent-shaped ridge with large rock
outcrops showing through a growth of brooms, gorse, and
brier tangles. At the foot of this ridge, and cut into it, was a
narrow doorway framed on either side by upright slabs of
stone with a thick wooden crosspiece at the top. In the center
of the clearing a large patch of ground had been cleared and
cultivated, the dark earth now marked with new bean growth,
rows of young cabbages, a line of vines, a patch of young
barley and a bed of glossy green-spiked spring onions.
Beyond the garden an apple and a fig tree stood close to a
low-roofed, long wooden-framed hut, the roof and sides
thatched with rush bundles. At one end of the hut was a small
wattle enclosure in which a cock and half a dozen hens
foraged. Nearer Baradoc a small spring welled from the
ground and ran in a thin rill through a marshy channel to the
far slope of the forest. Between the stream and the hut a fire
burned, a fire piled now with new kindling so that the fresh
flames leapt from it and the blazing wood crackled and spat
sparks and black ash that rose in the air like a cloud of flies.
Close to the fire stood Atro and Colta, each holding an arm of
a tall, thin-bodied old man whose long, girdled brown robe
had been stripped from the top half of his body. Standing in
front of the old man was Enghus, holding the light spear.
Already he had scored the man's bare chest with the spear-

53

point and now he thrust the spearhead almost fully into the man's left hip. Both arms already ran with blood from previous thrusts.

Baradoc watched, sickened and angry with disgust, as Colta, striking the old man's face with her fist, spat at him, shouting, "You old fool—talk!"

Enghus raised the spear to thrust again, crying, "Yes, talk, talk, talk! Where is the treasure?"

Atro swung his free hand and sent Enghus spinning away. "Enough, Enghus! Enough!" Then to the old man he said, "Listen, Father, be sensible and talk, and then we will leave you in peace. But if you don't we will surely kill you." He reached out, took the old man's long dark beard in his hand and jerked his head up. "Talk! V here is the treasure?"

Baradoc saw the slow bracing movement of the man's thin, bony shoulders as he drew breath. His dark eyes opened and he stared at Atro and his lean, weather-bitten face was stony with stubbornness. He said nothing.

Enghus lowered the spearpoint and held it against the old man's belly. "Let me, Atro. Let me!"

Atro shook his head. "No, he's had his chance. But now—you shall make him talk." He laughed gently. "Roast him a little. That'll start his tongue to wag."

"Yes, yes, roast him a little. . . ." Enghus dropped his spear and began to dance around, beating his hands in joy, like an excited child, chanting, "Roast him! Toast him! That'll make his old tongue waggle!"

At this moment, long before he caught the downwind scent of the hound, Baradoc knew that Lerg was close to him. And with Lerg would be the others . . . yes, even Tia, for he knew the dogs would never have left her so soon. He slowly turned his head and looked back at the near trees. The group around the old man were too busy with their own business to pay any attention to him now.

Enghus had taken a dry branch and was holding it in the fire, the end of it flaming in a great yellow-and-blue tongue. He whipped it from the fire and swung it around to kill the flame and fan the thick end into a living red coal. The

moment it glowed well Enghus danced in, cackling with
delight, and drew the red end slowly across the old man's
chest. The old man, his body jerking violently, threw his
head back and screamed, the echoes of his cry beating back
from the surrounding woods, setting pigeons flighting from
the far treetops.

Behind him on the fringe of the trees Baradoc heard the
shaking of a bush and a quick breathing as someone moved
behind it. Slowly he turned his head. Momentarily the sunlight flashed on a scrap of fair hair. As another scream from
the old man rang in his ears, Baradoc sat up so that the top
half of his body would cover any approach from behind. All
he wanted now was to feel the dagger thrust at the thongs of
his wrists behind him, and then to have the dagger in his free
hands to slash his ankle bonds.

The old man screamed again. Baradoc watched Atro and
Colta supporting the long, thin frame and Enghus dancing
back to the fire to heat up the brand for a fresh assault. Anger
burned in him at the wanton savagery of the three. Then he
felt his left arm grasped, heard Tia's heavy breathing and
took the warm body smell of her into his nostrils. He strained
at his wrists to stretch the thongs tight as, lying full length,
hidden behind him, she sawed at them with her small dagger. When they came free, he said quietly, "Stay where you
are." He took the dagger from her and brought his right hand
around quickly and began to cut away at his ankle bonds.

Across the clearing Enghus stepped back from the fire,
whirling his brand to make it glow. Colta was pulling at the
old man's beard while Atro supported him as his legs sagged.
The light spear lay on the ground, unheeded. Atro's bow was
slung across his back, the quiver and broadsword hanging at
his belt.

Baradoc's ankle binds came free. Dagger in hand, he
began to rise swiftly. The movement caught Atro's eye. He
turned full toward Baradoc, let out a loud warning cry, and
began to fumble to free his bow from his back.

Through Tia raced a sudden surge of fear as she saw Atro
beginning to unship his bow as Baradoc ran across the clear-

ing. Then she heard the racing Baradoc shout, *"Saheer! Aie! Saheer!"*

Lerg leapt from the thicket behind her and with him went Aesc and Cuna. Before Baradoc could reach the group at the fire, Lerg was past him and leaping at Atro as the youth freed his bow. They went over in a roaring, growling mêlée of arms and legs and twisting grey body. A long shriek of pain cut through the air. Colta let go of the old man and he fell to the ground. Enghus threw his burning brand at Aesc as the dog rushed in and bit and snapped at his legs as he tried to reach his light spear. Colta raised her fish spear and ran at Baradoc, but before she could reach him Bran dropped from above in a threshing at her eyes. Colta screamed, dropped the spear and ran for the woods, covering her face with spread hands. Enghus ran after her, away from the snapping, savage attack of Aesc and Cuna, abandoning hope of gaining his spear.

Baradoc shouted to Lerg and the dog drew back from the fallen Atro. Baradoc picked up the light spear and stood over him as Colta and Enghus disappeared in the woods. Tia ran forward and, hardly knowing she was doing it, pulled the old man away from where he had fallen so close to the fire that the hood of his gown was burning. She beat out the flames with her hands.

Baradoc stood over the fallen Atro, spear and dagger in hand. Blood was pouring from the side of the youth's neck where Lerg had taken him.

"Make one move," said Baradoc, "and I'll put the hound on you." Spear poised for action, he bent down and picked up the Parthian bow and threw it behind him. Grimly, he said, "Stand up and keep facing me."

Holding his hand to his neck, Atro rose to his feet. Then with a slow shrug of his shoulders, he smiled and said, "What need is there for all this? The talk of selling you as a slave was not in earnest. You should join us. Together nobody could face us." He nodded toward the old man. "There is treasure here. Everyone around knows it. We have only to make him speak and then share it."

Baradoc pressed the point of the spear against Atro's breast, pressed it hard so that it reached his skin and made him wince away. "Undo your belt and let it drop. And give me no more talk. After all I've seen—a wrong word could yet move me to kill."

Slowly Atro brought his hands to his belt buckle. The belt fell to the ground, an arrow slipping from the quiver, the heavy sword ringing against the stones.

"Now go," said Baradoc harshly. "And remember this—you are marked by me and by the hound. To see you again means a killing. Go!"

Atro, tight-lipped, faced him for a moment or two and then turned and began to walk to the trees. Behind him stalked Lerg and when Atro passed into the trees the hound still went with him.

They took the old man into his hut, stripped the gown from him and laid him on his bed, which was made of long, rough-hewn boards without over- or undercoverings. He lay. there, breathing faintly, making no move, his eyes shut.

Baradoc nodded to an earthenware jar by the door. "Get some water. Wash his spear wounds and find some cloths to bind them. Don't touch the burns." He went out of the hut, gathered up all the weapons and brought them back. Then, carrying only the light spear, he went toward the low crest above the hillside doorway.

Tia filled the jar with water. As she did so she noticed that Aesc and Cuna had stationed themselves on the forest edge of the clearing. Back in the hut she washed the old man's wounds and bound them as well as she could with some of the rags that Baradoc had found in the fishermen's hut. Since the rags were dirty she tore strips from her short undershift, which was reasonably clean, to go next to the wounds. When the dressings were done she made a pillow from the old man's gown, propped his head up and fed water to him from her beaker. Eyes closed, he drank a little and groaned sharply when her arm touched one of his burns.

Baradoc came back after a while carrying two handfuls of

leaves and herbs. With a stone he began to pound some of them into a pulp on a platter and said, "There's a hen run at the side of the hut. Get some eggs." He said it without looking at her, pounding away at the leaves. The old man was all his concern. She found four eggs in a bracken nest in a corner of the run and brought them back. She saw that Lerg had returned.

Baradoc broke the eggs over the pulpy herb mass and stirred them into it to make a paste. When the paste was well mixed he took handfuls of it and spread it over the old man's chest burns. Although he did it gently the old man twitched and groaned at his touch.

Over his shoulder Baradoc said, "Find something to cover him." Except for a rough loin wrapping, the old man had been naked under his rough woollen robe.

"There's nothing here. I'll have to fetch Sunset."

"Then get her. There's no danger. They won't be back to face Lerg."

As she left the clearing, Lerg rose and went with her without any sign or word.

When she came back with Sunset she unloaded the two panniers and freed her short mantle from the saddle rope. In the hut she spread the mantle over the old man, covering him just short of the lowest burn on his chest.

Baradoc said, "We must take turns to watch him. He's not in his proper mind and may try to pull the salves away."

"How do you know about such things?"

"By not running away from my master. From his words and from his books. And much from my own kind. Although the old man burns, water will not put out his fire. It is the air which gives us life that feeds a fire. The burns must not be allowed to breathe. Did you not know this?" He looked up at her and then, unexpectedly, smiled.

"There are many things I don't know. It seems there is much that is missing in me."

Baradoc stood up. "But much that I am grateful for. You can be fearful but not lose your courage. I owe you a life already. And now I owe you my liberty. Those devils would have sold me to slavery." He reached out, took her hand and held it between the palms of his own, pressing it firmly.

"Why do you do that?"

"As a sign. While we stay together nobody can harm you until my own power is broken." Releasing her hands, he grinned. "You came to me here, and I am free. Because of you, too, the old man lives and will live."

Tia shook her head. "I came because the dogs brought me."

"No. Without them you would have found a way. There is the mark on you. I know it and the beasts know it. They read your thoughts and know your heart. Before we reach Aquae Sulis I will teach you how to speak to them without words. Already the gift is in you. Now"—he turned to the hut door—"let us get unpacked and settled in. It will be many, many days before we can safely leave the old man to himself."

"Many days?"

Baradoc laughed. "Now your face grows as long as Sunset's. Do you think the old man will recover by tomorrow? He will be long on his couch and longer before he can work his garden and care for himself and his shrine."

"But that means—" Tia broke off suddenly, ashamed of her own selfishness.

Baradoc said easily, "Aquae Sulis will not run away. A little more rough living will make it seem like paradise. But if you wish you are free to go and to take Sunset with you."

Tia's face stiffened angrily. Then putting out her hand, she said, "This hand you took in gratitude has an itch to smack your face!"

Baradoc shrugged his shoulders. "Good. That means you will stay. Now, let us get things in order." He laughed, took her arm and tugged her gently toward the door, saying, "You have forgotten to bring the fish and I have lost the duck you were going to pluck. We will wring the neck of a hen. The old man will be better for a good broth to help him heal."

Looking back at the old man, Tia said, "He's very old. Might he not die from the burns?"

"He is old, yes. Just skin and bone. But he will not die."

"How can you know that?"

"Because we are here. Because the gods, yours and mine—*aie*, and his—joined together to weave the pattern that way. Now, come and I'll show you how to twist a hen's neck."

For the next few hours as the tree shadows lengthened across the clearing they were both busy. Baradoc killed the hen and Tia sat outside the hut and plucked it. The dogs drew back to the fire, and Sunset was tied on a long halter to one corner of the hut. Baradoc carried all their belongings inside and emptied the bundles. He made up two rough beds on the floor with cut rushes from a pile he had found behind the hut. Tia's bed was at the far end of the hut, next to the adjoining fowl run. Baradoc set his just inside the low doorway. All the arms were laid out in readiness. Atro and the others, Baradoc guessed, would not come back. By the time they had found new weapons their minds would be set to fresh mischief.

Sword in hand, standing over the old man, he looked at the wall above the bed. Hanging there was a rough tablet made of three pieces of board held in a frame. Painted crudely on it was the portrait of a beardless young man with a halo around his head. Above his head was the Christian Chi-Rho monogram. The shrine in the hillside was a Christian one, and the old man its keeper. There were many now in Britain who held to the new religion, worshipping the Nazarene and his Holy Father. Baradoc felt that it was the religion of slaves, no matter what its virtues. For him the gods of his people could never be replaced. Anyway, the world and the hereafter were wide and big enough for all religions.

He went out and began to help Tia around the fire with the cooking of their meal. They ate it in the fading light outside the hut doorway. Tia fed the old man with some broth, but he took little, most of it spilling down his chin and neck, matting his beard so that she had to wash it clean afterward.

Coming back to Baradoc and sitting cross-legged on the grass near him, watching the hawking flight of martins across the darkening clearing, the sky paling to a faint marigold

glow from the dropping sun, she said, "Why did they treat
the old man so badly?"

"Because they believed he had a great treasure hidden
here."

"Has he?"

"Who knows? He is a Christian shrine keeper. A holy
man. The country around will know him. He probably wan-
ders about preaching. His kind are always talking of laying
up treasures in heaven. Simple people get things mixed in
their minds." He took a chicken leg from his platter, chewed
at it until it was near clean and then tossed it to Cuna.

They went to bed by the light of the small length of tallow
candle which Baradoc had found in the fisherman's hut.
Lying in the darkness, Tia now and again heard the old man
moan, and from time to time he talked to himself briefly in
some language she could not understand. The dogs slept
outside. Once in the night she woke to hear the far-off howl
of a wolf. In the silence that followed there came the restless
padding of one of the dogs circling the clearing. There was no
fear in her. The hut around her seemed a fortress. Baradoc
guarded the door and the dogs stood sentinel. She drifted into
sleep again.

She woke to the sound of the cock crowing in the hen run.
First light came weakly through the open door. She got up
and ran her hands through her hair. The old man slept, and his
breathing seemed easier. Baradoc's bed was empty.

She went out and saw that only Cuna remained in the
clearing. He trotted behind her as she went to the spring and
washed herself. The fire, she noticed, had been banked with
new kindling. The wood was dry and burned low and bright
with little smoke. She collected eggs from the run, filled the
little cauldron with water and set it by the fire to have warmer
water to dress the old man's wounds. Some of the herb
plasters on his chest had cracked and fallen away in the night.
Baradoc would have to renew them and would need the eggs.
She would also hard-boil some for themselves. In the hut she
tidied their beds and then began to take stock of the place for
the first time with real attention.

It was poorly furnished but clean. A hazel-twig broom for

brushing the floor stood inside the door. On a shelf rested the few simple items of the shrine keeper's crockery and earthenware. There was also a big bronze skillet pan. In one of the earthenware jars she found three round goats' cheeses. Another robe like the one the keeper wore hung from a peg at the end of the bed, but it was much cleaner and the edges were trimmed with the white fur of winter hares. The grinding quern stood on the floor in a corner. Looking at it, she was taken back to the great kitchen of her brother's villa. For a moment a pang of grief touched her, but she pushed it away.

She stood in front of the bed and looked down at the shrine keeper. Outside, the forest was stirring with birdcalls. Blackbird and thrush she could pick out but none of the others. Baradoc, she guessed, would know them all. The sunlight, strengthening, flooded through the door and lit up the painting over the bed. She had seen many such portraits and mosaics in the houses of some of the friends of her brother. The young face with the shining halo had a tranquil yet slightly sad expression. Although none of her family had adopted the new Christian faith, she had sat often through the talk of her brother with others when they had discussed religion and had been without real interest. In fact, it seemed to her now, she had sat or walked or idled through many times, great stretches of her life, without interest in anything except herself and her pleasures.

The old man stirred and she saw that his eyes were open. For a moment the shadow of a smile touched his lips. With a slow movement he raised a hand. She took it gently in hers and felt his grasp tighten.

He said hoarsely, "You are?"

"Gratia."

"And the other?"

"Baradoc."

"In my memory their sounds are even joined . . . like the links of a golden chain. . . ." His voice faded and his eyes closed. Tia lowered his hand and turned away.

When Baradoc came back he brought with him, slung over

his shoulders, a young roebuck which Aesc had hunted downwind into the reach of Lerg, who had caught and pulled it down, holding it until his master had come to kill it with a spear thrust to the heart. In his tunic front he had a store of fungi and roots which he had gathered on the way back. As he gralloched and skinned the deer, he nodded at the fungi and roots and said, "There's little in the old man's vegetable patch yet ready for pulling. Today I will show you where to find the fungi and roots which are good to thicken broth. We must make a hanging bag for the meat we do not eat today. Even so"—he grinned—"a few bluebottles will find a way in, but their eggs can be washed away."

Tia made a grimace of disgust. "You say that to turn my stomach. And so you do."

Baradoc shook his head. "There's much that goes into a rich man's kitchen would turn anyone's belly. But at table it is eaten with pleasure. How is the old man?"

"He sleeps. But for a moment he came back and asked our names. I have dressed his wounds, but some of the plasters have fallen away."

"When this is done I'll make fresh salves." Baradoc went on cutting up the carcass. He threw each dog a portion, and each dog carried its share apart and fell to eating.

So began the run of their days in the clearing. Baradoc hunted when their meat and game fell low, and Tia learned the herbs for the plasters and tended to the old man's burns and wounds. She cooked and looked after the poultry, opening their run in the morning and closing them in at night. Between them, with an old wooden hoe and a rusty mattock, they kept the weeds from the garden, and all day long and at night the dogs watched and roamed the edge of the forest. Bran, who was sociable only when he could find no food for himself, was seldom seen but never far away. Nobody now came to make offerings at the shrine or to bring small gifts to its keeper. The nearest homestead and village were some miles away. Honest people hugged their own hearths and stayed together for safety.

Tia learned fast how to broil and roast and baste meat with

wild-boar fat (a young sow of that year's early farrowing, run hard by the dogs, had been killed with two bow shots from Baradoc) and to mill the corn between the quern stones and to bake the bread in the small stone oven Baradoc built and over which the hot fire embers were scooped and piled, using flat slabs of shale for shovels. She learned to ignore the weather, going lightly clad in the sun and meeting the rain with indifference if her work took her into it, finding the best way to dry wet clothes was to go on wearing them.

Also, and this pleased her most, she began to learn how to talk to the dogs without word or look. As Baradoc had guessed, there was in her a little, waiting for growth, of the magic he commanded so easily. She learned how, without seeing Cuna, Aesc or Lerg, though they rested nearby on the forest edge, to put one of them into her mind like a small picture. Then with a concentration, almost like holding her breath until she would choke, though she went on breathing easily, she would force herself into her own mind, making a picture of herself within herself, and there give a silent word of command or direction. Not always it worked, but as the days went by it became easier and more often successful and she knew that with practice she would soon always be able to reach them. But with Bran she could do nothing, though Baradoc could. When she questioned this he laughed and told her that Bran, named after one of his people's gods, would serve a woman only when it suited him and that was not often in simple day-by-day matters.

With each day, too, the old shrine keeper grew better, but it was to be seven days before he could safely take to his feet. For those first days Tia nursed him and helped him with his washing and toilet as if he were a baby, often wondering to herself that she could do this, the work of the lowest slave or infirmary servant. But slowly she came to think it of no more account than serving his broth or changing the rushes on his bed boards. The old man, she guessed, however, had a shame from this. Although he was clear in his head now, he spoke little, withdrawn from them both into some other world, as though to escape the humiliation his body put on him. Yet each night as Tia settled him comfortably for sleep, he would take her hand and squeeze it gently, then turn his head from her. With Baradoc, when Tia was not there, he was a little freer and made his thanks for all they had done and were doing, and told his name, saying, "Asimus is my name. Not Father or Brother, but a simple servant of our Lord Jesus Christ, who sent you to me, knowing I waited for you but"—he smiled faintly—"choosing the moment of your coming to remind me of my own weakness and pride."

On their first day Baradoc and Tia had gone into the shrine. Beyond the rough stone-and-wood door with a plaited hanging rush curtain covering the entrance was a small natural cave which ran a few yards back into the hillside. Hanging from the rock face at the end of the cave was a long wooden cross. Below it stood a table made from a wide slab of loose rock raised on two rough boulders at either end. Worn in the loose earth of the floor before this simple altar were two shallow depressions where Asimus and his visitors had knelt for prayer. On the table itself was an odd collection of gifts and tokens which had been placed there in thanksgiving: a string of blown birds' eggs, bronze and iron nails, a folded linen napkin, a small wooden model of a farm cart drawn by two yoked oxen, a little statuette of an angel made from beaten lead, some curiously shaped stones with coloured veins of quartz and minerals running through them, a bunch of dried thistle heads, an old slave whip, the worn leather thong tails spiked with rusty iron studs, their points broken and blunted, some cheap wire bracelets and bead rings . . . a dusty, odd collection but each object, Baradoc guessed, symbolizing or commemorating some accident or turning point in the lives of the givers which had brought or linked them with the worship of the Christian god. So, too, did his people lay their like tokens before the gods as gifts and the value of the gift lay not in itself but in the heart of the giver and in the all-knowing mind of the god.

Tia said, "It's cold in here."

"True, were it not a shrine it would make a good place to hang our meat."

Shocked, Tia said, "You shouldn't say that."

"Why not? 'Tis but the truth."

"But this is a holy place."

"Then there is room for truth here." He smiled. "Now—if I *were* to hang the meat here then there would be blasphemy, and that I offer to no god, mine or any other's."

At the beginning of their second week Tia woke one morning to find Baradoc already away hunting, for their store of meat had grown low. She washed herself at the spring and then went to the fire and began to warm up some broth for Asimus's breakfast. Squatting on her heels by the fire as she watched the pot, she listened to the steady sawing notes of a chiffchaff coming from the top of a tree beyond the clearing. With help from Baradoc she was now coming to know more and more of the birdsongs and calls, and through him, too, her eyes were becoming sharp and observant. The way the wind swayed the tall grasses or the hanging branches of bushes she knew as natural, but any break or change in the rhythm awoke an instant awareness in her. She could pick up the overhead passage of a squirrel or the quiet foraging of Cuna in the sedges and rising bracken growths of the shrine hillside, and sometimes the overbowed tip of brier or hogweed where some harvest mouse or wren or blue tit swung unseen, searching for insects and grubs. Until now, it seemed to her, she had passed through life hardly aware of this ever-present stir and change of colour and shade, of animal and bird movement and the shifting cloud patterns.

Sitting now by the fire, the broth almost ready, she was suddenly aware that she was being watched from behind. But there was no fear in her. She turned her head and saw Asimus, his brown habit drawn closely about him, standing in the hut doorway, leaning a little sideways as he supported himself on a staff.

He smiled at her, waved her down as she started to rise, and then began to walk toward her, stiffly but steadily. He came and sat down near her, upwind of the thin fire smoke.

He said, "The smell of the broth gave strength to my legs."

"You should have let me bring it to you."

"No, it is time I began to fend for myself again."

Tia filled a bowl of broth for him. He held it in his hands, blowing at it for a while to cool it, and then began to sup with an old horn spoon which Tia had found in the hut.

He said, looking at his garden which they had tended, "The beans have grown, and the weeds are hoed . . . all while I have slept and dreamt and found strength. You and the young man have been good to me at a time when there was little goodness to hope for in this land. Is he your brother or perhaps bethrothed to you?"

Tia laughed. "Neither."

Asimus frowned a little. "There is no tie between you?"

"Only that we are now both making our way to the west. He goes back to his tribe and I to my uncle in Aquae Sulis." Without emotion, for the recent past was a memory now imprisoned as surely as a fly in amber in her mind, Tia went on to tell him what had happened to her and how she and Baradoc had met. She finished, "When we get to my uncle, he will go on to his own people. I shall never forget him and my uncle will reward him well. But there is nothing between us."

The old man shook his head. "You saved his life and now he guards you to your uncle. Such acts of charity put ties between people which can never be broken, neither by time nor distance. While I live there will be no day when my prayers will not include you both. Thus, you see"—he smiled gently and the dark eyes were soft in the bearded face— "you will always be linked together by me until the good Lord closes my days."

Made a little embarrassed and uncomfortable with this talk, Tia asked, "Is it true that you have treasure hidden here?"

The old man finished his broth, set the bowl down and then, shaking his head at her move to help him, rose awkwardly to his feet with the help of his staff. He looked down at her, one hand slowly teasing his beard, and there was a slow twinkle in his eyes.

"You are a practical, forthright young woman. That is there for all to see. So to talk in riddles to you would make you perhaps impatient. Each day that God gives us—or that your gods give you—life and freedom to worship them is a treasure. Is that not enough?"

Tia, puzzled, shrugged her shoulders. "That kind of talk is beyond me. You know what I mean by treasure. The kind those people would have wanted to find. Silver, gold and jewels."

Asimus laughed quietly. "Practical and frank. Then so will I be because a dream and a prophecy have come true. Yes, I have treasure here, treasure you could sell in the marketplace for a few gold coins. But their weight set in the scales against it would be nothing. You would need the whole weight of the world against it to make the beam tilt. But when you go, you and your friend shall take the treasure with you."

Tia, feeling he was teasing her, grinned and, shrugged her shoulders, said, "Well, I just hope it won't be too heavy. We have to travel light."

Asimus shook his head at her, giving her up, and then turned and began to make his way slowly toward the shrine.

CHAPTER FIVE

The Centurion's Cup

FROM THAT DAY ASIMUS made an ever-quickening return to health and he would take no more personal service from either Tia or Baradoc. He gathered and pounded his own herbs and worts to make into salves for his burns and he kept his half-healed body wounds clean but refused all dressing for them, preferring to sit in the clearing by the fire, letting the air and the sun work on them. If Tia had not fought him over it he would have insisted on helping with the preparation of food and cooking. But she stoutly scolded him away from the fire and such tasks and he would retreat, chuckling gently to himself. At night, depending on the weather, they would sit outside the hut or just within the door to catch the last of the light, and talk.

Asimus was never without questions to Baradoc about his old master and the things he had taught him. His face would be masked with a grave, yet almost amused cast when Baradoc (who never lacked words or wild flights of fancy) turned sometimes toward the east in his excitement, shaking his clenched fist as though he held a sword in it and with one swing could annihilate the threat from the Saxons, who sought to swallow up the whole land, and, bursting with emotion, cried *"Aie!* their time will come!" And Tia noticed that he showed no shadow of his own thought, no sign of whether he agreed or disagreed with Baradoc.

It was this that one evening made her say quietly in a pause, as Baradoc stopped talking, "Master Asimus, these last nights you have turned us both inside out as though we were chests stuffed with trifles and odds and ends of our lives and opinions that serve only to brighten your eye like a magpie's or to raise a smile under your whiskers as though you were a cat who had been at the cream. Is your own chest empty?''

Baradoc said sharply, ''Tia. That is no way to speak to a holy man.''

''No, no,'' said Asimus, ''she is not to be scolded. First, because I am not a holy man. Only an indifferent servant of our Lord, Jesus Christ. Also, too, it is true that I am like a magpie or a well-fed cat for the brightness and richness of your minds give me joy . . . aye, and hope. Though none of these can escape the shadow this world casts on them from time to time. So''—he smiled at Tia—''you would know what I have to show? And so you shall and so you should. I was born in Antioch. My father was a steward in the house-hold of a general officer in the Imperial Army. Later, I worked in the household, too, and became the personal servant of a young son of the house. He was called John and was ten years younger than myself. He wanted none of the Army and studied law and I went with him when he left his father's house. But when he was little over thirty he turned from the law, became a Christian and joined the clergy in Antioch. I became a Christian, too. We had bad times and good times, and with the passing of the years my master became archbishop of Constantinople and people named him John Chrysostom, John of the Golden Mouth. And his mouth was golden always with words in defense of the needy and in condemnation of the intrigues in his own church. Aye . . . he had a mouth with a tongue of gold when he praised and preached the teachings of our Lord, and a tongue like the whip of a fiery lash when he faced wickedness. . . . I will not empty the whole of my chest for it would take too long. My master, the good John, died well over twenty years ago at a place you will never have heard of, near the River Irmak in Asia Minor, and I was with him at his death, which was a lonely one.''

''Then how did you come to this country?'' asked Tia.

"Because of a gift he gave me the day before he died, and because of a dream he sent me after his death."

"If all this happened over twenty years ago you must be very—" Tia broke off, suddenly embarrassed at her own impetuousness.

Asimus smiled. "There is no shame in age. I have seen far more than eighty summers. My only sadness is that I did not come earlier to the service of the Lord."

Baradoc said, "I believe in dreams. But the understanding of them is often difficult."

Tia said, "Bother the dream. Tell us about the gift first."

"Tia!" Baradoc frowned at her.

Asimus smiled. "There is no call to scold her. She is the practical one. Things must be clear in the right order in her mind. It is no scolding fault. I will tell you about the gift when I give it to you, and then of the dream—but neither until the day you leave for Aquae Sulis, for that, too, was part of the dream and—"

At this moment Baradoc jumped to his feet. Turning his head toward the forest, he said sharply, "Listen!"

For a moment or two the three of them were silent, listening. The fire burned low like a small red eye. The feet of the trees around the clearing were lost in black shadow, and beyond the fire the three dogs were alert, facing away from the hut, watching the forest. Through the stillness of the evening came the sound of a low, long-sighing throat rumble from Lerg, and then Cuna whined sharply once. Then suddenly from beyond the stony, bush-clothed rise that held the shrine came a sharp, racking burst of deep roaring. There was a silence for a while, and then the spasm of roaring broke through the night again and this time it was much closer.

Baradoc turned to Asimus and Tia and said quietly, "Get inside the hut." He reached down and pulled Tia up and then helped Asimus to his feet.

As they moved to the hut Tia said, "What is it?"

Asimus put his hand on Tia's arm and led her to the door, saying, "There is a time for questions—but it is not now." Then he turned and said to Baradoc, "I have heard the sound before—twice. The only thing you can use is a bow. A spear would—''

Baradoc broke in impatiently, "I know. Now, into the hut.''

He went in with them and took up his bow and strapped on the belt with its quiver of arrows and went back into the clearing, closing the rough door behind him. Though the door, he knew, would hold no protection against the attack to come. That had to be met and held before the bear could move across the clearing to it. The racking, angry roaring split the still night again and the dark wall of trees sent back its thunder in searing, pain-filled echoes. Only once before, while hunting with his old master, had Baradoc ever heard the sound; but the memory lived with him and he knew that the beast that was coming their way moved now in a frenzy of pain and hatred for all of the kind who had lodged that pain with it. Somewhere in the forest recently, he guessed, a party of hunters, eager for meat, for the rich bear fat and the warm skin which would ward off winter cold, had attacked one of the last few of the great brown bears that roamed the south-lands. Avoided and left to themselves, they were no threat to human life, content to live on honey from wild bees' nests, on leaves and forest fruits and grubs and insects. But attacked and not killed, escaping with broken spears and arrows in its body, such an animal turned killer, savaging with blind anger and pain-goaded fury anything that crossed its path, follow-ing the scent of homestead fire, of any human or animal body that came downwind, seeking only a berserk killing to as-suage its own agony.

Baradoc went to the fire and stood with it between him and the rocky rise. He called the dogs to him. Only in desperation would he send them in against the bear, and then only to harry and not to attack for not even Lerg could stand against such an animal. He slipped two of the short arrows from the quiver, held one in his mouth and fitted the other to his bow. When the bear came over the rock rise, following upwind the smoke and human scent, it would be outlined clear against the sky. The bear would see him and come straight for him . . . and he knew that he would have to wait until it reached the foot of the rise before he loosed the first arrow at the farthest killing range.

Behind him Cuna whined gently and from the corner of his eye he saw Lerg stretch his great jaws in a slow, wide defiant gape and he knew that while fear ran in him, drying his mouth and lips, there was no fear in Lerg. One silent signal would send the hound in.

The bear roared and then appeared as though by magic on the crest of the rise. It stood for a moment on all fours, its great head weaving and swinging. Then it rose on its hind legs, raised its head to the sky and roared its anguish and fury. It stood almost twice as high as Baradoc and against the long line of its belly he saw the heavy milk-full dugs . . . a she bear, her cubs now killed to swell her fury . . . and from the right side of her thick, pelted neck stuck out the splintered shaft of a great spear, and another broken spear shaft showed in her left flank, the blood from the wound thickly matting her fur.

The animal, seeing Baradoc and the dogs, dropped to all fours, roared, and began to lumber down the slope. As she did so Baradoc saw that an unbroken shaft stood upright in her back. He raised the bow and drew it, sighting along the arrow, knowing exactly where it must lodge, through the long fur a hand's span in from the top of the left foreleg to smash through bone and sinew and find the heart. To shoot at her head would have been to shoot at a rock. As he covered the lumbering downhill approach of the bear the pony tethered to the back of the hut whinnied and neighed suddenly with fear and then Baradoc heard the thud of her hooves as she reared and bucked in panic. At the foot of the rise the she bear, hearing Sunset, stopped and swung her great head toward the sound. For a moment the beast's left shoulder was wide open to Baradoc.

He let the arrow fly, heard its hornet flight across the clearing and saw it bury itself deep in the bear's shoulder. The animal roared with pain, rose full height and, her jaws flecked with white foam, the red mouth gaping, the great teeth flashing ivory dull in the lowering sunlight, came on in a lumbering run toward Baradoc. And Baradoc stood his ground, for there was only death in flight; and standing his ground, he cursed himself that he had not practiced more with the bow at close range. It pulled to the left but the nearer the target the less it pulled. All this swept through his mind as he stood, marking the spot which the bear must reach before he fired again; and, as he held the tensed bow, he prayed to the gods that they would put virtue and cunning into his hands and eyes to humour and direct the arrow in a true flight to the small target inside the left shoulder.

When the bear was two spear lengths from the fire, Baradoc loosed the second arrow, saw it find its mark, heard the heavy sound of its strike as the short length of shaft bore into the beast's body until the flight feathers were only a finger length from the rough pelt. The bear roared, dropped to all fours, and still came on. It charged across the small patch of garden and through the low-burning fire, scattering ashes, red embers and hearthstones, and Baradoc, as he fitted another arrow, knew that the gods had deserted him, for there was no time even to draw.

At this moment Cuna barked sharply and ran in at the bear. He ran from the side, jumped for the furred throat of the animal, and got a grip on the side of her neck. The bear, pausing in her foreward movement, rose to her hind feet and with one sweep of a forepaw brushed Cuna from her neck like a fly. Cuna flew through the air, yelping high, and landed in the soggy ground around the pool. Then, as the bear still came on and the signal was moving from Baradoc to send Lerg in, the great beast swayed sideways, halted, roared to set wild echoes ringing around the clearing, and then dropped to all fours and collapsed on her side on the ground at his feet.

Baradoc stood unmoving. From the poolside Cuna barked sharply and then came limping toward Baradoc. Lerg went forward slowly and his great muzzle dropped to the bear's head. He stood, hackles risen, and then turned away. Baradoc knew that the bear was dead; the second arrow had done its work. Then, feeling Cuna rubbing against his leg, he bent and picked him up, fondled him, and then felt his limping leg and found that no bones were broken. Silently he thanked Cuna because but for the pause the bear had made to brush Cuna away he might have been crushed and mauled beneath the bear in her dying seconds.

He went toward the hut and Tia and Asimus came out to him. Tia ran to him and for a moment held his arm, anxiety still high in her.

"You are all right?"

Baradoc nodded. "But we have lost Sunset. The smell of the bear made her panic and she broke loose. It is growing too dark now to go after her. If she doesn't come back I'll search for her tomorrow."

Asimus, looking down at the bear, said, "God give you good days for your courage."

Baradoc said, "Those who hunt should always kill. To leave a beast alive and full of broken spears would mark the name of any of my tribe with shame. A man should fetch fresh spears, take the trail and finish the killing. But now the bear is dead it is your gain, Father. I will skin and butcher it and Tia can smoke the meat and fill your jars with bear's grease, and the skin you can use for a bedcover on winter nights. So do the gods arrange bad and good into their own patterns."

Suddenly Tia said woefully, "Without Sunset I shall have to go afoot to Aquae Sulis. I give no thanks to the gods for that!"

Baradoc and Asimus, seeing the half-angry, half-rueful look on her face, eyed one another and then burst out laughing.

Asimus, chuckling, said, "Maybe your gods, seeing into the future, have their reasons."

And Baradoc said, "Sunset did not break the tethering rope. The knot was pulled free from the hut post. Who was it that tied the knot?" He looked at Tia.

Sunset did not return and the next day Baradoc went with Aesc in search for her. He found her in a small valley under the craggy face of a cliff that blocked its end, but before he saw her he knew that she was dead. When he was half a bowshot from the foot of the crag with Aesc well ahead of him a cloud of carrion birds rose into the air. Standing over

the fly-swarming carcass, Baradoc could guess that a hunting
wolf—for the packs were broken now for cub raising—or a
rogue band of dogs had driven her up the valley to make their
kill under the crag. He left the halter rope length on her and
when he returned to the clearing he told Asimus and Tia that
he had found no trace of her. The lie was guessed at by
Asimus but he knew that it was told for Tia's benefit. That
Baradoc should have this consideration for the young girl
pleased him and heartened the faith he had in the dream he
had dreamt so many years ago, lying under the cold winter
stars by the River Irmak.

A few days before Tia and Baradoc left Asimus two young
men from the nearby village came to the clearing for news of
the holy man. When they saw the great bear skin with the
head still on it, pegged out on an upright frame of poles, the
inside of the skin already three-quarters scraped clean by
Baradoc and Tia, their jaws dropped.

After they had gone, Asimus, who had sat by as Baradoc
had told the two the story of its killing, said, "Now the story
will grow in their minds with every step they take toward
home. So begins the rise of a legend. Baradoc and the bear.
In years to come in Venta and Noviomagus . . . aye, and
Calleva, there will be a drinking house or hostel called the
Bear of Baradoc."

Tia, running her fingers through the hair on the nape of
Cuna's neck as she sat by the fire, said, "Here is the real
hero, little Cuna. The drinking shops should carry his name,
too. I take no praise from Baradoc, but Cuna should have his
share."

Baradoc grinned and said, "Give him no praise. It will
turn his head. He is so foolish still that he thinks he is a Lerg.
But when I tell the story to my people he shall have more than
his full due."

"You see that you do."

Looking down at her, her short golden hair stirring in the
breeze, her blue eyes alight with the pleasure she took in
teasing him, the glow of the lowering sun touching her
cheeks with the soft blush of a blooming peach, Baradoc said

without thought, "If you doubt that I will—then journey west with me and do the telling yourself."

Tia rocked on her heels with sudden laughter. "The gods save me from anything like that! No power on earth will get me farther west than Aquae Sulis!"

On their last evening with Asimus, after they had eaten, Baradoc and Tia were sitting by the low fire when the old man came to them from the shrine, where he had been saying his evening prayers. In his hands he carried a well-worn doeskin bag gathered at the mouth with a drawstring. He sat down with them and put the bag on the ground at his feet. Then quietly and without any emotion he began to speak to them.

"In this country, as you know, there are many people who are Christians. And in the old Empire which is slowly dying there are many, many more. Neither of you is a Christian. And, as I have learned while you have been here, you know little of the martyrdom of the Lord Jesus Christ, who was crucified at Golgotha. Before He died a centurion of the Crucifixion guard dipped a sponge into a cup of vinegar and, sprinkling it upon a spray of the hyssop plant, put it to His mouth. And when He was dead, but to be sure of His death, the same centurion thrust a spear into His side and the life-blood ran from Him. The blood ran down His body and some of it dripped into the vinegar cup which had been put at the foot of the Cross. All this happened over four hundred years ago and the story changes in the mouths of men as they retell it, but the real truth never departs from it. It is said that as He hung on the Cross two black birds, common in the country and around its shores, perched on the Cross, and their feet were covered with the blood from His pierced hands. When they tried to preen the blood from their feet with their beaks, then they, too, were covered and the bloodstains have stayed with all their kind since. There are many such birds all around the eastern Mediterranean." He reached forward and pulled back the opening of Baradoc's rough shirt and exposed the tribal tattoo on his skin. "You are marked with such a bird."

"It is our tribal bird," said Baradoc; "and it is the bird of our sea cliffs. We call them choughs, but there is a secret tribal name which I cannot speak to you. It means 'the red crow of enduring.' To kill one is punished by death, for as long as the choughs lives so will our people."

Tia said, "What is in the bag, Father?"

Asimus picked up the doeskin bag. "It is the gift I have promised you. It is the little cup or chalice which stood at the foot of the Cross, holding the vinegar. It is made of silver, now old and battered, and it has been lost and found many times, and by some is still much sought after. The good John Chrysostom gave it to me on his deathbed. It is said that, warmed in the hands of a man or woman who is marked for great and noble duties, someone whose name will live forever, to be praised by all true and just people, the inside of the chalice though now unmarked will slowly begin to glow with the crimson stains of our Lord's blood."

"Have you seen that happen?" asked Baradoc.

"No. Nor have I tried it myself for I know my own worth. But it is my gift to you both, for that was the command I received from the good John in my dream."

"You mean you dreamt about us . . . all those years ago?" Tia's brows furrowed with a frown.

"So it would seem." Asimus smiled, knowing her skepticism. "My master's voice said that I would be in a wild place, in a country far to the north, and in a moment of great peril to myself there would come two people to save me. One would be a youth bearing the sign of the red crow and the other would be a fair-haired maiden dressed as a youth who wore as a fastener on her torn tunic a silver brooch bearing a design of clasped hands."

"You really dreamt that?" asked Tia. "Before we were born?"

"If the good father says he did then he did," said Baradoc sharply.

"But," insisted Tia, "what's the good of giving it to both of us? We part at Aquae Sulis. To whom does it belong then?"

Asimus smiled and shrugged his shoulders and then

handed the doeskin bag to her. "I do not know. You will find some way to settle that. I obey only the dream, and now tell you the last words of my master. The gift being made, the bag must not be opened before me, and the dream being told must not be told again until one comes to hold it and the inside glows crimson with the ghost of the Savior's blood."

"Does that mean it won't glow for either of us?" asked Baradoc.

Tia laughed. "Poor Baradoc—did you want to be marked for great and noble duties, your name to be praised forever?"

Baradoc said stiffly, "For the work I have to do I need no magic chalice. One needs only—"

"Spare us!" cried Tia. "Father, by now you should know that he goes back to his tribe to be an important man, to do great things. And so I hope it will be—but I wish he wouldn't talk about it so much."

Baradoc stood up. He was getting used to Tia's flattening remarks now, and could see, too, that they were often deserved. Though what could a man do if that were his nature and destiny? Then, with a warning look to Tia not to interrupt him, he said to Asimus, "Father, we thank you for your gifts and for your words. How the gift will be settled between us at Aquae Sulis I do not know. The gods will decide. But this I say for both of us, it will be cherished and protected until the right hands come to warm it to crimson life."

The morning of their departure from the clearing a soft drizzle was falling, the slow swathes of fine rain swaying before a mild southerly breeze. From his hut Asimus watched them go, taking the narrow path around the northern edge of the rocky bluff and soon disappearing into the massed trees of the far-reaching forest. Both of them carried bundles over their shoulders, the heavy sword thumping at Baradoc's side, his bow tied on top of his bundle and in his hand the fish spear. Tia carried the light spear, and the cowl of her mantle was hooded over her fair hair against the rain. Asimus smiled to himself as he watched her ungainly walk. The soles of her light sandals had worn and Baradoc had repaired them with pieces of hide, stitched on with sinews taken from the dead bear. Cuna stayed at her heels, the two other dogs went ahead and, for a fleeting moment, Asimus saw Bran the raven, with the southerly breeze under his tail, swing high into the rain and disappear over the far crest of the trees.

Asimus turned away and went into his shrine to pray for them and for a safe journey to Aquae Sulis. As he knelt to the ground and bowed his head he saw at once that there was a new offering on the stone table. It was the arrow that had killed the bear, the head and part of the shaft brown with dried blood. Tied in a small bow just above the feather flights was a piece of bright braiding which he knew Tia must have cut from the loose end of the belt that she wore about the waist of her tunic. He closed his eyes and began to pray.

The soft drizzle lasted until nightfall. Tia and Baradoc marched through it, and their clothes and bundles grew heavier with the weight of water soaking onto them with each hour that passed. A quiet misery took Tia as she plodded along. But it was a misery she could carry with the same fortitude as she carried her bundle because with each step she told herself that she came nearer to her uncle. But marching was at first awkward because she had not become used to the weight of her new-soled sandals. Now and again she would trip and sometimes cursed aloud only to hear Baradoc give a soft chuckle from up ahead. At midday they ate cold meat and hard corn cake, washed down with barley mead that Baradoc carried in a small leather skin slung at his belt—a present from one of the young men who had visited the clearing.

Through the afternoon the country began to change a little. At times the forest broke away into bare heathland over the high tops and the path was overhung with tall bracken growths and drooping new-flowered switches of broom. Here and there were patches of long-stemmed foxgloves, the lower buds on their towering stalks already in bloom. Late in the afternoon they came to a main road. It was banked up on a small causeway. As they came up onto the road Baradoc stopped and Tia halted behind him. A bowshot to the left a man and a woman stood on the high agger crown of the road. In one arm the woman carried a child wrapped in a blanket and with her free hand held the halter of a small pony. Below the shoulder of the road, in the broad scoop ditch from which the material for the road had originally been taken, was a small two-wheeled cart lying on its side. Thinly through the drizzle came the cry of the child that the woman held.

Baradoc said, "Stay here."

Tia dropped her bundle and sat on it, and watched Baradoc move down the worn surface of the road. It was, she knew, for she had seen many in her life, one of the old military roads. But it was many years since anyone had bothered to repair it. With Baradoc went Lerg. Aesc and Cuna sat at her feet and she fondled the stiff wet fur of Cuna's nape. She watched Baradoc go up to the couple and begin to talk to them. After a while he turned and beckoned to her. Tia plodded down the road, splashing through the puddles in its broken surface. No legions, she thought ruefully, would ever swing down this road again, the eagles carried high, the studded shoes of the legionaries thudding out their heavy rhythm.

The woman was young, wrapped in a russet-coloured gown, its skirt edges torn and muddy. Rain shone on her dark long hair and her face was drawn and thin and she held the child to her right breast, suckling it. The man was much older with a rough skin surcoat belted over a green tunic, his legs and feet bare. In the belt about his surcoat was thrust a small axe. He held his left forearm with his large work-engrained right hand, his face twisted with pain. But as Tia came up and Baradoc said something to him in his own language the man laughed briefly and there was a flash of pleasure in his dark eyes.

Baradoc said to Tia, "They are from Calleva on their way to Durnovaria. He is a fuller but there is no work for him in Calleva and he goes back to his people with his wife and child."

"What happened?"

"He slept as he drove and the cart went off the road. His left arm is broken. Even with his wife he can't one-handed get the cart back on the road. They are good people—but maybe a little stupid to take the risk of travelling the old road.'' He smiled. ''It is all right. They do not speak your language.''

Tia said, ''You and I can get the cart back, can't we?''

''Easily.''

They went down into the ditch and cleared the cart of the few goods still in it, and then between them they righted it. With Tia pushing from behind and Baradoc setting himself against the crossbar of the yoke pole, which was designed for two horses or oxen, they ran it up onto the road. While they did all this the man and the woman stood on the road and watched them as though they were rooted to the ground by some numbness of spirit which froze their bodies.

As Baradoc took the pony and yoked it to one side of the pole, he said, ''I think they both still live in a nightmare. They say Calleva has been half burned. They fled at night. They have a son of six but lost him before they left. If they ever reach Durnovaria it will be only at the gods' wish.'' He patted the lean flank of the pony and then dropped down into the ditch and began to hand up the couple's belongings to Tia, who put them in the cart. As she did this Tia, eyeing the two who watched them, suddenly felt angry with them for their helplessness. She felt like shouting at them to wake and stir themselves from their apathy . . . but then the feeling went. She saw a town burning, flames arching over the night sky, people screaming and shouting, panic reaching through the streets and houses and, somewhere, a small boy lost and frightened, crying for his parents.

Before the two drove off, Baradoc made a rough arm sling from a strip of cloth for the man. He made a remark in his own tongue and the man smiled and laughed again and now Tia realized that it was truly the laugh of the simpleminded. The man said something and then the woman laughed.

As they drove away Tia asked, ''Why do they laugh?''

Baradoc shrugged his shoulders. ''Because they have gone beyond tears and weeping.''

''Was his arm truly broken?''

''It felt like it. But it will heal with time and Nodons' help.''

''Nodons'?''

"Yes, Nodons'. He is our god of healing, the god with the silver hand."

"Did they say who burned Calleva? Oh . . . it was such a nice place."

"They don't know—but not the Saxons. There are plenty of loose-footed tribal bands in the country who would be greedy to loot such a town simply out of old hates against your people and the legions that made it. I think maybe they could have been people from Cymru, from beyond the Sabrina River—kinsmen of my own people who would do better to keep their spears and swords sharp for the real enemy. One day—"

"Oh, no." Tia laughed. "Not that again, Baradoc. This is no day to stand in the rain dreaming and speech-making."

For a moment Baradoc frowned, then he smiled and said, "You're right. Let's content ourselves with the day that is."

As they left the road, however, he was thinking to himself that one day these old roads would serve again for the marching of armies, but for armies from the west and the north. The men who had built them had long gone, but they were good men, true soldiers who knew discipline and purpose. Men with such qualities were needed again, but next time they would carry no imperial eagles; they would come under the banner of Badb, the goddess of war, and with the blessing of the great father Dis.

CHAPTER SIX

The Circle Of The Gods

MIDWAY THROUGH the next morning they left the forest and moved into a country of heath and smooth downland, some of the slopes cut with the long rectangles of fields and cultivation. A number of the fields were being worked and from the hollows of shallow valleys there rose here and there the smoke from the hearths of homesteads and villages. But although the land seemed at peace here Baradoc kept always to the high ground. Behind the face of peace there was no telling what might be hidden. Even honest folk could give a hasty, hostile greeting to strangers. To pass through or near such places these days travellers had to stand and call from a distance, to show themselves and then wait while the men gathered and came to question them. There were many who travelled these days who carried a hunting horn to blow when they came down the road to a settlement or move out from a forest fringe above a valley farm or village and, the horn sounded, stood and waited to know whether their way would be barred or opened.

Topping the smooth crest of a down they saw the land falling away below them to a river valley. Alders and willows fringed the river and the grass grew long and lush in a ribbon of pastures along its banks, and nowhere was there sign of human beings or their work.

The rain had stopped now and from the clearing sky the sun's warmth beat down against their damp clothes. Seeing the river below and the sheltering groves of trees that marked it here and there, Tia thought longingly of stripping her wet garments off and plunging into the water to clean herself.

Never in her life had she felt so damp, dirty and stiff. But she said nothing to Baradoc. He was the master and he would decide.

As he moved down the slope a few paces ahead of her he stopped suddenly and waited for her to catch up with him. He dropped his bundle and put a hand on her arm.

"Listen." He stood looking up the narrowing valley.

Tia looked in the same direction. At first she could hear nothing unusual.

"I can't hear anything."

"You will soon. Look at the birds." Baradoc pointed up the valley. Clear in his ears was a faint rustling noise overlaid with a thin half-squeaking, half-grunting, almost complaining sound. A couple of bowshots up the valley the air was slowly filling with the movement of birds, circling and wheeling low over the ground and gradually edging their way down the valley.

Tia said, "I can hear it now. Like a lot of tiny puppies whimpering in their sleep. And what are all those birds?"

"They follow the army of the little furred ones. Have you never seen the march of the shrews and mice and voles before?"

"No."

"Suddenly they all move. Nobody knows why. Perhaps the seasons have been good to them, the litters have increased and then, one day, there are so many of them they begin to move, looking for more living room, more food. As they move all the hunting birds follow them, the birds of day and the birds of night. Look, see them!"

He pointed up the valley and picked out for her the birds that wheeled and hovered and stooped and dropped into the tall grasses. Tawny, brown and barn owls swept low on silent wings. Kestrels hovered and drifted along the line of the march, sparrow hawks, merlins and hobbies cut and dashed through the air, and above them hung a ragged cloud of kites, ravens, crows and peregrines, and all of them in their own fashion dropped from the air to plunder and ravage the advancing army.

And now Tia could see the vanguard of that army and hear clearly its noise as the small brown and grey bodies rustled and squeaked and chattered through the grasses. It passed them on a wide front a few paces below them and stretching down almost to the river edge: voles, mice, shrews, all leaping and scuttering forward, calling and complaining in tiny voices that, melded together, grew into a low surging of sound like the slow roll of a wave over fine gravel. Like a wave itself the brown-and-grey mass flooded over the ground, twisting and breaking and overleaping itself, moving always onward; and as it went it left the tall grasses broken and flattened and filled the air with a sharp, pungent smell.

Together Baradoc and Tia stood on the high slope and watched the living flood pass, and with them stood the three dogs, set back on their haunches, quivering, their eyes on the moving mass. No sound came from them, except from Cuna, who, his body trembling with excitement at the sight of an occasional rat that fled by, whimpered as he longed for the chase. Of Bran, the lone one, there was no sign but Tia could guess that he was with the other birds and would stay with them until he tired of the sport. As though Baradoc had read her thoughts, she heard him say, "The gods have linked all dogs with man. But the fish that swims and the bird that flies choose always their own paths." He nodded at the last stragglers of the passing horde, and went on, "They move like a people driven from their own worked-out land by hunger. So move the Saxons seeking new tilling and cattle grounds—and there is none to stop them among our peoples until the day of the new leader comes . . . until the day when that god-gifted man arises and turns sword in hand to face the east and its fury. May Dagda, the lord of perfect knowledge, send that day soon and Tentates, the god of war, strengthen every sword arm."

Tia smiled to herself as he spoke. At that moment she knew that he was oblivious of her. He spoke seeing himself as the leader. She was well used now to these sudden heroic moods which carried him away. She said quietly, "That day will come. But at the moment it is this day that has to be lived. I want to get these wet clothes off. I want to swim and clean myself in that river—and then I want to eat cooked food and not hardtack cold meat.''

Baradoc turned and grinned at her. ''As the good Asimus said—Lady Tia, the practical one. All right, so you shall. We'll catch some fish and, maybe, I can find a clutch of duck's eggs in the reeds.''

At a place where the river divided into two channels they waded across the shallows and set up camp on the small island between the streams. They took off their clothes and laid them with their other possessions in the sun to dry. In the cover of a low willow Tia wrapped her shift about her loins and knotted it at her waist and then bound a cloth about her breasts before she joined Baradoc, naked except for a loincloth. The far channel was deep and they swam together, enjoying the mild bit of the river's spring-fed water on their skin. Tia washed her face and body with a piece of cloth, shutting from her mind all thoughts of warm bathhouses, and scrubbed her hands with the fine riverbed gravel and then sat in the shallows and cleaned her broken nails as well as she could with the point of her small dagger. But even when she had finished they looked, she thought ruefully, like the hands of a kitchen servant. Massaging her feet to clean them, she felt the soles harder than she had ever known them, and the sore place on her toe had healed to a hard callus.

Between them they caught three of the thyme-smelling grayling and a fat trout. Baradoc made fire and they broiled the fish on a green willow branch over the fire into which Baradoc threw wild sage and water-mint leaves to flavour the flesh. All that was lacking, thought Baradoc, was salt to spark the full taste of the fish and in his mind's eye he saw the salt pans cut in the flatland at the side of the river estuary near his home with crystals glistening like frost as the sun evaporated the water. Which would he rather have had happen—to stay free with his tribe and be there now with so much of the world's knowledge closed to him still or to have known slavery, albeit he had been kindly treated at the last, and the

teachings of his old master? Only the gods knew, for he had
no answer. He smiled to himself, watching Tia at the fire.
Without slavery he would never have met her, never be here
now and never seen the slight raising of her eyebrows and the
look of mocking amusement on her face when he became too
self-important and full of himself . . . *Aie!* she was not like
any of his tribe's girls or women. Her beauty came truly from
her own race. He eyed her now as she squatted by the fire,
dropping pale bluey-green mallard eggs into the pot to boil
them hard for the next day's journey. Her face and arms had
browned, but the rest of her body was as white as a swan's
and her loose, short hair shone under the sun like the rich gold
fire of his own cliffs' ragged tansy blooms.

At that moment a dragonfly hovered close about her face
and she put up a hand and brushed it away. The dragonfly
darted off jerkily and began to hover and hunt over the
running silver of the river. Without thinking Baradoc spoke
aloud in his own tongue.

Tia turned and asked, "What did you say?"

Embarrassed for a moment, Baradoc answered, "It was
nothing."

"If it was nothing why say it in your own tongue?"

"You would laugh if I told you."

"Then make me laugh. There's nothing wrong with that."

Baradoc shrugged his shoulders. "If you truly want to
hear."

"I do."

"Well, seeing you wave away the dragonfly I spoke
poetry in my own tongue."

"Then speak it to me in my own tongue—if you can."

Baradoc hesitated a moment and then as well as he could
he spoke the poetry in her tongue.

> "Over the silver stream hunts the four-winged fly.
> Each eye holds a thousand eyes;
> But he sees not your beauty."

Tia was silent for a moment. From Baradoc, she thought,
always something new. Then, turning to drop more eggs into

the boiling water, knowing that she was hiding her face from him, she said, "Which of your tribal bards said that?"

Baradoc laughed. "None of them. There is no man of my people who cannot say such things. The tongue speaks what the eye sees."

Tia her eyes on the boiling eggs, said, "And did you hear me laugh?"

"No."

"Nor should I. The words were good." She turned to him and her mouth was wreathed momentarily with a teasing smile. "And poetry is a change from warlike speeches about the future of this country. Now come and eat."

But after they had eaten and Baradoc had gone off with his bow, Aesc at his heels, to get a wildfowl for the next day's pot. Tia lay back on the grass and let the warmth of the sun flood across her bare body and thought about him. Even against his tanned face she had caught the flush of his embarrassment when he had spoken his lines. In herself there had been not embarrassment but a quick flush of pleasure to which she was no stranger. At her brother's villa there had been many visitors and friends from the neighbourhood and among them young men who she knew were attracted by her. Some she had liked and some she had avoided but, like or dislike, she was always pleased when she was complimented, when she was feasted with a string of flattering words. Why not? She was a woman . . . well, almost, and one day she would marry. . . . Dreamily, she tried to imagine Baradoc as one of her own kind. But it would not work. Dress him in no matter what clothes or uniform, there was something utterly un-Roman about him. Not even could he be taken for Roman-British. He was a Briton, a tribesman, and it stood out all over him like the true grain of his own country's oaks. Chance and tragedy had brought them together. She liked him and was grateful to him and she thought nothing now of the roughness of some of his ways, but in his heart she guessed that there was only one love, greater than any he would ever give to any woman.

She leaned forward and picked up from the ground, where their belongings were spread to dry, the doeskin bag which held the chalice Asimus had given them. Baradoc, she guessed, since he knew that it would never glow with the soft crimson of the ghost blood for him to mark him for greatness, had no interest in it. Not once since it had been given to them had he mentioned it or shown any care for it.

She opened the bag and took the silver chalice out. It was no larger than a drinking goblet with handles on each side curved and worked in the form of rams' horns. One of the horns was badly bent. The bowl itself was pocked here and there with dents and there were scratches on the fluted base. Around the outside rim ran a continuous Greek key pattern and on one side of the body of the bowl, worked in relief, was a large round boss in the shape of an almost circular wreath of bay leaves, enclosing the simple outline of a human eye. For a moment or two Tia was tempted to encircle her hands about it to see what would happen. Then she put the thought from her mind. If it glowed for her—even though Asimus had said it would not—she would be scared stiff because she had no wish to become a great leader. Anyway, there was no true belief in her heart for his story. Still, if Baradoc did not want it . . . well, cleaned up—for it was dirty and tarnished inside and out—it would make a nice ornament for her bedroom in her uncle's villa, and would look pretty with flowers in it.

She rose and went to the river, carrying the chalice. She had nothing to do until Baradoc returned and they started on the rest of the day's march. She squatted in the river shallows and scooped up a handful of the fine silver sand and began to clean the bowl, working the sand lightly over it as she had often seen servants working fine pumice-stone dust over her brother's silver. As she worked a dragonfly came upstream and hovered low over a drift of white-starred water crowfoot. Tia smiled to herself. *Each eye holds a thousand eyes; but he sees not your beauty.* One day, she thought, some woman, some tribal maiden, would be won by his poetry and find herself only a shadow against the power of his dreams and ambitions.

*   *   *

For the next two days the weather was fine and they travelled northwest at a leisurely pace. Now and again, and always approached with caution, they met singly or in small groups travellers like themselves, some going north, some south and some west, but none going east. From them they heard many stories whose truth it would have been idle to try to unravel. This year the Saxons were coming ashore in even greater strength and spreading and settling through the east. And with their coming all over the country many of the common folk, touched with a madness born of their fears and their deep-seated, generations-old resentment of their masters, had turned to pillage and murder. They told, too, of rumours that the far-western Cymric hill tribes, the Dobunni and the Ordovices and the Silures from beyond the Sabrina, were moving down from the mountains in raiding parties, bolder even now than they had ever been in the days when the ranks of the legions had thinned in the garrisons and forts, eager to take and hold what they could before the tide advanced to the foothills of their own homelands. Safety now for ordinary folk lay in the bigger towns where law and order still held, where men still kept to their businesses, paid taxes and travelled well armed and in strength, and where slaves still served them because there was no true freedom to be found in running away. Much of all this came to Baradoc in his own tongue and much of it he kept from Tia or trimmed down in the telling. Although Aquae Sulis lay on the banks of the Abona River, which flowed northwest little more than twenty miles to join the Sabrina, the place was large and would be well organized. No raiding party of freebooting tribesmen could touch it. All these tribes were tied by blood and history and common origins to his own people, and like his own people they were torn and divided by internal rivalries and feuds and had long forgotten how to stand together against a common enemy. Although they sang the virtues and valours of their ancestors who had faced the Fourteenth, Twentieth and Second Legions in the early days of the coming of the Roman invaders, they were a rabble now under many quarrelling chiefs, their destiny to be conquered unless they learned to hold rank-and-order disciplined battle skills against the new invader and dedicate themselves and their swords to a single leader and follow him without question or greedy turning aside for private plunder and rapine.

On the evening of the second day they came up from a river valley, followed the track of an old ridgeway for a while and then climbed the bare, grass- and thorn-covered shoulder of a rising down full into the light of a low westering sun. Black against the blood-red glow of the sun were silhouetted the circular double ranks of great rising stones, three times the height of a man, many of them joined together across their tops with long stone lintels and caps. A handful of wild sheep cropping around the stones galloped away from them as they came near.

Tia said, "What is this place?"

"A great henge of stones. There are some in my own country but not as big as this. This may be a place my master often talked of."

"Men raised these stones?"

"No. They were raised in the days before man—when only the gods walked the earth. They raised them as a temple for man to use when he came, as a place for worship and sacrifice. Only priests are allowed to go inside the circles."

"I don't believe all that."

Baradoc smiled. "I don't ask you to. But I do. And we do not go inside. We can camp on the far side, away from the ridge road."

Tia, looking at the stones towering from the ground, their shadows long and black across the grass, gave a little shiver and said, "I don't want to go inside anyway. All I want to do is to put up our shelter and sleep."

That night, before they slept, as they lay under the meager cover of a canopy made from their goat-hair cloak and a blanket, tied over hazel poles which Baradoc had cut, Tia said, "How many more days before we get to Aquae Sulis?"

"Three or four. Tomorrow or the next day we should come to the headwater of the Abona River. Then we can travel down it. Does your uncle live in Aquae itself?"

"Oh, no. In the country. About two miles outside."

"Which side?"

"I don't know. Just outside."

Baradoc sighed. "You mean once we get to Aquae you still couldn't find your way to the villa?"

"No, of course I couldn't. I've only been a few times and I was taken by my brother. We used to go in two carts with servants. But I remember the road. Up to Calleva and then down the legionary road through Cunetio—we used to stay there a night—and then on through Verlucio and so to Aquae."

"And when you got to Aquae—was the villa this side, or did you go through the place to the south, west or north?"

Tia yawned. "Oh, we always went into Aquae, but after that how would I know which direction? But it makes no difference. All you have to do is ask for the villa of my uncle and anyone will tell you. Everyone knows him."

Baradoc said nothing. It was useless to expect too much of a woman. But how could you go anywhere and not afterward remember the road you took? How could you, even if the gods whipped you up and set you down in the dark of the darkest night without stars to see or wind to smell, still not raise your hand and point to the north? To do that was as natural as breathing.

Suddenly out of the darkness Tia said, "You think I'm stupid, don't you?"

Baradoc laughed quietly. "No, I don't. You learn fast. You can shoot a bow well, you can silent talk the dogs, you can make a day's march and carry your load, and you can now strike fire from flint and iron. But you only learn when you have to. You don't learn because it is good just to learn."

"Women aren't supposed to. Anyway, what a lot of fuss over my uncle's villa. It is called Villa Etruria, and that because he was born in Etruria. In Aquae we just ask for it and we shall be told. And the sooner I'm there the better. And for you, too, because my uncle will show his gratitude for the way you have looked after me. And anyway, you wouldn't like it if women were as clever and good at things as men.

Though sometimes I think, the way things are now and man having made them so, it's a pity that they aren't.''

Indignantly Baradoc said, "The gods made man to fight and rule and to reason, and they gave him woman to bear his children and to keep his hearth, though sometimes, when a nation needs it, they give a woman the heart and brain of a man and then we have queens like Boudicca, who your people—'' He broke off for from Tia had come the sound of a gentle snore.

Baradoc woke at first light. He slipped quietly out of the shelter without waking Tia. He strapped on his sword belt and moved away over the dew-drenched grass followed by the three dogs. He turned and looked at Cuna, and the small dog, after a moment's hesitation, went back to the shelter. Northward from the stone circle the downs rose and fell in gentle swells, marked here and there with clumps of wind-twisted thorns. A light breeze came full into his face. In a little while the sun would be rising, but now the light was a pearl-grey flood muting the colours of trees and grass. A couple of bowshots away to his right he saw a flock of great bustards. For a moment or two he was tempted to go after them, but then he knew that he must have a truly ritual animal. The bustards, seeing him and the dogs, moved away, running awkwardly, and then took off heavily, flying low, their slow wingbeats stirring up the dust and dead grasses below them until they gained height and wheeled away out of sight over the crest of the downs.

He sent Lerg and Aesc ahead and for a while they were lost to sight. Then downwind came the clear sharp barking of Aecs. Baradoc whistled and dropped to his knees on the ground. After a moment or two he heard a thud of hooved feet and he whistled again. Over the low swelling of downland ahead of him suddenly appeared the close-packed ranks of a handful of wild sheep, heading downwind toward him, moving fast away from the dogs who had circled behind them.

As the dogs appeared over the skyline behind the sheep Baradoc stood up and marked quickly the beast he wanted. Seeing him, the small flock swerved caterways across the face of the down. It slowed, made an attempt to break away but was held by the dogs. The old ram leading it stopped and the rest bunched behind it. The ram lowered its head and stamped angrily with its forefeet, the thuds ringing across the hard ground.

While the dogs held the flock on the flanks Baradoc moved forward slowly, step by step without hurry, toward them, his eyes on a young ram he had already marked as the wanted beast. He whistled gently to Aesc with her own slow trilling call and she crouched, watching the flock. Lerg moved in closer from the other side. The sheep, packed tight now, moved uneasily, waiting for the signal from the old ram to break from the flock pattern and scatter in all directions. The young ram pushed out to the side of the flock and faced Lerg. Following the fashion of the old ram, it lowered its head and stamped. This was a flock made of strays and abandoned animals, the sight of dogs and man still without the full force of danger for them. As the young ram stamped again and tossed its head in threat toward Lerg, Baradoc whistled high and shrilly and made a quick movement of his hand.

The flock broke wildly in all directions and Lerg moved in fast and leapt at the young ram, knocking it over and then holding it down by the grip of his great jaws on the loose neck fleece and the weight of his body.

Baradoc ran in, pulling a long hide thong from inside his shirtfront. Seizing the immature horns of the ram, he swung the beast onto its back, clamped his knees around its forequarters and with a few quick movements looped its front and hind legs together and knotted them securely. Baradoc picked it up, slung it over his shoulders, the strong, aromatic smell of its dew-wet fleece sharp in his nostrils, and turned back toward the stone circle.

As he neared it the lip of the sun came over the eastern ridge of the downs and the dew on the grass was suddenly fired with its red glow, the shadows of the stones reaching long and black over the ground.

He carried the ram up to the circle. To one side of the entrance a grey, lichen-stippled lintel stone lay on the ground. Baradoc dropped the ram onto the stone, and stood back with Lerg and Aesc on either side of him. He drew the broadsword from his belt and, holding it before him by point and hilt, looked up at the great arc of the stones, their eastern faces flooded by the fiery sunrise, and began to speak aloud in his own tongue the call to the gods for their favour and guidance, the sacrificial prayer of his tribe, of the people of the enduring crow.

This, he knew now, was why his steps had been directed here. Never in all the years of his people had any of them made this sacrifice in the first morning light at the great stone henge, the temple made by the gods for men. . . . Over the levelled sword raised before his eyes, he called the prayer and then began to name the great gods so that none should be missed and work against him and his dreams—Father Dis; Taranis the thunderer; Tentates; Esus; Coventina of the sacred grove of Nemeton; Cernunnos the horned one; Epona the hooved one; Nonus the wise and forgiving one, who, when his wife deceived him with another, because he loved her, claimed the child for his own; Dagda; Nodons of the silver hand; Badb the goddess of battle, who had flown high above the chariots of the great queen; and Lug the fair-haired, who stirred the corn seed ot life and set the blossoms of all flowering trees to swell into fruit. . . .

As the great rim of the sun began to wheel above the horizon, he reached down, took one of the ram's horns in his left hand, drew the animal's head back, and with one fierce slash of the sword cut its throat. The ram kicked in its death agony and its blood ran dark over its tawny fleece and moved darker still across the rough face of the stone slab. Baradoc watched the ram die. Then he stepped back and looked through the great stone archway at the linked twin circles of raised stones over and through which the swifts were screaming and hunting the insects raised to flight by the new sun; and he looked for some sign that the gods had heard him and were pleased with his offering.

There was a flutter of wings from the top of a small thorn that grew close to one of the far stones. Baradoc, catching the flash of red-wings and the blue-black head, saw that it was a shrike. The bird settled on a side branch of the shrub. In its mouth it held a limp, dead wren it had killed. As Baradoc watched he saw the butcher-bird with a quick stabbing twist of its head impale the wren on one of the long thorns to rest there among the dead beetles and bees of its larder until hunger should bring it back to feed. For a moment or two he was sure that this was his sign, but his mind had scarcely turned to the reading of its message when from the top of one of the far stones a bird, at first a slaty-blue shadow against the darkness of the stone, winged down fast. It streaked low over the sheep-bitten grasses toward the thorn, the sun metalling its dark wings with a high gloss and lighting the pale, rufous patch of its gorge with a golden glow. The shrike, seeing it coming, rose with a cry of alarm from the thorn and flew away, hugging the ground and swerving in and out of the thorn patches. After it in fast pursuit, swinging and turning, and fast closing on the shrike, went the other bird, and Baradoc watched, knowing now that this was the true sign, for the other bird was a merlin, the smallest of his country's falcons. Baradoc saw the merlin strike and kill in midair, saw a great puff of feathers spread in the air and then, as the merlin disappeared below the crest, heard its distant exultant killing call. The gods had spoken plainly to him. Was not the bloody butcher-bird the Saxon threat from the east and the swift, sudden killing of the merlin the vengeance and victory which would one day come from the west?

He turned away from the stones toward the shelter. He saw that Tia was standing outside, watching him, and he knew that if she began to question him, maybe to mock or tease him, then he would be hard put to hold his feelings back. These things had nothing to do with women.

Tia said nothing. She had seen him make the sacrifice, but the killing of the shrike had been to her no more than part of the morning stir of nature. As he came toward her she saw his face set brown and hard and the dark intensity of his eyes and she guessed that he moved with his dream of the future glowing and blood-stirring within him.

She gave him the morning greeting and then, while
Baradoc began to strike their shelter and pack their belongings, went to their fire. Overnight they had banked the pile of
red embers with new wood and dry grasses and covered it
with turves. She pulled the turves aside and blew the slow
embers into fire and fed brittle, dead thorn kindling on it. She
put bear grease in the skillet and began to cook the last of the
fish that they had caught the previous day. A wind eddy blew
smoke into her eyes and mouth. Weeks ago it would have
made her cough and her eyes water. Now she was hardly
aware of it. All could be born because Aquae Sulis came
nearer each day. At this moment Baradoc came to the fire,
carrying their two wooden platters, and squatted down on his
hunkers. He smiled almost shyly at her, as though there were
only a few hours gone since they were strangers, and said,
"We should travel well today. The country is open and we
can keep to the ridgeways." He nodded to the westerly sky.
"I think, too, these parts are more peaceful. No scavenging
birds, crows, ravens or kites wheel in the sky and the wind is
free of rolling smoke clouds."

Wiping her sticky, floured hands on a cloth, Tia, her
words surprising herself, quietly said, "Since I've been with
you it seems to me that my body and my brain have been
wakened from a kind of sleep. Not so long ago I took my
pleasant life and ways for granted. Other people were
shadows that moved around me. I had no curiosity about
them and little about myself. Now my mind is full of
questions."

"That is the way it should be. Without questions there are
no answers. And without answers no truth, no progress, no
future."

"Then I am free to ask questions?"

"Why not?"

"If you choose."

"You have a living dream to free your country. Once your
forefathers had that dream and turned it against my people.
Time has settled that struggle. Now your enemy is a new one
. . . the Saxons."

"And your enemy, too."

"True. But tell me, why do you hate the Saxons with a hatred that is fiercer than a smith's furnace? Why do you have an anger in you that is harder than iron against them, so unbending that it must come from more than a love of your country and your dream for its future?" She leant forward and turned the frying fish in the skillet to brown their sides, hiding her face. "What did they do to you?" She looked up slowly after a while and saw his face unmoving, the mask set over it again.

Baradoc, each word a chip struck from an icy mass, said, "I had a father and was taken from him into slavery. I had a master and was his slave. But even while I was a slave he became my father. He taught me the arts he knew. He even taught me things about my own and other tribes I did not know. Everything I am and will be is forever marked by his wisdom and kindness. He gave me my freedom and understood, since I did not leave him at once, that there was more I wanted from him. And then the Saxons came. He hid me in the roof loft and, sword in hand, met them in the courtyard of the villa. I saw it all through a gap in the tiles. They ringed him and taunted him and baited him. Age made his movements clumsy. Slowly and savagely they speared and axed him. They made his dying long and a drunken sport. And when he was dead they hacked with their blades at his body, danced on it and kicked it, defiled and degraded it. That night I swore to the gods that I would take the sword against them so long as any rested in this land, and I made a vow that the first Saxon I ever killed I would dedicate to him." He paused for a moment, the mask slowly faded from his face and the thin edge of a smile wreathed his lips as he went on, "So that is the answer to your question—and, Lady Tia, it is not one which I expected ever to come from you. From today the people around you will no longer be shadows."

CHAPTER SEVEN

The Villa Etruria

FOR THE NEXT TWO DAYS, the country being open and untroubled, they travelled easily and finally reached one of the small branches of the headwaters of the Abona River. The valleys of the downland with their clear chalk streams held small settlements and farms. The southern slopes were worked with terraced strip fields, the greens of sturdy growths of wheat and barley and oats patchworking the land. Now, too, they came across flocks of cattle and sheep herded and guarded by family groups who lived and slept under rough shelters on the downs. Sometimes they talked to these people and bartered the game that Baradoc killed for cheese and milk. Money none of these people would accept as payment. True value lay in barter, goods for goods.

With the days an easier relationship sprang up between Baradoc and Tia. Something had awakened in her which gave her understanding and a growing admiration for his character and strength of purpose. In him, too, grew an acceptance of her which discounted all her race and breeding. She was a travelling companion, the two of them bonded in a growing friendship. One evening as they sat beside the slow-moving Abona where they were camped for the night, she asked him about his cousin who had been made a slave with him and why he had betrayed him and left him hanging from the tree in the Anderida forest to die.

Baradoc said, "When he was given his freedom he left my master but he stayed in Durobrivae and worked there for a smith and armourer. He had a cunning in his hands as great as the cunning in his mind. And he heard from meeting travel-

lers who came to the smithy that my father had died. At the
moment his father is head of the tribe—but only until I return.
What he did to me in the forest he did first for his father, and
then for himself. With me dead then one day he would lead
the tribe.''

''What's he called?''

''Inbar, and our tribal name is Ruachan. After the Saxon
raid in which my master was killed he came to me with a
friend and we all travelled together. Not until they strung me
to the tree did he tell me that my father was dead.''

''And you mean to kill him?''

''We shall fight and when he lies on the ground with my
sword at his throat his life will belong to me. Then I shall give
it to his father, who is a good man, and he will choose
whether the sword strikes or is sheathed.''

''And what do you think he will say?''

Baradoc gave a dry laugh. ''Lady Tia, the questioner.
How should I know? But if the word is to kill, then I shall kill
him and he will be laid in the burial grounds on the cliff hill.
But if the word is to spare him, then Inbar must rise and go
from our lands forever. Whichever way the loss is great—for
Inbar has many skills. With so much craft and cunning and
courage it is a great grief that the gods at his birth flawed
him.''

Tia lay back on the grass and stared at the evening sky.
High above she could see the black shape of Bran wheeling
slowly on a rising air current and then, suddenly in a moment
of play, falling quickly, twisting and turning, the searing
sound of the wind against his wings coming clearly to her.
Cuna came and sniffed at her face and she raised a hand and
fondled his muzzle. Tomorrow or the next day they would
reach her uncle's villa and this episode in her life would be
closed. But, although her meeting with Baradoc had sprung
from tragedy, she knew that for her, too—even as the gods
had flawed Inbar to bring her to rescue Baradoc from the
oak—the gods had fashioned time and movement to give her
this period with him so that her eyes should be truly opened
and her mind truly awakened. In her reverie she heard the

low, soft growling of Cuna as he played with a broken stick. Then she heard him yelp loud and Baradoc suddenly laughed.

She sat up to see that Cuna in play had attacked the loose roll of their fishing net, which lay near the shelter and was now tangled in its meshes. As he rolled and twisted she laughed, too. Leaping and jerking inside the web of net, Cuna lost his balance and began to roll down the slope of the bank. Before she could move he had gone over the edge and landed in the river.

Laughing still, Baradoc jumped up, took the long fish spear and lifted the netted Cuna out of the river. He held him up and Cuna yapped indignantly until Tia reached for him and, sitting down, began to disentangle him from the net. Free, Cuna shook himself, spraying her with water and then, as they both still laughed, began to race around in wild circles, leaping from one to the other in mock attacks, delighted with the attention he had brought on himself. While Lerg and Aesc looked on impassively, Tia caught Cuna and held him to her breast and calmed him down.

Baradoc, watching her and the dog, said after a moment or two, "Of the dogs he's the one you like best, isn't he?"

"Yes, yes, I do. He's so small, but so brave, and he makes me laugh."

"Then when I leave Aquae Sulis he stays with you. He is yours."

"Oh, no, I couldn't—"

"He is yours." Baradoc stood up, his eyes turning away from her. "The gift is made. Now I will cover the fire against the morning." He moved away to gather turves and grasses to damp down the fire.

The Villa Etruria was two miles to the west of Aquae Sulis. It stood on a gentle riverbank slope, well above the winter flood line. From the main arched entrance to the courtyard, stone steps ran down to a small landing place on the Abona. They had come to it by the road that ran west to the small port of Abonae, near the mouth of the river,

reaching it in the late afternoon, the lowering sun striping its
red tiles with black ridge shadows while the breeze rippled
the branches of a row of mixed limes and poplars that flanked
the slopes on either side of the building. Part of the bank had
been cut away and the villa had been built into it. A covered
way ran around the large courtyard, backed on one side by
the kitchen, servants' quarters and storerooms. On the other
side was a small bathhouse with the hypocaust that served it.
Between these wings the main rooms of the villa faced square
across the court to the river. In the center of the courtyard was
a spring-fed well, encircled with a carved stone parapet and
roofed with an ornamental canopy from which hung a large
bronze bucket. A little beyond it, giving shade to the yard,
grew a tall sweet chestnut tree, a tree, Baradoc knew, which
the Romans had brought to his country in their early days.
When corn was short the old legionaries had milled the
chestnut fruits to add to their scanty cornflour issue.

As he lay on his couch that first night it was a long time
before Baradoc could find sleep. Lerg and Aesc slept outside
his door, and outside Tia's bedroom not far away he knew
Cuna would by lying. When they had come down the river
into the bowl of hills that held Aquae Sulis he had been
surprised to see how small the town was. There had been no
sign of trouble or past disturbance and although they had
drawn some curious looks from people, mostly because of
the dogs and Bran on his shoulder, they had been met kindly
and given directions to the villa. But although the town was
small he saw, on their way to the villa, that there were many
more like it scattered along the Abona and on the hillslopes.

The villa itself had not surprised him. As a slave he was
used to such places. But for the first time in his life, because
of Tia, he was a guest. When they had arrived he had insisted
that Tia go by herself into the villa to her uncle. He had sat on
the river steps with the dogs, watching the swallows making
water rings as they dipped to the river surface and the flight of
the bronze, green and blue dragonflies hovering and darting
above the yellow flag blooms.

Finally, with his steward at his side, Tia's uncle had come

to greet him. Ex-Chief Centurion and Camp Prefect Truvius Corbulo walked now with slow, awkward steps because of his rheumatism, helping himself with a long vine staff, old and polished with use, a relic from his army days. His hair was white and he was a little bowed at the shoulders, but carried himself with a natural and professional dignity. His eyes were a deeper blue than Tia's, and although they looked warmly on Baradoc he could guess that in the past many an erring legionary had quailed before them. It was easy to imagine Chief Centurion Truvius of the Second Legion in the days of his prime—plumed helmet, armoured in mail cuirass and strapped shoulder plates, a pleated leather kilt, a senior officer's highly decorated boots, sword hanging on his left side, his staff of rank in his right hand and, sweeping from his shoulders, the folds of a red paludament, the cloak of authority.

He had greeted Baradoc and in a short but friendly speech thanked him for all he had done for Tia and had then put him in the care of his steward. For a moment as they had moved into the courtyard the steward, his eyes on the dogs and Bran, had begun to say a few words . . . a mumble about should the animals go to the stables and the young Briton . . . Truvius had jerked his old head round, eyed the man without words and had moved on. From that moment Baradoc had been looked after as a highly privileged guest. He was taken to the baths, where he stripped and—as he had often done in his old master's house and in the public baths at Durobrivae—passed through the cold and tepid rooms to the hot room, where, once the sweat had begun to break through his skin, he lay and was shaved and then his body scraped and currycombed by the bath servant, relishing the man's skillful strokes with the curved bronze blade of the strigil.

When he had come to dress it was to find a fresh-laundered tunic and undershirt awaiting him with highly polished sandals of soft green leather, the leg thongs worked with a running design in fine silver thread.

Lying now with the silence of the house about him, a soft down-stuffed mattress giving him the feeling of floating on

air, he realized the shock it must have been for Tia savagely
to have been thrust out of the luxury of her old life into the
wilderness with him. And this house *was* luxurious, though
small. It had been built of the local limestone. Even the
pillars supporting the roof of the open corridors that ran
around the courtyard were of stone. The wall openings of the
reception room and the dining room were glazed with green
and yellow squares of glass. The dining-room floor was
covered with a large mosaic; six hanging bronze oil lamps
gave light and on plinths along the walls stood family busts.
One angle of the courtyard corridor where Truvius had his
collection of birds had been faced, too, with glass, a rough,
green whorled glass through which the light came broken and
uneven as through water. But of all the things in the villa
none had surprised him more than Tia when she came into the
anteroom before dinner, where he and Truvius waited for
her, drinking a fine white wine the like of which he had never
tasted before.

In the darkness now the picture of Tia glowed bright and
vivid in his mind. Her short hair, combed and arranged in
tight curls, shone like a gold flame and was trapped by a red
velvet band that ran across her clear brow and behind her
ears. From one shoulder hung a blue silk robe, leaving the
other shoulder bare. A transparent, diaphanous short mantle
fell in light, moving folds to her waist, while on her feet were
soft blue-dyed slippers worked with a close pattern of small
seed pearls. The sight of her had made Baradoc catch his
breath. Gone was the forest-and-downland, dirty-faced
youth who had travelled with him. Here was a beautiful
young woman, perfumed and elegant, a young goddess coming into the room like a vision. The contrast shook him. A
memory of his tribe's settlement had gone darkly through his
mind—the men in their rough skins, the women, young girls
and children, sun- and weather-bitten, who worked over the
cooking pots, hands greasy and callused, and tilled the hill
plots and on the feast days could find for finery only a mantle
or cloak of cheap wool, for ornament some solitary armlet or
neckpiece, some brooch set with coloured stones . . . *Aie!*

He had come back to the present as Tia, teasing mockery in her eyes, had said, "Well, Son-of-a-Chief Baradoc—do I get no greeting? Did you lose your tongue as well as the dirt and sweat of travel in the bathhouse?"

Baradoc had smiled and said, "What could my tongue say, Lady Tia, that could match what my eyes see? Can the beauty of a bird be told by counting the colours that paint each feather, or the silver glory of a salmon be known by the tally of its scales?"

Tia had laughed and, turning to Truvius, had said, "I should have told you, Uncle, that Baradoc is a poet as well as a warrior who one day dreams of sweeping the Saxons from this land."

Truvius, handing Tia a glass of wine, had answered, "When a man sees beauty and cannot find poetry in himself, then he is a man, too, who finds no courage in himself when he faces danger."

For the first time in his life—for not even in his old master's house had this happened to him—Baradoc ate in Roman fashion, reclining on one of the three sloping couches set around the low table, waited on by the steward. Although Truvius showed little hunger, shifting often, too, in discomfort from his rheumatism on his couch, he and Tia did full justice to the stuffed olives and preserved plovers' eggs, the cold lobster—which had been brought upriver from Abonae—and the young broad beans and carrots, followed by slices of grilled venison, their appetite lasting right through to the dessert of dried figs and walnuts. Throughout the meal the steward had hovered round, refilling their wineglasses, bringing fresh napkins and water bowls for them to clean their hands, and watching always over the comfort of Truvius, ready to help him turn, prompt with a fresh cushion to ease his stiff body.

At the end of the meal Truvius, giving them a wry, humorous look, had said, "Twenty years ago I could have matched your appetite. Forty years ago, when I was still in service, after a day's march I could have eaten and drunk you under the table." Then looking at Baradoc, he said, "So—you go to the west to rouse your people? And why should you not, for my own have forsaken you? But remember this when you come of age to lead and fight. . . .'' He coughed a little, shifted stiffly on his couch and sipped a little wine. ''When Claudius sent General Aulus Plautius with the Second, Ninth, Fourteenth and Twentieth legions against your people, the Cantiaci, the Regnenses and the Atrebates, then man for man, courage for courage, there was no difference between defenders and attackers. There seldom is. But there was this difference in Plautius's men—discipline, one leader and one plan of battle. He wins battles who makes the enemy fight on his terms, on his chosen ground. Your tribes must find a leader, just and severe, whom men will love, and he must find for himself new battle skills and tactics that these barbarian Saxons have never known. . . .'' He had broken off in a fit of coughing and the wine spilled from the glass in his shaking hand, but when the steward came to him, he waved him away testily and after a while went on: ''I would ransom my soul if such a thing were possible to be your age again, and to fight for this country, for it has been good to me and I have grown to love it more even than my native Etruria. . . . Aye, I would gladly fight without rank as a simple bowman or spearman if the gods would will it. But the gods give but one portion of life to each man. When his eyes close for the last time they wait on the other side of darkness to greet him with his reckoning and his reward or punishment.''

In bed now, hearing an owl cry by the river and catching the stir of Bran, who roosted on the ledge of the window, Baradoc could remember every word the man had said, and he knew that the memory would never leave him. One leader and each man disciplined, and new battle skills and tactics that the Saxons had never known. Then, driving those thoughts away, there came into his mind the picture of Tia, a young woman who stirred his heart but who, now that their journeying was done, was as far above him as the stars. Somewhere he knew there was a woman he would marry and make his own . . . but already she had been betrayed. . . .

Aie! the heart was a house of many chambers and the doors of some once shut could never be reopened.

The next morning as he stood outside the kitchen quarters and saw to the feeding of the dogs and Bran, Tia came to him and when the dogs had eaten they walked down to the river.

With a brusqueness which he did not intend Baradoc said, "You are safe with your uncle, and this part of the country, too, seems settled. I must go on my way. Today."

For a moment or two Tia was silent. Then she said sharply, "You cannot leave today."

"Why not?"

"Because it would offend my uncle—and it would offend me. Would you treat him as if he were an innkeeper? And myself as a . . . a sack of corn you delivered for the kitchen?"

"I meant nothing like that."

"He is old. He has suffered two heart attacks in the last few months. His days are numbered, Son-of-a-Chief Baradoc. You will not shadow even one of them with the discourtesy of leaving so soon. You are a guest. We both owe you a debt of honour. That cannot be paid quickly as you toss a coin onto a tavern slab in return for a beaker of beer. And stop scowling. It puts ugly lines across your brow."

Baradoc laughed and shrugged his shoulders. "I meant no rudeness. But you're right to scold me."

So Baradoc stayed on at the villa for the next three days. On one of those days Tia and her uncle travelled to Aquae Sulis and made their prayers at the temple for the spirits of her brother and his wife, and Truvius gave orders to a stonemason for a slab to be carved, commemorating them. When it was made he intended to place it in the wall of the villa overlooking the river. Baradoc travelled with them but did not go to the temple. Instead he wandered around the town. Many of the wealthier people had already left it and from the shopkeepers and working people whom he spoke to it was clear that there was a deep feeling of unrest in them, a shadow of the fear which clouded the east already. But their chief anxiety centered on the Cymric tribes beyond the Sabrina River, and the tales that each new traveller brought that the hill tribes were moving. The Silures, Demetae and Dobunni, who had never been truly under the old rule, saw the prospects of easy and profitable pillage, the pleasure of wielding firebrand and sword, and the prospect of slaves to sell or to work their mountain farms and herds.

As he sat with Truvius that evening in the courtyard, the dogs lying before them, the sun firing the plumage of the birds in their aviary, the steady movement of worker bees about the flower urns and beds, the old man said to him, "Sulis is a town of shadows, and many of the villas around here hold nothing but ghosts. The gods have called a term to the bright days of glory and now we begin to enter the darkness of a changing age. A man can do no more than to cherish his own honour, to fight for it and to die for it. I have lived by war, and would that I had died by war. . . ." His words trailed away, his eyes closed, and his head dropped to his chest. He had drifted away into sleep, maybe into a dream of the bright, hard days of his manhood. Then one of the birds from the aviary screeched loudly. Truvius's head jerked up, his eyes blinking. He cocked a grey eyebrow at Baradoc and smiled. Nodding at Lerg, he said, "In my young days with the legions I would have given you a handful of gold for a dog like that. Aye, and I would rather travel with such a dog for companion than many a man I have known. My Tia was lucky to find you."

Baradoc shook his head. "I was lucky that she found me."

"You were both fortunate. She says that you must be well rewarded."

"I want nothing."

"This I know. But I make a gift from an old soldier to one who still has to face his first battle." He raised his right arm, letting the folds of his toga fall away from it. On his wrist he wore a thin, much worn gold armlet. He slipped it off and handed it to Baradoc. "This is the first battle decoration I won . . . when I was little more than your age. . . . Others and greater came later, the torques and disks and silver spearhead. But this was the first for no great act of bravery, more a moment of youthful rashness. Wear it.''

Baradoc took the thin, worn armlet and slipped it on. For him it would always hold the memory not only of the old Chief Centurion but also of Tia.

Each evening they sat in the courtyard, talking, before the time for bathing and dinner came; the three of them and the three dogs and the steward bringing them cool drinks and small dishes of salted nuts and sugared fruits to eat. It was an oasis of well-being and peace—which was shattered on the evening of the day before Baradoc was to leave.

They were sitting in the courtyard in the shade of the tall sweet chestnut when Cuna sat up and whined. At the same moment Lerg and Aesc rolled to their feet and both of them turned their heads toward their master.

Tia said, ''Why are the dogs uneasy?''

Baradoc stood up. None of them were armed. He signalled the dogs to keep their station. As he did so there was the sound of footsteps from behind him. He turned and saw the steward and his wife and the house servants come through from the reception room to stand in a close group at the top of the steps leading down into the courtyard. From the room behind them six men appeared and ranged themselves along the face of the covered walk, six men with long hair and bearded or moustached, six men wearing belted tunics of skin or wool, the cloth crudely striped in greens, reds and yellows. All of them were armed with spear and sword and all of them were weather-browned and hard-muscled, short, wiry mountain men. Before the three in the yard could make any move or sound, the man beside the steward, taller than the rest, a bronze torque about his neck, raised a hand as though commanding silence and then pointed beyond them to the archway that framed the top of the steps leading down to the river.

Baradoc swung round quickly. A tall man stood inside the archway, carrying sword and spear, a throwing axe thrust in his belt, a short cloak hanging from his shoulders over a finely dressed deerhide tunic, his legs bare of sandals or gartering. From behind him, rippling in like shadows, without sound, like some flawless movement of a dream, came six other men in hillman dress. They split on either side of him in even ranks. Each man carried a heavy hunting bow, raised and arrowed, the bows partly drawn and each arrowhead pointing at the group in midcourt. For a moment or two it seemed that the invasion was part of a dream.

Cuna broke the spell. With a sudden, short bark he raced forward to the man in the doorway. Before Baradoc could stop him, he leapt up and seized the edge of the man's tunic and hung on to it, swinging from its folds and growling. The man looked down at Cuna, then laughed, and putting his spear behind him against the archway wall, reached down and lifted Cuna by the scruff of his neck, pulling him free of the tunic skirt. Laughing still, he held Cuna aloft, yapping and growling.

Baradoc moved forward quickly, seeing the arrow points swing to follow him. He went up to the man who stood smiling with amusement at the suspended Cuna.

Baradoc said, "Put the dog down. He is young and bold and not yet fully broken to command." Without thinking he spoke in his own tongue. The man, no smile on his face now, tossed Cuna to him, Baradoc fondled the dog's ears for a moment and then dropped him to the ground, ordering him to go to Tia.

The man watched Cuna trot to Tia, eyed her briefly, and then turned to Baradoc and said quietly, "You speak my language, but not with a Cymric sound. You dress like a Roman landowner's son, but your hands are marked with hard work and you have the gift of silent talk with your dogs. Tell the big hound to come to me in peace, but say it in words, words that only I know in my tribe, words that in all the tribes are only given to the few."

From behind Baradoc the voice of Truvius came testily, angrily but bravely. "What does he say? What does the ruffian want? By the gods—that I should be so old and feeble . . ." He broke off suddenly in a fit of coughing.

Without turning Baradoc said in Truvius's tongue, "These

are hillmen from beyond the Sabrina. Their leader could be a man who prefers reason to force." Then, turning briefly, seeing Tia holding Cuna, the old man bowed forward, head doddering, in his applewood seat, he spoke briefly to Lerg.

The great hound moved forward slowly, the sunlight sliding over his rough pelt. He went up to the man in the archway and sat back on his haunches. The man put down his hand and with the back of it gently touched the black wet nose of Lerg. Lerg sat unmoving. The man withdrew his hand and said to Baradoc, "What did you say to the old man?"

"That you could be a man who prefers reason to force, a man who does not use the sword or spear without true cause."

"You speak their language well?"

"Yes. I served a Roman master as a slave for years."

"And still keep their company?"

"I did them a service. I go home to my people beyond the River Tamarus."

"*Aie* . . . now I know the strange notes in your words although they are mine. That you speak their tongue is good. You can speak for me and save the legs of old Machen, who nurses a mead-skin downriver with the rest of my men."

As the man was speaking Baradoc studied him. He was taller than most hillmen and he had a full handful of years more than himself. When he smiled there was no guile behind the eyes, but when he frowned there was force and authority in him.

Baradoc said, "I will speak for you."

"Good. But first I would know who you are."

"My name is Baradoc. I am the only son of my father, the son of great Ruachan, chief of the tribe of the Enduring Crow." He pulled aside the shoulder of the light tunic he wore and exposed the tattoo of his tribe's bird. He went on, "I return to my people to raise them and all our kind against the Saxons and . . ."

"Enough!" The man cut him short. "Such talk is everywhere among the tribes but it is no more than the empty chatter of house-safe sparrows as the hawk flies over. My business is of today—and here in this villa."

Anger was so strong in Baradoc that he had to hold down the words he would have spoken. Prudence alone moved him as he said, "I have named myself. Who are you?"

"I am Cadrus of the Ocelos." The man touched his right shoulder. "I bear their mark here. We are from the hills beyond Gobannium, and Eurium. But this day we are from Abonae, which my people hold after crossing the Sabrina."

"You go to Aquae Sulis?"

"No. We are not enough." He looked around the court-yard, smiled and said, "We are content to take the straying goslings. The fat goose can wait until another time."

Baradoc knew the joke had been made for him alone. The mark he carried on his shoulder was of the goose with the golden feet and bill, the Ocelos' tattoo.

"And from here? What do you take?"

"All weapons, save yours. All treasure and money. And some of the household for slaves. All this without force unless force is offered. Go to the old man and tell him this, and then stay with him and the girl while my men do their work. Who is the girl, his daughter?"

"No, his dead brother's daughter. She came with me from beyond the Anderida forest. She lived with her brother and his wife. Their villa and homestead farm were burned and pillaged by their own people . . . the ones who, fearing the Saxon coming, turn in madness on their own kind. The brother and his wife were killed. She escaped into the forest and I brought her here."

Cadrus nodded, and said, "Go tell the old man and then the three of you hold your place while my men do their work."

Baradoc went back to Tia and Truvius. Cadrus began to give orders to his men. Four were left spaced around the courtyard, their bows held ready, while the others began to go through the house. Cadrus stood in the archway and as the house was sacked the weapons and looted treasurers were piled alongside him, gold and silver plate spilling onto the stones, small leather pouches of coins from Truvius's room, a casket of jewels—nothing of good value was over-looked down to the smallest bronze brooch, the tiny hand lamps of

beaten copper—and amongst it all the silver chalice given by
Asimus, which had stood in Tia's bedroom.

Baradoc told Tia and Truvius what Cadrus intended. The
old man heard him in silence until the end and then he raised
his grey head and said, "So it must be, for the man who holds
the sword and the spear is master. What they take from us is
nothing. The years have made me helpless, and the times
have made victims of the innocent. All my servants are free
people. Now they go to slavery in some wild hill fortress."

Tia said firmly to Baradoc, "The man is of your kind. He
holds you in good faith. Go to him and ask him to spare the
servants."

Looking down at Tia as she sat on a stool at the old man's
feet, Cuna resting against her leg, Baradoc said nothing. But
the shadow of unease that had been with him from the
moment that Cadrus had glanced toward Tia was now grown
blacker in his mind. Truvius lived now in a dream of old age.
The world about him had long lost meaning. His life lay in
the past, his days now were a crawling serpent of slow hours
that wreathed about him and found him impatient for the
final sting. But Tia was at the beginning of her days. Cadrus's face had been unmoving as he had glanced at her, but
his eyes had mirrored the quick stir of his emotions.

Baradoc said, "This is no moment to ask for a favour
which will not be granted. The hillmen have no bellies for
field or farm work. Fighting and hunting are their work. A
slave is a high prize, to be put to the plough or the cattle folds,
or to be sold to the coast traders from Erin." But the more he
could have said he kept to himself, for a woman slave who
was fair in all men's eyes was a treasure not to be passed by.
Tia stirred angrily and began to speak. He broke in sharply
and said, "Stay here and say nothing. One wrong word could
put Cadrus out of humour." And then, as Tia looked up at
him tight-lipped, he saw her face slowly change and he knew
that she had read his thoughts.

From behind him Cadrus called sharply to the man who
guarded the servants outside the reception room. Prodding
them with the butt of his spear the man moved them down

into the courtyard and across to Cadrus. They halted before
him, the old steward and his plump wife, who worked the
kitchen, the strong middle-aged man who kept the bathhouse
and stoked the hypocaust for water and house heating, and a
younger man who did general work about the villa and kept
the small stable of two horses which drew the old man's
four-wheeled carriage when he drove to Aquae Sulis or went
to visit friends.

Cadrus raised a hand and beckoned Baradoc to him. He
nodded at the group and said, "I take the two younger men.
They are full of years and work. The old man and the woman
could not be worth the food they would eat. They can stay."

Baradoc turned to the servants and told them Cadrus's
decision. At once the steward and his wife moved quickly to
join Truvius and Tia. Of the two men the elder stood pas-
sive, but for an instant the head of the other turned, sweeping
round the courtyard, and he half moved as though to escape.
The movement was halted by the sharp hiss of a flighted
arrow loosed by one of the men near Cadrus. The arrow bit
deeply into the ground at the man's feet, the long shaft
vibrating savagely. From the men on guard around the courtyard and from the others who had now come from the
building rose a roar of laughter. Only Cadrus was silent. He
watched as his men, needing no signal from him, roped the
hands of the servants behind their backs and then fastened
heavy leather collars about their necks, each one joined to the
other by a long length of strong, plaited-hide rope. Cadrus
watched all this done and not until they were led away
through the archway toward the river did he turn to Baradoc.

He said, "What is the girl's name?"

"Gratia."

"You speak grudgingly. Tell her to go gather a warm
cloak and strong sandals and any woman's things she needs.
Tell her that in obedience she can walk free and unshackled
but if she kicks like a young heifer and would escape from the
path then she will be roped to the others for she now belongs
to Cadrus."

There was no surprise in Baradoc. He had now long known

in his heart that this moment was coming, had faced the dilemma and had known only one answer to make to it, an answer with the strength of tribal custom behind it, an answer with which all of his own race would keep faith, but an answer which Cadrus, his eyes trapped now by Tia's grace, might sweep aside with a single sharp word to bring a flight of arrows to destroy him. Tia's beauty shining in his eyes had blinded him.

Baradoc said coldly, "She cannot go with you. She is betrothed to me. Not even Cadrus of the Golden Goose can take the future wife of a man of the tribe of the Enduring Crow as a slave. The gods would mark your tribe forever with shame for the crime. She is promised to me, she stays with me."

Without hurry, no movement of muscle in his face to betray emotion, his eyes steady, Cadrus raised his sword and held it out point forward so that the sharply honed tip just touched Baradoc's breast. He said evenly, "Your tongue is swift in the battle of words and cunning. You are distantly of my blood and we share the same gods. If the feud fire had been lit between our tribes I would kill your father, slaughter your house and burn your huts, and there would be no shame for you would do the same to mine. There is no feud, and you speak fair that I cannot take for slave a woman who has promised herself to you." His hard face creased with a quick smile, and there was a touch of mockery in his voice as he went on, "But it is in my mind that you speak falsely for her sake. I would know from her without any word from you whether you speak the truth. From this moment you stay dumb as the slowworm. And, if she denies you, then I kill you as I would slaughter a young bull for the sacrifice!"

Without taking his eyes off Baradoc, the sword point always against the loose fall of his tunic, he called to one of his men, "Fetch me Machen here, for I need one who speaks the bastard tongue."

From the outer side of the archway he was answered at once by a slow, lilting voice, touched with the edge of lazy laughter. "Who sends for Machen when Machen is here fresh from mead sleep?"

A tall, thin middle-aged man, his face grizzled with long copper-coloured stubble, dressed in a rough habit of brown, its ragged skirts swinging as he walked, the loose cowl hanging down his back, came through the arch and stood alongside Cadrus.

With hardly a glance at Machen, Cadrus, sword never moving, pointed with his free hand to Tia and said, ''Tell the girl to come here. I would take her as slave, but this young bull denies me the right, saying that she is betrothed to him. She understands not our tongue but you will ask her the questions I give you in her own bastard language. If she denies the young bull, then he dies.''

''She knows you want her as slave?''

''No. They sit there knowing nothing—the ancient eagle of the legions and the sleek young falcon—and their world spins dying under them as yours spins when the mead takes you. You know their language and the gods have given you an ear for the music of song and the music of truth. If you tell me she says that he speaks the truth she can be no slave. If you hear the false note of a lie then she becomes my slave and this one dies.''

Baradoc felt the point of the sword prick him briefly as Cadrus finished speaking, and from the corner of his eyes he saw Machen move across the yard to Tia and Truvius.

Tia watched the man as he came to her. He moved slowly but easily and there was the ghost of a smile about his lips. Beside her sat Truvius, his hand in hers, mumbling to himself, staring straight ahead, his eyes blinking slowly with the fixed rhythm which marked his periods of withdrawal.

In her own tongue Machen said gently, ''Leave the old man and come with me. Speak no word to your young tribesman friend.''

Tia rose. Of all that had gone on between Baradoc and Cadrus she had caught only a few of the words she had come to know of their language. They gave her no grasp of the trouble between them, except that her own instinct and her knowledge of the ways of tribal raiders told her that there was some argument about slaves and herself. She went with Machen across the yard and up to Cadrus. He looked at her boldly, his gaze moving over her from head to foot, and she saw his mouth tighten, his shoulders tauten as he drew sharp breath and a sudden glitter fired his eyes. From her deep woman's instinct she knew at once that in some way she was a prize that Baradoc had disputed with him.

She stood at the foot of the semicircular steps rising to the archway and Machen stood with her, translating for her the questions that Cadrus made in their own language, and all the time Cadrus spoke and then Machen translated, Cadrus kept his eyes on her.

Machen asked her, "Cadrus would know how you met this young man."

"In the forest of Anderida after my brother and sister were killed and making my way to Aquae Sulis. . . ." There was a nervousness in her which she held down; but not entirely could she keep its note from her voice as she described how she had cut Baradoc down and they had then journeyed together.

"For how long have you travelled?"

"A month or more."

"Cadrus and our people have made this raid for weapons, treasure and slaves. He takes two of your good men and also he would take you." Machen paused, expecting some quick response or outburst from her. Women spoke or cried out before thought or common sense could govern emotion. This young woman said nothing. Her forehead slowly creased and her mouth tightened into a thin line. When she said nothing, he went on, "This man of the tribe of the Enduring Crow disputes his right by tribal law. He says that you are betrothed to him. If this is so then you cannot be made slave. Speak truly—are you promised one to the other and one by the other?"

With the question Tia, although she could not see him fully from where she stood and there was no sound or movement from him, knew the full reading of Baradoc's mind. It came to her now as it came from him to Lerg and the others, not words, not direct sense, but wholly in a magic that by its force turned the body and the brain to paths of understanding.

She said firmly, "It has been a secret between us which I was to tell my uncle this night. Yes, we are betrothed."

Machen turned to Cadrus and said, "She says he speaks the truth. They are promised to one another."

Without emotion Cadrus asked, "Does she speak the truth, my machen? Tell me and swear it by your faith, by the gods of the sacred oak groves, by the white purity of the tree-suckling mistletoe, and may your soul shrivel and there be no afterlife for you if you swear me false."

Machen without hesitation said, "I swear that she speaks the truth which is in her." But to himself, because the mead was still warm in him and there was a respect in him for the girl's bold and quick-witted response, he had no fear of imperilling his soul and his life hereafter. There were truths that grew between people which they could not know themselves until some sharp moment of destiny brought them to light.

Cadrus, his face suddenly softening to a smile, shrugged his shoulders and said, "Oh, Machen of the mead-breathing mouth, may the gods rack you if you lie because of her gorse-bloom hair and pretty forget-me-not eyes."

"I speak not falsely. There is no truth that lies so deep that my ferret mind cannot unwarren it."

Cadrus said, "Ask her if she knows what it is to marry a tribesman. She comes of high Roman blood. She knows only one way of life. This—" He waved his hand around the yard. "It is in me that she had deceived you, good Machen."

Machen turned to Tia and said, "Cadrus doubts you. Aye, he even doubts the truth in me. Answer now his question." He put to her the demand that Cadrus had made.

Tia, confidence growing in her, speaking as though some outside power and intelligence answered for her, replied, "I would marry him because I love him and he loves me. I would go to his people and their hard life because this country which my uncle and my father and all their kin before them helped to create now falls apart in misery."

She stood watching Machen and Cadrus as they spoke together, no more than an odd word of their talk having any meaning for her, and she kept her eyes from Baradoc, who stood wooden-faced with Cadrus's sword still at his breast. Then as Machen turned to her to speak again, she saw Cadrus lower the sword and slide it into the leather-and-wood scabbard that hung from his belt.

Machen, now smiling openly at her, said, "Cadrus, whose heart can be softened by a woman's ready wit as mine by good mead, salutes you. He accepts my word that you speak with a frank and true tongue. Now do as I say and he wishes. Go to the treasure which we take with us"—he nodded toward the piled weapons and household loot which lay heaped on the top of the broad archway step— "and choose any one thing you value and bring it back here to me. Go now."

Tia walked across to the piled loot and looked down at it. What of all she possessed was of great value to her? What of all the life she had until now was dear to her? Her family were all gone except Truvius and his days were few. These hillmen would go and the house would echo like a shell as she moved about it and the day would come when she would be alone in it. Baradoc would have gone to the west, and the lie she was living at the moment would have gained her only an empty freedom. Tears misted her eyes and almost without knowing it she bent and picked up the silver chalice and walked back to Machen. She gave it to him and he passed it to Cadrus.

Cadrus stepped up to her. He raised the chalice, touched his brow with it and then handed it to Tia. "Tell her," he said to Machen.

Machen, the dying sun threading his beard with copper glints, looked Tia deep in the eyes and said, "There is a long skein of kinship between the Ocelos people of the mountain and the people of the Enduring Crow. Before the wedding kinsmen bring gifts. This is Cadrus's gift to you. If times were different we should stay and make feast after the marriage. Now we stay only to make the gift and to join the ceremony. I am a priest whose power and authority no tribe, not even in the far north or the west, not even over the sea with the Scotti or beyond the first of all the great walls with the Picts, can question. Take now the hand of this man and go both of you to your uncle, and stand before him for his blessing so that I may join the hand of husband to wife.'' Then with a quick flicker of laughter in his eyes, he added, ''This must be so because the good but still-doubting Cadrus to know truth to be true would see it sanctified in deed.''

Cadrus turned to Baradoc and, his eyes now friendly, said, ''Go now—take your Roman filly, but think not that she will be easily schooled.''

Without a word Baradoc moved to Tia. And Tia, with a nervous shiver as though her body moved in the spell of a vivid dream, turned and took his hand. They went across the courtyard toward Truvius and the tribesmen with lowered bows and rested weapons watched them. Long evening shadows striped the paving and flower beds. The aviary birds took the last of the paling light on their enamelled wings, and the sound of the worker bees about the shrubs by the running springwater of the well made a heady droning. They walked, neither looking at the other, and behind them came the three dogs and from the end of the red-tiled roof Bran, his sable plumage lacquered with the sun's last glow, sat still and graven like a carved corbel. They stood before Truvius, who sat, his head sunk on his chest in sleep, his old vine staff resting across his knees. Tia reached out a hand and touched him. Slowly he raised his head and blinked the weight of sleep from them, then smiled and said, ''What has happened? What is it, my Tia?''

Tia, her hand in Baradoc's said, ''We come to you, my dear uncle Truvius, for your blessing.''

CHAPTER EIGHT

The Flood Riders

TIA WOKE JUST BEFORE FIRST LIGHT. As she lay in the darkness she heard Cuna whine gently from the foot of her bed. She spoke quietly to him and he was silent. About her the ravaged house was still. She saw the eyes of Cadrus on her as she had faced him. There was good and bad in the man. Her body shook with a spasm of remembered fear as she thought of the life which would have been hers had she had to follow him as a slave. Baradoc had saved her from that, but she could not guess at what cost to himself, to his pride and his deep sense of tribal customs. True, Machen—who for some hidden reasons of his own had taken her part—had guided and shielded her as she stood before Cadrus, and then had carried out the simple pledging ceremony in the courtyard, joining her hand with Baradoc's after Truvius had given them his blessing. Dear Uncle Truvius . . . sometimes she wondered whether there were not, as well as his true lapses into senility, also times when he pretended them either to cloak his own helplessness or from a deep wisdom which compensated for the vigour and mastery of his old days. And Baradoc? By his quick thinking he had saved her, had stood by her while Machen joined them, his face giving no sign of any emotion he felt. Strange Baradoc . . . with his burning dream of the future. As he took her hand, he would have been already rejecting the picture of himself leading a Roman woman into the homecoming gathering of his people . . . their wild and noisy greetings turning to silence as they eyed her. Well, he need have no worry. He had saved her from slavery. She would not nor could not make any claim on him. When he got back to his people he could say that she had refused to follow him, refused to be a wife, and one of his own holy men could with a few words break the tie that bound them.

Cuna whined again, louder. In the silence that followed Tia heard two sounds, the brief protesting *cark* of Bran from somewhere in the courtyard and the sharp note of metal momentarily striking against stone. Cuna whined again, a low muted note, and swiftly there was an understanding clear and vividly all-embracing in Tia. Baradoc was going. Sword or fish spear had swung against the stone parapet of the courtyard well as Bran, from the ironwork canopy over it, his favourite nighttime roost, had hopped to his shoulder; and Cuna had whined because . . . poor Cuna, who had been pledged to her, sensed that the others moved away and longed to go with them.

Tia got out of bed, wrapped a cloak about her shoulders and went barefooted from her room into the open corridor. Part of the yard lay washed in moonlight as pale as the underside of a willow leaf and the chestnut's shadow was dark as a thundercloud over the archway that led to the river. Baradoc, Bran on his shoulder, the two dogs at his side, dressed now in his rough clothes, the old sword at his side, his travelling bundle slung over his shoulder from the head of the fish spear, stood in the tree shadow at the foot of the archway steps.

She walked down the corridor, past the aviary where the bright birds were now, as they roosted, dark, strange-shaped fruit on the shrubs and twisting creepers, and out onto the uncovered terrace by the archway. Baradoc heard her, and was still as she came up to him. They stood in the tree shadow and their faces were stiff masks as though they wore them like the theater players of some high drama.

Tia said quietly, "So you go?"

"Yes." Baradoc's voice was thick as if some inner anger half strangled it.

"At night and without farewell?"

"Because of what has been and the way it has been, yes. I

come from a different world. There is no place in it for you even if we truly loved one another.''

"You would be ashamed to bring a Roman before your people as a wife?"

Baradoc was long in answering. Then he said, "Be content, Lady Tia. What was done was to save you from Cadrus. Not to gain you for myself. When I reach my people the priest will set all aside."

"You do not answer my question."

"No, I would have no shame before them. Our paths no longer lie together. I take the ford across the river and the mining road west to the hills."

"Then you shall take Cuna with you. I give him back."

Baradoc hesitated briefly and then, with a small shrug, he said, "If you so wish."

With an abruptness that surprised Tia, he turned sharply and moved through the archway, his bundle swaying on the spear, the dogs at his heels. When he was gone from her sight she went back into her room and lay in the darkness, seeing him moving through the night, the dogs around him, and Bran on his shoulder. What had been done had been done to save her from Cadrus. There was nothing more between them. He had his world and she had hers. . . .

When morning came, as she had done every day since she had arrived, she gathered flowers from the courtyard and went to Baradoc's room after the servant had cleaned it to refill the small earthenware jar on the table by the window. She knew that, until some new guest used the room, she would do so every day because this until then was Baradoc's room and much of him lingered there for her still.

As she arranged the flowers and stepped back to look at them she saw on the end of the table one of her uncle's flat ivory writing tablets, and she knew that Baradoc must have taken it from the reception room, where her uncle kept it at hand to make notes of household affairs. She picked it up and held it under the light from the window. The smooth wax bed was stylus-scored with writing in her own language. She read the words and at first there was a confusion in her mind through which they slipped, almost avoiding capture. Then she read them again. This time, although her eyes were slowly touched by tears, nothing of the message was lost to her.

> I would have built for you a house with a
> roof of green rushes and a flower-pied floor.
> A thousand seabirds would have greeted the
> golden girl with a brow like a lily, the
> young queen who rode the perilous paths
> without harm or hurt.

And as she stood there Truvius, leaning on his staff, came into the room. She turned and ran to him and he put an arm around her and held her as she wept.

A spear's throw from the rough road Baradoc sat with his back against a rock, facing the west, eating a handful of dried grapes and a piece of hard cheese. The sun was shrouded in a low, rolling mantle of grey rain-promising clouds. There had been little morning movement on the mining road, a few carts making for Aquae Sulis with country produce, a handful of miners on their way back to the lead mines in the low limestone hills over which the clouds now were close-wreathed. The men had given him news of Abonae. The hillmen had taken it some days before and most of the people from the settlement had fled into the country to hide. Cadrus and his men would go back across the river in their hide-sheathed boats, taking their spoils with them. One day some-one would have to arise with the strength and power to command Cadrus and his kind, to shape and wield their courage and skills and make of them an army with a mission and a true faith. He broke the cheese into small portions and tossed a piece to each dog and Bran, and he smiled to himself as he realized that to Cuna he had tossed the largest piece. The gifted dog. The twice-gifted dog.

But this thought was driven from his mind as Cuna suddenly leapt to his feet, barked and began to run toward the

road. Baradoc called sternly to him, but the dog took no
notice. At the same time, although Lerg and Aesc held their
place, Bran, from the top of the rock against which Baradoc
leant, took off, dropped low, his great wings almost sweeping the seeding heads of the long grasses, and then rose,
beating his way above the road. In those few moments a wild
hope swept through Baradoc which shook his body as though
a swift fever had gripped him, firing his blood. He jumped up
and ran toward the road. Far down it he saw a low cloud of
dust racing away like wind-flattened smoke. Clear to him
came the sound of horse hooves beating against the hard
ground.

Standing by the road, watching her ride toward him, he
knew that this was what he had wished for but had cherished
only as an idle dream that defied all sense and reason. Only
she was free to turn the ceremony of duress into the truth or
denial of love. Now she came riding the single horse, which,
being free at grazing, Cadrus's men had overlooked, and he
knew that even had he left the road earlier and moved without
benefit of track or path to the hills she would have found him
because, no longer to be denied, the heart had its own
knowledge of human courses as the swallow went unerringly
south in autumn to return to the same hut eave each spring.

With Cuna barking around the horse's legs she halted
before him, her growing hair free and shining in the wind, her
eyes smiling but uncertain with a soft shyness. Behind her a
bundle was packed across the horse's back and she was
dressed as he was in the old travelling clothes. Going to her
and looking up, he took her hand. With a touch as brief and
light as the wing of a passing moth he kissed her palm, and
the shyness went from Tia. Her lips upturned with a faint
touch of mockery, she said, "O Son-of-a-Chief Baradoc,
who was too cowardly to speak the truth, but wrote it on wax
in the night—is that how your love will be? Easily scribed
and as easily wiped away?"

Baradoc raised her hand, touched his brow with it, and
then, kissing it again, said, "No, Lady Tia. What I wrote on
the tablet was the shadow of a dream which I thought would

die at daybreak." He held her arm as she slipped off the horse and stood by him, and he went on, smiling, "Now we both have our feet on the ground and live no dream." He raised her hand and kissed it. "This is the kiss of my true love and the true pledge that joins us. From this day, as there is only one royal sun, so there is only one queen in my life. Your honour is my honour and any who misnames it shall have only the swift charity of my sword."

For a moment Tia said nothing. Then, the teasing in her eyes masking her joy, she said, "O Son-of-a-Chief Baradoc, your old master gave you a skill with words that snares my heart . . . aye, and did so, I know now, from our first day together. But this day I have ridden hard and far and without food. If you would not hear the belly of your love grumble then feed me." She leant quickly forward and kissed him on the lips. Before he could hold her, she bent and picked Cuna from the ground and began to fondle him.

Baradoc led the horse to the rock and made Tia sit on the ground on the goat-hair cloak, and he fed her from the small store he had brought from the villa with him. There were few words between them and when their eyes met it was as though a light passed between them too strong and too strange yet for them to endure its flame but briefly. Man and woman they would be but until that time came there lay ahead of them the groves of courtship to be threaded hand in hand, and a sweet and slow discovery of one another which would bring their love to full term.

They slept that night in a dry cave on the lower slopes of the hills, lying so that in the darkness they could reach out and touch one another. Until sleep took them, it was mostly Baradoc who talked, both to ease his own shyness and joy and also to have her begin to know about the journey ahead and the life that waited for them with his people. He told, too, about these hills which they must cross, where now most of the mines were worked out or abandoned, and the great stretch of marsh-and-lake land that lay beyond, which must be crossed before they would reach the coast where the barren moors ran down to the sea in steep headlands. Finally he heard Tia's breath-note slow and her body stir briefly to find comfort as she fell into sleep. Then as he lay awake he thought of old Truvius, who, Tia had told him, had sent her after him with his blessing, of Truvius who had once said to him as they talked in the courtyard together, "All countries are greater than the people who take them by the sword. They shape conquerors to their ways and work in them a new love which is a mystery above any human love." So it would be with Tia. One day she would know herself to be not only his wife, but one of his people, and their children would be of his country.

The high-summer rain fell steadily the whole of the next day. Because there was no hunting with success through the slow-driving swathes of rain as they climbed the long scarp to the crest of the range, they turned aside to the road and found a small mining encampment of meager huts and a rough tavern, where they bought cheese and oat cake and dried fish and six eggs for their evening meal. The tavern keeper told them that in the last week there had been few travellers coming or going through from the quest because the marsh people would boat none across the lakes and swamps. He advised Baradoc to take the long route around to the south, but Baradoc's mind was set on crossing the marshes for it would save them two or three days' travel and there was a growing eagerness in him now to reach his own people.

They crossed the top ridge of the hills in a grey shroud of rain cloud and picked their way slowly down the steep westward face through rocky ravines and sides of loose stones where the horse, laden with their goods, had to be led and sometimes forced to keep the track. That night on the lower slopes they found a herder's hut, its wattle sides and bough-thatched roof half burned away in some old accident or act of pillage. Baradoc cut fresh branches from a nearby thicket of alders and repaired enough of the roof to give them shelter. Even so, the rain drifted in upon them and they passed the night with more discomfort than sleep, but because they were together and their shyness was easing they made light of the hardship. Baradoc said, half in joke and half in earnest, "You could be lying warm and comfortable and clean in your bed at the villa, Tia. Even now I would take you—"

With a suddenness that startled him, Tia suddenly reached out and put her hand across his mouth, stopping his words, and she said without anger but with a sharp note of command, "Never talk like that again. I belong to you."

As she withdrew her hand Baradoc took it and said, "Then I never will. When you command I obey." He chuckled. "*Aie* . . . from that first moment after you had cut me down and I opened my eyes to see you I became your slave."

Tia, smiling shook her head. "You talk, and your tongue runs away with you, my brave heart. You will never be anyone's slave."

When they awoke the next morning the rain was still falling, driving before a strong southerly wind in dark, swaying curtains. They ate a scanty cold breakfast of dried fish and were wet through to their skins before they had travelled half a mile. The western slopes of the limestone range eased and finally levelled out at the fringe of the great river-and-lagoon-scored stretch of marshes that lay across their path. Skirting the first stretch of towering rushes and reed-mace growth, they came across a well-used path. In places the path had been firmed and strengthened with faggots of cut withy branches and bound bundles of reeds. After a time it brought them to an opening in the marsh growths and they stood on the edge of a small piece of cultivated ground, the tilled dark marsh soil green with lines of growing vegetables and lank rows of still unripe barley. Beyond the cultivated ground was a narrow lagoon inlet. Built on wooden piles a little way out in the water was a reed hut which was joined to the land by a rough wooden causeway. From raised poles along the causeway and at one side of the hut fishnets were strung. From the eaves of the roof hung plaited osier cages and coops in which fowls and pigeons were penned.

Baradoc shouted three times before any movement came from the hut. Then a short thickset man appeared and came to the head of the causeway.

Baradoc, giving the horse's halter to Tia to hold, walked

forward slowly a few paces, holding his hands above his head. The man on the causeway made no movement.

Baradoc drew the sword from his belt and thrust it upright into the ground and then walked forward farther. At this the man came slowly down the causeway. In one hand he carried a light spear, and his other hand rested on the haft of a long knife which was thrust into the belt at his waist. He was bearded and long-haired and dressed in a sleeveless tunic made of otter skins roughly thonged together, the garment worn and greasy and ripped in places. The man stepped off the causeway and walked to within a few paces of Baradoc, then stood in silence for a while, eyeing him suspiciously. The skin around his right eye was red and swollen. The rain ran off his bare arms and legs and the sour smell of his body came strongly to Baradoc. The man's gaze went from Baradoc to Tia with the horse and dogs standing at the fringe of the reeds.

He said gruffly, "What do you want?"

The words were in Baradoc's tongue, but heavy with the marshmen's accent and surly with suspicion.

"We go to my tribe in the west. We have money and will pay for a passage across the marshlands."

"Who is the woman?"

"My wife."

"The word has been given that none can cross the marshes." He gestured to the south. "You must go round. Besides, I have nothing that would take your horse."

Baradoc said "We want to cross quickly. To go round will take many days. The word was not given against your own kind. Marshmen have eaten in my father's hut many times. We have the same tongue, the same country."

"Maybe. Show me your mark."

Baradoc pulled his cloak and tunic aside and showed his tribal mark of the crow. "We want to cross now. If this rain lasts another day not even you could take us against the floods."

The man pursed his lips. "What do you know of the marshes and the rains? Nothing. This is the rain of Latis, who weeps for the return of her lover.'' A smile briefly touched his dirty, weather-marked face. ''She could weep for a day or a week. No man can tell.''

Baradoc said, ''Then let us leave Latis to weep long if she must. You could have us on the other side by nightfall. Also—'' he paused, for he had seen the man's eyes stray more than once back to the horse which Tia held, ''as well as paying you we would leave the horse. Two people with one horse travel no faster than a man alone.''

The man was silent for a moment and then, grinning, nodded his head, and said, ''Leave me the horse. I need no other payment.''

From that moment there was no trouble. The horse was handed over to the man, who told them his name was Odon. From his hut appeared his wife and son, who was a sturdy boy, his face still smooth and untouched by any beard growth. At a word from Odon the boy dived off the edge of the causeway and swam across the lagoon inlet to the fringing reeds. He disappeared into them. In a short while he reappeared, poling a strong, light-drafted boat made of overlapping hides stretched over a framework of willow poles. The inside had been roughly daubed with a mixture of marsh mud and chopped straw and sedges, all set hard by baking in the sun, and then given a coating of fish glue whose rank smell still persisted.

Between them they loaded up the possessions which Baradoc and Tia carried and the dogs, Tia sat forward in the blunt bows, while Baradoc was in the middle of the boat and Odon stood in the stern to pole the craft. At his feet lay a broad-bladed wooden paddle which he would use in deeper and more open water.

At first the boy wanted to go with his father and refused to leave the boat. After a few angry words between them Odon swung his pole menacingly and the boy jumped over the side and waded ashore, shouting defiantly at his father.

As Odon poled off he laughed and said to them, ''He's as wild as a wolf—but he's a good son. I had two others but they died of marsh fever.'' He shook his head to free his hair and eyes of the rain and went on to Baradoc, ''There's a bailing pot near you. The boat is sound. But with this rain it gathers water. You'll need to use it.'' He dipped the pole and they began to move down the narrow inlet.

For the next two hours Tia sat in the bows, the thick woollen cloak draped around her, growing heavier and heavier with the rain. Sitting there, she was, although wet and uncomfortable, surprised by the calmness and happiness of her feelings. She had no true idea of what lay ahead. But she had no dread or concern about it because her spirit was content with the calm knowledge that whatever happened now she and Baradoc were together, not as strangers held by chance, but as man and wife tied by love.

She sat with the dogs at her feet as the boat slid down the inlet and, after a while, Bran, who had been circling overhead, dropped down and perched on the low prow of the boat. Odon, seeing the raven, said something to Baradoc, who answered, but Tia could not understand what they said. Odon, now that the bargain had been made, seemed pleasant enough but there was something about the man that she did not like, something that had nothing to do with his dirty, unkempt appearance or the strange cast given to his face by the constantly twitching diseased eye. Baradoc had told her that the marshmen had long grown apart from all the other tribes. Nearly five hundred years of Roman rule had left places like this and the wild mountains from which Cadrus came much as they always had been. Beyond Isca no great military roads ran. Westward was an almost unknown land, and it was westward that she was now going.

Hour after hour they moved through the marshes, sometimes snaking through narrow channels that were overhung with high reeds and rushes, sometimes sliding out into stretches of river where the brown waters rolled and swirled so strongly with the rain flood that Odon had to fight his way with strong strokes of the paddle to ease the boat out of the mainstream and into a side channel to keep his course.

Tia grew used to the sudden upflinging of a fishing heron disturbed by their coming, to the quick fire-flash of

kingfishers arrowing away from them, to the noisy alarm
calls of mallard, teal and widgeon rising from their feeding
grounds, churning the water to a creamy spume with their
thrusting feet and beating wings, to the sudden shocks which
she had had at first when the weird booming calls of bitterns
rang through the rainy air. Now and again Baradoc pointed
out to her an otter sliding through the water, or the white
marked head of a water snake as it curved sinuously away
from them.

In the early afternoon they came to a wide weed-free
lagoon. Near the shore stood a small group of huts built on
poles over the water. From the causeways and platforms
around the huts a group of marsh people watched them pass
and Odon gave them a wild, ringing cry of greeting as they
swept by. Sometime after this they entered a track of swamp-
land where alders and willows crested the reeds of little
islands and the shallow stream they followed closed until the
rushes at times overhung the boat.

After a while the stream began to broaden, and eventually
the boat slid out to a small lake into which a river ran from the
south and emptied from the north end. Nearly halfway across
this lake, short of the main river flow, a solitary hut stood on
poles. It had no causeway because it was too far from the
shore, but there was a wooden platform around it.

Odon, taking the paddle, swung the boat toward the hut.
He said to Baradoc, ''The hut is empty. We rest for an hour
and eat.'' He looked up at the sky. ''Soon I think the rain will
stop. By nightfall I can put you on a safe path to take you
through the far side of the marshes.''

Odon edged the boat into the side of the hut, dropped his
paddle and held on to the timber frame of the platform. He
held the boat steady as Tia climbed out and the dogs jumped
up with her. To Baradoc he said, ''You go up. There's a rope
in the bows you can make fast.''

Baradoc climbed on to the platform, walked to the bows
and knelt to take the bow rope. As he did so, and before he
could reach the rope, Odon, giving a strong push on the
platform's edge, sent the boat gliding away from the hut. As

it drifted he picked up the paddle and turned the boat back in the direction from which they had come. Over his shoulder he shouted, "The word was given that none should cross. I would have taken you for you are a tribesman. But I take no woman who is not of the blood and who speaks only the foreign tongue."

Turning his back on them, he began to paddle strongly away. Baradoc and Tia, taken by surprise, stood and watched him. He was going and taking with him all they possessed, leaving them stranded in the middle of the lagoon. Then, angrily, Baradoc swore loudly, and the anger was at himself for his stupidity. For a moment his instinct was to dive in and swim after the boat, but he knew at once that Odon could easily outspace him. All their weapons and belongings were in the boat, except for the sword which he wore. Even if he got to the boat Odon had a spear. . . .

Then, the dullness clearing from his mind, he turned to Tia, unbuckling his belt and beginning to strip, and said, "Give me your dagger."

"But, Baradoc, you can't—"

"Give me your dagger!" he cried harshly as he stripped himself naked.

Tia handed him the dagger which she always carried. Baradoc took it and then turned toward Bran, who had flown up onto the rush roof of the hut. He called loudly, "*Saheer! Aie! Saheer!*"

Without another glance at Bran or Tia, the dagger between his teeth, he dived into the water and began to swim as fast as he could after the boat.

From the platform Tia, her heart thumping, watched him and she saw that he would never catch Odon. The man, seeing him coming, was paddling hard for a reed channel at the northern end of the lake. No man swimming could ever overtake the boat. Then, harsh and searing through the rain, she heard the strong wingbeats of Bran. Bran came down through the wind-driven rain and flew low over the water after Baradoc. Tia heard Baradoc whistle to Bran as the bird hung at his side. The raven wheeled away from him and began to beat quickly toward the boat.

Standing on the hut platform, the dogs about her, alert and quivering as they watched, Tia saw Baradoc swimming as fast as he could through the dark waters, saw Odon paddling toward the reed channel, and Bran moving after the boat. The raven rose in the air and then came down in a slow, heavy stoop at Odon, passing over the man's head, raking it with his talons, and then swung back to hover and beat with talons and great beak at Odon's head and face.

Odon raised his paddle and swung at Bran. The bird slid away from him only to come back, first from one angle and then from another, forcing him to twist and turn on his seat as he struck upward with his paddle. Again and again Bran dived at Odon, baulking and sideslipping to avoid the paddle blows. Once as Odon slipped on his seat, Bran landed on his shoulders and drove rapid thrusts of his great black beak at the man's neck and face.

Odon screamed with sudden pain and Bran, hovering away from him, called loudly "*Cark-cark.*" As Bran came in again Odon dropped the paddle and picked up his light spear. He stood up in the boat, blood running from his face, and slewed and turned as Bran attacked him, but Bran now kept well clear of the quick spear thrusts, circling and diving and calling loudly all the while.

As Odon could no longer paddle, the boat lost way and drifted, and Baradoc rapidly began to overtake it. He saw Odon glance around to mark his progress. When he neared the boat he circled away to the bows, well clear of any spear thrust that Odon might make, safe in the knowledge that Odon would not risk throwing it, for a frenzy now had taken Bran, who whirled and swooped at Odon. One unguarded opening given to Bran and the raven would strike for Odon's eyes. Baradoc caught the side of the boat and with a great thrust of his arm and shoulder muscles lifted himself over the side. The boat tipped as he rolled aboard and water swirled over the gunwale. He heard the hoarse bark of Bran and a sudden fierce cry of pain from Odon. As he scrambled to his knees Odon, with blood running down his neck where Bran had struck him, raised the spear and hurled it wildly at him. Baradoc threw up an arm to protect himself and the blade of the spear scored the length of his right forearm and flew past him into the water. Then Odon, to escape Bran as the bird came swooping at him, dived overboard and disappeared. Oblivious of his wound, Baradoc stood, dagger now in hand, and watched the brown waters while Bran circled slowly overhead. Suddenly he called and went downwind through the rain wreaths toward the distant fringe of reeds about the channel opening through which they had come into the lake. Odon's head and shoulders appeared above water, but as Bran dived at him he sank quickly below the surface and Baradoc knew that when he surfaced again it would be in the safety of the reeds. He called to Bran, and the raven, after a slow circle over the waters of the mouth of the channel, beat back to him upwind and dropped to the bows of the boat.

The wound in Baradoc's arm, though long, was not deep. Tia, tight-lipped, tore strips of cloth from an undershift and bound it. They had unloaded their possessions from the boat, which was now securely tied alongside the hut platform. Above them the rain beat steadily on the weathered and decrepit rush roof. The hut was empty except for an old pile of reeds laid out as a bed in one corner. Seeing Tia's anxious, drawn face Baradoc raised his free hand and touched her on the cheek. He said, ''Don't worry about Odon. He won't come back.''

''Why didn't he keep his bargain? You are of the same blood.''

Baradoc hesitated, then said lightly, ''The same blood, maybe—but his has become diluted with the fever water of the marshes. He was over-greedy for a good bargain.'' He looked up at the leaking roof, the sound of the rain beating on it mingling with the noise of the floodwater rushing against the piles below them. He went on, ''Odon was wrong or lying about Latis. She still weeps for her lover. I think we should stay here the night. In this rain and with darkness coming on we should be helpless. We can make an early start at daybreak. I'll see what food we've got.''

Tia shook her head. ''You do no woman's work. Sit and

rest your arm. And while I do it you can tell me about Latis
. . ." Her voice trailed away. Impulsively she moved to
Baradoc and pressed her face against his breast, holding him.
She felt his arms move around her and slowly the comfort of
his embrace eased the shaking in her own body and killed the
fear she had known for him when she had seen him climb into
the boat and Odon had flung the spear. She raised her head to
him and Baradoc touched her cheeks gently and then bent and
kissed her on the lips.

While she lay in the darkness before sleeping Tia thought
of the story of Latis, which Baradoc had told her as they had
sat eating, sharing their cold and short commons with the
dogs and Bran. Beside her, his arms ready at hand, Baradoc
slept. She drew close to him to find the warmth and comfort
of his body to join with her own. Latis still wept . . . Latis,
who, sitting by the side of a river, had seen a great silver
salmon swimming in the waters below her and had fallen in
love with it. To please her the gods had changed the salmon
into a young warrior who had stepped from the waters into
her arms. But each year in the winter the warrior lover moved
back into the waters, became a salmon, and swam away to
sea, not to return until the next year's floods brought him
again upriver to step silver-armoured into her arms. Latis,
who sits beside the drought-starved waters and weeps, flood-
ing the rivers with her tears to bring her lover back from the
sea, hastening to her up the spate-filled stream. . . .

Latis wept all that night and was weeping the next morning. When they looked out the floodwaters had risen so much
that the boat floated level with the hut platform and would
soon be in the hut itself. A brown torrent, carrying drift and
flood debris, swept through the lake, and the fringing rushes
stood now with only their flowering tips above water. They
could not stay in the hut and in this flood there was no hope of
finding a way across the miles of marsh they still had to cross.
They must follow the river down to the sea and then make
their way westward inshore until they were clear of the
marshlands.

They loaded the boat with their belongings. Baradoc

pulled one of the framework timbers from the hut wall and with his sword and knife fashioned a rough second paddle so that they both could sit in the stern and handle the craft between them. With the animals sitting up forward and their belongings stowed amidships they went downstream on the summer spate-filled river, a rolling flood of creamy-brown water running so high now that they could see far over the marsh stretches on either side. They had no need to use their paddles except to keep the boat on course. When Tia had got used to handling hers, Baradoc now and then left her to hold their course while he bailed the rainwater out of the boat. By mid-morning the simpleminded Latis gave up weeping. The wind shifted round into the east and slowly the sky began to clear of the low, heavy clouds which had dominated it for so long.

The farther north they moved down the river, the larger it grew. At noon they came to a wide lagoon. To one side of it they saw a hut with the water well over its platform. They paddled out of the mainstream and across to it. When there was no answer to Baradoc's shouts, they eased alongside the platform and tied up, and Baradoc splashed along the flooded boards and into the hut. The marsh family who inhabited it had clearly left from fear of the rising waters. Such stores as they could not take with them were lodged high up under the roof or on the rough shelving on either side of the door.

Baradoc found dried fish, a basket of wild duck eggs, a hard circular slab of bread, three smoked eels, a waterskin half-full of thin barley beer and a small wicker cage in which sat three miserable-looking hens. He loaded them all into the boat and left payment for his takings with some of the money which Tia had brought with her. As he got back into the boat and they pushed off, Tia said, "Look, the flood must be going down." She pointed to the wattled side of the hut where a dark, wet band showed a handsbreadth above the water.

Baradoc scooped some of the lagoon water into his hands, tasted it and spat it out. "No—the flood's still running high.

The tide is going out. We must be nearing the mouth of the river. The water's salty here.''

By midafternoon they were running down the looping estuary of the river. Mud flats were showing above the dropping tide and echelons of gulls and waders were beginning to work them. On either side of the estuary the marsh ground spread dense and high with reeds. To the westward, over this sea of moving greenery, they could just make out, like a brown mist in the distance, the hazy rise of the first low hills beyond the flatlands. A little while later they were free of the mudbanks and the bordering marshes, moving into the sea on the breast of the river that curved like a dark ribbon across the turquoise and jade waters of the sea, a ribbon that thinned and faded and frayed as the sea slowly took it and made it part of itself. When they were well clear of the land the tide, running hard, took them and swept them westward.

Tia, stiff and tired with the labour of their river ride, dropped her paddle and rubbed her sore hands. A seal surfaced briefly and watched them with lustrous eyes. Baradoc cut portions of the hard bread and smoked eel and handed them to Tia. As he did so he held one of her hands, raised it to his mouth and kissed the rough palm.

CHAPTER NINE

The Fortress Of Birds

THAT NIGHT THEY paddled ashore to a sandy beach walled by high dunes. Climbing the near dunes, Baradoc saw that they were backed by a wilderness of marshes which stretched inland and away to the west. They pulled the light boat ashore, well above the high-water mark, and, tipping it on its side, propped it up with their two paddles to make themselves a shelter in whose lee they could sleep. After some difficulty Baradoc made a fire, starting with dried grasses from a mouse's nest which Cuna dug out of the dune side. They killed a hen and boiled it in a mixture of their thin, musty beer and some rainwater that Tia had bailed from the bottom of the boat to fill their own waterskin as they came down the river. The duck eggs from the hut they found were already hard-boiled so they cut them up into the cauldron to thicken the broth and added some mussels that Baradoc had foraged from the low-water rocks. As soon as their meal was cooked, Baradoc smothered the fire with sand for while they were in the marshlands he knew it was wise not to attract attention to themselves.

Even so, as they ran the boat into the water at first light the next morning and began to paddle away, four marshmen came over the dune tops and ran into the water after them, shouting and waving their spears. Seeing that they could not stop them, they went back to the beach and began to throw stones at them from their slings. They paddled well out and then turned along the coast pushed by the tide which had just ebbed and was running out strongly westward. All that morning as they worked at their paddles they now and then saw small parties of men, women and children come over the dunes and down to the water's edge to watch them, all the men armed and from their manner hostile.

They paddled all that morning while the tide ran. When the water finally slacked and began to turn they were clear of the low stretches of dunes and marshes and moving along a coast where now the cliffs began, rising higher with each mile they passed. The cliffs were topped with trees and green hanging valleys, some of which held a few huts, and they could see the patchwork of small fields.

They turned in at low tide to a small beach, cliff-buttressed and with no sign of habitation, and they ate and filled their waterskins from a small cascading stream that came down the rocks. It was here that they decided that as long as the weather lasted, which had now set fair, they would stay with the boat and work their way along the coast by water. Ashore, the travelling would be hard because they were reaching that part of the coast where beyond the eversteepening cliffs the land ran back in a high moorland plateau, full of bogs and running streams, and without roads, a place of desolation which travellers avoided by going far to the south. On the sand with a stick Baradoc drew a map for Tia showing the river that rose on the moor and ran south to the old legion fortress of Isca and then on to the sea that separated Britain from Gaul. Then he outlined the other great moor that lay west of Isca, where two other great rivers ran northward, rising not far from Nemetostatio, an abandoned legionary outpost, to join each other before meeting the sea in the great bay guarded on the west by the high promontory of Hercules, beyond which the coast ran away sharply to the southwest toward his own homeland.

Watching him as he talked, the sunlight glinting on his newgrowing beard, marking the line of the fast-healing cut on his bare arm, Tia was aware that it was almost as though she had never really looked at him before. This Baradoc was her husband. He was leading her into a strange land beyond the Tamarus River, to a life which would close around her and claim her for the rest of her years—and she was not only totally unprepared for it, but hardly given it any serious thought in the happiness which had flooded her as she had galloped away from the Villa Etruria to join him. Searching to make some amends for this she said quickly, "From this moment we speak only my tongue in the morning. The rest of the day we use yours. I should be a wife without honour if I got to your people and cannot talk to them freely. And each night before we sleep you will tell me about their history, their legends, and their beliefs and their gods. I would not shame you with my ignorance or my dumbness."

Baradoc said nothing. He put his arms around her and drew her to him, both of them half upright, kneeling on the soft sand. He kissed her and felt her lips move with his, felt her arms fold about him as his held her tight to him. And they held together so moulded to one another until Cuna suddenly barked and jumped up at them, and then they collapsed sideways onto the sand map. From that moment there was no longer any Lady Tia and no longer any Son-of-a-Chief Baradoc, or any curtain between them.

The following days moved to a pattern which was brightened by settled fine weather, and the quiet swell and fall of the summer sea imposed on them something of its own easy rhythm. They moved with the tide when it began to ebb westward whether it was day or night. They slept sometimes in daylight, sometimes under moonlight, sometimes on the warm sands, sometimes in the boat as it rocked under the stars. Tia began to learn Baradoc's language fast, and she lay often with her head against his shoulder as he told her about his people and their history, spoke their poems to her and taught her their songs. One night they slept in the summer hut of a friendly old fisherman at the head of a small beach at the foot of a gorge through which tumbled and roared a swift moorland river. He knew nothing of the world outside his fishing station and the small settlements he served. From him they bought hooks, gorges, lines and a small net so that they could do their own fishing, and when they left he gave them a great slab of heather honeycomb, which they wrapped in dock leaves and kept cool in their cauldron.

Before they left, the old man, nodding at their boat, said, "The gods have been good to you with the weather. Not for many years have I known it so settled. But when you come to the mouth of the Two Rivers, even though the gods still smile take to the land." They left him and idled along the coast for many days, working the tides, or sometimes passing whole days sheltered on secure cliff-guarded beaches, wrapped in the laziness and bliss of the sun and their own happiness. Then came a day when the high cliffs, their tops flaming now with purple heather bloom, dropped away and before them was the wide bay of the Two Rivers curving southward in a great arc. Beyond the river mouth the land was shrouded in a heat haze, but Baradoc knew that somewhere close in the haze was hidden the great promontory of Hercules. He decided that they would cross the bay, abandon the boat, take to the shore and follow the coast westward to his homeland. But as they crossed the bay, although they had the tide with them, they met the spew of the strong waters of the Two Rivers. Paddle as they might they were pushed farther and farther out to sea and the pearl-grey heat haze, thickening over the distant shore, slowly began to roll in a cloaking mist over the water toward them.

Within an hour they were wrapped and lost in veils of heavy mist and the sea which had been kind for so long stirred and strengthened and began to run in a long swinging swell, deep and powerful, carrying them up its dark slopes and then drawing them down into wide valleys of foam-marbled water. Through the mist came now and then the cry of some solitary seabird and sometimes a glimpse of the black-winged, surface-hugging passage of shearwaters and shags.

The three dogs, hating this new movement of the sea, huddled together miserably in the bows. Within an hour Tia was violently seasick and Baradoc made her lie down on a couch of their spare clothes in the bottom of the boat. Although he spoke cheerfully to her, he was worried by this sudden turn in the weather. In the past days he had always been careful to hug the shore as closely as possible. Now because of the mighty outpouring of the river waters they were farther out to sea than they had ever been and in the mist he had no idea of the direction of the boat's drift. In a couple of hours it would be dark. By morning they could have drifted far out to sea, maybe out of sight of land. The prospect was not a happy one, but he kept his anxieties to himself. So far they had seen no ships but he knew at this time of the year that the foreign trading vessels from Erin and Cymru would be on their way west and south-about to clear the great toe of Britain around the promontory of Belerium to avoid the autumn storms, heading for Gaul and the Mediterranean. If they met one of them there was every chance that they could be taken up as slaves. Silently he put up a prayer to the gods that the mist would clear soon. . . .

By the time full darkness was with them Tia had recovered. The two of them sat in the stern, their cloaks drawn over them, pressed close together for warmth, the darkness now so thick that although they could hear the occasional stir of the dogs forward they could not see them.

Tia slept, leaning against Baradoc, his right arm about her. She dreamt that she was back in her brother's home and riding with him as he made his morning rounds, seeing the oxen drawing their ploughs across the long strips of lynchet fields, hearing the laughter from a shearing party as men clipped the early summer coats from the sheep, riding through the beech woods on the down tops where the swineherd watched his beasts rooting through the dead leaves for the last of the past year's mast, and looking forward to the moment when they would turn down the long home combe to the beach. Coming back through the fishing village, they would buy fresh lobsters and crabs, carrying them across their saddle fronts, alive and moving in their straw-plaited skeps. And as they turned from the beach they would rein in and watch the fishing boats, with crowds of gulls and terns wheeling and calling noisily above them. . . . In her dream the screams of the gulls rose until she was slowly drawn from sleep to find that the noise had followed her. For a moment or two she had no idea what had happened or where she was. Then slowly memory and the present came back to her.

She stirred stiffly and sat upright. The darkness of night had gone, but the mist was still with them. She could see the dogs sitting in the bows, their coats dewed with a fine rain. But the sea no longer rose in the swinging motion which had made her sick. It lay around the boat flat and calm. Not far from them came the screaming and calling of unseen sea-birds.

Baradoc, seeing her awake, said, "Take your paddle. The gulls are crying from cliffs, I think. A little while ago the sea calmed as though we had come into the shelter of land."

They dipped their paddles and began to move the boat toward the sound of the crying gulls. After a few moments Aesc rose from the bows, shook her coat and began to bark.

Tia said, "Aesc smells land."

Almost before she had finished speaking, the bows of the boat grated gently on shingle and the mist ahead of them darkened, then swirled apart and briefly they had a glimpse of grey rocks footed with a small stretch of pebble beach. Baradoc went to the bow, slid overboard up to his waist and then began to drag the boat forward. Lerg and Aesc jumped over and swam to the beach and disappeared into the mist. Baradoc let them go. If there was any danger close at hand they would soon give warning.

Tia, as the boat slewed sideways to the beach, jumped over. Between them they drew the boat up onto the beach clear of the water.

As they walked across the narrow scallop of beach Lerg and Aesc came to them out of the mist. The morning light was strengthening quickly and the air, which had been still and heavy, was slowly touched with the breath of an awakening breeze which began to shred away the veils of mist. They saw that the small beach was flanked closely by rocks on either side and backed by the steep broken rise of a cliff.

Baradoc said, "We'll make the boat safe and then find out where we are."

They took all their possessions out of the boat to lighten it, carried them above the high-water mark of sea wrack and driftwood, and put them safely on a wide shelf of cliff rock.

Then they pulled the boat well above the tide mark and to make it safe Baradoc tied the long bow rope to a heavy boulder. Then, wearing his sword and carrying his spear, Baradoc sent the dogs ahead and they followed them up a narrow, overgrown track which zigzagged up the cliff through screes of loose shale and patches of scrub and low windshaped thorns. Sea thrift padded the rocks and brown seed-headed foxgloves, willow herb and gorse filled the small gullies and gentler slopes. Before long they were above the last, dying trails of mist and out into the strong sunlight. The cliff line ran far to the northeast and the rocks were covered with colonies of seabirds, the air full of their cries. Here and there on the higher slopes they could make out the movement of grazing goats and sheep. To the southwest the cliff line, much shorter, ran sheer for a while and then dropped sharply to the sea, ending in a small island joined to it by a line of rocks which the dropping tide was now uncovering.

Without a word to Tia, Baradoc turned and began to climb higher and after a while they came through a narrow, twisting valley to the top of the cliffs. Before them stretched a wide run of grass and heatherland rising gently to the north. Just below the skyline stood a group of round, stone-walled huts roofed with weather-browned turves. Baradoc dropped to the ground and pulled Tia down with him, his eyes never leaving the huts.

Tia said, "What is it? Do you know where we are?"

"Yes, I think so. We're on the island of Caer Sibli—the fortress of birds. Only a handful of people live here and they don't welcome strangers. Look—" He turned and pointed southward where the haze over the sea had cleared. "That's the main coastline over there."

Tia saw, away across the growing sun sparkle on the sea, a faint hazy line of shadow against the lower sky. Then, looking back at the huts, she said, "I don't see any smoke from cooking fires or any sign of life. We're short of food and we come in peace. Why should they harm us?"

"Because they are the Lundi people."

"Lundi?"

"That is their name for their tribal bird. The birds you saw on the cliffs as we climbed, the ones with solemn faces and painted beaks that others call puffins."

"But why should we fear them?"

"Because nobody ever knows what is in their minds. The sea raiders and the trading captains know this island. They land and rob them and take those who do not hide in the cliff caves for slaves. Sometimes, too, when there is famine on the mainland the tribesmen come out in their boats and steal their sheep and goats and take their maidens. Once there were many of them. But over the years they have become only a handful. Wherever they are we would risk too much by meeting them."

Baradoc rose, took her hand and began to lead the way down to the beach where they had left their boat. Tia went with him without question, her legs aching from the long climb to the island top. Halfway down when they stopped to rest Baradoc said, "The tide is running out and the wind is in our favour. We can cross to the mainland by nightfall. The little food we have will serve us." He was happy, as he moved on, for if the gods were good to them, a handful of days would see them back with his people.

Walking behind Baradoc, her clothes dry on her now from the strong sun, Tia watched Cuna snap at a butterfly that crossed the track before him and thought of the Lundi people, whose hard life had taught them that there was danger in greeting any stranger. She smiled fondly to herself as the memory came back jewel-bright to her of Baradoc talking his daydreams to her one evening as they lay close together on warm sand, his dream—maybe his only dream—of a Britain proud and free of all Saxons, where one day any man might walk its length and breadth unarmed and unafraid . . . Baradoc the dreamer of peace—but also the warrior husband, the man she loved, whose sharp spear tines shone from the whetstone and whose sword never lacked its bright edge.

So they came down together, jumping the sea-smoothed beach boulders onto the tiny crescent of sandy shingle, grow-

ing now as the tide ran out—and both of them were suddenly
robbed of all movement.

Their boat was no longer on the beach. The large stone to
which the bow rope had been tied lay in its place, and from it
the shingle and sand were scored with the broad mark where
the craft had been dragged down to the sea, pulled by the
stern for there were no footprints showing. Tia looked out
over the waters. There was no sign of the boat, only the
winging and diving movement of the myriad seabirds and the
long, lazy rhythm of waves breaking over the rocks and
washing up onto the shore, seething and hissing softly.

With an anguished cry, Tia turned and ran back up the
beach to the rock ledge where they had left all their possessions. None of them had been taken. They rested, piled on
the ledge, just as they had put them there.

"Why take the boat and leave these?" cried Tia angrily.

Baradoc said nothing, but he stepped closer to the rock
face below the ledge. On its flat face writing had been freshly
scratched with the sharp edge of a piece of shillet.

Baradoc said, "Read the writing. The answer is there if
you can understand it." Then the passion of frustration in
him burst and he struck the rock with his fist and cried out
bitterly, "What have I done that the gods make sport of me
like this?"

On the rock face was written in Tia's own language:

> Cronos in the dream spoke thus
> Name him for all men and all time
> His glory an everlasting flower
> He throws no seed

Tia turned slowly to Baradoc, a frown marking her sun-
tanned brow. "What does it mean?"

"Ask the gods!" he said angrily.

"Who is Cronos?"

"He, too, is a god, but not one of ours. From my old
master I know about him. He was the god of all Time, the god
of the Golden Age and the father of Zeus."

"Why should someone steal our boat and then write
that?"

Stifling his rage, Baradoc said, ''How can I tell you? But it is said that many of the people who live here, because of their close breeding, are strange in the head.''

''To take our boat and leave our belongings they must be mad. What are we going to do?

Baradoc, catching the trembling note of anxiety in her voice, put his arm around her and said calmly. ''Accept what the gods have sent and face it. The boat must be hidden somewhere around the island shores. But we can't go looking for it without being seen by the islanders. So there is no choice left us but to go to them.''

''But they're dangerous, you said.''

''So they are. But if they had meant us harm they would have waited in ambush for us here and killed us and taken our boat and our possessions.'' He pointed to the rock ledge. ''Look, the boat is stolen but the bow and the arrow in their quiver are left. That is either a sign of madness or a sign of peace.'' He tightened the buckle of his sword belt, handed Tia his spear and picked up the bow and the arrow quiver, and said, ''I leave you with Lerg and if anyone—''

Tia interrupted him, her face taut, ''You leave me nowhere! Where you go I go. Until we read the truth of this mystery my place is by your side.''

Baradoc hesitated. Then, seeing the firm set of her mouth, the stubborn tilt of her chin and the light of defiance in her eyes, he shrugged his shoulders and said, smiling, ''What kind of wife have I taken that she overrules my words? The women of Enduring Crow are meek and lower their eyes when their men speak.''

Tia said, ''So they should when the time is right. But that time is not now, though''—she grinned—''the gods know I will take no pleasure in climbing that cliff track again.''

She turned from him and began to make into a bundle such food as they had left. As she picked up the almost empty waterskin Baradoc said, ''There will be no need for that. There will be water on the high heathland.''

That day, their first on the island, was a strange one. The mist long gone now, the sky bright and clear with a warm breeze blowing from the south, the sea a maze of serpentine currents below them, the air pierced with the cries of the seabirds, they climbed the cliff track. Near the island top where a small stream ran down a narrow valley they stopped and drank at a pool overhung with ferns.

When they reached the plateau they hid for a while and watched the nearest group of huts. They saw no sign of life. Before moving Baradoc sent Lerg on ahead. He loped away across the rough grasses, lost now and then in the tall patches of bracken, and they saw him move around the huts and disappear into one of them. After a while Lerg came out and sat on his haunches in the doorway.

Baradoc and Tia went forward with the two other dogs, while Bran circled in low flight above. There were four huts and they were all deserted. Their walls were made of piled stones; the roofs of driftwood poles—for there were few trees on the island—were thatched over with layers of heath bundles and turves. For protection against the strong sea winds the thatch was held by a network of twisted heath ropes from which hung large stones. All the low doorways faced southeast to cheat the fierce westerly winds that swept the island top in the autumn and winter gales. Outside each hut was a pile of old limpet and mussel shells, fish and animal bones and other cooking debris. Each hut had a stone hearth in the center, long cold now and the ashes blown about the floor. Above the hearths was an opening in the roof to take away the smoke. Each hut, too, had a raised platform away from the door which served for bed, and three of these still held piles of sewn sealskins and rough woollen coverings. And each hut looked as though the owners had suddenly, in the midst of their normal life, just walked out and left everything. Earthenware pots still held stale, dust-filmed water; skillets and cauldrons stood by the cold hearths, some with dried and rotten fish and porridge in them; a string of coloured clay beads lay on the floor by one of the beds and from the walls hung fishing lines and nets. In niches were set scallop-shell holders full of congealed seal oil with rush tapers for lighting. The floors were covered with soft, dark

peat earth which still held the footprints of the people who
had lived there.

Beyond the huts was a large granite-walled enclosure for
cattle penning, the gateway of driftwood and latticed rushes
broken and lying on the ground. In a sheltered corner of the
outside wall stood two wind-crabbed and -twisted damson
trees on which the fruit was slowly turning colour.

All that day while the light lasted Baradoc and Tia
explored the island, moving always with the three dogs well
out ahead of them. The island was almost four miles long
and, in its widest part toward the southern end, a mile broad.
It ran narrowing to the north like a roughly shaped flint
dagger, the cliffs on the westerly side so steep and sheer that
Tia drew back with fear as she looked down at the breaking
waters and the white stippling of seabirds on the rocks and
coasting above the sea. On the easterly side the land was
gentler, sloping through bracken combes and small hanging
valleys to much lower cliffs.

It was in one of these combes toward the tip of the island
that they came upon another group of huts, lying below the
crest of the plateau, the doorways looking out to sea and to a
great rock outcrop far below where a colony of gannets
roosted. All the huts were deserted, but here the insides
showed signs of violence. Some of the roofs had been
burned, the cooking vessels about the hearths were smashed,
bed platforms broken and the nets and fishing gear strewn on
the floors. Grain storage pots were broken and cracked and
corn and flour lay yellow and mouldy over the trodden peat.
Behind the huts a walled field held crop strips, long neglected, the pods on the rows of beans now black and split,
the barley in full ear smothered with poppies and weeds and
thrusting bracken growths.

On the seaward side of the field, in a small marshy hollow
from which a stream ran thinly, a great rock outcrop thrust up
from the short turf before the fall of the true cliffs, and here
Baradoc and Tia found some of the islanders.

They were all men, and there were eight of them, and they
lay as they had fallen in battle with their backs to the craggy

face of the rock pinnacle. Sun and weather had worked on their raggedly clothed bodies, and rats and foxes and seabirds had picked their bones clean. All their weapons had gone except for a broken spear, a sword snapped short almost to the hilt, and two round padded bucklers, skin-faced over wooden frames, their centers crowned with wide bronze bosses. One of them had been split almost to its center by some weapon stroke, and in the bleached skull of the skeleton alongside it was wedged an iron head of an axe with the wooden handle broken off short below the socket. Bracken and yellow ragwort had grown up around the men, mildew had spread over their rough tunics and the rain and sun had stiffened board-hard their cloak skins.

Without a word Tia and Baradoc turned away from the scene of past violence. They knew what must have happened . . . Tia seeing it all in her imagination, though she would have wished to close her inner eyes on the sight: the long keels of sea raiders or traders who would barter and sell human or any other goods, ghosting into the island by night, the sudden assault maybe at first light when all the men, women and children would be in or close to their huts . . . and here, this handful of men who had found time to snatch their weapons and make their stand, choosing death to the slavery which would await them in far places.

Suddenly Baradoc said vehemently, "What kind of thing is man that he does this to other men? To kill in a true cause is a just thing. To kill and enslave for a handful of gold is an evil, a poison which must be stamped out as a man brings the sharp of his heel down on the head of the adder in the path before him."

They passed that night in one of the huts at the southern end of the island. The three dogs kept watch outside and Baradoc lay on the sleeping platform with Tia, awake and with his weapons close to him. Tia slept and sometimes talked in her sleep and Baradoc guessed that she was haunted by dreams of the men who lay, bleach-boned and fleshless, under the tall rock. Every little while he went out and joined the dogs. The night was clear and the great stars of Orion's belt blazed in the heavens. Southward, hidden in the darkness, lay the mainland. Anger stirred in him as he thought that in a handful of days they would have been back with his people . . . and now, until they found their boat, they were trapped on the island. Although tomorrow he would make a closer search around the whole shoreline, his common sense told him that there were a hundred places among the tall cliffs and rugged bays and inlets where the boat could be hidden without much hope of discovery. He wanted to be back with his people, to present his wife to them, to take his place with them, to deal with Inbar, his cousin, and to be free to take up the true cause which stayed ever with him, like an always open wound when he thought of the Saxons and of the night they had circled his master and hewn him down, shouting and jeering and laughing in their drunken sport.

But the gods, as he slowly came to acknowledge as the days that followed slipped from the coil of time, were against him. By himself he searched the island, climbed down the sheer cliffs, risking life and limbs, swam across inlets and gullies that boiled with surging, foaming waters to explore caves and clefts, and lay sometimes motionless for hours on a commanding rock point, watching for some betraying sign of human life, until with the passing days the fire of his impatience died.

They settled in the largest of the huts and furnished it with their own possessions and pickings from the other huts. They lacked neither shelter, food nor water. There were fish to be netted or hooked from the rocks, and wild on the island roamed the feral animals of the islanders, sheep, goats and pig. After a few days a handful of the islanders' fowls made their way back to them to scavenge their scraps and stayed to lay eggs for them. Now and again Baradoc stalking with his bow, shot a seal basking on the rocks, and they had its flesh to eat, its pelt to repair clothing and its blubber to render down to oil for the lamp sconces in the hut's wall niches. There was peat to be cut and driftwood to collect for their hearth fires and as the year waned they took the islanders' abandoned short-handled sickles and cut the weed-choked grain crops, and they collected the hard beans from the rows of blackened pods and Tia ground them on a stone quern to add to their flour when they made bread or to thicken their fish and seal broth. As autumn came in they found a small valley where blackberry bushes grew, and feasted on the fruit and pulped some with the meager crop of damsons and stored it in earthenware jars to sweeten their bread in the days to come. Salt they scraped from the dried hollows of the sea rocks where storm pools had long evaporated.

While the good weather lasted they both kept their eyes alert for any sign of ship or passing craft and often looked longingly at the distant mainland, and wherever they were along the island coast they searched always for some sign of their boat or of the stranger who had taken it. They wore little clothing, swam together from the rocks and hid from each other the core of longing they held to escape from the island.

Against the coming of winter they laid up in one of the other huts a store of cut peat turves, dried strips of goat and sheep flesh, smoked fish and the small harvest of grain they had garnered. Baradoc repaired their hut thatch and twisted new ropes to hold more stones so that when the first gale did sweep over the island the hut stood firm and secure.

It was after this gale that Baradoc, hunting with his bow at the northern end of the island, had his first glimpse of the stranger. Lying in the bracken watching a herd of goats, waiting for them to crop closer so that he could take one, he saw them suddenly scatter and move quickly away. Distantly over the skyline close to a sheer cliff drop a brown-clad figure appeared and stood looking out to the western sea approaches.

Aesc raised her muzzle as the scent of the stranger came downwind and from the throat of Lerg at Baradoc's side came a low rumble. He gave the dogs the word and they went upwind fast and steadily. Baradoc held his pace, knowing that once they reached the stranger they would hold him until he arrived.

The two dogs raced across the plateau to take the stranger from either flank. Whether the man—for he was clearly such—was aware of their coming or not Baradoc could not tell. As the dogs closed silently on the man Baradoc rose and began to run after them. But before he was within two bowshots, he saw him drop quickly below the skyline.

When he reached the dogs there was no sign of the stranger. The land dropped away into a small bowl that stood at the head of a great landslide of rocks that ended in a cliff face that dropped sheer and unbroken by path or by any ledge or shelf wider than would give scant roosting or breeding place for the seabirds.

Far, far below, the great westerly swells of the dying storm rolled and thundered against the cliff foot. Yet more surprising than the sudden vanishing of the stranger, who could have had no escape route, it seemed, than over the cliff edge, was the behaviour of the dogs. They stood a few paces apart where they had come to a halt to hold the man and when Baradoc commanded them to the search they ignored him. Aesc, the wind ruffling her long coat, gave a tired yawn, then sat and began to scratch her flank with a rear foot, and Lerg under Baradoc's angry gaze lowered his head and avoided his master's eyes. For the first time since he had trained them they were refusing to obey his command. . . . A high wave of anger swept through him and he would have shouted at them, berating them, but he checked himself. Some power greater than his own held sway over them. There was no fault in them which merited his anger.

He left them and searched about the bowl and the cliffside, but could trace no way by which the stranger might have escaped him. In the end he gave up the search. As he walked away the two dogs turned and followed him. Back with Tia, not wishing to worry her, he said nothing of having seen the stranger.

Two mornings later Tia, rising early while Baradoc slept, went out to collect eggs from the hens. On the threshold of the hut she found an earthenware crock, a looped thong handle about its neck, full of goat's milk and by its side wrapped in broad dock leaves a large piece of goat's cheese.

CHAPTER TEN

The Island Parting

WHEN TIA TOLD BARADOC about the milk and cheese, he said, "It must be a gift from the stranger. Some days ago I saw him, but he slipped from me by casting a spell over the dogs."

After Tia had got the full story from him, she said, "Although he may have taken our boat and destroyed or hidden it, I can't think he means us any harm. Why leave such a gift otherwise?"

Baradoc shrugged his shoulders impatiently. "What you say is true. But he has stopped us from reaching my people. Even if we had the boat it would be dangerous now to put to sea. At this time of year a single cloud in the sky which would be the pride of a summer's morning grows to a storm before hot broth can cool. By myself I would take the risk, but in winter I would never put you in such peril."

For a moment or two Tia was silent, looking down at him where he sat on the edge of the bed platform, pulling on a pair of rough goatskin sandals he had made and binding the broad thongs about his sun-browned calves. For her he had made soft sealskin sandals on which with his own hands—for when he needed he could work as fine and surely as any woman— he had sewn a beaded outline of the Enduring Crow, the bird of his tribe, now the bird of her tribe, and a bird which haunted the island's cliffs in pairs, their jet wings flashing in sun and rain, the scarlet of their legs brighter than rowanberries. The sun glinted on his tawny beard which she had close-cropped for him with her finely honed single-edged dagger. As he looked up at her, his dark eyes warm and as lustrous as bloom-free damson fruits, she knew that she loved him and could love no other. She moved to him, put down a hand and softly ran her finger across his rough, weather-cracked lips, and said, "You would not only put me in peril, my brave heart."

Baradoc, tugging at a thong, raised his head to her, kissed her finger, and asked, "Who else?"

"You do not know?"

"All I know is that this spell-weaving stranger acts out some madness which, with so much waiting to be done elsewhere, holds us here till spring comes. *Aie* . . . we are well set enough with food and drink and shelter, but time passes without true action and golden hours are lost forever." He struck his hand irritably against his head and went on, "In here I have already schemed the way and the means. We begin small, smaller than a mustard seed, but the growth will come. First, with my own people, and then gathering a good company of men of reason and courage from other tribes, we must train and learn to love discipline as did your people's armies. We shall need men with the grain of your old uncle Truvius as he was in his prime and—"

Tia suddenly pressed her hand across his mouth. Holding it there, she said, "Crow man—cease your cliff-top croaking and listen. Maybe this stranger acts out some madness. But in my mind it is more a wise magic, far beyond that which you hold over Lerg and Aesc. Milk we have not had for many weeks. And for long now there has been in me a craving for milk, aye, and cheese. Does that mean nothing to you, that a woman should have such cravings?" She took her hand away and, laughing, said, "Now you look moonfaced at me, empty-eyed and empty-headed like some simple wit sitting on the Forum steps understanding nothing but that the sun shines and he is warm. Did your great master teach you nothing about women and their terms?"

Baradoc frowned at her. "Now you talk in riddles."

Tia shook her head and, reaching down, held his tawny hair, gently tugging at it. "You, whose eyes are like a hawk's and can mark the stir of the far grasses as a vole makes passage foraging, it seems, are blind when you look at me. Do I have to grow as round-bellied as a full moon before—''

"By the gods!'' Baradoc leapt suddenly to his feet and grasped her shoulders. ''You're with child!''

Smiling teasingly at him, but trembling with her own happiness which she had had to contain until there was only certainty in her, Tia said mockingly, ''My lord Baradoc, my brave heart, I have never met anyone so quick at understanding. Yes, I am carrying your child and have done for these last few months.''

Baradoc drew her to him and, holding her, smothering her face against his shoulder, hugged her. Then he kissed her, stood back, looking at her, his face creased with joy, and said, ''It will be a boy, won't it? It must be a man-child, to grow to arms and courage and honour and—'' He broke off abruptly, shamefaced, and took her hands gently in his. Then, his voice low and shaking, he went on, ''Tia, my Tia . . . boy or girl, it matters not for there can be no shadow of difference in my love for either, and no shadow ever over the love which binds you to me and me to you.''

''That I know. But I know, too, and you need have no shame in it, that you would if it were possible bribe the gods with ambrosia, nectar and high sacrifices to grant that our firstborn be a son.''

Shaking his head, Baradoc put his hand about her cheeks, and said, ''You tease me and for my slowness you are right to do so. But you are wrong. I go now to make a sacrifice to the gods, but I shall ask them for one thing only—that when the day comes they keep you safe, for you are the bright bird of my life.''

From that moment there was a fire and an impatience in Baradoc which made even the shortening days of winter seem long. To ease the itch in him for action as the old year rolled slowly toward the new, he set about building a boat which would carry them to the mainland when the spring came. He took driftwood and poles from some of the huts and slowly thonged them together with hide strips to make the framework of the hull. All this he did on a slope above the beach where they had originally landed, well out of reach of the highest tide or winter gale. He worked sometimes from first to last light, and the hours he had to lose to hunting for their pot he grudged. Most of the seals had moved away from the island now that the breeding and rearing seasons were gone, but he killed them whenever he could and scraped and cleaned the skins until, with other skins that he foraged from the bed platforms of the abandoned huts, he had enough to fashion an outer and an inner skin about the framework of the boat.

There were times at night as he sat in their hut, lashing the skins together with thin strips of hide and sinew, when Tia would rise and deliberately blow out the sconce lights and scold him to bed. There were nights, too, when he woke in the darkness and thought about the child which Tia carried and saw them returning to his people. Yet more often he lay working out some problem in his boat-building. He had no pine pitch or clay to caulk it. Between the inner and outer skin, he decided, he would pad the space with a mash of chopped-up reeds and rushes to be gathered from the bob patches in the middle of the island, working into the cut rushes pig fat and seal blubber rendered down in a cauldron over a fire. The mess would harden after being laid on and should make the boat water-tight enough to take them to the distant coast. Not a day passed, except in the fiercest gales when to step outside the hut into the shrieking wind and rains was to be buffeted to the ground, that he did not labour at the boat with knife or axe or a small broken saw which he had found in one of the huts.

As Tia grew bigger with her child, he made her keep close to their hut and he took from her all the work he could. He grew even harder and leaner of body, but his spirit flamed bright and steady, and Tia, knowing and understanding the passion in him, made no complaint. She loved him, knew his love for her, and knew the truth of him that under the warrior he would be lay also the poet and dreamer. There were few mornings when she woke to find him gone in the dark to catch the first light by the time he reached the boat that she did not find scratched with a stick on the smoothed-out-peat-and-earth floor some message from him. On a rainy morning he wrote, "The day weeps its sorrow for the summer suns that are gone, but in my heart like a wren in its moss bower my love for mother and child is the warmth of a hundred suns." And on a morning of rare frost which white-laced the grasses and dead bracken, she read, "Three things that are wondrous fair—winter silver on the spider's web, the moon's broken gold on the moving waters, and the smile which is a rose on the lips of my sleeping love."

There were times after the turn of the year when Baradoc sensed often that he was being watched as he worked on the boat. Whenever the feeling struck him he would see, too, that the dogs had marked the scent of another, but they would stand near him and make no move of their own or at his command. Although he searched the cliffsides and the rocks he could see no one, but he knew that the one who watched must be the stranger who still occassionally left small gifts outside the hut, a stranger who clearly meant them no harm and who—although he must have taken their original boat—showed no concern that he should be making another for one morning he had left outside the hut a sharp-pointed, stout thonging needle for which Baradoc was grateful because he had been sewing his skins together by making a hole in them with the point of Tia's dagger and threading the thongs through by hand.

Sometimes, lying warm under their skins, holding Tia in his arms before they slept, he talked about the man and once Tia, who needed no words from him now to read his mind, said, "Since he means no harm and by his gifts shows kindness why do you worry about him?"

"Because I don't like mysteries. I have seen a man walk to the edge of a cliff five hundred feet high and disappear over it where none but a seabird could know safely. He takes our boat . . . . aie, and I'm sure cast it adrift to keep us here. Yet now he does nothing to stop me building my boat. Even helps us with the gift of the needle. Is he mad or is there purpose in this?"

"I don't know." Tia stirred in the darkness to ease her burdened body. "Maybe he's someone like Brother Asimus. A priest or dreamer, someone perhaps who has been shown the future. Asimus had a dream and waited for us to come. Maybe this man had a dream, too. From his writing on the rock it would seem so. The gods use such men." She gave a little chuckle. "It is no good you saying you don't like mysteries. The gods won't change their ways for you."

Baradoc said, "If I were not so busy with the boat and the hunting I would find him and speak boldly with him because the child you carry would have been born amongst my people, and there would have been women to serve you when the time came."

"I would have liked that, yes. But I am not frightened. You are here. That is all the comfort I need. Birth is a natural thing, a tide which takes a woman so that she needs do no more than drift with it. Now sleep."

She lay in the darkness when he was asleep, listening to the sough of the wind over the thatch and the singing notes it made through the ropes from which the great stones hung. There was suddenly a bright picture in her mind of the child—boy or girl, no matter which, though she prayed always for a son out of duty to Baradoc—a child tumbling and playing with the dogs, their child. Would it have her eyes and Baradoc's hair? Then, feeling the child move within her, she put her hand to it and drifted into sleep.

In the end it was the stranger who revealed himself to Baradoc. The year had long turned and spring was moving and awakening. The migrating birds were flocking back from the south and Tia made Baradoc take down the old bird-catching nets left by the islanders for there was sorrow in her with each small bird that got caught in the narrow meshes. The seabirds were nesting, and the boat work was finished except for the making of two paddles, and there was a fire of impatience in Baradoc to haul the boat to the water so that he could lay the flat stone ballast in it to settle its trim.

One morning as he sat in the sun outside the hut, shaping

the last of the paddles from a length of rough plank—the flotsam from some ship's wreck—Tia came to the doorway, her long hair caught back with a piece of braided wool, a loose robe, leaving her arms bare, sweeping almost to her feet, and said the wish was in her to eat fresh eggs. Of their few hens three had died, two had been killed by a fox, and the last had been taken by a golden eagle which had coursed it across the cattle fold, made kill and was away before the dogs could reach it.

Baradoc, absorbed, said, "I'll get some gulls' eggs when I go down to the boat."

Tia, her chin set stubbornly, reached down and took the paddle board from him. "I want eggs now, my brave heart. A dish of beaten eggs and herbs. The desire is with me and with the babe." She smiled, putting her hand to her front. "He kicks from the need and greed for eggs. And we want not gulls' eggs but the eggs of the lapwings on the northland heath."

"But I have work to—"

Throwing the board from her, Tia cut him short. "You have no work that will not wait. We need eggs. If we do not get them the babe will kick me to death." She eyed him teasingly for a few moments, and then went on slyly, "He kicks as only a man-child could kick. Would you have me tell him someday that the first time he asked his father a favour it was denied him?"

Baradoc sighed, stood up, put his hands on her shoulders and kissed the tip of her nose. "Lady Tia, I am your servant. Should you ask the eggs of a phoenix I should find them for you." Then, looking across the bright waters to the mainland and the distant shoulder of Hercules' Promontory, he went on, "If the weather holds, then we shall soon be across. You have enough time to run yet to see us with my people and the babe born where he should be born."

"The child will be born where he is born—and that is in the hands of the gods. Now fetch the eggs."

Baradoc went north with the dogs to the downland where the lapwings flew, their cries sharp and wailing as they

circled and tumbled close above his head, their broad wings
cutting the air with a hissing and searing sound like water
steaming and spitting from red-hot stones. But before he
could find any of the nesting hollows Lerg growled and Aesc
gave a sharp warning bark.

A bowshot away Baradoc saw the stranger, and saw him
more clearly than he had ever done before. The man stood on
a hummock beyond a shallow, marshy depression which held
a broad pool whose waters flowed in a stream to cascade
thinly over the nearby western cliffs. He wore a long, brown
coarsely woven habit, its hood lying back over his shoulders,
while about his waist was wound a thick rope girdle.

Baradoc began to hurry forward. The dogs went with him.
The man turned and walked from him and, without a glance
backward, his pace kept measure with Baradoc's so that the
distance between them remained the same. Something told
Baradoc that this was no pursuit, that the man had decided
that he no longer wished to avoid him.

The man moved across the downland toward the edge of
the western cliffs and passed out of sight over a rocky rise in
the ground. Baradoc, following, crested the rise in the
ground and hurried down its far slope along a goat path he
had often used. Old bracken growths with the first green of
the new crosier heads breaking the earth covered the slope
and amongst them lay a scattering of large weather-and-
lichen-marked boulders. There was no sign of the man, but to
the left of the path Baradoc saw at once a large flat rock which
was tilted at one end toward the sky. Since his memory held
now a familiarity with this place and many others on the
island, he knew that the rock had never so pointed skyward
before.

He ran to it and saw that the rock, working on a natural
pivot against other rocks buried in the ground, had been
swung upward at one end and downward at the other to make
a pent over an opening in the ground, a cavity with a stony
floor away from which, through a boulder-framed archway,
ran a tunnel.

Baradoc lowered himself into the hole and looked through

the stone archway. Light seeped through it. Leaving the dogs
at the top of the hole, Baradoc began to move down the
tunnel, which after a few paces grew in height so that he
could stand with ease. He moved forward, hand on the hilt of
his sword, through a light which grew stronger and stronger.
From ahead there came to him the growing sound of the call
of seabirds and the low thunder of waves breaking at the foot
of the cliffs. The tunnel ended with a down flight of wide
steps.

Baradoc stood at the top of them, looking down in amaze-
ment. Below him was a wide, rock-vaulted chamber, lit by
sunlight that came through a great fissure in the rocks on the
far side. On one side of the fissure hung a long, heavy curtain
of skins, thong-looped to a pole along which it could be
pulled to close the entrance. The floor of the cavern was
strewn with dried bracken and rushes, and a wall embrasure
held a bed close to which stood a rough table flanked by a
long wooden form. Around the walls rock ledges and ship's
timbers formed shelves and cupboards. To one side a turf-
damped fire smoked feebly on its hearth. Near the curtained
opening a goat, her udder milk-full, was stalled in a pen made
of rough driftwood timber. Standing by the pen, one hand
scratching the head of the goat, was the stranger.

Before Baradoc could take in more, the stranger moved
across to the foot of the flight of steps and looked up at him.
He was of no great height, but stoutly and strongly built and,
Baradoc guessed, had seen twice the years he had. Jet-black
hair hung to his neck and he wore a close-cropped beard. His
eyes were friendly and had the wet brown shine of closed sea
anemones.

Baradoc, his anger against this man stirring anew, said,
"Who are you who stole my boat? And why at last have you
brought me here when at other times you disappear like a
wild goat over the cliffs, or watch hidden and cast spells over
my dogs so that they take no heed of my commands?"

The man smiled and the whole of his face was briefly
wrinkled and lined like the skin of a hoarded russet apple.

"I give no name in answer to a question. But the questions

not asked are answered. Between these two lies the virtue of patience. One sees the fire and the smoke at a distance but the warmth is not felt until the hearth is reached. But since questions stir always in your mind like angry wasps and there is an impatience of desire in you like the unending breaking of sea waves against a rock, I give you some ease of the mysteries.''

''You talk in riddles.''

The man nodded affably and began to unloop from his waist the thickly plaited girdle until he held in his hands a long length of stout rope. He walked to the rock cleft over-looking the sea, saying, ''Come and see a mystery answered.''

Baradoc crossed the cavern and, standing at his side, looked out. For a moment he half drew back to kill a sudden stab of vertigo. The cliff face fell sheer to the sea hundreds of feet below where the long swell thundered and crashed at its foot. The waters, foam- and current-marked, heaving and moiling, were alive with the swimming and diving seabirds and overtraced with the flying lines of others as they passed between their feeding grounds and the roosts and new sea-son's nesting places.

The man said, ''A rope is no mystery. You double it, put the loose loop over a cliff-top rock and then move down it to swing like a spider at the end of its thread, and enter. Then you pull on one end of the rope. The whole comes to you—and the mystery is dead.'' Smiling, his eyes mischievous, he turned and put out his hand toward the hearth. ''I breathe the fire to full life at darkness. Only the eye of the night owl could see the shadow of smoke against the sky and the stars. Learn, then, that a question is answered not by speaking it for another to answer, but by seeking the truth of it in yourself.''

Momentarily Baradoc, though the man was being friendly enough, felt higher anger spark in him at the manner of the man's approach to him. He said brusquely, ''I am no child to be teased with idle riddles, or plagued first with the theft of my boat and then puzzled by your gifts and spells. You chide me without cause.''

To his surprise the man said, "I speak for your own good because I have read the runes and dreamt the dreams."

"Forget the runes and dreams. You took our boat. Why?"

"Because it was written so. Listen—for many years I lived here with the islanders. When they were killed or taken by the sea raiders I alone escaped for the gods in my flight led me to this cave, and here at night they speak to me. But I am no islander. My feet have trod many countries from Asia to Gaul and Erin. But this is my country and there is no part a mystery to me from Vectis to the far north to the lands of the Cornovii and the Carnonacae, to the far Orcades and Ultima Thule. I have read the papyrus rolls of Londinium, Lutetia and the Great Empire City . I have talked with devils and demons and magicians and sorcerers and taken no harm but much wisdom. I have learned that while the past is a jewel fixed forever in its setting the future is a river which the gods have set in its course but which time and man's works can loose from its bed to new courses. The gods have dreamt it, but man with his waking dream of power, conquest and greed mars all." He paused and the red gleam of his lips showed through his beard as he smiled ruefully. "Keep faith with the true dream. Misshape it not by impatience and greed for false glory. One day men will call you Pendragon as many before have been called. But the true king comes to meet glory and betrayal and then to sleep until all lands groan with the labour and distress of chaos and he comes again and the true march of the centuries begins anew. . . ." He broke off and moved slowly to one of the cupboards on the cavern wall.

Listening to him, Baradoc knew that for all his quiet speech, his sober, even manner, the man was mad; not mad with any violence of talk or manner, but mad with the innocence of one touched with the disease of the gods, one for whom the air was full of voices and for whom the shape of solid things—a bush, a rock, a tall pine, a running stag— wavered always as though seen through water and became the fabric and fancies of a phantom world.

He said stubbornly, "You set our boat adrift."

"I did. But now you have built another." The man spoke

without turning as he opened the cupboard door. "But if you would leave this island safely with your woman and child put the boat not to the water until the first red-gorged swallow comes winging north, and until that times comes say nothing to your wife of our meeting." As he finished speaking the man turned and came back toward Baradoc. In his hands he held a shallow basket made from woven heath stalks and lined with a soft bed of moss. Resting in it were eight mottled lapwings' eggs and a slab of soft, creamy goat's cheese set about with a thin garland of snowdrop blooms, the white petals flushed with faint green like new grass breaking through melting snow. He gave the basket to Baradoc and said, "Take these to your wife. And remember, the war steed, which is the heart of man, smells the coming battle and stamps for the charge, but the warrior which is the wisdom of man must check the reins and draw the curb until the horn is sounded high and clear. Now return to your woman and wait for the first swallow to come hawking and winging over the cliffs of Hercules."

Baradoc said nothing to Tia of his meeting with the stranger. This not so much because of the man's injunction, but because as the child grew in Tia she had moods that flighted from periods of high gaiety and laughter over small things to times when she sat silent, touched with some hidden anxiety which she would deny if he questioned her. He guessed that at such moments her thoughts were on the day of labour and birth to come, when from wife she would become mother. To tell her of the stranger and of the nonsense he had talked would only give her food for brooding. When he gave her the gift basket, he said that he had found it nearby on the wall of the cattle fold.

"But how could he have known I wanted lapwings' eggs?"

"He didn't. There was only the cheese in it. The eggs were the ones I collected." It was the first time he had ever lied to her, but though he did it for her sake there was an unease in him for the rest of that day.

On the day he finished the shaping of the last paddle, the fine weather withdrew. For three days a gale blew from the northeast with a wind so strong that the spindrift from the waves breaking over the rocks sheeted across the high island top in swirling veils of salt mist and spume. Unable to make a trial of his boat and settle the ballast stones, unable to hunt, Baradoc sat around the hut full of impatience. He wanted the child, which they both had decided had a full month yet to reach its time, to be born amongst his people. The warning of the stranger that he should not try yet to make the crossing he had quickly put from his mind. Although some birds were already in passage, it would be weeks before the first swallows came skimming across the sea. Once let the weather settle and they would make the crossing. Since he would then be in country he knew and with people who were friendly and near to his own tribe in faith and kinship he would take loan of a quiet mare and Tia could ride in comfort.

After a few days the gale wore itself out as the sun went down. When Tia woke in the morning and sat up on the bed platform, sunlight was streaming through the open door and Baradoc was away. She smiled to herself, knowing exactly where he would have gone. His impatience to try the boat had been like an itch covering his whole body while the gale had blown. She rubbed the sleep from her eyes and stretched her arms. As she did so the child kicked hard within her and a swift pain shot through her stomach of a kind she had not known before. She put her hands on her swollen flesh and spoke aloud to the babe so that Cuna, who never left her now, turned his head and looked at her. She slipped off the platform, threw off her bed gown, and went to the wooden tripod holding their shallow washing bowl. Baradoc had long ago made the tripod for her and before he had left he had roused the fire and put the caldron on it full of water for her washing. As she bent to fondle Cuna's ears she saw that Baradoc had scratched a message for her on the peaty floor. It read:

The gods raise the door latch of night
To let the silver morning in

Sleep veils the brook-lime blue of your eyes
The gay bird of love in my heart begins to sing
Returning, I will lay a chaplet of purple vetch
                    about your hair
And, kneeling, call you queen

She smiled to herself, but even as he love for him stirred
her she relished the wifely pleasure of knowing that in the
reading of his lines she could read also the small guilt behind
the offering. She liked him near her these days but the pull of
his boat was strong. Stripping to bathe herself, the sunlight
through the door gilding her brown body, the fine down of
her arms and legs trapping its brilliance in a soft golden mist,
she said to Cuna, "Our master Baradoc weaves a net of fine
words to hold us content while the gay bird of love in his heart
sings of his dreams." The child kicked hard in her again and
she leant forward to ease the quick pain that flared in her
loins.

On the beach Baradoc placed lengths of trimmed tree
trunks he had beachcombed along the shores to make rollers
over which he could run the heavy boat down from the
sloping bluff on which it had been built and across the shingle
to the water. Stripped to a loincloth, he hauled the boat down,
watched by Lerg and Aesc. The sea was gentle with the last
of the dying swell from the storm, and for the first time that
year the sun was almost summer-fierce on his body.

He slid the boat into the water and, holding it by the bow
rope, let it float free. It swung gently on the swell, riding high
but listing to one side. He pulled it half out of the water and
packed stones in it to trim it even. Three times he pushed it
out, and then pulled it back to make the balance just. Finally
it floated on a level trim and with enough freeboard to take
himself and Tia safely out to sea. But before he could risk that
he knew that he must prove its caulking sound. They could
not safely leave the island in a leaking boat. He climbed into
the craft and, taking up a paddle, began to work along the
shore. A bowshot to the south was the small island promontory that sheltered the cove from the westerly winds. As he

moved, the dogs followed him along the rocks. The boat answered true to the paddle and a surge of pleasure filled him as he thought of the long days of work he had spent on it, and, now, here was the reward of his labour and determination. If the weather turned fine and steady, then in a few days they would be moving to the mainland, to the place of his people, to the birth of his child.

As the little island drew nearer he swung the boat away from the shore on a tight turn to take it back to the beach, but the bow came only partly round and then fell away against the push of a current that curved along the shore and swept seaward along the projecting island. Fighting the thrust of the current with his paddle, Baradoc turned the bow of the boat into it at last, only to find that the thrust was so strong that the current still took him, sweeping the boat stern-first along the island shore and dragging it out to sea. For one wild moment he was on the point of abandoning the boat and swimming ashore. The thought of losing all his past labours held him. He decided to round the island point, find calmer water in its lee and beach the boat in the first cove or inlet he found.

At the moment when Baradoc cleared the point of the island, Tia was sitting in the sun outside the hut, plucking a mallard duck which Baradoc had taken with a slingstone in the marshy hollow around the midisland pond. The light breeze set the soft breast down floating into her face. She sneezed suddenly against its touch in her nostrils and, as her stomach muscles contracted, pain hit her so hard that she dropped the bird and clamped her arms about herself tightly. The child kicked and the pain came again and then again quickly.

As the pain went she heard the sound of footsteps over the hard ground between the huts. She looked up quickly, thinking it was Baradoc. A man came up to her, walking slowly. He was dressed in a brown habit and as he came to her he smiled. There was no fright in her. She guessed he must be the stranger for he carried in his hand a thong-looped jar down the sides of which ran goat's milk that had slopped free as he walked.

Straightening up as the pains left her, Tia said, "My husband, Baradoc, is down at the beach with his boat. It would be another great kindness if you would fetch him." She smiled. "I think my child has his father's nature and is impatient of the long wait."

The stranger looked westward to the sea, which ran like beaten silver to the hazy line of the horizon, and for a moment his eyes closed as though some remembered grief overpowered him. Then he turned back to Tia and, smiling, said, "All will be well with you. Your husband will come in full time. But now it is written that it is your term and there is no waiting for him. Go to your bed and I will stay by you. Yours will not be the first child I have brought into this world. You need have no fear of me, nor have any shame that a strange man helps you. I give my name, which is Merlin, freely to you and so all strangeness dies."

He took her by the arm, led her into the hut to the bed platform and put the milk pot down at its side. Then he turned to the hearth fire and began to fill the cauldron with water from the hanging skin.

Tia said, "You could go to the cliff top and call my husband. It is better that he comes."

Merlin shook his head. "There is not time enough. Be brave and be patient. Baradoc will return and when he does it will be to be greeted by his son. Now undress and lie beneath the covers. Your son as you say is impatient like his father. He will not wait for him, for there are many who already wait for the child's coming."

As Tia began to strip Merlin went out of the hut and although she could not see him, she could see the shadow of his body cast across the doorway and, without her knowing why, the sight of it was a great comfort to her.

As she pulled the bedcovers over herself the sharp pains came again; and then began for her a time when all thought and feeling and the march of all her senses lost shape and sequence, a time when she lived in a dream through which loomed always the calm and comforting face of Merlin, and the touch of his hands on her was that of a woman, and the sound of his voice as peaceful and lulling as the rustle of aspen leaves under the breath of an idle breeze until finally, as though from a great distance, came Merlin's voice with a high note of happiness in it, saying, "Take your son in your arms. He was hard on you in birth, for the birth of great ones makes the gods jealous of losing them to this world, but in life your son will never be less than gentle with you."

At the moment that Merlin placed the child in Tia's arms, Baradoc saw the vessel bearing down on him. It came riding toward him on a freshening northeasterly wind. The great mainsail was set and curved like an arching yellow shield as the craft ran free before the wind. At the bows the white foot waves creamed high and flared in a great spate along its sides, below the long row of lodged war shields that lined the gunwales. At first Baradoc had thought it a trader coming down from some Sabrina port, but as it drew nearer, the island from which he had long drifted low on the horizon behind it, he saw from the sail and the shields that it was no peaceful ship. As it raced down on him, already fetching a little from its course to reach him, he knew that it brought no hope. Black anger was added to the misery already in him as he sat, naked except for his loincloth, watching the ship overhaul him, seeing the long line of multicoloured shields hung over the freeboard, and clear now the two men at the long stern oar and other man in the bows, their heads all turned his way, the sun and sea glitter reflected on spears and swords, and above them, swollen and straining in the wind, the great curve of the saffron-coloured mainsail blazoned with the wingspread of a great black raven across its full breadth. From the bitterness of despair in him rose the memory of the stranger's words . . . *if you would leave this island safely with your woman and child put the boat not to water until the first red-gorged swallow comes winging north.* . . . What kind of black sorcery, what fine cunning with words from the gods or the stranger's madness was this? He had put the boat to water, but not to leave the island, only to ready it for leaving . . . *Aie,* but face the truth, there would have been no waiting for the swallow.

The great ship passed him, an order was shouted loud,

ringing across the waves to him, and then it came about
sharply. The high sail boom was lowered quickly and the fine
leather sail gathered safely by the crew. The ship ghosted up
to him and three long-handled boathooks grappled him to its
side. As he looked at the men, leather-and-wool-jacketed and
tightly long-hosed against the weather, they were none, he
knew, of the kind he hated, the land-hungry Saxon men, but
Viking sea raiders who had probably overwintered in Erin or
Cymru.

They took him aboard, cast his boat adrift, and marched
him, held securely between two crewmen, to the high carved
bows where stood a man he had met before, a tall powerfully
built man wearing a silver-winged bronze helmet, a saffron-
coloured tunic with the raven device, and a broadsword
swinging from his whale-skin belt. His face was black as sea
coal.

The man looked at him unmoving for a long while as the
wind whistled softly through the rigging and the waves
slapped idly at the ship's sides. The man smiled and bit his
underlip with fine white teeth in pleasure, and then he said
gently, ''By Thor, what day of omens is this that out of the
sea is thrown up an old friend, my young horse thief with the
great wolfhound?'' He laughed and cried mockingly for all to
hear, ''Have you turned then penitent and paddle now to Erin
to join a Christian monastery?''

For a moment Baradoc was silent, mouth and chin set
stubbornly, and the blackness stayed sourly in him but
through it came now the dim touch of hope. He said, ''I go to
my people beyond the point of Hercules, a few hours' sail for
you. Put me ashore, Master Corvo, and you can name your
ransom money. I am the son of a chief.''

Corvo was silent, while the crew watched and the ship
rolled gently. None moved except the two men at the stern
oar who kept the bows dead up into the wind with their
strokes. Then the man spoke and he said savagely, ''The son
of a chief? And what am I? The son of a black slave woman
begotten by a drunken sea raider—and gold means nothing to
me until we reach the warm southlands to spend what we
have. But this trip death has trimmed our crew and I need

men—not money.'' His voice rising fiercely, he called, ''Put
a collar on him and chain him to the rowing benches!''

Baradoc was led aft. As he went he saw far, far to the
northeast the sun gilding the green tops of the island. He
clenched his hands and bit his lip until blood flowed to hold
back the anguish that engulfed his heart.

Grief had paced out its first fierce measures, encircling her
heart and shadowing her mind with the heavy folds of its
sable mantle. Baradoc's boat at the whim of the tides and the
caprice of the veering winds had drifted back to the island.
Merlin had swum out and brought it into the little cove where
its keel had first touched water. When Tia saw it and wept
Merlin told her that Baradoc still lived and would return to
her, for he had seen the future in the dreams the gods gave
him.

Now with the passing days warming the rocks and all the
island balmy under the touch of growing spring, the young
bracken a foot high, the sea samphires and the thrift pads
moving toward bloom, and the sureness of Merlin's faith that
one day Baradoc would return becoming her courage and
strength, Tia found a peace and a fortitude that served her
strongly.

She lived now, for safety against sudden raiders and for
human comfort and companionship, in Merlin's cave, where
Lerg and Aesc slept each night under the boulder entrance
and Cuna at the foot of the child's small wicker crib, while
Bran roosted on a rock spur outside the curtained fissure
opening. At night the brazier glowed like a red eye and the fat
tallow candles, their light flickering in the drafts that idled
through the high curtain, cast moving shadows over the
rough vault of the cavern's roof. Sometimes before she slept
and Merlin moved to finger-snuff the lights she would look
down at the child in the crib at her side and find him awake,
watching the shadow play on the vaulted roof. She would put
out a hand and gently touch the warm cheek and smooth the
down of his pale, mouse-coloured hair, already flecked with
the copper glints he drew from his father, and the down-soft
touch under her fingers always brought back the morning of

Baradoc's going and she saw the rough writing on the peat floor . . . *Returning, I will lay a chaplet of purple vetch about your hair and, kneeling, calling you queen.* And she remembered again the moment when bearded Merlin leant over her and put her son into her arms, the early-born, the longed-for son, and, standing back from her, said after a while, "How shall he be named?"

Without hesitation, for this had long been settled between herself and Baradoc, she said, "He is named after the father of his father, and is called Arturo."

Merlin nodded, smiling, and said, "It is a good name. A name for all men and all time."

And so she lived now, cared for and protected by Merlin, waiting for the time when Arturo should be grown enough to make the crossing to the mainland. She would go to the people of the Enduring Crow and claim her place among them and rest with them until Baradoc returned. So, while she waited for Merlin to name the day of the crossing, she lived with him as she had once lived with her brother, in openness and companionship. He knew her mind and learned of her past and the story of her meeting with Baradoc. But the one thing she kept locked in her mind, hidden even from Merlin, was their meeting with Asimus and his gift to them, because the true ending of that story belonged only to her and to Baradoc.

She used from the first bathing of Arturo the silver chalice to hold the warm water with which she sponged his body and cleaned his apple-bloom cheeks. When the child was a month old, sitting cradled by her arm on her knee, his naked body shining in the sunlight through the sea entrance, the cry of the seabirds and the slow booming of the swell against the rocks echoing around the cavern, it happened that Arturo, crowing in baby delight, reached out his small fat-wristed hands and put them on the sides of the chalice. Through the water, seen only by her, the ice-bright silver of the bowl was misted and clouded with a crimson flush as pure and unflawed as the rosy gorge of the swallow which had made it nest above the cavern's sea opening.

PART
II

THE
CIRCLE
OF THE
GODS

CHAPTER ONE

The Brooch Of Epona

ARITAG SAT IN THE SUN, looking down over the village, its huts stone-walled, the roofs turf-and-heather-thatched, weighted with boulders against the winter gales. The river, running down from the distant moorlands, was low with late-summer drought. Where the river met the sands of the small cove it fanned out in a shifting web of shallow channels. Some of the younger children, naked, their brown bodies gleaming like polished oak wood, played in the water, watched by a small group of women who sat in the shaded lee of the tall rocks which ribbed through the white sands at the foot of the cliffs. He caught the sound of their laughter as they worked at their spindles, teasing the wool of the moor sheep into yarn. At the edge of the sea, docile under summer zephyrs, older boys and their fathers were working on two of the fishing curraghs. From time to time, despite the summer's heat, he coughed and shivered under the striped cloak drawn close about his shoulders and, with each cough, felt the chest pain stab him, a pain which had grown fiercer with the passing of each year.

Among the women he marked the fair, gorse-bloom hair of the one named Tia who had come to them with her babe, claiming it to be the child of Baradoc—the son of his long-dead brother; Baradoc who—if he lived still—was chief of the people of the Enduring Crow. With her had come Merlin, whose word no man doubted, Merlin who with one eye looked into the past and with the other into the future; Merlin who had said that one day Baradoc would return and speak

179

the truth of the villainy which the woman Tia had laid against Inbar, his own son. But, since he, Aritag, now stood in Baradoc's place, he had refused any judgment until Baradoc should come himself and, amongst them all in the boulder-flagged village circle, should speak the evil to Inbar's face. *Aie* . . . but in his heart he, Aritag, knew the truth already for he knew his own son.

A shadow stretching over his shoulder from behind darkened the close-cropped grass, and the scent of crushed marjoram and thyme rose briefly in the air as Merlin sat down cross-legged. Merlin ran a hand over the jet-black hair which fell long to his shoulders and then scratched at the tangle of his thick beard.

Merlin said, "The corn is ripe for gathering, the fleeces are stacked and the heather ready to cut for winter. All that lacks now is the silver shoaling to fill the great jars with salted fish against the winter."

Aritag said, "If the gods are good I shall live to see it."

"You will see it, Aritag."

Aritag smiled. "How many times?"

"Only the gods know that."

Aritag nodded and said, "I would live long enough to see Baradoc return. Do the gods tell you about that, my friend?"

"He will return. That I know."

"Then let it be before I die. Without me here, when Inbar is chief he will take the woman, Tia."

Merlin picked up a ladybird from the grass and watched it crawl across his palm. "Because of this woman it is written that he will come to his death." He blew gently at the ladybird and it took clumsily to the air.

"Say more."

"I cannot."

"Will not?"

Merlin laughed. "You think I live in the belt pouch of the gods? Good Aritag, when in my dreams I play cupbearer at their feasts, there is too much laughter and noise to catch more than scraps of their talk. Anyway, I came not to talk of the future. I came to say that my time here is ended and I go this day.'' He stood up and briefly brushed dried grass and dust from his loose trews and long tunic.

Aritag smiled. ''For a man who can hear the beat of a moth's wings above the roar of the wind and the waves in gale time it is strange that in dreams the laughter and noise of the gods' feasting makes you so deaf. . . . Go to Bada and he will give you all the stores you need and a moor pony to carry you.''

Merlin shook his head. ''I need nothing.''

''You will be back one day?''

''One day.''

''But I shall not be here to greet you?''

''If not''—Merlin nodded his head westward to the great run of the sea that met the horizon in a silver haze—''there will be a greeting one day in the Blessed Isles.''

He raised a hand in parting and turned down the grass slope, following the narrow path to the cove. He walked across the white sands to the rocks where the women sat working. Before he reached them Tia saw him coming and left her companions.

In the years since he had brought her with her babe to the people of the Enduring Crow she had grown a little taller, and her body had lost some of the slender suppleness of a young girl and found the beginning of the dignity and maturity of a woman. Her hair, short like a boy's when he had first seen her on Caer Sibli, was long now, worked into gold braids that hung loose over her shoulders. Watching the movement of her body under the belted working smock of dyed coarse linen he knew how Inbar must feel when he saw her. The gods, he thought, gave men their desires and had created women to inflame them. The gods, he felt, sometimes expected too much of mortals.

Tia came up to him and he briefly set his hands on her shoulders in greeting.

Tia said, ''You are going.''

''Yes.''

''And leave the boy and me—and no man to stand by my side?''

"You will come to no harm."

"How can you know that?"

"It is written."

Tia gave an impatient shrug of her shoulders. "You are like Baradoc. Something calls you and you must follow it. To excuse yourself you say that the gods have decreed it. But you use the gods for your own ends. You put words in their mouths."

Merlin laughed. "Or they in mine. I have done enough for you. Now you must do everything for yourself."

For a moment or two Tia was silent. Then she said in a softer tone, the hint of a plea in her voice, "I am strong and can look after myself and Arturo so long as Aritag lives. And without him I have friends who would stand by me. But friends may not be enough. If you can . . . then, before you go, give me some word of comfort."

Merlin shook his head. "When Baradoc took you to your uncle at Aquae Sulis you could have stayed in comfort, but you left all the pleasures of a Roman villa to follow him westward and be his wife. For you comfort lies in the giving, not the receiving."

Tia laughed suddenly. "Oh, Merlin, whose tongue is as twisted as a unicorn's horn, sometimes I think that for the moment the gods made you their occasional cupbearer you have mourned the comfort of being as other men." She gestured to the far group of working women in the shadow of the rocks and went on, "Look—there are single women there who would join their lives to yours and give you comfort. I have seen you eye them with the eye of a man. Stay here and wait for Baradoc's return."

Merlin, grinning, shook his head. "Not for me, my Tia. I must move as the seasons and the stars move." He gestured with one hand down the beach to where the five-year-old Arturo, naked and brown, was rolling in mock fight with old Lerg the great hound, splashing in shallow water and scuffling up the white sand, and said, "There is another who will never be content at any hearthside for long, nor ever be full held by any woman and will rouse wrath in men before he gains their love. Take the withy switch to his brown hide when he offends for there is an arrogance in him which ill fits the young but will serve him well when the gods open his eyes to his destiny.''

Tia shook her head, her eyes narrowing with mockery. "You spawn fine phrases careless of whether they die or live in the memory—or even make sense. Now be on your way, for I see your feet shuffle the sand with impatience. But take with you my gratitude for all you have done for me.''

Without a word, laughter in his eyes, Merlin half bowed his head, touched his forehead in salute, and turned away. Tia watched him go across the sands and up the narrow path that climbed the cliffs to the north while above him the seabirds wheeled and called in the bright air, among them the black choughs, red-billed and red-legged, the tribal birds of the people of the Enduring Crow. She watched him until he reached the cliff top and his figure dwindled and finally disappeared over the headland.

When she turned it was to find Inbar standing behind her with Arturo squatting on the sand beside him, digging into it with his hands to build a barrier across a small rivulet of the spreading river.

He was taller than his cousin, Baradoc her husband, and darker of hair and colouring. His bearded face was long, strong, and pleasant so that it was hard to believe any villainy of him. He stood looking at her, smiling, showing the edges of his white teeth, his lean, hard body, sea- and sun-tanned, bare except for the rolled-up trews, held by a leather belt which carried a short sword in a whale-skin scabbard.

Inbar said easily, "So Merlin goes. What mad dream does he follow now?"

"Only the gods know."

"He makes too much of the gods, and fills people's heads with nonsense.''

"You don't believe in the gods?"

He laughed and, putting out a leg, rolled Arturo over into the rivulet with a flick of his foot. Arturo laughed and threshed the water with hands and feet like a stranded fish.

Inbar said, "I live in this world. The gods in theirs." Then, nodding at Arturo, he went on, "Baradoc will not return. Merlin cossets you with that dream because he is against me. But one day soon you will be my woman, my wife, and I will give you sons as strong as this one."

Tia said evenly, "There are plenty of unmarried women over there." She nodded at the group in the rock shade. "None would deny you."

Inbar smiled. "Show me one with hair like the turning wheat, with eyes like the blue flash on a jay's wings, with the body of a goddess and the pride of Rome in her blood, and I might be tempted. There is none, and no need for you to tight-draw your red lips into a bow of contempt. I am a patient man. The tribal law sets you free by summer of next year if Baradoc does not return. By then I shall be chief for my father has little time left in him, and the tribal law says that no woman may turn away from the honour of being the chief's woman."

"To marry her husband's would-be murderer?"

"It is a lie."

"I have Baradoc's word for it, and there is no standing against that."

Inbar shrugged his shoulders and smiled. "Baradoc has no true love for this tribe. His eyes have always been fogged by his own dreams of greatness. He would have come back here to gather what young fighting men he could. He would have turned back to the east, impatient for battle against the Saxons, impatient for his own glory. . . . *Aie*, maybe for a kingship which lies for the taking beyond our Dumnonia and Isca. He made you his woman, his wife, because he wanted sons to carry his name and glory after him."

"And you?"

Inbar scraped a rough line in the soft sand with one foot, his head lowered momentarily, his eyes hidden from her briefly. Then raising his face to her, a wooden, expressionless face, he said quietly, "I want no more than to be chief of the people of the Enduring Crow with a woman of my own choosing to bear me sons, a woman whose love for me and mine for her will forever be lodged in my heart like a wren in its moss-bowered nest.''

"A woman you would take by force?"

He stared at her boldly for a moment or two and then a slow smile bloomed faintly around his lips. He turned abruptly and began to walk away across the sands, following the river channel upward to the long hanging valley and the huddle of huts and village buildings from which rose the blue haze of hearth fires.

Tia turned and went back to the women working on the rocks and Arturo followed her, clutching at the hem of her belted smock. Following them came the three dogs, Lerg, aging now, his muzzle whitening, Aesc, the water dog with the long-furred red ears, grown stout and limping on one foreleg a little from an old bite from a sea otter, and Cuna, small, short-legged and wirehaired, now in his prime.

Joining the other women, taking up her hand spindle, Tia watched the dogs settle close to Arturo as he curled up on the sands and dropped into the quick sleep of childhood. For a moment Tia glanced up to the sky as though she might see, circling heavily up there, the black, diamond-tailed shape of Bran, the raven. But Bran had gone on the day that Merlin had brought her here with Arturo from Caer Sibli, now lost in the summer haze far out to sea. The dogs had held to her as once they had held to Baradoc. But Bran had gone. And Baradoc had gone. Maybe when Baradoc returned then Bran would come winging back.

A shadow fell across the sands at the rock foot and Tia turned to see Mawga settle herself in the lee of the limpet-covered rocks.

Mawga was her own age, dark-haired, red-lipped, her summer shift leaving one sun-browned shoulder bare, her long body large-breasted, her eyes dark and shining. From a rush basket at her side she took cheese and a flat wheat cake, broke them and passed portions to Tia. When they worked on the beach or at the tilling or cattle watching on the slopes above the village they always ate together and they shared the same hut where Mawga lived with her mother. Her father and only brother had put to sea four summers ago to follow the mackerel run and had never returned.

Mawga said, "I have an uncle, Ricat, who is horsekeeper to the Prince of Dumnonia in Isca. He is a good man and would welcome a woman to manage his house." She smiled. "No more. He has but one love and that his horses. When he next comes here you could go back with him."

Tia smiled. "You think of me—or yourself?"

Mawga laughed. "Both. Before you came Inbar was always at my heels, and there was an understanding. Now . . ." She shrugged her shoulders.

Tia put out a hand and touched Mawga's bare shoulder. "I stay here until Baradoc comes."

Mawga sighed. "When Aritag dies, you will see a different Inbar. Ever since he was a boy there has been a madness in him which breaks like a summer storm without warning. You would be safe in Isca until Baradoc comes back. Think about it. Think also Baradoc may never come back."

Tia shook her head. "He will come. Merlin has said so. But more than that"—she touched her breast—"in here I know so."

Mawga shrugged her shoulders. "Then the gods grant that it is before Aritag dies."

At that moment from the high cliffs behind them came the slow wailing of a horn, three long-drawn-out blasts that echoed back from the crags and sea-lapped rocky heights.

Mawga leaped to her feet, spilling cheese and wheat cake, and cried, "The shoaling! The silver shoaling!"

From the cliff top the horn rang out again, but this time calling and echoing in fast, quick notes that set the seabirds clouding into the air from their roosts and perches and turned the long run of sandy beach into a scene of frenzied activity. Men and boys abandoned their boats at the water's edge and ran for the village, and the working women left their spinning and joined them, and as they ran the cries of "The shoaling! The shoaling!" rose and mingled with the now sharp imperative blasting on the bull's horn.

High on the cliff edge above the village Aritag stood by the horn blower and watched the scene below. Men, women and children were all running from the sea, boat work and net-mending abandoned, running fast up to the tribal huts, and from the huts came the old women and the old men, leading or carrying the very young babes. For a while he watched them as the trumpeter filled the sunbright day with fierce horn blasts. Then Aritag's eyes turned to the sea. A bowshot offshore he could see the movement of the fish, countless sprats swinging in great silver swathes as they twisted and curved through the water. Shoal after shoal came crowding into the shore until the sea began to hiss with spume and froth like a great cauldron boiling. The bright bloom of the fish hung in an eye-dazzling mist over the sea as they flung themselves into the air to escape the marauding mackerel and herring that followed them in. From above the gulls and seabirds cried and wailed so that at times they drowned the noise of the insistent bull's horn, as they dived and flung themselves into the feast of the waters.

Aritag raised an arm and the trumpeter lowered his horn and wiped his aching lips with the back of his hand. Aritag turned and went down the path to the great stone-flagged circle around which the huts were grouped.

Inbar came to him, the tribespeople crowded behind him, carrying rush baskets and panniers, old cloaks and earthen-ware pots and bowls, throwing nets, anything and everything that could be used to scoop up the harvest of fish which now thrashed to creamy spume all the waters fringing the shore. This was a harvest which none could gather until Aritag should walk into the sea waist-deep and scoop the first cropping in the bowl of the hide-faced, bronze-bossed cere-monial tribal shield of the people of the Enduring Crow.

Inbar handed his father the shield and Aritag, slipping his left hand through the thonged arm-crotch and gripping the short crossbar, began to walk to the sea, following the fall of the shallow river, while the tribe followed him in silence, watching the leaping waters ahead. Behind them came some of the youths, pulling the great wooden sleds into which the shoaling fish would be loaded to be drawn up to the drying and salting grounds about the village. Two good shoalings in the worst of poor corn-cropping years could hold off starvation, while more meant salt fish for bartering inland as far afield as the markets of Isca.

Aritag walked into the sea, the spray and splashing of the shoal rising about him like a mist. Merlin, he thought, had said that he would see the shoaling again, but not how many. Merlin, he thought wryly, would probably say anything that came into his head that he fancied might feed his reputation. But there was something in the man that tied him to the gods. Some even said that he was the son of the great horned stag god, Cernunnos, born to a mortal maid in the far past. The edge of a smile touched Aritag's thin lips. More than likely Merlin had spread the story himself.

Waist-deep, he turned in the sea and faced his tribespeople who lined the strand. All about him was the clamour of the feeding seabirds and the hissing and seething of the sea as the shoals silvered it into a mad turbulence. Slipping his left arm free of the shield, he held it like a great bowl in both hands above the water. He dipped it into the water and raised it up full of the living, leaping, writhing fish. A great shout went up from the tribespeople.

"The shoaling! The shoaling!"

Then, as Aritag began to wade slowly to the beach, his back bowing beneath the weight of the shield and its living load, all the men, women and children rushed into the water and began to scoop up the catch, filling baskets, cauldrons, looped kirtles, tunic skirts, nets, and lengths of cloth. Between sea and shore they rushed, shouting and laughing, to fill the great wooden sledge. Aritag handed his shield to Inbar to empty and then walked up the beach toward the village without looking back, followed by the horn blower.

As they breasted the steep path a spasm of coughing took Aritag. The attack was so severe that it made his head swim with a giddiness he could not control. Bada, the horn blower, caught him as he swayed.

"Sit and rest," said Bada.

Aritag breathed deeply and fought the giddiness in his

head, slowly forcing it from him. "No," he said, "it passes."

He walked on. His time was not yet, he sensed. But it was not far away. This year there would be other shoalings. He would see them through. But the first shoaling of the year was the most important. Maybe the good god Nodons of the silver hand would give him time to see another.

There were two more shoalings that year before summer passed and Aritag lived to see both of them, and the winter that followed was mild and there was no hunger among the people of the Enduring Crow. It was during this winter that there sprang up between Aritag and Arturo an affection which Tia found pleasing. Generally the children of the tribe were in awe of Aritag and came to him only when bidden. But Arturo, in his sixth year, had a boldness which in other children would have been greeted with a quelling look. Even when Aritag sat in a circle talking with the other men Arturo would work his way to his side and squat by the old man, listening to the talk without fidgeting or drawing attention to himself. And when Aritag walked the cliffs with Bada, Arturo would join them or, if the weather was too bad, slide into Aritag's hut and squat across the fire from him, so that the time came when Aritag, growing used to his company, favouring him above all the other children because he was the son of Baradoc, would talk to him and tell him the tales of the people of the Enduring Crow and of the other peoples of Dumnonia, tales that went back over the years into the mists of past times.

There were hundreds of these tales and Arturo began to learn them by heart, a frown or a disdainful spitting into the red heart of the turf fire by Aritag marking any deviation from the strict form of their wording. The boy had a quick mind and memory and learned easily. He had, too, a quick temper. If any of the other boys teased him about being Aritag's favourite, calling him nose-wiper, toe-licker, he would waste no words but take to fists and feet no matter the odds against him.

In Mawga's hut Tia would scold him sharply for his quick temper, though her anger never lasted long. She was privately proud of his ready learning and quick mind and tongue. During the long winter evenings she began to teach him her own language; not only to speak it but to write it, filling a shallow osier basket with fine beach sand and tracing the letters with a stick. As Aritag gave him the history of his father's people, so she gave him what she knew of the history of her people. Always, too, before he slept he had to be told—though he knew it all by heart now—some part of the story of the way she had met Baradoc in the far-eastern forest of Anderida in the land of the Regni and had journeyed with him to Aquae Sulis, and how she had finally married Baradoc and journeyed westward with him.

"Tell me the bit about the bear and how Cuna helped to kill it. How big was it really? As tall as a rearing moor stallion? Like this?" Excitement building in him, Arturo would leap to his feet, arms stretched high above his head, brown fingers curved into raking claws, and prance around the hut like a pain-maddened bear, growling and roaring so that Cuna, sleeping by the fire with the other dogs, would leap to his feet and, barking furiously, would circle around him.

There was, however, one part of the story of her travels to the people of the Enduring Crow which Tia had not told Arturo yet, knowing that he was too young to understand it fully. This was the story of the silver chalice, which she kept, wrapped in an old piece of doeskin, in the ash-wood chest which stood at the end of her bed platform. One day she would tell him of the good Christian hermit Asimus who had given it to her and of the prophecy he had made about it . . . but it would be many years yet she knew before Arturo would be ready for the tale. Sometimes, as she looked down at the boy as he slept, her longing for Baradoc would rise to a high peak, a longing now which was often—despite Merlin's word—shadowed with a growing doubt about his return. Arturo showed only a little interest in Baradoc. His world was too full of the people and things around him to leave room for concern over a figure as remote as an unknown father.

On a night of wind and rain toward the end of the year, Inbar, heavily cloaked against the storm, came into the hut where she sat by the fire thonging a small hide jerkin for Arturo, who slept in his bed. His entry set the flames of the oil lamps in their wall niches briefly wavering and guttering. Mawga and her mother were away for the night, death-watching one of their relatives in another hut. Inbar, she knew, was well aware of this. He stood for a moment smiling at her, his cloak rain-beaded, his dark hair rain-plastered to his head like a moleskin helmet.

He said, ''I come from the beach watch. There is a cold in me which fire and a beaker of mead will warm.''

''Both of which you could find in your father's house a spear throw from here.''

''True . . . but he holds a council there, haggling with Ricat, the Prince's horse master, and the elders over the tribute of young stallions from the moor.'' He slipped the throat clasp open at his neck and dropped the wet cloak across the rough beechwood table. The flame from the wicks of the lamps steadied and the light lay across his bare brown arms, gleaming like polished bronze.

Tia rose and went to fetch the mead jar from the storeroom at the far end of the hut. She passed close to him but he made no move to touch her. Coming back, she set the mead and a slab of goat cheese before him. He cut himself some cheese with his dagger, ate, and washed down the food with a draft of mead. When his mouth was free, he said, ''Ricat and his men go tomorrow. It is known that he has asked you to join him, to keep his house in Isca. You go with him?''

Tia shook her head. ''No. My place is here.''

Inbar shrugged his shoulders and grimaced. ''Any woman of this tribe in your place would have gone.''

''This is my tribe. But my blood is my own.''

''And good blood, too. Proud blood. But Isca is a fine place even these days, and Ricat is an honourable man who has given all his love to his horses. So why do you stay? Baradoc will never come back and next year is the seventh of his going, and you know that the need in me for you grows stronger every day.''

"Baradoc will return. I shall never be your bed-warmer, wife, or bearer of your children."

He finished his mead and then, shaking his head, laughed and said, "No other woman would ever dare say that to me." He stood up and, reaching out suddenly, took her by the right wrist. With his other hand he pulled free from its sheath the small dagger she wore in the belt about her working shift. Still holding her wrist he held the dagger in the flat of his palm. "You would kill me with this on the night I took you?"

"If not you—then myself." Tia looked down at the hand that held her wrist, and said quietly, "Free me."

For a moment Inbar hesitated. Then he released her wrist. In a quiet, almost puzzled voice, he said, "Why should you not like me? When the seven-year term is spent I would come to you in honour to take you to wife. You would have silver and bronze dishes in your house, the finest furs for the sleeping couch, and silks and linens of the best from the sea traders . . . *Aie,* and gold torques and enamelled clasps for your robes, and a table that would never lack for food. My father is a rich man and hoards his riches to no point. After him I shall have his riches and would shower them on you like the windfall of hawthorn blossom in spring."

"You would be kind, no doubt. But there is no gift you could give me great enough to make me forget that once you hanged Baradoc high and left him to die slowly."

A smile suddenly flashing across his lean, handsome face, Inbar said lightly, "Then let it be understood that when the time comes I shall take you and tame you to my ways and my love." He flicked Tia's small dagger downward suddenly and it lodged, quivering a little, in the rough wood of the table. "And you will find that you have no heart for dagger work."

He reached for his cloak, flung it about his shoulders and left the house.

Tia picked up the mead jar and the remains of the cheese and took them back to the storeroom.

When she came back Arturo was awake, though still fogged with early sleep. He said, "I thought I heard Inbar talking."

"You did. He came for mead and cheese." Tia paused and then, following a prompting suddenly alive in her, went on, "Do you like Inbar?"

Arturo rolled over, stomach downward on the soft fleeces of the bed, and, resting his chin on his hands, said, "Only for some things. The things he makes me, like spear and bow, and the things he shows me how to do . . . like . . . well, using a stone sling and how the wind takes off line spear or arrow in flight." He yawned. "Oh, yes . . . he's good to me. But I would drop a boulder on his head from the cliff top if you told me to."

Tia frowned. "Why do you say that?"

"You know why. All the boys know he wants you to wife if father comes not back and—" He broke off, turned directly to her, and grinned broadly.

"And?"

Arturo scratched at his tousled fair hair. "And that you do not want him."

"The boys know too much and talk too much."

"So do the girls." He rolled over on his back and, yawning, rubbed his eyes. "So, when you want a boulder dropped, tell me. To kill your first man in your mother's honour would be a great killing."

Suddenly out of sympathy with his precocity, Tia snapped, "Arturo—talk not like that!"

Arturo made no reply. Eyes closed, limbs loose in returning sleep, he snored gently, yet although Tia knew that he could fall into sudden sleep, she was far from sure this time that his sleep was genuine. But she was sure that, despite Aritag and Inbar's care, he needed the harder hand of a father. He was growing fast and overknowingly.

Before Ricat left he came to see Tia. She was in the great cave in the hillside above the village where the rush panniers and earthen crocks of wheat and barley were housed and with three other women was labouring at the two large milling querns, grinding into flour the oven-dried ears. When he called to her she came to him at the cave entrance, her working shift looped up at one corner into her belt, her face flushed, her hands and bare arms powdered with flour.

A short, stocky man with the wrinkled face of an overwintered apple, his belted tunic and gartered trews of the finest wool, the short red cloak of a chief servant of the Prince of Dumnonia open over his shoulders, Ricat laughed, and said, "If your uncle Truvius were alive to see you now he would not believe it."

"You knew Truvius?"

"I did. He often when he first retired to Aquae Sulis came to Isca to buy horses and would have none of the moorland breed, only those still bred of the true cavalry strain, though few of those are with us now. Give a moorland stallion freedom and he will mount any mare he can find. You knew Truvius was dead?"

"No. But I long since guessed it. The gods have gained good company."

Ricat nodded. "He once did me a favour that put me in good standing with my Prince. *Aie*, at a moment when I needed it. I would return that favour through his kin. I say again that there is now or at any time a place for you and your son in my house at Isca—and a safe passage there though you should travel alone if you show this token."

He reached to the scarlet fall of his cloak flap and unpinned from it a brooch, which he handed to Tia.

"What is it?"

"It is the badge of the Prince's master and keeper of horse. Once you are over the River Tamarus and out of the lands of the people of the Enduring Crow, not even Inbar would touch you, and" —he smiled—"the headwaters are a day or a night's march to the east from here. Show the brooch—there is none other like it—and safe passage will be given."

Looking down at the brooch, Tia, who over the years had learned much of the beliefs and customs of her husband's people, said, "It is the goddess Epona."

Ricat nodded. "Truvius would have known that, too, as would any legionary cavalry commander in the old days."

On the bronze brooch, inlaid in silver gilt, was the figure of the goddess, holding in her arms a wide bowl full of ears of corn. Behind her stood an arch-necked horse. Around the rim of the brooch were set garnets backed by thin gold-leaf foil to give added luster to the stones. It was a beautiful piece of work, worth many head of cattle. Tia's eyes misted momentarily at the thought of the man's kindness and concern for her. To part with the brooch, his sign of office, would mean a lot to him.

She held it out to him. "No. I cannot take it."

Ricat reached out and closed her fingers over the brooch. "Keep it. I need no such sign to mark my rank. Every man in Dumnonia knows my standing. An honourable welcome waits you in my house whenever you find the need for it. But I think you should come with me now. Put aside the pride which comes to you from your Roman blood."

Tia shook her head. Ricat eyed her for a moment or two and then, giving a little shrug of his shoulders, touched his forehead in salute and turned away.

Late in the afternoon Tia carried up to Aritag's hall a shallow, straw-plaited basket full of flat bread rounds. Pulling the leather drawcord thong to lift the heavy inner door bar, she went in to find the living quarters occupied only by Inbar, who sat sprawling by the turf fire from which a lazy spiral of smoke curled away to the roof opening. From one of the sleeping booths at the far end of the hall came the sound of heavy snoring. Beside the booth Bada, the horn blower, sat on a small stool, keeping watch over his master.

As Tia sat the basket down on the long table Inbar slewed toward her and, smiling, said, "Ricat has gone."

"Yes. He is a man of great kindness—and honour." Tia made no attempt to mute the edge in her voice.

Inbar laughed. "I agree. I rode with him awhile to see him off the tribal grounds. He wore in his cloak a plain bronze brooch."

"So?"

"So—you have the goddess Epona to give you safe riding to Isca should you ever need it."

"If I ever need it, yes."

Inbar shook his head gently. "Your eyes are the mirror of your temper. Now they are the bleak blue of ice under a clear winter's sky. But then, who would want a woman whose eyes never betrayed her feelings? You will have no need of the brooch.'' He nodded toward the far booth where his father snored in sleep. ''When my good father dies you will come to me willingly.'' He eyed her for a moment or two and, when she made no reply, turned slowly to the fire, resting his elbows on his knees, cupping his chin in his hands, and stared into the red heart of the slow-burning turves.

Tia, as she left the hall and walked toward Mawga's hut, felt for the first time the chill beginning of fear. This country and the world outside it, she knew from her own experience, and from the tales which came with the travellers and merchants from Gaul, was in a turmoil where none now knew the security which had marked the days of her father and even her own early days. For the first time, no matter what Merlin might have said, she faced the numbing fact that Baradoc could be dead, that the life ahead of her might have to be paced out without him. She could admit to herself now that she should have forsaken her pride and ridden to Isca with Ricat.

CHAPTER TWO

The Moorland Meeting

THE FOLLOWING SPRING came reluctantly. Cold winds and gale-raised seas lashed the northern coasts of Dumnonia. Leaf buds were salt-blighted by the fierce drift of spray on the high winds, the young corn blades were yellow-tipped and the inland pasture grounds were slow to growth so that there was no good early grazing for the over-wintered cattle and sheep. Of fresh fish there was little, for the sea was too fierce on most days for the small boats to risk a passage to even the nearest fishing grounds.

But the weather did not stop the spring raiding of the Scotti bands from Erin for they came in their large boats, indifferent to the rage of the sea, making their camps on the wild coast of Demetae across the Sabrina Sea, and also on Caer Sibli, and raided near and far for loot, slaves and food. Three times before the seas began to grow calm, the sun to find cloudless skies to pour warmth on the cold earth, and the first of the choughs to begin to brood a full clutch of eggs, the Scotti came to the settlement of the Enduring Crow and Bada's horn wakened the settlement to arms. The men and older youths sprang to their weapons and swept down to the beach and formed a barrier across the narrow valley mouth leading to their homes and cattle.

The first time, although the Scotti were beaten back, they took with them two youths as slaves. The second time the valley mouth defenders broke against their pressure and, before they could reform, the Scotti looted and then burned three huts and bore away the wife and young girl-child of

Garmon the chief cattleman, who was away with his beasts on the inland pastures. The third time they came unwisely on a night of full moon and the cliff watchers saw them long before they landed. An ambush was set for them and a third of their force was slaughtered and one of their longboats captured. It happened that on this night Tia was one of the two women whose turn it was to sit at the couch side of old Aritag, who had fallen ill and could no longer look after himself.

Not long after the sound of Bada's horn had filled the valley with the sharp calls that signalled the retreat of the attackers, Inbar returned to the hall. His short cloak was thrown back and blood ran from a deep cut in his sword arm. He sat himself at the long table and called for water and cloths. The woman with Tia rose and went to look after him. As she began to clean his wound he turned to Tia and said, "This time the Erin dogs were mastered. Those who live will tell the tale and leave us free next year. Twenty now lie dead on the sands that are black with their own black blood. And we have a fine boat, planked and masterly built, which they must have plundered from some sea raider, for there is none in their parts who could make such a craft." He smiled at Tia. "When the summer comes you shall ride in her on a down-stuffed silken seat and—"

At this moment a small figure slipped through the partly closed hall doorway and Arturo, clad only in a coarse short shift, rushed toward Tia. He stood before her, his eyes shining, his arms and legs bespattered with blood and sand, and, holding up his right hand which held a bloodied single-edged knife, cried, "Look! With my own hand I have killed a man. *Aie! Aie!* I've killed a man!" He began to dance around, shouting and waving his knife in excitement.

Tia jumped to her feet, seized his wrist and shook the knife from his grasp. With her free hand she hit Arturo across the cheek, abruptly quietening him, and as Arturo froze, his face clouded with sullenness, she said sternly, "Back to the hut, clean yourself and go to bed!"

Arturo made no move, his lips tightening stubbornly.

Before Tia could make any move or speak, Inbar said firmly, "When your mother gives an order, obey it."

For a moment Arturo still made no move. Then with a slight shrug of his shoulders he turned and walked slowly from the hall.

Tia turned to Inbar and asked coldly, "Was this your doing?"

Reaching for a beaker of mead that the other woman had set at his side, Inbar drank and then said slowly, "That he was on the sands? No. There were other boys his age. There always are when the fight goes with us. How else do they get their first sight of battle and their first smell of blood?"

"And the killing of the man?"

"A kindness the gods would approve. He was already dying of a spear thrust. I told Arturo to cut his throat to hasten his passage to the Shades."

"And you gave him the knife?"

Inbar laughed. "Now your eyes have the blue flame of burning sea-wrack wood. No, I gave him no knife. It was already in his hand. Where he got it would be idle to question. Theft, barter? What boy of his age in this tribe has not a knife hidden somewhere and longs for his first killing?"

That night when Tia, her spell of vigil over Aritag finished, returned to Mawga's hut she stretched herself out on the bed platform alongside Arturo. From the single night-light of the wall lamp she could see that he had washed himself. He slept with the even breath of the young. Looking down at him, his face smooth and unmarked, she found it hard to believe that his hand had helped a man to death and that already there was in him a growing impatience to reach manhood. Lying back, she drew him gently to her, holding him in her arms. In his sleep Arturo made a few puppy grunts of protest and then turned and snuggled against her.

The first silver shoaling of the following year was still to come when Aritag died. Spring was fast giving way to summer. There were new-feathered young in the seabirds' nests, the sea samphire and patches of thrift along the cliff edges were moving into bloom, the cattle and swine were fattening, and the early lambs of the now scanty sheep flock were well grown and long past all urge to frolic and sport about their elders. There was little news of the rest of the country for there were few travellers, and no trading ships came creeping along the now storm-free seaboard. From the few passing travellers there was no more to be gained than rumours that King Vortigern, who had married a Saxon princess and become the pawn of the men of the long keels, now faced the threat of a rival, another Ambrosius who some said was the son of the old Ambrosius, the western king who had once held the long line of the Sabrina River and the lands and hills about it. Only one thing held with certainty and that was that the young Prince of Dumnonia still held Isca firmly and that while no man could claim that peace reigned in the east along the Saxon shores or through the long, looping valley of the River Tamesis, the old Roman road that ran northeast from Isca, through Lindinis to Aquae Sulis and on to Corinium, was once more safe to travel in well-armed company.

Aritag died as dawn broke with Tia sitting beside him, and while Inbar with the night patrol kept the cliff watch. He died quietly and peacefully as the tide began to ebb. Bada came in, looked at him and then, blank-faced, turned and left. A few moments later all through the still air of the early-summer dawn came the notes of his horn, wailing the passing of the leader of the people of the Enduring Crow. Tia held the still hand of the old man and prayed to the gods of the Blessed Isles far out in the Western Sea to welcome him with the honour he deserved and to give him good life in the Shades and fair greeting from his friends and fighting companions who had made the passage before him.

Two days later Aritag was carried in procession on a bier of three shields supported on long shoulder poles up the valley to the first slopes of the near moors to the tribal burial ground. They laid him in a shallow grave and piled it with rocks and boulders to stay the burrowing of foxes and wolves. No grave goods were buried with him for he had already gone to another life and needed nothing there. The earth held only the husk of his manhood in this world. The Druid priest, Galpan, who lived a hermit on the moor, placed a fresh-cut oak branch on the pile of stones and spoke aloud for him to the gods. When he had finished, the priest placed a sprig of mistletoe with the oak branch and turned and moved away up to the moor top. Inbar, without arms, followed him while the rest of the tribe turned away and walked back down the valley to the settlement.

Mawga, alongside Tia, said, "In seven days Inbar will return. Seven years have gone now since Baradoc went from you. You are free to be wife to any man who pleases you, but Inbar will not wait upon the trifle of your pleasure. Bada will find you a good mount. You have but to pin the Epona brooch to your cloak and ride away."

For a moment or two Tia was silent. She knew that Mawga spoke nothing but good sense, but there was a stubbornness in her which hardened her against flight. Baradoc lived and would return. Merlin had said so. Her place was here with Baradoc's people. Inbar had stolen Baradoc's birthright. Although she could claim no common sense for her stubbornness, to leave would be a betrayal. Inbar would use no force with her for he knew that she would kill him no matter how long she had to wait for the moment to do it. Death in battle would do him honour with the gods, but death at the hands of a wronged woman, forced to his bed, would condemn him to the dark wandering of endless time.

She said, "I am a freewoman by tribal law. I stay because my heart says stay although there are times when my mind urges the comfort of cowardly flight."

Mawga shook her head. "You are wrong. You are a young wife who has been seven years without her man. Your heart and body have become strangers to your mind. They seek comforts and means which they hide from you. But when the time is ripe they could betray you."

"You talk in riddles and I have no time for them."

"Then I talk no more of this, except we say only that Bada will always find you a good mount."

At the end of seven days Inbar came down from the moor and in the long hall there was a great feast for all the men to celebrate his chieftainship. At the end of the feast all the men rose one by one and swore faith to him. Tia, who had been helping in the serving and cooking for the feast, watching them, knew that had the womenfolk been called upon to swear the same oath, no power on earth could have made her step forward.

In the following weeks, when Tia took the weekly store of fresh-baked bread to the long hall, always Inbar awaited her there. Because he was the chief and to be obeyed, upon his invitation they sat and drank a beaker each of mead and talked. Because there was, almost unconsciously, a growing nostalgia in Tia for her old life, she was always glad when he spoke of his days in service with his old Romano-British master. He made no movement to court or woo her, though he always went through the ritual of asking her to marry him and she without feeling always refused him. When she left he would always open the door for her and, unfailing, before she passed would pay her some compliment that arose from his desire, phrases that reminded her of the way Baradoc, too, had found a poetry to match his love . . . *My heart is a bird without song because there is always winter in your smile . . . I walk the moor through the blaze of gorse bloom and know that, like yours, it is a beauty masking a snare of thorns . . . What man needs a summer house of laced ash boughs and a sealskin couch if the calm of the night knows not the love sigh of his beloved?*

Apart from these brief meetings he took no notice of her when he saw or passed her in the business of daily life. More and more, though, he kept Arturo close to his company as he worked with the other men, and openly favoured him above any of the other boys as though he would say, "One day this will be my stepson and more to be favoured than any son of my own loins."

Yet, for all he favoured Arturo, he had no hesitation in punishing him, for Arturo in his eighth year was already growing in thought and deed beyond his age. There was a small cove, not far from the main settlement beach, which was the place where twice a week the women and young girls bathed naked and washed themselves and sported with one another. One day Arturo, who could now swim like a fish and dive like a cormorant, covered his head with seaweed and, drifting offshore, let the tide take him down to the cove so that he could watch the naked girls and women and was discovered by Mawga's sharp-eyed mother. He was taken before Inbar and Inbar beat him with a hazel switch and raised weals across his rump. Watched by everyone, Arturo made no cry. When the beating was done he drew up his ragged trews and walked from the open space before the long hall and up the river toward the moor without word or look at anyone.

As he lay at Tia's side that night. Arturo out of the darkness said quietly, "One day I shall kill Inbar."

Tia smiled and turned to him where he lay face downward to avoid the smart of his weals against the bed boards. "Why? Because he beat you for a deserved reason?"

"No. I think nothing of that."

"Then why?"

"For the same reason that you will not marry him. Because—be my father dead or alive—I should one day be chief of this tribe. If my father does not return to kill him, then when I am grown the duty becomes mine."

For a moment Tia was silent and then she asked, "If your father never returns and I should marry Inbar as he wishes—what then?"

"I would still kill him—and find you a worthier man."

Tia laughed quietly, but as she did so it came to her that this was the first time she had ever put in words to anyone the thought that Baradoc might never return and that she might marry Inbar.

From that day on Tia noticed that although Arturo behaved as usual with Inbar he spent less time with the other boys and was always ready to go up to the moor and take provisions to the hermit Druid priest, Galpan, who lived alone in a turf shelter, and that there were nights when she woke to find him gone from the bed alongside her and to answer for his absence would only say, teasingly, "I could not sleep so I sat on the cliff top and watched the rock foxes dance." Or, "I lay by the Big Bend pool and the king salmon who waits there for spawning time put his great kype from the water and taught me a song the mermaids sing."

"Then sing it for me."

"Nay—it is not fit for the ears of my gentle mother."

Galpan, the priest, meeting Tia on one of his rare visits to the settlement, stopped and said to her, "Your Arturo has the gift of memory and the fault of imagination. When he comes to me with bread and meat I teach him all the stories of this tribe and the other tribes of Dumnonia and of our country and he learns them word-perfect, for so only should they be remembered lest time and man's memory abuse them. He learns fast and accurately but sometimes, to anger me so he thinks, he will tell them in his own fashion. Would you know what that fashion is?"

"You would have me know or you would not be speaking to me."

"True. He retells the stories and always the great priest, the great warrior or prince he calls Arturo. And always the feats of bravery or acts of piety are more wonderful than they were in life, and always—which is why to my shame I allow him the license—his words are, even for such a child, golden with the gift of the true bards and his phrases so beautifully wrought for one so young that I forget to be angry."

"Tell me why you say this to me. All children embroider a story in the telling."

"As children, yes. As men only the truth must be spoken. But as a man, unless my years and wisdom already fail me, your Arturo though he act with valour and skill will make of his acts and the feats of others a false wonder."

"Then he should be curbed or beaten free of the failing now."

Galpan shrugged his shoulders and rubbed one bare foot against the dusty ground. "No. The cock crows to the rising sun. The lark cannot soar from the bare heath without song. There is no altering them. Your Arturo will become what he will, but few men will ever learn from his own lips the full truth of what he is, or does, or dreams. For my own peace I have told him to come no more to me for I would not have my calm and meditation corrupted by his bright fancy and golden tongue.''

''He has shown none of this to me or others here.''

''Why should he? Until its wings are flighted the young plover is a stone among stones.''

So Arturo stopped going to the priest and instead attached himself to Garmon, the chief cattleman, and became herdboy, spending his days and many nights on the high moor slopes, and since Garmon rode his distant rounds on a spirited mealymouthed pony it was not long before Arturo was riding some of the rounds for him and for this Garmon was well content. He grieved still for the loss of his wife and daughter to the Scotti raiders and often his grief found comfort in a goatskin of mead or barley beer. He was content to lie fuddled in the sun and let Arturo do his rounds and always with Arturo went Cuna, alone, for the other dogs, Lerg and Aesc, were now too old for long days and hard going.

But although Arturo had joined Garmon mainly for the chance to learn to ride and for freedom from the small but constant dull tasks which the settlement boys were set to, his natural inquisitiveness, sharp eye and brain could not stay idle. He fast became a good herdsman; and long before high summer saw the yellow flowering of bog asphodel and the sloughed skins of adder and grass snake on the granite rock slabs, he could pick out from three bowshots away the sick animal in a flock or, running his eye over a herd of cattle, know at once which one was missing since to him they all had personalities. In the evening when he came back and had fed and watered and hobbled the pony, he would sit with Garmon over a meal and then, enjoying his ration of two beakers of mead if any remained, would regale the man with highly coloured stories of his day's doings—mostly to the accompaniment of Garmon's drunken snoring.

There were other times when, doing the rounds alone, if Arturo should find the herd harboured close to Garmon's hut he would use the spare time on his hands by riding southward across the heathland and moor to a lonely tor from whose summit he could look down on to the dusty, rough road which ran from Isca in the east through the old Roman outpost of Nemetostatio and so westward to link hamlet and settlement all the way down to Antivestaeum and the great land-ending promontory of Belerium. But Arturo's young eyes turned mostly to the east, for that way lay the world of which his mother had told him so much, the world of fighting men, of great woods full of wolf and bear, and the high mountains beyond the Sabrina River and the rich lands of the Catuvellauni and the Coritani, where great chiefs ruled and fought, and where a man who could handle spear, sword and bow could gather others to him and find adventure.

One day Arturo watched a small party coming along the road, travelling eastward. A man walked at the head of a horse which was pulling an open cart in which sat two cloaked figures pressed close together against the bluster of wind and rainsqualls which were sweeping the moorland. Tethered to the rear of the cart was a milch cow and a spare horse. When the party was directly below Arturo, the cart lurched in one of the deep ruts and the sudden movement alarmed the tethered horse.

It reared on its hind legs, tossed up its head and broke the halter rope. The animal galloped off the road and took to the moor ground in alarm. Faintly on the wind Arturo caught the sound of the shouts and cries of the party and for a moment or two he sat his pony, grinning at their plight. Before they could unhitch the cart horse to go in chase of the escaping animal it would be well away into the moor and an easy prize for him to capture.

Impulsively he kicked his heels into the flanks of his pony and began to ride fast down the tor slope on a line to bring him to the escaping animal. Behind him, barking and losing ground, came Cuna. Excited now at the easy prize which lay before him Arturo, as a squall of wind and rain beat into his face, cried, "*Aie! Aie!* The gods give and Arturo takes!"

Thighs and legs gripping tight on the pony's sides, Arturo swung the animal around rocks and heather and gorse clumps and fast overhauled the horse, which had now dropped to a slow canter. On the far ridge of the tor Arturo drew level with the horse and, pulling the pony back to match its gait, he rode alongside, talking and calling to it until it dropped to a slow amble. Arturo leant over and caught the free-flying halter rope and drew horse and moor pony to a halt.

Flushed with his prize, he sat back and looked down at the road party. The man was making no effort to unhitch the horse from the cart to follow him. But one of the two people in the cart had jumped to the ground and was running quickly up the long slope toward him. Arturo grinned as he watched. He had but to turn and canter away with his prize and none could stop him. Mischief rising in him, he waited, planning to hold his ground tantalizingly until the figure neared him before riding away. The runner was a bowshot away when the passing of the fierce rainsquall allowed him to see clearly. He saw that the pursuer had thrown off his cloak and now came toward him, wearing only a rain-damp red tunic, and carried no arms. Then, as the gap between them narrowed, he saw more—that the pursuer was no man or youth, but a girl with long black hair and that she ran faster than he had seen anyone run before and with the surefootedness of a deer. He was on the point of turning away with his prize in escape when the impulse to kick his pony into action died in him. He sat and waited for the girl to come up to him.

She drew up before him and stood, squaring her shoulders as she took deep breaths before speaking. She was, Arturo guessed, little older than himself and more beautiful than any of the settlement girls. Her hair was as black as a raven's wing and lay now plastered to her head and neck with wet like a sleek helmet, and the same rain had drenched her tunic so that it clung to her body like a skin, firming into bold prominence her apple-small young breasts. Her legs were bare except for light leather sandals, the thongs between big and second toes cross-gartered high up her bare legs. But more than the boldness of her young body, which Arturo covered unbashfully with his eyes, was the beauty of her face. Her skin had the soft, dull polish of a hoarded hazelnut, her eyes were a bright, clear, piercing blue and her lips were red as the wild rose hips which grew on the banks of the lower combes of the moor. Arturo had never seen a girl so beautiful and the sight made him clear his throat with a grunt as though his gullet were dry with sudden thirst.

Her breath recovered, the girl stepped forward and laid her hand on the halter of the escaped horse. In an accent which told him that she had never been born or bred in Dumnonia she said, "I thank you, stranger, for catching our horse."

Tempted by some demon of mischief, Arturo answered, "And I say no thanks are needed since I do not mean to give him up."

The girl laughed and tugged gently at the loop of the rope that curved between horse and Arturo's hand. "Then you must get down and fight for him—but watch as your feet touch the ground lest I fairly slit your gullet with this." As she spoke she pulled up the long hem of her tunic and drew from a sheath held by the top-gartering of her sandals against her thigh a long single-edged knife. Seeing the look of surprise on Arturo's face as he still sat his pony, she laughed and said, "I see you have no stomach for knife work!" With the last word she jerked the free end of the halter from Arturo's unresisting grasp.

Arturo, confused and suddenly no master of himself, said, "You are not of these parts?"

"No, nor wish to be if it is peopled with horse thieves." She spoke harshly and then as though from her mastery she had decided to be magnanimous, went on, "We come from Gaul and landed two days since in the bay which is named after the island of Ictis and we make our way to Lindum."

"Where is that?"

The girl smiled. "To hear my father tell it—where every other spring flows wine instead of water, where the birds on the trees have golden wings, and the cattle grass grows knee-high and lush through winter. You want to leave your bog hut or beach shelter and come? You would be welcome, less for the company of yourself than the gain of your pony and the friendship of your dog." She stooped and fondled the ears of Cuna, who sat at her feet.

Arturo, slowly mastering the unusual confusion which had spread quickly through him, said with a return of spirit, "One day I will come to Lindum and seek you out. You shall see—when I am grown I shall come and woo you and we shall lie in the long grass, listen to the golden birds sing, and drink the new wine. This I promise you."

The girl laughed, shaking her head so that the raindrops sprayed from her long black hair, and said, "You have a boy's build but a bard's tongue. How will you ask for me since you know not my name?"

Enjoying himself now, excited by her presence and the day's adventure, Arturo grinned, then spat like a man over his pony's neck and said, "I shall ask for one who has eyes like the blue bellflowers, lips redder than the thorn berry and hair like polished black serpentine."

The girl rubbed the back of her hand across her nose as the rain, which had begun again, ran down it and said, "There could be many such."

"*Aie . . .* so. But not any who can lift a tunic skirt to take knife and show a red birthmark like a swallow's gorge on her thigh."

The girl was silent for a moment, then shook her head and asked, "How many years have you got, boy?"

"Ten," liked Arturo.

She shook her head, and said, "I doubt the truth of that— but one thing is true, your tongue outruns your years."

As she finished speaking there came through the wind and the rain from the road below the high, winding sound of a horn.

"Your father calls," said Arturo.

"Then I go. But"—she grinned impishly—"to save you trouble in the years to come I give you my name for I would not have you wandering the streets of Lindum lifting the skirts of every dark-haired girl looking for a swallow's gorge birthmark. 'Tis Daria, daughter of Ansold, the sword smith."

She turned from him, as the horn blew again, leapt to her horse's back, kicked him with her heels and set him at a canter down the slope.

"And mine," shouted Arturo after her, though the rain and wind drowned his words "is Arturo, son of Baradoc, chief of the people of the Enduring Crow and . . . and . . . and . . ." He spluttered into silence as a sharp squall burst into his face.

He sat then, still on his pony, watching Daria rejoin her father, seeing the escaped horse retethered to the cart, and unmoving still sat on, watching, until the slow-moving party disappeared over a far crest of the moor.

Two days later Tia walked the river path from the cave up to the long hall. She was smiling to herself because Arturo had returned from the moor that morning with Garmon and had come straight to her in the cave where she worked, stuffed himself with two of the fresh-baked wheat cakes, and had insisted that she draw a map in the sand of the cave's floor to show him where Lindum lay. But when she had asked him why he wanted to know he had been evasive and she had not pressed him. In the last few months, since he had spent less time with boys of his own age, and had frequented first the priest and then the herdsman, she had sensed a growing impatience in him, a restlessness of spirit and body, and a precocity which far from pleased her. When he slept at home now it was no longer to share her bed platform but to lie in the long-empty bed of Mawga's father. The children of the tribe grew faster and matured earlier than the Roman and Romano-British boys and girls of her own childhood. Since most of the youths and maidens of the tribe moved about in the good weather half-naked it was a development to be expected—but it was an early ripening which, she felt, needed the control more of a father than a mother so far as Arturo was concerned. Had she a daughter she could have dealt with her, but Arturo was fast slipping beyond her grasp. He needed the firm hand and sharp tongue of a father to guide and school him. For a moment or two her heart was full of

fierce longing for the return of Baradoc. By all the gods, she
needed him for Arturo's sake and for her own. . . .

When she entered the long hall Inbar was sitting alone at
the table, lashing the three-tined head of a fish spear into the
socket of a new ash pole with waxed leather thongs. To one
end of the table was set the customary mead jug and by its
side two beakers. He rose as she came in, holding the door
wide to let her pass with the great rush basket of new bread,
and stood watching her as she carried it through to the
storeroom. When she came back, without any word or greeting, he motioned her to sit at the table. He went to the door,
glanced around as she sat with her back to him, then closed
the door and with a flick of his fingers drew the leather latch
thong inward through its hole so that none could open the
door from outside. He came back around the table and sat,
facing her. He lifted the jug and filled the two beakers and Tia
saw at once that instead of pouring mead he was pouring
wine. Seeing that she had noticed this, Inbar smiled.

"There is a reason," he said.

"And for these, too?" Tia touched her beaker with a
finger. Like the other it was not the usual earthenware beaker
but two fine glass drinking cups each engraved with the
snake-wreathed head of the gorgon, Medusa. Such
glasswork, she guessed, could never have been made in this
country.

"For those, too," said Inbar. "In his time my father
traded for and hoarded much treasure. But he seldom used
such things as these—unless someone as important as the
Prince of Dumnonia or his high steward came this way."

"Then who is honoured today?"

"You."

"Why?"

"Because this is the day of my birth." He smiled. "That is
if Galpan, the priest, in his keeping of the calendar is to be
believed. So I make you my birthday guest, and for this
meeting plague you not about marriage, but ask in its stead
that you pledge my health."

Tia smiled. When he was in this mood, despite all he had

done to Baradoc, she could find herself easier with him. She took the glass and breathed in the bouquet. How many years had it been since she had last drunk a fine Falernian? Besides his treasures old Aritag had hoarded wine, too; wine bartered for in the peaceful days when the trading ships came coast-creeping all the way from the Mediterranean.

Tia said, "In return for a truce to marriage talk, I drink willingly."

"You do me honour. 'Tis but a small glass, so drink deep."

As she put the glass back on the table Inbar raised his own glass.

He said, "From this day I ask no more that you should be my wife, but wait only for the time when you shall look into my eyes and I shall know that the thirst I have for you lives also in the woman who for me is the woman above all women."

He drank, emptying his glass, and as he set it back on the table he touched its rim against the rim of Tia's glass and a small, silvery note rang high and then died through the silence of the long hall. Then he stood up and moved slowly around the table to come to Tia's side. As he did so Tia's head began to swim and, smiling at the conceit, she fancied that suddenly there was not one but three Inbars who approached her, three that swam first apart and then merged into one and then broke again into three, and then, as almost uncaringly she began dimly to know what had happened, the middle Inbar came to her and lifted her from her seat. As he drew her to him, knowing now that the wine had been drugged, she tried to push him from her. His arms encircled her and his lips came down to hers and took them, and he held her until there was no resistance left in her.

He lifted her from her feet and carried her, kissing her face and neck as he walked, to his sleeping booth at the end of the hall. He laid her down on the great white spread of bearskin, the pelt of one of the northern monsters which dwelt among the icebergs and frozen seas which only the Viking sea raiders knew, and rested her head on the red of the damask cushion stuffed with the nesting down of eider ducks. She lay there, breathing gently, with her eyes shut, and her fair beauty fogged his eyes with tears of joy.

Yet to himself, as his hands began to unlatch the buckle of his deerskin surcoat, he said, the edge of regret in his voice, "A little more of patience and gentleness, good Inbar, and she would have come to you freely, tamed by her own desire. Now loving itself must be the shy mare's gentler."

His belt dropped to the floor, but as he moved to slip free of his surcoat there came from outside the distant sound of people running and calling, the noise growing louder with each second.

Then clearly through the still summer air burst the fierce, insistent clarion calling of Bada's horn, beating and searing and wailing, as he heralded the first shoaling of the year.

As the sound of shouts and racing footsteps came nearer and the horn's clamour grew fiercer and fiercer, Inbar looked to the indrawn latch thong of the door and then down to Tia. Slowly a wry smile spread over his face. A man could plan, he thought, but there was no escaping the intrusion of the gods. As chief of the people of the Enduring Crow there was no escape from honouring the great gift from the sea.

He picked up his belt, rebuckled it, and then went to the wall and took down the great shield. He opened the door as Bada and a gathering of tribespeople swarmed across the forecourt. Seeing him, they rushed forward and eager hands began to pull him away, across the court and down the valley while the horn blower paraded before him, waking the cliffs to wild echoes and setting the seabirds awing and awailing.

Only one of the tribe loitered and turned back to the long hall. Mawga, before the opening of the door, had seen that the latch thong had been pulled inside. She went in and saw the wineglasses and jug on the table, and Tia lying clothed and untouched on the bed.

CHAPTER THREE

A Chaplet Of Purple Vatch

INBAR GUESSED THAT MAGWA had helped Tia to escape. Two nights later he took her to the long hall, dismissed the old woman from the cooking quarters and the other house servant. Then he flung her on the bed and beat her until she confessed (which she did soon enough) that she had brought a moor pony to the long hall, set the partly recovering Tia on it and led her until long after nightfall across the dark upland until they had reached the Isca road. Here, recovering fast, Tia could manage the pony herself. Wearing the Epona brooch of Ricat, she had ridden off eastward.

Four days later Inbar had married Mawga, and she, despite her weals, was well content. To Arturo he said nothing for long since there had been no lack of boys and gossips to tell him the story. But he took Arturo into his household and treated him as his ward. Arturo, behaving himself and docile, took advantage of being lodged in the hall as the ward of the Chief to avoid any task that displeased him. Within himself he nursed the promise that he would leave the settlement as soon as he had grown to self-sufficiency and, if chance could be wrought, would kill Inbar before he left for attempting the dishonour of his mother.

In Isca, Tia was met by Ricat, the horse master, as she rode down in the pearl haze of a summer morning to the shallow ford across the river. Beyond the river rose the great Mount of Isca topped with the long abandoned Roman fortress. It had been beyond the memory of most men since any Cohort Commander had made the night rounds of legionary sentinels, and the fortress now was slowly lapsing into ruin as the townspeople robbed it for its quarried stone, its well-wrought woodwork and the great red tiles which had roofed stables, barracks and officers' quarters. Beyond the Mount at the foot of its slope was spread out the British town, a huddle of squalid reed- and straw-thatched dwellings. A haze of cooking smoke rose in the still morning air, cattle grazed in the water meadows, and pigs rooted and foraged through the middens that spread around the skirts of the lower town. Above all, flying from the topmost rampart of the old fortress, the scarlet standard of the Prince of Dumnonia hung from a stout pine flagpole like a lazy flame as the idle wind now and then unfurled it to show the Dumnonia symbol of a great oak tree.

Ricat greeted Tia warmly and then, without asking her for any explanation of her coming, took her right hand and pressed it to his forehead briefly. "You are welcome, Lady Tia."

He took her to his house, which was stone-built and tile-roofed and stood at the side of the old Forum. Its entry was through a small courtyard where roses grew in red earthenware urns, and across its front straggled an ancient vine which held now small clusters of green grapes. He led her into the house and showed her around and told her that the top room, which was approached by an outside flight of stone steps, was hers. He handed her the key bolt to its great wooden lock, and said, "You shall do such work as you wish, but each day there comes Berna, an old woman from the lower town, who will help you. I am often away on the Prince's business, but when I am, a night watch will keep the courtyard."

Tia, her spirits still in slow turmoil from her escape from Inbar, took his hand and kissed it. As he stirred with embarrassment, she said, "You are good to me, Master Ricat. The day will come when you shall be rewarded for your goodness." Then, unpinning the brooch, she held it out to him, saying, "I thank you for the loan of this."

Ricat shook his head, smiling. "Keep it as a gift, Lady

Tia. A gift to welcome you in my house.'' Before Tia could
protest he had gone.

Touched deeply by his kindness, she went up to her room
and, putting the cloth-wrapped bundle of her few belongings
on the low table which stood in the center of the room, she sat
at the window and looked out over the untidy sprawl of the
town beyond which the slow curves of the river shone like a
silver ribbon. The thought of Ricat's goodness laid the beginning of a slow balm over the misery of her own feelings.
Arturo stayed with Inbar, but she had no fears for his safety.
Some strange god, she fancied, watched over Arturo. For
herself, stronger now since she had known how close she had
come to abandoning it, lived only one faith, one
conviction—that someday Baradoc would return to her.
Never again would her woman's body or weak woman's
mind ever waver from that belief.

Ten months after her marriage Mawga gave birth to a
girl-child, which was given the name Sabele. By this time
Arturo was well into his ninth year and grown taller and
thinner as though his strength and bulking were hard-pressed
to keep pace with him. Inbar showed no impatience that the
child had not been a boy. There was time and plenty for that.
Eleven months later, when Arturo was into his tenth year,
Mawga gave birth again and this time to a man-child, who
was called Talid.

Inbar gave a feast in the long hall to celebrate the birth and
long before he and the other men were too drunken to talk or
understand sense he called for silence and then told the men
of the tribe the changes he was going to make in the running
of the settlement. He had now, he said, a son to follow him,
and a man of wisdom and goodness had a duty to lay up not
only treasure for the son's future, but a future which should
be peaceful, industrious and well-ordered. This was the duty
of all men. He then told them the changes which were to be
made in the settlement life. All the middens were to be
cleared away and one main midden set up on the beach verge
where the high spring tides would scour it away periodically.

The river would be rock-dammed at the foot of the valley beyond the last of the huts and there and only there should the women do the washing. There would be cattle and pig pens well-fenced for the winter folding. Crops and cattle were to be held in common and each family to draw meat, fish and flour according to their size and their standing. Every youth would be trained to arms for defense against raiders, but no man or youth was free to take leave of the settlement without his permission. If any did so his family would be punished in his stead. When traders came whether by sea or land then a council of elders from the settlement would negotiate the bartering and there would be a fair division of all the goods purchased. There was talk, he said, of war and raiding and the rise and fall of new warlords throughout the land beyond Isca and as far as the shores of all the Saxon seas, but such trouble was no concern of the people of the Enduring Crow. If such trouble did eventually come then the Prince of Dumnonia would call the levies from each settlement and lots would be drawn among those of fighting age to determine who should go.

There was more he said, but in truth few of the men paid much attention for not only had they heard most of it before, but they knew in their hearts that many of the things would not be done and that life would go on much as before. It was idle to speak against him and delay the moment of feasting and full drinking.

Some time after this Inbar's manner to Arturo began to change. When Arturo approached Inbar one morning, after the Chief had spent most of the night drinking, to ask permission to go out with one of the fishing boats Inbar refused him. Arturo began to argue and in the midst of the protest Inbar struck him and knocked him to the floor. Arturo, tight-lipped, picked himself up and left the long hall. He went down to the beach and sat on a rock, staring at the sullen grey sea of late autumn. He was no fool and knew that Inbar's changing manner toward him came from good reason. He was held now in the settlement always under the eye of one of the tribe be it man or older boy. He was allowed no more to the cattle and horse grounds on the moor, nor even permitted to visit to old Galpan, the priest. Although no one had ever said so, he was a prisoner in the settlement.

As he sat there, brooding, and watching a handful of black-headed terns diving for fry in the shallow water, Mawga came across the sands with two other women and, seeing him, left them and came to him. In the crook of one arm, wrapped in the loose folds of her gown, she carried her babe, Talid. The gown was of good stout linen, dyed blue and sewn with black beads around the hem and throat. Mawga now wore such clothes as she had never known in her life before. She gave him greeting and sat beside him.

After some idle talk she said to him, "Arturo, you are grown now enough to know better how to approach Inbar. When he drinks and after drinking is no time to ask him for favours."

Arturo answered, "There is no proper moment for me to ask anything of Inbar. Every time he sees me he thinks of the shame he would have done my mother. *Aie* . . . and more than that. He sees that I am the son of Baradoc and the rightful one to be chief of this tribe when I reach full years."

"Nay. There is goodness in Inbar. Speak him fair and hold yourself proper to him and one day he will name you to be chief after him."

Arturo looked at her, his eyes widening a little, and the line of his lips slanted wryly. Mawga was good, but she was simple. He said with a nod to the babe in her arms, "You know not Inbar. He waits but to see that Talid grows into sturdiness and health. *Aie* . . . maybe he waits for more than that. For the time when you bear him another healthy boy-child. Then will come the thing he wishes for me."

Mawga's face clouded with anger. "Speak not so. You are his ward. The gods would mark him if he harmed you."

"'Tis a small point. He will not kill me himself—any more than he could boldly kill my father. But I can be killed by the chance fall of a rock from the cliffs. Or the mischance of a badly aimed hunting arrow. *Aie* . . . or from the sudden movement of a boat as I help haul the nets while fishing." He leaned forward and placed the tip of his forefinger on the soft nose of Talid, and went on, ''He is pink and soft and helpless like a newborn harvest mouse in a straw nest. And so, for the moment, am I.''

Mawga shook her head. ''Your mind is full of black images. Inbar is a good man.''

''That you must say—for he is, to you. But if he is so good, then ask him for permission for me to go and join my mother in Isca.''

''That I cannot do for it is not my place to meddle in Inbar's affairs.'' Then, seeing Arturo grin broadly, she went on, ''Why do you smile so?''

''Because—and I do not blame you—you did not draw back from meddling the day you helped my mother. Tether me a pony in the thorn scrub at the valley bend and one night be careless with the lock key of the great hall. Inbar would never suspect you, though he might beat you for carelessness with the key.''

''You ask too much—and without reason. But for love of your mother what I have heard I have not heard.''

Mawga rose and walked away, and Arturo watched her without emotion. He had not expected her to help. Nobody would help him for none was rash enough to meddle in the affairs of Inbar. Raising his eyes from watching Mawga, he saw that on the high cliff behind him one of the older youths was sitting on an outjutting crag, looking down at him. So they watched, he thought, day by day, and the nights saw him safe within the long hall. Well, then he must use the cunning of the cliff fox, the patience of the fishing heron, and find his own way out, for to Isca he would go. He picked up a piece of dried bladder wrack and began to pop the black blisters in its strands. As he did so it seemed to him that suddenly the gods were speaking to him and giving him the sign which would show him the way to escape. He lay back on the rock, watching the grey scud of clouds sweeping eastward up the coast, and began to chuckle to himself. Yes, the gods had spoken and given their sign. Yes, he would go to Isca, but not to stay for long, since even the Prince might for his own reasons send him back. What matter that he had so few years? The years would come, and there

were always travelling parties that would take him as horse or
mule boy. He would find his own way, make his mark and
when manhood was with him he would come back . *Aie! Aie!*
. . . the whole world lay to the east and a man should see it
before he came back to his own people to settle down.

That evening in the long hall Inbar was good to him, sat
him at his right hand to eat and allowed him an extra beaker of
mead, and Arturo showed a due gratitude and cheerfulness
which he did not feel. He knew quite well that Mawga must
have spoken to Inbar on his behalf and urged him to show
more kindness to him.

The next morning Arturo set about gathering the things he
wanted to make good his escape and since he did not stray
from the settlement area little notice was taken of him. Not
once did he go down to the beach or beyond the settlement
bounds for the next week. He loafed about the cave, watching and talking to the women baking bread and grinding corn.
He spent time each day to sit and talk to Bada, who, apart
from being the horn blower, was a skilled bowmaker. Arturo
took delight in the man's adroitness in shaping and fashioning the layers of wood to make bows, and learning from him
how to tell by look, feel and hand-tensing the best lengths of
gut and sinew for use in finely plaiting drawstrings. Since
autumn would soon pass into winter, and selected cattle and
swine were now being taken to the slaughter pen for killing
and curing against the hard days to come, he would sit atop
the fence of the killing pen and watch and talk with the
tribesmen working at the skinning and quartering of beasts.
He was polite, ever cheerful with everyone and willing
always to humour Inbar and to serve him. But though this, he
knew, pleased Inbar, he noticed that always someone, man
or boy, and different every day, watched him.

Only at night, as he lay on his bed, did his face show his
real thoughts, stubborn thoughts that matched the stubborn
lines of his face and which made him clench his teeth and
grind them slowly. But when everyone else in the hall was
asleep, he would sit up quietly and, by the dim light of the red
glow of the turf and peat fire, he would draw from inside the
straw-stuffed palliasse of his bed the things he had quietly

filched during his loafing days. He needed little light to work by for his preparations were simple.

By the near end of October when the new moon was passing to its first quarter, Arturo had everything ready. He only needed Inbar to sit after Mawga, himself and the servants had retired to bed, as he did sometimes, warming himself at the night-piled fire and drinking a last beaker of mead or wine before retiring.

When the right moment came he was favoured by the weather and the tides. As though, he thought as he lay abed, fully dressed and with his needs for escape concealed under his tunic, the gods were on his side.

Through his partly open bed-curtains he watched Inbar sitting on a stool by the peat fire, leaning forward with his elbows on his knees and a great beaker of mead cradled in his hands as he warmed it. The thought had been in his mind during his planning that he could kill the man, but he had decided against it. Inbar could have engineered some accident to kill him and there would have been no trouble. But if he killed Inbar without honour like some assassin, then the blood-mark would have been put on his name by the Prince of Dumnonia and no man in the west would have given him aid or shelter. No matter, he thought, as he watched Inbar raise the beaker and drink, the time for an honourable killing of Inbar would come. This was no moment to use the knife which he carried bound to his right leg under his long trews.

Inbar coughed and hiccoughed as he swallowed his drink and his body swayed a little as he was lulled between part sleep and part intoxication. Arturo slipped from his bed platform and with no attempt to quieten his movements walked toward the fire.

Inbar heard him and half turned. In a good mood from warmth and drink, he smiled and said, "What, not abed and fully dressed, my Arturo?"

"I was cold and couldn't sleep, my lord."

Inbar said nothing for a moment or two, but the smile stayed on his lips. He held out the beaker and Arturo took it and drank a little of the mead and then handed the beaker back.

"It puts warmth in the gut," said Inbar.

"And dreams in the head," said Arturo, thinking that if the opportunity he needed did not come then he would try again some other night and there would, because of this night, be no suspicion in Inbar.

Inbar belched gently and said, "And what dreams does my Arturo dream?"

Humouring him, Arturo answered, "That the days between me and manhood were gone."

"And if they were?"

"Then, my lord, I would ask you leave to take my arms and go east to fight against the Saxons now that the troubles have started again."

"How do you know that?"

"From every peddler and packman who passes. Ambrosius and Vortigern are in arms again."

"More likely against one another than against the long-keel men." Eyeing him for a moment in silence, Inbar gave a sudden laugh. "And which would you serve? Vortigern, who to save his life once married the harlot daughter of Hengist? Or Ambrosius, who, like his father once, dreams of wearing an emperor's purple?"

"Ambrosius is of our race. I would serve him and, by serving well, do honour to the people of the Enduring Crow."

Mellowed by the mead, Inbar handed him the beaker and said, "Here, cool your hot blood with this and wish not your young years away so readily."

"Nay, my lord. I have had enough."

Inbar nodded his head and withdrew the beaker. "And so have I. Enough so that my bladder calls for relief." He rose slowly and, putting his hand on Arturo's shoulder, said, "Go to bed, and dream not of fighting."

"Aye, my lord."

As Arturo began to walk to his bed Inbar moved to the main door and drew from his belt pouch the long key of the heavy wooden lock. He unlocked the door and went out. The night air swept in and sent the grey fire ashes swirling. The door swung almost closed behind him. As it did so Arturo turned quickly and went to the fire. He picked up the stout length of oak plank which lay there for prodding the turves and ran to stand against the wall so that the inswinging door would hide him.

Outside he heard the sound of Inbar relieving himself, and from the far end of the hall came the light sound of Mawga snoring. Without harming Inbar he could have slipped out and run for liberty, but Inbar would have raised the alarm and every man, boy and dog in the settlement would have been soon hunting after him. Such a shift would have served him nothing.

Holding the oak post two-handed, Arturo waited. He heard Inbar belch outside and then the shuffle of his feet as he turned to enter. As the door swung open slowly Arturo raised the oak plank, stepped forward to clear the swinging door and crashed the long post down onto the man's skull.

Inbar collapsed to the ground and lay still, and the door swung back to be held by his prone body, which sprawled across the threshold. Arturo, moving now without excitement or clumsy haste, bent over Inbar and pulled him free from the threshold and then took the key from the lock. He went out and locked the door from the outside and began to run toward the scrub and bracken growths that grew up the side of the valley. When he reached the first of the bracken he sent the key flying deep into the now dying growths.

Reaching the crest of the valley side, keeping well below the skyline to avoid being seen by any of the settlement patrols, he dropped his pace to a steady trot, heading always east and on a parallel line to the cliffs. He had long discarded the temptation of striking inland and making a bid overland for Isca. His best chance of escape was by a route which none would dream that he would risk.

He moved steadily along the line of a wide gully that ran parallel with the sea on his left. There was light from the stars and the thin slip of the new crescent moon. After a time the gully sloped upward and was lost in a maze of rocks and broken ground not far from the cliffs' edges and here Arturo

followed a narrow path which took him out along a headland
which he knew well. When he reached its point he climbed
down its face, disturbing the roosting seabirds, until he
firmly stood on a flat rock at its foot. Some way below him
the rock foot disappeared into deep water, the sea heaving
and swinging as the tide, which some time before had been at
full ebb, was now setting in flood eastward along the coast.
Under the light of the stars and the moon Arturo could see the
dark line of current streaming away from the headland out to
sea. It was a current which the men of the settlement used in
their fishing for one could work the tides to go west or east on
the ebb and return on the flood. Arturo knew that many,
many miles away to the east the current swung inshore again
and would carry a man with it if he humoured it. To fight it
was to ask for an early drowning, and to ride with it for the
long swing out and back called for the strength and endurance
of more than most men since the body weakened fast with
just the effort of keeping afloat.

But, as Arturo had realized when his bursting of the
bladders of sea wrack had set him thinking of escape, that
which a man could not achieve by strength he might well,
with some risk, bring to fruit by artifice.

He sat down and began to work fast. From beneath his
tunic he pulled out three pigs' bladders stolen from the
slaughtering pens and, blowing them up, trapped the gut ends
with thin but strong lengths of old Bada's bowstring sinews,
leaving small loops in the thonging through which he ran a
long length of thickly braided gut to fasten the three bladders
together so that he could slip them over his head and secure
them under his armpits to keep him afloat without any effort
on his part. Inside his tunic he had, wrapped in a large piece
of pig bladder, two flat rounds of hard bread and a slice of
smoked neat's flesh. The tidal current would eventually bear
him safely to shore but, although the sea lacked yet its biting
winter cold, it could sap strength and the body's warmth.
Against this the blood's fire must be stoked with food. As for
thirst . . . well, that must be endured if there were not juice
enough in a handful of small crab apples which he carried
with the other food in the blouse of his belted tunic.

His preparations complete, the bladders securely about him, he went to the rock edge, waited awhile to judge the surge of the slowly heaving seas, and then jumped as a great swell rose below him, keeping his arms stiff at his sides to hold from slipping the braided thonging that joined the bladders. He landed backside first and as he went under felt the fierce tug of the thonging cut into his armpits as the bladders dragged above him. Then he surfaced, riding high and comfortably, and the current took him and bore him away from the cliff point seaward, swinging him gently up and down in its long-paced swell.

One night late, long after Ricat's guests had departed. Arturo came to Tia. She had dozed off to light sleep when she awoke to hear voices in the courtyard. One of the voices was Ricat's but the other meant nothing to her, dulled with sleep still. Then came the sound of footsteps on the outside stairs, a knock on her door, and Ricat's voice called, "Mistress Tia, you have a visitor."

Throwing a cloak over her shoulders, Tia went to the door and opened it. Silhouetted against the star-strippled sky stood Ricat and Arturo.

"Arturo!"

Tia reached out her hands for him and Ricat with a chuckle pushed the boy forward and said, "When you have finished with him, send him down. There is food and drink enough on the table board still." He turned away and clattered down the steps.

Tia drew Arturo into the room and embraced him. Even in her joy she smiled briefly to herself, for he stood within the embrace patiently like a well-schooled pony and his lips only briefly and shyly touched her cheek.

Their greeting over, she stood back from him, fetched a pinewood taper spill and from her bed light set the wall-sconce lamps to flame. Turning back to him, she asked, "You are well?"

"Yes, my mother."

"Thank the gods for that."

"*Aie . . .* they helped somewhat. But we must not forget

the pigs." He said it solemnly, but the lamplights marked a
familiar and brief ironic smile:

"Pigs?"

"Forget them, Mother. I am safe and sound and have been
well fed these last five days since I came ashore." Then, with
a touch of maturity and command, he reached forward, took
her arm and led her to the bed. "Sit down, my mother, and I
will tell you all."

Tia sat down on the bed and Arturo straddled himself
across a stool and began to tell his story. As she listened Tia
had it borne into her that despite his lack of years, not yet in
his twelfth year, he was fast outstripping boyhood. Close
about him hung the shadow of the man to be, fairly set up,
holding himself with quiet pride and sureness. Aye, she
thought, maybe too sure, too proudful. His rough tunic and
loose trews were torn and dirty and about his waist he carried
a tightly buckled leather belt in which, without benefit of
scabbard, he wore a short double-edged sword, its cutting
edges keenly honed.

Without hurry he told her the story of his escape and again,
despite her joy in his presence, she hid a smile now and then
as he fell victim to garnishing truth with fancy.

". . . So I was cradled by the tide and carried safely far up
the coast beyond the Point of Hercules. As I went I ate crab
apples and neat's meat and the mermaids sang to me to while
the night away and with the rising of the sun the pearl-bellied
dolphins made a ring about me and amused me by their
sports."

Coming ashore on the estuary sands close to the mouth of
the Two Rivers, he had gone inland, walking the high divide
between the rivers southward toward Isca, and had found no
lack of food or friendship.

"Most gave me food gladly for I told them that I had been
taken for slave in a Scotti raid and had seized my chance to
jump overboard to escape in bad weather. At other times, if I
could not eat by charity, I filled my belly by theft, mostly by
taking eggs from the hen roosts and sometimes a hen for
roasting over the embers of a friendly charcoal burner's fire.
And one night, as I sat by a river pool, a dog otter came up

from the dark waters, carrying a salmon. It killed the fish with a bite across the neck, feasted but briefly and left the rest for me. The taste of raw salmon curd and its red-berried spawning seed is in my mouth still."

"And the sword you carry—which here you must not wear for none of your age may openly bear arms?"

Enjoying himself and genuinely glad to have arrived, for, in truth, his travels had been far less than comfortable, Arturo grinned and was momentarily all boy, the shadow of manhood gone from him. He asked, "Would you have the truth or some comforting fable, my gentle mother?"

Delighted with his coming, Tia said, "No matter which I ask, you will give me the tale of your own choosing."

"Then hear the truth. Two forenoons gone I sat in the sun by the river and, lo, the same dog otter came from the water and laid the sword at my feet and for gift fee accepted one of my stolen eggs. And if you doubt there is enchantment about the sword see the finely sharpened, bright cutting edges. In a day and a night of rain they took no rust to mar their keenness. It is a sword of magic and shall ever be with me, awaiting the day when I shall cut the dog's throat of Inbar with it and send him to the Shades."

"Arturo! Enough! Either tell me the truth or say nothing."

"I have told you the truth, but now I would eat and then sleep." He stood up, reached for her hand and kissed it, and went on, "I will go down to Master Ricat." Then for a moment or two he paused, his face slowly clouding, and in an uncertain voice asked, "When the Prince Gerontius knows I am here, will he take Inbar's part and send me back to the settlement?"

"The Prince is a man of honour. Through Master Ricat he has given me sanctuary, and the same will be done for you—but you will get sharp punishment if you walk Isca carrying that sword. Give it to me." As Arturo hesitated, she repeated sharply, "Give it to me. I will guard it until you are of age even though I shall never know the truth of your gaining it."

Arturo shrugged his shoulders and then, drawing the sword from the hanging loop on his belt, handed it to her hilt-first. Tia sat with it on her lap as Arturo clattered down the outside steps, whistling gently to himself. He needed, she knew, a man's hand on him and a father's authority to curb him for he grew too fast and fanciful despite his courage and mounting strength. He was built of dreams and fancies . . . liar she could not call him for she knew that a boy's imagination was shaped of finer stuff than common deceit. The flushing of the clear water in the silver chalice to the soft pink of a swallow's gorge, the pale stain of blood, had marked his destiny. Maybe to achieve it, for it must needs be great if Asimus were to be believed, then the coming years would put him beyond any man's control. There was no standing against the gods if they in their wisdom took one from so many to be their chosen instrument in this world.

Though Inbar of the people of the Enduring Crow sued for the return of Arturo, Gerontius, the Prince of Dumnonia, refused to send the boy back and made Ricat—who had spoken strongly in his favour—his ward and responsible for his sober behaviour.

But first Arturo was taken before the Prince and left with him in solitary audience. Arturo stood straight and manly before him and listened to his words with a serious face, though in truth he paid little heed to them. They held mostly only a due formality and, he guessed, had Gerontius a real friendship or need of Inbar he would have been sent back under escort. More interesting to him were the man and the room in which he stood.

Once the audience room of the Roman commander of the Isca garrison, its floor was clean and cool with black and red tiling. A long window flanked by tall wall niches which had once held statues looked out from the castle heights over the town and river. The wooden shutters were wide open now and the fine kidskin curtains were drawn back to let in the light of the westering sun that slowly marked the dying of a mild late-autumn day. A long table held bowls of fruit and a silver tray on which rested a blue glass flagon of wine and silver drinking cups. A fresco ran round the walls in a running design of stiffly prancing and galloping horses.

Gerontius sat in a high-backed throne chair. He was a man in his late thirties, dark-haired and with dark eyebrows that merged with one another over the high bridge of his hawklike nose. His eyes were half-hooded as though burgeoning sleep sat waiting full capture of him. He wore a long tunic of fine white wool and over it an open toga of green linen, under the hem of which showed a pair of soft red sandals fastened with gold cord laces. He looked, Arturo thought, as though he had no interest in the world except to fall gently into sleep, a look which must be deceptive, otherwise in these times he would never be sitting where he was.

The Prince, after Ricat had retired from presenting Arturo, stared at him for a while from half-closed eyes and then, taking a slow, deep idle breath, said, "You are?"

Arturo said, for in truth Ricat had warned him of some of the Prince's manner, "I am, my Prince, Arturo, son of Baradoc, chief of the people of the Enduring Crow." He touched his left shoulder and went on, "And bear their tattoo mark here."

"Your father could be dead."

"Then, my Prince, I am rightful chief of my tribe and not my uncle Inbar."

Without any change of expression Gerontius said flatly, "Then why not thrust a knife in his gut and settle the matter?"

For a moment or two Arturo was confused by the man's sudden bluntness. As his face showed it the Prince chuckled slowly to himself. He rose from his chair and walked across to the table and poured himself a cup of wine. Behind Arturo's back, he went on, "Don't tell me that one who had the courage to escape as you did—though I gather the sea-maids and the dolphins helped you and even the otters of the river provided you with fresh salmon and a fine sword—lacks the wit to use a knife in the dark?"

As the Prince came back to the chair Arturo said, "It could easily have been done, my lord—but it would not have been fairly done, face to face. And more, my lord, if my father lives and returns it is for him to do. When there is no more hope of that and I am youth no longer then I shall do it."

The Prince nodded and asked, "You believe that your father still lives?"

"It is enough for me, my lord, that my mother believes it and has the word of the wanderer Merlin for it."

"Ah, the words of Merlin are well known for being so cunningly shaped that whatever he prophesies comes true, though it is not always the truth that one has expected."

"Maybe so, my lord. But for my mother's sake I pray that the words of Merlin about my father bear only one shape and one truth."

The Prince nodded, sipped at his wine and then said, "Well spoken. Now go to Master Ricat, who will set work for you. But for two hours each day before sunset you will come here and be tutored by the good priest Leric." He waved a hand in dismissal and Arturo touched his forehead in homage and left the chamber.

So began for Arturo a period of hard work and happiness that was to last until he was almost fourteen, and his eyes were lifted skyward each morning to seek the first sign of the returning swallows—the birds of his birth month—and, as he worked at the schooling of horses in the river meadows, his ears were cocked for the first notes of the cuckoo.

Ricat and his overseers worked him hard and after a few months had grudgingly to admit that he had the true gift of the Epona-marked. When he sat a horse there were no longer man and beast, but one entity. Iron-thighed, gentle or masterly handed, he could bring the most wayward steed to obedience, and there were many horses which were so, for their bloodlines were long-mixed from the days when the first Roman cavalry units had come to the country. The old priest Leric (who worshipped horses a little less than his country's gods, and seldom lost a wager on a horse match on fair days) explained to him (strictly in his history lessons) that the mounts of the cavalry wings of such units as the *Ala Hispanorum Vettonum civium Romanorum,* stationed as far back as the time of Trajan in Cymru at Brecon Gaer, and the *Cohors I Nerviorum,* mounted by Gallic auxiliaries, had often escaped; or badly guarded mares had been covered by the wild hill-pony to the high-blooded eastern mounts which many a young *tribunus* or *praefectus* had brought to Britain on his first cavalry command. The bloodlines were a maze which no man's memory could now thread.

Arturo was content with his work and his station. He was content, too, for the first time with the comradeship he found with the youths of his own age who also worked for the Prince. Like himself they had been hand-picked for one quality or another, though there was one trait—apart from their skill with horses—that they all shared and which often brought them a flogging or a week's stay in a cell on bread and water. They knew no fear so could not resist a challenge which might put their courage or ribald sense of humour in question.

For Leric—a lapsed Druid priest with tentative leanings toward Christianity, who had escaped from Gaul and been given sanctuary within the bounds of Isca by the Prince—Arturo had an odd mixture of high regard, occasional contempt and, rare for him, pity. Leric was far more learned than Galpan in the Druidical mysteries, far more widely travelled and educated in the Roman and Greek tongues, but he was plagued by doubts still over the religion he had abandoned and, too, over the one he lacked the courage yet to embrace fully. To escape this dilemma he often sought comfort in drink. From him Arturo learned more fully his mother's tongue and adequate Greek to cope with the exercises that Leric set him. But of far more interest to Arturo were the lessons in the history of his own country which Leric gave him: a history going back far beyond King Cunobelinus and the great Queen Boudicca, and the days when the Emperor Claudius invaded Britain or the first Saxon shore fort was built on the island of Tanatus.

As for Tia, she was well content with Arturo's progress and paid not overmuch attention to his occasional lapses into bad behaviour because on the whole he worked hard and his company was a joy to her. On the day he was fourteen and the swallows and house martins had returned she gave him a hound puppy which had many of the markings and much of the build and stance of old Lerg.

To her surprise, although he thanked her and showed

pleasure as he stood in her room cradling the puppy to his chest, she could tell from the brightness of his eyes and a restlessness in him that his mind was far from presents. It was evening and still light and he had just come from his lessons with Leric.

He said, "Put on your cloak, my mother, and come with me. *Aie* . . . I know well 'tis my birthday, but it is also a day of other importance. And ask no questions; for I give no answers."

They left the house and walked down the hill to the river and then took the road southward. A little outside the town the land rose. At the top of the rise stood an old oak, its branches blasted long ago by lightning. Arturo stopped at the foot of the hill, and said, "Go to the tree. There is one there who would speak to you." His face which he was holding solemn broke suddenly into an impish grin. Then, without another word, he turned and left her, making his way back to the town.

It was then that Tia knew the truth as surely as though it had been announced with a fanfare of trumpets and a proclamation by the Prince himself. She hurried forward through the growing twilight, her heart beating rapidly, her lips and mouth drying with excitement.

A wiry pack pony was tethered to a bole sapling of the oak and a man stood by it. He was tall, with a lean, strong body, wearing a short-trimmed, tawny-red beard, his clothes dusty from travel, his belt carrying a scabbarded short sword and a dagger. For a moment or two he watched her coming. Then, the impatience in him matching Tia's, he moved forward swiftly down the slope and, without word on either side in that first ecstasy of reunion, took her in his arms and kissed her.

From a distance, Arturo watched them, his heart pounding with excitement and his mind active with speculation about this man, Baradoc, chief of the people of the Enduring Crow . . . his father, who, mindful of his own safety and the courtesies due to his Prince, had halted outside the town and sent message asking for a yea or nay to a free and unmolested entry to Isca. While Arturo had been at his lessons with

Leric, the Prince had come into the room, told him the news and said, ''Go now to your mother and lead her to your father, and when their greetings are made tell him there is welcome here for him.''

That night as Tia and Baradoc lay abed, the pale sky showing through the window cut with the erratic movement of hawking bats and distantly the occasional screech of hunting owls breaking the silence, Tia said, ''Oh, my love, the moment you landed you should have sent a messenger ahead of you and I would have made a feast and a great preparation for you.''

Baradoc, holding her in his arms, kissed her eyelids gently and said, ''I came as swiftly as any messenger and for feasting what needed I more than to glut my eyes on your beauty and to feel beneath my hand the joy throb of your heart.''

When she woke the next morning to find herself alone, but hearing his voice and that of Arturo as they spoke in the courtyard below, she found beside her on the old wax stylus pad she used for making household notes the same lines which Baradoc had written for her in the hut on Caer Sibli when he had been taken from her:

> The gods raise the door latch of night
> To let the silver morning in
> Sleep veils the brook-lime blue of your eyes
> The gay bird of love in my heart begins to sing
> Returning, I will lay a chaplet of purple vetch
> > about your hair
> And, kneeling call you queen.

At that moment the voices in the yard ceased. She heard his footsteps on the stairs and the door opened to show him, framed in sunlight, smiling, and holding in his hands a circlet of purple vetch which he had gathered from the river meadows.

CHAPTER FOUR

Between Sword and Sea

FOR NEARLY TWO MONTHS BARADOC and his family stayed in Isca. Each day for the first week Baradoc was closeted for hours with the Prince, who had a hunger for the tales of his long years of wandering and slavery, and when the telling was done a friendship had sprung up between the two men, who were much of an age, both in their growing thirties.

At night as they all sat around Ricat's table, eating, Baradoc gave his family the story of his wanderings, which not only held Arturo spellbound but slowly excited his envy and longing for such adventures. Lying in bed at night, he would fancy himself in the place of his father . . . captured at sea by the northern long-boat men, those who had no hunger for land like the coast-creeping Saxon keelmen, but sought only quick plunder or slaves for marketing and knew the world's oceans far beyond the bounds of shipborne traders and merchants.

Passing into the Mediterranean through the Pillars of Hercules, Baradoc had been sold as slave on the African shore to a band of desert traders and had passed through the hands of many masters, escaped and been recaptured often, but in the end had become a mercenary soldier in the service of the Eastern Empire under Marcian. Later, since he was always seeking to return home (though Arturo and certainly Ricat guessed, if Tia did not, that as there was so much to see and hear there had been times when the call of hearth and family had given way to his passion for learning and lust for experience), he had made his way to Rome and fought with the forces of Ricimer, captain of the German federates, who had overthrown the Emperor Avitus. Eventually he had found his way into Gaul and finally back to Britain.

Listening to him talk, Tia waited at times for some sign of his youthful flaming hatred of the Saxons, for some show of his old ambition to raise men and take arms against the barbarian keelmen. That he gave no sign of these passions, however, did not deceive her and she guessed that his long sessions with Prince Gerontius must have held more than an account of his adventures. When he learned of the treachery of Inbar, his face showed nothing except a thin tightening of the lips and he said, "Soon the Prince will give me leave to return and then Inbar shall be made to answer. Arturo did well to run from him for as soon as his own sons had grown to health and years he would have killed him."

"And now that you have had time to learn something of your own son—how like you him?" asked Tia.

Baradoc smiled, his dark-brown eyes lit with a teasing light. "He is a brave and kind youth, and the Prince reports well on his learning, his skill with horses and his training at arms. But there is a willfullness at times in him which needs schooling. For that I am to blame by my absence. But it shall be remedied. There are times, too, when almost unknowingly he speaks fable for truth. That, too, must go for it will serve him ill when his full manhood comes."

Tia said, "What you say is true. But treat him gently at first for through your absence he comes late to the breaking pens."

And so, in the first of the two months they spent at Isca before returning to the settlement, Baradoc after his own manner was forbearing with Arturo, but the past years of his own slavery and then the iron disciplines of soldiering had made him readier to punish than to forgive.

Three times in that month was Arturo flogged by Baradoc (though if his father had not been there the flogging would have been carried out by one of the Prince's men). Once it was for taking horse and spear on his free day without permission and riding with three of his working companions,

who had been given permission, to hunt boar in the low hills
to the north of Isca; and another time for spending an evening
in a low drinking house in the poorer part of Isca and being
too fuddled to do his work properly the next morning; and a
last time for brawling with the son of a trader from Lindum in
the castleyard in broad daylight.

Tia could see no sign of resentment in Arturo for his
punishment by Baradoc. The beatings done, he forgot them,
though to his working companions he boasted, "In a dream
long ago the god of healing, Nodons of the silver hand,
revealed to me a magic word which, chanted to oneself
during a flogging, makes the hardest swipes but feather
strokes and all wounds to heal without pain." Offered payment for revealing the word, he had explained, "Nay. To do
so at once kills its magic."

They rode back to the settlement of the people of the
Enduring Crow in high-summer weather. There were four of
them: Baradoc, Tia and Arturo, and Ricat, who went as the
Prince's surrogate. The Prince would have sent more men,
but Baradoc disclaimed need of them. From reports that had
already come from his people Baradoc knew that they waited
his appearance with loyalty and that Inbar stood his ground
from pride and the knowledge that his one hope of escaping
being an outcast from his people was to stand and contest by
arms Baradoc's right to the chieftainship.

Except for Tia, they all rode armed and Arturo was proud
of his right, now that he was free of Isca, to wear on his belt
the keen-bladed short sword which Tia had held in keeping
for him. The larks sang high in the warm air currents over the
moors, and the tall grasses, ripening to seeding, swayed like
a restless sea in the westerly wind. At the heels of his mount,
Anga, Arturo's hound puppy, now growing fast to legginess
and strength, loped until tired when he was lifted to couch
between Arturo's thighs.

They passed one night on the road, taking lodgings at a
homestead by a ford across the River Tamarus. Although
they could have reached the settlement by the following

nightfall they stopped on the high moor above the settlement valley and passed the night in the open, camped near the hermit refuge of the priest Galpan.

As they rested here Bada the horn blower came up to Baradoc with a message from Inbar. Baradoc and Bada walked apart from the camp and sat on a rock close to the stream's source, the bank behind them thick with whortleberry growths over the pale flowers of which the night moths hovered.

Bada said, "Inbar says that he will stand and give you answer only by arms. By your long absence he declares you have forfeited the right to lead our people. Inbar will await you on the fighting ground and give you choice of weapon, spear or sword."

"I take the sword."

"So be it." Bada was silent for a moment or two and then with something like a sigh shrugged his shoulders and went on, "You were good friends once and shared many trials before he wronged you. Should it come to it, there is a strange goodness in him which might stir you to mercy."

Baradoc's face muscles tightened. "No. When he lies disarmed his heart shall know my blade."

"So be it." Bada rose, touched his forehead in farewell and began to move down the streamside.

Later as Baradoc lay by Tia's side under the rough canopy which made their shelter, she said quietly to him, "You remember Mawga?"

"A little. But her father more. He taught me the art of braiding horsehair to make fishing lines."

"She was good to me when I needed help."

"For that she shall have a reward and high place amongst us."

"What reward or high place will heal the grief in her heart if you kill Inbar? As kill him you know you can, with all your years of fighting skills such as I have seen you display at practice with the guards in the Prince's yard."

Baradoc said coldly, "He and a companion strung me to an oak to die. He would have dishonoured you and killed my son in the fullness of time. Sleep now, and trouble yourself no more.'' But it was long before Tia found sleep.

Unsheltered under the stars against the dew, Arturo lay sleeping with Anga curled between his drawn-up knees and arms, and his sleep was untroubled by dreams for Arturo rarely dreamt by night since his days were oversurfeited with them. Long before the first sunflush in the east roused the larks to rise and sing he came awake and walked with the hound puppy to the stream. He stripped himself and washed in the cold water and then sat on a boulder and stared down the long valley whose turns and twists hid the settlement and the sea from him. Though today held the coming excitement of the fight between his father and Inbar (and Inbar would fight well but must finally be overcome) he wondered what excitements could really exist for him in the settlement when all was put in order under his father. He had the feeling strongly that he would soon miss the work with the Prince's horses, the smell of the stables and the blood-stirring gallops and tussles with wild, unruly mounts in the breaking pens . . . *Aie*, and the good companions of his own age with whom he worked. Here, his father would school him to the chieftainship which would eventually be his, a future which held no relish for him unless first he had proved himself in lands and countries far beyond this Dumnonia.

Footsteps sounded behind him and he turned to see Galpan carrying his drinking bowl to take water from the stream. The old priest dipped and drank and then, squatting on his hunkers, the edges of his rough robe trailing in the water, looked up at him and said, "How was my once-good friend Leric?"

Arturo grinned. "Scholarly and in good health when sober, but unruly as a drunken pig when not. He sent you greetings."

"Which I may not welcome." Galpan spat into the clear stream.

To tease him Arturo said, "He taught me much about the Christ religion. I did not know that once it was so strong in this country."

"Aye, with the strength of bindweed which under a

canopy of white, innocent-seeming flowers throttles all that grows. Now the land is hoed clear of it in most places. What did you think of its teaching?''

Arturo shrugged his shoulders. ''Nothing. It is a religion for women, not men.''

''Aye, and Rome learned that too late.'' Glapan rose, rested a hand briefly on Arturo's shoulder and added, ''You are a good youth, though a little too full of spirit. It may be that our gods have marked you for great things, but let that not blind you to small things. Your hound dog's ears carry sheep ticks which suck its blood and you have not seen them.''

He moved away and, after watching him for a while, Arturo called to Anga and began to nip free the swollen sheep ticks in his ears, whistling gently to himself. Priests were all the same . . . Galpan and Leric . . . full of mysteries and prophecies which he was sure they invented to mark their own importance. As he finished clearing Anga's ears the voice of Baradoc called to him from up the slope. He rose, stretched himself and went to him. Today, he thought, Inbar would die. For a brief moment the stir of some emotion disturbed him . . . there had been things about Inbar that he had liked. One thing at least had to be said for him, evil at most he might be, but he did not lack courage to stand and face his father. The gods would show him some kindness for that, maybe, when he went to the Shades.

Baradoc and his party rode down the valley to the rock-paved open space before the long hall. The sun from a cloudless sky gilded all with its brightness and charged with changing colours the spray of the stream's falls. Baradoc drew rein before the silent tribespeople, who had lined themselves in a great crescent between him and the path to the sea. They gave him no greeting or raised-arm welcome. For the moment Inbar's challenge lay between them and the joy in their hearts at his return. Over the heads of his people Baradoc could see the sharp cleft that opened the view to the beach and the sea, the beach from which, boys still, he and

Inbar had by the treachery of visiting traders been snatched to slavery. He watched for a moment or two the white, combing curl of the breakers and his eyes followed the flight of the seabirds, while on the dark cliff crags he caught the quick, restless foraying of his tribe's bird, the black chough with scarlet legs.

The party dismounted and a group of boys and youths came forward and took their mounts. Bada came from the crowd to Baradoc and said, "Inbar waits on the trying ground."

Baradoc nodded and, as Bada turned, he followed him. The crowd parted before them as they took the path to the cliff tops and then followed behind them. They climbed the track through gorse patches where bees and flies feasted on the golden pollen, across the sheep-bitten grass fragrant with milkwort and marjoram, to the high headland which thrust its steep fall into the restless waters below.

On the flat turf, his back to the sea, Inbar waited for Baradoc. He wore short leather breeks and his feet were bare to give him true fighting grip of the ground. From his waist upward he was bare, his torso and arms brown by the sun, the wind stirring his dark hair and beard. He held himself tall with a new dignity which came strange to all who marked him now, and although his lean, thoughtful face was firm-set there was the twist of a bleak smile about his lips.

A few paces in front of him there lay on the grass two broad-bladed long swords and two small fighting shields, wooden-framed and covered with layers of stiff, hard-cured leather. In the center of each shield the sun struck dull fire from the high rounded bronze bosses. As the tribespeople made a wide crescent behind Baradoc to enclose from cliff edge to cliff edge the fighting space, Bada went forward and stood over the swords and shields. Baradoc halted a couple of spear lengths from Inbar and looked at him. If there was to be speech between them he knew that by tribal custom it could not come first from the man who claimed to have been wronged. Baradoc slowly stripped himself of his belted tunic and the coarse shirt he wore below it. As he tossed the shirt away Inbar's eyes marked his naked, weather-tanned and hardened body and saw, too, the puffed lines and pale furrows of battle and slave-whip scars.

As he saw these, there was a strange, sudden stirring in Inbar that roused the sharp memory of their old friendship when as youths they had served as slaves to the same wise master. Raising his eyes, he saw beyond Baradoc, on the edge of the waiting crowd, the figures of Tia and Mawga, standing close together. His eyes passed quickly from Tia to Mawga. The golden-haired beauty of the Roman girl who had once stirred him to lust meant nothing now, for over the years Mawga had moved into his heart; and Mawga, her eyes moist with waiting tears, lowered her head as though she would not with her womanly fear dull the edge of his courage.

Inbar's gaze came back to Baradoc and in a steady voice he said, "It is long since we met last. The gods ruled that day as they rule all days and gave its outcome. Now I am content that they shall judge this day and give life to rest with him who shall be proved to hold their favour." He stepped back a pace and nodded to the weapons which lay between them.

Baradoc said evenly, "So be it."

He stepped forward, picked up one of the small shields, slipped his left forearm through the thonged loop on its inner side and grasped the wooden handhold on the far edge. Then he took up from the ground the sword nearest to him, swung it once or twice to get its feel and balance, and then stepped back and watched Inbar ready himself with shield and sword.

From the edge of the crowd, his throat drying already, Arturo watched them, saw them raise their swords high to one another and then spring back and, half crouching, begin to circle warily. The shock of their first meeting took him by surprise, for suddenly they were closed and the clash of their swords struck fire sparks in the bright air and the thud and hiss of sword against shield seemed to fill the morning with a noisy venom and anger which seized his own body and tensed every muscle in his limbs.

They came apart from that first clashing and, holding

fighting distance, swung and cut and lunged as though they sought now only to test and prove each other's qualities and courage. Their breath grunted and sobbed from their lungs as they circled and stamped and parried, and slowly over their naked torsos the sweat rose and lacquered their skin so that every movement was marked with the fierce ripple of sunlight running like fire over them.

Suddenly, without any eye keen enough to mark the swiftness of the blade that scored it, a crimson line of blood marked Inbar's left cheek. As suddenly again, as though the gods would match their favours, a great chip of leather flew from the edge of Baradoc's shield and the glancing blade of Inbar turned course and cut into the soft under flesh of Baradoc's sword arm. From then, as he fought, his forearm grew red with the blood that came from him to seep over his hand and the pommel of the heavy sword. But from the moment of his wounding it seemed that Baradoc, resenting even such a minor injury, lashed himself with some inner chastisement for undervaluing the prowess of his adversary. He became as a man demented with cold contempt for Inbar, and as a man exalted and so much at one with his weapon and so much in accord with the skills that had come to him over the years that fighter and sword were one whirling, probing, taunting, invulnerable singleness. A low sigh of wonder came from the watchers as they saw plainly now and again as Inbar left himself open that the slashing edge of Baradoc's sword was turned at the last moment to strike flat-faced in brutal arrogance. Again and again, for further humiliation, Baradoc forced Inbar step by step back to the cliff's edge and held him there while all knew that he had the power and mastery now to send him toppling and spinning to the sea below with a thrust to his body. Yet, each time, Baradoc drew back and stood with sword point lowered while Inbar held his ground, shoulders heaving, his mouth gaping and sucking at the salt air to give him breath for fresh fight.

At such times Tia was forced to turn her head away to shut the sight from her until she heard the clash of swords again ring clear above the cries of the seabirds below. At her side Mawga had no power to turn away. She prayed to the gods either to give Inbar quick end or to give their favour to soften Baradoc's heart when Inbar finally lay at his feet.

Then as the swaying, breath-hungry Inbar came forward in weakening attack, Baradoc gave ground until they were in the center of the open space.

There, in a gesture of contempt, Baradoc slipped his left arm free, tossed his shield from him, and leapt forward. His sword drew two fine blood lines across the man's chest within his laggardly guard. As Inbar winced with the pain and his head jerked skyward with muscle shock, Baradoc smashed the flat of his sword down viciously across the knuckles of his opponent's fighting hand so that his weapon was beaten from it to drop at his feet. Inbar swayed, then fell to the ground and lay there.

A great cry went up from the watching tribespeople. Baradoc, his body gleaming with sweat, unheedful of the blood that coursed down his sword, darkening the dull gleam of its blade, stepped forward and put his broad sword point to Inbar's chest above his heart. Mawga turned away to find Tia's arm wrapped around her and Tia's hand pressing her face gently to the comfort of her breast. By Tia's side, while the tribe sent up cry after cry for the kill, Arturo stood wooden-faced, watching, loath to move or speak or by any sign betray a strange shame for his father, who, despite his wound, must have known that he was always more than Inbar's match and had played with him like cat with mouse and who now, in easy victory, would show no mercy for this humiliated man in whom much that was good outweighed the bad.

Inbar, lying at Baradoc's feet, opened his eyes, felt the small bite of the sword's point against his chest, and saw the red-bearded, muscle-taut face of Baradoc above him, the deep-brown eyes still and dark as the darkest bog pool. Then with a slow sigh he said, "*Aie* . . . you have learned fine skills and feints in your wanderings. But before you press home the sword and send me to the gods I pray one charity from you. Take my wife, Mawga, into your house and treat fairly my sons who had no part in my doings.''

Looking down at him as he spoke, Baradoc felt no pity for this man who would have left him to a slow death to make pickings for the carrion birds and the scavenging beasts. Behind him he heard the stir and low voices of the tribe and he said aloud so that all should hear clearly, ''Though you would have dishonoured my wife, yours shall live under my roof in peace. Though you would have killed my son when yours were well set, your sons shall live and serve with the tribe without fear of me.''

Inbar said, ''I am content. So now, send me on my way.'' As he finished speaking he closed his eyes and lay waiting.

Baradoc stood above him and his hand firmed on his sword to make the thrust true and clean. But it seemed to him then as though some power beyond his control was slowly possessing him, staying his sword hand and, against his will, invading his whole mind and body. Through their dead fathers they shared blood, he and this man, and their fathers had only known love and comradeship with one another. Then, as though not he but some other voice new-lodged in him spoke, as though not he moved but some inexorable will commanded him, he knew himself to raise his sword point. He stepped back from Inbar to the close-by Bada and said, ''I rest it in the hands of the gods who suddenly move within me. Let him make the cliff run, but if he have not courage for it, let him be stoned, for he is not worthy of my blade.''

Almost before he had finished speaking, a great shout went up from the crowd. ''The run! The run! Let him take the run!'' While they still shouted Baradoc turned away from Inbar and moved through his people, seeing for a moment Tia's face, her eyes moist with tears, and by her side Mawga, who would have moved to him but was restrained by the hand of his wife. He walked alone down the cliff path, hearing the shout of voices and the stamping of feet behind him as all was prepared for Inbar's run. He climbed the streamside path to the long hall and, entering, called to an old, half-crippled woman servant to bring him water and cloths to clean and dress his arm wound. As he sat and was tended by her he heard distantly a great shout arise and he knew that Inbar had taken the cliff run. Once, as a boy, he had seen a tribesman take it and go to his death. In the living memory of the tribe out of a score of men to make the run no more than two or three had been known to live and escape to banishment from all the tribal lands of the Cornovii here or with their cousins in the far north of the country.

Sometime later, when Tia and Arturo had returned to the long hall and Tia was insisting on redressing his wound after her own fashion with a salve of healing herbs and the whites of fresh eggs, he said, "He took it. I heard the great shout."

When Tia made no answer, Arturo said, "Yes, my father. He took it. But though we waited he did not show."

Tia, finishing his fresh bandaging, said, raising his right hand to her lips and kissing it, "I was glad in my heart that you found that mercy for him."

Baradoc grunted. Small mercy it had been and that never lodged knowingly in his own heart. He said, "Where is Mawga?"

"Tonight she keeps her place with her children on the cliff to mourn Inbar. She will come here in full time."

That night, lying on his bed, the window slit above him unboarded to let the cool air in, Arturo lay thinking about Inbar. The crowd had formed a long open lane which led to the cliff's edge. Inbar had stood at the end of it while two tribesmen stood a spear's length behind him armed with the broad-bladed fighting swords. Once a man began to run along the lane to the cliff brink, from there to take the outward jump and the long drop to the sea below, there was no holding back except to be overtaken by the following swordsmen and to be hacked to death. There had been no hesitation in Inbar. He had run, outpacing the followers, and had leapt clean and far out. Arturo could see him now . . . dropping feet-first and then, as the wind took him, cartwheeling and sprawling while the dark sea rushed up to meet him and the cliff birds rose from their roosts in their hundreds, their cries drowning the shouts of the tribe as they lined the cliff and watched. Far below as Inbar had hit the water a plume of foam had spouted and been ragged and teased to nothingness by the wind. Inbar had gone under and had not shown again. Had he shown none would have helped or hindered him. The tribal law was that he must go where sea and tide took him, but seek the shore he must not until darkness came.

That night, too, as Tia lay alongside Baradoc it was long before sleep came to her as she thought of Mawga with her children, keeping vigil on the cliff top. The grief which she knew clouded Mawga's mind took from her the secret joy which she, herself, had come to know in the last few days. She was with child again. Although she had waited to be certain before telling Baradoc she knew that it would be many days yet before she would speak to him. He had been as merciful as tribal law allowed him to be toward Inbar and for that she honoured him, but she wanted no telling of her joy while Mawga dwelt in the first dark shadows of loss and despair from Inbar's death.

During the next two years Arturo never left the tribal lands. He grew in strength and height and in longing for the life that he had known at Isca. On the few occasions when Baradoc went to see Prince Gerontius he was refused permission to go with him. There were times when he sat alone on a cliff top staring out to sea, brooding over his grievances and the dullness of life in the settlement. Even the Scotti raids had now grown few and far between so that there were only rare times when, sword in hand, he could join the tribesmen in their stand on the beach at night or early morning to beat off the sea attacks. Sometimes he wondered whether Baradoc's firm refusal to allow him to go back to Isca came from his own, though never expressed, bitterness at the loss of his fighting powers. The wound that Inbar had given him had refused to heal properly. It had festered and sent him into a fever for many weeks. Tia and Galpan had treated him, but when with the passing of the months the wound had finally healed it was only to reveal that the arm muscles had wasted so that he could no longer wield a heavy sword. Baradoc had made light of it, no matter what his inner feelings might be, and had trained himself to use his sword left-handed but with only a shadow of the dexterity and skill he had known before.

A man so burdened, Arturo guessed, must always know bitterness or regret, and would want to keep a growing son, his heir, close to him, to fight at his right hand against the Scotti. *Aie,* he thought, watching a peregrine stoop from on high above the cliffs to take a rock dove, but what of the son? Each day here, except for the changes of weather and season, was the same as another and his body and mind itched for the excitements and adventurers of Isca and all the lands beyond.

So it was that out of boredom and restlessness as he reached his seventeenth year Arturo began to find himself more and more in trouble with his father. He would steal out at night to meet a girl and then have to face an angry Baradoc. If one of the other youths spoke to him carelessly he would waste few words but take to blows and then accept stoically a beating from his father for brawling. Once he stayed away for three days high up on the moors, hunting and roaming with only the now full-grown Anga for company. When he came back he stoutly maintained that he had been bewitched and held captive in a cave, and went on to invent some fanciful story which even made Baradoc secretly smile to himself. Of words and inventions to excuse or defend himself Arturo never had any lack.

One day as he sat on the cliff, brooding over his pinioned life, Tia came to him. She sat beside him, holding in her arms Arturo's sister, Gerta. Arturo leant back on his elbow and stroked her warm cheek and said, "She has your eyes, my mother, like the blue flower that grows among the corn, and your hair, brighter than the bunting's breast. One day she will marry a great chief and men will sing about her beauty and her goodness."

"That she be a good wife to some man is all I ask," said Tia.

"And what do you ask for me?"

"That you pleased your father more."

"So I would if he gave me liberty to do what I must. And if he does not give me that liberty then soon I shall take it, for the gods command more obedience than any father."

Tia laughed. "Now you begin to talk in your riddles again."

"No. I say only what has been said. In the cave where I was held on the moor by enchantment the gods spoke to me plainly."

"Arto! Tia shook her head, smiling. "You dreamt with your belly empty from hunger."

"No. I have few night dreams. I saw and heard. The gods have put their mark on me and, when the time comes, I must obey them."

"And do they tell you to chase the maidens here and brawl with your companions and—"

"No." Arturo sat up. "They tell me only that when the sign is given I must go."

"And what is the sign?"

"I shall know it when I see it." He plucked a grass stalk and began to tickle Gerta's nose, making her crow with pleasure. With a glance at his mother, he said, "You do not believe me? You think I am no more than a fledgling whose growing flight feathers begin to itch and make it long to take the air? No. It is more than that. There are things for me to do."

"What things?"

"The gods will show." He rolled over on his back and stared at the sky. "You have all power over my father. Ask him to give me leave to go . . . back to Isca and then when the sign comes to where the gods will."

For a moment Tia said nothing. She was thinking of the old Christian hermit, Asimus, who had placed the sacred silver chalice in her hands and told her that one day held by the right hands it would blush crimson within to show one—the words of Asimus rang clearly in her memory—*who is marked for great and noble duties, someone whose name will live forever, to be praised by all true and just people* . . . Often, since he was now grown almost to manhood, she had thought of telling Arturo this but had decided against it for it would have only increased his longing to be away from the settlement. Yet now that he had begun to talk of signs from the gods himself, and she herself had once seen the chalice cup blush pink as his baby hands held it, she wondered whether there was not a duty in her to tell him.

Standing and cradling Gerta in the crook of her arm, she said, "Carry yourself patiently and keep from all wildness until the winter comes and I will speak to your father for you. But expect nothing from me if you once play the hellion or the bully or" —her lips tightened to hide an impulse to smile— "seek to frolic with any maiden in the bracken."

Arturo jumped to his feet, seized her hand and kissed it and cried, "I shall be as patient as the plodding ox, as forbearing as a priest . . . aye, and as untouched by any maiden's charms."

So, through the rest of that summer and autumn until the first of winter's gales pushed great curling combers far above the summer drift line on the beach, Arturo was of good behaviour, though sometimes to give ease to the pent-up longing and excess of natural spirits in him he would get leave to ride on herd duty on the moor. Then, with Anga at heel, he would set his pony to wild galloping among the tors, and sing and shout to himself like a madman. Also, when he was on the moor he would spend time with old Galpan and make him tell all he knew of their country and draw maps with a stick in the heath sand of all the tribal lands that divided it. There were times when Galpan, squatting with his back against a rock in the sun, would lose his words in a mumble and drop off to sleep. Then Arturo would lie back and stare up at the sky and watch the great clouds drift in from the west and, of all the places of which Galpan had spoken, his mind would go flighting northward to Lindum and he would remember Daria, the black-haired daughter of Ansold the sword smith. One day, he told himslef, he would ride into Lindum and find them and Ansold would make him a sword that all men would fear. Then he would take Daria to be his wife and somewhere carve himself a domain and a kingdom so that all men should call her queen and bow their heads to him for permission to speak just as all men did to Prince Gerontius and that old windbag Ambrosius and to ailing Vortigern. *Aie*, and maybe the day would come when the long-kennelled Angles, Jutes and Saxons of the east would have their days numbered and be driven into the sea. That, at least, would give his father pleasure.

On a night of hard frost when the stars seemed fixed like chips of ice in the sky and the winter grasses were so hoarded with rime that the cliff tops seemed snow-covered, Tia spoke to Baradoc about Arturo. She had chosen her time well. That day she had told him that she was certain that she was with child again, and also a messenger had arrived from Prince of Dumnonia, calling him to a council at Isca.

Baradoc listened to her patiently, watching the firelight play over her face and draw sharp glints from her fair hair.

She finished, "He has curbed his ways and shown all patience. To be a man among men he must now go from here. Take him with you to Isca and leave him with Prince. Things are afoot there and I ask nothing about them. That you show openly now little of your old hatred of the Saxon kind means only that your anger is now appeased by some great hope for the future. Make Arturo part of that future. Although I think he talks too easily of signs and miracles which live only in his imagination, maybe that is how the gods work. But with my own eyes I saw the water in his silver bowl turn crimson as he held it."

Baradoc smiled. "It was but the reflection of the red sunset."

"No. It was midmorning, and you know so for I have told you the story often."

"I tease you."

"Then please me also. Take Arturo with you."

Baradoc reached out and took her hand. "It was already in my mind. He shall go."

So Arturo rode to Isca with his father. But before he went Tia took him aside and told him of the silver bowl and the words of the good Asimus and how, as a babe, he had held it and the water had flushed with crimson from the blood of the Christ who had died on the Cross, and she gave him the bowl to take with him since it was rightfully his.

Looking at it as he held it in his hands, he said his thanks and then added thoughtfully, "I would it had been one of our country's gods."

"There are many in this country who claim him as the only god."

"So I know. But for my taste there is overmuch gentleness and forbearance talked about him unless, of course" —he gave her a quick grin— "he uses that as a cloak to hide his real strength and power. *Aie* . . . maybe that is it. He waits for the day when, perhaps through me, his true majesty and power shall be shown to all. Maybe, too, this is the sign the other gods have chosen to test me. Instead of Badb I have this Christos, for they know that one day he will be even greater than Badb."

When Arturo was alone he filled the bowl and cupped it in his hands. He held it until the silver was warmed by his palms but there was no flushing of the water. He gave a careless shrug of his shoulders, tipped the water to the ground, and then stowed the chalice away in the baggage pack he was making ready for his trip to Isca.

CHAPTER FIVE

The Road To Corinium

ARTURO SAT AT a bench in the tavern courtyard, elbows on the rough table, staring at the sparrows that quarrelled over a scattering of scraps Ursula, the tavern keeper's daughter, had just thrown out of the door. Spring sunlight filtered through the leaves of the ancient elderberry tree which grew against the courtyard wall. Anga lay in the shade under the table, snapping at the flies which teased his muzzle. Discontent and boredom showed plainly on Arturo's face. If anyone, he thought, had told him almost three years ago when he came here that he would be tired of Isca soon, he would have laughed in his face. He was, he knew, out of favour with the Prince for his occasional bouts of brawling and outspoken comments on military affairs. The Prince, he felt, with all the men and horses at his command should have moved east long ago. The minds and spirits of the cavalrymen yearned for action, and being denied it they grew bitter and sullen— though not so outspoken with their discontent as he.

Ursula came from the tavern and set before him a jug of beer and a beaker. She was a dark, tall girl of his own age, her cheeks the colour of ripe spindleberries, a strong, large-breasted girl who knew how to look after herself when the young men of the Prince's household grew overbold from drinking. But with this Arturo she had never had trouble . . . more the pity for everything about him found favour with her. In his twentieth year, broad-shouldered and tall with a closely cropped beard and his pale hair fired with red glints—a young man to make any girl's mind flower with romantic fancies—he had, it seemed, only two loves, the aging hound which lay at his feet and the horses of the Prince's pastures.

Arturo fumbled in his belt pouch and dropped a small silver piece on the table. It was one of the coins that the Prince had started to mint in the last year for the use of his household in Isca and the surrounding country.

As Ursula picked it up Arturo said, "Bring another cup. Durstan joins me soon."

Durstan came into the courtyard before Ursula returned with the extra beaker. Thickset and dark-haired with sharp, yet smiling brown eyes deeply set in his weathered face, he was dusty from exercise in the schooling pens. Of the same age as Arturo, he was much shorter and seldom given to brooding. Life for Durstan was a brightly moving pageant which gave him constant delight. It was said that where others sometimes groaned and talked in their sleep Durstan always laughed.

He sat down opposite Arturo, reached for Anga's lifted head and briefly fondled and teased the hound's ears. Then he filled the single cup and drained it in one long draft, his Adam's apple working against the throat.

Putting the beaker down, he said cheerfully, "You look like a crow in moult, Arto."

"Who would not when life here is the same thing every day?"

"Nay, the day will come." Durstan turned and grinned at Ursula as she brought the second beaker and pinched her bottom as she turned away, though ducking swiftly to avoid the backhand swing of her arm.

"The day has come and gone. How many times has the Prince sent the Count Ambrosius's plea men away with an empty answer? I think he means not to join any fighting but to make all secure here and stay within his bounds until—and then it may be too late—the fighting comes to him. Meanwhile, what do we do? We breed and break horses and drill and sharpen up our men—and then give them nothing but exercises in mock attacks and battle skills. And when we have finished with one lot we send them back to their tribes where they soon forget what they have learned while we go to work on a new levy. Do we sit here for ever, fighting imaginary battles?''

''And is this the feeling of your good father, Baradoc?''

''I know nothing of his thoughts. He keeps them as secret as does the Prince. Once it was well known that his hatred of the Saxon kind was like a fire in his belly. And now, so Leric has told me in confidence, the Prince has sent for him. He arrives in a few days, and it is in my mind he comes to take me back to the settlement.''

''Why so?''

''Because I have asked the Prince to give me a horse in return for my service here and leave to ride to join Ambrosius—and have been refused.''

Durstan laughed. ''Then go without a horse.''

Arturo frowned at him. ''How could I? I am the son of the chief of the tribe of the Enduring Crow—''

''Now in full moult.'' Durstan laughed.

''Aye, maybe. But Ambrosius would do me no favours if I arrived without horses and without men. He would do me no honour since the Prince has refused him more help to take arms against the Saxons.''

''The news is that they sit quietly, content with what they have. Why stir up the hornet's nest?''

''No Saxon sits quietly—except to let his wounds heal—when over the hill there is plunder and land to take. In this, for all his vanities, Ambrosius is right. Do you tell me that you are happy to be here, sweating and riding and shouting all day at sour-faced tribesmen who come only because the Prince has ordered their levy?''

Durstan shrugged his shoulders and filled his beaker. ''No, I am not happy. But I am patient, where you are not. Here there is good living, horses and work, and drink and girls in the evening. When the gods will it, then things will change.''

Arturo smiled suddenly, and said, ''Sometimes the gods feign sleep, I think, to give us the chance to arrange our own lives for a while.''

Durstan was silent, but his eyes were on Arturo. He had

the same discontent as his friend, but more patience and, for all his carefree manner, more caution since, where Arturo was the son of a chief who was close to the Prince, his own father was long dead and had never been more than a horse trader from neighbouring Lindinis, in the country of the Durotriges. Only his eyes for and skill with horses had brought him to the Prince's service.

Finally he said quietly, "So the gods sleep. How would you have us arrange our lives?"

"We have our own arms and the right to carry them. We buy two horses at the next trading fair and then go north to Ambrosius."

"But he would give us no welcome. This you have said."

"Not us alone—but with men well mounted he would. Twelve men, nay, six, well horsed and armed he would accept."

"And where would we find these others and their mounts?"

Arturo sipped at his beer, and then said, "The gods must wake sometime and give us a little fortune. You think that between here and Corinium or Glevum there are none such as us waiting for the prick of comradeship to bring them forward? No horses to be found or plunder to be taken to pay for them? We shall come as no ragged band. You and I between us can train them and when Count Ambrosius sees us, there will be no heart in him to turn us away. He needs fighting men."

"The next trading fair is but three days hence. When we have these horses where do we keep them so that none knows they are ours?"

Arturo nodded to the tavern. "Ursula's father, Durno, will stable them and say he has bought and holds them for resale. Which he often does at fair time."

"The Prince will make trouble for him when we are gone."

"No. He will say that we stole the mounts."

"You speak as though you had already arranged all this with him."

"I have, Durstan." Arturo grinned.

"And he does this out of friendship for you alone? Or maybe you have promised to marry his daughter?"

"I make no promises, nor does he deal in them. You go to the fair with him. You pick the two horses and he buys them and holds them until we are ready."

Durstan shook his head. "All this is wild talk, Arto."

"I have that which will get us two good horses and also leave enough to pay Ursula's father for his trouble." As he spoke he reached into the loose front of his tunic and brought out the silver chalice that his mother had given him. Seeing the look of astonishment on Durstan's face, he said, "It was a gift from my mother and is mine to do as I wish with. Take it and hide it until fair day."

Durstan picked it up and turned it about, examining it. Then, whistling gently as he put it under his short cloak, he smiled at Arturo and said, "For this we should get two good mounts and Durno be well satisfied with the barter balance."

"Aye, he can use it as a dowry for Ursula."

"For myself I would take her without dowry."

"For yourself, Durstan, there will be no marriage for many years. I want no men with me who are thinking always of home and wife and children. All those who join my company must be free to fight without care except for themselves and their comrades. . . ."

Durstan said nothing, but his eyes grew round and a smile faintly touched his lips. Arto was away again . . . and without benefit of a beaker too much of beer or Gaulish wine. He moved away to seek Durno. As he went through the tavern kitchen, Ursula, bare-armed, was mixing flour in a great bowl on the table, her back to him. He pinched her bottom and darted through the far door to the rear courtyard and the stables where he knew he would find her father.

On the first day of the horse fair Durstan went with Durno and the two horses were bought. One was a black stallion of seven or eight years, well-schooled, which had been shipped from Gaul two years before, and the other a grey mare, older than the stallion but smaller, with a touch of dun and mealyness about the ears and muzzle which showed some not-far-distant moorland strain.

They were lodged in the big courtyard behind the tavern and kept there for three days. Arturo and Durstan made their preparations to leave on the night of the fourth day. Since the tavern was well outside the fortress area and on the southern side of Isca, the two had decided against the risk of riding north through the town. They would go south down the river road and, when they were well clear of Isca, begin to make a wide semicircle to the east which by daybreak would bring them around to find the northeasterly road running up to Lindinis. They left their lodgings in Ricat's house just before curfew. Both wore their long Cavalry cloaks over their leather tunics and trews and their thick belts, from which hung their swords and side daggers. The weather had blessed them by bringing an evening of soft rain with a fair breeze so that there was nothing odd-seeming in being abroad heavily cloaked.

But if the weather had blessed them the gods—perhaps waking from their sleep—had not. Durno had betrayed them, following the prompting of his own fears and wisdom. He was a prosperous tavern keeper, but the worm of anxiety had eaten into his mind, growing more active as with each hour he foresaw the strain that would be his when the Prince's men began to question him and the horse trader who was still in Isca. That morning he had gone to the castle, told all and in return been given his part to play.

When Arturo, with Anga at his heels, and Durstan came into the darkened yard Durno was waiting for them, holding the two horses. The only light came from a pine-faggoted torch thrust into a wall bracket, its flame flattening and swirling in the breeze.

Durno held the stallion while Arturo mounted. But, as Arturo settled to his mount, three men came swiftly out of the stable, all armed with drawn swords. Two of them moved to Durstan, who was still unmounted, and the other came swiftly to take Arturo's horse by the reins while he held his drawn sword ready to strike. His back to the others, the man said, "Sit firm, my master, and no harm comes to you. It is the Prince's order."

As he spoke there came the first clash of swords as Durstan was backed against the stable wall and faced the two other guards. Arturo sat firm, knowing that one movement to reach his sword would set his guard free to strike. Helpless, he watched as Durstan, back to the wall, fought the two guards. Durstan gave no cry for help, no look toward Arturo. He was a good swordsman and for a time kept the guards at a distance, but for Arturo, watching, it became clear as the courtyard danced with the leaping shadows from the wall torch that the two were taking their time and enjoying themselves awhile before finishing their business. It became clear, too, to Arturo that Durno had betrayed them from the start and that Durstan was to be sacrificed because he was nothing, the son of a dead horse trader, a man of no importance. Durstan was marked for death—but he, since he was Baradoc's son, would be spared and sent back in disgrace to the tribal lands. A black fury suddenly possessed him. He drew breath and shouted angrily, "*Saheer!* Anga—*Saheer!*"

From behind the stallion which suddenly curvetted and moved nervously came Anga, his hound, like a great shadow, swifter and truer than any of the dancing torchlight shadows, rising in a long curve from the ground beneath the guard's raised sword arm to take his in the throat. Man and hound rolled to the ground together and the scream in the man's throat was brief-lived.

Arturo swung the stallion round, drew his sword from under his cloak and rode down on the two guards, who turned to meet their death at the noise of his coming, one from a thrust in the back from Durstan and the other from the sweep of Arturo's blade slashing into the side of his neck.

Holding in the stallion only for time to see Durstan swing himself onto his horse, Arturo called to Anga and rode hard for the open yard gate. He went sweeping out into the rain and wind, riding fast through the maze of hovels and huts that fringed the southern side of Isca. Behind him he could hear the sound of Durstan's mount following hard.

They galloped without halt or speech between them and

took the road along the left bank of the river which led to the sea, but three miles from the town Arturo swung his horse off the road to the left. Dropping pace a little, he began to thread his way through a broken country of small, stream-lined valleys and over the rises of the sparsely forested hill tops to make a half-circle which should take them around well to the north and east of Isca.

They both knew this country, for they had ridden over it at exercise many times and on their free days had hunted boar and deer here with the Prince's hounds. As he rode, Arturo carried on his mind a picture of the maps which old Galpan had drawn for him in the sand and, more accurately, those which Leric treasured in the Prince's chambers limned on faded and brittle papyrus. Lindinis was forty miles from Isca on the old legionary road which ran northeast through Aquae Sulis and on to Corinium and farther Glevum; and beyond, if fortune and the Prince's and Count Ambrosius's displeasure forced them to it, there were roads that ran north to Lindum and Eburacum. But there was no wisdom in taking the Lindinis-to-Corinium road yet for they had killed two, maybe three, of the Prince's men and the warrant against them would be passed from post to post quickly.

Pulling up to breathe their mounts, they sat side by side, the steam and sweat of horsehide strong in their nostrils. Their cloaks were heavy with the soft rain, and their baggage rolls lashed behind their thick felt saddles hung limp and bulky like badly made hogs' puddings.

Durstan wiped his face and eyebrows with his hand and said lightly, "Arto, my thanks."

Arturo nodded at the aging Anga, who lay flat on the wet ground, panting. "Give me no thanks, but you owe a cut of good venison to Anga."

"He shall have it." Durstan sighed slowly, shook his head and went on, "By the gods, the Prince is a fox."

"And Durno a serpent."

"Nay, a frightened man, tempted by silver and then made faithless by fear. Your true villain makes a bargain and sleeps sound. There will be no welcome for us from Ambrosius."

"That is to be tried."

Durstan shook his head. "No. It comes to me that there is something between the Prince and Ambrosius that they only know. Against it, you and I are nothing. The Prince would have had me killed and you sent back to your people. Now the word will be out against us. I am for death and you to go back and serve the tribe and stay fast within its boundaries."

"Be the Prince what he may. The gods serve those who serve themselves. If there is no welcome for us at Glevum then we will find a welcome elsewhere. But for now you are right about the Lindinis-to-Corinium road. We go farther east to Sorviodunum and then north through Cunetio and Durocornovium. For a time we ride by night and rest by day."

"And draw our belts tight when our bellies grow empty."

Arturo laughed. "That never while we have Anga." He pulled his horse's head around and began to move off at a walk, heading more sharply east. There was no need for hard riding or haste for they were going into a wild, thinly peopled country of few roads.

The next morning Baradoc, long since summoned by the Prince, arrived in Isca. Tia had come with him and they were lodged in Ricat's house. He stood now in the sunlight by the open window of Gerontius's audience room and the anger in him against Arturo smouldered still. Smoke rose in the still air from the homesteads below the castle. A skein of swans came in heavy flight from the river and the jackdaws quarrelled over their nesting sites along the broken ramparts.

He turned to the Prince, who, red-robed, heavy-eyed sat in his chair, one hand drooping to scratch at the head of the hound which crouched at his side.

Baradoc said, "Withdraw the warrant. Have him back here. Have them both back. They have had their lesson and will come to heel."

The Prince shook his head. "Three of my men are dead. The warrant stays. The word has gone to Count Ambrosius. Against Durstan I would withdraw it and he would stay kennelled. But there is no taming Arturo. Time or the gods must do that."

"And if he is killed and someone claims the head price?"

"He shall have it."

"How then shall he free himself from the warrant?"

"Can I read his future? If there is a way, then the gods will show it. Too many of the young men are restless against the discipline and the long wait. Many have felt as Arturo did, but have stayed content. But now they have to be gentled again to a patience which is not in their true natures. There is no place for Arturo in this matter. For you, my good Baradoc, I would do much. But three men are dead, and their price must be paid or I shall have my hands full of further trouble from their comrades."

Baradoc's lips tightened. Not for the first time Baradoc found himself wondering which of the two men, Ambrosius or Gerontius, held mastery and called the tune for the other to dance. Count Ambrosius was older, and vain for the day when a campaign could be fully carried against the now quiet Saxons, who kept to their own enclaves in seeming peace. Ambrosius at Glevum looked only for the day when his dream of wearing the purple of an emperor should come. But this Prince had his dreams, too, though he babbled them to no man in the way Ambrosius did.

Now, once more, for the sake of his son, he said stubbornly, "Count Ambrosius can refuse you nothing. Call back the warrant. Banish Arturo from your lands for a term, but let the Count Ambrosius know that he can take my son into service. He will weather in time and he is the kind men will follow when the years have steadied him."

Gerontius shook his head. "No. To do so would encourage others into impatience and rashness. But for you, out of my love—aye, and also my need of you, good Baradoc, for there is only frankness between us—I make the warrant of outlaw for a term of three years. After that your Arturo, if he lives, is free to come and go and serve either here or with Ambrosius. More I cannot do."

"And Durstan?"

"Is he then also your son from some happy chance?" The thin lips curved slightly.

"No. But he is Arturo's man, and Arturo will not accept

for himself that which is denied his comrade. This I know.''

"Then Durstan shall be given the same grace.''

"I thank you, my Prince.''

Gerontius nodded and then, rising from his seat, walked across the room and took from the long table, on which stood a great bowl of pink apple blossoms, a cloth-wrapped bundle. He came to Baradoc and handed it to him.

"You have someone who will find Arturo?''

"Yes, my Prince. Myself.''

"Then take this to your son and give him this message. In three years' time if he brings me the bowl that is wrapped in that cloth he is a free man. Until then death waits for him in my lands and those of Count Ambrosius. Also, since you are his father, you will pay the death price to the families of my guards who were slain.''

"So shall it be.''

Baradoc slipped the wrappings from the bundle, but already he knew well what lay within, the silver Christos chalice which old Asimus had given to Tia and him over twenty years ago.

On his return from the Prince to Ricat's lodgings, where Tia waited for him, she said, "Who will you send to find Arturo?''

"I go myself with two of my men.''

"How will you find him?''

Baradoc smiled and, reaching for her hand, said, "He is my son and though wild and without sense his mind when his skin is at stake works as mine would. I shall find him.''

"The gods protect him.''

Holding down a sudden movement of bitterness, Baradoc said softly, "Why should they not? Already he talks with them like a familiar. The otters will feed him with fish and the ravens bring meat and the sparks from his flint will kindle wet tinder to give him fire and warmth. . . .''

Two days later in the early forenoon, while Arturo and Durstan rested their horses just off the old track that ran up to the north from Sorviodunum to Cunetio, Baradoc rode up to them, leaving his two companions on the track below. Both

Arturo and Durstan had long since seen the party approaching but when Durstan had looked inquiringly at Arturo he had merely smiled and shaken his head, saying, "It is my father."

"How can you know?"

"The gods told me as I lay awake last night with my belly rumbling from half-cooked pig meat." But the truth was that he could pick out his father riding a horse from a far distance because of his stiff right arm, which he liked to ease by thrusting it into the front of his tunic to hold it like a sling.

Durstan grinned. "Did the gods tell you how he would find us and why?"

"They had no need. He would read my mind and know we would never take the Lindinis road. Each day it has rained and the tracks of two horses and a hound have given him our line."

They stood at their horses' heads as Baradoc rode up to them. When he halted, Arturo gave him greeting and Baradoc acknowledged it, grim-faced, with a nod. He said, "For two who have a blood price on their heads in all the lands of Prince Gerontius and Count Ambrosius, you travel leisurely."

"A man without destination has no need of hurry, my good father. That there should be a blood price is unjust for arms were drawn against us and we had the right to protect ourselves."

"I am here for no dispute. The warrant runs for three years. If you are alive then you are free of the now forbidden lands."

His face tightening with sudden stubbornness, Arturo said, "We are free of them now if we care to take the risk. There are many who live so . . . aye, both Saxon and British."

"I give you no counsel but this. To live you will need companions. Pick them well for the blood price is high and a temptation. Your mother's heart sorrows for you. Mine knows only stiffness. The Prince from some fancy of his own sends this." Baradoc tossed a cloth-wrapped bundle to Arturo. ''At the end of the three years there is no pardon unless you return it, so guard it well.''

Arturo loosened the cloth and took from it the silver chalice. Then, seized by pride and deep anger, he said with deliberate contempt, ''Your Prince, my father, is a man of windy fancies and little action. He plays at war with his horses and men but sweats with fear at the thought of a wound. For him even the quick buzz of a wasp is too like the feathered hiss of an arrow for comfort. Against him pompous Ambrosius is Mars himself. So speak thus to him from me—for the gods have said so—that one day he will sue me to return. Aye, the day will come when this country will cry for Arturo and his voice and that of Ambrosius shall not be the least among them in clamour.''

For a moment or two Baradoc said nothing. Emotion played within him like summer lightning. Anger, despair and bewilderment and the faint flicker of pride possessed him. There was a madness, he felt, in Arturo that made him stranger, not son. Then, in a weary voice, Brardoc said, ''If I live to see the day that Gerontius or Ambrosius sues for your return, then I shall have lived into the age of miracles. Yet, because you are my son, I pray the gods to bring you to reason.'' With a jerk at the reins with his left hand Baradoc wheeled his horse away and called over his shoulder, ''Until today I had two sons. Now I have only one.''

Arturo said nothing. He watched as his father rode away to join his companions on the trackway and they turned and put their horses to a steady trot, and he watched still, his face grim, until they disappeared over the smooth shoulder of the chalk downs. He knew quite clearly that he had been boastful, arrogant and vain with his father and there was not pleasure in him from it. He knew, too, that the warrants of outlawry would make life hard and dangerous for him and Durstan. But there was no turning back now. He was in the hands of the gods, who would show him no favours unless they saw him proving himself . . . *Aie,* and maybe then not give their help too readily at first for they knew too well that the early spring of courage could be the false growth of anger and pride. For a moment, as brief as the flick of an eyelid, he wished he were safely back in Isca, dust and dung and horseflesh smells about him as he rode to exercise or drill. Then the wish was gone, leaving a dying ripple on his mind like the fading water ring where a swallow stoops its breast to the stream in swift flight.

Behind him Durstan said quietly, "And did the gods truly say that one day our lords of the west would sue for your return?"

Arturo turned, smiling, and shook his head. "No. But they will."

They turned their horses' heads northward, moving toward the distant sanctuary of the forest and marshlands about the headwaters and upper valley of the River Tamesis, a lawless land between the Saxon east and the sprawling enclaves of the west, a land of low-caste men of both sides who tilled their patches, tended their cattle and when times or seasons grew bare took to plundering their neighbors.

As the light began to pale in the western sky they came over a smooth curve of the downs and saw before them the great ring of standing henge stones which men called the Circle of the Gods. They came to it unexpectedly for neither of them knew this country except by repute, but Arturo recognized the place at once from his mother's stories of the great journey she and his father had made over twenty years ago, when the country had been torn with civil strife following the ravaging westward movement of the Saxon armies.

They spread their pack blankets and made camp outside the circle and ate what remained of their cold pig meat. They lit no fire, for the night was mild and they had nothing to cook and no desire to draw attention to themselves. Lying on his back, staring up at the brightening pageant of the stars, Arturo found it strange that he should be here where all those years ago his mother and father, not so old then as he was now, had made a shelter and slept. A little way from him Durstan lay with his head cushioned on Anga's flank and played on the small elder-wood pipe he always carried with him the slow, lazy tune of a stableyard song. He broke off as

Arturo suddenly stood up and began to rummage in the loose pack at his side.

Arturo took the silver chalice from the pack and then drew his dagger from his belt. When Durstan raised an eyebrow questioningly he said, ''Where we go and what we do—how long should we keep a silver bowl safe?''

''There are those who would slaughter a handful of home-steaders for it. Aye, or murder their mothers, fathers and brothers.''

''This place is under the protection of the gods. Come.''

Durstan rose to his feet and, followed by Anga, they moved between two of the great cross-lintelled henges into the circle. At the foot of one of the great stones, against whose side a fallen lintel leant half-propped, Arturo buried the chalice, cutting a square of turf clean from the chalky soil and then digging the hole deep with his dagger and hands. When he had finished and stamped the turf back into place Durstan said, ''The gods have it in their keeping. Would that they could name to us the day of its recovery.''

''No matter the day. It will come in good time. I ask the gods only that on the day we shall both be together.''

Arturo looked up into the star-scattered sky and Durstan smiled to himself, knowing that his companion looked for a sign from the gods of their approval. *Aie*, he thought, the smallest of shooting stars would do, or the slow drift over the stones of a pale-winged owl, that bird of omens. For his friend's comfort of mind he hoped that chance would favour him. But there was no open sign from the gods.

CHAPTER SIX

The Villa Of The Three Nymphs

FROM THE CIRCLE of the Gods the two went northeastward, travelling slowly, following the line of the old road to Cunetio. The town, lying on the far slope above a tributary of the River Tamesis, was largely in ruins, and almost uninhabited. Only a handful of old people existed miserably among the abandoned and despoiled houses.

As they left the town and began to climb the slopes of the downs beyond it on a line which would take them to the River Tamesis, Arturo fell into a silent mood, riding ahead of Durstan with Anga at his horse's heels.

So they rode for a long time while the midday sun began to slide down the sky. Then, as they crested the long curving shoulder of the downs, Arturo pulled up his horse and waited for Durstan to come up with him. Without a word he pointed to the valley below, where from a clump of thorn trees a billowing of thick black smoke rose into the air. Some of the land around the trees had been cleared and was now bright with the green of growing crops. As they watched, an old man came stumbling and running from the thorns pursued by another man, who in a few paces overtook and felled him with one sweep of the sword he carried. The old man screamed and the noise carried faintly to them on the wind. Then the noise was gone as the swordsman thrust his blade in his victim's throat.

Arturo said, "To help others in trouble is the best way to forget one's own. Come."

He drew his sword and began to ride fast down the valley side, and Durstan followed him. The swordsman below saw them coming and ran back into the thorn trees. With Anga racing at their heels the two swept down to the trees and, dividing, went one round each side of them to come galloping into a small hollow in which flames and smoke roared up from the burning of a brush-thatched hut. Beyond the hut two men, with their backs against a small cart, were fighting off the attack of four other men, using spears against the swords of their attackers.

As Arturo and Durstan rode into the fight from either flank the men turned to face them. They were Saxon outcasts, wearing sheepskin tunics and short trews and armed with scramasax swords and daggers. As Arturo bore down on his man, the Saxon began to run in quickly, hoping to get under Arturo's sword and find a way to take him in the groin. Arturo wheeled away to escape the threat and flat-bladed him with a backhand sweep that sent him to the ground. One of the men who were being attacked jumped forward and thrust his spear into the man's heart. Another Saxon ran at Arturo, seeking to chop at the horse's forelegs to unseat him, but this time, anticipating the move, Arturo levelled his sword at the man's throat, riding hard down on him until the man was almost under his guard, and then, thrusting the sword point into his throat, sent the man toppling, screaming in a strangled death agony.

In a few moments the whole affray was over. Two of the Saxons lay dead on the ground and the others were racing fleet-footed up the downside, choosing the steepest scarp where the horses would have been hard put to follow them. Arturo watched them go, but his attention was less on them than on the significant and always to be remembered fact that he had killed his first Saxon.

From behind him a voice said, "The good Lord give you thanks for coming to our help."

Arturo turned in time to see the man, one of the two whom they had rescued, cross himself and knew that he was one of the Christos followers. He was a young man, lightly bearded, wearing a long shirt whose ragged hem fell well below his knees. He had a pleasant, open face, the deep brown of his eyes the same colour as his long hair.

Arturo said, "Who are you? And why do the Saxon men attack you while the crops are still in the ground?"

"My name is Marcos. And this is my brother, Timo." He nodded toward the other man, who was the shorter of the two and looked also the younger. He had the same hair and eyes as his brother, but his face was solemn and tight-lipped. Marcos went on, "He, too, would thank you, but he has no speech though he understands all that is said." At this Timo nodded though his face remained unchanged. "As for the Saxons . . . there is one crop they can gather all the year round. They came to take us for slaves. Many of our kind have been taken down the river and sold to the people of King Hengist. They need slaves since for the barbarians the only work worthy of a man is fighting."

Arturo looked at the now smouldering remains of the thatched hut. "This is your home?"

The lips twisted ruefully in the pleasant face. "Was."

"And the old man who lies dead beyond the thorn trees?"

"Our father."

Arturo nodded and then said quietly, "We remain here tonight. Go bury him."

Marcos nodded and then turned to his brother and said, "Come."

Still sitting their horses, Arturo and Durstan watched the two brothers go to the rough cart to which a small, sturdy pony was yoked. They took a well-worn wooden spade, its blade iron-tipped, and an axe from the back of the cart and made their way to the thorn trees.

As they disappeared Durstan said, "We have given our help. Why stay here tonight? The Saxons will not return."

For a moment or two Arturo said nothing. He watched a kestrel wind-hovering above the downside. It has been there when they had ridden down to attack the Saxons and it was still there. It was an inhabitant of another world than the world of men; and above and beyond the world of the kestrel

was the world of the gods who marked and controlled all life
, . . the movement of chance and time which had brought
them to the aid of Marcos and Timo. But only men of small
vision called it chance and time. Life was patterned more
intricately than the interknotted serpentine designs of a jewel
marker's brooch and the gods ordained the pattern of men's
lives.

He smiled suddenly and said, ''These two are homeless
and dispossessed. So are we. A single stick breaks in the
hand easily. Bind ten together and they defy the strength of
most men. They owe us their lives so they would never sell
ours for a handful of blood money.''

''True—but what can you offer them? This is their home.
We have nothing.''

. Arturo smiled. ''But we shall have, Durstan. If they agree
we shall be four bound together . . . the gathering of
strength begins. First men and then''—he nodded toward the
dead Saxons—''their arms and their clothing, though the
gods know it will take hard washing to clean the stink from it.
And in the cart there I see tools, hoes and axes and homesteading gear. The pony, too, is young and well fed so they
are no men to neglect their animals. With all this we need but
a place to settle and soon others will come to us.''

''And you will tell them who we are and why we are
without any true state?''

''Is there an enduring companionship and faith built on
other than the truth?''

Durstan smiled and shook his head. ''And, so, in the end
you will have a comitatus, a gathering of companions, that
will grow into an army which will one day bring both Count
Ambrosius and Prince Gerontius to sue for your help? You
dream, Arto—but I like the dream.''

''Everything in life begins as a dream. That is how the
gods speak to us. First the dream and then the reality. Believe
that and work for it and then the gods are on your side. Today
I have killed my first Saxon. It is a day of portent. I should
ignore it at my peril.''

They ate that evening with the two brothers, who produced

eggs, cheese, cabbages and two chickens from their cart, and a bronze cauldron for cooking with water that came from the still running source of a winter bourne that flowed away down the valley from the edge of the thorn brake. When they were done Arturo spoke frankly to Marcos, first of the state in which he and Durstan found themselves and then of their need for comrades, of a great company of comrades which should eventually grow into a great army to be the envy and the awe of all men.

At first, Durstan noticed, the two men were plain-faced, showing nothing of their feelings, but slowly the spell of Arturo's words began to touch them. For the first time, too, Durstan found himself listening to an Arturo he had never heard before. Although he stayed quiet-voiced there slowly grew an enspelling magic about him. Never in all their time in Isca had he known this Arturo and never before had he found himself, as now, won over to the slow, powerful faith which Arturo had in his own god-favoured destiny. . . .

When Arturo had finished speaking, Marcos said, "Our father is dead and neither Timo nor I am married. Living here grows more dangerous for"—he nodded to the distant bodies of the dead Saxons—"more and more small parties of the men of the South Saxons come up the river valleys since they can find neither living space nor good plundering in their own kingdom. When you arrived our cart was loaded for we were going to abandon our young crops and move away. But where we move and whom we serve rests not with me. My brother and I are as one. I go nowhere nor accept any service unless we are together. For myself I would join you." He looked at Timo and said, "You have heard the words of this Arturo. How do you find them?"

For a moment or two Timo gave no response, but slowly the corners of his solemn mouth moved to a wry smile. Then suddenly his hands came to life, fingers touching palms, fingers playing against each other, and sometimes a hand flighting to make some expressive movement about his forehead, and all done so rapidly that to Durstan, watching, it seemed like a flight of two wide-winged birds steepling and playing together in some intricate courtship display. Then, abruptly, his hands collapsed and lay still on his knees.

Arturo said, "What does he say?"

Marcos smiled. "That we are fatherless, and you shall be our father. That we now seek a home and a new life and the bond of comradeship, and that he is ready to serve you. But he says also, and so do I, that we serve only one god, while you serve many. We are Christos men and must remain so."

Arturo answered, looking directly at Timo, "In my camp all men shall be free to serve their gods, be they one or many. We swear but one oath. That of comradeship. He who breaks it shall himself be broken."

So Marcos and Timo joined Arturo and Durstan. They slept that night in the open, close to the warmth of the slow-dying embers which were all that remained of the hut. But Arturo lay awake for a long while before sleep came to him. Today was the beginning, but he was wise enough to know that the passage of a dream into reality would be a long, slow birth. Before men could be drilled and shaped into a fighting force they must eat to live and not all the hunting skills of a band of comrades could feed them. Both Timo and Marcos were good husbandmen and with time their fighting skills could be sharpened. But it was for now as sowers and reapers of crops that he needed them most; and before any ground could be turned or cattle herded a place had to be found where they could dwell securely. From talking to Marcos he knew that only the Noman's-land around the source waters of the Tamesis far south and east of Corinium and Glevum, where Count Ambrosius's mandate did not yet fully run nor the slow upriver creep of small Saxon bands yet reached, offered hope of some haven which would give them, and, with the help of the gods, others to come, shelter and time to grow into an ever-increasing company.

At his side Anga growled softly, catching the scent of the marauding foxes about the bodies of the dead Saxons on the hillslope. From the thorn trees a little owl shrieked suddenly and, for a moment, the noises echoed the dying scream of the Saxon he had killed. Everything about this day, he thought as sleep began to take him, had been touched by the gods.

Two days later, having crossed the weed-grown, slowly breaking-up Londinium—Calleva—Corinium road close to Durocornovium, they found a ford over one of the tributaries of the Tamesis. Some miles to the north of the ford they discovered an old abandoned Roman villa. It lay at the head of a small valley, screened by a new growth of trees and bushes. Its large courtyard was surrounded on the west side by the ruins of the steward's office, the kitchens and the latrines. Linking this on the north side to the east wing were the weed- and bush-covered remains of the foundations of the hot and cold bathhouses. Only the east wing with the old reception room and a series of private rooms fronted by a covered corridor remained partly roofed. Here from time to time travellers or temporary settlers had made a home. Much of the villa had been pillaged for building stone and roofing tiles and all the wooden and iron piping long since taken.

At the side of the courtyard a spring—the source of the stream that ran away down the valley—broke from the steep hillside to cascade into and overflow from a circular basin of marble. This was backed by a pillared and arched shrine holding the figures of three nymphs.

Riding into the courtyard, followed by his companions, Arturo drew up and looked around him. The villa was hidden from the lower valley to the south by screening trees and from the north by forest land which came right up to the back of the old bathhouses. As he sat on his horse, his eyes going over the litter of shattered red tiles, the rubble of broken masonry, the air full of the sound of the springwater flowing from the marble basin, he saw not the ruin before him, but the villa as it must once have been, and the thought came to him that this was the kind of dwelling place which his mother's people had once known. All over the country lay such ruins, shabby, broken and despoiled reminders of the now-faded and shrunken Roman Empire. Well, empires flourished and died, but empires could spring again from their own ruins. Surely it was for this that the gods had directed his steps this way? Here was a refuge and a beginning, here was a place and a moment opened to him as a challenge from the gods. Bracing his body proudly as he sensed the truth and significance of this moment, he looked for the sign which he surely knew the gods must make him.

And the sign came. The black stallion he sat suddenly moved restlessly under him, curvetted, and called for all his strength to hold it. The horse threw up its head and neighed, setting the echoes beating back from the surrounding trees. From the trees beyond the ruined line of bathhouses came an answering whinny and out into the sunlight, stepping proudly, her head turned toward them, came a white mare, neck arched and mane flowing as she broke into a gallop across the tree front and then, with another whinny, disappeared into the forest.

Calming his restless mount, Arturo turned to his followers and said, "This is our place, for the goddess Epona has marked it with her sign. There is water for all our needs, wood in the forest for our fires, sun-facing ground in the valley to break for our crops and"—he smiled—"a roof over our heads from the simple task of picking up these fallen tiles."

So the Villa of the Three Nymphs became their home. Although it was growing late in the season they broke the ground on the south-facing slope with Marcos and Timo's simple plough and sowed the little that remained of their barley seed. They all worked through the lengthening days from morn till night, retiling and refurbishing the east wing into living quarters and a secure stable for their mounts. At night they stood guard duty in turn, but for two months none disturbed them. Arturo and Durstan set up a small shrine to Epona at the end of the pillared corridor and welcomed with grace the homage Marcos and Timo made to their own god when they carved the Greek letters Chi Rho above a niche outside the door of their room and kept the niche adorned through the seasons with wild flowers. And their gods seemed to favour them for the crop lines showed quickly and they were lucky enough, or god-graced enough, to round up four sturdy winter lambs and a milch cow which they found straying in the forest. A hen they had brought with them, squired by a great black cock, sat a clutch of twelve eggs and brought off eight chicks. There was pasture in the valley for

their hobbled horses and the rich promise of hay which would
see the beast through the coming winter. In Marcos and Timo
they found two men of skills which they envied. Marcos
made a turf-covered charcoal-burning stack in the forest and
a pair of deerskin bellows to fuel and work a small forge,
where with heavy hammer he repaired broken ploughshares
and hoes and grubbing picks and mattocks. In the rubble of
building material he found an old sharpening stone so that
their weapons and the Saxon seax knives and scramasax
swords they had brought with them never lacked a bright
keen edge. Timo, too, had his skills for he made hunting
bows and knew the right wood to shape fire-hardened throwing spears and he was a true herdsman, maybe because his
dumbness reached out and gentled the dumb animals in his
care. His hands, too, with which he spoke—and whose
language Arturo and Durstan began slowly to read—had a
deftness with which he shaped fishhooks from bones to take
trout from the broadening valley stream and horsehair lines
not only for fishing but to fashion bird nets, which they hung
like a fine, faint mist between trees to take pigeons and doves
and wild geese and ducks in the marsh at the far end of the
valley. So, as the days passed, they moved from short to
good commons and from poorly to well-lodged, and their
beasts and poultry thrived, and the milch cow proved to be in
calf and, dropping at high summer, brought milk for all and a
store of cheeses to set against the coming of winter.

All this time they lived without going far from the villa.
They had their own small world to make before there could
be any far venturing beyond it—though there were times
when the itch of impatience took Arturo like a fever and he
longed for the blood stir of a more manly work than careful
husbandry. When these moods came on him he would go
through the forest to its limits and sit overlooking open
country and the dim shape of the hills that lay to the northwest, knowing that there lay Corinium and Glevum and men
and horses and weapons without which the design of his life
which the gods were slowly patterning could never be
completed. Though it was hard for one of his nature, he
schooled himself to patience, telling himself that these days

were being set for him by the gods to temper the iron of his ambition.

Then, on a day when autumn was whitening the forest glades with the fronding curls of willow herb seeding, Arturo came into the courtyard in the early morning as his companions readied themselves for the day's work. He was dressed in rough cross-gartered trews, wore open shabby sandals on his feet, a long belted tunic which had belonged to one of the dead Saxons, a dagger in the belt, and a short cloak caught at the throat with a rough circular brooch which Timo had found in the ruins and repaired. Over his shoulder he carried a small store of provisions in a knotted cloth.

Marking his dress and provisions sack, Durstan said, "So the time has come?"

"Yes. Last night the gods spoke to me in a dream."

"What did they say?"

"Go north to where the hills fall away into the great valley of the Sabrina. There one waits for you."

Durstan would have smiled broadly but he deemed it wise, sensing Arturo's stiff mood, to keep his face unmoved.

"You take your horse?"

"No. Nor Anga."

Marcos said, "There is a price on your head and men may recognize you."

"No. I ride no horse. I dress like a peasant. Who is to recognize Arturo, son of Baradoc of the tribe of the Enduring Crow and a troop leader in Prince Gerontius's cavalry?"

Timo stirred and, looking at Arturo, moved his long, thin hands in a brief flutter of finger play.

Arturo, his mood changing suddenly, laughed and said, "Good comrade Timo, if by ill fate I am killed then that is the will of the gods and this place will be yours for the grace of a prayer for my soul. But that time is not for now. The gods in my dream held up before my eyes a red banner on which was blazoned a white horse and the white horse carried a rider, fully armed and capped with a war helmet, and the face of the man was my own face. Would they have shown me this if I am to die in the near future?"

Marcos said, "There is no doubt in my mind that your

gods have spoken so and shown you this sign. But you go into bad country. So I tell you this. If he still lives my father's brother, Paulus, who is a carpenter, is settled in Corinium. He lives near the east gate. If you should need help or shelter go to him. You will not be turned from his door.''

Arturo nodded. ''This I will remember.'' He bent and fondled the ears of Anga, who stood at his feet, then gave the hound a word of command. Anga hesitated and then moved from him and went to Durstan. With a farewell movement of his hand Arturo turned and made for the forest boundary beyond the west wing of the villa. As Arturo disappeared into the trees Durstan, with a shrug of his shoulders, turned and followed the others, who were already moving to their work.

When he caught up with them Marcos said, ''I have nothing but honour and gratitude to Arturo—but do you believe the gods truly speak to him and show him their signs?''

''Does your god never give you a sign?''

''Yes, but it is nothing that the eye can see. When I pray I feel him move in my heart and thoughts, and I feel his strength comforting my weakness.''

''From each god his own way of revelation. And for each man his own way of marking the shadow which his god casts.''

For a moment or two Marcos was silent. Then he said, ''A white horse on a red banner. White and red, those are the true colours of Christos.'' He nodded to the villa. ''It would look well flying from the rooftop yonder.''

''But better carried before a well-armed host.''

Arturo travelled for five days without haste, and each day he moved into more settled country where men worked their fields and tended their herds in peace. Seeing him come, armed only with a dagger and poorly dressed, they gave him welcome and food and shelter for the night. None asked him from whence he came or where he was going for if a man made no move to explain himself then all knew that he remained silent out of good reason.

He passed through the deep-valleyed country well southwest of Corinium and on the morning of the fifth day came out of a thick wood that covered a valley ridge to find before him a great fall in the land. The ridge side plunged steeply away from him, dropping almost sheer in places to a wide plain far below. Through the clear air of the autumn day a vast panorama was spread before him and he saw it as though from the eyes of an idling falcon borne up on a steady air current. Beyond the plain ran the broad, snaking ribbon of the Sabrina River in full tide, the sun taking the silver of its waters with a keenness which hurt the eyes. Far to the northeast it ran until it was lost in the encroaching folds of the long ridge line on which he stood. To the southwest it broadened slowly and was swallowed by the sun sparkle from the waters of the sea into which it ran. Beyond it, purple and mist-hazed, rose the hills and mountains of Cymru and Demetae. Far away up the river on his right hand, hidden from his sight, the Sabrina waters came down through Glevum. For the first time, he became aware of the vastness of his land, and the immensity moved him. All this, and more and more to the north and the east, was Britain . . . a country torn and divided by the quarrelling of the tribes of his own kind, harried by Scotti and Pictish raiders, and threatened by the slow, barbarian march of the Saxon warriors and settlers from the east.

He sat down and began to munch on one of the wild apples he had gathered in the wood, melding their sharpness with goat's cheese and flat bread which he had brought from a homesteader with one of the silver coins from his still remaining store of Prince Gerontius's money. As he ate he was slowly seized with a dullness of mind and lack of spirit, rare for him, and which he would never have confessed to any man. For the truth was that now he was here he knew that he had come, not at the bidding of the gods, but because of the tedium which had grown with him week by week at the Villa of the Three Nymphs. Homesteading gave him no joy, no fullfillment. He had dreamt of the white horse on the red banner. But such a dream could easily have arisen from his longing for warlike action. The truth, sharp in him now, was that he had gone awandering for his own pleasure and relief.

With a sudden spate of self-disgust he threw his apple core out into space and heard the sharp click of bursting seedpods as it fell into a broom bush. As he reached for another apple, a long shadow fell across the grass at his side. He looked round to see a short, strongly built man, dark-eyed and with long black hair, who wore a rough, long brown robe girdled with a thin belt of plaited leather thongs, and who carried a well-seasoned ash stave.

The man smiled at him and said, "Greetings. 'Tis a long time since we last saw one another."

Frowning slightly, Arturo said, "We know one another?"

The man sat down, placed his stave across his knees and reached out for one of Arturo's apples. "I know you. I knew you from the time of your birth until I last saw you as a bare-bottomed infant splashing in the sand at my feet on the day I left your mother and your people. My name is Merlin."

"Merlin? Ah, yes, of course . . . My mother often spoke of you. You are the—" Arturo broke off for fear of offending the man.

"I am the ageless, the wandering one. Or so men say. But then it is seldom that I agree with what men say. And what do you do, brooding here like an eagle on its eyrie?"

Arturo hesitated for a moment or two. He had heard many tales of this man. But mostly he knew that it was said that Merlin spoke like a brother to the gods.

He said bluntly, "I was outlawed with a companion by the Prince of Dumnonia with whose cavalry I served. I have been hiding for many weeks in a small homestead with my companions—but my feet began to itch for better occupation than following the plough and my eyes to smart for sight of new country. To the others I lied that the gods had told me to come here where I should meet a man who waited for me."

"And what will you say when you return to them?"

Arturo smiled. "No doubt I shall lie again, though what the lie will be must rest unknown until the moment comes."

Merlin laughed. "At least your frankness should please the gods. You could say, of course, that you had met me." He reached out, broke a piece from Arturo's cheese round, put it in his mouth and mumbled as he chewed, "And that I

had a message from the gods for you—which I have not, of
course. Our meeting is pure happen-chance. I am on my way
to Glevum from Aquae Sulis and often take this way along
the ridge. So you are young Arturo who sent message to the
Prince Gerontius and the Count Ambrosius that one day they
would sue for your return?''

"How did you know that?"

"The message was given in full council by your father.
Many heard it and the tongues of man wag faster than any
woman's when a Prince is so defied that he hurls a full wine
cup from him in anger at the words. The discomfort of the
great is ever a delight to the small. From Dumnonian Isca to
Deva and Lindum the story runs . . . aye, and to Saxon
Cantawarra and the island of Tanatus to make the barbarians
roar with laughter over their rude mead. My young captain
Arturo, the country knows you and''—he stood up and
brushed cheese crumbs from his robe—''now for any who
pledges beyond his performance call it an Arto promise—''

"Then the gods damn them!" Arturo was quick on his
feet, his face stiff with anger. ''They shall see the truth of it
one day.''

Merlin shrugged his shoulders. "Such a truth would not be
unwelcome to many. Now cool the fire of your anger. There
is a foolishness about your boast that warms me, and for this I
give you my own message—for sadly''—his mouth moved
to a mock mournful twist—''I am out of grace with the gods
this long time and they favour me with little of their dispositions. You know the Roman tongue?''

"At my mother's knee and by the hammering of old
Leric's fist between my shoulder blades.''

"Then know you suffer not alone from acedia. There are
many such in the growing army of Count Ambrosius, and
none more bored than in the Sabrina cavalry wing which he
has stationed near Corinium. Many there grow stale with
drills and maneuvers and might be tempted from their barracks and the taverns of Corinium with an Arto promise—
even, if at first, the promise showed no more warlike gain
than petty raiding against the Saxons down the Tamesis. But

remember this, speak not your heart to any man until you have proved him.''

"And how should I do that?''

''If you know not that, then you are not one to command men. Now, I thank you for the apple and cheese. I would have thanked you more had you carried a wineskin. The gods be with you.''

As he turned to go Arturo said, ''It is in my mind, for all your talk, that the gods did indeed send you to me. How else could you have recognized me whom you last saw as an infant just able to stand and walk?''

Merlin smiled. ''You could have answered that for yourself were your mind not idle. You sprawl on the grass cudding your cheese, your tunic flung wide open to cool yourself from walking. Need I say more since I have seen you naked many times in your mother's arms?''

Arturo smiled ruefully, and said, ''No.'' With one hand he rubbed the strawberry-coloured birthmark below his left ribs. Then with a frank, friendly smiled, he went on, ''I thank you for chiding me. Your words will stay with me.''

He stood for a long while watching the receding figure of Merlin move away along the tree-edged ridge. When the man was finally lost to sight he turned and gathered up his gear. A glance at the westering sun gave him the direction he wanted and he set out.

He reached Corinium on the evening of the next day while there was still a couple of hours of daylight left. The streets were crowded with people and the troops from the nearby camp. Market booths and stalls were open and the rutted roads were busy with the carts of country folk and packhorse trains carrying army supplies. As he made his way toward the east gate he was with other people pressed back to make way for a patrol of cavalry moving through the city. A young man who led the party was wearing a leather war helmet plumed with dyed horsehair, a bronze-plated cuirass taking the dying sunset light dully, and knee-length boots, and was armed with a scabbarded broadsword. About his neck was knotted a blue scarf with its ends swinging freely to the motion of his horse. Similarly coloured scarves were worn by all the men in the patrol and also by the dismounted cavalrymen who walked the streets on leave. Arturo had no need to ask about the scarves for he knew that they were the mark of the man of the Sabrina wing of Count Ambrosius's army. He decided that when his day came all the men of his army should wear the white and red scarves of the banner he had seen in his dream. . . .

A small boy, his skin as brown as sun-dried earth, wearing only a ragged pair of short trews, directed him to the house of Paulus the carpenter. It was a dwelling place that stood with its back hard against a section of the ruined city wall and was no more than one large living room and cooking quarters with a rough ladder that led to a communal bedroom above. The workshop was a faggot-thatched open shed to one side of the house.

He introduced himself to Paulus, a white-haired man in his sixties, wearing a leather working apron, the stubble of his face hoared with sawdust and all about him the sweet smell of worked wood and shavings. He was accepted at once and with few questions. Paulus lived by himself, but a neighbour's wife came in once a day and cooked a meal for him in the evening. The old man made a place for him at the table and while they ate questioned him about the welfare of his nephews. When he heard of the death of his brother at the hands of the Saxons, he said, "God rest his soul."

Arturo said, "You, too, are of the Christos people?"

"Yes, and there are many in this city. It is said, too, that Count Ambrosius is one of us, but I doubt it more than pretense, for the Count is ready to be all things to all people so long as they will serve his ends."

"And those ends?"

Paulus paused from dipping a bread crust into his stew and said, "He dreams of a conquest of all Britain with himself wearing the purple of emperor."

"And what is wrong with such a dream?"

Paulus shrugged his shoulders, poured ale into Arturo's cup and said, "Nothing—except the man who dreams it."

"Men say that openly here?"

"Go into any tavern or drinking court and you will, as the night lengthens, hear many of his own soldiers and cavalrymen say it. They long for action and he gives them drills and marches and mock battle—and now that autumn is well with us it is clear that there can be no campaigning this year. This winter many men will drift from him back to their homes. It is two years since the army marched east and south. Two years—and that is a long time for warriors to content themselves with sword and spear drill. Go into the country to the villas and the farms and you will hear strong words against Count Ambrosius. Although the land is rich and is tilled in peace the crop levies to feed his men are high. I ask nothing of your business here, but take heed of your speech in this city. You like this stew? 'Tis hare . . . I have a friend who passes through often who always brings some fine gift. . . . So, my brother Amos is dead, eh? And by a barbarian. Thank God they come not this way. Hare stew, I like it well. But not so well as venison—though 'tis seldom my friend brings that. Such game gets rarer the longer the army stays . . ." The old man suddenly broke off, leant back and smiled, saying, "I ask your forgiveness. I rattle away like a gossip from the pleasure of company for I am much alone."

Arturo raised his cup to the old man and said, "Talk, my friend, for there is much that I would like to know about this place and the cavalrymen here."

Chuckling with pleasure, Paulus drank with Arturo and began to talk again, never flagging, but always ready to take a new line when Arturo put a question to him.

That night Arturo lay long awake while the old man snored gently in his cot. He was in Corinium and here, and in the country around, were cavalrymen, many of them owning their own mounts, who longed for action. But he had nothing to offer except a share in his dream to create a company whose fame and success would eventually bring the Prince Gerontius and Count Ambrosius to sue for his help. How many men, he wondered, would have the vision to see what he dreamt and for the sake of it go into the wilderness with him? He groaned gently to himself. If ever a man needed the help of the gods to direct him he was that man.

The next morning he left Paulus to his work and wandered abroad in the city. It was market day and the old ruined Roman Forum was crowded with stalls and benches on which vegetables, game and meat, crockery and pots and pans, and woollen cloths and belts and buckles and leather goods were laid out for sale. Wandering through the crowd, Arturo noticed that there were few army men about. Most of them were held at stables and cavalry drills until late in the afternoon . . . the same training exercises which he, as a troop commander, had known endlessly at Isca.

Walking now from stall to stall, he saw clearly that there was more for sale here, and a richer variety of goods, than had ever appeared in the Isca markets. The penned poultry and cattle were plump, the cloths and fabrics rich, and much of the pottery and bronze and iron pans and cauldrons of a finer work than the people of Dumnonia knew. Count Ambrosius, whose writ ran from the Sabrina plains north to Glevum and beyond to Deva, held in his power a fat and rich land. Maybe because of all this the Count had grown over-content and was loath to stir away—but amongst his men there had to be those who suffered a restlessness and a lust for war and action which full bellies could not assuage.

As he turned from a stall hung with loops of gaily coloured clay beads his eye was caught by the bright blue of a long, belted robe worn by a young woman who worked her way through the crowd, a straw-plaited basket hanging from the crook of her right elbow. A stallholder shouted some pleasantry to her and as she turned her head to reply her eyes were briefly met by Arturo's. For a moment or two, like the sudden glare of sun between racing clouds, she smiled at him, a warm, friendly and, he imagined, a beckoning smile. As he met it the whole purpose of his business here in Corinium was reft from him. The sharp thought went through him that it was long since he had held an Iscan girl in his arms, or felt the warmth of full red lips beneath his own. Hardly aware that sudden impulse was moving him to action, he moved forward through the crowd to follow the young woman. But at this moment the market throng pressed back upon him, trapping him against the side of a stall, to make ground for the passage of a herd of cattle being driven to the slaughterhouse on the far side of the Forum.

When he stepped free from the press at last the young woman had gone and he made no attempt to search for her. He needed no woman. Men and horses were his need. He turned away towaard the north gate and left the city. A little way along the Glevum road he climbed a grassy knoll crested with two beech trees and sat down, looking across at the camp of the Sabrina cavalry wing through air which was hazed with the dust kicked up by three troops of horse at drill. He was angry with himself for even momentarily being stirred by the sight of a pretty face. The gods had brought him here for matters of far higher import.

CHAPTER SEVEN

Horses and Men

ARTURO SAT ON HIS KNOLL for over an hour, watching the cavalry drills. He heard that Count Ambrosius had formed his cavalry into wings—the old Roman *alae*—of sixteen troops with each troop holding thirty-two men and had even named the commander of a wing in the old style of *praefectus*. From the size of the camp and the number of mounted men drilling he guessed that this Sabrina wing was no ordinary *ala* of around five hundred strong. This seemed more like an *ala milliaria* of twenty-four troops, each of forty-two men—around a thousand men in all—and no doubt commanded by a *tribunus*. Maybe it was yet far from its full complement of men and horses, but it was a larger force by far than any that Prince Gerontius could muster. Clearly the ambitions of the Count ran high and matched his pride in the ancestry he claimed for himself. He was a man full of nostalgia for the great days of past Roman glory, of Roman blood himself (though that was common enough now in this country), who longed to restore the glory of the old Empire.

Tired of watching the cavalry and overwarm under the midday sun, he slipped off his tunic, made a pillow with it for his head, and lay back, staring up at the sky. Men there must be, he thought, drilling out there on the plain, who longed for real not mock action and must know that it could not come this year for it was far too late for campaigning. To tempt any of them to his side he had nothing to offer. Now, if ever before, he needed help from the gods or some sign from them that there should be no death of hope. He shut his eyes and silently called on them, willing them to hear him, his teeth

grinding with his fervour as he mutely named them . . .
Epona, Nodons, Coventina, great Dis, father of all . . .
great gods and small gods he named, battle gods and household gods . . . Badb and her brothers, and was tempted to
call, too, to the Roman gods, for surely they held lien and
interest still in this land, but turned away from the thought for
fear of offering his own native deities.

He was brought from his silent fervour by the sound of
horses' hooves behind him. He sat up to see a man riding one
pony and leading another up the knoll and, after a brief nod to
him, dismount and hitch the ponies to a beech branch.

He came across to Arturo, carrying a drinking skin, and sat
down by him. Without a word he drew the stopper from the
skin, drank, wiped his lips with the back of his hand, then the
mouth of the skin, and handed it to Arturo, saying, "A gift is
the best greeting. Drink."

Arturo took the skin and drank. Expecting mead, he found
that it was wine. Handing the skin back, he said, "I thank
you." Then prompted by a wry sense of humour, he went on,
mocking his own newly passed fervour, "If you bring a
message from the gods then I will give you double thanks."

For a moment or two the man eyed him without replying.
He was small of stature with a pear-shaped face, brown as a
ripe chestnut and, as Arturo had noticed when he had walked
across to him, bowlegged as though he had come into this
world riding a pony and had seldom set foot on ground since.
His eyes were as dark as polished sloes, his hair darker and
tightly curled, his cheeks cleft with deep wrinkles and his
thin lips, at this moment, drawn back tight over firm white
teeth in an amused, houndish smile. Driving the wineskin
stopper home with a quick smack of his palm, he said, "And
what kind of message wants young Arturo, son of the Chief
of the tribe of the Enduring Crow?" He nodded at Arturo's
bare shoulder as he spoke. "Nay, look not surprised. You
would not know me, but many a time I have seen you at drill
in the river readows below Isca town. And many a mount
your old friend, Master Ricat, has bought from me."

Arturo pointed a finger at the long knife which the man

wore in the belt about his hide surcoat and said, "What charity stayed your hand as I drank? You could have slit my throat and claimed my blood price."

"Stolen or honest-come I deal in horses, not men's lives, no matter the price. But you would do well when you take the sun to keep your tribal sign and the birthmark below your ribs hidden."

Ignoring this, Arturo asked, "What do men call you?"

The man shrugged his shoulders. "A hundred names, mostly vile. But seldom my own, which is Volpax."

"Then, Master Volpax—and I have indeed heard of you—the gods sent you. They know I need horses." He nodded toward the beech trees. "Not mixed-breed ponies like your dun-coloured mare there with a black tail."

"You shame my mare. On a long march she would outlast many of those overstuffed, overcosseted cavalry horses out there." He nodded to the plain where the last of the dust was settling as the troops rode away to quarters. "So you need horses? Have you found some silver hoard that you can afford to buy them?"

"We have no need to buy them."

"We?" Volpax's eyes widened and he grinned wolfishly.

Arturo smiled. "The gods have sent you to an honest and reliable partner. There are hundreds of horses quartered around the barracks of the Sabrina wing. You could work alone and take a few, or you could work with some rogue helper who would betray you when you trimmed his share—which you would."

"It is always a temptation, I agree."

"With me it would be different. I can betray no man without betraying myself. And we would draw no daggers over sharing for out of every three horses we take I would keep one. Remember this, too. I know a horse from an overstuffed hay bag. And, like you, I can talk their soft language at night to gentle them and cut their hobbles or headropes while you ride a mare in season down the lines for them to follow."

Volpax chuckled. "You know the tricks."

"Why not? You probably played them at Isca against us. I say, although you do not know it, that the gods have sent you."

Volpax pursed his lips, his eyes hooding with thought, and then said, "I would not quarrel with that—for it is a sign of distinction. But it is beyond their power to make up my mind for me. I will think on what you say." He stood up, the wineskin swinging from his left hand. "You stay in Corinium?"

"I do. At the house of Paulus the carpenter."

Volpax shook his head. "You are too open—even with me. There is a blood price on your head. Every man knows the taunt you have flung at Gerontius and Count Ambrosius."

"I am open with you alone—for the gods sent you."

"Let us from now keep the gods out of this. I have an affair which takes me to Glevum. I shall pass this way again in three days' time. Be here then at midday and I will give you an answer."

"You have my promise. And I thank you in advance for your answer, Master Volpax."

For a moment Volpax seemed on the point of protest. Then with a slow shake of his head he turned and went to his ponies. But as he mounted the dun, he called, "Stay close to Master Paulus. Keep away from the drinking places and wenches, and forget that you ever met me or heard my name, Comrade Arturo."

Arturo sat and watched him ride away down the Glevum road. He could have wished to be going with him for he would have liked to see the city. Then he rose and began to make his way back to Corinium. The gods were with him. There was no doubt of that. One horse in three. That meant stealing sixty to gain twenty mounts. And three hundred to have a hundred . . . *Aie,* but that was looking too far ahead. All great matters began small.

He began to whistle gently to himself. The gods had truly marked him. But for all that, they were stern and devious masters. Had they not momentarily tempted him that morning with a glimpse of a young woman in blue? He could have pressed after and searched for her and never have met Master Volpax. No, until he came again to the beech knoll in three days' time, he would keep close to old Paulus.

For the rest of that day and the one following, Arturo never went beyond the yard where Paulus was content to have him either helping or sitting on a stool as he worked. Toward sunset on the evening of the second day, while Arturo helped Paulus stack a pile of rough-cut planks, a voice from behind them called, "Master Paulus!"

Arturo and Paulus turned. Standing in the open front of the thatched shed was a young woman and one glance told Arturo that it was the girl in the blue robe whom he had seen in the market. Unaware almost that he did it, Arturo ran his fingers through his sweat-tousled hair and then drew his open tunic about him and belted it.

"Mistress," said Paulus, shuffling past Arturo, "if you come with a complaint from your father about his tool racks tell him that they will soon be ready."

The young woman shook her head and said, "He sends no complaint. But a summons to a meeting of the city's tradesmen and craftsworkers called now because of a new demand by the Count's warden to raise the levy once again on the free work we give to the calvary camp." She smiled. "They meet now and will talk until dark and drinking time and it will all come to naught."

"Aye, that is so. And I shall wake with a sore head from drinking in the morning. So be it." He shrugged his shoulders and moved away to his house.

But when he had gone the young woman stood her ground, her dark-red lips curved in an almost mocking smile which, for some reason that baffled him, suddenly irritated Arturo so that he said, ignoring courtesy and ceremony, "Some mornings since you smiled at me in the marketplace, and now you stand as though there was something you expected from me."

Her smile broadened, and she said, "And why should I

not? Or are your promises like blowing thistledown to be
carried away and lost? Have you forgotten then that once you
said to me that one day you would come and woo me; that we
should lie in the long grass, listen to the golden birds sing and
drink the new wine? That seeking me you would ask only for
one who had eyes like the blue bell-flower, lips redder than
the thorn berry and hair like . . . ..*Aie* now that escapes
me—''

"Like polished black serpentine," said Arturo suddenly,
for now memory was back with him like the sudden sweep of
light from the sun breaking free of dark clouds.

"True, that was it. So why should I not smile at you in the
marketplace—since I would know your face anywhere, or so
I thought until you greeted my smile with a face as blank as a
mouse-stuffed owl's? But now I know you as all folk who
have heard the blood price called against you would know
you with your tunic drawn back to show your tribal tattoo and
birthmark. Would you, too, have me immodest enough to lift
my robe and show you the swallow's gorge mark on my
thigh?''

"There is no need," said Arturo quickly, recovering from
his confusion. "I would have known you at any time except
this when—as you must know—there are other matters
which bear heavily on me. You are Daria, daughter of Ansold the sword smith. But it was to Lindum, not Corinium,
that you were travelling."

"True—but my father changed his mind when he saw the
work which was here with Count Ambrosius's army. You are
a fool to work with old Paulus half-naked for all to see your
marks and so make a high blood price an easy picking for any
man who passes. Such heedlessness will never bring you the
years to make good your boast to Gerontius and Count
Ambrosius. Perhaps those who called that an Arto promise
were wiser than I thought.''

As she finished speaking she began to turn away, but
Arturo, anger rising in him, stepped forward and held her by
the arm and said pugnaciously, "You do right to mock me.
But you do wrong to taunt me with talk of empty promises.

They shall sue me for help for the gods have ordained it."

Daria frowned down at the hand which held her arm and, as Arturo released her, she said, "And the golden birds and the new wine—when shall they be heard and drunk?"

Arturo smiled. "There will be time and place for them. You think you stand here and talk to me out of chance? Nay, even though I had forgotten you the gods had not. I take my shame for a misty memory. But it is written that on the day of my triumph you shall come riding into Glevum with me on a white horse, wearing a cloak of scarlet with a lining of blue silk and about your waist a golden belt with a clasp of two singing birds. And when Count Ambrosius comes out to greet us he shall hand to you a silver goblet full of new wine, and then—"

"And then, and then," Daria interrupted him, mockingly, "will be the day when pigs shall be flying and the salmon coming up the Sabrina shall wriggle ashore, their mouths full of sea pearls to lay at my feet. But for now, be wise. Keep your tunic drawn and your god dreams to yourself."

Without other word or look she turned from him and walked away. Arturo watched her go, knowing now that he would never again lose her from his mind, and wondering how he ever could have forgotten her and that rain-drenched day on the high moors when she had slipped a quick hand to the dagger in the garter sheath beneath her tunic.

At noon on the following day Arturo waited for Volpax under the trees on the little knoll that overlooked the cavalry training grounds. When he arrived it was as before, riding the dun pony and leading another. He came over to Arturo carrying his wineskin and a knotted cloth in which were six cold roasted quail.

He set the food between them and this time offered the wineskin first to Arturo and began talking as though there had never been any break in their conversation.

"The affair is settled. I have a friend who keeps cattle in a valley far to the south of Corinium. He will lodge and find fodder for up to thirty horses. No more. We take no more than four horses a night—and that at long intervals—and never travel the same path to my friend's valley. Nor when the ground is soft from rain to show the hoof marks. When we have the thirty, you take your ten and I take my twenty and we go our own ways. When you have the men and need for more mounts all you have to do is to pass a message to my friend and I will come to you.''

Volpax smiled wolfishly, flicked his hand at a bluebottle which buzzed above a roasted quail, and said, ''Also from today you see no more of Corinium. We stay together, not from lack of trust on my part—but for each other's safety.'' He lifted the wineskin and drank deeply.

Speaking almost to himself, Arturo said, ''We shall steal our horses. Would that it were as easy to steal men.''

Rubbing a hand over his wine-wet lips, Volpax shook his head, and then, grinning said, ''You and I are in the business of horses. No more. But this I say—once it is known that you need men and can promise them what they want they will find a way to you.''

Arturo lay back on the grass, staring at the slow march of the heavy clouds above, and felt a heaviness, too, in his heart. Now that the moment was on him for action he suddenly felt helpless and undecided and astray. So far he had done no more than make Arto promises. Now was the beginning of the time when, gods or no gods, he had to work and scheme and make a beginning to bring to truth the words and dreams which had comforted him for so long. He sighed suddenly. ''Well, 'tis with one step after another that a long march is made. We will take the horses and then I will think about the men.''

''So be it.'' Volpax flung a picked quail carcass into the grass. ''Be here at nightfall, fair weather or foul, and we will walk around the camp. Then tomorrow night, if the weather is kind, we will take our first horses. For now you can go for the last time to Corinium. Tell Paulus you travel back to your friends. Then steal charcoal from his firepot to blacken your face and hands for tonight.'' He stood up, taking the wineskin, and went on, ''I leave you the rest of the quail. When you come back tonight give me a curlew's whistle three times. If I do not answer, then you must find some other to help you with mounts."

Arturo stayed until he had finished the quail and then went back to Corinium. That night, with blackened faces and hands, he and Volpax made themselves familiar with the cavalry horse lines. Some of the beasts were penned inside wooden-palisaded yards but more were hobbled and tethered to picket lines. Guard fires burned at intervals around the camp and sentries patrolled each sector of the great space that the cavalry wing occupied. They made the circuit of the camp twice to familiarize themselves with it and then, withdrawing to a safe distance, sat in a patch of low broom scrub and watched the movement of the patrolling guards. As the night began to wear away they saw that the guards often hugged their fires and missed a patrol, and saw, too, that the guard officers were lax in their duty rounds. Inaction, Arturo knew, bred carelessness and indifference in the best troops.

Long before first light the two withdrew to their ponies, which they had left tethered in a wood far up the Glevum road, and Volpax led the way to a small bothy made of hazel boughs and roofed with dead bracken in a small dell deep in the wood. They slept and ate their way through the long day and there was little talk between them and no passing of the wineskin. A nearby stream gave them water to drink. When Volpax was about his business he remained sober.

The next night they took the first of their horses. Volpax left Arturo near the picket lines and went to the far end of the camp. Here, between midnight and dawn, standing in the cover of some trees, he drew his bow and shot four arrows at the three guards who sat around the watch fire. The first stuck the three-legged ion brazier and sent sparks and burning wood high in the air. The others thudded into the ground about the guards. The men scattered, shouting and drawing their swords. Expecting an attack, one of them blew the alarm on his horn. The blowing of the alarm brought the main guard turning out from their hut and they ran toward the danger spot. Arturo smiled to himself as he saw the two men guarding his length of picket line jump to their feet and hurry toward the alarm call. Crouching low, one hand holding his dagger and the other two stout rope halters, he went quickly to the line of horses where the animals moved restlessly. Talking softly and soothingly to the disturbed animals, he slashed the hobbles from two of them and slipped the halters over their necks. Then standing between them, gentling them, crooning the love talk and caressing noises which bond all good cavalrymen to their mounts, he waited. In a few moments Volpax, running low, crablike on his bowed legs, came scuttling across to the line and freed another two horses. He swung himself onto the back of one of them and rode, leading the other, out into the darkness of the night and away from the pandemonium and shouting from the far end of the camp. Close behind him rode Arturo.

By daybreak they were well south of Corinium in wooded, steep valley country, each man now riding his own pony with a haltered stolen horse on either side of him. As the sun, glowing red through a misty autumn sky, climbed high Arturo rode with a light heart. Here, by the gods, was a beginning. Horses first and men later.

A week later they took four more horses, and this time without causing any disturbance since it was a night of thin brume, lying waist-high over the ground under clear starlight. They worked their way on their bellies to the lines while the guards huddled about their braziers, cut the horses free and, mounting, galloped them away, separating and twisting and curving through the mist to defy all hopeful pursuit.

On the next foray, two weeks later, and now there was the nip of sharp frost in the air and the camp drinking troughs were plated with a thin layer of ice, Volpax and Arturo wormed their way to the pens at the northern end of the camp where unhobbled horses were quartered. Volpax surprised the single guard at the gate, laid him low with a blow from a wooden club and then freed the horses to stampede them through the camp while he and Arturo roped two horses each and rode off with them. After that they kept away from the camp for three weeks, and then made another raid, using the same strategy as they had employed on their first raid.

By the time the year was well on the turn, they had taken twenty horses. Since a fall of snow then made raiding unwise Arturo took two of the six horses that had fallen to his lot and, riding a pony borrowed from Volpax, led them back to the Villa of the Three Nymphs, where he found all in order but his friends becoming overanxious about him.

When he returned to Volpax he brought Durstan with him so that his companion could take by turns his remaining four horses back to the villa. Now, because the weather was worsening, snow and rain often making raiding impossible for fear of their tracks being followed, Volpax and Arturo spent many a long day lodged in their bracken-roofed bothy, waiting for the right conditions to favour them. Sometimes, since tedium was an enemy which Arturo was least fitted to combat, he left Volpax sleeping or nursing his wineskin and wandered off through the woods by himself, close-wrapped in his cloak against the cold or the rain. He would stand at the edge of the wood and look across to the smoke of the cooking fires rising above far Corinium. The day came when, the impulse strong and irresistible in him, he made his way there. If a man's feet itched, he found excuse for himself, then might not that be a sign from the gods? If they could colour his mind with visions why should they not as surely direct his footsteps past denial?

Avoiding the main gates, he entered the city through a gap in the broken walls. A heavy squall of rain made him draw the cape of his cloak over his head. He ran across the Forum and took shelter under the colonnade which fronted the Basilica. There were very few people abroad and those that were hurried about their business. Arturo sat on a stone bench and watched the puddles forming between the broken paving of the Forum square. As he sat there his eye was caught by some graffiti marked with the soft edge of a slate on one of the colonnade pillars. A long inscription amongst them ran vertically down the length of the column. As he read it anger grew suddenly and sharply in him.

Between the empty promise of Arto and the
sloth of Ambrosius where shall a warrior
blood his lance?

Impulsively, heedless of any who watched, he stood up
and went to the pillar. With a piece of the charcoal which he
carried for night raids he wrote:

Arto has taken your horses. Are all the
warriors of Ambrosius dormice to sleep
through winter? Come south with your swords
and claim your mounts.

A few minutes later, careless of whether he had been seen,
he left the city and made his way across country in the
gathering gloom and rain toward the forest shelter.

A few nights later with the ground iron-hard from frost he
and Volpax took another lot of horses, but this time things
went wrong for them. As Volpax crouched, cutting the
hobbles of a horse, the animal, frightened by the noise of the
alarms sounding, reared and a forehoof struck Volpax to the
ground. A guard came running through the darkness, saw the
two men and threw his spear from a distance. It struck
Volpax in the side of his neck as he rose, tore deeply through
his flesh, and then fell away from him. Abandoning the
horses he would have taken, Volpax ran from the picket lines
and caught up with Arturo, who, ignorant of what had happened, was leading his two horses away at a fast trot. As
Volpax called to him he pulled the horses up, saw the blood
streaming from Volpax's neck, and without word—the night
behind them loud with the cries of men and the blowing of
horns—he hoisted Volpax to the back of one horse and
swung himself on the other and they rode hard into the
darkness. When they were well clear of the camp they pulled
their mounts up and Arturo, ripping lengths of cloth from his
cloak, tied them about Volpax's neck to stop the bleeding
from the wound.

Choking over his words, Volpax said, "'Tis nothing. A

glancing blow that will leave but a ragged scar and—''

He swayed and Arturo held him on his feet. From the way the blood had spurted from the wound he knew that it was far from nothing. Life was pumping fast from his friend.

He said, "Save your words to spare your breathing."

Suddenly Volpax's eyes closed and he fell heavily against Arturo and, before he could be held, collapsed to the ground. As Arturo tried to staunch the blood flow Volpax opened his eyes. They shone dully in the starlight and Arturo knew with a heavy heart that the death look was on the face of his friend.

With his next words Volpax showed that he knew it, too. He raised a hand and held Arturo's, gripping it tightly, and said, fighting for breath, "There is an end to every road. Mine stops here, Arto. *Aie*—'' a weak smile touched his lips, and he said, "and I go without the comfort of a wineskin. May the gods be kind and greet me with one. . . ." He coughed and swallowed violently as the blood gorged his throat. Then, in a moment of ease, he went on, "Leave me. Take the horses—they are yours now—all of them. A parting gift from Volpax. In return say a prayer for me when you ride to Ambrosius to make your promise good. . . ." Then, with the faintest of sighs, his head dropped and he lay still in Arturo's arms, his dead eyes staring up to the frost-bright stars.

Because of the comradeship which had been between them Arturo wrapped the body of Volpax in his cloak and bound him crossways on the back of the second horse. He had no means of burying him and would have thought it scant respect to leave him to be picked clean by scavenging birds and beasts. He rode the rest of that night, leading the spare horse on its halter. The dun-coloured and the other pony they had abandoned near the camp in their flight. There was nothing in him now but sorrow. Horses he might have now in plenty, but for the first time he knew the measure of the loss of a friend. If the gods granted him his wishes he knew that the time would come when he would mourn other friends, but none, no matter how dear, would cloud his mind with the blackness of the grief he felt for Volpax.

At daybreak he stopped by a small forest pond to rest and water the horses and to eat the hard bread and cold meat which he carried in his pouch. The night had brought a thick hoarfrost which now, as the sun strengthened, dripping from the bare tree boughs. Deep in his own misery, sitting with his elbows on his knees, staring at the black surface of the pond, he was taken by surprise when from behind him a voice said, "Reach not for your dagger. I come in friendship."

Arturo swung round and half rose. His hand went for the knife in his belt, gripped it, and then was stayed from drawing it by the sight of the young man who stood on the fringe of the trees. He was on foot, a sword hanging from his belt, his hands held wide and free from any weapon. He was bareheaded, his hair, the rich colour of a polished chestnut and fired with sharp red glints from the rising sun, running down the sides of his checks to a small, bushy beard. He wore a close-fitting surcoat and tightly gartered trews while about his neck was tied a blue Sabrina wing cavalry scarf. He smiled as Arturo now stood slowly upright.

Arturo said, "Why should one of the Sabrina wing offer me friendship?"

The man came forward a few steps, his eyes going from Arturo to the two cavalry horses standing by and then to the cloaked body of Volpax on the ground. He said slowly, "Because if you are, as I truly think you to be, that Arturo of the famous promise, and also that same one who has set Corinium and all cavalrymen talking about your message written on the Basilica pillar, then I am no longer of the Sabrina wing." He raised a hand to the knot of the blue scarf, tugged it free and threw the cloth from him to rest pinned on the thorns of a leafless brier.

"I am that Arturo." As he spoke Arturo's eyes went from the man to the thickness of the trees and scrub behind him. Soft words and friendship's appearance could be the forerunners of treachery.

As though he had read his mind the young man said, "There is none behind me. I come alone, riding your dun pony and leading the other. 'Twas my comrade's spear that sent your friend to the Shades—the gods celebrate his coming. I followed on foot and found your ponies, which you dared not stop to untether. *Aie* . . . and then there was another trail plain to follow . . . wet and shining on grass and leaf under the stars. And when that went the gods gave a quick night frost to bear your marks. The gods have grieved you with one loss, and now—if it is your will and you are truly the man I seek—offer you the gain of myself and others like me. If I talk overmuch be not surprised. My father was a bard in Lavobrinta in the country of the Ordovices and I would have become one but that I loved horses more. My name is Gelliga.''

''You would offer me service and bring others of the same mind?''

Gelliga shrugged his shoulders. ''Why not? Three weeks past you stole my mount, a grey mare. We were both tired of empty drills and empty words. I come to join her. And there are others like me.''

For a moment or two Arturo said nothing, but there was in him now, growing fast, a rising exultation. The gods took and the gods gave. But in loss or in gain a man should never cease to honour and trust them. Volpax was gone. But was it not true that the very lifeblood he had shed on grass and leaf had brought one to stand in his place and he, a man from whom trust shone without flaw, one who should bring others?

He said, ''I am Arturo, and the gods have been kind. Go back to your friends. Tell them of this place and be here with them at the next full moon. I shall come to greet you and lead you to those who have already sworn service.''

''You will come alone?''

Arturo smiled. ''Why should I not? The gods have marked me, and now they have marked you. I give you and your comrades my trust. To do other would shame me before the gods.''

CHAPTER EIGHT

Comrades Of The White Horse

ARTURO FOUND DURSTAN waiting for him at the horse keeper's steading. Between them they led ten of the horses back to the Villa of the Three Nymphs through two days of wind and rain. On hearing of the death of Volpax and the promise that Arturo had made to go back and meet Gelliga and such men as would follow him, Durstan tried to argue Arturo out of such foolishness. But when he saw that Arturo was adamant, he shrugged his shoulders and said, "So be it."

Arturo, heavily cowled against the driving rain as they rode side by side, said, "The gods have willed it through the death of Volpax. While I am gone there is work for you to do. Ride eastward down the river. Talk to the farmers and the headmen of the villages. Take a good horse, dress well and carry a sword, and tell them Arturo sends his greetings, and that soon he will be riding with his comrades to clear the banks, the swamps and the woods of the upriver lands of all Saxon bands."

Durstan's eyes widened in surprise. "In midwinter?"

"Aye, in midwinter. Is it not then that Saxons find their bellies empty and begin to raid our people to rob them of their corn and root stores? I shall have a company which has long itched for true action, already drilled and sharp-set for fighting. Tell our river people that we come to protect them and to clear the headwater valleys of the Saxons."

Despite himself Durstan smiled, recognizing the note of

exultation in his friend's voice. He said, "And in return you will take tribute for your protection?"

"That would be to do as the Saxons do. I take nothing, but accept whatever is offered freely for the service and protection we give."

Twelve days later Arturo rode down the forest path under a full moon to the pool where he had first met Gelliga. He had dressed himself as proudly as he could from the meager possessions of himself and his friends at the villa. He wore a woolen cloak caught at the throat with a bronze brooch donated by Timo, long trews cross-gartered with deerskin hide thongs, his own tunic and belt from which hung his sword, sharply honed by Marcos, and on his head a leather cap with a stiff plume of white and red goose quills—the red quills so dyed by Dursdan in the dark blood of a winter hare which had been trapped for the pot. He rode a chestnut stallion, the best of the stolen horses, and carried for lance a seasoned length of ash, the tip fire-hardened and capped with a sharp iron point fashioned by Marcos from a piece of scrap metal scavenged in the villa's ruins.

The moon threw ebony tree and branch shadows across his path, the stallion's breath plumed in the frost-sharp air and the ground rang under its hooves. Arturo came openly, armed and alert, but fearing no mischief; for this night, this meeting, he knew had been long ordained, and the knowledge—whose provenance he never questioned or thought to prove—filled him with a controlled but commanding arrogance. Openly he rode down to the hollow, came out of the cover of the winter-stark trees and brought the stallion to a halt at the side of the white-rimed reeds of the black waters of the pool. He sat and waited, curbing the horse firmly as it fidgeted. An owl called from the trees far up the valley side and the star reflections on the water were shattered into a maze of shifting silver as a water rat swam across its breadth. He sat there facing across the clearing, his eyes on the path by which Gelliga had first come to surprise him.

The owl called again and the waters of the pool grew calm.

A voice from behind him said quietly, "Greetings to Captain Arturo."

Arturo wheeled his steed about to find Gelliga standing at the foot of the pathway which had brought him into the clearing. Touched with a moment's irritation at the conceit of the man's maneuver, Arturo said, "Greeting, good Gelliga. You come alone—and without horse?"

Gelliga shook his head. "No, my captain. There are six others with me and we bring four horses. There is a high wind of suspicion blowing through the camp now. Guards have been doubled and a curfew keeps all men in barracks after nightfall. There were those who would have come but could find no way. But they will with time." Then with a slow movement he drew aside his long cloak, pulled his sword from its scabbard and thrust it upright into the hard ground before him, saying, "Here is my sword which I, Gelliga of Lavobrinta in the country of the Ordovices, pledge to you in true comradeship."

He stepped back a few paces from his sword. As he did so another man moved out of the trees to his right. Heavily cloaked, tall and with a deeply wrinkled face, he, too, drew his sword, fisted it into the ground and said in a voice which was like the low growl of a bear, "My captain, I, too, Garwain from Moridunum on the banks of the River Turius in the country of Demetae, pledge myself to you."

After him, and before Arturo could stir or say word, another man stepped out from farther along the ring of the trees and stabbed his sword into the ground. Short, lean and bowlegged, he said in a high voice, "Lacto of Calcaria in the country of the Parisi, my captain, gives his sword to you." Then, clear in the moonlight, his face broke into a broad grin as he went on, "My horse you have already for you sit upon it now."

Arturo answered, "It is yours again when we reach the Villa of the Three Nymphs."

Then from beyond Lacto another man moved into the moonlit circle and, announcing himself, gave his sword and pledge, to be followed by three others so that Arturo sat the stallion within a crescent of swords. After Lacto came Borio from Deva, fresh-faced and big-handed; Tarius from Olicana of the Brigantes, lean, hard-bitten of face and older than all the rest; then Netio of the Catuvellauni with a hawkish, hooknosed face marked to one side by an old sword scar; and last of all one, the youngest of them all, Lancelo, short, broad-shouldered and with a round moon of a face set with smiling eyes, who came from Corinium.

Arturo sat his horse and let his eyes swing from one to another and slowly there rose in him the beginning of a deep pride. Here was the seed which would grow fast to bring him a great company of men, a comitatus, a firm brotherhood which in a few years could become an army. Truly now he was poised on the brink of a god-marked destiny, and he saw now that the drama staged for his benefit by Gelliga must surely have been put into the man's mind by the gods. Seven men to pledge their seven swords. There was magic in the number, and magic in this moment which he must meet appropriately.

He dropped his horse's reins, holding it firm and controlled by the clamping pressure of his knees alone, and he drew his sword with one hand, holding it upright before his face, raised his lance with the other hand and began to speak without thought because he knew the gods would put the right words into his mouth.

His face tight-drawn from the fervour which stirred in him, he said boldly, "With this lance I give you welcome and will be with you as straight and true in comradeship, in valour and in faith." Then drawing his up-pointed sword to his lips, he kissed the broad, cold blade, and went on, "On this blade I make the oath-kiss and swear that I shall never ask of you that which I would not dare myself. I shall be your true captain and you my beloved brothers. Neither in distress nor want, nor in courage nor in victory shall there ever be shadow or stain on the love and duty which I hold dear toward you. Swear then to accept but one destiny, to rid this island of all those who do now and would further oppress us, to bring back the glory and the peace which once were lodged with our fathers and their fathers. Swear this by the god or gods who rule your hearts!" He kissed his sword again and raised it high.

Before him in one movement seven swords were drawn

from the ground, flashing in the bright moonlight; seven swords were raised as one to take on their cold blades the oath-kisses, and as though in one voice the seven cried, "We swear! We swear!"

Then began, in the raw and savage days of midwinter, Arturo's true time as a captain of men. Durstan had returned to say that while he had been received with friendship by their own people none of them would move to help them or freely provision them. They had been left alone so long without help that the poverty and hardships of their life and the sudden attacks of raiding Saxons formed a pattern of their days which they met now with a practical stoicism. They hid in storage pits, cliff caves and woodland dells most of their harvest corn and lodged their lean cattle in secret pastures. When the Saxons came they withdrew to the woods and hills, the raiders took what they would from their poor huts, and when they were gone the homesteaders came back to repair the damage and to mourn wife or child or the aged who had been butchered. They lived in fear on the knife edge of want and prayed only for the coming of spring, when they could open their furrows and sow what seed corn was left and look to the farrowing and calving of what swine and kine they still held. Spring and summer were the easeful seasons, for the barbaric Saxon robbers had enough sense to leave them undisturbed to their cropping and folding against the fat time of autumn harvests and full cattle pens.

For a few days while his new comrades settled into the villa, Arturo sat for long periods in his room, planning his first move against the Saxons. More men would soon come to him, of this he was sure. But to hold a company of any size together he knew that he needed not only the friendship of the settlers, but a supply of stores and services from them. He had to find some shift by which, swiftly and surely, he could bring the settlers to his side and gain from them a confidence which would turn them to him in true gratitude. Slowly he came to a decision, but once reaching it he threw all doubts from his mind and moved to action.

Leaving Durstan and Lancelo with Timo and Marcos to

guard the villa, he took the rest of his men and they rode out, scantily provisioned, on a morning of heavy, cold rain. They rode down the left bank of the river, skirting the swamps and the low-lying, winter-flooded pastures and when darkness came turned their horses into the marshes and swam them across the river. For the rest of the night they moved down its right bank. When dawn came they made camp in the shelter of a tree-covered knoll. That evening as early dark fell they left the knoll, each man knowing now the moves to be made.

The river Saxons, unlike those in the settled lands, who preferred to build their huts apart in widely scattered communities, lived in small groups by the waterside where they moored their boats for upriver raiding. At midnight, circling around such a Saxon village, Arturo's men took it by surprise from the east. Arturo rode at their head and with a great cry of "Arturo comes! Arturo comes!" he lowered his lance as they swept by the rough log-built and reed-thatched huts and speared from the heart of the watch fire a burning brand and lodged it in the roof of a hut. Behind him came Gelliga and his iron lance tip caught the throat of the startled, bemused Saxon on watch as he rose from sleep beside the fire. Behind Gelliga came the other comrades, spearing brands to fire the thatched hovels of the Saxons and then to wheel, following their captain, and with drawn swords cut down the Saxon men as they came tumbling, hands groping for seax and fighting axe, from their sleep into the flame-lit circle of huts. The victory was swift and bloody. No fighting man was spared. Most of them stood and fought, back to back, and died from lance point or sword's edge almost before their minds had time to clear. Spared only—and this long ordered by Arturo—were the women and children and the young boys whose chins had yet to know the roughness of a growing beard. These survivors were marshalled to the riverbank where the raiding boats were drawn up. There were seven boats and four were put to the flames. Into the others were hustled the women and children and two old men. Before these were pushed out onto the dark bosom of the racing stream Arturo spoke to one of the old men who, like many of

them, understood his tongue and said, "Know well that I am
Arturo and hold my words firm in your memory. This night
has begun the cleansing of the valleys of all your kind. Go
down the great Tamesis and to all your race give warning
that, under the gods, I, Arturo, begin now the purging of the
upper river lands. . . ."

Listening, watching the fire-lit faces of the people in the
boats, Gelliga smiled quietly to himself. He was content—
for, this night he and his comrades had tasted action which
had long been denied them, and this night, too, Arturo had
begun to make good his promise. But there was this about
Arturo which all his comrades now understood and were
content to accept—behind the high words lay the iron will
which took men into battle ready to give their lives for him
and his god-touched passion. He looked across at Netio, his
hawk face wet with sweat, the blaze from the burning huts
shadowing the great scar on his cheek, his blooded sword
resting across his knees, and there was no surprise in him as
the warrior gave him the winking flick of an eyelid and his
tongue ran slowly along the underside of his top lip. Aye, he
thought, they had found a man who would give them all the
battle and bloodshed so long denied them by Count
Ambrosius.

They watched the three boats move downstream and slide
from the light of the leaping flames into the murky curtain of
night. Then they searched the houses and grain pits for all
they could bundle and carry. They took plunder of bronze
and silver armbands, and brooches and torques. They
stripped the dead of their weapons but touched none of their
clothes for the Saxon men with no love of cleanliness stank
like polecats. Then in darkness they made their way upriver.
They swam their steeds across it at dawn, laden like peddlers
and baggagemen.

At midday they rode up the slope of a wide valley through
which ran a narrow tributary of the Tamesis. Just below the
crest a poor stockade of thorns and loosely piled turves
enclosed a group of huts. Seeing them coming, the villagers
ran to the ridge crest and there halted to watch them.

Arturo, his men following, rode into the stockade and there unloaded the stores and plunder which they had taken from the Saxons. As they did so an old man came limping from one of the huts and approached Arturo.

Greeting him, Arturo said, "You come without fear, unlike the rest of your kind. Look at us. Do we seem like Saxon robbers to you?"

The man shook his head. "No, my lord. But know that had I the full use of my old legs I would have run, too. It is not only by the Saxon kind that we are plundered and robbed and killed. In these parts are men of our own race who do the same."

"The times are changing. Know now that all the valleys of the river from here to the high wolds are the domain of Captain Arturo, who now speaks to you. These last days we have taken war to the Saxons and this is our booty"—he nodded at the corn sacks and baskets and the piled Saxon plunder and weapons—"which we now give to you and your people. In return we ask for nothing that you cannot find a willingness in your hearts to give. We are to be found at the Villa of the Three Nymphs."

Without waiting for the old man to reply, Arturo wheeled his horse and led his companions from the village. Riding at his side, Gelliga said, "No forced levies, no pressed labour—they will think us witless, my captain. We should at least have taken a pannier of seed corn."

Arturo shook his head. "No. We are not Saxon robbers, or some thieving band of cutthroats who have forgotten their own race. The gods will touch their hearts with the finger of faith to rouse them to new hope and true generosity."

Whether indeed the gods did this or, more likely, the villagers acted from a policy of caution scantily endowed with goodwill, the upshot was that four days later a pony-drawn cart on wooden runners came up the snow-covered valley to the villa, attended by two youths whose curiosity showed clearly through their faces. In the cart were two earthenware pots full of flour, a basket of flat bread cakes, two skins of beer and half a deer carcass.

After Arturo had thanked them the two youths stood awk-wardly by the cart without making move to leave the villa yard. Seeing their hesitation to go, Arturo said, "You would eat and drink before you leave?"

One of the youths shook his head and then answered hesitantly, "No, my lord. . . . We are to say that pony and cart are yours and . . . and we go with it. To stay here and serve you."

For a moment Arturo said nothing but he knew that in the most wretched of men there was always one heart spot that the gods could touch. For slaves he had no use since forced labour was the seeding ground of treachery. But a willing man was without price. Now, smiling at the two, he said, "You look alike."

"We are brothers, my lord. We will stay and work for you . . . and—" the taller of the two, who was speaking, hesi-tated and then smiled. "And perhaps one day you will arm and horse us to fight against the sea people."

"For which we are impatient, my lord," said the other with a sudden grimness, "for the Saxons killed our father and carried away our sister."

His face forced to severity to hide the sudden joy in him, Arturo said commandingly, "So be it. Work hard and drill hard and the day will come."

From then on through the slowly lengthening days until the first primroses began to push pale buds from their green leaf rosettes and the rooks in the leafless trees began to bicker and fight over their winter-ruined nesting sites and the trout rested thin with spawning in the valley stream, Arturo and his companions carried war against the river Saxons.

They struck in short fierce raids mostly by night. When they attacked a Saxon village by day it was always just as the light was going and the men were settling to their eating and drinking and the cooking fires flamed high and made the flinging of firebrands onto the hut roofs easy.

Of his own men Arturo lost two. Lacto of Calcaria in the country of the Parisi was killed by the thrust of a scramasax into his groin, and Tarius of the Brigantes, the oldest of the companions, had his horse hamstrung, to be stabbed to death as, earthbound, he tried to fight off his enemy. But against these losses there came fresh cavalrymen to join them; for innocent-looking, moon-faced Lancelo returned secretly to his family home in Corinium and there recruited willing men from the Sabrina wing and brought them through the high wolds and forests to the villa.

Since the death of a comrade was to Arturo like the death of a brother, he sought all ways to protect them. He took from the Saxon war booty the small round shields which were easier to handle than the large, cumbersome shields that Ambrosius's men were drilled to use. The Saxons facing mounted men came in fast and ducked the lance to make a great stabbing thrust at the rider's groin; but the small buckler could be quickly dropped to turn away the upward jab and leave the comrade free to ride the man down. Later too, the lances were discarded. In a set battle charge they would have their use, but in quick night-raiding they were more nuisance than they were worth. Sword and small round shield were enough.

In two months Arturo had cleared five miles of the upper river valley and the closely adjoining lands. Tribute came now willingly from the British villages and farms that knew a peace and safety long absent. In far Glevum Count Ambrosius had heard of Arturo's exploits and for a while had considered sending two troops of cavalry against him, but had discarded the idea since he feared the men might desert and join Arturo and their comrades who had already gone to his side. At the moment Arturo was no more to him than the bite of a flea in his sleeping blanket. When the fine weather returned, he promised himself, he would move against him. Now was not the moment to risk the ridicule of an open desertion of a troop of cavalry to the outlawed son of the Chief of the tribe of the Enduring Crow. Already enough of his men had gone over to Arturo to make him quick with anger when his name was mentioned.

. As spring broke over the land Arturo could look with pride at the force he commanded at Villa of the Three Nymphs. He had enough men for a full troop of horse and, beyond fighting men, there were another dozen who worked and serviced the villa and the warriors. The villa itself was fast being repaired and warmed again to human life. The stables had been extended for the horses and a smithy set up for the repair of tools and arms. A wandering Christian monk called Pasco—who would give no details of his life, though he spoke their tongue with the heavy brogue of a Scotti—had settled with them unasked and finally welcomed because of his skill with wounds and ills and his reluctance to preach or proselytize.

Among the comrades there were occasional small quarrels but none so troubling that they went beyond the usual barrack-life jealousies and mead- or beer-stirred sudden resentments at imagined slights. One bond held them all firmly together, their love and admiration for Arturo. Smile though they might, and joke amongst themselves at their captain, there was none who would deny that Arturo's sure knowledge of being god-touched and god-directed was as real to him as the sword he carried and the horse he rode. Unmarked by them, legend was slowly growing about him and the full truth behind his own words escaped even Gelliga when at night in the long eating hall, full of food and flushed with drink, he would sing:

"The knife has gone into the food
And the good wine fills the horn
In Arturo's hall . . .
Here is food for your hound
And corn for your horse
In Arturo's hall . . .
But none there shall enter unless he be
Swift with a sword and comrade to all."

But with the passing of the evening and the drink Gelliga's and the other comrades' moods would change and then he sang of the yearning that not even battle and the chance of death waiting at the opening door of each day could smother:

Take my true greeting to the girl of thick tresses
The sweetheart I lay with in the glen of green
willows. . . .

It was of this sentiment that Pasco, the priest, spoke to
Arturo one morning when the first burst of true lark song rang
brittle from above the pastures, and the woods were awake
with the fret of the calls of the returning chiffchaffs.

He said, "You dream a dream, my son, for this country
which I, too, hold dear in my heart. But that dream must be
made real by men of human clay. Your comrades are clois-
tered here without the full and fulfilling submission to God's
love alone which men of my kind know. Already now when
the people around send tribute there are women who find
reason to walk with the carts. As foxes fight over vixens in
the spring and the gentle doves grow fierce in courtship, so
stirs the same passion in the hearts of men." He smiled,
rubbed the tip of his nose, his eyes quizzical, and went on,
"The gods you worship may have made you in a different
mould from your comrades—though I doubt it. You order
things well here. Now you must order this, not as Count
Ambrosius does with loose camp followers at Corinium, nor
as your own Prince Gerontius with the stews of Isca. You are
the captain of a brotherhood—but not a brotherhood of
monks."

Acknowledging the wisdom of Pasco's words, Arturo
talked the matter over with Durstan and Gelliga. Each week
now two or three men filtered through the valleys and woods
to the villa from Ambrosius's forces. Some brought horse
and weapons, and some came on foot with naught but a
dagger in their belts. But with these reinforcements, all of
them well-trained, there were now more men than mounts.
So Arturo announced to his comrades that some of those who
come from far lands could return to their people to visit
sweethearts and wives. They would be chosen by the drawing of lots so that the main force of the brotherhood was not
depleted beyond the number of horses they owned. For those
whose homes lay around the eastward side of the Sabrina

basin permission was given for their womenfolk to visit the villa for limited periods. Quarters would be set up in the west wing of the villa, but at the first sign of discord or quarrelling then all the women would be banished.

Over all these concessions Arturo laid one adamant condition. All men would be back by the feast of Beltine, which was the first day of the month of Damara, the goddess of fertility and growth. At the end of this month—though Arturo kept this secret between himself and his two closest comrades, Durstan and Gelliga—he meant to move from the villa, for this was a time when he guessed that Count Ambrosius might be tempted to strike at him. But more to his concern, it was also the time when he meant to make his own move which would send his name echoing widely over the country and bring even more men to his side.

Among those who were unlucky in the first drawing of lots was Lancelo. But one of the comrades, who had neither wife nor sweetheart, nor immediate wish for either, set his lot up for bid and Lancelo gained it in exchange for a pair of old but serviceable bronze greaves taken as plunder in a Saxon raid.

Seven days later Lancelo rode out of the forest and into the countyard of the villa. There were only two men in the courtyard at that moment, for the rest were either at their work or exercising and drilling their mounts in the lower valley pasture. One of the men was Arturo, who sat in the sunlight on the edge of the fountain of the nymphs with old, grey-muzzled Anga at his feet.

Lancelo rode up to him and dismounted. He saluted Arturo and said, his face grave, "I bring no sweetheart or wife, my captain. Sweetheart I had, but on my second night in Corinium she betrayed me to Count Ambrosius's men. But one of the Sabrina men, an old friend, sent me warning in time so that we were able to escape."

"We?"

"My family, my captain. Had I left them they would have been butchered by the troopers in their anger at my escape. I ask your permission for them to stay here until such time as they can move on to a fresh place of safety."

"Where are they now?"

"They wait in the wood for a signal from me."

"Then make it, good Lancelo."

Lancelo's face beamed with pleasure. He put two fingers to his mouth and blew a piercing whistle. A few moments later an elderly man rode out of the wood on a small pony. He was small, bareheaded, and almost bald and wrapped in a great square cloak of sewn furs. Across the withers of his mount hung two bulky, awkward packs of stained and patched cloth. At his side on another pony rode a woman wearing a cloak and cowl of red wool, and her mount carried two slung panniers of plaited withy branches.

They rode up to Arturo and as they halted the woman pushed the folds of her cowl free of her face and a pair of clear blue eyes regarded Arturo solemnly. In that instant Arturo knew with a certainty that this moment was god-touched. At three different times in his life he had looked into those eyes, and now, this time, he knew that here was no capricious play of time and chance but the deliberate hands of the gods as they moved their pieces on the playing board of his destiny. Although he would have returned the smile he kept his face calm and turned to the man.

He said, "I did not know that the father of Lancelo was Ansold the armourer and smith, for here we ask nothing of a man's past or family so long as he brings loyalty and a ready sword. But you, good Ansold, are more than welcome. *Aie* . . . and would be even without your hammers and tongs." He nodded to one of the packs, from which protruded the handle of a long pair of forging grips.

Ansold blinked happily and rubbed a worn, charcoal-grained hand across his chin, saying, "Your welcome warms my heart, Captain Arturo, for the truth is that, although the lying will be harder here than at Corinium. I would rather serve you than Count Ambrosius, who pays poor for good work and that only after long waiting."

Pushing the cloak cowl free of her dark hair, Daria, straight-faced except for a slight curl at the corners of her berry-red lips, said, "And what welcome does my lord Arturo give me?"

Arturo, smiling now, speaking without thought as though the words flowed from elsewhere through him to her, said, "You have no need of welcome for my heart has given it before to you. And now—although you speak teasingly—I know there is a true kindness to me in your heart since the faces of your father and Lancelo tell me that they have never known until this moment that we had met before. Though I count that caution not needed."

Daria laughed and shook her head. "Then you count wrong. Give my good father too much mead and in some moments his tongue grows too loose. As for Lancelo, I wanted for him no more favour than rested in his own body and skills. Nor now do any of us ask for undue favours. So long as we are here we are at your commands, knowing that they will always be just."

Before Arturo could reply, Ansold said gruffly, "She is right about the mead loosening my tongue. But smithying is hot work and hard and a man's throat gets parched."

When Lancelo led them away to find quarters for them, Arturo went back to the fountain and sat, one hand teasing at Anga's ears. The gods had sent him a master sword maker . . . a man who could wander the breadth and length of the land and always find a welcome in any camp. And the gods had sent him Daria. In so doing there was no doubt in him that they moved him and the dark-haired, blue-eyed young woman in some pattern of destiny not given yet to the eyes or mind of man to know.

CHAPTER NINE

A Gift From The Gods

THE WINTER SPENT its strength at last and spring began swiftly to spread its coloured mantle over the land. The woods grew green-budded and primroses and white and purple violets studded the mossy alder thickets along the valley stream, and the gold of daffodil blooms was spread like largesse over the meadow banks.

There were times now when Arturo, quick with the restlessness of the season, found himself turning away from the ordering of men and horses, from drills and cavalry exercises, to forsake the villa and walk by himself in the surrounding woods. Sitting alone in a clearing, he would become lost in a dream of the campaign that he meant to start as soon as the first days of summer came. Ill-provided and rash he knew it had to be, but there was no doubt in him that the gods would approve his daring. With a handful of men he would do what Gerontius with all his forces had talked long of doing but still had not found the will to effect. Active though his mind was with this dream, there were the times when its place was usurped by his second passion. From thoughts of coming renown and glory, he found himself slipping into thoughts of Daria.

Again and again the gods had put her in his path. He was in love with her and knew that she, for all her challenging and teasing spirit, looked with more than ordinary kindness on him. Yet one doubt tangled his thinking about her. Through her the gods might be tempting and testing him. Many men in history had been drawn from the path of greatness by their love for a woman. Because of this uncertainty in him he had more and more in the past weeks avoided the company of Daria.

Sitting late one afternoon in a small glade above the villa, idly stripping the young bark from a hazel wand with his thumbnail and frowning to himself as he teased his mind with the dilemma which Daria posed for him, he saw her come out of the trees on the far side of the glade and walk toward him. She sat down close to him. He gave her no greeting and kept his eyes from her.

Smiling, Daria said, "There was a time when you had no lack of words boastful or bardlike to greet me. *Aie* . . . even in my first weeks here. Does the beginning of greatness which all your men claim for you begin to move you away from ordinary courtesies?"

Throwing the hazel wand from him, Arturo said, "You are right to chide me. But do not think because I lack words that there is no greeting in my heart. You know what is in my heart as I know what is in yours. The gods have brought us together, and for a purpose."

"But you cannot read that purpose, is that it?"

"Can you?"

"I do not try."

"But I must."

"Why?" She leant forward and cradled her brown arms around her knees, and her dark hair fell about her cheeks.

"That I cannot tell you."

"Then I can give you no help. But when the feast of Beltine is over and the women go from here I shall go with them. There is one who has offered me a place with her people."

"Your father goes with you?"

"I cannot speak for him. Nor he for himself until the moment comes. I think that you, too, are much like him. You do not know what you will do until the moment comes. But when it does you find good reason for your actions. Like a hare disturbed from its form you bound away and even when you are moving you do not know why you have taken your line."

Despite himself Arturo smiled, and said, "What need to know till then—since the gods will have put it in my mind?"

"The gods control us, true. But not every moment of the day. There are times when they are too full of their own affairs."

"For most men, yes. But not for me."

To his surprise Daria threw back her head and laughed. "Oh, Arturo! You have such faith in the gods. And true— there is that about you which speaks of greatness. Your men mark it and respect it. But the gods cannot be with any man for every minute of his life."

"The gods are always with me when the moment is of great importance. Since no man would talk to me as you do, then I will talk to you as no man would to a woman without shaming himself. I love you and would make you my wife—but this I cannot do unless I know it is in the will of the gods that it should happen."

In a low, angry voice Daria said, "My lord Arturo, you forget one thing. Gods or no gods, when a woman takes a man for husband it is a matter of her will, and hers alone." Then standing up, her eyes narrowed, her cheeks flushed with emotion, she went on, her voice almost contemptuous, "I am no woman to wait on the will of the gods for a husband. *Aie* . . . I would have been wife to you if you asked me frankly out of your own true love for me. But now I am as far out of your reach to master and to cherish as is the wild white mare that roams these woods!"

She turned from him and walked away through the trees, and Arturo, watching her go, was suddenly filled with a great elation and joy which almost made him call out to bring her back for he knew that through her the gods had spoken and given him the sign he needed.

For the next two weeks he spent much of his time away from the villa camp. He went on foot into the woods, by day and by night, and the only company he had was Anga. He searched the valleys and dales, the remote clearings made by long-dead charcoal burners, the places at streams and pools where deer, boar, fox and other forest animals came to drink.

On the high meadows and swampy river pastures he marked the hoofmarks and the cropped patches of sweet new grass that told of the passing of the white mare. He followed the trails that she used, found the resting places where she couched at night, and the bare sand patches among the wild heathlands where she rolled in the dust, and from fresh and stale dung droppings he began to have a clear picture of her movements about the country around the villa. Sometimes he heard the distant thud of her galloping as she scented him and Anga and hurried away. Once he saw her break free from a copse of young beech trees and canter away from him down a valley side, her long tail and full mane floating in the wind of her passage like silk, the sun turning her white coat to moving, polished ivory; her beauty made him catch his breath with its wonder. A joy rose in him at the sight of her. She was a fit steed for a great commander and she was god-marked to be his. When the first days of summer came he would ride out on her at the head of his company. But before that he would come astride her, her master, into the villa courtyard and Daria, seeing him, would need no words to know his mind, and to know that he came to claim her as wife, the wife the gods had ordained for him.

Knowing now the ways of her coming and going, he waited three nights running for the break of dawn, lying above a narrow forest track, stretched out on a stout over-hanging oak branch, a rope halter thrust inside his tunic, and Anga hidden at his command in a thicket a little way ahead of the oak at the track side. For two dawns the mare kept away from the track, but on the third as the sun lipped the eastern sky and the birds began to sing, the mare came down the track, trotting gently and tossing her noble head so that her mane was wide-flung like a floating web. When she was almost under his branch Arturo spoke his will silently to Anga with the art which belonged to all men of the tribe of the Enduring Crow.

Anga came out of the thicket and stood in the trackway. The mare shied a little and halted. Then, seeing that she faced no bear or wolf, she moved forward and stamped her right foreleg on the ground. At this moment Arturo rolled from his branch, twisted his body and dropped squarely onto her back. As she began to rear with fear and surprise under him, he jerked the halter from his tunic, slipped it over her head and held its loop in either hand as he clamped his legs and thighs iron-hard to her sides.

From that moment Arturo was translated into a world that held only himself and the wild movement of the white mare. There was no thought in him except to master the white mare, and no art in him except the savage skill of muscled purpose which inhabited legs and knees and thighs and hands to make him one with the racing, plunging, rearing animal beneath him. Neighing with anger and panic, the mare, blind to open track or glade, raced through the forest. Thorn and branch ripped at Arturo's hands and face, and the blood from his cuts dripped and ran from him to stain the white hide of the mare.

Time and place lost their meaning. He lived in a world of savage motion as the mare sought to unseat him. She came out of the forest, bursting through a great bank of gorse thicket like a wind devil to set the new bloom scattered high in a golden drift. She thundered down a valley side and, as though with deliberate malice and intent, raced with long neck outstretched under the low branches of an old yew to sweep him from her so that Arturo, laid low across her back, his face pressed close into the sweet horse smell of her wild mane, felt the slash of scaly branches rip and tear the cloth of his tunic. They went, man and horse like one beast, through copse and pasture, hooves throwing sand clouds high across wild heathland, and the mare's angry neighing filling the bright morning air. He knew the great gathering and surge of her muscle as she jumped brake and stream and when she reared and plunged and swung round on her hind legs the world spun before him in a mist of green and blue chaos. Then, as no sign came of let or stop to the mare's wild panic and anger, there slowly crept over Arturo the black humiliation of knowing that his strength could never outmatch hers. His body was bruised and battered and his hands and thighs grew weaker. He found fresh anger and determination to fight his growing weakness, but only for a while. Silently within himself he cried out to the gods to be with him, but all that rested with him as the mare raced plunging and kicking beneath him was now the certain knowledge that she would master him. The gods were with her and not with him.

The moment of defeat came when the mare, galloping wildly through a forest clearing which held a sedge-ringed pool, suddenly from full pace, her hooves scoring great marks in the soft ground, pulled up to a violent halt such as Arturo had never known horse to make before. His body slid forward with its own momentum, but before he could fall the mare reared suddenly to full height and, as her forelegs pawed and threshed the air, twisted herself in violent pirouette and flung Arturo from her.

He lay on the ground close to the pool's edge, face and hands bloodied and cut, his clothes ripped, and he was lost to the world. The old hound, Anga, long left behind, came loping into the clearing and sat near him, panting with exhaustion, his great tongue lapping free over his jaws, and whined when Arturo made no move. Time passed and the moorfowl which had taken cover in the new sedge growth came out onto the waters of the pool. Anga moved closer to Arturo, sniffed at his face, and then settled beside him and snapped at a fly which teased his muzzle. The sun climbed higher, clearing the treetops, and a shaft of light began to warm Arturo's face. He groaned and moved.

Slowly he sat up and, seeing the pool, crawled toward it on all fours and like a dog lowered his head and lapped at the water. With the easing of his thirst memory came back to him. He sat back on the grass and, resting his aching head in his hands, knew that he was truly forsaken of the gods. They had seen his pride and arrogance and had set him to a task that would break and humble him. For a moment or two he was near to weeping but before his manliness could be breached a new pride suddenly flared in him, starting him to anger and the fire of bitter challenge. This country, his country, torn and parcelled by warring tribes and ravaging Picts and Scotti, knowing no true leader or destiny except the greed and self-seeking of petty princelings like Gerontius, Ambrosius and the discredited, aging Vortigern, was at the mercy of the growing strength and arrogance of the Saxon Hengist. Gods or no gods, from this moment he was dedicated to the cause and the great matter of Britain and would follow it and master it and all his country's enemies so that as the name of the great warring Caesar could never die from men's minds, nor should his. Forsake him the gods might, but there was that in him that forced him to scorn their desertion.

He pulled himself to his feet and turned away from the pool, but as he raised his eyes across the glade, he saw that which was a humble and wild joy in him and a never-to-be-forgotten sign. The gods had tried and tested him, humbled him in misery, but from that misery they had sparked a fire to kindle in him the life flame of his destiny. Never again would he deny them, for clear against the bright green of new forest leaf stood their sign of favour. Cropping peacefully at the lush spring grass was the white mare, her brier- and thorn-raked hide flecked with her own and his blood, the halter hanging slack from her lowered neck, and the long white tail switching across her quarters to break the tease and bite of worrying flies.

Sure of himself, Arturo walked slowly across to her, and the mare stopped cropping, raised her head and looked at him from her dark-pooled eyes and showed no sign of fear or flight. He stood by her, put out a hand and stroked her muzzle, and she took his touch with a gentle blowing of breath through her nostrils. He spoke to her gently then and called her white one, called her queen of all horses, breathed and crooned the low love talk of a horse master and ran his hand along the proud line of her neck and promised her cherishing and honour for all the days of her life.

He took her halter and led the white one back through the forest paths to the villa. He could have mounted and ridden her but would not on this day for he knew her pride was like his own. They came together down the slope to the Villa of the Three Nymphs. And when his people and his comrades came running and hurrying to gather about him, the mare stood quietly and without fear.

He said to the crowd about him, "She is the White One, the Shining One, and wherever we ride against the enemies of this country she shall be known and seen as the White Horse of Arto and all the shields that follow shall be marked with her emblem and all our scarf and helmet colours shall be the white of her shining hide and the crimson of her blood and mine, which dapple it now."

Then, from the crowd, he called a small boy who had come with one of the visiting families and he handed the loose halter end to him and said proudly, "Lead her to the stables and remember always that after Arturo you were the first to have her gentle obedience."

The boy led the White One away and she followed without let, stepping like a queen along the lane which the crowd fell back to make for her passage. As she went Arturo turned away from his people and walked across the yard to the ruined steps which led up to the colonnaded open way which ran across the face of the west wing of the villa where Daria stood, the morning breeze flicking free the tendrils of her dark hair and moulding the soft wool of her blue gown about her tall, full body.

He took her right hand and said humbly, "You know what is in my heart, and I know what is in yours. Although I have mastered the White One, to you I say I would take you for wife and between us for all our days there shall only be cherishing."

Daria was silent for a while. Then, raising a hand and brushing her dark hair from her face, she said, smiling, "You do me honour, my lord Arturo, in the asking. *Aie* . . . I will gladly and lovingly be wife for you. But though we shall lie in the long grass and listen to the golden birds sing and drink the new wine, those times will be few and far-spaced for I know that there will be often the loneliness of longing for you when the White One takes you away. And now"—she smiled broadly, mocking and teasing him with her eyes— "you must do grace to my father and go ask him for leave to make me your bride. I doubt that he will refuse you, but should he, then make him a gift of a jar of beer and ask again when he has drunk it."

Inbar of the tribe of the Enduring Crow had been well drilled by the captain of the guard on how he should behave before Count Ambrosius. Stiffly drawn up to his full height, he stood before the low wooden table at which the Count sat on a folding stool and waited for the man to raise his head to mark his awareness of his presence. All he could see at the moment was a bald head with fluffy wings of greying hair over the ears, bowed low over a sheet of new parchment covered with writing. On a bed against the far wall of the room lay an old but well-polished cuirass, a red cloak, and a horsehair-plumed bronze helmet as old as the cuirass. Count Ambrosius, all knew, kept to the old Roman ways and ordered his army so. The word from some was that he was a fool who lived in a dream, but there were many more who knew the real truth of the commander. It was that truth of the man which Inbar was hoping to use for his own advantage now. *Aie* . . . and many a long week it had taken him to get this audience.

After a while, and Inbar, whose judgment of men was shrewd, gauged the waiting imposed on him to be deliberate, the Count pushed the parchment to one side and raised his head. As their eyes met, Inbar lifted his right hand in a military salute but said nothing, remembering the words of the guard officer who had been one of the last he had bribed to get this interview. A pair of shrewd, narrow-lidded, pale-blue eyes fixed themselves steadily on him and a bare arm was raised to jerk the folds of a white toga to comfort about the thin shoulders. A small, hard man, thought Inbar, with no comfort in him for others and need for none himself . . . a shadow Roman, dreaming of the past, but a weasel of a man, swift and deadly. And on that he was placing his hopes.

"Name yourself and your business." The voice was low but gritty like the rub of sandstone on sandstone.

Inbar said, "I am Inbar of the tribe of the Enduring Crow, cousin to Baradoc its chief, and uncle to Arturo, the son of Baradoc."

At the mention of Arturo's name Ambrosius's lips thinned and from his hands, which he held locked together as his elbows rested on the table, came the crack of his knuckles as his fingers tightened. He said, "I have heard of you from Prince Gerontius and know you to be a dead man for shaming the wife of Baradoc."

"Shame there was none, my lord, for the woman would have been willing and I would have made her my wife. Dead I should be, but am not for the gods were on my side when I took the long run and the death drop. Out of their bounty I hit the water cleanly feet-first, sank deep and then swam under-water to the cover of the cliff foot, where that night my wife came—"

"Yes, yes, the gods were with you, but spare me the rest and come quickly to your matter with me."

"Arturo has taken men and horses from you, my lord, and his company grows."

"You tell me what I already know, man. Come to your point."

"I would kill Arturo for you."

Ambrosius raised his head and the cold blue eyes widened in surprise. With an impatient wave of his hand he said, "What need to come to me and waste my time? Any man is free to kill Arturo for he is outlawed and then the blood price will be paid."

"So it would seem, my lord. But beyond the seeming is now the truth that there is not a man in this land who would kill Arturo for a blood price that he could not live long to enjoy. The blood price must be claimed openly before you or the noble Prince Gerontius and proof given of the deed. Such openness would mark a man for life, but that life would be short for there are those among his companions who would make it so."

Count Ambrosius was silent for a while, the thin fingers of one hand fidgeting with the neck yoke of his toga. Then quietly he said, "It is true that must be the manner of the paying of the blood price. It is true, too, that I would have him dead. At the moment he is a gadfly but others begin to gather with him. So, what is in the mind of Inbar of the Enduring Crow?"

"Much, my lord, which I would wish to rest secretly between us. Alone, unmarked, and unknown to any, I will

kill Arturo for you. As return I ask little. First I would have a
small command in your army for I am tired of wandering like
a lone wolf. After that, and I can be patient over the years, I
ask that when his father, Baradoc, dies you should through
your friendship with Prince Gerontius have me named as
chief of the tribe of the Enduring Crow.''

"Baradoc's death would not clear the road for you. He has
another son by the Roman woman Gratia he married, and
could have others.''

"No, my lord. From my own wife, who still lives with the
tribe, I know that the woman Tia is now barren since the birth
of a fourth child, a girl-child.''

Ambroisus gave a thin smile. "And it is to your wife—
since you are forbidden to go west of Isca—that you would
look for the end of the second son . . . a wasting disease, a
destroying fever? So, so, and if needs be—for barrenness is
no more a certainty in a woman than her affections—she
would see that no future man-child lived long?''

"Yes, my lord.''

Count Ambrosius lowered his head on one hand and with
the other fingered the edges of the parchment on the table.
Arturo and his companions were an annoyance to him. He
was a young man of spirit and wild dreams and loud boasts
with thirty or forty men at the most (but *his* men and *his*
horses). For a moment or two he was on the point of dismiss-
ing Inbar. He had greater worries on his mind than Arturo.
Vortigern, sunk in senile debauchery in Demetae, had sent
no levies this spring and Prince Gerontius had cut his levy
heavily. The great sickness over the eastern lands was passing, though slowly; and wily Hengist, who had once fought
as a Roman auxiliary, was fast-drawing fresh men from
across the northern sea and would soon begin to move, for no
Saxon warrior sat content in camp for long. Against all this,
while he sat here, lacking men still to make his move, waiting
on promises, Arturo surely was a single gadfly. Then the
thought quickened in him that the great Caesars and conquerors were ever at the mercy of time and chance. The sting
of a single gadfly could make a mount rear or stumble and a
noble captain fall to his death.

Raising his head, he said curtly, "Let it be as you promise, and it shall be as you wish."

"I thank you, my lord."

As Inbar went out through the anteroom the captain of the guard said, "How was the old lizard?"

Inbar smiled and said, "In the mood for taking flies." He reached into his belt pouch and handed the man a worn and clipped silver piece of the reign of the Emperor Gratian which had been in the baggage of a trader he had murdered for loot on the Salinae—Glevum road, coming south. So, too, would he serve young Arturo, striking suddenly and without warning.

During the handful of weeks which led up to the feast of Beltine, which was on the first day of the month dedicated by the Romans to Maia, their goddess of growth and fertility, Arturo lived in two worlds. There was the world of his love for Daria and hers for him, and the world of the passion in him to set out on his first campaign—though he knew in his heart that with the forces at his command it would be no more than a demonstration of audacity to make his name widely known and bring more men to his side.

In the world of men and horses he passed most of his time, and this without chiding from Daria, for she knew the temper of the man she was marrying and secretly approved it. But he rode most afternoons with her on a hide saddle before him and old Anga trotting at the heels of the White One. They went to a withy bower on the far fringe of the water meadow below the forest which the companions had made for them. There they lay in the long grass and drank, not new wine, but the fresh stream water and listened truly to the golden birds sing, for the hawthorn thickets on the forest edge were full of yellowhammers in full song. It was there that they talked and caressed one another and between the long sweetness of kisses learned those things which make the sturdy frame and sheltering roof to house the heart and strength of true love.

One afternoon Pasco the priest came to them and, sitting down on the old grass-covered anthill, spoke to them of marriage.

He said to Arturo, "The Lady Daria has told you that she is of the Christian faith?"

Arturo nodded. "Yes, but not long since."

Daria said, "Why should I talk of something which, in good time, Pasco could talk of far better than I?"

Pasco said, "It is logic—of a womanly kind. Which means, contrary to most people's thinking, that it is wise. So, my lord Arturo, you know that I cannot marry a follower and worshipper of Christos to one who worships all the heathen gods?"

Arturo nodded, unconcerned. "Yes. I know that, but it seems to me that you threaten to close a gate against a young ram when he is already within the pen. I worship my country's gods and those of my race. Are not your Christos and his great father gods like other gods?"

"They are indeed, and more so than any other gods."

"That is no uncommon thing among gods. Some are greater than others. So I am happy to worship your Christos and his father for they are gods and I worship all gods. How else can a man live in grace and under heavenly protection unless he gives homage to all gods? From my mother and my teachers I learned long ago that all the gods the Romans worshipped were but our gods with a different name. Great Bellenus was their Apollo. Our great Credne, who made the silver hand for the god Nodons, was their Vulcan, and so with all of them to the highest. Our all-powerful Dis was their Jove. A name is nothing. There must be as many names for the gods as there are races on this earth with different languages. Have no worry, good Pasco. You can marry me to the lady Daria with a clear mind since I will happily worship this Christos and his great father."

Pasco rubbed his chin and sighed. To argue with Arto further was to invite a spreading of confusion and trouble. The lady Daria would have Arturo for husband for she loved him. For that, if need arose—since her faith was not well-tempered—she would unhesitatingly declare herself no longer a Christian. It was better, he gauged, to keep the sheep in the fold than lose it forever to a young ram from a strange

flock. And was it not true that Christos often chose to bring
the heathen by strange paths to grace?

Seeing Daria's eyes attentive on him and her hand holding
Arturo's in union which his common sense told him, since
the season was spring and young blood was young blood,
must soon be celebrated, he said, "Then I will marry you.
But there is one small rite of the Christian god you must
make."

Arturo smiled. *Aie* . . . I know of that, too. You would
have me stand in the fountains of the three nymphs and duck
me under in baptism? So be it. Cold the water may be, but
what could be colder than a heart denied its love? And know,
too, good Pasco, that I shall take pride in being a follower of
your Christos. Many of my men are such. Was it not the
great Christian bishop Germanus who gave our people the
miraculous Alleluia Victory over the Saxon and Pictish
forces of the young Hengist when he first came to these
shores?"

So it was that, in a courtyard crowded with all his followers, Arturo, stripped to a loincloth, was baptized in the great
stone bowl of the fountain of the three nymphs. The water
which he had expected to be ice-cold seemed warm to him
and he gave thanks, as Pasco spoke his ritual words over him,
to the goddess Coventina for her favour.

They were married and feasted and then taken in procession by torchlight to the bower in the water meadow, and as
the first slip of a late-rising moon paled the sky the nightingales began to sing from the hazel beds. The next morning,
when the two came out from the bower to face a morning
lively with a fresh breeze from the south, Arturo was greeted
by the sight of a tall lance fixed firmly in the turf. From it, its
folds curling and uncurling in the wind, flew a red war banner
which had emblazoned on its center the device of a rearing
white horse, mane and tail flaring as though the breeze itself
were giving the animal life.

Daria said, "This night you have had my bride's gift. This
morning I gave you my first gift as your wife. May the gods
protect you whenever you go into battle with it."

Arturo, putting his arm around her, his eyes fast on the waving banner, said, "If ever I bring dishonour to it or to you may all the gods desert me."

Three days later in the early afternoon came the high warning call of the horn of the watch guard on duty at the southwestern edge of the camp lands. The call was three high-pitched blasts which told of the approach of strangers. As the guard men of the day came running from their quarters and the companions working and training about the villa grounds began to muster to arms the horn called again. But this time it was the long, high sustained note which told that the strangers came in peace.

Shortly afterward a small party rode into the villa court-yard, where Arturo and his men stood waiting to greet them. Arturo's face lit up as he watched them approach. At their head rode his father, Baradoc, with his mother, Tia, at his side. Behind came three of Prince Gerontius's men as body-guards, followed by two youths leading heavily laden bag-gage ponies. They greeted each other affectionately and Arturo presented Daria to them as his wife and saw the quick gleam of pleasure and approval in his mother's eyes. Tia, now in her fortieth year, had grown matronly. Time had not flawed her beauty, but the years had given her the noble bearing of a queenly woman. Her hair was still corn gold and her eyes quick and all-embracing as she looked around her. His father looked much older and there were iron-grey streaks in his russet hair. His sword arm had grown stiffer and when he embraced Arturo it was only with a clasp of his left arm around his shoulders. His face was stern but more now, Arturo guessed, from habit than mirroring any immediate emotion. But his directness of manner was still the same. Daria led Tia away to the women's quarters, and the guard of the day took charge of the comfort of their mounted guard and baggagemen. Baradoc, left alone with Arturo, walked to the edge of the fountain basin and sat down. He accepted the cup of wine which one of the camp women brought to him. When the woman had gone, he said to Arturo evenly, "We stay not the night, for we are in Count Ambrosius's country and that would be a discourtesy to him."

Arturo, smiling, answered, "This is my country—but I take no issue with you, Father. That you are here, and my mother, too, is a joy to me. But I would be foolish to think that you come simply as father to greet his son."

Baradoc nodded. "That is the truth. I would it were otherwise." Then looking around him, he went on, "You have things well ordered here. Your horses in the pastures are a delight to the eye. The crops show fair, and your men walk and hold themselves with dignity and pride. You and your time here are wasted, though. You live in a dream of defiance."

"I live to make a dream come true. And the gods are with me."

Baradoc smiled and, rubbing his stiff right shoulder, said wryly, "You are as ever, I see, a familiar of the gods and enjoy their favour. Well, I will not argue with you about that. I come from Prince Gerontius on other business. He has entrusted to me a task of great importance—I go now, in fact, to persuade Count Ambrosius of this. For this task I would have one at my side whom I can trust. Someone to take the place of this. . . ." He half raised his stiff right arm.

For a moment or two Arturo said nothing. From the companions who had come to him recently he had heard that Prince Gerontius planned to raise in the country of the Durotriges, west of Lindinis, an armed camp to be a bastion against any future westward move of the Saxons. Then seeing his father's eyes shrewdly watching him, he said, "I have heard something of this work. But to me . . ." He shrugged his shoulders. "Well, my father, it is one thing for a hedgehog to roll itself into a ball of spikes until the fox walks away. But Hengist and his Saxon kind are not to be so easily baulked. They will sit themselves down around your hedgehog and wait for it to starve to death."

Baradoc shook his head. "There is more to it than that. I would have you know it and work for it with me. That is why I am here. Prince Gerontius will withdraw the warrant of outlawry on you. When I have seen Count Ambrosius he will do the same—for in return he will get a levy of troops he thinks not to have. The Prince expects no humbling of yourself before him. You give him your allegiance truly. In return, you are free, and you come with me to help in this great work and you bring your men and horses and all your people as your command.''

Arturo, tight-lipped, shook his head. ''In a fashion he sues for my help. But now the wind blows from another quarter. I have men here who have only one thought in mind—and that is not to sit them down and protect the building of this great fort which you would raise. Nor have I such thought. Within a month I would have no men. They are hungry for war and defiance—and so am I. We begin small, true, my father. But after the flowering of one blood-red poppy who can count the seeds that burst from the pod? With the gods we can dare all. But sitting on our backsides about a great fort would invite their mockery.''

Baradoc shook his head and sighed. ''You think too much of the gods. But, remember this, there are those they touch with madness in order to destroy them. Still, your answer is what I expected. Nor, in truth, would I have pursued it this far were it not for the urging of your mother.''

Before the little party left, Tia walked alone with Arturo along the terraced plots below the villa, where now the young bean shoots grew high and the spring cabbage fattened, to say her farewell to her son. Another son she had and two daughters, but this one was the marked one. Her sole joy was to have seen him again and to know an increase in that joy in learning that he was married to Daria, to whom her heart had warmed so immediately that, putting aside any thought of a last plea that he should join his father, she said to him now, ''The woman you have taken to wife pleases me. I know that she shares the dream you have. But remember this, Arturo, for I speak to you as a man and not my son, the constancy of a woman's heart-troth for her man is no polished jewel to be untouched by time and absence. It is a living plant which can wither under the killing frosts of long ab-

sence while her lover dedicates himself to an all-consuming
love for his country—or selfish glory.''

Arturo took her hand fondly and said with a present hon-
esty and passion, ''I shall never cease from cherishing Daria,
nor ever give her true cause to turn away from me. Do I not
remember how it was with you during the years my father
was away? Your virtue was a sword which went before
you.''

Tia made no answer for she knew that he spoke as he
would want things to be and, knowing only the strength of his
young manhood, had yet to learn how weak and barren the
spirit and body of a woman could be who lived in loneliness.

CHAPTER TEN

Under The Banner Of
The White Horse

AFTER THE FEAST OF BELTINE all sweethearts, wives and children left the villa, except for Daria and Ansold, who were to go to the nearest forest settlement when Arturo and his men left. Of all the men who had gone away to visit their homelands and their families only two never returned, and it was known much later that of these one had been killed in a drunken quarrel and the other had died of the slow sickness in his hometown of Ariconium, west of the Sabrina River. This sickness had been spreading now for over two years from the north. It came slowly and unevenly. It broke out in one village and left its neighbour unplagued, and turned one town into a desert while another a few miles away went unscathed. It was no new thing. The oldest of men could remember it in their boyhood and held the memory of their father's memories of it. It was accepted as the seasons were accepted, and this year it was being said that it was as bad as any could remember and was the cause of Hengist and his fellow chieftains showing no signs yet of moving their war bands westward across its direct path.

Arturo gave it little importance. Disease was the lot of man and beast. A beast was at the mercy of the good keeping and feeding of his master, but a man was his own master. He should drink clean water, eat good meat and bread, and—in his camp—keep the privies clean and, except in the coldest of seasons, wash the body thoroughly every two weeks.

Each day now was filled with preparations for the march

eastward and, although he knew that it would be no great army he led, he was fired with the thought that from the exploits and daring of his handful of men an army would grow and, with its growth, the renown of his name.

On the night before the morning of his leaving the camp with his company of comrades, he lay awake on the bed in their chamber at the villa with Daria. Holding her hand, he leant over her and kissed her and then said, "I say my farewell to you now. While I am gone, pray to your god for me, and know that everywhere I go I carry you in my heart. In my dreams I shall walk with you beneath the sweet yellow apple tree by the stream and there shall be no sadness in the voice of the storm thrush, or melancholy in the call of the blackbird from the bower of the white-blossomed thorn tree. I shall see your bright cheeks, red lips, eyebrows as black as a chafer and your teeth bright as the noble colour of snow. . . ."

Daria made no answer, though she smiled at his words, knowing that with the comrades in his hall he had feasted and drunk the last of the over-winter mead. But her heart was full with her love for him and she needed no words to show it. She drew him down to her and when he slept she kept him harboured within her embrace.

They rode out the next morning to leave the Villa of the Three Nymphs to the foxes and the birds, to the basking lizards and snakes, and their growing crops to the care and mercy of the surrounding settlements. At their head rode Arturo on the White One, wearing a leather war cap from which the red and white horse plumes swayed in the morning breeze. About his neck was knotted a red-and-white scarf and tight around his leather tunic a studded belt which carried sword and knife, his trews cross-gartered with braided deer-hide thongs, his legs guarded by a pair of old bronze greaves. Over his shoulder he carried, as did all the companions, a small round buckler painted red with the device of the rearing white horse on it, and he held himself proudly, his head high so that the low sun set dull fire-flecks amongst the growth of the campaigning beard he had grown. At his side rode

Daria's brother, Lancelo, red-and-white-plumed and -scarved, armed with shield and sword, and carrying high the war banner of the White One. Behind them came the companions, all plumed and scarved and armed and bucklered, but clothed for war variously. Some wore the clothes of the Sabrina wing from which they had come. Some were cuirassed fore and back with padded leather plates, and a few proudly bore old bronze cuirasses which had seen service nearly a hundred years before, in the days of Stilicho and Constantine.

They mustered near sixty horse, and Arturo had divided his force into two troops of twenty-four horse each. The first troop was commanded by his closest friend, Durstan, with Garwain of Moridunum as his second-in-command. The second troop was led by the bearded, sweet-singing Gelliga from Lavobrinta, who had for his deputy the young fresh-faced giant-handed Borio from Deva. Behind them came the remount section of six horse, ridden by two other companions, the brothers dumb Timo and Marcos and the two young men—Barma and Felos—who had first come to the villa bringing tribute from the surrounding Britons. Behind them came a string of pack ponies, led and ridden by the priest Pasco and other workers who had attached themselves to the community of the companions over the months.

It was a small force but a brave one, well trained and disciplined, and now fully aware of what was in Arturo's mind. The only man who travelled unarmed was Pasco, and as the column rode out of the courtyard he intoned in a loud voice a prayer, to which for Arturo's sake he added a few unorthodox touches:

"O chaste Christ well-beloved, and all the native gods of this great country, to whom every verdict is clear, may the grace of the Seven-fold Spirit come to keep and protect these Thy servants.

"Let neither sword nor spear restrain them, nor the enemy slip from their grasp like an eel's tail, so that under Thy banner neither barbarian, bond, fortress nor bare waste can stop their course.

"O powerful Creator, and Protector, rule our hearts, that Thou mayest be our love, and that we may do Thy will."

And so they went down the hillslope to the pasture and into the water meadows to follow the streamside which would take them by midday to the valley of the young Tamesis River. Here, they would turn eastward until they came to the ford which carried the Corinium road that ran to Spinis and Calleva and beyond into the heart of the wastelands waiting yet to be fully claimed and held by Briton or barbarian.

High up the valley side, on their right flank and hidden in the woods, Inbar watched them move, sitting his horse which switched its tail lazily against the summer flies. He wore a long brown woollen cloak which hid the sword he carried from his belt. Across his back was slung a hunting bow and a plaited-straw sheath of arrows, and lashed behind him was a roll of baggage to serve him in the slow hunt which was now beginning. Only the gods could number its days, but he knew that it would be long.

Two days later Arturo and his company rode into Calleva of the Atrebates. In their progress, riding along the old road, its ditches ruined, its surface broken and long despoiled in places, they had met no travellers. In the crop fields their fellow countrymen watched them from a safe distance, offering them no friendship, and the cattle minders, seeing the cloud of dust that rose about them, drove their beasts fast to distant safety. They trotted in over the old earthworks, the setting sun rose-tinting the ruined walls, and through the west gate opening, bare now of the great portals which had once swung close to protect the town at night.

Except for a few old people, spinning out their handful of days in misery and hunger, the town was a place of the dead. There was nothing of value left. Here no man pursued his craft, no merchant his barter, no housewife her marketing. No children played and even the sparrows and kites had deserted the place. Between the Saxons of the east and the Britons of the west and north, the country was a No-man's-land where safety lay in forest and river marsh or the openness of the high downs.

They slept that night in the old, almost ruined *mansio* close to the south gate. The horses were quartered in the inner courtyard and the company either slept in the surrounding lodging rooms of this old official inn of Roman days or lay rolled in their blankets under the balmy night sky. A courtyard well held good water still for men and horses. Doing his rounds that night to the sentries he had posted, Arturo, his footsteps echoing through the ruins, could imagine the days when travellers and staging Roman officers and officials had made the place a hive of warmth and talk as they passed through on their way to new postings in distant legions or to fresh markets as far north as the Antonine Wall. His lips tightened as he thought of those ordered, prosperous days and of his country now. A country which was being torn apart by so many forces and made a ruin and a desert to offend the eyes of man and the hearts of the gods.

The next morning he had his men round up all the miserable people who still stayed in the town, bringing them limping and halting into the old Forum through the ruins of its monumental east entrance, to be greeted by his companions, mounted on parade and drawn up in line along the front of the shell which had once been the Basilica.

Riding out from the center of his companions, the White One curvetting and restless beneath him, and with Lancelo holding the red banner of the white horse behind him, he spoke first in his own tongue and then in the tongue of his mother to them. Listening, Pasco smiled to himself for it amused him to recognize that in the warrior a great preacher had been lost. The smile went as he wondered why it was that war and bloodshed could silver a man's tongue so readily where love of God and one's neighbour so often left him dumb.

Arturo spoke as though he were addressing a crowd of able-bodied, just-minded citizens and seeking recruits and support to his cause, which he called the Great Matter of Britain and for which, he proclaimed with sincerity, the gods of his country had fingered him as the chosen one to achieve.

To his side must come the warring and jealous princes and kings and warriors of his own country, all men of good intent, to revive the greatness of the past, to restore peace and prosperity, and to order justice and free passage for all. But to this end there could be only one beginning—the barbarian Saxons of the east must be swept away, driven to the sea to seek their ships and the safety of their own countries.

Although his companions had heard it all before, when he had told them of his dreams of this great progress which would give them fighting enough and also carry his message abroad, and had mostly latched their minds to the prospect of battle, there was something in his manner this morning, as he spoke to the miserable handful of old crones and broken men before him, that kindled a new fire in their spirits. A horse and a sword, the dust and sweat and blood of war had been promised and would be given them. But now they began to see the shape of a greater glory than their passion for battle had ever promised. They saw themselves now, each according to his faith, the picked of the gods or God. From that moment, though none showed it openly, there was a new dignity of the heart and a bolder, nobler edge to their allegiance to Arturo.

As they rode out of Calleva, Arturo, loosening his neck scarf against the morning's growing heat, turned to Pasco, who had come trotting up to give him company on his right side, and said, "And what does the good Pasco think of my preaching in the Forum?"

Pasco smiled, wetting his lips with his tongue, and said, "The preaching was good. But the congregation was poor. What gain will you have for your cause in such few and wretched hearts? There was not a man among them with strength to raise a sword or any woman with her mind on aught but the hope of good pickings to fill her supper pot."

Arturo nodded his head. "*Aie* . . . that is true. But they have that which I need. Each mouth has a tongue and when they go into the countryside to steal or beg amongst the scattered country people they will talk of the strange company in Calleva this day. The story will pass and pass until it begins to blaze like a summer fire through dry grasslands.

Although we quarter no more in towns, for their ruin and misery sickens my heart, there is none we shall pass without a herding of its wretched people to hear my words.'' He paused for a moment and then added slyly, ''Does it not say in your religion that in the beginning was the Word?''

Pasco, surprised, raised an eyebrow and asked, ''How do you know the disciple John so well?''

Arturo laughed. ''From a Druid priest who taught me well when he was sober enough to sit his stool without falling.''

''Do not forget that since you have been baptized it is your religion as well.''

''Nor shall I. A man cannot have too many gods to watch over him.''

Pulling up his horse sharply, Lancelo said, ''Then let us hope they are all with us now.''

From the top of the gentle hill which they had just crested he pointed ahead down the slope. At the bottom of the broad valley where the road crossed a small stream a body of about thirty men on foot barred the way in three ragged ranks.

Arturo, reigning in, said, ''They would have done better to have chosen this hilltop than the valley bottom. Sound the horn for Gelliga's troop.''

From inside his cloak Lancelo pulled his bullhorn and blew the four sharp battle notes and then a long fifth which was the call for Gelliga's command.

Without looking back Arturo sat on the White One and watched the men at the valley bottom. Many a time the maneuver which must come now had been made in mock attack from the forest hill down to the stream at the Villa of the Three Nymphs. Many a time this situation and others had been drilled and redrilled into men and horses. But now across his path stood his first real enemy, and on this bright morning there awaited him his first real attack. His breath quickened a little with pleasure. The moment had come sooner than he had thought, but it was more welcome for that. He looked back and saw Gelliga leading his men at a gentle trot away from the road and up the hillslope to the left to stop just short of the skyline. Keeping to the road came

Durstan's troop, to ride openly onto the crest and halt in four ranks of six behind Arturo. Farther back the remounts and baggage horses were being taken well away to the right flank.

Durstan rode to Arturo's side and said, "They cannot know our strength or they would not stand so bunched and ready for plucking."

"There are many things they will learn. Now let us see what days and nights of aching backsides and sore thighs have done for us."

Pasco, steadying his restless, sturdy hill pony, sat and watched. The men were Saxons and were a rabble, though well-armed. They were, he guessed, the war party of a scattered community of outcasts or adventurers who had moved away or been banished from the settled lands of the Saxon shore. There were many such pockets along the line of the valley of the River Tamesis and these communities often lived in uneasy peace with the native British of the district. The rumour of Arturo's coming must have spread ahead of him. They stood now to dispute his way.

The skirmish was brief and to be repeated with variations dictated by ground and chance many times to come in their advance eastward. Lancelo's horn sounded the long, high, whickering call to advance. Durstan's troop put their horses to the gallop and charged down the slope toward the Saxons, who waited their coming with heavy, sharp-pointed, single-edged scramasax swords drawn and their small round shields raised, not for defense so much as for striking at the face of their enemy once he was brought to ground to fight foot to foot. Arturo and Lancelo stayed on the hilltop.

Seeing him restraining the impatient White One, Pasco smiled to himself. This was no full battle that needed him at the head of his force. Both Durstan and Gelliga knew his mind, and he would take away no part of their pride of command. Also, too, Pasco guessed, more than the pleasing blood-surge of moving into action, he would be drawing a greater pleasure from seeing the long hours of cavalry attack-drills at the villa now pass into reality itself, where a hamstrung horse could send a man to the ground to meet the swinging scramasax and the face-smashing shield and—if the gods were unkind—have a ready seax dagger sharp-slit his throat.

The dust clouds rose behind Durstan's troop as it swept down on the Saxons, and the unruly barbarians, eager for fight, broke ranks and ran to meet it. But the moment the troop was within a spear's length of the foremost Saxons, every horse swung to the right and raced across the front of the enemy as though their riders had suddenly lost heart. A great shout of triumph went up from the Saxons as they turned and chased them, calling taunts and bellowing their derision.

It was then that Gelliga's troop came over the hilltop and charged at full gallop down the slope to take the Saxons in the rear. Hooves thundering, tails and manes flying, the morning sunlight bright on drawn swords and helmet crests and streaming crimson-and-white scarves, the troop, with Gelliga and the great-handed Borio leading its center, spread out into a horned crescent and scythed its way into the rear of the Saxons. Some turned to meet their foes and died with wound in throat or chest, but most were killed from behind and went to their end not knowing they carried the death mark of those who die with their backs to the enemy to be banished forever from Woden's hall.

In a short while the attack was over and the few Saxons who had survived were running away from the road and along the stream and over the marshy ground where they were left free from pursuit. Amongst the companions there were few injuries. One had taken a spear thrust in the shoulder, another a slash from a seax which had cut through the hide cross-gartering of his leg and scored his calf with a long though shallow wound, and others had cuts and bruises of no importance. But one horse had had its windpipe and neck artery slashed with a sword and died as Gelliga's troop re-formed. It was left for the crows and kites and foxes and rats to pick clean. None said a word to the companion who had ridden it, for there are no words that can pass with any comfort to a man who has lost a loved mount. He sat by it, stone-faced, until the party moved on and then took his remount and cantered to his place in his troop column. Behind the troop came the baggage party, its cart and pony packs loaded with the pick of sword and knife and axe and the meager plunder taken from the bodies of the dead Saxons.

From that day they moved no longer directly to the east. Staying south of the Tamesis, which hereabouts took a great loop northward, they travelled in zigzag fashion, meeting little opposition. Wherever he could find a British village or settlement, no matter if it contained only a handful of people, Arturo would stop and, with his companions on full parade behind him, make his declamation as he had done at Calleva, so that the news of his presence and progress ran before him. To his delight now and again men of worth who had long deserted Count Ambrosius and Vortigern to return to their homes came to join him. Welcome they were when they came mounted and armed, but those who carried only the clothes they stood in and the itch for action were mounted and supplied with arms and such war gear as Arturo's force took from the Saxons in their path.

By the time Arturo reached the town of Pontes and the now south-curving Tamesis he had almost the makings of a third troop of horse under his command. Sitting one evening on the riverbank by the side of the ford which they would cross the next morning—for the old timber bridges had long been wrecked and pillaged for the sake of their timbers—he knew that far and near now the name of Arturo and his companions was working in the minds of more and more of his country-men like a ferment in the honey and water of new mead. On this progress he commanded no force large enough to fight great battles, but he would have blazed his name and intent across the country to catch the eyes and ears of every man who longed for true leadership and an end to his present misery, and so bring many of them to his side. With that, for this year, he would be content.

As he sat there a thin summer drizzle began to fall and suddenly from the smooth surface of the rolling Tamesis a great salmon, running the river to the spawning beds of the headwaters, leaped like a great bow of silver into the air. Seeing the fish, he remembered the story of the goddess

Latis, who wept and brought the rains to fill the rivers to bring back her warrior lover who deserted her each year to go to the sea as a salmon. Remembering this, he thought suddenly of Daria, who sat now and waited for him—Daria, who grew more and more absent from his mind if not from his heart.

He had then a black sense of shame that he, whose eyes watched always for signs from the gods who controlled his destiny, saw now a sign from the peaceful, gentle Latis which should not have been necessary.

He rose and with the Latis rain dewing his face went into the camp and found the youth Felos.

Arturo, the shame still clouding him, said, "Go to Marcos. Tell him to give you a horse, weapons and food. Ride back to the lady Daria and give her all the count of our days and progress. Then, returning, bring with you all news."

"Yes, my lord."

"Say that I am well and bear her always in my thoughts and heart."

"Yes, my lord. And where will I find you, my lord?"

Sharply, Arturo said, "Only the gods can say. But"—he smiled, to ease his tartness—"find me and from that day you and your brother Barma shall ride as companions."

Felos, beaming, raised his hand in salute and was gone at a smart trot to find Marcos.

Three weeks later they rode out from the great elms which crested the high ground to the northwest of Londinium. They were now a company of two troops of thirty-two horse, each still commanded by Gelliga and Durstan, and a reserve troop of fifteen horse commanded by one of the new companions, Cuneda, from Lactodorum in the country of the Catuvellauni, a man of forty, built like an ox, black-bearded but without a hair on his head. Their camp servants had increased and they now had two carts, the second taken from a burned-out farmstead which they had repaired and fitted with runners to carry their food supplies and grain for their horses—though, the grass being abundant and sweet at this time of the year, their mounts needed no more than a few handfuls of corn a day. Five of the companions bore wounds which, under Pasco's care, were fast healing; and two companions had been killed the day after leaving Pontes when, riding ahead of the column as scouts, they had been ambushed by a band of robbers and cutthroats who stripped them of clothes and weapons and disappeared into the thickness of the surrounding forest where none could follow them. They were buried where they lay and, as Pasco finished his prayers for them, Arturo turned aside and rode alone with his grief, knowing it to be the beginning of a burden of the soul which he must from now on learn to endure as the never-ceasing lot of a commander of men.

Below them now the silver loops of the Tamesis snaked away eastward to the sun-blazed spread of its estuary, and at their feet lay the once great city of Londinium. Only a few wisps of smoke rose from its houses. It was a dead city; for these days, without true commerce or trade, there was no gain or security to be found in it. People in these times drew away from towns and settled where a living was to be found, in their hovels and sparse communities close to their poorly cropping fields and cattle grounds.

Arturo sent two of the companions to ride down to the city gate close to the ruined fort at the northwest corner of the walls to bring him back news of the place. When they returned they reported that the two western gates, though unmanned, were open and in good repair, that the fort was empty and that the great wooden bridge over the river was broken and gapped in many places and would give no crossing. There were people in the half-ruined city still, but they were a miserable set of wretches. Where there had been greatness and the noisy bustle of commerce and trade, and the ring of horses' hooves and the clank of armour as well-furbished and well-ordered troops had garrisoned the great fort and the walls, there was heard now only the scavenging cries of the kites and the carrion birds and the barking of dog packs that roamed the alleyways and deserted houses. And that they were there was due to one thing. The slow sickness had swept through the city since the beginning of summer and although it was now almost abated, the streets and houses still held the corpses of the dead, lying as they had fallen to make a feasting for all the city's carrion eaters.

Hearing this, Arturo was for a while in two minds whether he should risk his company in such a place, but then the conviction came strongly to him that since the gods had led him thus far under their favour, that favour would still run only if he entered the place and raised the white-horse banner for all to see so that the report of his coming would spread like a great ripple across the country. This was Londinium Augusta, once sacked and burned by the great Queen Boudicca, greater than Camulodunum or any other city, the capital, and his country would one day become great again.

He left the reserve troop of horse to guard the baggage train and with the rest of his companions, Lancelo carrying the white-horse banner before them, he rode down to the city and entered it through the most southerly of the two western gates. Men, women and children, dull-eyed from the slow sickness, lay in the gutters and doorways and gave them no greeting as they waited their deaths. Hooves clattering on the broken paving and rubble of the streets, the crows and kites rising in wild flight from the bodies that here and there littered their way, the dog packs retreating from them, snarling and barking, they moved along the Tamesis side, past the ruined warehouses and collapsed river stockades, the gulls and river birds, disturbed from their low-tide feeding, flighting from the beaches. Past the broken and burned and pillaged Londinium bridge and the ruin of the great river palace they went, and then swung north to breast the rising ground and finally rode in proud formation into the old Forum and drew up in a long line of horse across the face of the ruined Basilica. With them came a growing drift of miserable men and women with nothing to lose but their lives, which for most would be a happy release, ragged, half-starving and moving like famine-weary cattle.

Arturo rode forward a little and to these, as though they were proud, well-set citizens he made his declamation. When he had finished there was for a while a low muttering amongst them and then it died as the sound of a slow flurry of passing rain dies before the wind. Arturo and his men rode away and the crowd stayed where they were, no strength or curiosity in them to fire their wasted limbs and weak spirits. Helmet plumes tossing, the white-horse banner before them, the companions passed from the city, splashing over the summer-low river, past the ruined baths, past the shells of once noble buildings with their broken statues and defaced and cracked tablets of dedication, and out into the clean air and the green grass of the hillslopes where the rest of the company awaited them.

At Arturo's side Lancelo said, "Can such a city ever live again?"

Arturo, stiff-faced, moved by all he had seen, said with curt emotion, "Under the gods, someday, it must and will."

The next day, at low tide, they forded the river well above the city and the column turned south to begin a great sweep which should bring them westward to move along the fringes of the great forests that rolled northward from the shore line of the country of the Regnenses, from the sea towns of Anderida and Noviomagus.

Twelve days later they fought their first and only true battle of the progress. In the early hours of the morning, as they were camped below the crest of a steep scarp of the hills, it started to rain heavily. Since they lay in the open, rolled in their blankets without cover, Arturo gave the order to break camp and move. Every campaigner amongst them knew that the misery of rain soaking through blankets and clothes is abated if it can be met marching rather than lying on wet ground.

The companions formed into their two troops and moved off while the baggage train followed them more slowly with the half-troop of reserve horse in their rear to prevent surprise attack from behind. As the morning wore on, the ground became soaked and soft and slowed up the movement of the two baggage carts and the rear guard screen of cavalry. Little by little the leading troops gradually drew out ahead. Two troopers rode wide on each flank of the column as scouts, their cloak hoods drawn about their heads against the still driving rain. At midmorning as they rode along the crest of a broad upland sheep run, the two leading troops dropped down into a great dip in the land and disappeared from the sight of the following reserve troop and baggage column.

At this moment, from the bushes well to the left flank, there arose a party of fifty or sixty Saxons, who came running hard, howling and shouting and brandishing their weapons, to drive a wedge between the head of the baggage train and the forward two troops of horse now lost to sight. Then, too, from the right flank more Saxons ran from their hiding places and raced to the rear of the train to form a barrier between it and the following guard troopers.

Long before Cuneda, the rear guard commander, could reach for his horn and call the alarm the two parties of Saxons had swept around and amongst the baggage carts, killing all those who had not escaped at the sight of their coming. As the first notes of Cuneda's horn wailed the alarm the Saxons formed a circle about the carts and stood firm in three ranks to defend their position and their plunder.

That morning as Arturo, the alarm horn sounding in his ears, forced the White One hard back up the slope to the down top and saw the Saxon force surrounding his baggage carts, he learned a lesson he was never to forget. Hard rain makes a man seek, even on the move, what comfort he can. His scouts had ridden with their cloaks cowling their heads, their eyes part-blinkered, their minds on their discomfort rather than on the country around them. The situation before him now was none that had ever been faced in mock attack at the Villa of the Three Nymphs. He acted from impulse and instinct without time even for a prayer to the gods to be with him.

He shouted a command to Lancelo at his side and as his horn began to sound, he drove the White One forward into a gallop with the troops of Gelliga and Durstan following him in a combined wedge-shaped formation.

Pasco, who had been riding his pony with the leading troops, came back up the slope onto the level ground in time to see the tight wedge of flying horses, great scuds of turf flung up behind them by their pounding hooves, burst into the ring of massed Saxons, the swords of the companions swinging and flashing in the rain.

But the Saxons, shouting insults, held their ranks as the cavalry swirled round them on either side, the horses neighing with excitement and others squealing with pain as they were cut down or hamstrung, leaving their riders to fight on foot. Around the baggage carts men and horses circled like a great whirlpool. Watching, Pasco realized—for he had travelled far and seen much in his time—that these were no cutthroat, outcast, plunder-hungry men such as harried the valley of the Tamesis. They stood and fought like warriors and there was one among them, towering head and shoulders above the rest, who wore an iron-banded leather helmet and a short white sheepskin cloak that fell to his waist and was caught by a sword belt with a silver clasp, who was clearly the leader. These men were Hengist's men from the settled Saxon lands to the east, seasoned men who would stand their ground so long as the faintest flicker of victory burned for them.

Lancelo's horn blew and the two troops drew back and re-formed, and then the horn blew again to send in the rear guard troop under Cuneda. Arturo watched Cuneda's attack break against the Saxon ring, swirl about it and pass by, and then, his anger passing and his brain clearing, he realized that cavalry could only do so much against men who stood and fought and kept their ranks.

Durstan's troop followed Cuneda's to the attack. As it went in, Arturo dismounted, followed by Gelliga, Borio and all their men, to attack on foot. The cavalry swung left and right of the Saxon ring to harry its flanks and the dismounted companions flung themselves against its front. Leading them was Arturo, sword swinging, his buckler held low to prevent the swift Saxon thrust to the groin, cutting and hacking his way into the ring of men, forcing his way toward their leader in the sheepskin cloak. The Saxon chief, seeing him come, recognizing he must be the leader of the companions, pressed forward through his men to meet him. They met with a great clash of sword and scramasax, Arturo silent while the Saxon shouted taunts and insults at him. In the few moments before the lust of battle claimed him Arturo called silently to the gods to be with him, and then all thought deserted him as he became one with the flash and hiss of his sweeping, jabbing sword.

Pasco, watching them fighting face to face in the confused and bloody throng of men, saw the swing and thrust of cavalry sword and scramasax flash above the sea of heads and straining bodies, lost them, saw them again while the air rang with the fierce shouting of men and the screams of those who fell. Then suddenly, the white-fleeced cloak was gone. A great shout went up from the companions and, like the concerted movement of a raiding flock of crows taking wing in alarm from a field of young corn, the Saxons broke and ran. Pasco, who had seen battle against Saxons many times, knew their mind and their temper. With hope of victory they would fight and stand and die, but when hope or strong leadership went, they would turn and run. Only if they were hopelessly surrounded would they bunch and face their enemy and fight to the end, taking their wounds from the front and going gladly to their death to claim a warrior's welcome from Woden.

As the Saxons ran, the cavalry re-formed and harried them along the down top until Lancelo's horn blew the recall. Pasco, riding up on his pony into the carnage and destruction that surrounded the baggage train, found Arturo standing over the dying Saxon chief.

Blood running over his white fleece cloak from a great sword thrust in his chest, he lay with his eyes closed. But after a few moments he slowly opened his eyes, looked up at Arturo and said something in his own language. Then his head dropped to one side as life passed from him.

Arturo, leaning on his sword, said to Pasco, "You know their tongue?"

Pasco nodded. "Yes, my son. He said that now in Hengist's hall the name of Arturo of the White Horse will no longer make men laugh in scorn."

Arturo, after a moment's pause, said solemnly, "May his

gods honour him, as this day we humbly honour ours for the victory they have given us.''

That evening they camped beside a muddy, slow-flowing stream and Arturo, after eating, sat by himself on the bankside in a brooding mood which kept his companions from him.

The day that was passing had taught him many things and amongst them those which he knew he should have long marked from his own understanding. Ten of his troopers had been killed, and six of the baggage train, among them Timo the dumb one. Six wounded horses had had to be destroyed. If his name were not now to be held in scorn in Hengist's hall there was much about his own conceit of himself which gave him self-scorn. The gods, though they had kept his side, had given him lessons which he would never forget. Chief among these was that cavalry by itself was useless against men who would bravely stand and fight on foot. He had to have such men, men who would march and fight afoot, to come behind the cavalry and hold the ground or pour through the breaches made by his horse. He knew now that he had fed too long on his dreams. From this day the hard work began. He had made his progress and the name of Arturo had spread and was spreading. Behind the word now he had to work and build and shape the reality of a great command.

CHAPTER ELEVEN

Dawn Meeting

FOR MORE THAN a month Arturo and his company moved westward and wherever there was town, hamlet, settlement or village to be found they would stop and Arturo would draw up his companions and address the people. The news of the manner and purpose of his coming running ahead of him, there was now no fear of him so that on the high downs when they rested for a night the cattle and sheep minders would come from their runs to see and hear him, and in the wooded valleys he drew the lonely charcoal burners and swineherders wonderingly from the trees into the clearings. Now, when he called for men to join him, there were those few who stayed after their fellows had left. He went south down the river valley to the outskirts of Venta, which, although a shadow of its former self, was more prosperous and inhabited than most towns, and although the gates were closed against him there were those who came over the walls secretly by night to hear and see him. He moved like a man in a dream and spoke like one possessed and there were many of his companions who were hard pressed to keep patience and face with him. But others, like Durstan, Gelliga, Lancelo, Garwain and Borio, who knew his mind and purpose and read them right, knew, too, that Arturo meant to raise his own army and own no master but himself. When the day came to league himself with Gerontius and Ambrosius it would be as equal and with his own troops.

From Venta they turned northwest and at the end of that day's march Felos rode into camp. He found Arturo grooming the White One after feeding and watering her for he would let no one serve her but himself.

Arturo said, "Greetings, good Felos. You have been so long gone that I had thought never to see you again."

Felos, smiling, shook his head. "I would have been with you sooner, my captain. But your lady Daria kept me many weeks at her side."

"She is well?"

"She is, my lord, and full of deep content."

"Then why should she keep you so long and deny me the happiness of this news?"

Felos grinned. "Because she would be certain that I might bring you the happiest news you could have."

Arturo, stroking the neck of the White One with his hand, knowing that for days on end his mind had held no place for Felos or Daria, said, "What news could I have greater than to know she is well?"

"That of which she would be doubly certain before my return. She bids me tell you that she carries your child and all is well with her."

Arturo's hand dropped from the White One's neck and his face stiffened with the quick spasm of his inner joy and pride. Then, with an impulsive movement, he reached into the pouch of his sword belt and drew from it the silver buckle which he had taken from his first true Saxon foe and gave it to Felos, saying, "Such a great gift as you give me with your news deserves a return. Take this in token of my joy. And now go attend to your horse first and then yourself."

Felos moved off happily, and smiled to himself at his master's last words . . . *your horse first and then yourself*.

When he was gone Arturo stood alone in thought for some time, and there was a mixture of emotion in him which tinged his joy with shame. His love for Daria was deep and true, but it was of a different nature from his love of his country and his desire to see it become great again. But now Daria carried his child. . . . *Aie*, more than that, his son it must be if the gods were truly with him; and as though they were and would have him know it there came to him the bright conviction that without delay he must ride to their place and give them his thanks; and more than that, to show no disrespect to the god of Pasco, in whose name he had been baptized, he would take from the place of the gods a gift for the child from this other god to bear home with him.

Impatient now, he called for Durstan and said, "I saddle and ride this night to the Circle of the Gods for there is a thing I must do to set my mind at peace."

"Alone?"

"Alone, yes. Our company moves that way tomorrow and I shall be waiting for you. Give me no talk against it for my mind is set. Felos will give you the news he brought me and from that you shall, since our thoughts keep pace together, know my reasoning."

For a moment or two Durstan hesitated, but the look on Arturo's face told him there would be no shifting him. He said, "There is a moon tonight and you ride through peaceful country. Go, and the gods watch over you."

"They will—for I go to give them all thanks."

Losing no time, Arturo saddled the White One, armed himself and rode out of camp. The night was still and balmy and the full moon was passing to its last quarter. He rode north away from Venta to the high ground and then swung westward. But well behind him, trailing on his left flank, another marked and followed him, a man on a dark horse, heavily draped in a cloak which had grown ragged and torn and hid the sword he carried. Behind him was slung a bow and a sheaf of arrows hung at his side. The man's face, under its unkempt growth of beard, was drawn and haggard, but there was a dark gleam in his eyes which seen close would have told his joy. Many a time had Inbar in the past been on the point of turning from his hunt, but now he was joyful that hunger and thirst and hard lying and the perils of following the companions had not drawn him from his quest. Why Arturo should leave camp and ride into the night alone he did not know or care. One desire only burned in him and he waited now only for the meeting of time and place to give him the reward and the reformation which his manhood demanded.

Toward dawn, with a light ground mist rising knee-high over the land, Arturo came from a belt of trees out onto open ground and saw ahead of him on the sheep-bitten slopes of the down the great circle of henge stones silhouetted blackly against the westward-dying moon. As he had ridden through the night his thoughts had been full of Daria and the coming child, and of Daria and his days with her. Sparse though they had been, each one now seemed like a wondrous jewel inlaid with precious stones and enamelled with flaming colours. The gods had marked him for greatness to serve his country and he would make her by the grace of the gods a queen for all men, as she was now queen for him.

He rode into the great circle of stones and, slipping from the White One's back, took his knife from his belt and walked toward the fallen slab where long before he had hidden for safekeeping the silver chalice which had once held the blood of Pasco's god. As he moved away the White One lowered her head and began to graze on the sweet downland grass and herbs.

Kneeling, Arturo dug into the turf and quickly unearthed the chalice. He brushed it free of soil with his hands and the moonlight touched it so that it gleamed dully. At this moment Inbar, on foot, his horse left tethered to a thorn bush out of sight, stepped noiselessly from behind one of the tall stones. In his hands he held the drawn bow and the goose-feather-flighted arrow, armed with its sharp iron tip. There would be no honour in this killing, and he needed none since honour had been long lost to him. To his right the White One raised her head from cropping and looked at him. The sun, yet to show itself over the edge of the eastern land, already paled the sky with light and touched the underbellies of the low morning clouds with red and gold wash. The kneeling figure of Arturo was clear against the growing light, and already overhead a lone lark sang and the meadow pippits looped their way in morning flight across the juniper-tufted down-land.

As Arturo slowly began to rise to his feet, the White One whinnied gently and uneasily. Arturo, knowing her moods and manners, swung round, suddenly alive with an instinct of coming danger. The arrow, meant to take him below the left shoulder blade, sped true across the stone-encircled grass, the hiss of its feathered flight one long, low note against the morning quiet, and the deadly point sank deep into his body below his right ribs. He cried aloud with the sudden shock of pain and staggered backward, the silver chalice dropping from his hands. He would have fallen but the great stone behind him held him up and through the mist of pain which briefly dimmed his eyes he saw Inbar racing toward him with his sword drawn.

They fought then, without shield or buckler, sword-armed, and no words passing between them while the blood ran dark over the linen shirt under Arturo's open tunic. The sparks leapt blue and gold from the clash of their swords and the White One, disturbed and frightened, raced round the great inner circle and whinnied high. In a moment of withdrawal Arturo reached down with his left hand to the hampering shaft of the arrow lodged in his side and snapped it short. His hand came back, dark as ebony with the spurt of his own blood, and he prayed to the gods, if it were his destiny to die, to give him lifeblood enough and strength to kill Inbar before he fell himself.

And the gods were good to him and gave him this boon. He fought with the blood-veil fast clouding his eyes and, fighting, he remembered how his father had faced and fought this man, and of the dishonour which had been planned for his mother. They fought without words in the growing light of the burgeoning morning. The grass about them was trampled and scarred and bloodstained and, when the moment came that his sword slashed across the neck of his foe and Inbar fell with his death cry bubbling from his blood-filled throat like the wailing cry of an upland curlew, all reality passed from him. He fell to the ground and passed from violence into the calm of a dream of fair days and love's delights. He walked with Daria in the river pasture and plucked for her the scent-heavy meadowsweet plumes. He rode the forest paths with her lodged between his arms, riding before him on the White One, her dark hair in the wind making a moving lattice before his eyes and the sweet warmth of her woman's body filling his nostrils with a headier perfume than any that could come from the flowering summer blooms. With time out of joint, he walked with her through the villa courtyard to the fountain of the nymphs and she held in her arms the man-child which was his, and the child, seeing the splashing waters fling a veil of drifting, jewelled spray to trap the sunlight in rainbow colours, stretched out his hands to take them and crowed with delight; and with the sound of his son's voice in his ears and the sight of Daria's red lips parted to touch the child's warm cheek with a kiss, lips redder than the breast of any spring-fired robin's, he drifted further into the dark shades of oblivion.

A long-haired, shaggy moorland pony grazed close to the White One within the circle of great standing stones. The pack which had been on its back lay open on the ground beside the body of Arturo, which was half-propped against a fallen lintel, his head cushioned by his own bloodstained cloak and tunic, and his body naked above his trews except for the tight binding of torn strips of cloth that circled his body below his ribs and held, tight-pressed, a great moss wad which blocked and staunched the flow of blood from his wound.

At his side sat the man Merlin, whom he had last seen on the high scarp above the Sabrina River, the dark-haired, stocky, brown-robed man known as the ageless, the wandering one. On the ground lay a half-empty waterskin and a piece of old cheese resting on a great dock leaf. The man ate and, from watching Arturo's face, he turned now and then to look at the body of Inbar lying a little way off, the flies and bluebottles crowding the wound in his neck, the eyes up-turned and open, staring sightlessly at the midmorning sky.

A pair of grey-polled jackdaws, scavenging and eyeing the cheese below, sat atop one of the great stones and called noisily. At the sound Arturo slowly opened his eyes. He lay without moving for a while and there was a weakness in him that made him feel without body or contact with the turf and

stone which supported him. But that he lived he knew, for
slowly there grew in him a raging thirst which fired his throat
and slowly brought him to an awareness of his own flesh and
blood. His mind clearing, he said weakly, "I live."

Merlin smiled. "It is the wish of the gods. Why else would
they have set my steps this way? Once by happenchance we
met. But now they stir themselves and begin to meddle with
my affairs and give me dreams to plague my path. Yes, you
will live. While you rested in limbo I cut the broken
arrowhead from you."

"Thanks I give you, and more thanks would for a drink.
My . . . my throat is like a smithy's furnace and my body
burns."

Merlin reached for the waterskin and then took from the
ground at Arturo's side the silver chalice. He filled it and,
with an arm around Arturo's shoulders, lifted him a little so
that he could drink in comfort.

Arturo took the chalice in his weak, trembling hands and
drank. The water went into him with a coldness that suddenly
made his body shake. He half lowered the chalice and
coughed, holding it in his cupped hands against his breast,
closing his eyes against the shock. When the spasm passed he
opened his eyes, felt strength stirring in him and moved to
raise the chalice to drink again, but slowly stayed his hands.
Within the silver bowl cradled between his palms the clear
water was slowly flushing with a crimson hue that deepened
and, as the water stilled, took the morning light and glowed
with a high brilliance to show his own bearded, fight-sweated
face mirrored in it.

He raised his eyes in wonder at the sight and saw that
Merlin, too, had seen the colouring. They looked at each
other without words and then Merlin smiled gently. The
White One, suddenly raising her head, whinnied high and
fiercely and cantered across the marjoram- and thyme-laced
turf.

From the dip in the land to the east there rose then the
sharp, echoing call of a horn. Over the crest of the land came
the leading troop of Arturo's companions with Lancelo at its

head, the white-horse banner streaming in the rising morning breeze, and behind him, cloaked and scarved and helmeted, moved the ranks of the companions with scarlet and white plumes tossing and swaying.

Merlin, speaking almost as though to himself, said, "Your people come and there is no more need of me. But there will come a day when I shall be with you in an hour of your own choosing when the war horns shall blow neither for victory nor for defeat, but to set echoes rolling forevermore over this land to give your name everlasting life while you take the long sleep which the gods have decreed for you."

But as he spoke, a great weariness and weakness seized Arturo and the chalice fell from his hands as he passed into the first sleep which would stage him well on the road to full force and proud intent again.

PART
III

THE
IMMORTAL
WOUND

CHAPTER ONE

The Coin Of Hadrian

IN FULL COMPANY they came riding across the flat headwater meadows of the infant Tamesis River and breasted the growing slope to the wide mouth of the wooded valley at the head of which lay the Villa of the Three Nymphs. It was a day of high summer, the blue sky cloudless. Early morning rain had lacquered the beech and ash trees and brought the valley stream into a foaming spate. At the head of the company rode Arturo on the White One, the mare's long mane and tail swirling in the strong breeze, her hocks mud-splashed, while at her side loped the great hound Anga.

Arturo held himself stiffly in the saddle to ease the slow-dying pain in his right side and to lessen the chafing of the tight bandages of coarse linen that bound his midriff. But for him the nag of the arrow wound meant little against the growing pride and joy which filled him at this time of triumphant return. Behind him rode Lancelo, carrying the wind-streamed red-and-white banner of the White Horse, and following them came the full company of companions, their red-and-white scarves and war helmet crests tossing and winging. Every man among them was straight-backed with pride and tight-lipped with deep pleasure at the thought of the long, hard weeks of the progress they had made down the Tamesis River to Londinium and then of the long return which had taken them, fighting and triumphant, through the lands of the Regnenses to give taunt and despite to the Saxon people of the southeast. Yet with the prospect of comfort and rest so near in this friendly territory there was no relaxing of their hard-taught discipline. The slow-moving baggage train was shielded by two ranks of protecting horsemen and along the rising valley sides flanking patrols threaded their mounts through the thinning trees.

Arturo himself, glancing skyward, seeing there for the first time a slow circling of hawks and kites, frowned as he watched them. The bite of sharp instinct born of grim campaigning suddenly roused him. He reined in and called a command to Lancelo.

A horn blew, the sharp notes whickering and echoing from side to side of the valley. The company halted and its flanking troops formed an *hérisson* about the baggage train. The outriding patrols on the valley sides changed formation and strung themselves in a wide protective bow across the front of the company.

At Arturo's side now, Lancelo, his eyes skyward, said, "When the carrion birds gather they come for feasting."

Arturo nodded. "Stay here. I go forward with Gelliga and his troop."

Lancelo raised the command horn to his lips and at its call the dark-bearded Gelliga with his second-in-command, giant-handed Borio, came riding up with their men.

With a glance at the far sky and its circling birds of prey Gelliga said, "Maybe the wolves have taken but a single cow somewhere and the carrion wait for the pickings."

Arturo said nothing. He put the White One to a trot and rode forward through the thinning wood, and the troop followed him. After a while they came out of the trees into the wide, sloping bowl of the valley which rose to the Villa of the Three Nymphs. He reined in his mount and raised a hand. The troop spread behind him in a half-moon and, as they did so, the feasting carrion birds rose in alarm from the slaughtered cattle and swine, whose carcasses littered the stock pens. A thin plume of smoke rose still from the smouldering ruin of a thatched cart shed. The dead thorn fences around the crop strips were gapped and the high-standing barley and bean vines lay trampled and flattened.

Tight-lipped, Arturo raised his eyes to the villa itself. The red-tiled roofs were gapped and the gaunt fire-blackened timber frames of eating hall and sleeping quarters still smouldered. Sword-sharp anxiety coursed through him. He had come riding back in triumph, waiting for the moment when, free of the forest, he would raise his eyes to the villa and see standing at the top of the wide steps that led down to its lower terrace the figure of his wife, Daria, who carried his child. As he would have kicked the White One into a gallop he was halted by the appearance of two horsemen who came round the eastern edge of the villa, picking their way over the rubble of the long eating hall, and began to ride down toward them.

Behind him Gelliga said, "They come in peace, my captain."

The two men rode down to them slowly. One was elderly and the other a young man. They carried their shields slung over their shoulders, their swords at their sides. They were war-capped, their tunics and gartered hose worn and marked with rough living, their hair long and lank over their shoulders.

Lancelo said, "They are Cymru men and they ride the cavalry crossbreeds of Ambrosius, but wear not the blue scarves of the Sabrina squadrons."

Arturo said nothing. The destruction he saw before him he knew could be at Ambrosius's orders. If harm or death had come to Daria, he swore to the gods that Ambrosius should pay the debt with his own blood.

The two men came down to them and now Arturo saw that the cloth of their belted tunics was crudely striped in greens, yellows and reds. The elder man—who was much the same age as Arturo's own father—wore a bronze torque about his neck, partly hidden by his unkempt beard. The young man at his side carried the other's features with a faithfulness that marked him as a son.

Reining in before them, the elder man raised a hand to touch his brow in friendly greeting. Then, smiling, he said, "Arturo, son of Baradoc of the tribe of the Enduring Crow, let my first words be of happiness. Your wife, Daria, is safe and well and awaits you at the villa.''

"May the gods be blessed for that. And you, too, if it is so because of your protection.''

The man smiled. "The gods, it seems, have fated me to bring happiness of this kind first to your father and now to you. You do not know me?''

Smiling now from the joy which was in him, Arturo said, "Aye, I know you now. My father has spoken often of you and of the time when you would have carried off my mother into slavery when you raided her uncle's villa in Aquae Sulis many years ago; but since you were of the Ocelos tribe, all of whom are distant kin to his own, he denied you the right since he claimed that my mother was already betrothed to him.''

"Aye, he tricked me to save her, not knowing that he spoke the truth then of their love. Yes, I am Cadrus of the Ocelos.'' He pulled aside the front of his tunic and showed, tattooed on the brown skin of his shoulder, the symbol of the goose with the golden feet. "And this is my son Anwyl who would take service with you. He brings with him my blessing and ten good men, mounted and armed, who wait in the woods beyond the villa. For myself I go back to my own lands beyond the Sabrina for I campaign no more with Count Ambrosius.''

"Whose work this was?'' Arturo waved a hand over the dead cattle, the stricken crops, the ruined villa.

Cadrus smiled. "You should have foreseen it. You are not only banned from all his lands and those of your own Prince Gerontius, the blood price on your head for any man's taking—but you have made of Ambrosius a figure of shame by drawing some of his best men from him. Aye, and now you have marched your warriors east to Londinium and south-about to taunt and fight the Saxons while Ambrosius has stayed close to Glevum and Corinium and seen his own men grow restless for action and loud with complaint. To ease their grumbles a little''—he half turned and held out a hand toward the ruined villa—"he sent troops of the Sabrina cavalry to destroy all you had created here and to take your wife captive. And would have taken her if we had not ridden ahead and saved her.''

"For which you have my thanks, yet may well suffer from the hands of your own king Vortigern, with whom he is leagued.''

Cadrus shook his head. "Vortigern is dead. There will be no more levies from his lands until Ambrosius or some other proves his worth—''

"And that man,'' Anwyl, despite his father's frown, broke in sharply, "is you, my lord Arturo. Men speak openly in the barracks of Corinium that now there is only one way to manliness and true action against the Saxon kind, and that with the companions of Arturo. And I . . .'' He stopped suddenly and looked at his father.

Cadrus smiled and with a cock of his head toward Arturo said, "My wolf cub has much to learn, not least that he steps out of place from overeagerness. But take him and his men and see them blooded. They are all of the Ocelos and will serve you well when you have schooled them.''

"I take them willingly. But now I would go to my wife wherever you have lodged her.''

Cadrus wheeled his horse about and pointed up the long valley slope. "She waits for you.''

Standing on the steps, the sound of falling water from the spring that filled the broad basin of the fountain of the three nymphs making quiet music for her ears, Daria waited for the coming of her husband. The eager breeze moulded the soft stuff of her blue woolen gown about her body and, against the constraint of the yellow band about her head, lifted and toyed with the fall of her ebony hair. One hand ran nervously with pleasure along the amber beads which strung her neck and the sun dully fired the bronze clasps which ringed the dusky skin of her arms. Gown, beads and armlets were all tokens of his love, all plunder spoil sent ahead of his coming, but none so dear or precious as the gift which she held now for him, that life which in the last few days had begun to move with increasing vigour beneath her heart, the child of his begetting.

Arturo reined in at the foot of the steps, and the horse tang of the White One came to her on the breeze as her eyes marked Arturo's bearded face. He had lost weight and his skin was dark and tight-stretched like the leather of a worn belt. Yet the shine in his eyes was the old shine and for a moment his lips showed pale and pink in the purse of a private smile for her. But she knew the pain and wound-stiffness in him as he dismounted, came to her and took her hand and kissed it, saying, "You wear my gifts."

"There is no gift greater than your safe return. So—you have moved against the Saxon kind at last. May the gods make you content enough to stay by my side until you are whole again."

"The wound is clean and heals fast."

"That I would see for myself."

She took him by the arm and led him across the courtyard, through the rubble and desolation, to her room in the south wing of the villa, the walls fire-scorched, the roof gapped and its beams roughly propped with new-cut timbers, and then out to the open portico. Here, untouched by fire, a great growth of yellow roses rambled up the pillars, surviving still from the days, long distant now, of the peace and prosperity of the villa. Close to the roses stood a table and two stools, the table bearing an earthenware jug of wine and drinking beakers.

Daria poured wine for him, but before she could pass the beaker, he put his arm around her and kissed her and the trembling in her body was matched by the shaking of his own hard frame.

Releasing her, Arturo said, "Now tell me that you and the boy are well."

Smiling against the certainty in him, she said. "The child and I are well, my lord. To know that it is a boy you must"—the tip of her tongue flicked teasingly between her full red lips—"as usual have had private word from the gods."

Soberly Arturo said, "It is a boy. In a dream the gods have promised it."

"Aie . . . those dreams of yours. Then there can be no doubt. Now drink and then strip. Your wound to me is of more account than anything else."

Arturo hesitated, then grinning and shrugging his shoulders, he began to strip to humour her, saying, "The arrow missed its true mark. It was loosed by my uncle Inbar, long cast out of the tribe for his villanies." Dropping his short cloak to the portico balustrade, Arturo reached within his shirt and pulled out the silver chalice which his Roman mother, Tia, had given him when he had left the tribe as a youth to go to Isca. As Daria took it, he said, "I bring a gift for our son-to-be. There is a story to it which I will tell you the day that he is born and I place it between his hands."

Daria smiled. "A story, no doubt, of gods and magic."

Running the back of his hand down the soft bloom of her cheek, Arturo grinned. "In truth, yes. But not one of my dreaming."

Daria turned the silver chalice in her hands. It was little larger than a drinking goblet with handles each side, curved and worked in the shape of rams' horns. One of the handles was badly bent and the bowl was marked with dents and had become tarnished from burial in the ground. Around the outside rim ran a continuous key pattern and on one side, in bold relief, was a large round boss in the shape of a circular wreath of bay leaves enclosing the outline of a human eye. The wish was suddenly strong in Daria that the child should be a boy. For that she would pray, but to her own God.

At the sight of the wound she was relieved to see that it had begun to heal cleanly. As she washed and fresh-salved it, Daria gave Arturo the news of Count Ambrosius which old Ansold had gleaned by secret visits to nearby Corinium. Ambrosius would have marched eastward at midsummer against the Saxons. But Prince Gerontius at Isca had sent only scant and poorly trained levies, and from the now dead Vortigern had come no levy but a straggling of small chiefs and independent young warriors. So Count Ambrosius had sat tight, too wise and cautious to mount a great campaign with a doubtful force.

Sipping his wine and listening, Arturo felt at once contempt and compassion for the man. Ambrosius dreamt still of the past glories of the Empire and was impatient to rid this country of Pict and Scot and Saxon kind and call himself emperor. He lacked no passion for that end, but the glory would be forever denied him. Caution inhabited the center of his heart like a frightened harvest mouse huddled in its grass nest high in the summer corn, scenting the coming of hunting marten or polecat. There was scorn in him at the pettiness of the man who, hearing of his own small progress with a handful of men, could give vent to it by raiding the villa and destroying crops and cattle. *Aie* . . . but already, he knew without arrogance, the gods looked elsewhere to place their favours. Men would come, and come quickly now as the noise of his name spread and the story of his long-spanned foray was told and retold and carried far and wide. And what bard or traveller was there who would not add his own wonder touches? Then let it be so. There was a power in the sword which showed only in the heat of battle. But there was a power in the word which worked without let and spread fast like bright morning over the land.

At his side Daria said, "Now you smile. But I doubt it is from the pleasure of returning."

He said affectionately, "Then you are wrong. I smile because the gods have been good to me in linking your life with mine. As lovers we lay in the uncurling bracken together and the high larks sang our happiness. As man and wife I have lain at your sleeping side and your soft breath has touched my cheek like a silk-winged moth. I smile because each day I have wakened beside you, the morning light borrowed brightness from your opening eyes. And I smile now because—"

"Because, my Arto," Daria interrupted him, "you have finished your wine and it fills your head with fancies." She leaned forward and kissed him on the brow, and went on, "My Lord, I am content to see you back. You will rest and recover, and that will be all my happiness."

The smile went from his face and slowly he shook his head

and then said flatly, "No, there is no rest for me, not for many a long year." With a gesture of his hand down the valley to the ruined crop strips and to the carrion birds that still fought and bickered over the dead cattle, he said angrily, "The gods arranged this welcome for us. You think it was to daunt me? No—it was to show me clearly their will. Tomorrow at sunset we ride for Corinium. No man, now, not even Count Ambrosius, can offer injury to Arturo and his companions without knowing that it will be returned in full measure . . . firebrand for firebrand, slaughter for slaughter."

Eye widening, Daria said, "You would move against Corinium, where Ambrosius numbers a hundred and more men for each one of yours?"

"Against Corinium, no. I have no quarrel with honest citizens and work folk. But against Ambrosius and the Sabrina cavalry which are camped outside it. Their food stores and their cattle shall know fire and slaughter. Their barracks and their eating halls shall be gutted and left roofless. And when all is done there will be those of the Sabrina squadron who will hide their smiles and their joy and will ride to join me."

Tight-lipped, Daria held back the protest within her. When the madness of the gods touched this man, her lover, husband, father of her child-to-be, she knew that there was no crossing his purpose. She lifted the wine jug and refilled his beaker.

When they had ridden out long weeks ago to make their progress down the Tamesis River into the Saxon lands they had numbered two troops of twenty-four horse each and a remount section of six horse—scarce sixty horses and fighting men. They had lost and won men and horses along the way and now mustered three troops of thirty horse and a remount troop of ten horse. The company of companions had grown and with it, too, had the baggage train and the number of men who manned it.

At sunset the next evening they paraded for their foray

against Count Ambrosius. Arturo took with him but two troops, and there was not a man among them who did not know the hard country ahead of them, and knew, too, the cavalry camp of the Sabrina wing at Corinium. The rest of the companions stayed to guard the villa camp with Anwyl, son of Cadrus, and his ten men. Cadrus himself went with Arturo, not claiming the honour as a return for the service he had rendered him, but pointing out that Corinium lay on his route to Glevum, where he must cross the Sabrina to reach his homelands.

Standing beside the courtyard steps, Daria watched them go. Arturo had given her his love and protection. But neither to her nor to any other woman, had she not come into his life, could he ever truly give himself. The gods had claimed him long before she had met him on the rain-swept western moors beyond the Tamarus River. Ambrosius dreamed of the past glories of the Empire and ached to clear this country of its foes and then take to himself the imperial purple. . . . The dream was void of reason for time could not be turned back. Only Arturo held the true dream: to clear this land of its invaders, to make it one country and to give its peoples peace and prosperity under the sign of the White Horse. The dream the gods gave him called for a son to follow him and to make fast the bright future for which he laboured now. With this she was content, but she knew she would be less than a woman truly in love not to have grieved in the dark stretches of night for that part of him which was forever beyond her understanding and cherishing.

Three nights later, as she lay on the furs of her couch while the quiet of the valley was broken now and then by the call of nightjar and owl, Arturo and his companions raided the cavalry camp which lay a little off the Glevum road to the north of Corinium.

They had waited in the thick woods some miles from the camp, the woods which had once sheltered Arturo and the now-dead horse trader Volpax in the days when they had made horse-stealing raids on the cavalry picket lines for mounts. They came down on it in the hour when sentries and guards yawn and rub their eyes and nod with sleep, when the fighting men off duty were filled with dreams or sunk in the lingering stupor of the past evening's wine and mead drinking, when the brazier fires of the picket watches along the horse lines burn low; and they came, spread wide across the heath- and meadowland in a great front of two lines of horse shaped like a crescent moon. They bore down on the camp, with no shout or war cry, with only the pounding beat of hooves drumming the hard ground in a rolling tattoo of endless growing thunder. They came, the extended double ranks of horses and warriors, sweeping from the north like the onward rush of a great tidal flood, and they overwhelmed the camp in a wave of destruction. But no companion killed unless to protect his own life. Arturo had given this order, for among his own men were many who had come to him from the Sabrina cavalry wing. They lit the heath-and-straw torches they carried from the picket fires and took flame to huts and brushwood stockades. They stampeded the picket lines, setting the hobbled and tethered Sabrina horses rearing and kicking and squealing with panic so that they broke free from their tethers to run or stumble or roll loose into the camp to add confusion to confusion. They fired corn sheds and stores and set ablaze the year's new hayricks and burst through the folding pens of sheep and cattle to send them stampeding into the night and the surrounding countryside from which—since town and country folk never hesitated to take the gifts the gods sent—less than a third of them were ever recovered. They swept round the great blue tent of the *praefectus* of the Sabrina wing, slashing the guy and straining ropes so that it collapsed like a stricken monster over the cavalry commander as he lay in his bed and trapped him there until long after the great crescent of Arturo's men and horse had wheeled at the far end of the camp and swept back and through the camp again as the fires of destruction now turned night to day. As they went the horns of the crescent curved more sharply inward and the charge took ahead of it all loose and stray mounts, herding them northward into the night as booty.

They left behind them firmly planted in the earth, so that it was the first thing the *praefectus* saw when he wormed his way out from under the loose tent cloth, a tall standard pole driven into the ground by Lancelo as he galloped by. From it in the freshening night breeze flew the banner of the White Horse, snow white and blood red, streaming in the wind. Tied to it was an old piece of vellum on which Arturo had written—in the Roman tongue as a touch of mockery to the imperial dreams of Ambrosius—this message:

> Arturo and his companions of the White Horse thank Count Ambrosius for the courtesy of his virtuous concern for the well-being of all those at the Villa of the Three Nymphs who do now humbly return it in somewhat fuller measure—Arturo, War Duke of Britain.

Later the following afternoon in the fortress at Glevum, which was Ambrosius's headquarters, the *praefectus* of the Sabrina wing stood stiff-faced before his commanding officer and watched him as he read the message. Ambrosius, wearing a red cloak over a well-polished cuirass, raised a hand and smoothed one of the greying wings of hair which tempered his growing baldness. After a moment or two he lifted his head. From the large, severely lined face a pair of narrow-lidded faded-blue eyes fixed the *praefectus* coldly. Then he said in a quiet, bitter-edged voice, "So, he calls himself Dux Bellorum. In jest or in earnest?"

"I know not, my lord."

"And maybe neither does he. But no matter. He has made a fool of you, a laughingstock of the Sabrina wing, and a mockery of me. More than that, wherever men sit and drink and gossip, wherever peddler or packman stops to beg crust or drink at farm or hovel, the story of this night's work will run and grow and grow and grow!" With each repetition of the word *grow* he thumped the table before him angrily with his fist, his face stiff with anger.

"Maybe, my lord. But he should not live long to enjoy the pleasure of it. I wait but your order to take my men to the villa."

Thumping his fist on the table, Ambrosius almost shouted, "You are a fool, Corbulo! By the time you get there he will be long gone. No, go back to Corinium and I wish you joy of the looks and laughter of the townsfolk—which you have well earned. Go!"

Without a word Praefectus Corbulo saluted and left the room to seek the ease of the large goblet of wine which he badly needed.

Alone in his room, Count Ambrosius picked up the tattered piece of vellum and read the message once more. Then slowly he began to smile to himself and shake his head. Dux Bellorum, he thought . . . and all the message in the Roman tongue. That at least was courtesy . . . by Mars, the man had spirit to match his courage and arrogance and he dreamt high. Well, that were no failing given the right schooling to go with it. What should he do? Smoke him out wherever he might now seek to lodge himself? Or let him run under whatever favour the gods might show him? And then use him? More and more men were beginning to be drawn to him. Did they sense that he had that divine afflatus, that magic which he himself had never known? Well, then, why not let him run until his power and his followers had grown and then cut him down and step into his place, grieve for his loss, honour him in death, and gather into his own command the army which he would have created? . . . Aye, even leave his men the white-horse banner under which to fight for him still, every man going into battle knowing that his ghost rode ahead of them, that his magic still armoured and protected them.

He reached forward and beat with his bare knuckles on the hanging gong which stood on the table. When the guard outside the room came he gave him an order. Then he rose and went to the window. Looking westward over the partly refurbished Glevum walls, he could see a great loop of the Sabrina River and beyond the rise of the wooded hills that rose and died in the mist haze of summer, a mist that hid the mountains of Cymru . . . mountains and valleys which were full of fighting men who could be drawn across the Sabrina by a leader with the magic and appeal of an Arturo.

He turned as the guard came to the door and announced

Decurio Aulus Venutius, the troop commander of Ambrosius's personal mounted bodyguard, a Roman of full blood still, although his family had been domiciled in Britain for eight generations, a proud young man who shared Ambrosius's imperial dreams and served him faithfully without questioning or seeking for the reasons behind any order given to him.

Ambrosius sat down while Venutius stood before him, a young man in his early thirties, sandy-haired, clean-shaven, a pink-and-white complexion which the sun never affected, something a little plump and boyish about his face still, the pale jade-coloured eyes frank and marking a seeming guilelessness which masked, as Ambrosius knew well, a ruthless devotion to him and his aspirations.

Gently Ambrosius said, "You know my faith in you?"

"Yes, my commander."

"Three nights from now you will desert from your command here in Glevum. You will take your horse and arms and ride south and find Arturo of the White Horse. You will join him as so many of the Sabrina cavalry wing have done. You will give him faithful and loyal service. Aye, if it comes to it you will die at his side in battle as any of his other companions would do. You will love and honour and obey him in all things."

"Yes, my commander."

"All this you will do—until one comes to give you my wishes." Ambrosius leant back a little in his seat and felt beneath his toga for the belt which he wore around his under tunic. His hand came free from the belt pouch and he tossed onto the table between them a coin. It lay on the boards, shining dully in the sunlight which came through the window. "Whoever comes will bring the coin with them so that you will know he comes from me. You will do whatever is ordered. And think not that my messenger will come only once. Time will show how long my need for an ally in Arturo's camp will last. But when that time is past you will come back to stand first at my right hand."

"Yes, my commander."

"Good. Take up the coin now and look at it for I would have you know it well."

Venutius reached out and picked up the coin. He knew it already, though not in detail, for when Count Ambrosius was in council he often absently took it from his belt pouch and toyed with it as though the play of his fingers over it aided his thoughts and decisions. It was an aureus of the Emperor Hadrian, a gold coin much worn. Still clear on one side was the head of the great Emperor and on the other a seated goddess figure wearing a Phrygian cap and holding in her left hand an upright spear with the words *Roma Aeterna* encircling her, and the rim was marred in one place by a deep nick in the soft metal.

Venutius handed the coin back and said quietly, "I shall remember it and wait for it, my commander."

Ambrosius took the coin and, fingering it in thought for a moment, suddenly smiled, and said, "Then go and become a good companion."

"Yes, my commander."

Decurio Aulus Venutius saluted and left, and Ambrosius sat slowly fingering the gold coin of Hadrian and said quietly to himself, "Rome Eternal . . . Rome Eternal. . . ."

CHAPTER TWO

The Camp Above The Cam

FOUR DAYS AFTER the raid on the Sabrina cavalry camp they left the Villa of the Three Nymphs. They took with them the few cattle which had escaped slaughter and the small supply of food and grain which was left to them. The ruined crops, so near to the point of harvest, meant that they faced a lean winter. They loaded the wheeled carts and the few pack animals with the most vital and precious of their household and war gear. What they could not carry they left to the settlers and the people of the district who had befriended them. Arturo rode ahead with Durstan, and Gelliga was left in command of the progress of the slow baggage train and the full complement of cavalry troops. Daria pressed to be allowed to ride ahead with Arturo but he forbade it. She was near five months gone with child and rode a quiet pony. When she tired of that, she was carried on one of the baggage carts and always close to her hand were her brother, Lancelo, and her father, Ansold.

They went south over the Tamesis River and then across the country of the headwaters of the Abona River, which flowed through Aquae Sulis and finally found the sea at the mouth of the Sabrina estuary. As he rode, Durstan smiled to himself for they were now retracing almost exactly the path he and Arturo had taken in the days when they had escaped from Isca Dumnoniorum after being outlawed by Gerontius.

He said now, "This place you have chosen will bring you no favour with Gerontius, nor that of King Melwas of the Summerlands, in whose country it lies."

"We shall see. But since—no matter how remote it is at the moment—they both fear the threat of any Saxon approach from the east they will take some comfort from knowing that we stand first in their path.''

''It will be many a long day before the Saxons thrust so far west.''

Arturo smiled. ''Long days become long years. But well within our lifetime you will see it. The gods will favour them to give us the trial of proving our manhood and right to hold what is our own.''

''The gods have told you this?''

Unexpectedly Arturo grinned. ''They had no need. Hengist and the other Saxon leaders might now be content to sit and hold what they have south and east of Londinium and northward along the Saxon shores—but each spring more of their countrymen arrive in their long keels. And they are land- and plunder-hungry men. A bucket can only hold so much water. The Saxon bucket is almost full and must soon overspill.''

''This place we go to has already been marked by Gerontius. Your own father works on it still?''

Arturo shook his head. ''The work was hampered by Melwas. He wants no fortifications overlooking his country.''

''What greeting then can you expect from him?''

Arturo shrugged his shoulders. ''All those who stand against me—even in good conscience—must know that the gods are with us. All that is needed is courage and patience.''

Durstan said no more. There was no man in the company of the companions now who would say or argue more once Arturo said that the gods were with him. The gods of his country had Durstan's reverence but he sometimes wondered . . . aye, occasionally felt sure . . . that the will of Arturo was more often than not remote from any dictation of the gods. Arturo lived in a dream of his own creation, the great dream of a Britain freed from the faintest taint of Saxon intrusion. But, by the gods, one had to admit that once set on course there was no stopping him.

Late in the afternoon of the fourth day of their travel they came to the borders of the Summerlands held by King Melwas. Here the country was gentler. For the most part men worked their plots in peace, game was plentiful and when the gods gave good harvest only the improvident had to pull the drawstrings of their trewtops tight in winter to still their bellies' grumbles. Long before sunset they reached the edge of the smooth downland and, following it, saw slowly rise from the green country ahead a great hill which stood on its own in a sweeping bight of the downs. A long loop of a river called the Cam curved around the foot of its westward flanks to run away to the north through the heart of the Summerlands on its way to the Sabrina Sea. They rode up the mount, following a track from the northeast, through the thin skirting of trees around its base. Finally they came out on to the great ridge-backed plateau of its crest, the whole of whose perimeter was enclosed by a triple line of ancient earthworks and ramparts long neglected and falling into ruin.

On the top of the plateau ridge, where stood the remains of a Roman shrine to the god Mars, raised there to mark the conquest of the hill fort by the westward thrust of the legions when they had first come to the country over five hundred years before, Arturo and Durstan sat their horses, slacking their reins so that the mounts lowered their heads and grazed the sweet grass. To the northwest lay the Summerlands, the country of King Melwas. In the still lucid light of early evening they could pick out the green slopes of Ynys-witrin, the glass isle, at whose foot Melwas had his summer quarters for he delighted in the abundance of game and fish which filled the rivers, streams and meres and the wide spread of marshlands. And far beyond the glass isle, backed by the sun sparkle on the waters of the sea, there stood up, too, the great knoll of the raven god Bran.

That night, as Durstan slept rolled in his heavy cloak, Arturo kept watch with Anga at his side, and he was full of content. This hill above the river Cam would serve all his wants. The plateau top was large enough to house more men and horses than he would have under his command for a long time to come. There was room, too, for the growing of crops and the building of shelters, for which there was plenty of timber to be cut from the steeply wooded western side of the hill. For water there were two spring-fed wells, one within the perimeter and the other a little way down the slope on the northwest side. As he sat there listening to the call of a little owl from the wooded slope and the steady cropping sound of the hobbled horses as they grazed in the warm night, he knew that the coming winter would be hard, and made harder if he found turned against him the anger of Prince Gerontius and King Melwas. They could harry and plague him at a time when the real hardships up here would be hunger and the fast need for warm quarters. There was nothing he could do to appease Gerontius, but the Prince would never move against him into King Melwas's lands unless Melwas gave leave. The first thing he had to do was to make some sort of peace with the King—and a man who came suing for peace, no matter for how short a period, must bear gifts and the promise of more. The main body of the companions would not arrive for at least another three days. The peace must be made before they arrived. To ride with only Durstan as companion to King Melwas was to offer the man the chance of treachery. Chewing on a sweet grass stalk, he considered the wisdom of this move. As he pondered this the sky to the northwest was suddenly and fiercely afire with the burning streamer of a falling star which curved earthward and finally burned itself away high over the twin summits of Ynys-witrin. He knew that the gods had spoken.

They rode into Ynys-witrin the next morning over the long causeway which spanned the marshes at its foot, and were halted by the guard at the stockade which blocked the entrance to the small settlement. Arturo asked for an audience with King Melwas. A messenger was sent to the King and after a long delay—deliberately prolonged, Arturo was sure, to stamp upon them his authority and power—they were conducted through the settlement to the edge of a wide mere on whose bank had been built of withy poles and rush thatch a long hall which Melwas used as his hunting lodge. Children played and frolicked about the water's edge and a guard of long-haired, half-naked marsh warriors armed with swords and spears formed a half-circle about a rough wooden table outside the hall. Here Melwas sat, bareheaded, the sun firing the red tints in his fair hair, wearing a short cloak of otter skins across his shoulders, his chest, tanned brown, bare to the top of his trews. The man wore no finery, and carried no mark of kingship: a man who had twice Arturo's age, a man powerfully built with a large, pockmarked face, whose eyes were hidden as he bent over a fishing net spread on the table and his fingers worked skillfully with waxed thread, repairing a hole in it.

Arturo and Durstan dismounted, and Arturo, standing at the head of the White One, dropped a hand and touched Anga's head as the hound, sensing some stress in the air, began to growl low and deep in its throat. The growling stopped at Arturo's touch and Melwas raised his head to show grey-green eyes, the skin about them deeply creased from years of sun glare on the waters and marshes of the Summerlands.

Unexpectedly Melwas smiled and said, "So at last I meet Arturo of the White Horse, son of Baradoc, outlaw of Prince Gerontius, thorn in the side of Count Ambrosius and"—his tongue flicked between his lips like a lapping cat's—"the scourge of the eastern long-keel men. All these to so many. And what are you to me?"

"One who comes in friendship and asks for sanctuary on the hill above the Cam until such time as I can turn against the Saxons again."

"And if I refuse and hold you now to send to Prince Gerontius?"

Arturo smiled. "Would I have come, King Melwas, had that thought held truth in my mind?"

"But it may be the truth in my mind."

Arturo shook his head. "Last night the gods spoke to me and gave sign that I should come to you. So I am here and make you the gifts of friendship." Arturo stepped forward, ignoring the tensing of the Melwas warriors who stood around, and drew from within his surcoat a cloth bundle which he put on the table before King Melwas. He unwrapped it to display the gifts he had brought, all of it plunder taken from the Saxons: an old Roman gold chain, two bronze armbands with their bosses intricately worked in enamels that flashed with kingfisher brilliance, a silver ring fashioned in the form of a snake, and, last of all, a small bronze wine flagon whose handle was shaped in the form of a hunting dog which stalked a pair of finely modelled ducks which adorned the spout. It was no surprise to Arturo when Melwas picked up the flagon first and ran his fingers over the moulding.

Melwas looked up at Arturo and his eyes were suddenly shrewd beneath their bushy, sandy brows. "Fine gifts . . . aye. Well, then, you shall have my leave to stay on the hill if you add to them one other." He glanced from Arturo to Anga, who sat on his haunches at his side, and went on, "Two days ago I lost my best hound to a boar. Give your hound the word to come to me and serve me and, even though Gerontius and Ambrosius give me commands and threats to deny you winter sanctuary, I will defy them. *Aie* . . . give me the hound and you can take back these other gifts."

For a moment or two Arturo said nothing. The noisy, happy cries of the children bathing and playing by the mere filled the air. A heron flapped low and clumsily across the water and at his side Anga snapped at a bluebottle which teased his muzzle. Then, slowly shaking his head, Arturo said, "There are three things which the gods deny any man the right to gift to another, a virtuous wife, a horse which was the first to carry him into battle, and a hound which would stay by his dead body till death for itself gave it release to follow him into the Shades. No, my lord—you ask too much."

Melwas was silent for a while and then, with a shrug of his shoulders, said indifferently, "Then my young warrior, Arturo, it seems that the gods have betrayed you and have sent you here to rid themselves of you." He raised his right hand and pointed his forefinger at Arturo. With the movement, each of the men in the half-circle about him lifted his spear and held it poised ready to throw. Melwas went on, "They wait but one word from me."

Arturo dropped a hand so that it rested on Anga's head and he answered in a level voice, "There may come a day when the gods will desert me, King Melwas. But this is not the day. Give the word and you shall see the spears turned aside from me in full flight."

Melwas's lips tightened and his brows almost hooded his eyes as he faced Arturo's defiance; then suddenly he gave a great shout of laughter and smacked the table before him with his fist and cried, laughing, "Lower your hackles, you fighting cock! You think I would tempt the wrath of the gods by the death of one they love so much? But know this, for a hound such as yours I would trade any of my wives—though to be fair none of them are virtuous. The hill is yours and we will drink to it." He turned and shouted to his womenfolk who stood bunched about the doorway of the long hall to bring wine, and at this his bodyguard lowered their spears.

As they rode back to the hill fortress through the early afternoon Durstan said to Arturo, "The gods were truly with you."

Arturo nodded. "As they always are. But also a man has his own wits. No man of pride names the gift he wants. Melwas did but follow a humour to test me."

Durstan said no more. Still, it would be a story to tell the others when they arrived. Arturo and the Spears of Melwas. The spears that were thrown only to be miraculously turned aside in midair by the gods. . . . When the mead flowed, the stamp of feet and thumping of fists on the boards would set the wonder alive to spread through all the land.

Within the week the full company had arrived at the hill and every daylight hour was spent in establishing themselves there. Trees were felled to make living quarters, stables and cattle pens. Furrows were turned to make crop strips across the gentler slopes of the hilltop and the little of seed corn left was sown. They cut late hay and carted it from the free land to the south, and each day game was hunted along the downs and river valleys for fresh meat and also for salting against the winter. Deer, boar and small herds of escaped or abandoned kine, swine and sheep roamed in the woods and heaths.

There was a small settlement of King Melwas's people nearby and Arturo gave strict orders that none of them was to be molested nor their goods or cattle taken. As the weeks passed traders and peddlers were to learn of the camp on the hill above the Cam and found that they could come and go freely to offer their wares. But even so, it was clear that the winter would bring lean times. If there were any doubts in Arturo's mind about the near starvation they would have to face as the months passed he showed none of it. The future was in the hands of the gods. And already the gods were on their side for warriors hearing of the camp began to drift to them and most of them came carrying a sack of grain or roots across their horses' backs. But of all the men who gathered to him Arturo was most content with the first to ride up the hill. This was Decurio Aulus Venutius, the commander of Ambrosius's personal mounted bodyguard.

He was escorted to Arturo by Gelliga, who still could hardly believe that such a high-ranking Sabrina officer should choose to join them. Arturo was sitting on a rock outside the rough shelter which had quickly been made for himself and Daria. Daria, refusing to overcherish herself, was away with some of the other women, gathering hazelnuts from the hillslopes to be ground into flour for the winter.

When Gelliga had left them, taking Venutius's horse to be watered and fed in the lines, Arturo said, "And what brings Aulus Venutius to my side?"

The plumpish, fresh-complexioned face of the man creased into a smile. "Aulus Venutius grew tired of being barrack-bound and bodyguard to Count Ambrosius. I am a cavalryman and, like my horse, have grown stale and restless for the need of action."

"All I can give you here is a tight-belted winter."

Venutius shrugged his shoulders. "After the winter comes the spring."

"No matter your rank in Glevum you will serve here as a trooper."

"That will be no hardship. There are many here who have known me as such. Although I am of full Roman blood this is my country and my family have served it faithfully for many generations."

"So be it. Now go to Gelliga and he will assign you to a troop and your duties."

That night, as Arturo lay by Daria's side in the darkness,

she said, "Your Venutius gives up a great deal to come here. Ambrosius could have sent him."

"All things are possible. But had I been Ambrosius I would have sent someone of lesser rank and importance."

"Maybe that is how Ambrosius has reasoned."

"Then I will keep that in my mind, too."

Smiling to herself, Daria went on, "Maybe the gods will give you a sign to prove him faithful."

Arturo laughed gently. "If he comes to kill me—and what else could Ambrosius wish?—then he shall have his chance, and soon."

Four days later on a day of great heat, as though summer were making a last gesture in defiance of the onthrust of autumn, Arturo rode down from the hill to the river Cam with a party of men to set osier traps in the river to take the eels which with the coming of autumn were now beginning to run seaward. He took with him Venutius. When he had seen the men set to their work Arturo rode up the river to a spot where it broadened into a wide pool, its far side thickly matted with tall mace reeds and beyond them a tangled scrub growth of willows and thorns.

Pulling up the White One, Arturo nodded at the pool and said to Venutius, "It is too long since I had a proper washing." He dismounted and began to strip free his clothes. "Keep guard on me."

Naked he dived into the pool and swam for a while. Then he came back to stand below the bank, where he began to scrub himself with handfuls of sand and small gravel as he had used to do in the moor streams of his own tribelands. Above him Venutius sat his horse, sword hanging from his belt and his long cavalry lance held upright, and said, "In Glevum the Roman baths are still in use, for as far as he can Count Ambrosius keeps all the old observances."

Arturo laughed as he stepped naked out of the water and began to dry himself on his undershirt. "He puts the cart before the horse. First there must be fighting to bring peace—then with peace a man has a just need for comforts." As he spoke—naked and defenseless, an easy mark for the swift dipping and thrust of Venutius's lance, a quick heart blow and then an easy escape for the man—he heard Anga snap at a worrying fly and his eyes held his companion's.

Green and guileless were Venutius's eyes as they watched Arturo and he said, "The wound in your side, my lord, has healed clean. Is it true it came from your uncle Inbar?"

"It is. He was a man of many parts, courage and craft and greed. The gods twisted his nature at birth." He turned away from Venutius and bent to recover his clothes, knowing that he was fair mark for a swift downward thrust of the lance to spit him through the heart if the nature of this man, too, had been twisted at birth. But no thrust came.

As they rode away and began to breast the rising ground to return to the camp, Durstan, bow in hand, the arrow still strung in it ready for use, stepped free of the scrub on the far side of the pool and watched them. His brow was beaded with sweat but not from the heat of the day. One muscle movement of Venutius's lance arm and the arrow would have been winging toward him. . . . *Aie,* but even so, the risk had been great.

That night as they lay together Arturo told Daria of the testing of Venutius, and she said, "And you mean to try him no further?"

"No. To do so would be to doubt the gods."

A month later, when the first of the fierce autumn gales blew hard to set the browning tree leaves spinning and flighting through the air and the first prick of green from the winter corn began to stipple the worked soil of the crop strips, a party of peddlers and traders came into the camp to barter their salt and seed and cloths and their leather hides and rough pottery wares for the few young foals already dropped by the mares of the cavalry mounts. Venutius, who had been made horse master, was wrapping a dressing of strong herbs over a festering cut in the near forehock of a stallion. As he squatted at his task he heard someone come up behind him and, glancing over his shoulder, saw one of the peddlers. The peddler stood watching him until he had finished his work and then said, "The bellies of horses and companions will be full of loud grumblings before this winter is out."

Venutius grinned. "Maybe, but the remedy is tight belts,

tight girth and a patient notching away of the days to spring.''

Looking down the picket line of horses, the peddler, who was middle-aged, thick-bearded and warmly clad in a heavy woolen surcoat over strong leather trews, said, ''It is known that you have more mounts than men. Sell me one of your spare mounts and I will pay well.''

''We part with nothing but the foals.''

The peddler said, ''I can pay you in coin which will buy you corn and fodder to keep a dozen horses from dying through winter lack.''

He reached into the wallet of his surcoat belt and flicked a coin through the air for Venutius to catch. Looking down at it, Venutius's face stiffened as he saw the sun glitter rise from the golden face of the aureus of the Emperor Hadrian, one edge of which was deeply nicked. Then, without a word, he tossed it back to the peddler. A horse whinnied high, and there was a sudden bright burst of laughter from a handful of the few women who still stayed with their men in the camp. He said sharply, ''Speak that which you have come to speak!''

The peddler said, ''The lady Daria carries the child of Arturo. If it is true the gods favour him, then it will be a boy.''

''Boy or girl, what matters it to Count Ambrosius which she drops?''

''I am not in his counsels. But his mind is not difficult to read sometimes.'' He waved his hand around the hilltop. ''This is the beginning. Come spring Arturo will move again and more men will come to him and suddenly a handful of deserters becomes an army. Armies have leaders, and given enough victories the leaders become kings. Kings have sons so their deaths solve no problems when a line of inheritance is secure. When Arturo dies then our noble Count would have none alive with right to claim his place.''

''Then why not have Arturo killed now—before there is any army to win victories?''

The peddler shook his head. ''Even a simple man like me can read that riddle to its end. Count Ambrosius knows that none of the tribes and their leaders will fully rally to him. His military caution offers them no glories, no plunder—only drills and, for the most part, the irksome rub of camp life. But, if he lets Arturo run until all this country knows his name and the bards sing the renown of his victories, then there is a rich tree in full bearing to be cut down for the ripe harvest of its fruit. He will mourn Arturo and praise him—and then take his place for there will be no son to follow him. Believe me—Count Ambrosius will let no woman, be she wife or concubine, come to full term with any child seeded by him."

He felt again in his wallet and pulled out a small alabaster amphora no larger than a pigeon's egg, its top thickly sealed, and handed it to Venutius. "When the right moment comes—which must be soon for the lady Daria is near seven months gone—see that the liquid it holds goes into her wine or water beaker. It has neither taste nor true colour."

"To kill the child but not the mother?"

The peddler said shortly, "Why kill the foal and leave the mare to be served again? Both will die, but slowly so that it will have the look of nature."

Venutius was silent, his lips tight. At any time he might have been ordered to assassinate Arturo and save himself as best he could. A sharp coil of disgust tightened his guts at the thought of becoming poisoner of a mother and child.

He said, "And, this being done, I still stay at Arturo's side?"

The peddler said, "You would leave when she is dead and so sharpen all men's minds to the truth? No, Venutius, you are bound to Arturo for many a long year."

He raised a hand in parting and moved away into the heart of the crowded camp to join the other traders. Venutius slipped the amphora into his tunic breast. He was a man whom the Fates had fingered. He prayed then that in the turbulent times ahead he might find honourable and gallant death in battle and so never know the shame of seeing the aureus of the Emperor Hadrian again.

Two weeks later he poured the liquid from the amphora into Daria's drink. The ease with which he was able to do it might have been arranged by the dark gods. It was a night when he was guard commander, a night of sharp frost and a cloudless sky which blazed with bright stars. As he made his rounds in the late evening, he could hear the singing of some of the companions in the open hall which lay beyond the ridge of the plateau. He knew and loved them all now, troopers and troop commanders, hard men, many of whom, since there were too few shelters to roof them all, wrapped themselves in their cloaks and slept in the open or huddled close-packed under skin-covered lean-tos.

As he crossed the far neck of the plateau, from high above him came the distant calling of geese and he looked up and saw a wedge-shaped skein of flying birds against the great stippling of stars. He moved on and spoke briefly to the guard who kept watch at the foot of the small rocky rise on which Arturo's quarters had been built.

The guard, a stocky tribesman, bowlegged from riding almost before he could walk, was from the country of the Ordovices, far south of Segontium. Looking up at the geese, he said, "By morning they could be harbouring on the flats of the Tisobis River, where I have taken many of them with bow and arrow as they cropped the eelgrass."

Venutius smiled. "You would you were there now?"

"Not for my sake." He grinned and leant on his lance. "But for my wife's, yes. A woman needs a man to keep her warm at nights. Cold nights try a woman's virtue hard."

Venutius laughed and moved on. As he came to the front of Arturo's hut a figure, heavily cloaked, moved out of the doorway and he recognized the lady Daria.

He saluted her and said, "You should be warmly asleep, my lady."

Daria smiled and said, "So I should good Venutius, except for two things. There is too much noise from the men's hall and I have a raging thirst from the salt meat at table this night." Her hand lifted to show him a bronze beaker. "I go to the spring."

Venutius reached out for the beaker and said, "You stay here, my lady. This is no time for you to be scrambling down the path."

Without waiting for a reply, not wanting to see the star-shine in her dark eyes, he turned away. As he stood at the thin overflow from the small well he pulled out his breast pouch and took from it the amphora. With his knife he cut off the wax stopper and then pierced the tough goatskin cover of the amphora's mouth. He filled the beaker and then poured the liquid from the amphora into it. He turned back to the hut and Daria took the beaker from him and drank. She paused with the beaker half empty, gave a little sigh of contentment, and said, "You come from Glevum, don't you?"

"I do, my lady."

She gave a soft chuckle. "Once Arturo said to me that one day he would ride into Glevum in triumph and I should ride beside him on a white mare, wearing a cloak of scarlet with a lining of blue silk and about my waist a golden belt with a clasp of two singing birds, and that Count Ambrosius should come out to greet us and hand me a silver goblet full of new wine." She raised the beaker and drank, finishing the water, and then went on, "You warriors throw your promises about as lightly as you venture your lives."

Venutius shook his head. "My lord Arturo breaks a given promise to no one."

Venutius finished his round of the camp sentries and then went back in the shelter of the little lean-to of hazel poles. He put the amphora between two cloths and with the heavy pummel of his sword smashed it into chips which he flung out into the night.

That night as Arturo lay at Daria's side and her breath warmed the side of his face, she took his hand and placed it below her breasts and said, "Feel, the child moves." Underneath his hand he felt the faint kick of his son. Aye . . . son it had to be for certain. Placing her hand over his, Daria went on, teasingly, "It will be another mouth to feed this winter but there shall be no lack for the babe for already I begin to grow as well stored as the finest milch cow."

"But lack there will be for all others, you think?"

"There must be. We are here without full corn bins or pits well stored with smoked fish or meat. The time will come and—" her voice changed to a serious note, "I say this, my lord, because you will not say it to yourself—when horses will be put to the slaughter and men, before they will starve,

will leave you for their homelands or to forage for themselves."

Arturo stirred angrily and said, "None shall starve and
none shall so leave. We have come here under the gods who
turned aside the spears of Melwas to name this our sanctuary.
Tight belts we shall have, but for the rest the gods will
provide."

Daria said no more, but she smiled in the darkness to
herself. The gods had spoken. His faith suddenly warmed her
with a sweet flush of love so that she slid her hand about his
neck and pressed her lips to his and made silent prayer to her
own God that out of His charity the child she carried should
be a son.

Two weeks later, when the sun rose to show the hilltop
covered with a thin fall of early snow, Daria woke to find her
body heavy with a lassitude which with the passing of the
days was to grow to a weakness that finally held her to her
couch and slowly began to waste her body. Within a month
she was dead, passing away with her hand in Arturo's as the
first owl call of night echoed through the wood on the western
slope of the hill. They cut a deep grave for her in a dell of the
hillside, bowered by young beeches which still held their
brown leaves against the winter gales. Pasco the priest spoke
the burial rites of her own religion and old Ansold, her father,
and Lancelo, her brother, filled the grave, and after them the
companions piled stones and rocks to a cairn over her whiile
all the time Arturo stood by with his face graven and speaking
no word. When all was done Arturo turned and took the reins
of the White One. He mounted and rode slowly away down
the hill, followed by Anga. None doubted that he would
return, and a few like Pasco and old Ansold and some of the
older companions moved with him in spirit for they knew that
with the death of true love a man must move for a while into
the wilderness and seek solitude before he can return to the
world and live again.

CHAPTER THREE

The Return To Isca

IT WAS FIVE DAYS before Arturo returned. He came back leaner and with his beard grown matted and shaggy and with a
hard, tempered look in his blue eyes which he was never to
lose even when making merry with his companions, a look
which, when he wished, could throw an icy veil between him
and all others and make all men choose their words with care.
Only when he laughed and played with children or spoke to
the camp women did the look become remote. He began to
organize the camp for the winter ahead with a grim and
inflexible ordering of life on the hill which none questioned.
The daily mess issues were cut to a point where no porridge
bowl was left until licked clean and no bone tossed to a hound
until it had been picked bare and the marrow sucked from it.
The dogs foraged for themselves and as the game around the
hill grew scarcer so dogs and men foraged wider afield, the
hunting parties often being away for days on end.

Every night before Arturo went to his bed he would walk
with Anga to the small dell which held Daria's grave. There
was no inner rebellion in him against the bereavement which
had been placed on him. He understood it and accepted it.
The gods had schooled him with this loss lest he should forget
that he and all those he loved and cherished were mortal.

By the turn of the year the camp was a place of lean men,
lean women and lean children and of rib-straked horses.
Prayers and hopes for a mild winter went unfilled for the
snows came early and stayed and the nights were either clear
with iron frost or wild with the blanketing and drifting of

snow. In the mornings crows and owls could be found dead and frozen stiff to their perches and the river Cam was quietened by a covering of thick ice. These were mornings when men, women and children found it no shame to gather the fresh dung in the horse lines and, wrapping it in old cloths, hug it under their clothes to their bare bellies to give them heat and the false relief of food-warmth in their guts. Men and women in the sharp agony of cold and hunger called on their gods and goddesses for help, to Bellenus and Dagda and Lug, the fair-haired one, to Nodons of the silver hand, to Taurus the bull, Epona the horse, to Artio the bear, to Cernunnos the stag and to Dis, the god of the underworld, from whom all mankind had descended. For the followers of Christos, prayers were made to Him and His Father. And Pasco, the priest of the divided heart and faith, called on them all for he knew that all were one and the same God.

In the middle of the first month of the new year when, in a night sky of pale ice-blue, the moon was passing to full and Orion's great belt hung high near the meridian, Lancelo came to Arturo's hut, where he sat outside, cloak-wrapped, before retiring.

Lancelo, who, next to Durstan, could speak most informally to Arturo, said, "I have just made the round of the sentry posts. Cuneda is dead. He was lying where he fell— struck through the heart by the cold."

For a while Arturo said nothing. Cuneda had been one of the companions who had joined him at Pontes when he had been making his great progress to Londinium. Just as the winter's killing frost could rive the stoutest oak so had sturdy Cuneda been riven. That there would be others he had no doubt.

He said, "Bury him in the beech dell."

"The ground is iron and will not yield."

"Take iron to iron. The gods have his spirit. The wolves and foxes shall not feast on his proud heart or bones."

"It shall be so, my lord." Lancelo was silent for a time and then went on, "No man living can remember a winter like this. A man on his own or with wife and child would fare better in his homeland or tribal town."

"Have any asked to leave?"

"No, my lord. They would die first. But if you gave the word . . ."

Arturo, stern-faced, said, "The gods are with us and in the time of our greatest want they will provide. No battle is lost until the standard falls. When the moment of cruellest pinch-belly comes you will see . . . the gods will send us a winter harvest. But any who wishes is free to leave."

Going back to the companions, Lancelo said to them wryly, "Without leave from you I have spoken to Arturo about our state here. He says two things. Any who asks is free to leave and seek warmth and food elsewhere. Against this the gods have told him that at our moment of greatest need they will turn winter want to summer bounty. The trees shall fruit, the corn shall grow and ripen overnight, the wild duck shall fly in and lay their eggs for us and then submit to killing and roasting. The gentle does shall climb the hill to be slaughtered and the red hares lollop to our cooking places and wait their turn to take the pot—"

Durstan gave a great roar of laughter. "My mouth waters. And who would miss such a time? Have I not seen the spears of Melwas turned aside? Why then miss the sight of the sky clouded wth quail and pigeon falling ready-plucked and drawn to the waiting cauldrons?"

When the laughter died Lancelo said soberly, "Who would ask to leave?"

Speaking for all of them, black-bearded Gelliga said firmly, "There is no leaving for any of us except by the hard road already taken by Cuneda."

The next morning they took mattock, pick and spade and before the early sunset reddened the sky above distant Ynys-witrin they buried Cuneda alongside Daria and raised a cairn of ice-coated rocks above him; and Pasco, who knew him for a Christos man, commended his soul to the mercy of God.

Within the next three weeks a woman died in childbirth, and another companion, wrapped in wolfskins and huddled deep in a bed of bracken under his lean-to shelter, died in his sleep. That same night, a roving lone wolf broke into camp and attacked the horse lines and, before it was killed by a spear thrust from Venutius, so badly mauled a bay stallion that the beast had to be killed and so provided meat for the pot for a handful of days. When the last of the horsemeat was gone, the snows came again to lay a fresh mantle over the pocked and broken surface of the old snow and ice on the plateau top.

After the snow the days were clear and bright as though the sword-sharp sweep of the frosty air had forever purged the skies of all cloud. Hunger and cold each day took toll of some living thing on the hill, a hound, a child, a woman, a camp servant and, twice, a companion. Although Arturo by word and manner held them firm and denied the death of hope and confidence, he hid his growing heaviness of spirit until it could be borne no longer. There was no trial the gods could put on him which he would not accept. But the death and misery of others now defeated him.

He called Durstan and Lancelo to him and said, ''Tell the others that I go away for two or three days. When I return it will be with plenty for all.''

After a moment or two of surprise from them both, Lancelo said, ''You journey where, my lord?''

Arturo answered, ''To seek the charity of the gods. They have tried us hard and, for my part, could try me harder. I take no shame in becoming supplicant to them for others.'' He smiled and there was a swift glint of his old teasing spirit in his eyes so that Durstan at least knew that what was to follow would be no truth. ''Last night I dreamt that the gentle goddess Coventina spoke to me and said, 'Since great things are destined for you and your pride grows stiff and ironbound I tell you for the sake of the others with you that the gods wait for you to become a humble beggar. Before they grant you a kingdom you must come begging for a crust.''

''You ride alone?'' asked Lancelo.

''Yes. I shall give the White One loose rein and the gods will govern her going.''

For a moment Durstan would have spoken. Always the nearest to Arturo, he could read him in a way hidden from all the others. There would be no loose rein, he knew, for Arturo would head for Ynys-witrin and ask for charity from Melwas and the answer of Melwas no man could predict. He kept his own counsel.

When the White One was saddled Arturo led her, slithering and slipping, down the steep hill path. With him went the now ancient Anga, gaunt-framed, and his coat staring with hunger roughness.

At the bottom of the hill Arturo mounted and gave the mare slack rein so that she moved toward the river. Soon the reins would come firmly into the command of his hands for indeed he knew no other place to go or other charity to seek than that of Melwas, and knew, too, that all the king's people would be on tight belly-strings for this winter had spared no one, and knew further that if the gods gave him any bounty there would never again be woman or child in any camp or army train of his. A man could gnaw the ice-cold ash bark in winter . . . *Aie,* and even take a handful of earth to his mouth and cud it for comfort, but women and children were gentler creatures. Light-headed a little from his own deprivation, he thought now that gentle Coventina had truly spoken to him in a dream for her heart had been moved where his had remained untouched. . . .

As they reached the Cam, he took the reins firmly and turned the mare's head downstream. All these troubles came from the sacking of the Villa of the Three Nymphs, where all could have lodged without lack this winter. One day Count Ambrosius should be given back in double score the misery and loss which he had heaped on the companions. . . . And so he rode on toward Ynys-witrin, knowing that he would get from Melwas not even a handful of oats enough to make a bowl of porridge. For this he could make no grudge against the King. A man must look after his own people when want held the land as hard and iron-fast as did the snow and frost.

For two hours Arturo travelled slowly, letting the White One pick her own gait. His eyes, narrowed against the blinding sun-glare on the snow-covered earth, now and then played him tricks, creating the vision of things long forgotten and of desires long now unfed. A willow tree seemed suddenly to be loaded with a crop of fat yellow plums. A hollow in the ground ahead was a coolness to the eyes with a rich spread of new spring grass, but as he rode down into it there was only the hard crunch of the frozen snowdrifts under the White One's hooves. He talked to himself and also talked as though there were others with him. The waters of the Cam were suddenly free of ice and he thought he saw a fish leap high in the ecstasy of a fast spring run from the sea, just as he had seen the salmon leap in the Tamesis River at Pontes on the day when Cuneda had joined him. But all the while there was a detached presence in him which understood all mirage and held firm to the burning truth of his real state. The gods, for their own purpose and his future greatness, were humiliating him. Arturo, the great one, the outlawed defier of Count Ambrosius and Prince Gerontius, going abegging to a fish-reeking marsh king. . . .

It was then, as he sat his saddle, head drooping as the head of the White One drooped, that he heard Anga growl. He looked up and another mirage danced before his eyes and he watched it, wondering at the power of the mind to create fantasy from the weakness of his body and the loss of his pride.

A man, heavily cloaked and cowled, was riding toward him on a sturdy moorland pony. His robe was belted and from his right side hung a leather-scabbarded sword. In the midst of his vision Arturo smiled weakly to himself, touched with the arbitrariness of the mirage which sent him a left-handed man. He lowered his head and shut out the hallucination, seeing only the White One's dipping head before him and hearing only now the slow bite of her hooves into the crisp snow crust.

Then clearly through the frost-purged air a man's voice said to him, "You would pass without greeting one who holds you most dear?"

Arturo raised his head as the White One came to a stop to see that the horse-and-rider mirage now blocked his path. The man drew back the loose edges of his cowl and Arturo knew then that the gods put further mockery on him. The other rider, lean-faced and his beard a rusty-tan colour, was a man well in his forties with eyes the colour of ripe hazelnuts, and he was smiling with his face full of welcome. Arturo knew him, though he had not seen him for more than a year, and he knew, too, that this other lived only in his fancy as had done the ripe plums and the sweet meadow grass.

He said, ''If you were true man and not my brain's fancy I would give you the warm greeting of a son. Aye . . . and even hold my hand out as though to feel yours in mine and be warmed by the blood which we both share.''

As he spoke he held out his hand and the other took it and said, ''I am Baradoc, and I am flesh and blood and your father.'' As their hands were clasped it was as though Arturo had been struck a sudden blow for, beyond all doubt of mirage or the mind's deceit, he knew his own flesh to be grasped by true flesh and blood.

In that moment of truth before the gods gave him release from their trial they abased him with a final chastisement. He swayed in his saddle, his hand slipping from his father's, to topple to the ground in a fit of oblivion, and as he lay there Anga stood over him growling, the soft skin of his mouth drawn back to bare the aging teeth and fangs. But when Baradoc dismounted and squatted on his hunkers alongside his son, he spoke gently to the hound and, slowly, the growling died in Anga's throat like the passing-away of distant thunder.

There were his father and two other men whose ponies were heavily pack-laden. He lay propped against the bole of a great oak close to the river. Above him the bare branches were hung with icicles. They would have built a fire and made a meat-and-barley soup for him, but he refused for he knew now, though nothing had been said as yet by his father, that the days and weeks of starvation were over, and there was nothing which could make him fill his belly until he saw his own companions and camp people succoured first. He accepted only a pull at the mouth of a mead-skin and the honey bite of it went through him like fire, a warmth that cleared his head and waked his weak body to the stir of new vigour. A little way from him the two men fed oats to the White One from an osier skep and Anga lay full-length, chewing at a piece of smoked deermeat.

Baradoc, squatting at his side, said. "You would have had nothing from King Melwas for he is not at Ynys-witrin. He has taken his people over the marshes to the hills where they live warm in the old lead workings but eat poor because the ice holds rivers and marshes hardbound and all the marsh fowl have gone south. If the gods sent you this way then it was to me. Half a day's march behind us comes a pony-and-sledgetrain with supplies for you from Isca."

"Why should Prince Gerontius give me, whom he outlawed, such charity?"

"He gives nothing. He is dead and now his son reigns, young Prince Geraint, and I am made Pendragon of all the tribes of the Dumnonian lands and stand at his right side."

"And, knowing of our wants, you begged for me?"

Baradoc laughed. "Damp the fire of your pride a little. I begged nothing. Prince Geraint remembers you and was ever trying to persuade his father to pardon you. Now that he is Prince he has given the pardon himself—though since his writ does not run with Count Ambrosius at Glevum you are still outlaw under his mandate."

"From Ambrosius I would accept nothing. Neither pardon nor provisions."

Baradoc shrugged his shoulders. "Time brings changes. But we live now and there is this winter lack on the camp hill which must be met. But Prince Geraint has more in his mind than present charity. He would meet and speak with you."

"To what end?" As he spoke Arturo was remembering Geraint. He could give him a handful of years and there were many times when he had schooled and drilled the cavalry horses of Prince Gerontius when the boy had first watched and then ridden with him, a quiet youth with a pleasant manner who spoke little but clearly thought much of matters beyond his years for he sought seldom the company of those of his own age. And now he was Prince of all Dumnonia though in years he could scarce yet be twenty.

"That rests with him. As Pendragon I am his counsellor

but I am far from knowing his true mind. The pony train that follows us comes from him out of his good bounty."

Arturo nodded. This news and the presence of his father already refreshed his body and spirit and he began to feel a new man. He took another pull through his cracked lips at the mead-skin and let its fire seep through him like a slow peat-burn. "How," he asked, "did Gerontius die?"

"He was trying a new mount that had been shipped from Gaul with others of its kind—an overmettlesome creature which threw him so that he struck his head on the ground. It seemed no more than a bruise a man would rub and forget but he was found dead on his couch the following morning."

Pulling himself upright slowly, Arturo said, "For all those who love horses, death is the distance between the saddle and the ground. May the gods keep him."

As he began to move toward the White One with the clear intent of mounting, Baradoc said, "You ask not of your mother and the rest of your kin?"

Arturo paused with his hands on the reins, ready to mount, and he smiled. "No harm can have touched them for the gods this day have done with trying me. But I take your scold with humility, and I ride now to take good news to my people on the hill of the Cam."

The baggage train arrived the next morning. There were twenty sturdy packhorses fully laden and two great sleds teamed by lank-shouldered, long-headed draft mules which Gerontius had bred from Gaulish imported he-asses on his moorland pony mares. The train brought food and stores in no great plenty but of a sufficiency to see the camp through the rest of the winter and early spring, no matter how hard the weather should stand. Within a week, starvation's marks began to pass from men, women and children and the horses and hounds, and where there had been little chatter and less laughter about the campfires there came a singing and a gossiping and shouting which filled Arturo's heart with lightness except when he paid his nightly visit to the beech dell. Of Daria's death he had no need to tell his father for the news had reached Isca by one of the camp-visiting peddlers and Baradoc, knowing the nature of true grief, said no more than a few words about her going and then talked no more of Daria.

Thin though the commons were they represented feasting to all. The hounds now had vigour to fight and quarrel and forage afield. Wet mash and oats began to put a new bloom on the horses. When Venutius walked the picket lines and pens at night and saw their eyes bright in the starlight and their breath pluming in the sharp air he knew a happiness which brought him for a time forgetfulness of Ambrosius and Glevum. Arturo and Baradoc spent much time together walking the old, broken and overgrown ramparts and defenses of the hill. Baradoc, during his travels, had made himself a master of forts and defenses and towers and knew from his own experience of them the art of making *ballistae*, which could throw a flight of arrows or flaming iron bolts coated with tarred tow to flare through the air farther than any spear could be thrown and knew, too, the setting-up of large catapults—the *onagri*, which the early Roman legions had used against Britain in the days of the great Queen Boudicca—that slung with ease large boulders to a distance far beyond any arrow flight.

Arturo knew that his father would have made this hill impregnable and many others like it to give a secure base from which the tribes and factions now holding the long spine length of this country could move forward to meet the Saxon's westward creep. But that dream could never flow as his father saw it. When the Saxons came in sufficient numbers they would flow around each fortress like the tide around a standing rock. The true answer, he sensed, though the vision was far from clear with him, lay elsewhere. But a well-protected winter base when none would move to fight he knew to be wise. Armies that gathered in spring, fought through the summer and then scattered, each man to his own holding and fireside during the winter, were no more than flocks of mad starlings who had lost all sense of due seasons. For himself he knew that the gods had sent him to this hill above the Cam. On this hill they had tried him and his people with the cruellest winter men could remember and, at the

point of despair and disaster, had redeemed him. This hill
was his and none should take it from him for already he began
to see the glimmerings of the way he would use it.

In the first week of the month of the Roman god Mars, the
great thaw came, as a robust and warm westerly wind blew
across the land. Every gully and rivulet ran high with water.
The ice sheets that had covered the Cam melted and broke
into floes which went racing downstream on a growing spate
which in two days reached high over the banks and flooded
the low-lying lands. All the country which had been a waste
of whiteness now delighted the eye with the sweeps of green
hillside and the lush growth of the first new grass. The
thickets, woods and skies which had been bereft of all creatures now stirred with their return to renewed life. A
stormcock sang with high melody each morning in the beech
dell. Robins and sparrows and jackdaws and crows came
back to the camp to forage for pickings about the cooking
fires, and middens and kestrels, sparrow hawks and high-
winging kites and buzzards and higher-pitched peregrines
took toll of the life below them or tore and gorged themselves
at the thawed carcasses of hind, hare, and boar which winter
starvation had claimed and the snow and ice had until now
held locked fast under their iron pall.

The rain lasted three days and when it passed Arturo and
Baradoc left the hill camp and set out for Isca. With him
Arturo took Marcos, whose dumb brother, Timo, had been
killed in the fighting of the previous year. Marcos now was
no servant but a fully trained and seasoned trooper. He left
Durstan in command of the camp.

Some days later at noon they rode into Isca. They came
along the old road westward from the Fosse Way, a road
which long ago had known the steady tramp of cohorts of
Roman auxiliaries beating out their twenty miles a day, their
raised standard going before them, gilded and wreathed with
their battle honours.

They rode through the town and up to the fortress over
which flew the great scarlet Dumnonia standard with a green
oak tree in its center. Arturo and Marcos were shown to their
quarters and Baradoc left them to go to the house of Master

Ricat, the Prince's horse master, with whom Arturo had always been a favourite, though this had never saved him thrashings as a youth for wild conduct.

Before Baradoc left he said to Arturo with a smiling twist to his mouth, "The Prince is young. Speak fairly to him. To be overbold will serve you nothing. So, keep well bridled"—he grinned openly—"the arrogance you draw from the gods. At the moment you have more need of him than he of you—and so it is with me. I would see your camp well fortified, and you need quickly more men and mounts than will come from other parts this spring." He paused for a moment or two and then said straightly, "Until now I have thought you a dreamer and a maker of your own myths— god-touched but in the way of men with disordered minds. Now I know better, and now is the time for you to lay the strong foundations of your desire which is also mine—to turn the Saxons back to the sea and heal this country of its long sickness."

Arturo said quietly, "Have no fear, my father. This winter the gods have schooled me well."

Later that afternoon Arturo was given audience by Prince Geraint. They spoke together in the large room where he had had his first meeting with Prince Gerontius when he had been a boy. Its floor was paved with black and red tiles. A long window flanked by wall niches looked out over the town and river, where the day was dying into the last red glow of sunset. A long couch held a tumbled cloak and a pile of papyrus reading rolls. An oak table held a great silver tray on which stood a glass flagon of wine and two drinking cups. At the head of this table sat the young Prince, dressed in a surcoat of finely cured doeskin over a white linen shirt, and red woollen trews whose bottoms were stained and still wet with mud from riding the water meadows.

He had his father's face and complexion, dark hair, and dark eyebrows that merged with one another over his high-bridged hawklike nose. But whereas the father's eyes had always seemed, under their heavy hoods, to be burgeoning with sleep or suspicion, Geraint's eyes were warm and frank.

Ignoring all formal greeting, the Prince put out a hand to warm it from the heat of a charcoal brazier which stood near his chair and said pleasantly, ''You remember me?''

Arturo nodded. ''Yes, my Prince. The last time I saw you, you sat in a meadow puddle, having been thrown there by a bay stallion that had far to go to be broken.''

''But in the end broken it was.'' He nodded to the bench by the table. ''Sit—when I want formality you shall know it—and pour wine for us.''

As Arturo did this, he said, ''The whole land has known a cruel winter. I give you the thanks of all mine and myself for your bounty, my Prince.''

Geraint smiled, shrugged his shoulders, and took the wine cup which Arturo passed him, saying, ''Without it you would have held place. The gods would have sent ravens with meat, and the corn would have pushed through the ice and snow to come to full ripening between dawn and dusk.'' He drank a little of the wine, and went on, smiling broadly, ''Tell me, is it true that the spears of Melwas were turned aside from you in full flight?''

Arturo laughed and said, ''Is there any warrior when the mead flows who does not sing his leader's deeds in bold words, forsaking truth for fancy? No, my Prince. The spears were stayed by the command of King Melwas.''

''There are times when men, weary of the hard truth, look only for miracles. This is such a time. So now, tell me what is in your mind. I have freed you from outlawry where my writ runs, but you have made an enemy of Count Ambrosius and with a handful of men have given Hengist's red beard a more than gentle tweak. Where do you go now?''

''Where the gods lead, my Prince.''

The Prince shook his head and a hint of a frown marked his face. ''Let us now leave the gods from this for a while. They will stay or give their favours. Tell me in plain words what you have in mind.''

Arturo's hand tightened a little around his wine cup. For all his father's warning he found it hard to take the Prince's reprimand. Although he could only give him a handful of years they held all the difference between unfleshed youth and scarred warrior. Then, aware of his own arrogance and the great service the Prince had done him this winter, he said quietly, "You shall have it plain, my Prince. I have dreamt a dream for this country and shall live in discontent until I have brought it to truth. . . ."

So, while Geraint sipped his wine now and then and listened patiently, Arturo spoke his mind and clothed his dream in simple words of good sense, and the Prince heard him through without interruption. He heard him, too, without irritation because Arturo held now to facts, suppressing all fancies or god-predicted certainties. But though this was so there came into Arturo's mind as he spoke of practical things—of levies of men and garrisoning over winter, of stores and the weapons of war, and the need for armourers and smiths and the careful selection of good mounts and foot soldiers—the one prime argument which might hold this young Prince Geraint and all others like him as allies, and that thought he knew came from the gods.

He finished: "This is a country now of great chiefs, princes and kings, many of whom, although they fear the Saxon threat, fear more the loss of their own high states. They give no full levies to Count Ambrosius because in their hearts they know that by giving him victory they would be raising him high above them in full sovereignty. And this is true, for Count Ambrosius—aging and waning as he is—sees himself as the coming Emperor and will never relinquish that dream."

"And your dream?"

"I am of no royal blood. With victory in my hands no one has cause to fear tyranny from me. In anger I not long since underscored a message to Count Ambrosius, calling myself Dux Bellorum. War duke of this country to give it freedom. When the victory is won and there is no more war then the title, like a morning mist under the rising summer sun, vanishes. I shall be content under my father or as chief myself to return to the people of the Enduring Crow to improve my lands and the lot of my people. You have been kind to me, my Prince. Be kinder. We are both of Dumnonia so it is fitting that you should be the first. And by your example in a few years others will follow.''

For a moment or two Geraint was silent, tapping his fingers against the side of his drinking cup. Then he smiled and said, "You will find this hard to believe, but not long since, I sat where you are and listened to my father speaking and he said much that you have said. More, too, he spoke of you and the things you have done this last year. Hearing you speak now, I know that he had read much that was in your mind. Had he lived he would have soon pardoned you and called you to him. That is why you have your pardon and are here now. If this thing is to be done and achieved by you, then it is right that the first to aid you should be the Prince of your own country. Prove yourself in the coming years and the others will follow.''

"Even Count Ambrosius?''

Prince Geraint stood up to show that the audience was over, and said with a sly smile, "Since the gods are so strongly on your side what need have you to overconcern yourself with him?''

That evening Arturo walked down to the house of Master Ricat, where his father was lodged. Here, to his surprise, for his father had not mentioned her, he found also his mother, Tia. She rose from a couch by the glowing brazier that warmed the room and embraced him. Then stepping back but still holding his hands in hers, she looked at him and said quietly, "I loved Daria and know your grief. I say no more.''

Looking at her—a tall, handsome woman in her forties, her periwinkle eyes bright, her fair hair, caught with a braid of red silk, still untouched by any dull tint of time—he knew that she spoke from her own heartache during the long years when his father had been torn from her to serve as slave and then mercenary in distant lands.

He said, "To you I can speak of her, for you will know the truth in me. There is none ever that can take her place.'' Then dropping her hands, he said, looking beyond her, "But who is this?''

On a stool, her lap full of simple embroidery work, sat a

girl of about eight or nine years: a dark-haired, brown-skinned child with a solemn face.

The girl without bidding rose, her embroidery work spilling to the ground, and came to him, holding out her hand in greeting as she said, "I am your first sister, Gerta. Is it true that the spears of King Melwas were turned aside by the gods?"

Arturo laughed, his spirits lifting at the pleasure of being with his family, and said, "Of course it's true, and to feed us on the hill during the snows the ravens brought meat each day."

"Ah, then that, too, I shall work into my embroidery."

"Enough," said Baradoc. "Once he starts his stories there is no knowing where truth begins or ends." But when he brought a mead cup to Arturo there was a shine of pride in his eyes.

That night when Arturo returned to the fortress he was summoned to Prince Geraint.

The Prince said, "Not long since a trader who for years gathered news for my father arrived. He travels freely in our lands and the Saxon shorelands because"—he smiled—"he takes news to both sides though he would deny it to either. But he is a man of true news. He tells that Hengist is dead and that his son, Esc, rules all the lands southeast of Londinium in his place."

Without thought of any irk it might give Geraint, Arturo said, "Then truly the gods begin to move. They stir you to forgiveness and bounty and now they take away the one man who held the first place over all the chiefs of the Saxon shores from the Ocelli point in the north to beyond Lemanis in the south. Each chief now will struggle and fight for leadership over the others since Esc is not the man his father was. Truly this is the time to begin to harry them. Aye, they will find a leader in time, my Prince, but long before then I shall have an army trained and battle-blooded by harassing them; an army which will, when in the years to come they find unity, meet and break them with bloody slaughter and drive them from our shores. The gods are with us!"

A spasm of irritation reaching near anger touched Geraint as Arturo spoke. The gods, the gods . . . always the gods. Aye, he had belief and faith in the gods, too, but was not blind as this Arto seemed to be that they worked their ends, shaping the destinies of men and nations, in a pattern that mortal eyes were slow to pick out. Then, oddly, he remembered the times when he had watched this Arturo school and break horses, had seen his love and care for them and the men in his command, and knew from Baradoc, too, the downing of pride that he had forced on himself to go seeking charity from King Melwas. In this moment he found a truth which he needed to keep countenance and temper with Arturo. He was not one man, but two, a dreamer and a warrior—and the one could not live without the other. So he now said evenly, "Tomorrow we will talk more about this."

CHAPTER FOUR

The Taunting Of The Boar

A WEEK LATER ARTURO rode back to the hill camp with Marcos, but on the way he turned off and went to Ynys-witrin. As they rode to the settlement the floodwaters lapped over the causeway still in places. He was escorted to King Melwas, who with his people had now returned from his winter quarters in the old lead mines. The air was balmy with the first promise of spring and he found Melwas—who like all true marshmen was most at ease with the sky rather than a roof above—sitting in the courtyard of his palace.

Melwas, who was having the thick winter growth of his beard plucked and trimmed by one of his women, made him welcome. He sat at the rough plank table with him and a jug of crab-apple brew was set between them. As their beakers were filled and Melwas waved away the woman tending his beard so that he could drink, he said, "So you have charmed the young Prince—and now comes my turn?"

"News runs fast. But I have come to use no charms. Plain speaking serves us both best."

Melwas laughed. "Your tail is up. You begin to feel your oats after the winter fast. My answer is, Nothing of charity will be found here."

"Nor do I ask it. I need your leave to keep quarters on Cam Hill and to make the place secure. The need will be with me for many years."

"You speak plain . . . aye, even a little rough for a beggar. Now, to your plain need add the golden tail."

"One third of all loot we take. From this you pay the fighting men you bond to me."

"First my land—and now my men! How many men?"

"Fifty."

Melwas laughed. "Young, of course. And able to take bow and shoot the eye from a crow at fifty paces, and to throw a spear that will slit the throat of a bounding deer and so not spoil good carcass meat. This, too, at fifty paces?"

Arturo smiled. "Is there any marshman who cannot do that?"

"No." He scratched at his beard. "But go on—the morning was dull until you came. Did Prince Geraint suffer your humour as pleasantly as I do?"

"He has seen how this country's needs must be served. He supplies horses and men and provisioning and asks nothing in return."

"He is young and generous with his new inheritance. Even so you will have no great force."

"Success will bring the growth I want. But I must have a safe stronghold for winter quarters for the next few years to come. This I ask you to provide, not from charity, but on fair terms. If I speak boldly it is because I know the gods will govern your heart."

"You talk of the gods as though you supped with them on their feast days. People already sing the tale of my spears being turned from you."

"And will sing it for a thousand years to come. Would your name live so long had not the gods brought us together? And longer still will it live when men sing of your wisdom and foresight in giving me Cam Hill for leaguer to begin the great progress against the Saxons."

Melwas leaned back and roared with laughter and then, thumping the rough table boards, he said, "There's a boldness in your begging which puts me on the edge so that I know not whether to smile and say yes or shout to my men to throw you in the mere. Though, of course, should they do that the gods would see to it that you landed on your feet and walked the surface of the water."

"Would you have me go elsewhere so that people in years to come will say that Melwas was—"

"Enough! You make my mind itch more than my winter beard does my face. I am a fool to like you and more fool to listen to you, but I have a son your age who shares your spirit and dreams and nags me like a gadfly to be allowed to take service with that old fool Ambrosius. You shall have what you want if he comes as leader of your bow- and spearmen and all others of the same like who may join you in the days to come. He dreams of nothing but battle and wastes his days here in fishing, hunting and tupping the marshmaids."

"He shall have command until the day he proves unworthy of it."

"If that day comes he is no son of mine. Now go your way before the gods put it into your mind to ask further alms of me. Coroticus will bring his men to you within a few days and the hill is yours and your good father, Baradoc, can fortify it."

"I give you thanks, and thank, too, the gods who sent me to you."

Melwas shook his head slowly and with a sly smile, his lips wet red through the tangle of his beard, said, "So, so—but think me not deceived. You would have come gods or no gods."

Coroticus arrived with his men five days later. He was of much the same age as Arturo, but with a marshman's small, lean figure. He was dark-haired, with a tightly trimmed beard, and his face was grave and brooding and seldom showed any emotion, a dark pool of peat water showing nothing of the depths below. He spoke quietly and pleasantly except when he would be obeyed in exercise of command and then his voice could take on a rasp like the scything of a winter wind through the frozen sedges of his own marshlands. Pride went with him, too, Arturo saw, for all his men came dressed alike. They wore leather skullcaps, their hair bound tightly over the napes of their necks, and soft leather tunics belted over thick woollen shirts. On the left breasts of the tunics copper studs pricked out the rude shape of the Summerlands and King Melwas' emblem of a hovering fish eagle. Below the tunics they wore leather aprons over short woollen trews and their legs and feet were bare each year from the first spring thaw until the first winter snow. Each man had a slung bow, a quiver full of arrows, and a long knife in his belt and carried a heavy fighting spear. That the men were all dressed alike told Arturo much about Coroticus. Not only pride went with good appearance but the beginning of hard military discipline—and discipline was a rare virtue among the marshmen.

He said, "You are welcome, Coroticus."

Coroticus answered quietly, "We are proud to come, my lord Arturo. There is no man with me not of his free will. Show us some piece of this hilltop for our quarters and the rest we will do for ourselves. And so it will be on the march and in fighting camps."

Arturo smiled. "And will it be the same the day your fifty men become five hundred?"

Coroticus said, "If I lead them then—yes, my lord. I wish only to serve you and fight against the Saxon men, and in all things to be obedient and faithful to you."

From that day Coroticus and his men were as he had said they would be. And from that day there was a new beginning for all on the hill. They were days of drilling and exercises, days of training in battle and surprise attacks, when troops of horse went thundering down the long slopes of the neighboring hills and valleys in mock attack and the marshmen came fast behind them to learn to take advantage of the confusion and panic in the ranks of imaginary Saxons. They were drilled for one long, hard month in all the tactics and feints and battle moves which Arturo could devise, and there was not a man from Arturo down who came riding back from a day's training who, fatigued though he might be, did not still sit proud in the saddle or trot lightly, skin sweat- and dust-coated, with long spear at rest on his shoulder. The hill now was a company of men, for Arturo had sent all women and children back to their lands and settlements. He drove the men through all the lengthening daylight hours. When darkness came there was only rest in relay for those who came from guard and camp duties for they lived now as though they were deep in hostile country and attack could come at any time. No man grumbled, for it was clear to all that in these days the discipline was building habit and instinct on which their lives would rest when they moved away from Cam Hill to face the killing reality of bloody warfare. Their pride, too, blossomed in pace with the bursting sprays of blackthorn bloom on the hillside. They were Arturo's men, companions and fish eagles, the men of the west and all the other free lands.

One day only they rested—though not from guard duties. This was the seventh day of the week. Then Pasco gave service and preached for those who were Christos men, and later for those who held to their country's gods did equal duty, though far fewer of these came to him because most of those who served the gods gave worship each in his own fashion before one or other of the many little rock-piled altars which had sprung up among the ancient, broken ramparts.

At the end of the first month there came from Prince Geraint two troops of mounted cavalry volunteers and with them a fresh baggage train bringing supplies. The new horsemen were put to exercise and drills and within a handful of days ten of them were sent back to Isca (though their horses were kept) with the returning baggage train, for under the eyes of Arturo and his troop commanders their worth was quickly weighed and found wanting.

Venutius said to Arturo, ''Returning these men, my lord, could anger Prince Geraint.''

''Then angered he must be, Venutius. These are men of good enough nature but there is no true bottom to them. They came because they seek the excitements that come after victory . . . boasting and drinking and raping. Any bright lure of the flesh or appetite would draw them aside from duty.''

''How can you know this?''

''You forget that Durstan and I served with the Isca cavalry. We know these men . . . aye, and were friendly enough with them. But no man rides or marches with me in this great beginning who looks to the spoils and lusts of victory before victory is won. We begin a struggle which will eat up many years. I need none who looks no further ahead than a summer's span.'' He paused and then with a smile asked, ''You think me hard?''

''No, my lord. Determined.''

''Then take this for comfort—to each man I have sent back I spoke the truth of his going. You shall see that a half of them will return to find us when they have chewed the cud of their rejection.''

Before the end of April Baradoc arrived at the camp with more provisions and a party of workmen to begin putting the ancient hill defenses in order and to raise new ones. The carts and horses he brought were taken over by Arturo to add to his own to make the baggage train for his force. Army it could not be called, nor did he see it as such. This first year, he knew, could only be a probing, proving campaign. The baggage train would travel well in their rear. He was seeking for swiftness and suddenness. Every man would carry with him, in saddle pack or back sack, that which would keep him for a week—dried meat, hard biscuit—and if pack or sack hampered him in fighting, it would be abandoned until the fight was over and then sought afterward.

At the beginning of May, two days after the feast of Beltine, and the night before Arturo's men were to move from the fortress of Cam Hill, he walked in the half-gloaming to the beach dell where Daria lay. As he sat there a nightingale began to sing from the nearby thickets of elder and was answered by another from the valley of the Cam. The gods he knew held all men and women in the hollow of their hands, and they had taken Daria from him to make the long passage to the Blessed Isles cradled in the Western Sea where Cronos slept his long sleep. For himself he knew the years would be long before he followed her, and knew, too, that this was the ordering of the gods for they had reft him of the full joy of human love so that the seed should spring and flourish of another love far more demanding of his devotion.

As he sat there in the beech dell there was one who at the same moment had Arturo much in his thoughts, and this was Count Ambrosius.

He sat in his command tent at the Sabrina camp outside Corinium. A fair breeze coming over the distant river from the Cymric hills lifted and flapped the blue folds of the tent cloth above him and set flickering the flames of the two oil lamps that stood in tall holders at each end of his table, the smeech of their burning wicks strong in his nostrils. Standing before him, waiting for his attention while he studied a map drawn on fine parchment, was his *praefectus castrorum*.

Without looking up Ambrosius waved a hand to a chair and said to the Camp Prefect, "Sit—and take some wine."

Grinning briefly to himself since Ambrosius was not looking at him, the Prefect sat and helped himself to wine from the flagon and glass on the table. Both flagon and glass were old and each held an engraving of the god Bacchus. The old man, he thought, must be in a good mood, for except on feast days he seldom touched wine.

As though Ambrosius had read his thoughts, he now pushed the map aside and with a thin-lipped smile reached for the flagon and poured wine for himself, and said, "We make no great campaign this year."

"It will be hard for our regular troops to sit in idlenss, my commander."

"There will be no idleness. We go first west through Cymru to show our strength to these hill chiefs and then north to Lugovalium on the Wall to show our strength." He sipped his wine and added pleasantly, "You think we waste a year's campaigning now that Hengist is dead? That this is the time to march against them? There is no need—for our young Arturo will do that for us."

"True, my commander. But in so doing will draw more men to himself and new glory to his name."

"Which serves us well, though he may be long in seeing it. He shall make an army and a name for himself, and in a few years we shall shake the fruit of his growing into our basket. No, I would have the Saxons finish their quarrelling with the rise of a new leader—be it Esc or some other—and then we shall have again a head and heart to strike at."

"And Arturo and his army?"

Ambrosius flicked a fingernail against the rim of his glass

so that it rang, the high note trembling and then dying. He said quietly, "At heart he's a raw western savage, full of courage and blood-thirsty, but his brains are in his backside and only work when he sits a horse. I have handled his kind many times, chiefs of the Brigantes, the Ordovices and the Dobunni in our own country here. They think only of the glory of fighting and the triumphs of victory. The building of a great state and the craft and judgment which that demands are beyond them. When they meet their limits they come to hand like broken horses. It is for this I have called you here. You will send an envoy to him to say that he is outlaw no longer and, more, that I give him free right of passage throughout the land. A handful of sweet oats to feed his pride." He paused for a moment and pulled from his hand one of the rings he wore, and slid it across the table to the Camp Prefect. "Let this go to him with the pardon."

Outside the tent the Camp Prefect eyed the ring in his palm. It was gold, a signet ring with the seal worked into an intaglio of Ambrosius's head, laurel-wreathed. For a moment or two he wondered whether the Count practiced some wisdom beyond his seeing. Arturo was more than likely to throw pardon and ring back in the face of Ambrosius. But on one score his commander was right. There was no gain in marching against the Saxons this year for they would never come out to fight in full strength until they had another leader who could call and gather them to full battle unity.

Some days later a Sabrina cavalry troop leader with an escort of two of his men arrived at Cam Hill. Olipon, the troop leader, left his two men at the foot of the hill and rode the path to the battlements alone to show his peaceful coming. The sight that met his eyes surprised him. Work was going ahead on the great ring of fortifications and inside them was a well-ordered camp, full of bustle and preparations for the coming campaign. The horses were sleek and well fed, every fighting man moved with a spring and alertness which showed growing zest for the fighting days ahead. Here was no rabble of disorganized tribesmen under an impetuous, plunder-hungry chief. Things moved here with almost as much order as they did in the Sabrina wing at Corinium. And

why not, he thought, since as he was led to Arturo he saw
many a former Sabrina man among them? Aye, and was
called to and jested with by men who had been his friends and
companions in arms so that it was hard for him not to wonder
whether they had moved to a wisdom and understanding of
this Arturo which escaped him. Momentarily the urge took
him to deliver his message and then ask to be allowed to join
this company for nothing but a long dull summer of parades
and show-of-strength marches lay ahead of the Count's
army.

He was led to Arturo's hut, over which flew the white-
horse standard. Outside on guard stood a short, dark-haired,
dark-skinned marshman, resting on his spear, the copper
studs of his fish-eagle insignia burnished to catch the sunlight. Arturo came out to him and he was at once less and
more than he had expected: a young man wearing a loose
linen shirt belted over his leather trews, smiling, fair brown
hair and blue eyes, his beard tightly trimmed, who could
have passed without notice on the Corinium drill grounds
until at second look the force of the young face and the depth
of the blue eyes suddenly spoke of some tight-bridled passion. It was all there to see if a man had the eyes and wit to see
it. There was iron in this man and an age beyond his years.

Olipon raised his right arm in the old Roman salute,
announced himself and gave his message and then handed
Ambrosius's ring to Arturo. Arturo nodded, his face un-
changing as he rolled the ring absently in his hand after
giving it no more than a glance, and then said, "How many
days are you from Corinium?"

"Three, my lord."

"Hard riding. You would stay the night to rest yourself,
your men and your horses?"

"You are kind, my lord—but no. I give my commander's
message and return with your . . . your—" Olipon broke
off.

"My thanks, you think, to Count Ambrosius?" Arturo
smiled.

Recovering himself, Olipon said, "I shall speak, my lord,
as you shall command me."

"Then say this to Count Ambrosius. When I and my good companion Durstan were first outlawed by Count Ambrosius I swore a promise that men now call Arto's promise . . . aye, they still call it so to make any idle boast." His smile was frank and good-natured. "Tell your commander that promise was made under the gods and still holds faith with me. I come only to Count Ambrosius when, as equal to equal, he sues me for help. On that day I will ride to Glevum and be with him in good faith to serve this our country." He handed the ring to Olipon. "Take back this, too. He wears the laurels of victory well ahead of due season, but to spare you his anger you need not give him those words."

As he rode down the hill to rejoin his men there was a moment when Olipon was half tempted to turn back and ask leave to join the companions. Then his good sense prevailed. Plenty of chiefs had gone their own way before and made fight against the Saxons, refusing to league with Count Ambrosius. Few still lived and those that did held to their wild homelands and sent the Count their sparse levies with bad grace.

When Olipon was ushered into the Count's presence some days later to speak Arturo's words and return the ring —though he said nothing of his wearing the laurels ahead of season—Ambrosius merely nodded and showed no emotion. But when Olipon had gone he slipped the ring back on his finger and smiled broadly to himself. Had Arturo accepted the pardon gratefully then he would have known that there was no hard-lasting in him. But last this western hothead and dreamer would until the day when he should decide on his going and with no mark of infamy on him gather up his victories and his army for himself.

On a May morning with the high soaring downland larks filling the bright air with their song, the companions of the White Horse left Cam Hill and began their long march westward. They numbered three troops of thirty-two horse each. The first-ranking troop was commanded by Durstan, who had for second-in-command Garwain. The second was headed by Gelliga with Borio at his side, and the third by

Netio, the right side of his face puckered with an old sword scar, with Marcos to second him. Behind the two baggage trains was the reserve troop—mostly men and mounts from Prince Geraint—commanded by Venutius in the place of the dead Cuneda, and served as next in command by an Iscan trooper called Branta. Holding the flanks, split into two detachments, were the marshmen of Coroticus. In the baggage train, ridden by the camp servants, were twenty remounts. In all there were close on one hundred and fifty horse and cavalrymen—for no servant rode a remount unless he could turn fighting man, too—and fifty spear and bowmen.

At their head rode Arturo, and Lancelo carrying the white-horse standard. Anga, the aging hound, kept pace stiffly at Arturo's side. It had been in Arturo's mind to leave the hound behind for the days ahead would be long and hard but if death were to come to Anga, he decided, then it should not be pining on the hilltop. He should die on the march or in battle.

They rode out red-and-white scarved and fish-eagle-studded, all weapons and fighting gear true, a rising lust in them for action and triumph; and with them went Pasco on a moorland pony, Pasco, who had wearied them with a too-long sermon and blessing before they left the hill.

Watching them go, Baradoc, stiff-faced with pride in his son, swallowing the gall of his own envy to be fighting-fit and to go with them, remembered the day when he and Tia had landed on Caer Sibli, where Arturo was to be born, remembered, too, what the hermit, Merlin, had written of him, scratched on the face of a rock:

> Cronos in the dream spoke thus
> Name him for all men and all time
> His glory an everlasting flower
> He throws no seed

Then thinking of Daria lying in the beech dell, he wondered if the gods would deny Arturo the common gift of a man's love for a woman because they would keep him bound indivisibly to them for the full length of his days. There was always for such men some great tribute to be paid. He raised his eyes to the far downslopes and saw the cavalcade strung out and spread across it and the red-and-white scarves and banners burned like a slow flame over the new grasses.

In the following days the companions rode down the old road to Sorviodunum and on to Venta through peaceful country, the news of their coming running fast ahead of them. In Sorviodunum, where the citizens were slowly rebuilding their town which had been sacked in a raid by sea pirates some years before, they were welcomed and freely provisioned during their stay. At Venta the same greeting met them. They then at Arturo's orders—and none knew what they would be beyond the day's march ahead—turned southeast toward the coast and rode to Noviomagus. Here was a strong community of Christos people and also the seat of the bishop of the diocese, an ancient, not fully witted man who believed that the rule of the Great Empire still ran through the southern lands. He gave Arturo and his chief companions lodgings in his palace. Hearing from the priest Pasco that Arturo had been baptized in the Faith before his marriage to Daria, though not that he had done so because he held all gods in reverence and some, because of their greater powers, in more reverence than others, the bishop came out at their departure and gave his Christian blessing to the little army. He also presented Arturo with a rich scarlet sleeveless surcoat embroidered with the blue-robed figure of the Virgin Mary, the halo about her head formed by clusters of small seed pearls cropped from the oysters that flourished in the nearby sea creeks and tidal flats. Arturo wore it until they were out of the bishop's domain. After that it was put with his spare gear on one of the baggage carts.

As they went eastward between the shore and the rising slopes of the great forest of Anderida to the north, Durstan dropped back to ride with Arturo. After a while he said, "We ride gently, as though in triumph, all victories won. This way what shall we meet but a handful of raiding sea pirates now that the good season makes fair passage and landing for their keels? The true Saxons from the Cantiaci lands seldom come south through the forest."

Arturo nodded. "We ride gently—but far slower than the

news of our coming. The forest is full of eyes. The word goes swiftly from charcoal burners' stands to swineherds' huts, and to the boothies of fish and bird trappers and so by smoke signal and fast runners to Durobrivae and Durovernum to find Esc and his warriors. Last year we were a war band, no more than a thorn in the side of Saxon pride. Now we come as an army, a sword thrust which must be met. Though it draw not Esc himself, he will send men to meet it. If he would hold his father's inheritance this is no moment for him to lose the smallest part of his valour.''

Two days later, when they were almost on the borders of the lands of Eleutherus, who held the fortified British town of Anderida and called himself King, but stayed in power because he had compounded an uneasy pact with Hengist, they turned northward up the valley of a sluggish river which cut through the thick forest. Two days later they broke free of the trees and thickets on to the stream-laced highland of the river's watershed. Here, as they marched in battle order, with outriders ahead and on their flanks patrols of Coroticus's men, a horn sounded loud and clear from the front, giving the warning for the sighting of the enemy.

Riding ahead to the leading troop, Arturo saw that the Saxons had placed themselves well. The land fell away into the narrow mouth of a steeply cut valley. Three lines of Saxons held the valley bottom and its steep sides. No cavalry charge could take the steep valley sides for no horse at speed could safely assault them from the front. The Saxon lines at the valley bottom were equally well protected, for any charge down the sharp slope—if the Saxons opened ranks to let it through—would take men and horses into the marshy quagmire which was the nurturing ground of the stream that flowed north down the valley. The soft ground would hold a man with ease. But horse and man would sink and founder in the quaking bogland to become easy victims to the long saber-curved scramasax swords of the Saxons.

Looking down at the enemy, Arturo saw that they were no hurriedly gathered band of undisciplined settlers and townsmen. Few of them wore any body armour, being clothed in short leather trews and tough skin-and-pelt surcoats belted tight to carry axes and the sharp, deadly seax knives with which to cut the throats of a fallen enemy. Many of them were leather-helmeted and all of them carried small round shields with which to strike into the face of an opponent while their swords went into his guts below. Arturo realized, too, that behind this confrontation lay the warcraft, if not of Esc himself, then of one of his trusted local commanders, warcraft which was designed to tempt him to disaster or give to him the humiliating choice of turning aside from them. But to turn aside from them would be all the victory needed, for the news would run like a summer heath fire and his name would be shamed before the gods and all men.

With Lancelo at his side, the White One moving a little restlessly under him so that Anga stayed away from her, Arturo ran his eyes over the Saxon lines—the warriors unnaturally silent for usually they shouted taunts and abuse—and knew that the gods were putting him under trial. There was no choice for him. Now was the time when the long days of drills and exercises back at Cam Hill must be shown to serve them all in bloody reality.

He turned to Lancelo and said, "Give the call of the Taunted Boar."

Lancelo put the horn to his lips and sounded the call. It was one among many that had been born of their training days, and all of them were named . . . the Taunted Boar, the Coiling Snake, the Wolf Circle . . . and there was not a fighting man or a baggageman who did not know as the notes rang out exactly what was demanded of him. The horn wailed, high and screaming, changed to a quick succession of sharp blasts and then was suddenly silent as its echoes rolled down the valley still.

Curbing the restless white mare, Arturo watched the pattern of his men and horses move and swirl and heard the shouts of the baggage train handlers as the end of the column closed up and the reserve troop rimmed it in a double-rowed crescent.

The two forward troops went wide on each flank, well above the valley head, and held their mounts champing and restless in double lines, the forenoon breeze teasing their red-and-white scarves and helmet crests, the sun striking points of fire from the scabbard-freed swords of each front rank and sparking the lancetips of the second lines.

Then into the forefront of the battle formation came Coroticus and his men, spears slung behind their backs, their bows drawn and arrowed. They trotted down the slope in two lines abreast and when they were within easy bowshot of the ranks of Saxons Coroticus called an order. The first line of marshmen dropped to one knee and the second line stood two paces behind.

For a moment or two there was no movement save that of restless horses, no sounds save those of the high chorusing larks. Not even from the Saxon ranks came taunt or shout for they were meeting now a move which puzzled them, for they had expected an onrush of cavalry to cut through them and throw them into disorder while the marshmen followed up behind with their spears.

Coroticus, who assumed no commander's privilege in the fighting itself and knelt at the right end of the first line of bowmen, gave a low curlew's whistle and, flexing his arrow-charged bow, took aim at the throat of a man on the right flank of the center line of the Saxon warriors in the valley bottom. The arrow sped true to take the man in the gullet and with a high choking scream he toppled backward. As he did so the marshman on Coroticus's left sent his arrow through the left eye of another warrior. And then the next marshman, unhurried, following the well-learned drill, fired another arrow, the goose-feathered shaft sinking deep into a Saxon's left breast. Deliberately, without hurry, a few moments between each shot, the marshmen picked their targets and fired, and not until twenty of their men were down did the Saxons stir and break their silence. The taunting of the boar had begun and Arturo, watching, knew that the Saxons barring the marshy ground would not long hold themselves in check for it was the nature of these men to go to meet the enemy eagerly, filling the air with their battle cries.

So it proved. As man after man went down, now from the middle ranks and now from the valleyside flanking ranks, the cries came and grew louder and angrier, and those Saxons with spears flung them at the marshmen. But Coroticus had gauged his front well and they all fell short. Then suddenly like the onrush of a tidal wave, in a great burst of noise, the three ranks of Saxons, on the steep hillside and valley bottom, enraged that they should stand like sheep to wait the arrow which should sent them to Valhalla, broke ranks and surged forward, shields high, scramasaxes swinging, eager to come to grips with their foes.

Arturo at Lancelo's side smiled as he saw their coming. Thus was the taunted boar goaded to break cover and offer itself to slaughter. He nodded to Lancelo and the horn called, echoing down the narrow valley.

Coroticus's men, as the Saxons rushed for them, turned and ran back and as Coroticus passed Arturo he looked up. There was a gleam in his dark eyes and—seldom seen in a marshman except in drink—a broad grin on his face and the faces of all his men.

As the Saxons raced after them, leaving their boggy ground far behind, Gelliga's flanking troop came galloping down upon them, the heavy swords of the first rank swinging and slashing and cutting into the enemy, killing and maiming. Behind them came the second line of lances to bring death to those wounded warriors who from the ground on their knees or backs tried to hack and stab at the legs and bellies of the horses. Then, after the passing of Gelliga's troop, there came down from the opposite flank, charging through their already-blooded companions, the troop of Durstan to hack and hew and carry their killing lances through the shouting rabble of Saxon warriors.

Arturo watched as the two troops wheeled, re-formed and charged again. This time the Saxons broke and ran hard for the safety of the lower soft ground from which they had been tempted and kept running even as Lancelo's horn sounded behind them the call to break action. Watching them go, Arturo knew that this was a beginning, a good and god-given beginning, a gift from Badb, the god of battle, and an offering to Andraste, the goddess of victory, and proof that—great fighters though the Saxons were when they saw victory coming to their grasp—they were no men to stand and die in defeat if any loophole of escape still offered itself to them.

Close to a hundred men lay dead or dying, their arms to be plundered, and their small wealth of rings and torques, brooches and armlets which they wore into battle to be taken into the war chest of the companions against the wants of the long campaigning days ahead. The news of this first clash would run fast and far and wide. Looking up, Arturo saw in the clear afternoon sky the beginning of the first circling of the prey birds, kites, eagles, the diamond-tailed ravens and the already bickering crows mobbing the stately circling buzzards to ease their impatience to arrive at the waiting feast below.

That night, as Arturo made his round of the sentry posts with Lancelo, he heard from the downland hollow where his men sat around their campfires the voice of Durstan singing:

"The boar in the east does not call.
No more in his bracken lodge does he sleep.
The hornet flight of the arrows of Coroticus
Have taunted him to rage
And the swords of Arturo
Have stayed the strength of his red anger.

"Under the moonlight his saffron tusks
Makes perches for the ravens who feed on his eyes
And on the dead pine branches
The eagles sit heavy from feasting."

CHAPTER FIVE

Girl With A Harp

For the rest of that spring and summer they sat nowhere in camp for long. For the first part they stayed south of the River Tamesis, moving, sometimes in small bands and sometimes in full strength, along the borders of the Saxon lands, harrying and destroying the outlying settlements.

They came and went with no pattern of movement or settled strength which the Saxons could anticipate. They were a wolf pack, marauding now in force and now in small groups. They leaguered their baggage train well to their west and then for a week the cavalry troops of the companions would disappear to the east with Coroticus's men to attack at dawn or as last daylight faded, until the time came when they mounted a strong assault on the heavily settled outskirts of Durobrivae, the next-largest town after Durovernum. They came at night and set fire to the hovels and round huts and squalid log cabins along the river so that the flames turned its waters to blood. When daylight came—for the Saxons had no taste for night marching, and the warriors had gathered in the dawn to pursue them—they had melted away, splitting into small parties of eight or ten horse and a few marshmen, each group going its own way back to the baggage train. Then, when at last Esc, who had other matters on his mind, gathered a force to overmatch them and marched westward they were nowhere to be found on the borders of his land for they had gone north around Londinium and were sitting openly and in force on the road to Durolipons, which bordered the land of the Trinovantes held by the East Saxons.

Now, too, though Arturo never gave explanation of his overall strategy, the shape of the design that lay in his mind began to come clear to most of his leading companions, and—since he had served under Ambrosius as a staff officer—abidingly clear to Venutius. This year and for a few more years the pattern would be fixed. Harry and raid and go. They would stand and fight when the battle was fairly matched, but not otherwise. A man or horse lost in a useless foray or an overmatched confrontation gained Arturo nothing. This was the first sowing of a rich crop to come and the sowing would be not of one year but many. Already fighting men were coming to them, seeking them out, and to all of them the answer of Arturo was the same: to ride to Cam Hill come the autumn, where a welcome would await them. None joined him now who did not know the ways of the companions and had not their training and discipline. Venutius saw readily the virtue of this demand. One man accepted by Arturo would be worth ten reluctant levied men. He saw, too—perhaps more than any other companion—that patience was now yoked with Arturo's warlike, eager spirit. The dream he dreamt was not to be accomplished in a few years.

Against the East Saxons that year they pursued the same tactics as they had done with the South Saxons. Then as summer began to pass they moved farther north through Causennae to Lindum, where the news of their coming had run fast ahead of them. Here, where the city and surrounding country were precariously held by the Coritani, they were welcomed warmly by the townsfolk and the bishop. The companions made camp on the gently rising ground to the south of the town, but the bishop insisted that Arturo should take quarters in his own palace, and on his first evening they supped together.

The bishop, a small, spare man of fifty, with a dark, cheerful glint in his eyes, entertained him alone, and was full of eagerness to hear of his progress along the borders of the Saxon lands.

He said as they ate a dish of stuffed carp, "I shall be in bad grace with Count Ambrosius for making you welcome but 'tis long since he was here and may be longer before he comes again. But who am I to deny hospitality to one who brings a gleam of hope for this wretched land—and one, too, who is a Christian? Is that not so, my son?''

"It is, your grace."

The bishop smiled. "But have, too, I am told, a great respect for this country's old gods."

Arturo, who liked the man, and had measured quickly his nature, said, "This is my country. Without its gods it would be nothing. For love of my dead wife I became a Christos man. For love of my country I also worship my country's gods. A warrior, your grace, needs all the help he can get."

"I will not argue that point with you. Time will make a better argument than I can." He sipped wine from his silver-mounted glass and went on, "It is a pity that there is bad blood between you and Count Ambrosius. God knows you are welcome here for we live dangerously and are raided often by the fen Saxons beyond the great Car Dyke."

Arturo shrugged his shoulders. "The Count is a dreamer of dusty dreams. He waits for a miracle. I work for an end and, if the gods spare me, will come to it. While the South Saxons are all in disarray he should have gone against them, but I hear that he holds back because he thinks they will not come out against him, lacking a strong leader. Why wait? If I had had a thousand men this summer I could have swept through the Cantiaci lands and driven them into the sea from Tanatus round to Lemanis, could have smoked them out of their holes like rats. But the day is coming when I will have those men, and this summer I have made a beginning under the gods—" he paused for a moment and then added, "—and under the banner of Christos."

The bishop nodded, his mouth pursed with a wry smile, and said, "You have an interesting approach to theology—but a very direct and admirable one to the great matter of this country. In a man who loves his country so ardently many things can be forgiven." He sighed. "Ah, me, yes. The good Lord works in a fashion not always easily understood. But we grow too serious. We shall have music to sweeten the rest of the evening."

He spoke to the servant attending them, who left the room

to come back a few moments later with a young girl who carried a small harp. Sitting on a bench by the open window, she began to play and sing for them in a sweet though not oversure voice at first, as though she was nervous. But after a little while she grew confident and assured.

Leaning back in his chair, Arturo listened to her as his eyes marked the evening hawking outside of the young swallows who were beginning to flock together for their southerly passage. Summer was fast deferring to autumn and his first campaign was almost done. The stone had been thrown into the still pond and the ripples were spreading. How many summers, how many campaigns before. . . ? He sighed, touched for a time by a sudden sense of weariness. In that moment, seeing his return to Cam Hill, he knew a brief and bitter flare of sorrow for the one love who could give him no greeting.

Through that moment of rare self-pity the young girl's voice came to him, clear and sweet. She was singing an old song which he knew well; a song the companions sang around their campfires. Daria lay in the beech dell. Ten of his companions and as many of Coroticus's marshmen would see no return to Cam Hill.

> "I have a hut in the wood.
> None knows it but my love.
> An ash tree this side,
> A hazel on the other,
> A little hidden lowly hut
> Where waits my flame-haired love . . ."

For the first time Arturo looked closely at her. She was a girl of twelve or thirteen years, her young breasts scarce challenging the soft material of the short white linen robe she wore. Her bare legs were sun-browned and on her feet were red sandals of soft doeskin. Sensing that the two men were now listening to her song, she raised her head, her fair hair caught with a ribbon of the same colour as her sandals, and smiled at them. For a moment the pink tip of her tongue ran like some small soft animal between her teeth and there was a momentary widening of her blue eyes.

"The black cock calls from the high heather.
  We eat sweet apples under summer's mantle,
  Her lips the red of the ripe bog-berries . . ."

A child still, thought Arturo as he sipped his wine, but with already something of boldness in her eyes. In five or six years' time she would turn the heads of young men and many would sigh for love of her.

When she had finished the song, the bishop said to her, "It is a song fit for a resting warrior. Play once more for us, child, and then away to your couch."

On the word *child* Arturo saw the flick of her eyebrows, momentary as the beat of a bird's wing, mark a fast-passing frown.

She lowered her head over the harp, her face hidden from them, and touched the strings strongly so that the notes came boldly and arrogantly.

"The boar in the east does not call,
  No more in his bracken lodge does he sleep . . ."

Beside him the bishop began to chuckle with pleasure and looked at Arturo for approval.

Arturo smiled, too, as she played on and when she had finished he said, "From where do you get such a song?"

Without shyness she said, "From your men, my lord, who walk the city. I would have liked to have been there to see the taunting of the boar."

Arturo laughed. "It was no fit place for a girl." Then seeing the brief tightening of her face, he went on, "But you sing sweetly enough to shame the nightingale at dusk and when the words are of war you have all the music of the dark torrent."

She laughed then and said, "You tease me, my lord."

"And I tease you more straightly," said the bishop, smiling. "Get you to your couch and be glad you will become a woman and have no part in wars. Away with you."

The girl rose from her chair, bowed to them and went to the doorway. There, her face full now of mischief and spirit, she drew her fingers across the harp to sound a full, loud run of chords, bowed and went out.

Both men laughed and then Arturo asked, "Who is she, your grace?"

"She is from far north of Eburacum. Her father, one Loth, is a good friend of mine. She visits here with her mother, who is my sister, for there is some talk of placing her with the nuns here though—" he sighed a little, "I doubt that it will serve her much. She is high-spirited and wayward when she chooses. But also full of womanly charms and guile when she needs. She cajoled me to be allowed to play and sing for you. Arturo of the White Horse and his companions are more to her liking than the sparrow chatter and strict life of a nunnery."

"And her name?"

"It is Gwennifer."

That night as he lay on his bed Arturo was long in finding sleep. In a few more days the companions would turn and take the road south to find Cam Hill. There were many good welcomes to await a returning warrior, but none sweeter than that of the woman of his heart. He dropped a hand over the side of the bed and his fingers found the hoary head of Anga sleeping alongside him. He remembered the day of his fourteenth birthday in Isca, when his mother had given him the hound puppy as a present to take the place of old Lerg, remembered, too, his grief when the old hound had died. Some griefs passed so that memory ran without pain but others endured, their season unending.

He slept and the memories slept with him.

He woke to hear the lowing of heifers being driven up the street below, the cries of their drovers and the ringing of the high-towered bell of the nunnery, a bell which rang the alarm when over the green marshes and low willow thickets to the east beyond the great Car Dyke the lookouts marked the approach of raiding Saxon bands. This morning the bells served as a farewell to Anga, for the old hound had died in his sleep. Arturo buried him under a mulberry tree in the bishop's garden. Three days later the small army left Lindum, marching southwest down the old imperial road of the legions, a road broken, neglected, but still serviceable that ran in a long diagonal across the land through Crococalana to Ratae to Corinium and from Corinium to Aquae Sulis and then through Lindinis to Isca Dumnoniorum.

Not long after they had left Lindum there were cries and shouts from the rear troop and the baggage trains. Slewing round in his saddle at the head of the long column, Arturo looked back. Coming down the road was a youth on a small skewbald pony, galloping fast, and laughter broke through the bright morning air as now and then he was forced by baggage cart or troop formation to veer to the side and take to the rougher going of the roadside vallum.

Arturo, signalling to Lancelo to keep the long-strung column moving, pulled aside free of the road to a bank where already the tall spikes of sweet balsam were being harvested by the bees and wasps. The youth rode up to him, his face flushed with sweat and dust. He wore a loose cloak that reached to the knees of his short leather trews and a red scarf wrapped like a turban about his head to trap all but a few loose curls of his fair hair.

Arturo, smiling, knowing that the deceit of habit was not meant for him, but to fool—though it scarce could have done—the gate sentries of Lindum, said jokingly, "We seek no recruits who are not of age—especially one who rides so awkwardly." There was no mistaking the deep, dark-blue eyes and the fair hair and poppy-bright lips of Gwennifer.

The girl was silent for a moment, catching her breath. Then, dropping her reins, she pulled the scarf from her head and her hair fell in a tangle which the breeze teased so that it was a moving web of gold threads under the sun, and she said solemnly, "My lord Arturo, I ride not to join you, but to bring you that which may ease a little the sorrow in your heart."

Then, urging the pony forward a little so that she was at the side of the White One, she fumbled beneath her drawn cloak and drew out a brindled, white-throated puppy which squealed as she held it from her and from fright piddled a little so that the liquid sprayed one of her bare legs. She said urgingly, "Take him, my lord. He is of the best blood and will be a good hound. The bishop would have none other in his kennels."

Touched by the gesture, Arturo covered the quick emotion rising in him, and said chaffingly, "The bishop will give you no thanks for pillaging his kennels and I would not see you in trouble for your kindness."

Gwennifer frowned and said firmly, "But he is mine to give. My uncle made present of him to me when I came here with my mother. Take him, my lord."

Arturo hesitated for a moment, then reached out and took the puppy—which could scarce have had three months since its whelping. Its belly was warm against the palm of his hand, and the sweet hound smell strong from its pelt. He said, "I take him and give you thanks. What is he called?"

"Cabal, my lord, and he will be a hound above all hounds for the gods have told me so in a dream."

Cocking an eye in open doubt, Arturo asked, "The gods speak to you in your dreams?"

"Sometimes. They have shown me many things that will happen. Some I like and some I like not, but then"—she shrugged her shoulders lightly—"there is no changing the fall of the dice they have shaken."

"You talk old for one so young. The Christos nuns will have their hands full with you."

She shook her head and laughed. "I shall make them such trouble, my lord, that they will cry out to be rid of me." Then eyeing him boldly, she said, "Why wish them that trouble? I can keep these clothes and come with you to Cam Hill to serve you as well as any other. I can do—"

"Enough." Arturo shook his head and his lips tightened severely. "I thank you for your gift and for the gentleness of thought that provoked it. But now you go back to Lindum to your mother and the good bishop. And to make sure you do I send two men with you. Back to Lindum. This I command.''

"Then I shall go. But this I say, my lord, and further risk
your anger. One day I shall ride into Cam Hill and you will
welcome me since in a dream—''

"—the gods have shown you this,'' finished Arturo for
her.

"Aye, my lord, and more.''

"Then I believe you. Now ride for Lindum.''

He turned from her back onto the road and called for
Marcos to give her escorts and handed him Cabal to find
lodge for on one of the baggage carts. Then he rode to take his
place at the head of the main column alongside Lancelo.

Lancelo grinned when Arturo told him what had happened
and said, "All Lindum and Eburacum, it is said, know her
for her wildness and, although she is a girl, her father has
taken the birch to her for some of her doings.''

Lightly Arturo said, "Some women are born with the
hearts of men, and some men with the hearts of women, and
for the making of trouble there is no choosing between
them.'' He said no more but as he rode and looked down to
where Anga had for so long padded alongside him, he knew
gratitude for the gift she had brought.

They marched that day to the outskirts of Ratae, where
they made camp. That evening as Arturo sat outside his small
tent Durstan came and joined him, bringing a bowl of goat's
milk for the hound puppy. As they watched the puppy drink
Durstan said, "You mean to keep this road for the full
march?''

"I do.''

"We march through Corinium?''

"We do. The more we are seen the more will men come to
us this winter.''

"And what of the Sabrina wing? We are no match for them
as yet.''

"There is only a small holding force at Corinium. Count
Ambrosius is still making his progress, so the bishop told me,
and is at Deva.''

"He is well informed.''

"You do not stay bishop long otherwise. I learned much from him. He is with us, and will make and find friends for us among the chiefs north of Eburacum." He picked up Cabal and stroked his white throat. "We are only at the beginning of things. We need the friendship and the help of his kind over the years to come. The Christos bishops and their people grow stronger in this country. The more a country suffers . . . aye, and they with it, the more their strength grows and we have chance to turn it to our advantage."

Durstan plucked a tall grass stalk, chewed its end for a moment or two and then, even he not knowing what reception his words might provoke, said quietly, "But you are no true Christos man, Arturo. They will come to know this."

Arturo frowned. "I am as true a Christos man as any for he is a god with other gods. When you are with fever you do not pray to Epona. You send your prayers to Nodons of the silver hand. In battle you cry on Badb, not Lug, who blesses the seed of man in woman. But when a whole nation suffers then you call on all the gods."

Durstan said nothing. There were times when the reasoning of Arturo escaped him. He prodded the flank of Cabal and the puppy turned and began to worry at the hard leather of his campaign boot.

The silence between them was broken by the first evening churring of a nightjar, and the flames of the bivouac fires from the camp spread around them on the sandy heath they had chosen for the night were cut by the black shapes of the sentries who patrolled the limits of their resting place.

Four days later they marched through Corinium. The small holding party which Ambrosius had left at the Sabrina wing camp had advance news of their coming. When the dust of their marching showed, the commander called his men to arms and two troops of cavalry were deployed in battle formation along the eastern front of the camp, which was flanked by the Ratae—Corinium road. Ambrosius had left him without orders for this happening. But he was a man of good sense and not without admiration for Arturo. When the long snaking column of Arturo's companions came into view

with Coroticus's men and mounted scouts guarding its
flanks, he put his horse to the trot and, leaving his men, made
for the place in the long column where the white-horse
standard flew in the soft breeze.

Seeing him coming, Arturo rode away from the road and
across the bare, hoof-pocked training grounds to meet him.

Reining in the White One, Arturo said, "We come in
peace. We fight the same battle and follow the same cause as
Count Ambrosius."

The commander's mouth twisted to a wry smile and he
said, "Aye, that is true, my lord Arturo. Then pass peacefully. I can give you no provisioning or quartering here for
under the writ of Count Ambrosius you are outlaw still." He
shrugged his shoulders, and with a firm hand gentled his
restless horse. "A pity . . . for otherwise we could have
shared wine, and I would have had pleasure in good talk with
many of my old friends whom I now see among your ranks."

Smiling, Arturo said, "A pity, true—but if you feel their
loss so much, you could join us."

The commander shook his head. "Not me, my lord. I am
one of the old Ambrosiaci. When you were a boy I fought
with the Count in the days of the great raidings of the south
coasts. We were young then and fought at Anderida and
Noviomagus to tame the sea raiders. My battle scars were
suffered under him. I carry them with honour and—though
he grows old now like me and, in truth, less venturesome—I
am his man. So pass in peace, my lord."

"We pass in peace, and may the gods give you honour for
your loyalty."

So Arturo and his men passed in peace, over the clear
waters of the river that curved gentle around the northeastern
side of the city, a river where the trout grew fat on the
jettisoned offal from the market slaughterhouses, and the
citizens opened the newly built heavy portals of the Verulamium gate. A great crowd lined the streetway that led
through the city's heart to the far Aquae Sulis gate and
Arturo—now at the head of the column—smiled to himself
as they passed the Forum on their left where, on a rainy day

now seeming far into the past, he had scrawled with a piece of charcoal words of defiance at Ambrosius when he had first been outlawed. *Between the empty promise of Arto and the sloth of Ambrosius where shall a warrior blood his lance?* Bold words, but seeded with truth. The gods had set him on his way and he knew that he was in their hands for the rest of his years.

They came to Cam Hill on a day when an early and sharp frost had set the leaves of the riverside willows and the ash trees on the camp slopes falling. His father, Baradoc, was there to greet him, and had been there with his workmen for all the spring and summer months. Work on the plateau fortifications was running fast; a great hall, troop quarters and stables had been built of wood and roofed with reed and hazel-bough faggots and there was now a small set of private quarters for Arturo. New ground had been broken in the valleys, crops sown and harvested, and hay gathered and stacked for the horses against the winter so that they would have to make no great call on Prince Geraint and King Melwas for provisioning. Ansold had set up a smithy and forge for the repair of arms and armour, and stores of charcoal had been bartered for with the cutters and burners in the woods to the west. But most pleasing to Arturo was the sight in the valley to the south of a camp, where was quartered a force of near a hundred men and horses—free men and trained cavalrymen and their mounts, and two men, sons of a chief of the Durotriges, who had come, provisioned and armed, to beg leave to join the companions.

The following night a great feast was set to celebrate their return. The chief companions filled the long table in the new hall and all the men sat at rough tables or squatted on the ground around the fires that ringed the hall and whose blaze could be seen afar on Ynys-witrin top and the sea-dominating knoll of Brant. They roasted three heifers, two pigs and long spitfuls of trussed wildfowl taken from the Cam River marshes. Six goatskins of new mead and apple ale matched their thirst, and flat cakes of fine-querned corn flour were spread with sweet thyme-and-marjoram-tanged honey which had been brought as a gift by the two sons of the chief of the Durotriges.

Much later when the men still held to the long hall tables and the lowering fires, laughing and singing and overgilding the tales and exploits of their campaigning days, Arturo left them and with Baradoc at his side sat outside his own private quarters, teasing the ears of the sleeping Cabal in his lap.

Baradoc said, "My son, you have begun what I would have done when I was your age if the gods had been kind."

"I know, my father. But the gods have marked you for as great a work. There are other hills like this which need your art and provisioning. To campaign is one thing, but when Latis weeps and the rains come and the snow denies passage to man and mount then we must have harbour to hold us through the winter. We must have such places set from south to north across the country, from Lindum down to Noviomagus."

"You talk of many years ahead."

"Aye. Of a full lifetime. Next year, if Prince Geraint give you leave, we must find such a place set back from the front between Lindum and Londinium from which in winter and all seasons the Middle Saxons can be held, and then between Londinium and the Gaulish sea to hold the others. And Londinium must be held and garrisoned to bar all land passage between Esc and the Saxon shoremen to his north. Aye, the thing is a loose tangle in my mind still but with patience and years the yarn shall be spun and the good cloth woven. . . ."

Listening, Baradoc felt the force of the passion that worked in his son and without harsh regret he knew that the dream he had dreamt at Arturo's age had been put into the hands of this fair-haired, lean-faced warrior of his own seeding to accomplish.

He rose and, touching Arturo on the shoulder, gave him goodnight and walked away, rubbing gently at the stiffness of his injured right arm. As he went laughter and shouting ceased from the long hall and through the sharpening air of the night came the voice of Durstan singing to the clear, vibrant notes of a harp.

> "The knife has gone into the meat
> And the good wine fills the horn
> In Arturo's hall . . .
> Here is food for your hound
> And corn for your horse
> In Arturo's hall . . .
> But none there shall enter unless he be
> Swift with a sword and comrade to all. . . ."

Long after his father had gone but while the singing and playing still made bird and beast uneasy over the hilltop and slopes, Arturo rose and, holding Cabal warm under his cloak, went down to the beech dell where Daria lay.

He sat still and brooding for a long time, so still that once a disturbed hare came lolloping past him within spitting distance. The gods had taken Daria from him and the taking had place in the pattern of the life they had marked for him. On the march and in skirmishing and forays a man had no thoughts of women. But when the winter came and there was all to refurbish and peaceful nights to lie abed in warmth, a warrior's manhood called for companionship and close harbouring under the warm furs and thick woven covers, Even as he thought this it was as though the mood of his companions matched his own for the sweet voice of Gelliga came clear to him.

> "Take my true greeting to the girl of thick tresses,
> The sweetheart I lay with in the glen of green
> willows . . ."

He sat listening as Gelliga sang on of the hot yearning that not even battle and the chance of death waiting at the opening door of each fighting day could smother. To tumble a willing girl in the high quake grass, its falling pollen sweetening all kisses, to slake the blood's hot fever in the arms of some milk-breasted matron . . . *Aie*, these the gods would permit him. He had paid the full barter price in the loss of Daria.

The next morning Coroticus came to Arturo to take his leave and return with his men to Ynys-witrin. His warriors were drawn up in line on the plateau grassland and with them were two ponies laden with the share of plunder spoil that went with Coroticus for his father. Arturo walked with Coroticus down the double line of men and there was pleasure in him at their appearance. Pride they had always had for few marshmen were born without it, but now they had added to it a sense of brotherhood and a spirit of discipline which he knew would mark them out from all other marshmen and fire more men to join them in the years to come. Although their dress was marked, as were their bodies, with the scars and rubs of fighting, they stood proudly, the sun flashing on the copper studdings of their fish-eagle emblems. Standing back from them with Coroticus at his side, he spoke to them, giving them his thanks and warming their pride with a fair eulogy of their prowess. When he had finished, Coroticus called on them for the marshmen's salute and—all of them moving as one man—they drew their bows, notched their goose- and heron-feather-flighted arrows and with a great shout sent them high into the air above their heads, the song of their flight a great keening through the morning brightness. Then the arrows turned at the top of their flight and came hissing back to earth to form a circle of trembling, feather-plumed wands about Arturo and Coroticus.

Coroticus stepped forward and pulled one of the arrows from the ground and with a quick movement snapped it in half across a raised knee. He handed the feather-tipped half to Arturo and said, "My lord Arturo—you are the first man not a marshman to be given the royal salute of the House of Melwas. With that broken shaft in hand you are free of the Summerlands and marshes for all time and wherever you show it, my people will know it and give you welcome and safe passage for all the years of your life."

He touched his forehead in salute and then, moving to the head of his men, led the company of marsh warriors, the proud wearers of the fish eagle, away. Arturo stood and watched them go until the last man had disappeared down the wooded slope of Cam Hill.

CHAPTER SIX

The Woman Of The High Rocks

FOR NEAR SIX YEARS ARTURO campaigned, building slowly to
the great plan which now lay clear in his mind, to hold the
Saxons behind the line that ran from Lindum in the north
down to Londinium and thence southwest to the fringes of the
great forest of Anderida. Behind this line the Middle and East
Saxons—denied any leaguing with Esc—and the South Saxons of Esc himself sat and stirred themselves only occasionally to make token forays. It was as though a great sleep had
overcome them from which now and then they waked and,
petulant at the disturbance, made a brief show of strength.
But Arturo—though he was content over the years to see his
forces grow and new camps organized by his father—knew
that the day would come when Esc or some leader of the
Middle and East Saxons would take the field to try and break
him. Nothing could stop this happening because their own
kind still came over the seas to them, though in smaller
numbers since eastern Gaul and the great prizes lying to the
south and beyond the Alps drew most of the land- and
plunder-hungry warriors. The Saxon enclaves in the land
were like leather waterskins which were slowly filling to
overflowing point.

During these years Count Ambrosius kept strict intelligence of all he did, and of the growth of his forces, to which
more and more men flocked. To avoid conflict with him—
since Arturo was serving him without knowing it—he limited
his own campaigns to the country well north of Eburacum
and to the western and southern parts of Cymru, where now

growing Scotti raids and encroachments had to be met and contained. There were times, too, when he acknowledged that the young Arturo, now near his thirtieth year, for all his passion and lust for war carried a wise head on his shoulders and schooled himself with a patience beyond his years. Where there were small peaceful Saxon outlying settlements to the west of his line he left them untouched and forced tribute and stores from them. If unwisely they took to arms and raiding, he rode down on them and there was a burning and a slaughter to signal a flaming and bloody warning to their fellows. But the passing of the years now began to build an impatience in Ambrosius. Each day now the itch for the great triumph, the lust for the day when he could ride, laurel-wreathed and wearing the purple toga to the full inheritance he claimed in this land, bit and worried him, denying him sleep and forcing upon him an impatience which ate into him as the passing of each day ate into the dwindling years of life left to him.

On an autumn evening as he walked in the rose garden of his headquarters at Glevum and his feet sank deep in the first frost-fall of leaves from the great walnut tree which some long forgotten Roman commander had brought from mid-Gaul, his Camp Prefect came to him with the news that Arturo, instead of returning to Cam Hill, was staying with a small army to winter in Lindum. Walking stiffly, aware of the rheumatic ache in his legs which had come over the years from hard lying and campaigning, he decided that the time had come to make the throw which would win him the game which he had played for so long with patience.

A week later, as Venutius sat in his lodgings in Durobrivae, where he had come with Arturo to make an inspection of the small force of cavalry and foot soldiers who were to garrison it for the winter, a travelling horse dealer came to him to make an offer for some of the foals that had been dropped by the mares of the companions but which had been rejected by him as horsemaster as unworthy of their winter keep. When the bargain was struck the man, a pleasant-faced, affable fellow, took a coin from his belt pouch and dropped it on the table before Venutius, saying, "This is payment and more for the foals."

On the table between them lay the nicked golden aureus of the emperor Hadrian. Venutius looked without emotion at the coin for he had known for some time now that its coming could not long be delayed. He said, "Say what you have been told to say and say it quickly."

"It is to be done, and done quickly and with no loss of honour to your reputation or forfeiting of your standing with the companions. The room that Arturo's going makes is to be filled by you under the Count."

He spoke the truth for over the years Venutius had slowly come to stand closer to Arturo—not in friendship, but in military worth and the ordering of large commands of men—than any of the companions who claimed his warmest friendship. He could turn them to Ambrosius and with that done Ambrosius would move Prince Geraint, King Melwas and the ever-growing ranks of tribal chiefs and overlords to acknowledge him while doing honour to Arturo's memory and greatness.

He picked up the coin and said, "Tell Count Ambrosius it will be done."

After the man had gone he sat on and, pouring himself a beaker of wine, drank absently. There had never been any escape for him from the day when, in all ignorance of Arturo, his loyalty to Ambrosius had sent him on his way to Cam Hill. Nothing now remained to him but that loyalty and its rewards and the slow, enduring stain of his own self-disgust that there was not the courage in him now to fling the golden aureus from him, take his side dagger from his belt, and make an end to his already crippled life. But the power that stayed his hand from the dagger was beyond his changing for it had true place in his nature. Raising his head as he drank more wine, he saw that outside the first heavy snowflakes of the onsetting winter had begun to fall.

The snow fell all that night and in the morning lay deep on the ground. Since the road from Durobrivae to Lindum was safe and picketed by winter-quartered patrols of Arturo's men, Arturo and Venutius rode it alone with the hound

Cabal, now grown to prime, at their heels. A few hours after leaving Durobrivae the snow thickened and with this came a strengthening wind which swept it into growing drifts and white-pelted their tight-drawn riding cloaks. Horses, riders and the great hound moved through it with their heads lowered. After a couple of hours' slow going both men knew that they would be hard put that day to do more than reach Causennae, a small town little more than halfway to Lindum.

Drawing up to breathe their mounts, Arturo looked across at Venutius and, laughing, said, "Where is road, and where is sky, and where the good earth? We move through the biggest goose-plucking ever made in the halls of the gods on high. They must make some great feast tonight."

Venutius said, "We must keep moving. The wind blows from the north and that way lies Causennae. And where is Cabal?"

Arturo looked around and then shrugged his shoulders. "He will find us. The snow balls up on his pads and he sits to chew and worry them free, but even in this his nose will bring him up to us in time." He stirred the White One to a walk and moved ahead.

Following him, Venutius knew that the gods had chosen this day for more than feasting. Although they headed into the wind, they were soon lost to the road. The snow was so thick-falling now that there were times when it was hard to make out the shape of Arturo and the White One ahead of him. The thought came to him that a man alone on his horse on such a day could be thrown by a stumble, crack his head against tree or rock and lie unconscious while the snow covered him and froze him to death. Truly the gods were setting to his hand the time and the season for his work. No man would doubt his word that in the blizzard they had become separated.

Ahead of him Arturo pulled up to rest the White One. The snowdrifts now were almost to their mounts' knees. To their right Venutius caught a glimpse now and then of a tall craggy rock face, the wind sweeping the bare falls and slabs free of snow. He rode up behind Arturo, who was leaning forward, sweeping the matted snow from the ears and long nose of the white mare. He pulled his sword from its scabbard and, raising it, struck hard with the flat of the blade at the back of Arturo's head. Arturo cried aloud, made to turn and then fell sideways from his mount. He lay still on the ground face downward.

Venutius eased his horse into the shelter of the rocks and dismounted. He moved to Arturo and squatted by him and there was a coldness in his mind far greater than the icy bite of the blizzard wind. The only small crumb of grace granted to him was that Arturo's face was pressed into the snow so that he could not see it. Within an hour the freezing wind would have leached all warmth from his body and within the next hour all life would have gone from him. Any who found him would know that his horse had stumbled and when he had fallen to the ground the startled mount had kicked him . . . The gods had given him the day and he had done the deed. But at this moment Arturo stirred and, from shame that even for a few moments Arturo should turn his face and see him, he raised his sword and struck with the flat of the blade again. Arturo groaned and lay still and in that moment the gods, needing sport and cruel jest before they feasted, brought savage irony into play.

Limping in the lee of the rocks came Cabal to see the sword blow. Silently the great hound came across the snow and leapt at Venutius to take him by the neck with his strong jaws. Venutius screamed and fell sideways and the scream was fast choked as Cabal clamped his great teeth through his throat, worrying and shaking as if he were holding down an overrun stag. The sword dropped from his grasp in the first assault, Venutius beat with his fists at the hound and twisted and rolled to find freedom, but Cabal held him, his life-blood running from the hound's iron-fast jaws to carmine the snow while the two horses, frightened at the screams from Venutius, stampeded and disappeared into the blizzard.

Growling low now, his jaws set fast, his weight holding down the now weakening struggles of Venutius, Cabal stayed bound to his prey until all movement died in the man. Then he rose and went to Arturo, sniffed at his head and body, nudged him now and again with his iron-grey muzzle and then, with a low whining, couched himself down alongside his master, pressing close to him. They lay together as the light went fast from the day and the snow laid a mantle over them and the red stains of Venutius's lifeblood.

From a cleft at the foot of the cliff a woman watched them, as she had watched from the time the White One had first whinnied on reaching the rock face. But for the hound she would have shown herself long before, but she feared the animal. Now as she watched, Cabal, who had long scented her and knew her presence, slowly rose from Arturo's body and came toward her. She would have turned and gone back into the rock shelter but Cabal stopped a little way from her and, lowering his head, whimpered softly. Hardly knowing she did it, the woman spoke softly to him and Cabal came forward, whimpered again and swung his tail in friendship. He raised his muzzle to her hand and, taking heart, she stroked his head and spoke to him with soft words. Cabal turned and moved back toward Arturo, stopped and looked over his shoulder and then moved on.

No fear in her now, the woman moved out into the deep snow. Under her belted greasy furs her body was strong and full, and her bare arms and legs were weather-tanned. Her long black hair flared in the strong wind as she came to Arturo. Kneeling by him, she turned him over. His eyes were shut, his face grey with cold and his dull copper-colored beard matted with snow. She had recognized him and the White One when he had first ridden into the lee of the rocks. She put her hands under his armpits and dragged him across the snow into the narrow cave which was her home. A small peat fire burned dismally at the back of the cave, the smoke wreathing up through a fissure in the roof. Close to the fire, on a low bed of rough boards, was a thin mattress stuffed with dead bracken that spilled loosely from a slit in its side. At the foot of the bed rested an untidy bundle of hides and furs. She pulled him to the bed and then rolled him on to it with ease. Many a man among those who visited her she had rolled, limp with drunkenness, onto the bed.

Talking to herself and to Cabal, who had couched himself by the fire, she stripped Arturo to his undershirt and won-

dered whether he would live, for apart from the blows to his
head, the freezing cold was set into his body, and when she
put her ear to his mouth there was no moving touch of warmth
from breathing. And this, she thought, was my lord Arturo
who rode the White One and had made this part of the country
safe for men to travel in peace, and whose name rang through
the land like the calling of a great brazen bell. The gods had
served him badly this day, but they had set her in his path
. . . a worthless woman, trapped long ago by her own
wildness and beauty . . . beauty of which only the coarse
mockery now remained. Yet woman she was and her body
was a fire which could fight off the killing clamp of the death
cold which was taking him.

She went to a rock ledge and found a hard corn cake which
she threw to Cabal, who nosed it but refused to eat, his eyes
on Arturo. She dropped the leather curtain over the rock face
opening. Then, in the darkness shot only by the dull-red eye
of the peat fire, she stripped the furs from herself and lay
down on the bed with Arturo. She pulled the furs and hides
over them and took him into her arms, shivering herself at the
first touch of his ice-cold flesh and then conquering it with
the fierce animal heat of her own naked body and limbs.

She lay awake all that night while the snow fell and the
wind screamed and howled and there were times when she
knew that she lay with a corpse, cold and stiff, and she
mourned the passing of one who above all others would be
most mourned in this country. But as dawn put grey fingers
through the rent and torn hide curtain and she held him tight,
feeling his coldness now begin to overcome the warmth of
her own body and arms and legs, her chill cheek was touched
by the feathered brushing of his faint breath as he returned
slowly from the limbo to which the gods out of their un-
fathomable reasoning had sent him.

And while that night passed the White One, separated
from Venutius's mount, ploughed the drifts and found shelter in the open-fronted shed of a reed cutter. But wolves
found the other horse and killed it, and toward dawn they
came to the high rocks and, while Cabal growled and stood
guard at the curtain opening, they found easy prey in the body

of Venutius, dragging it away, fighting and quarrelling over it as the blizzard matted their pelts, so that what had been the shape and shame of a man was no more than a butchered, bleeding hideousness, and the golden coin of the Emperor Hadrian, falling from his fang-ripped belt pouch, sank into the trodden snow to find lodging when the thaws came in the moss and reeds of a swamp.

The snow lasted three days. On the fourth the skies cleared and a warm thaw set in which filled the air with the running of snow water and swelled the streams and meres with flood while the sun shone and the birds found song again.

Those days were a dream through which Arturo lived and of which he was never to have clear memory. He knew the warmth of the woman that brought him back to life and sustained his growing strength. Warm broth and porridge made from the black peas of vetch were fed to him and then the mists of delirium passed and clearness came slowly to his mind as strength grew in his body.

He sat now on the edge of the wide bed, wearing his shirt and long leather cavalry trews, and chewed on a corn cake spread with honey while the woman squatted by the fire, broiling dried fish in herb-spiced mead. The beauty which had once been hers was clear to him, and he knew that it was her body and warmth which had brought him back to life—but he knew little else.

He said, "What do people call you?"

She smiled. "Genara—and much else besides at times, my lord Arturo. My husband is long dead, but I would lie if I said I lack men to comfort me."

"For saving my life you shall have reward which will take you from this place."

"No, my lord. I need nothing but the truth of knowing that the gods put me here for a purpose. You have no need to do me great favours."

Putting a hand to the rags which wrapped his wounded head, Arturo said, "Then let me call on you for a favour."

"If it is in my power, my lord."

"These things you tell me you saw. The way of my wounding and the death by Cabal of my friend Venutius—

you would do me favour if you keep silent about them always."

"That I will, my lord. But what do I say, and you, my lord, about your wounding and being here?"

Arturo smiled. "That I fell from my horse in the storm and wounded my head and you found me close by. As for Venutius—you never saw him or his death by Cabal. I shall say that we were separated by the blizzard, and the wolves found him."

"Which they did, my lord—on my threshold." She stood up and came and took his eating bowl and smiled down at him with a sudden boldness. "You will go this day, my lord? Causennae is close by."

"Aye, I go this day."

"Is one day more lost of great account even to my lord Arturo?"

Arturo laughed and, standing, began to pull on his long overshirt. "No. The days are ours to squander, but I would not cap these last days in which you have served me better than you can ever know with a final one which would not be god-touched. But remember this"—he picked up his riding cloak from the bed—"if you should ever want aught that I can fairly give you in the future you shall come and ask and it will be given."

Genara, her dark eyes bright with teasing, came to him and, drawing the cloak close across his shoulders, fastened the holding brooch. "Maybe, my lord, in these last days you have already given me the gift I ask and I would but know it again before you leave."

Arturo took her hand and kissed it. "It could be, but if it were so then it was of the gods' doing, not mine."

"Let it rest so. I will walk with you to the Causennae road. You are still a sick man and should have company at hand."

And Arturo was still a sick man. A few hours after reaching Lindum and being installed in the bishop's palace he was taken by fever and passed into a delirium which lasted for seven days. When he woke, his head clear but his body still weak, on the morning of the eighth day it was to find Lancelo standing at the room window and to hear the steady fall of rain from outside.

Hearing him stir, Lancelo turned and came to him. He grinned and said, "Welcome back, my lord. And to give you more heart I tell you that the White One was found four days ago and is now in the bishop's stables."

"I give thanks for that." He sat up, shaking his head to stop Lancelo's offered help. "I've been too long adreaming. Now there is work to be done."

Lancelo shook his head. "The season is too far gone for campaigning."

"There are some campaigns served better by pen and parchment than men and horses. Get me the stuff for writing and I would have Durstan and a troop escort ready to ride at noon for Glevum."

Knowing all Arturo's moods, Lancelo recognized this one as not to be crossed.

When the writing materials were brought Arturo sat up in bed and wrote with the fine goose quill in the Roman language. When he had finished Lancelo brought him braid and wax for its sealing and then wrapped it in a sealskin pouch for protection against the weather.

"Durstan will ride the white flag of peaceful passage, but fully armed, to Glevum and will himself see the message into the hands of Count Ambrosius and await his reply. If mishap falls on the road and there is danger of the loss of the writing he is to destroy it without looking at it. And now have sent in to me a jug of wine and bread and goat's cheese. I have been absent from this world too long and return with sharp-set appetite."

A little later there came into the room a young woman in her late teens, fair-haired and tall, wearing a red gown caught about the waist with a silver-linked belt, each link fashioned in the shape of some running animal . . . hare, wolf, horse and charging boar. She set a large wooden platter of wine and cheese on the table at Arturo's side.

Stepping back, she said, "If you need aught else, my lord,

you have but to call. I am within earshot.'' She smiled. ''It is good to see your old force returning to you at last. The priests and nuns of the bishop have prayed for you without let—and to their prayers have been added mine.''

''Then I thank you and them, mistress—'' He paused, and then added, ''What do they call you?'' He reached for the wine jug, but his hand was stilled as the young woman gave a laugh.

''My lord Arturo, you ask my name? Am I so changed in six years or so?''

For the first time Arturo looked at her with attention. Then, shaking his head, he said pleasantly, ''You ride a few lengths ahead of me.''

''Then I am set down. Why, even in your fever sleep you called my name, though there again your memory faulted you a little, but I do not grumble for in these last years there have been many things to crowd your mind. I am Gwennifer, though your swollen tongue could do no better than Genara. Yes, my lord Arturo, I am that pony-riding Gwennifer who brought you Cabal''—she nodded to the window where the hound lay full-stretch—''and I am that Gwennifer-Genara who combed and trimmed your rust-red beard while you slept and fed you broth. And when you complained of the cold in your fever and called me I brought you more wraps to heat your body.''

Arturo laughed suddenly and shook his head. ''Of course . . . ah, Mistress Gwennifer, you have my apologies and my thanks. The good nuns trained you well in the care of the sick.''

''They trained me in nothing, my lord, for I did not stay long with them.''

''Then what do you do here now?'' As he spoke he was thinking that she had grown in beauty but nothing of her spirit had changed. Behind the self-possessed young woman was still the tomboy, restless and wayward, waiting chance to show.

''My mother is dead these two years and my father stays little at Eburacum for he winters and fights in the north against the Picts to hold the lands he owns there. So I am here to run my uncle's household. And rare tedious work it has been until you came. When you have leave you should make me master of your household and I will doff these''—her hands plucked at the folds of her gown—"for trews and tunic and serve you well.''

Smiling, Arturo shook his head. "I can find no such service for you. Our ways are rough and the sermon the bishop would preach me for harbouring you rougher.''

"Maybe . . . then marry me and all will be proper—''

Arturo laughed, cutting her short, and the wine in his cup spilled to the bedcoverings. "You talk wild and willfully and frank—the nuns were well saved from you.''

"Nay—you put me off. Maybe you called not me but some other named Genara in truth, one who claims your love.''

Arturo eyed her in silence for a moment and then said firmly, "There is no living woman that I love and call for.'' Then shaking his head, a smile touching his lips, he went on, "Where do you find this bold way you think and speak?''

"My lord, that is easily answered. What I feel I show. What I think I speak. So the gods made me, and I have no quarrel with them.'' Before he could move she bent over and kissed his forehead lightly and then, laughing, moved from the room.

The room was warm with an even, steady heat for the old hypocaust system had been repaired and was fired now with sea coal that came upriver from the mouth of the Sabrina. The wall sconces gave a steady light and on the table in a bronze holder burned a fat tallow candle which threw its full glow on the parchment which held Arturo's letter to Count Ambrosius.

Munching a russet apple which he took every evening with his wine before retiring, Ambrosius, flattening the stubborn creases of the parchment, began to go again through the message from the Dumnonian warrior. In places it was tedious and his eyes skipped the passages of no real intent. The young Arturo wrote as he lived and fought . . . often with an undue waste of effort. But the truth of the overall matter lacked nothing in good sense.

> . . . and this Venutius, being your man, served you well and, but for the protection of the gods, would have faithfully worked your purpose. Dead he is now, and no stain against his name for none but I, and now you, know the dark truth. . . .

Ambrosius sipped his wine. Aye, lost in a blizzard and torn to death by wolves and now—he touched his greying hair and smiled wryly—the young Arturo, standing on the advantage of his growing popularity and increase in forces, could make the truth known to spread through the country to raise a cry like the howling of wolves against his name and bring an even shorter fall in the raising of levies and a jibing at and cursing of his name. He knew now, too, how to seize his advantage with the smooth shuttle of changing policy.

> I will come to you as long ago I said I would when you sue me for return. This done I will serve you faithfully as *Dux Bellorum* and acknowledge you as *Comes Britannicus* for I have no wish for king or overlordship of this country—only to fight and win its true liberty under the gods and then return to my people. . . .

Ambrosius smiled and picked an apple pip from his teeth. Aye, likely so. But the truth in a man of thirty was only one season. In twenty years, success would bring on a different fruiting. Still, by then his own seasons would have wintered into death's unending keep. He smoothed the parchment and reread the fine hand. The man was no barbarian. He wrote with the smoothness and polish that few now brought to the Roman tongue; and, writing, asked now for that which was to feed the young pride in him.

> This is how I would ride to join you at Glevum and

this is the manner of your greeting and none shall know that it is other than the true courtesy of a father welcoming a son, none other than the measure due to a well-serving War Duke come to be honoured by his noble Commander. . . .

Though in truth it was much other . . . aye, but why not so? Few in this country would fail to follow Arturo, where many now grew tired of him and withheld their men and loyalty. Leagued with Arturo, he would still hold supreme power. Many Caesars when young had fought in the field and many, when age and success came, had been content to leave the war grounds and work for the peace and prosperity that followed victories. Of one thing he had no doubt. For this country both he and Arturo wished and lived for the same thing, that it should rise to freedom and greatness again. And truth it was that his aging bones and body found no joy now in hard lying and the eating of hardtack, and the supping of cold ale or springwater on the black and windy nights of mountains and bare heathland.

With a sudden pleasure and a curt dismissal of all irony he freely gave ground to the run of time and chance. The promise of Arto should be made good. He pulled his purple cloak to proper set over his long-sleeved white toga and beat twice on the gong which stood on the table. His *praefectus castrorum* came in, the man Olipon, who had once visited Arturo on Cam Hill. He said, "Send to me Arturo's man."

When Durstan entered and was alone with him, he said, "You are the man Durstan?"

Durstan nodded. "Aye, my lord."

"Who was outlawed by me with Arturo?"

"That is so, my lord."

"You are no longer so."

"I am so, my lord, so long as the writ runs against my lord Arturo."

For a moment Ambrosius would have been angry. Then he laughed and said easily, "Aye, you are a stubborn lot, you Arto men. But you have no need to be now. The writ against Arturo no longer runs. There is peace between us."

"Then I thank you, my lord."

"Return to your lord Arturo and say from me that all shall be as he wishes and that he shall find true and warm greeting from me."

When Durstan had gone Ambrosius took the parchment—which could have been washed and scraped clean for further use—and reluctantly burned it in the flame of the big candle, the smell of its burning acrid in his nostrils.

So it was that in the year of Christ 480 on a morning when the hawthorn bushes showed scarce green with yet-to-open buds, and the past year's leaves of the beech were burnished copper and gold on their branches, defying the new growth, and the first swallows and martins were yet to come, Arturo made good his promise to his dead wife, Daria, to ride in triumph with her to Glevum.

He came riding the White One, his war cap red-and-white-plumed and wearing—in honour of his wife, who had been a true believer—the rich scarlet surcoat with the blue-robed figure of the Virgin Mary given to him by the bishop of Noviomagus, his sword sheathed, his lance raised high and his small red-and-white battle buckler slung on his back. Behind him in mounted troops came five hundred companions, red-and-white plumes and scarves flaring in the robust breeze, and five hundred marshmen with Coroticus at their head, their spears over their shoulders, the fish-eagle device on their breasts, their bows slung on their backs and their quivers showing blood-red-dyed goose feathers as flights for their arrows. There was no man among them not tried and proved by battle. Behind them on the rising slope to the south the rest of the army, save for those who still kept winter stations along the far-east line, lay in camp and cursed the draw by lot which kept them from place in the proud company on this day that the great war duke Arturo made good his Arto promise.

But none, except those closest and dearest to Arturo of his first small band of companions, knew the meaning of the great white mare that, riderless, her hide gleaming like polished ivory, kept place alongside and made pair with the White One. Across the mare's back was laid a cloak of scarlet with a sky-blue lining caught about the waist with a golden belt with a clasp of two singing birds and from it hung a small soft leather pouch which held three locks of Daria's dark hair which Arturo had taken from her before her burial.

As Arturo rode at the head of the column to the east gate, where Count Ambrosius with a guard of honour waited to greet him, in his memory coursed clearly the words he had long ago spoken to Daria in Corinium while yet his bold promise was a thing of wind and angry boast. *It is written that on the day of my triumph you shall come riding into Glevum with me on a white mare, wearing a cloak of scarlet with a lining of blue silk and about your waist a golden belt with a clasp of two singing birds. And when Count Ambrosius comes out to greet us he shall hand to you a silver goblet full of new wine.* . . . And then, curbing the smile that touched his lips, came memory of her reply. *And then, and then will be the day when pigs shall be flying and the salmon coming up the Sabrina shall wriggle ashore, their mouths full of sea pearls to lay at my feet.* . . .

Before him now, a spear's throw away, stood Ambrosius, not knowing or caring to know the reason for the coming ritual, knowing only that it was small price to pay for this alliance and that the wagging of tongues in the years to come would give it meaning or myth, for this stalwart warrior knew the power of riddle and mystery from the god-touched side of his nature.

Ambrosius waited, helmeted and cloaked, his ancient well-burnished cuirass shining in the sun, purple-cloaked and leather-belted and highly honed, heavy legionary marching boots on his feet, studded and unchanged in design from the boots worn by the fighting men of the Twentieth and then the Second Augusta legions who had first built and held Glevum, the *colonia Nerviana Glevensium*, under the governorship of Julius Frontinius when the Son of the Virgin that Arturo wore on his surcoat had been dead little more than seventy years. And now, mused Ambrosius, here came one who served willingly any and all gods and was mad—or shrewd?—enough to make his own rituals, though there was no denying the sense in him which understood and used the power of mystery to carry his name through the land and bring men to him and enslave the affections and loyalties of those who looked and longed for greatness to return to this country.

As Arturo drew up a few paces from him and the long column halted behind him, Ambrosius went forward with his bodyguard while at his side came, too, his Cam Prefect, carrying a great withy-plaited tray on which rested a fresh-run Sabrina cock salmon, its partly open jaws stuffed and overflowing with sea pearls. Beside it, couched on its belly, its hide smooth-scrubbed, lay a young dead pig with a pair of dove's wings fixed wide-spread to its back and a goblet of wine held between its fore trotters.

The two men gave greetings to one another and then Arturo leant forward and took the goblet from the tray, half turned and poured in libation some of the wine over the scarlet cloak on the mare at his side and then spilled the rest to the ground.

Arturo raised his right arm high and from the long column of warriors behind him came a great shouting and chanting. "Ambrosius . . . Ambrosius . . . Great Count of Britain!"

Erect, shoulders tight-drawn in pride, Ambrosius smiled and, drawing his short, broad-bladed, double-edged legionary sword from its wood-and-bronze scabbard, raised it high to return the salute. As he did so he knew that the gods had served him well in sending Venutius's treachery and his own awry, and knew, too, that in Arturo he had found the first warrior ever in this land who read his mind and guessed his dreams and had the spirit to bury other men's evils if in that way lay true service to his country. Whatever the future held, their names would live and for once—touched by a rare humility—he knew that he cared not which name time would prove the greater.

CHAPTER SEVEN

Elegy For A Warrior

ARTURO AND HIS MEN stayed ten days at Glevum, and in that time he became convinced that not only had the gods intended this alliance, but that it was meant to show him how much still he had to learn and to understand about the art of warfare which lay behind the straightforward marshalling of men into fighting positions when the enemy, in large or small bands, was sighted. His respect for Count Ambrosius increased when he realized that not only did the man share his dreams for the future of the country but he faced the task with an industry that covered every least aspect of the enemy. He gathered news of the Saxons from a discreetly organized network of peddlers, traders, disaffected Saxon warriors, and from their own countrymen who lived as slaves or worked barely tolerated in the Saxon lands.

While they sat in Ambrosius's room until late in the night the Count brought out for him maps and reports which for the first time gave him a picture of his own country to which he had been almost blind before. Seeing and understanding this, Ambrosius smiled and said, "Before the first sword is drawn or spear thrown if any army leader has done his work well then the battle should be half won. Would you waste time besieging a Saxon hilltop knowing that they hold stores and water for a month? No. Pass them by and then they must follow you and somewhere come to equal terms. You know why Esc lets you parade along his borders and only a few glory-hungry bands of his young men come out to find

honour or a welcome in Valhalla by swarming like hornets
around you? I tell you—because he sits content knowing you
have not the force to come to him. So, he farms and harvests
his lands and waits to make the move on the playing board
which will surprise and defeat you.''

"What move?"

"Of that later, my Arturo. But remember this, Esc is the
true son of his father, and like his father he makes others
work for him." He smiled and sipped his wine. "Now—for
he will have had the news—that we are drawn together he
will know that time is short for him and the move he would
make must soon be played."

A little roused, Arturo asked firmly, "Why should I not
know of this move now? Tell me so that I can prepare to meet
it."

"And find that naught waits for you to meet? Esc has his
men here as I have mine with him. If I seem unduly secretive,
unfitting our new friendship, it is because I wait for more
news to be sure of Esc's mind. For now take one half of the
men you have with you and go to Cam Hill. Send the others
east to Lindum. Draw such extra men as you can from Prince
Geraint and—if things move as they should—my Camp
Prefect, Olipon, whom you know, will be with you within a
few weeks to tell you my mind." He paused for a moment,
watching Arturo's face, and then went on gently, "So soon
after my treachery and our new accord you take this caution
well. But—though it give some shame—who is to know that
there is not among your men . . . aye, and mine . . . some
new Venutius? All great commanders dwell on a peak of
loneliness. Until the day comes to march trust no one for
there is no man living who has not his price."

Arturo's mouth tightened as he held down the momentary
anger at this cynicism and the shame it held for him to
withhold trust in any of his near companions. But remembering Venutius, he saw the wisdom of it. Nevertheless he said,
"Under the gods then there is no true trusting between man
and man?"

"Nor between man and woman—when the man has been

marked by the gods for his work. You are now in truth and all
honour Dux Bellorum of this country. You will find the wind
blows chill on your high peak. When I was your age I had all
to learn and none of true wisdom to help me.'' He smiled,
scratching the tip of his beaked nose. ''Now you have me,
and with our coming together a force far larger that I ever
had. And more will come. In time we shall be victorious and
this country will stay as it is now, the last part of the great
Roman Empire never to be overrun by the barbarians.''

''And then you will call yourself what? King? Emperor?''

Ambrosius shrugged his shoulders. ''What matters the
name? King or Emperor? It is the power that counts. Since
my remaining years are few I may not live to make the
choice. That will fall into your hands.''

''I seek no such titles. The work done, I would go back to
my lands and live in peace.''

Ambrosius shook his head. ''So you think now. The
thought does you honour, but you will find that the years you
have to spend on that cold high peak will change you. To
warm your loneliness you will have need to wrap yourself in
the cloak of majesty.''

Arturo rode back to Cam Hill with his men and for a month
he sat waiting for word from Count Ambrosius. In that time
he drew fresh men from Prince Geraint and put them into
training and schooling to the ways of the companions.

Toward the end of the month Prince Geraint rode into the
camp with a bodyguard. Talking to Arturo as they ate together in Arturo's small dwelling, he said, ''I stay with you,
my lord Arturo, to march with you and my men.''

Wiping grease off his lower lip from the chewing on a roast
wild duck leg, Arturo was silent for a while, studying the
man. He was now in his late twenties. He grew each year
more like his father, dark-haired, dark-browed, a smouldering warmth in his eyes and a restlessness in his body as
though he held down deep impatience.

Quietly Arturo asked, ''Why so, my Prince?''

''For two reasons. One—you wait the coming of the

Prefect Olipon. The second—I am young and have sat at Isca too long without true taste of battle.

"I wait for Olipon, it is true—but how could you know this?"

"Because by direction of Count Ambrosius I come in his place. Olipon we shall join in good time where he waits for us. For now I speak for him."

Straight-faced, thoughtful, Arturo said, "It was to me that Olipon would come, and for me to wait for him by command of Count Ambrosius. I trust and honour you, but—"

Prince Geraint laughed. "You raise your hackles? There is no need." He put his hand in his belt pouch and laid a gold ring on the table between them. Arturo knew the ring for Olipon had once brought it to him from Ambrosius and he had in defiance handed it back to him. "This is from the Count to show that I truly speak for him. Matters have moved fast and Olipon was needed elsewhere. Now will you hear me?"

Arturo nodded, his face easing into a smile, but even so he felt the bite of the truth which Ambrosius had so recently spoken to him. The high peak was lonely. Never would he have believed that he would have spoken so to his own Prince. Reaching over, he refilled the Prince's cup with ale and said, "You could have given me the rough of your tongue first and the ring after. The ways of the field and fighting I know. Now I begin to learn new arts and observances."

"It is forgotten. Now listen to the words of Ambrosius."

For more years than most men could remember, around Noviomagus and to the lands south and close up to Venta and along the shores of the Vectis sea and on the island of Vectis itself, explained Geraint, there had long been settled sporadically small Saxon settlements that gave little trouble and an uneasy truce ran through all these parts. More trouble came from the pirate raiders from the Gaulish seas once the seasons turned fair. At this time there was as leader of this straggling, ever-changing territory, a leader called Cerdic, still a young man, whose birth lines were unknown but variously described. His name was clearly British, and British he might have truly been, or as truly—as many claimed—either the son of Saxon born in or out of marriage with a British woman, or—and his name was strong argument for this—the son of a Briton got with a Saxon woman. Whatever his birth his ambitions had grown with the coming of manhood and his loyalties and ties were all with the Saxons. This man had been chosen by Esc to lead the first of his moves against Arturo and Count Ambrosius. As soon as the spring brought the right weather, Cerdic—who was already secretly marshalling the local Saxon settlers into a fighting force—would be joined by the arrival of a seaborne band of Saxon warriors, five or six hundred strong, all adventurers eager for plunder and land who would sail into the Vectis sea and make a landing somewhere between Noviomagus and Clausentium, on the long, broken coastline full of deep inlets and creeks. All this Prince Geraint explained, and finished:

"These Sea Saxons will come on the first good wind and tide as the season betters. That cannot be more than a few weeks distant. If Cerdic is successful then Noviomagus and all the lands right up to Venta and the western limits of the Anderida forest will be his. Then will come a linking up with the South Saxons who under Aelle now hold Anderida itself. With the creation of this new territory of West Saxons the whole right flank of this country is open and the way clear right up through Calleva to Corinium. Would you be happy to fight or even hold the line you have now, knowing that Esc would move out against you while Cerdic can march north and take your rear?"

Arturo, who had been toying with the bare-picked duck leg, frowned and tossed it to Cabal at his feet. The hound rose and went out into the night with it and the sound came clear of his teeth crushing the fragile bone. So this, he thought, was one more lesson among the many to be learned, the lesson of the value of foreknowledge which gave a commander long sight to prepare his moves. So far, although he had done much and made the country ring with and rise to his name, he had, compared to Ambrosius and his secret gathering of news, been no more than like some lucky, impetuous, feck-less raiding son of a tribal chief, adventuring the good sea-sons away to cure the itches of an idle winter.

He said, "Only a fool would wait for the dagger thrust in his side as he crosses swords with the enemy. Where is Olipon now?"

"He sits with a small party well north of Venta, a handful of men that will cause no tongues to wag and word to run to Cerdic. We go to join him at the full of the moon and march by day through Sorviodunum and take the Calleva road as though making for Londinium, there to move north to Lin-dum or south to the borders of the Cantiaci lands which Esc holds."

"Which all men would expect of me." Arturo said it wryly, not without a sense of amusement, for he was truly being taught a new lesson in the craft of warfare and with it a light touch of the switch from Count Ambrosius to his high mettle by making all this plain to him through another and so—to which he had good and acknowledged right—reminding him that he served a master. He scratched gently at his beard and went on, "And when we meet with Olipon? Am I still to be under instruction?"

Prince Geraint laughed. "No. You will hear what Olipon says, take the news of his gleaning about Cerdic and make your own decisions. I come with you from here on my own will. I have two sons now, the older, Cato, now in his sixth year so the Dumnonian line is secure should aught happen to me. If the gods take me then your father becomes his ward until he is of age and if anything happens to your father before then you will take his place. But I pray the gods spare me for I have that still to do in Dumnonia which one day you shall see and for which you shall give me thanks."

"You talk a riddle, my Prince."

"Aye, a riddle of time and blood." He rose to take his leave, and as they walked out into the night for him to go to his own quarters, he put a hand on Arturo's shoulder and said, "Prince I am, but from now on I march with you and take your commands without question as you would those of Count Ambrosius."

As he walked away in the moonlight Arturo watched him, moving with the ground mist knee-high about him, and he knew then that the fashion of all his future days was to be changed. He had new and hard lessons to learn . . .*Aie*, and would learn them fast and use them with the years better than any other before him.

He looked up at the moon and an owl called from the trees. The moon was just moving out of its first quarter; the month of Mars and Badb, the gods of war, was with them. In eight days it would be at the full.

The weather until the full moon brought days of heavy rain. The rivers ran bank-high and the meres and lakes rose until only the tips of the rushes and reeds showed above water. The short turf of the downlands was sodden so that the passage of men and horses turned it into quagmires and even the amadou tinder a man carried safe-wrapped in his pouch for fire-making became useless as it breathed and caught the dampness from the air.

Three days after the full of the moon, the rains now ceased, Arturo moved out with his company to meet Olipon. He had with him two hundred mounted companions, nearly the same number of Coroticus's marshmen and eighty mounted Dumnonian men under Prince Geraint, who had yet to prove themselves as companions. They met Olipon ten miles north of Venta on the Calleva road close to the headwaters of the river which ran south through Venta to find the sea at Clausentium. Olipon had with him a company of sixty-odd men, all tried foot soldiers, which was split—for Ambrosius still clung to the old Roman divisions—into self-contained parties of eight men who shared a tent or made their own from brushwood and ash poles, managed their own cooking and provisions and had a horse to pack their gear. They carried a heavy spear and either a short broad-bladed gladius sword or the longer spatha and wore mostly heavy leather helmets, surcoats and short trews. A few boasted ancient pieces of chain and scale mail and counted themselves fortunate for there were few armourers left in the land.

That first evening in camp Olipon gave Arturo his report.

Cerdic had mustered nearly three hundred foot soldiers from the local settlements and these were lodged halfway between Noviomagus and Clausentium, split into small parties and hidden away in the marshes and along the creek sides, waiting the arrival of the long boats. As he spoke he drew with a stick in the heath sand the dispositions of Cerdic's men. On the high ground north of the Noviomagus—Clausentium road he had placed lookouts to light a smoke fire at the sighting of the long boats and another party on the downland to the east of Venta to make smoke fire when the first signals were seen.

"How many warriors will there be to a long boat?"

"Since they come as warriors and not as settlers with wives and family there could be fifty to sixty a long keel. With at the most six boats—say, three hundred and sixty men. With Cerdic's army you have rising seven hundred men against you and you have well less than six hundred."

"It is enough."

Olipon said nothing, but he knew that the words were not made in boast.

That night Arturo lay long awake. The gods were testing him where they had first tested Ambrosius. To meet the keels as they grounded would be a child's folly, for Cerdic would long have known his coming and there might be no landing. Even if there were, then he would be fighting with only half his force, for the creek lands and marshes were no place for his mounted men. He knew that now he faced in truth the real understanding of many of Ambrosius's words to him. The winning of battles must be shaped long before the first spear was flung or the first troop of horse thundered into action.

The next morning he called Olipon to him and said, "Send word to your smoke-fire parties. They are to keep place after the landing and send fresh signals when Cerdic's men and the sea warriors have crossed the Clausentium—Noviomagus road and are well set on their march to Venta."

Two days later the first smoke signal billowed and plumed into the air southeast of Venta. The next morning the smoke came again, rising high and flaring away like the streaming of a horse's tail in the wind.

That evening Arturo marched southward. By the time they were below Venta the sun had long set and they had the light of the dying moon. Coroticus's marshmen went ahead in a wide crescent-shaped screen. None could move faster or with more ease and quiet than a marshman at night. Behind came the troops of cavalry while Olipon's footmen were split to march on their flanks.

Before dawn while the first bird had yet to sing the coming daylight and the last of the beetle- and root-grubbing badgers had returned to their holts, they saw below them the dying night fires of the Cerdic forces and, with the first pale wash of light in the eastern sky, could pick out the stir of the Saxons as they rose and began to prepare themselves for the coming day.

That day was one of triumph and bitter sorrow for Arturo. Without the cry of battle horn or wild shouting Arturo led the cavalry of the companions. They came down with the gathering dawn like a horde of wolves and were on the camp before most of the Saxons could buckle on their sword belts or reach for scramasaxes. Those that were armed stood and fought and made time for their fellows to seek their weapons.

The companions streamed through them, killing and maiming and, once through them, turned and rode back around the flanks of the camp to re-form on the higher ground as the marshmen ran forward and from a safe distance poured a swarming flight of arrows into the camp. When their quivers were empty the battle horn of Prince Geraint blew and the marshmen drew aside as his company of Dumnonians rode down and carried sword and lance to the Saxons. But by now the Saxons were past their first surprise. They formed a ring about the camp and faced their foe, shouting and crying, their swords finding many a trooper's groin, their seax knives quick to cut the throat of any that fell. The bright morning air was full of the screaming of maimed horses and the last calls and shouts of dying men.

As Prince Geraint's troopers spent themselves and turned away to re-form, Arturo led his companions to the attack again, closely followed by Olipon and his footmen and Coroticus's spear-carrying marshmen.

On this attack, their lances tossed aside for they were of little use now, Arturo's men took the fight to the Saxons with their swords and with their small round bucklers held low to protect their groins. Riding hard, knowing that the surprised Saxons must soon break and run, the air full of the bitter tang of sweating men and horses and sharp with the bite of dust and blood, Arturo saw beyond the camp the first of the enemy to run and knew they would be Cerdic's men, the tolerated settlers who had no real heart for battle.

Again the companions broke the Saxon ring and rode it through while the foot soldiers came hard behind them. As he fought and hewed with his sword, Arturo knew again what he already knew: that, once the fight was joined, a man could see nothing but confusion and know nothing but the shock of iron and flesh; yet knew *now* what had been beyond him before: that each man and trooper in this battle must hold to his place and to his duty under his commander, following even unto death the design of battle scratched out in bare dust and loose sand the day before. And many there were who found death, and many more among them who lay open to it and were saved by their comrades. Among these Arturo took company, for as he cut and slashed his way free from the heart of the camp a wounded Saxon, lying on the ground, half raised himself and thrust with his heavy spear at the breast of the White One. The mare screamed and reared high, throwing Arturo to the ground where one of the White One's flailing hooves struck him on the side of the head and sent him into oblivion. Lancelo and Durstan jumped from their mounts and stood over him. They were joined by four others of the companions, tight-pressed, fighting off the crowding Saxons, and stood fighting them off until Prince Geraint and his countrymen came again at the charge and broke a great passage through the ring into which Olipon and Coroticus led their men.

They fought while the prey birds began to gather above, spiralling on the soft southerly wind. They fought while Prince Geraint and his men re-formed and charged again, and they fought on when they saw the Prince go down as a great axe broke the left foreleg of his mount. He fell to take a spear thrust through his throat and then, as his dying cry burst from him, the Saxons broke and ran. Those who were Cerdic's men ran, throwing arms and war gear from them, to seek the safety of their marsh huts and wood bothies, and those who were sea warriors ran for their long keels and prayed to Woden that the news of their defeat would not outstrip them and give courage to the country's natives to come out and burn their craft.

Seeing them go, Olipon, who now stood in command, gave orders for the marshmen to gather their arrows and harry the enemy to the coast. The rest of the army re-formed and stayed where they were to make camp, to collect their dead and mourn and bury them, and to shelter their wounded and care for them. As darkness came the cooking pots simmered over the wood fires, the guards were mounted and the horses hobbled and fed and watered, and those that lived blessed their God or gods but, having little stomach for food, took the pack train ale and drank to those who would drink no more on the sweet turf or in the shady thickets of their green land. And Borio, who beneath a warrior's sweat-and-blood-soiled shirt carried the heart of a bard, gave rein to the spirit in him and sang of the day and its triumphs and its sorrows.

His voice was the first which Arturo heard as he came out of the blackness of coma, where he lay under a canopy of laced willow boughs with Olipon sitting outside, watching the dance of men's shadows around the campfires. Arturo, his head throbbing, lay still, and Borio's voice coming to him told him of the day's victory and its grim losses.

"At the battle of the men of the long boats, I saw
    Arto's men who flinched not from spears ·
    Under the thighs of the companions, swift chargers
    Long their legs, wheat their fodder, swooping like
      eagles
    Men in terror, bloody their heads
    At the battle of the men of the long boats, I saw
    Great Geraint, Lord of the land of the west

Before Geraint, the enemy's scourge
Loud the clash of swords, bitter the war cries
Lovely to behold, the glory of the west
When Geraint was born, the gods touched him
At the battle of the men of the long boats, I saw
Geraint slain and Heaven's gate open
The gods give him welcome, the Bright One
Lovely to behold, the glory of Britain.''

Arturo closed his eyes and, to stiffen himself against the
sorrow in him, ground his teeth. The gods gave and the gods
took and there was no tracing the pattern of their ways. They
gave men friendships and broke them by death and, since the
pattern of his days was clear to him, he knew that grief must
be a silent thing for there were no words to speak its truth.

Olipon came in to him and Arturo sat up. Before Olipon
could speak, he said, ''I have heard Borio singing of Geraint.
I saw the spear go into my White One.''

''She is dead, my lord, and buried deep where no vermin
can touch her.''

''And now tell me the rest.'' His voice was level and his
hand unshaking as he took a beaker of water which Olipon
carried for him.

''Coroticus's men followed to the long boats. Men from
Noviomagus had set fire to two of them. Three got away with
less than a hundred to crew them. . . .'' He went on, telling
the run of the day and the toll of losses, and finished, ''You
have done what Count Ambrosius wanted done. Esc will
squat like a broody hen for a long while yet.''

''Cerdic?''

''He was not among the dead. He will lie safe for a long
while. The story of this day will run for more years than any
child of living man will ever see. I leave for Glevum tomorrow, my lord, with your permission, to give a full account to
Count Ambrosius.''

Arturo nodded and, sliding his legs from the bed, stood up,
massaging the back of his head with his palm, saying, ''And I
for the east.''

He moved out of the shelter and saw the thin slip of the passing moon above. Borio's voice came again clearly to him.

"At the battle of the men of the long boats, I saw
Men who did not flinch from spears
Great Arto's men who now drink wine with the
gods. . . ."

Cabal walked at his side and he dropped his hand to the hound's head. Anga was gone, and now the White One. The White One it had been who had brought Daria to him when, running wild and free in the forest, he had caught and broken it and brought it to her for betrothal gift. True love, though it was mortal, raised a man near to the gods. But it was a once-given gift. All love that followed was no more than the broken reflection on the face of troubled waters of joys past.

That year Arturo took his men north to Lindum and on to Eburacum along the borders of the northern Saxon enclaves. Few came out to meet them. Twice he rode to Corinium to meet Count Ambrosius. At Glevum and Corinium men now came flocking to join the army of Arturo, the great Dux Bellorum, the fame of his name and exploits drawing them from their craggy tribal lands in Cymru and north as far as Lugovalium on the Great Wall of Hadrian.

By the end of the good season the men were trained and sent to increase and strengthen the growing line of armed camps and stockades that formed the long-stretched frontier against the Saxon east, leaving Arturo free to withdraw the bulk of his cavalry to Cam Hill and the west for the winter.

A week before he and the companions were to leave for Cam Hill, Arturo with Lancelo and Durstan rode into Lindum to take their farewell of the bishop. In the place of the White One Arturo was now mounted on a black stallion which was a gift to him from Count Ambrosius, a beast with a fiery war temper and a willfulness at times which brought hard bridling from Arturo, and often made him long for the smooth understanding needing no words, no hard mastery, only the pressure of knee or foot to know his will, of the White One.

As they entered the palace courtyard the bells from the monastery and nunnery rang for them and the bishop came forward with his household to greet them. Arturo dismounted and embraced the bishop. After their greetings were made, Arturo was shown to the room which stood always ready for him in the palace. A bowl of warm water, scented with the oil of honeysuckle, was brought to him for his washing. As he stood alone, combing his beard after washing, he heard the door open behind him, and he smiled to himself for by now he knew the ways of the lady Gwennifer.

Without turning, he said, "I had been told that you had gone north to your father."

"I did, my lord. On two matters of importance. But now I am here and you grant me only a view of your dusty tunic back. How could you know it was me?"

Arturo turned slowly. "When I hear the scolding of a wren in the wild clematis, the sweet plaint of the nightingale in the hazels, or the complaint of the chiffchaff on the poplar top—do I have to see them to know them? When you move, the silver bells of your bracelet ring—and more, there is none in this town but you would pass through my door without knocking." He gave her a little obeisance of his head. "You should be schooled to small courtesies."

"It is of a schooling already done that I come to you."

The sun through the window burnished the long sweep of her fair hair, and the blue eyes which seemed to shade or brighten with her moods now had the depth of the wood-bowered columbine. She stood proudly, of good height to match his own, the long white gown close-collared about her neck, its folds caught smooth across her breasts with a crossing of red silk ribbons, its looseness below her waist moulded in the draft from the open window to caress the run of her legs. She had a beauty which had been in his mind often this campaigning season. Seeing his eyes on her, she was caught in a rare moment of uncertainty and raised her right hand to touch the side of her sun-browned face so that the bells of her bracelet broke again into soft, sweet sound.

With a sudden gruffness that served to cover a rare stir of desire in him, Arturo said, "I am in no mood to tease myself with your riddles."

She laughed quickly, knowing her power to move him, and came forward and took his hand. "Then come, and an end to riddles. Please come . . . humour me in this, my lord."

They went down the flights of curving stone steps and she led him through the bishop's herb garden and into the stable yards. Standing in the middle of the yard was a white mare, bridled and carrying a red leather saddle and strong-braided girths of the same colour. At its head stood her personal manservant, Lacus, a dark-haired, bow-legged, middle-aged man whose right eye sat askew from the healing of a dagger cut underneath it.

Her hand still in his, Gwennifer said, "My lord should always ride the White One for all men know him as Arturo of the White One. My father bred her in the lands below the Wall and would neither sell nor make gift of her to anyone. Mount her, my lord, and see how well she has been schooled. She moves to the whisper of a voice between her ears. The scratch of a fingernail on her proud neck will tell her your mood and her mouth is as soft as the inside of the nest your wren makes in the wild clematis." Her eyes shone with teasing and excitement.

Arturo went to the White One, holding down the choking in his throat as he thought of the day of the battle of the long boats. She stood like a queen and her eyes were pools of peat-stained mountain water, and the curve of her arching nostrils marked her spirit and her pride. He put a hand on her withers and felt the pulse and strength of her body and he caressed her bowed neck as a lover might smooth the white flesh of his beloved, and he spoke to her in the soft language that came from birth to all the Epona-blessed and she tossed her noble head and curled her lips back from her strong teeth and neighed softly.

He took the reins and Lacus knelt and made a cradle of his hands for him to mount. He walked her around the yard and felt the movement in all her muscles which he had known with the White One, and he was thinking how Gwennifer had brought him Cabal to take the place of Anga, and now brought him this god-fired beast to take the place of the White One. Because all good fortune came by threes there was no escaping the impulse that took his eyes to Gwennifer as she stood watching man and mount move over the great flags of the yard.

He rode back to Lacus and dismounted, handing the reins to the groom, who said quietly, "My lord Loth, the lady Gwennifer's father, says her lines go back to the great horses of the Syrians who served on the Walls three hundred years ago."

"Can history be told so true over so many years?"

Lacus grinned so that his right eye closed. "History with my lord Loth is known by its horses. Her sires have borne Caesars and now, my lord, she will bear another."

Laughing, Arturo went back to Gwennifer and, taking her hand, kissed it. "First Cabal and now the White One. I thank you but there are no words fitting to mark your bounty. But one gift deserves another. Come."

He took her hand and led her back through the herb garden and up to his room.

He sat her down and poured wine for them both and asked, "Who schooled the mare?"

"I did, my lord."

"And the matters of importance you had with your father?" As he spoke he went to his saddle pack.

From behind him Gwennifer said, "The first was of the White One. Of the second I cannot yet speak without immodesty."

Smiling, he came to her and laid across her lap the scarlet belt with the clasps of two golden singing birds which had ridden with him to his triumph at Glevum. "Your present calls for this return. It was my wife's. Now it is yours."

"I thank you, my lord."

He raised his wine cup and drank to her and Gwennifer drank, too, lowering her head. This, she sensed, was the time when she stood waiting the sweet or sharp turn of her destiny and must keep her eyes from him so that no shadow of change on his face should give her forewarning of his words to come.

Arturo poured the wine which was still in his cup to the ground. "The wine is spilled and now so freely runs my desire. Two things greatly loved you have given back to me. There is a third still in your gift. If it is in your heart to grant me that gift then there is no need of words. Share your wine with me and I know that the gift is to be given."

Gwennifer looked up at him then and her eyes were bright now with the clear blue of the flax flower and she stood proud and radiant before him and slowly held out the wine cup.

"Drink, my beloved lord Arturo."

Arturo took the wine and drank. Making no move to her, his eyes narrowing with gentle mischief, he asked, "And now tell me—what was the second matter of importance you had with your father?"

She was silent for a moment, then, throwing her head back a little, she laughed, and said, "It was to ask him that if you should speak for me in marriage he would give his leave."

"And his answer?"

"That the likeliness was as remote as pigs flying, but if it should happen then he would be proud of the honour done to both of us."

"You are both wrong. The honour is done to me."

He reached out and took her hand and drew her gently to him and embraced her. As they kissed, Cabal, who lay by the window, rose, stretched his long body and gave a half-yawn, half-whine and then thumped back to the floor and beat his tail against the boards.

The return to Cam Hill was delayed for two weeks.

They were married by the bishop of Lindum and, to do the God of the Christians honour, Arturo wore the surcoat given him by the bishop of Noviomagus and a ceremonial sword

sent him as gift from Count Ambrosius. At his side Gwennifer wore a white silk robe with a saffron-coloured cloak and
saffron-coloured shoes. About her hair was a circlet of bay
leaves and she stood at Arturo's side as the bishop joined
them in marriage and her lips were dark red as the hawthorn
berries that grew on the great dyke which rimmed the city on
the east.

The night of their wedding Arturo and Gwennifer withdrew early from the feasting and as they lay abed, she full
woman now and he no longer lacking manhood's joys, the
soft breeze of the warm late-autumn day which had favoured
them stirred the window drapings through whose opening
the full moon, hanging low over Lindum, silvered the floor
and tipped the grizzled pelt of Cabal with ivory points. Clear
to them as they lay in each other's arms came the singing
from the feasting hall and Gwennifer kissed the hard muscle
of his shoulder as the words came to them.

> "Set your strawberry-coloured mouth against my lips,
>   O skin like foam; stretch your lime-white arms around
>   me . . ."

And later, when Arturo slept but Gwennifer lay awake and
the singing still lingered:

> "She's the white flower of the blackberry,
>   She's the sweet flower of the raspberry,
>   She's the best herb in excellence—
>   For the sight of my eyes . . ."

Lying there, she knew she had gained that which she had
wanted from the first time of setting eyes on Arturo as she had
played her harp to him. Her need for him was passionate and
absolute. Sensing the glory that with the protection of his
gods must come to him, she desired no more than to bear his
sons and one day be his queen. No woman in the land should
have claim on him or issue from him but her. As she thought
this, there came back to her the stable talk and camp stories

freely spread of the woman Genara, whose ill fame was known in Causennae, who claimed birth of her son from the fathering of Arturo when she had spread her body over him to drive the killing cold from his heart. . . .

Thinking this, she stretched her love-eased limbs in the great bed, knowing that no woman or child should live to lay claim to the smallest part of Arturo's coming glory or prove blood claim for any male child. She yawned with pleasure and the joy of long-sought possession.

Three days after Arturo rode out of Lindum on the White One with Gwennifer at his side and the companions raising the dust behind them, Lacus went at night to drink with Genara of the cave. The boy babe whose age was yet to be numbered by years slept under cloths in an old corn pannier. Lacus was good to the woman, drank and ate with her and praised the babe, whom she had called Anir. Because there was a mustard-sized grain of compassion in him he waited until dawn while mother and child slept, the one in drunken stupor and the other in innocence, and cut their throats with less noise and little more thought than he would have given to the butchering of pigs.

CHAPTER EIGHT

The Horses Of The Gods

THEY RETURNED TO CAM HILL for the winter, where now on the plateau top there were stout log-built quarters for men and horses, and the store huts and barns were well stocked with fodder and provisions to take them through to spring. Northward toward Aquae Sulis two more fortified camps were almost completed and here—since the growing army of companions could not be held at its full strength on Cam Hill—were lodged garrisons of four troops of cavalry each under the separate commands of black-bearded Gelliga and Netio of the sword-scarred face. To the southeast not far from Vindocladia another camp—under the command of Garwain—had been fortified with the help of the Durotrige people, who, thankful for the victory at the battle of the long boats, now acknowledged the overlordship of the Prince of Dumnonia.

That Prince was now the six-year-old Cato, for whom Baradoc stood ward in Isca. To Isca at the turn of the year Arturo rode with Gwennifer and a small band of his men to be welcomed and lodged in the old fortress. Here Arturo found Baradoc and his mother, Tia, and his eldest sister, Gerta. Gerta, now seventeen, was six months married to Adipo, the son of the chief of the Durotriges, and in this Arturo saw the hand of the dead Prince Geraint and his father, Baradoc. Blood bonds were the stoutest ties between tribes. But looking at the tall, slim, dark-haired Gerta, seeing the happiness in her face—and the slight burgeoning of her body beneath her green gown that spoke of a child to come—and the pride in the stance of young Adipo beside her, he knew that matching the diplomatic union was that of love given and love returned.

His mother, nearing her fiftieth year, proud of Baradoc's position and her son's fame, held the beauty now no longer of a woman's summer, but the fullness of ripe autumn. Her golden hair was touched with the silvering tints of time, but there was still a defiance of her years in her bright cornflower-blue eyes and in the bold vigour of her body. Baradoc had aged and looked more than his years. The hard, weathered face held sometimes a weariness at odds with the vigour of his speech and his actions and his troubled right arm had grown stiffer.

That first night in Isca lying awake beside Arturo as he slept, Gwennifer thought of the beginning of proudness in Gerta's belly and her hands smoothed the flatness of her own. Maybe, she thought, the ache of longing to be full with his child by its own force delayed the fruiting of the wish. If the love of the gods held, then king Arto would be of this country and she his queen and she would bear him children so that his blood and glory should live forever. Tight-lipped with sudden impatience, she knew that sleep would be long coming.

The next morning as Arturo came down to the fortress courtyard, the jackdaws calling and quarrelling on its ivy-covered walls, it was to find his father and Master Ricat, now greying and, though crabbed by age, still sitting horse as though he and beast were one, mounted and waiting for him while old Ansold, Daria's sword-smith father, held the White One already saddled for him.

Without ceremony Baradoc said, "Mount and ride. We have things to show you."

For a moment Arturo eyed them all, then, knowing his father's humour, mounted the White One. They rode off with Ansold following, his lean legs flapping loose over the back of a moorland pony, out of the fortress and down the southern hillslope through the old town and took a path that led seaward along the River Isca. Herons stood among the sere reeds, fishing.

Following a turn in the river, he saw now that which had

never been here in his time. A small meadow held in the
river's bend had been palisaded around with a high stockade
fence. Guard platforms marked its perimeter, all manned,
and at its only gate, spanned by a log-faced watchtower,
other guards stood on duty.

The gates opened as they rode up. Inside, the great enclosure was lined about with stalls, stables and storehouses.
Piped water ran into the drinking troughs from a small
aqueduct that tapped a stream coming down the slope to the
east of the stockade. In the center, shut off by barred rails,
was a large tanbark ring.

At the entrance of the ring they halted. Baradoc, who
lacked no sense of the dramatic, Arturo knew well, nodded to
Master Ricat, who put two fingers to his mouth and whistled
shrilly.

From the far stalls there came then twelve stable servants
each leading a horse. They filed into the tanyard, the servants
straining back against the leading bridles to curb those
mounts touched by mettle.

The prick of surprise and wonder needled Arturo's cheeks
as he watched. Roan, black, grey, chestnut, bay, piebald and
skewbald, mares and stallions . . . these he knew were the
horses of the gods. Now and again he had seen great horses
and the White One he rode could match them, but here were
twelve and over the stable and stall half-doors around the
enclosure he could see the heads of others. In all, his quick
glancing eye told him, there were no less than a hundred of
these animals.

He turned to Master Ricat and he said, "Master Ricat . . .
this is the dream of Prince Gerontius come true."

Master Ricat, lips pursed, nodded his head, and then said,
"Thank the gods he lived to see it. For years he worked at
this. Aye, and the secret of it has been well kept. Until this
year the horses were lodged in a well-guarded valley near
Nemetostatio. Whenever there came news of a great horse in
this country, it was sought out and bought. And not in this
country alone. Some of the sires and dams of these you see
were shipped from Gaul, bought in the great horse fairs of

Hispania. It was horses like these that served in the legions that Caesar brought to this country and—'' He stopped suddenly and smiled. "I can see that your mind is less on history than on the beasts before you."

Arturo grinned. "My mind is on history to be made, not that which is dead. These are the horses of the gods. How many is the tally?"

With the precision characteristic of him Master Ricat said, "One hundred and seven of age and ready for battle, and eighty-five that run from yearlings to four- and six-year olds. No big increase but Prince Geraint, like his father, would have none to live not truly thrown to his standard. Of broodmares that have stood to the stallions this autumn there are thirty-one." He sighed a little wearily. "And sore hard have been the loads for feeding and care and the guarding against robbery."

"With horses like this, one charge against the standing Saxons would be as the fall of a cliff to crush them," said Arturo softly.

"There is more," said Baradoc. "Now, when you charge, you have your lance or spear which you must thrust into your enemy by your own strength and that finely gauged so that the shock does not unseat you from the saddle. When you abandon or lose your lance and take to your sword, with how much of your full strength can you use your blade edge or point since you must clamp knees and legs to your beast to keep your seat? The full vigor of your sword arm must be tempered to the firmness of your seat. Sit astride a thick tree branch and throw a stone. Stand on the ground and throw a stone. Which goes the farther?"

"From the ground to be sure, my father."

"On the back of the White One now, you are as on a branch. But need be no longer. Ansold with others has made for you that which will turn the White One's back from branch to ground."

He called to the groom who held a chestnut stallion in the middle of the line. As the man began to lead the stallion to them, Baradoc went on, "I show you something now that I

remembered from my lost days soldiering along the southern
and eastern shores of the Middle Sea. Lost, too, from my
memory it was until you and your companions began to grow
to strength and triumph.''

The groom halted the stallion before them and Arturo saw
that the saddle on its back was of thick leather, plentifully
padded on its underside and that fore and aft it rose into a
wide high pommel or saddlebow which would cover a man's
groin before and the base of his spine behind and thus give
protection from the thrust or swing of sword or scramasax.
He saw, too, that hanging from each side of the saddle in line
with the girth bands hung thick leather straps to the ends of
which were looped heavy iron rings with their lower rims
flattened out to fit flush to the sole of a man's boot. At once
he understood all and marvelled at the simple good sense of
these devices and marvelled more at the blindness that the
gods could put on men to stay their fashioning of such.

He would have spoken but Master Ricat said, ''Watch,
my lord Arturo, and you shall see the power given to a man
who rides with his feet on the ground. The man who rides the
bay mare wears leathers and stirrup rings. The other rides his
saddle with his feet free even as you do now.''

Ricat called to the line of horses and two men carrying
heavy swords mounted their horses, one a grey and the other
a bay which bore the new saddle and stirrups. They trotted to
the far end of the enclosure and then turned. Putting their
mounts to a gallop, each man holding his sword free, they
came thundering down toward two stout ash posts which had
been set firmly and deeply into the ground in front of Arturo
and his party. As they swept by, each man struck at his post
and circled away. The force of the sword blow by the man
riding the grey cut deep and sent a great chip flying into the
air. The sword blow of the bay's rider swung into his pole and
sliced clean through it.

Before the horses could rejoin the line on parade Arturo,
his face stiff with pleasure at the vision of power to come,
said sharply, ''How many of these new saddles with their
hanging irons do we have?''

Baradoc said, "Ansold and the other craftsmen have made eighty-four."

"I want one hundred and fifty before the feast of Beltine and as many each month after that as can be fashioned. The increase of the great horses comes slow at Epona's pace, but even the horses we have now will with these saddles give a man double the strength in his sword arm." As he began impetuously to wheel away, he called, "The gods give you glory, my father and Master Ricat—for this day, too, they have given the promise of triumph to our arms!"

They watched him as he cantered out of the stockade and Master Ricat turned and looked ruefully at Baradoc. "I would have told him . . . aye, in a pretty speech, that all, horses and new gear, was a gift from Prince Geraint, sworn before he left here to join him."

Baradoc laughed. "You shall see him fret this winter away, eating his heart out for the moment to ride against the Saxons again. I know him. He rides now alone down the river and, maybe, prays to the gods to turn winter to spring in a day. Aye, and though he must wait like all mortals the due change of the seasons he will live this winter with a fury in him to leave only small part of his mind to others."

Later, on the afternoon of that day, when Gwennifer came into their chamber it was to find Arturo seated in a chair with his feet up on the broad ledge of the window opening, brooding and staring out at the great curve of the Isca River far below. She came up behind him and kissed him gently on the neck and he absently reached up a hand and caressed the side of her cheek.

She went and sat at a small table which caught the light from the window and, loosening the braids from her hair so that it fell loose about her shoulders, began to comb it, studying her face in a large polished bronze mirror that stood on the table.

"I have heard, my lord, about the great horses. Some rumour of these had reached my father. . . ."

Arturo grunted, his thoughts far away. Knowing his remoteness and its reason, Gwennifer smiled and began to pluck at her eyebrows with a pair of silver tweezers, studying her face closely in the mirror and taking pleasure in her beauty. Leaning forward, she touched the skin under one of her eyes. It was rough and the lower rim of her eye was a little inflamed and swollen, a common complaint when one rode much and wind and dust blew in one's face. She reached for a silver goblet which she had filled with a scented salve and, dipping a fingertip into it, smoothed the ointment close under her eye. A man, she thought, would scarce heed the beauty of a woman's face or body when his mind was full of affairs and dreams of the future. And clearly this was the way with Arturo now. To tease him from his mood, the turn of the new-minted words coming easily from her and making her long for her harp to enrich them, she sang, half turning to catch his response:

"Proud on the meadow, great horses,
    Grey of the winter mists,
    Black of the raven god Lugus,
    Brown as the new-turned ploughland,
    Epona's children, Badb's delight,
    Great horses for the Chosen One,
    Great horses of all the gods."

To her gratification the words reached through Arturo's mood and he turned, smiling at her, and, rising, came toward her. But, as he was poised to bend to kiss her, he halted and a frown darkened his forehead, a cloud over the sun of his smile.

His voice sharp, he said, "Where did you get that goblet?"

Surprised at his curtness, she looked at the silver goblet in her hand, and then, confused, said, "I did my duty to you, my lord, by unpacking your campaign chest and found it. Look''—she smiled, hoping to overcome the anger in his face—''I have cleaned it for you with fuller's earth and the polishing of my own warm breath."

"Take the ointment from it," said Arturo curtly. "It is not

a chalice to be used for any ordinary service. Clean it and put it back in my chest.''

Without another look at her Arturo walked to the door and she, stung by his uncouth manner which rode her high mettle hard, called after him angrily as he went from the chamber, ''Command me to anything, my lord—but not in the voice of master to servant!'' She raised the chalice high and flung it after him. It hit the long curtain over the door opening as it fell back on his going and dropped without sound into the softness of trailing folds on the ground.

She sat, hearing the sound of his footfalls on the stone stairs fade away, and then with a shrug of her shoulders, anger quickly gone from her, she got up and retrieved the chalice. It was the size of a drinking goblet with handles on each side, curved and worked in the form of rams' horns. She held it, the spilled salve sticky against her fingers, and wondered why Arturo had been so moved beause of her found use for it.

That night after Gwennifer had retired to her bed, Arturo stayed long below, talking with his father and Master Ricat. There was no sleep for her as she lay watching the long shadows cast across the chamber by the tall candles whose flames swayed in the drafts like yellow crocuses in a spring breeze. When at last Arturo came to bed she pretended sleep. But as he lay alongside her he was not deceived. After a time, without touching her, he said, ''I have offended you and rightly you give me no welcome. For this I ask your forgiveness. I was harsh to you, who are gentler than the soft-breasted dove on the red rowan trees, but that only because the chalice you used for your salve has a holiness that comes from the blood of the Son of the Great Father in the heavens whom the Christos followers worship. When he was crucified it was this bowl which caught the blood that dripped from the spear wound in his left side—so the story runs from my mother, who was given the chalice in return for her goodness by a hermit. It is said that if it is filled with water and held by one marked for greatness the water flushes to the colour of the Christos blood. Twice this has happened to me.

First when I was a babe without understanding, and again
when I was newly in manhood and near dying from an arrow
wound of an enemy. I am the offending lover. Between us
lies the winter of hasty speech. Turn then and speed the
seasons to the clover-scented warmth of summer.''

In the darkness Gwennifer smiled to herself. When he
chose his tongue could drip honey. She turned and put her
arms around him and her lips to his.

The following fighting season, during which Arturo began
the clearing of the valley of the lower Tamesis to make the
approaches to Londinium secure, he made no use of the
heavy horses. The Saxons about the river, he knew, would
never come out in sufficient force to warrant their use—and,
additionally, he was in no hurry to apprise Esc of their
existence. The time would come when the Saxons made a
real show of strength. Enough horses were drawn from Isca
and taken to Cam Hill to form two troops and left under the
command of Gelliga, with young Borio and enough men to
mount them and to begin their training.

Nearing the end of the summer the approaches to Londinium were secured and the city, which had long recovered
from the plague, was lightly garrisoned by local recruitment.
But, as the Romans in the long-past years had seen, it was
no place to be heavily fortified and manned to stand as a
strongpoint. It was slowly coming back to its old position as a
trading center and port, which even the Saxons of Esc used
through the offices of merchants and craftsmen who put
commerce higher than patriotism. Nevertheless Arturo left it
strongly enough held to stop any movement by land between
the Saxons of the south and those of the east and middle lands
reaching up to Lindum. At the end of the season he left a
troop of cavalry there under the command of Netio, hawk-
nosed, face sword-scarred, who had been early among the
companions to join him from the Sabrina wing at Corinium.

He rode back in the autumn to Cam Hill and then to Isca,
where he found that, of his mother's three other children,
Gerta, the elder of his sisters, had given birth to a boy whom

she had named Mordreth, that his young brother, Gareth, had died of the summer fever, and that his younger sister, Amla, was fast moving from childhood to girlhood and growing in looks more like her mother every day. His mother's hair was greyer and there was a calm and serenity about her face through which her true feelings seldom showed. Baradoc was alert and vigorous when anyone was near him and still improving the Cam Hill defenses and those of other hill sites running north to Aquae Sulis. But caught when he left that none observed him, the weariness in him and the growing pain of his right arm seemed to mark his face and body with far more years than he could claim.

For Gwennifer, his wife, there was only wonder in Arturo. The blaze of her beauty and the warmth of her love for him were like the light and heat of a never-setting sun. And her wish—which was his, too, for a son—he humbly prayed to the gods to be granted. A son he needed as much as she did for the day would come when all that he should create would, at his going, need his own flesh and blood to take from his hands and build to even greater glory. For this he prayed to the gods, and not always with modest patience.

And Gwennifer prayed, too, and while that autumn, as though the march of the seasons had been stayed, ate well into the last months of the year she watched for the signs of the springing of his seed within her and sometimes, in moments of disappointment, alone in her chamber at Isca or in the now comfortable lodge at the top of Cam Hill when none could see or hear her, she would vent her impatience in strong action or words, striking her fists against the top of her toilet table, and sometimes smashing unguent or salve pot. Arturo would be king of this country and where was there king who did not yearn for a man-child to carry his memory and greatness forward into the future?

But the day came when this passion of frustration passed from her. Going from their chamber one late afternoon to the eating hall of the Isca fortress, she passed the door of the room in which Baradoc and Tia were lodged. The door was ajar but covered on the inside by the long hanging doeskin draft curtain which was also partly drawn. Clearly to her came the voice of Baradoc and his words made her halt.

He said, ''There is a recklessness in the lady Gwennifer which Arturo should curb. She took one of the great horses yesterday and insisted on riding it in battle drill with the troop. *Aie* . . . and in wildness and indiscipline left them all trailing, riding like one of the Furies.''

''She is high-spirited, true. But she rides as well as any man.''

''This I know. But the time could come—or may have come now without her knowing—when she could be with child, and by her wildness lose it. Arturo will say nothing to her, even if I ask him—but you could speak to her and she would listen for there must be in her as in us a longing for a man-child.''

There was silence for a while and then the quiet, firm voice of Tia said, ''Have you forgotten the words that Merlin wrote on the cliff rock the day we came to Caer Sibli?''

''What words?''

Tia laughed gently. ''You know well, but do not wish to remember. He wrote of Arturo, even yet to be born but carried within me.

> Cronos in the dream spoke thus
> Name him for all men and all time
> His glory an everlasting flower
> He throws no seed.

So there will be no child, no son, no daughter. It is the price which our Arturo has already without his knowing paid to the gods for his coming greatness.''

Baradoc grunted intolerantly. ''Who believes Merlin and his nonsense?''

Tia said quietly, ''You should for he warned you, as you have since told me, that you should not put your boat to water to leave the island until the first swallow had come north. But you did—and were gone from me for many a long year. There will be no child of Arturo born to Gwennifer and my heart aches for her.''

Stiff-faced from the sharp turn of emotion in her, Gwennifer moved on down the stone steps.

The year lingered, mild and unseasonable. On a morning when Baradoc's men, still labouring on the defenses of Cam Hill, worked stripped to the waist under the sun a messenger, covered with sweat and dust, riding a hard-pressed mount, came to Arturo with a message from Count Ambrosius at Corinium.

The North Saxons, who held all the shorelands running south from Petuaria on the Abus River to the great fens and marshes below the Metatis estuary, reinforced by sea from the East Saxons of Esc, had broken out of their enclaves and were besieging Lindum and Durobrivae of the fenlands.

That evening Arturo rode out of Cam Hill with two troops of the great horses and two of his original gathering, and with them went a hundred marshmen with Coroticus. Each man took with him his short commons to last until they reached Corinium. Seven days later they rode into Corinium as the sun was dropping low over the distant Cymru mountains and took quarters in the camp of the Sabrina squadron—a camp which Arturo saw at a glance was held by only a beggarly handful of Ambrosius's cavalry.

As he dismounted and Lancelo took the reins of the White One and led her away Arturo saw Count Ambrosius standing at the opening of his blue-dyed square tent to greet him. The meeting was short of ceremony for Arturo was in a mood of angry bitterness which had built in him as he had ridden these past days. He knew his Ambriosius overwell now and had easily filled for himself the gaps in the scanty information brought to him by the messenger.

Ambrosius poured wine for him, but Arturo did little more than touch his lips with it. Seated across the table from his commander, he said without ceremony, "The weather holds fair still—too good for the season—and if we had been ill-prepared at Lindum and Durobrivae might have tempted the Saxons to break out and breach the line we hold from Lindum to Londinium. But both towns and all the armed camps along the line were left full-manned. What gives them then this sudden courage and hope of success, my lord Ambrosius?''

For a moment or two Ambrosius closed his eyes and breathed deeply. Arturo was all fire and anger and would need careful handling. Even so, he resented his arrogant mood and, but for the tiredness in him, would have bridled it with sharp words. Before he could answer, Arturo spoke again sharply.

''I ask, my lord, what gives the Saxons this boldness since between us we had left the line and its cities fully garrisoned and patrolled?''

Smoothing the grey patches of hair over his ears, Ambrosius answered, ''The reason, Arturo, lies in the craft of Esc and—I admit it—a lack of foresight in me. He has leagued with the Scotti and they have made landings with many craft from the Mona island as far south as Moridunum and Nidum in Demetia. Without time to warn you I have had to withdraw men from the Lindum line and from here to send west as reinforcements. Would you have done differently?''

''Aye, I would. The Scotti could wait. They have always harried the coasts of Cymru. The mountains would have held them long enough to give time to deal with the Saxons first. You can only hunt one stag at a time. Esc is our stag. The Scotti would take slaves, plunder and cattle and perhaps settle in a few sea valleys to await our coming. What is the last news from the east?''

''That Lindum and Durobrivae are surrounded but still hold. That was seven days ago.''

Arturo stood up. ''Then there is no time to be lost. The companions of the White Horse ride tonight. I pray the gods keep this good weather flowing for us on the ride. What it be when we arrive I care not.'' He smiled suddenly, and went on gently, ''There is much to be done, my lord, so I ask your leave to go. We stay but to water and feed our mouths and ride this night.''

For a moment Ambrosius was on the point of finding words to curb the mastery in Arturo and to bring him back under control, and he knew well, too, that the gentleness in his last words held no true respect for him. Then with a tired shrug of his shoulders, he said mildly, "You will do me one last courtesy before leaving. Drink your wine with me."

As he reached for his beaker Arturo took his and when they had both drunk Ambrosius said, "May the gods give you success."

"If they do not it will be from no lack of manhood in the companions."

When Arturo had gone Count Ambrosius poured more wine for himself and sat sipping it. Wine he found more and more these days drove the tiredness of mind and body from him for a short while, but he was under no delusion about the true meaning of its comfort. His days were slipping from him.

Then, with a sudden flux of pride, he called for his servant. Two hours later as the first stars began to take brightness in the sky, he sat his horse at the great gateway of the Sabrina camp, wearing his plumed war helmet, polished cuirass and greaves, his blue riding cloak over his shoulders and his broadsword held in salute to the companions as they marched out, near a hundred and fifty horse and a hundred marshmen: the cream of all the fighting men in this country, the pride in them clear as they went under the banner of the white horse because they knew themselves to be Arturo's men and knew Arturo to be chosen of the gods.

They were four days on the road to Lindum. On the third day the morning broke with a clear sky and a shift of the wind from the west to the east, a wind that blew strong with an icy, biting savagery as though winter, long deferred, had arrived with a freezing fury at its long delay. Within an hour the roadside ditches were surfaced with ice and the breaths of men and horses plumed in the air and set their sweating beards brittle with its cold grip.

On the fourth day as they came down off the high ground before Crococalana and passed through it they could see, far ahead of them across the flatlands, tall plumes of smoke rising from the direction of Lindum. Now, too, they began to meet people who were fleeing from it with their small posses-

sions hastily salvaged, and learned that after a long siege the
Saxons had broken into the city five days ago, killing all who
could make no escape. The garrison had died fighting. The
bishop and the monks and nuns had been slaughtered. The
Saxons had spent three days ravaging, slaughtering and
plundering and then a day and a night of feasting and drinking
and were now—three hundred or more of them—moving
down the river Dubglas on their way south to join their
fellows, some two hundred strong, who were still trying to
take Durobrivae.

Arturo drew his force off the road to the east and made
camp. He sent three of Coroticus's marshmen up the river
Dubglas to bring back reports on the Saxons' movements.
The river which was close by their camp was slow running
and heavily reeded along its banks. Parts of it were already
iced over and the soft ground of its marshy verges had frozen
hard enough to take the weight of man and horse.

Long before dawn the marshmen returned with their report
on the Saxons. Hearing it, Arturo gave the order at once to
break camp and move. Now, he blessed the hard times of
night riding and marching at Cam Hill during training. With
the marshmen scouts leading them they went five miles
northward up the river and then drew away from it and made
themselves ready for the morning to come. Through the
darkness they could see the campfire flames of the Saxons
two miles away in the direction of Lindum. All men stood to
their arms and their mounts and long before dawn came there
was no troop commander or trooper who did not know the
part he must play with the full rising of the sun. Coroticus and
his men had already moved off into the night, which was
bitter with the east wind blowing a gale, setting dust and dead
leaves and rushes swirling into the air, and numbing bare
hands to a stiffness which only the coming heat of battle was
to warm.

When dawn came, cloudless and biting cold with the
wind, the troopers standing to their horses saw that they were
lodged in the cover of a thin growth of pines which covered
the low summit of a stretch of heathland a mile from the river.

Beyond the pines at the edge of the heathland Coroticus's marshmen lay hidden in the trough of an old road that led down to the river. Three bowshots beyond them, on the slightly lower ground by the river, was the Saxon camp. The warriors were already breaking camp to begin their onward march down the river to Durobrivae and the plundering and ravaging of any farm or small settlement that came between.

Coroticus, lying on the lip of the road bank, saw that they were well armed and clothed in heavy furs and thick woollen clothes, and unlike most roving Saxon bands moved in a disciplined manner about their business. Clear in their midst, ordering and commanding them, was a warrior, tall for his race, who wore a winged helmet and a surcoat of black sheepskins. None of the Saxons were mounted for they had no use or skills for handling horses in battle, but they had with them ponies and mules now being laden with their supplies and spoils of war. From behind him there came clear to Coroticus the signal he awaited: the high, whistling pipe of a greenshank. He rose, but gave no order for all his near hundred men knew their parts in Arturo's battle plan. As he stepped into view clear of the sunken road ten men followed him on either side. They walked without hurry toward the Saxon camp, spears slung over their backs to free their hands for the bows they carried. They were so small a party that they excited no great interest, except for a few shouts and bursts of laughter from the warriors who were now forming up raggedly to begin their march.

Within bowshot of the camp Coroticus and his men knelt to one knee and then one after another they shot their arrows. As the flighting hiss of one arrow died so another whistled to life and followed it, and each arrow found its mark in throat or chest or groin. They shot five arrows each and then as the roars of anger and shouts of the wounded filled the air, forty or fifty warriors, like a roused swarm of wasps, came running up the gentle slope toward them with swords drawn and spears poised for action.

Coroticus and his men turned from them and trotted without hurry back to the edge of the sunken road and, on the lip of the bank, knelt again and without hurry string-notched their arrows and sent them flighting toward the Saxons. Stung by this taunting affront from so few men, the Saxons came charging up the gentle rise, roaring with anger and filling the air with their oaths, leaving eight of their men on the ground behind them. When they were half a bowshot away the rest of the marshmen rose suddenly over the edge of the road bank with their arrows ready-strung to let them fly into the packed ranks of the attackers. The Saxon attack broke and withered like wheat under the sickle. Then, as another flight of arrows thinned their ranks, they turned and ran back down the slope.

Coroticus licked his lips with pleasure as he saw the fresh stir from the far Saxons as the survivors rejoined them, and grinned at the howling and crying and milling movement in the camp as their black-coated leader began to draw them to some kind of order. Here was, he thought, the beginning of the firing of the wasps' nest. He watched as the swarm below took ragged order and then wide-strung rank after rank of warriors, led by their wing-helmeted leader, came charging up to the road.

The marshmen stood their ground until their last arrow was spent and then, as though content with their wrought havoc, they turned, crossed the road and began to trot for the far cover of the pine-studded heath crest.

Seeing them turn and run, the Saxons, breaking ranks and raging to avenge their fallen, came pack-hunting after them, swarming across the road.

As the marshmen came through the pines and past the waiting cavalry, Lancelo's horn blew and the long note made the cheek skin of Arturo tighten with joy. Here now was the first day of the Great Horses and the power that came from safe saddles and body-bracing stirrup irons. With himself at the center, faithful to the White One, they came out of the pines at a growing gallop, Gelliga and his troop to the left and Durstan with his men on his right. Behind them, in a thick driving column, came the long-tried smaller horses of the companions. They burst down on the Saxons who had crossed the road, lances lowered and strongly couched, and Arturo led them, marking the figure of the black-surcoated Saxon leader. The shock of their meeting was like the sudden breaking of an angry sea, and for the first time Arturo and his men knew the real power of their new mounts and horse gear. The Saxon leader ran to meet him and threw up his small shield high to hammer aside the lowered lance while the blade of his scamasax drove hard for Arturo's groin. Arturo dropped the point of his lance and felt the great arm and body shock as it drove through the man's chest. He fell to the ground, screaming, his sword flying from his hand, and lay there with the lance spitted through him. As he passed Arturo drew his sword and knew now with certainty that although the lance could only serve but once there was a new strength and sureness in the sword's blade. The battle lust took him and all his companions as for the first time they knew the bloody, death-giving strength that lay in their sword arms. The swing of the blade which before had cut deep now sheared through flesh and bone like a butcher's cleaver taken to quartering carcasses.

If it was a morning of joy for the companions in their newfound strength, it was also a morning of blood and relentless carnage, a massacre without mercy to avenge the people of Lindum, a great killing to claim blood price for the murder and rape of the gentle nuns, and a hunt to the death of the sea wolves which would make the memory of the battle of the river Dubglas live forever. Over the hard, frost-bound river lands they harried the fleeing Saxons, driving them to the water's edge either to turn and meet death or to fling themselves in to sink or swim to the far bank. No mercy was shown. Behind the fast-scouring cavalry group there came Coroticus and his men with their spears and their daggers drawn, seeking the hearts and the throats of wounded and living.

When the killing was done and the last Saxon had found safety across the river, the companions re-formed and buried their dead, of which there were few, and the march began upriver to Durobrivae, which was to prove luckier than

Lindum. The town still held, and the Saxon survivors from the Dubglas battle had reached their comrades with the news of Arturo's coming. The siege was quickly lifted and the Saxons marched in haste to the east and the safety of their flat mere- and river-cut lands.

Arturo stayed three weeks at Lindum, setting the city to rights as the citizens who had escaped came back, re-forming the patrols and strongpoints along the Lindum—Durobrivae line, and pressing to service any youth or man able to bear arms. They would serve until the spring came and then be free to return to farm or settlement; but he knew that there would be no real fighting for them to face. Esc had made this throw and the gods had turned the dice against him. It would be long before he cradled the marked ivories in his palm to make another cast. Arturo left Gelliga in command of the city and the defenses of the line with a troop of horse and fifty of Coroticus's men to give heart and fire to the local forces.

He rode back to Cam Hill through Corinium. The news had long been sent ahead of his victory. But there was no welcome for him from Count Ambrosius. He had died two days after receiving Arturo's messenger.

Sitting in the Count's quarters at Corinium with Olipon, the *praefectus castrorum,* Arturo asked, "What was the manner of his death?"

The campaign-hardened Olipon, who now had a real affection for Arturo, though not greater than his love for his old commander, shrugged his shoulders. "Some men know when their time comes to die. He had a seizure, but he had known them before and overcome them. But this time . . . the wish was no longer in him to live. He had been buried at Glevum which was his wish. Long before spring the whole of this country will know of his going." He paused and grinned ruefully. "You will then be set high as target for the rivalries and enmities of many chiefs. You must win them by your boldness if you wish for kingship over this country."

Arturo said curtly, "There is no lust for kingship in me— only a wish for the return of the greatness of this country and the flowering of peace when we have driven the Saxons from us."

Olipon shrugged his shoulders. "True lust or not, my lord—you must assume the shape of it. He who commands must be king, for where else does authority rest?" He reached within the loose robe he was wearing and brought out a folded piece of parchment fastened with the seal of Count Ambrosius. "These are Count Ambrosius's last words to you. Since he wished it I have read them. He speaks as father to son, and he speaks with the wisdom which came with his years and their bitter experience."

The words of Count Ambrosius, written on the parchment, read:

I salute you:

Be king and above all men. No throne can
be shared.

Give your trust to no one except for a season.
The summer of a man's loyalty is often followed
by the mischievous winter of his pride.
No matter the warmth of your heart, keep the
cold sword always at your side.
Treachery respects no blood bonds; look for it even
seated at your own hearth.

The gods have claimed you for this country and
freed you from the wrack of conscience.

I give you the inheritance of Ambrosius.
Enrich it so that in the years to come all men
will shout "Arto" while my name will be whispered
like a brief echo, the gentle fall of ash from
the fire of your kindling.

CHAPTER NINE

The Holly On The Hillside

ARTURO RODE BACK to Cam Hill, leaving Durstan with horses and men to stand in command for him at Glevum and Corinium. His course was set by the words of Ambrosius; all that remained was to test the tides and perils of the voyage ahead. King he would be, but the proclamation should come from others. If any stood in his way they should fall for the gods had freed him from conscience.

The man changed and lived no longer for himself but for his dreams. At Isca he talked long and late with his father, who, standing ward for the young Cato, held control of the Dumnonian treasury. Baradoc, knowing the change in him, would have tempered some of his demands but saw the darkness of rising frustration in his eyes and gave him his way. Arturo sent messengers to all the chiefs of the north as far as the Wall of Hadrian, to all the chiefs of Cymru and the ruler of Demetia, calling for their presence at Glevum by the feast of Beltine. He rode to see King Melwas at his winter quarters on the slopes of the limestone hills above the great swamp. When he left Melwas—enriched by presents from the Iscan vaults—it was with the firm promise that Coroticus would come to him in the spring with three hundred armed and provisioned men.

After he had gone Melwas said to Coroticus, "The old wolf has died. Now the pack gets a new leader but there are many who will wait to tear him down."

Coroticus rubbed his nose and grinned. "What other leader is there? There is not a man amongst us who does not know his mind and is with him."

Melwas grunted. "I am no fool to sit overclose to the fire and burn myself. I give him the men, but for your glory, not his. *Aie* . . . though I like him well, and he is no fool to call himself king yet. He will be, and will work that royal yeast differently."

Three weeks after Arturo's return, and he lodged now more often at Isca than Cam Hill, the gods sent him an unexpected gift. A young man who had crossed from Gaul to the estuary of the river Isca with a shipload of horses and returning refugees asked for an audience with Arturo and would name nothing of his business. In the end after much pestering of the fortress guards he was brought to Arturo by Borio, who had searched him for hidden weapons.

Arturo saw him in the great chamber where he had once been taken to see first Prince Gerontius and then his son, Geraint. Without opposition from Baradoc, Arturo had taken the chamber into his own use.

Alone with Arturo—for he had refused to speak in the presence of any other—the young man said, "My lord Arturo, I am Oleric, the son of Theodoric from the land of the Visigoths below Gaul."

"And so?"

"My father's name means nothing to you, my lord?"

"Nothing." Then seeing the youth's surprise, Arturo smiled and went on, "In this country we have our own troubles. The Franks, the Goths and the Visigoths are known to me from my studies but of their present men of fame I know little."

The young man smiled boldly. "How did you know that I spoke of a man of fame, my lord?"

"Because you stand proudly and speak as would the son of a man of high state. Now give me plain facts and the reason for your coming."

"I will, my lord. But I should say to you that on crossing from Gaul it was to Count Ambrosius I travelled. Now, since I learn he is dead, I speak to you who have taken his place, so all men tell me."

Momentarily Arturo frowned. Then with a shrug of his shoulders he said, "Speak to me then."

"Very well, my lord."

Arturo sat and listened and, within a very short while, he knew that here being offered to him by this Oleric son of Theodoric was a part of the inheritance from Ambrosius of which he could never have guessed the existence but whose richness made him long for the moment to come when he met the war chiefs of this land at Glevum.

When the youth had finished Arturo said, "Return to your father and tell him that I accept that which he offers and the first price shall be paid when he comes ashore in this land at the time and the place you have named."

"I thank you, my lord."

"My thanks are to you and your father. The gods keep you on your journey back to him."

A little after Oleric had gone Gwennifer came into the chamber to him. She had been riding and still wore dusty men's clothes, her long hair part-freed from its nape ribbons.

Teasingly she said, "You look like a cat that has been at the cream bowl, my lord."

Rising, Arturo went to her and kissed her hand and said, "I smile because of the sight of you now, as wild and tousled as the morning you first brought Cabal to me. I smile, too, because it is now hard in me that I have had enough of affairs here and the closeness of this fortress and the streets and the midden smells. Tomorrow we ride for Cam Hill and you come with me. We will lie in our hilltop lodge together and hear the fox bark through the frost-thin air to his vixen and walk by the Cam and see the sun take the silver of the leaping salmon as he comes to the call of Latis."

They went to Cam Hill, where in the hard bright winter weather they rode by the Cam and, siting their horses by the bank, could look down through the clear crystal of the waters and watch the hen salmon arching and curvetting their long bodies as they cut their redds for spawning while the great cock fish kept station at their sides. Sometimes, unseen by Arturo, Gwennifer's white teeth would bite frettingly at her lower lip from longing for the boon for her body which was still denied her.

They rode the high downs with Cabal and a span of chase hounds and with the setting up of a winter-coated hare they followed hare and hounds, shouting and calling and laughing as though they were youth and maiden charged with the wonder and passion of a first love which gave all the world a freshness unseen before.

On their last night at Cam Hill they sat by the turf fire and drank wine, shared from the same cup, and Gwennifer took her harp and played and sang for him and the words that came from her were, he could believe, a gift from the crook-nosed god Maponus, who fired the heat of true-tempered words in the minds of all bards. . . .

> "Arto the spearhead in battle,
> The Saxons will cry woe
> As they flee before the Britons.
> Arto will hunt them down,
> A pillar of flame, king over men,
> High the banner of the White One,
> Under its linen border, great Arto
> From Isca in the west
> To the great wall in the north,
> King over men, beloved of all."

Lightheartedly Arturo said, "You sing too soon of future things."

Gwennifer shook her head. "No, my lord. In men's hearts you are king already. Only the word is lacking and that comes soon. King you will be and sons I shall bear you to be princes."

But, as the year's shortest day came and went and the feast of the Christos people to celebrate their Lord's birth passed, Gwennifer knew that her deep wish to bear Arturo a child still showed no sign of being granted, and she came fully to believe the truth of the words of Tia which she had overheard. Anger and frustration turned in her like two serpents, so that when Arturo and Baradoc went back to their tribal lands on the north coast below Caer Sibli to order affairs there, she—at her own wish—stayed in Isca. There were times then when she paced her chamber restlessly and others when she took her harp and played airs of sweet melancholy so that the tears misted her eyes.

On one such day as the winter-burnished sun hung low, reddening the waters of the Isca in its setting, she sat at her window playing when Borio, now commander of the fortress and its winter garrison, came down the winding stone steps from the broad walks that ran around the fortress walls. Her door was partly open and, seeing her playing the harp, he stopped and listened. When she had finished and raised her head to see him, he smiled and said "You play a sad melody, my lady. But sing no words. Are they then even sadder?"

"Good Borio, there are no words to match its sadness."

"Then it is a tune which must be teased to cheerfulness."

He came across the chamber, took the harp from her in his big hands, and began to play the same tune in a brighter vein, raising from the same sad notes she had struck gaiety and liveliness, and because the bard's gift was in him and words and music came to him as easily as breathing, he sang:

"Her hand and eye are gentle,
Walking under the vine.
The nightingales salute her.
She will come over the high crag
To sit me under the holly
Until there be no green leaf over us.
So long will be the season of love."

When he finished Gwennifer laughed with pleasure and went to the table and poured him a goblet of wine. As she gave it to him she asked, "And where is the one who waits under the green holly tree for Borio?"

Borio's face puckered with a wry smile. "If she waits, my lady—which I doubt—then it is beyond Deva by the wide sands of the estuary where the wild geese will now be wintering and where"—his smile broadened—"the holly trees are few.'' He touched the wine to his lips and saluted her.

When he was gone she took the wine goblet and, standing at the window, sipped gently. He had been with Arturo from the beginning; one of the youngest of the companions. When he was campaigning he grew a beard, but during the winter he went clean-shaven, a fresh-faced young giant, big-handed yet with fingers that caressed the harp strings with a light and magic touch to match the easy spring of his gift for words. That faraway maiden beyond Deva, she thought, would be a fool not to wait and keep herself for him to bear his children. . . .

That night she lay awake for a long time, her mind twisting and turning. The conflict in her between her love for Arturo and her own needs for him and his wide-ranging ambitions drove sleep far from her, and sometimes, while her face stiffened in the spasms of her resolution, she felt the touch of tears in her eyes. No man would doubt her honour. No man would talk loosely of her for fear of Arto's wrath and the safety of his own life.

Two nights later when Borio, who had his chamber at the top of the tower above Gwennifer's room, retired, he found lying on his bolster a sprig of green holly, its dark leaves silvered by the dim light from a single wall sconce. Because of the poetry and music in him and the memory of the parting look which Gwennifer had given him he knew the meaning of the holly and felt at once the stir of loyalty to Arturo move strongly in him, warring against the sharp onset of his manhood's desires.

She came to him long after the watch had called midnight from the fortress gate tower. Her hair was braided into plaits, the long tresses coiled in a golden wreath about her head. Her long white gown was close-caught about her neck, but her arms were bare and she moved, he thought as swift dryness took his throat, like a golden-crowned swan.

Curbing his troubled spirit, he said gently, ''My lady, you would do me a great honour. But this must not be. Many years ago I came to Arto and pledged him my sword and my faith and swore to serve him with all my honour.''

"You do him no dishonour, my Borio. The gods have brewed the draft of this night's drinking. Arto would have a son to match his greatness when he goes, but there is no living seed in him. Since you have sworn all love for him and I carry none but love for him and his desires, the gods have marked us thus to serve him, and the secret stays between us for all time." She came close to him and, reaching up, touched gently with her fingertips the weather-browned firmness of his cheek. "Arto's companions are Arto's flesh, and Arto's wife is the vessel that must hold the everlasting wine of his greatness. The gentle breath of a woman's sigh can blow the candlelight to death and darkness. But tonight the boon of darkness lies with you, and I ask it of you from my love for Arto."

For a moment or two Borio stood, unmoving. The gift of words was in her as in him, but the truth of her words and her pleading was like summer lightning, coming and going in proud many-hued flames, turning the world to brief wonder and blinding him to set free all the coiling desires of his manhood.

He turned, took three steps to the solitary wall sconce and blew the tallowed wick to darkness; but, in that darkness as he came back to her and his arms went round her and the stir of her body wakened to full life the desire in him, he knew that he did this alone as Borio and for no other reason than Borio's because Borio was a man and Gwennifer was a woman, and both were caught in the snare of the gods.

They were lovers until Arturo's return, which was on the last day of the month of the two-faced god Janus. That evening Borio, with Arturo and Gwennifer, ate in full company in the fortress hall. Borio drank heavily to kill the shame in him, while Gwennifer laughed and drank at Arturo's side and teased him gaily. After midnight when, for all his drinking, the gods had withheld from him the least edge of oblivion's cloak, Borio walked the ramparts on his rounds as the rain fell steadily, and—so it was thought when he was found later, though the truth died with Borio—he slipped on the wet planking bridging a parapet gap and fell sixty feet to the cobbled yard to break his neck. They buried him off the roadside along the Isca, where a stream ran down to serve the aqueduct for watering the horses in the great stockade and where the sound of their neighing and the thunder of their hooves in exercise would reach him. But it was not with this in mind that Gwennifer had chosen the place. He lay beneath an old holly tree, its berries red as the robin's breast, red as his blood which had marked the fortress cobbles.

A few days before the feast of Beltine, marking the coming of spring, Arturo, leaving Gwennifer at Isca, rode north with a full company of companions drawn from the hill forts and Cam Hill and with three hundred marshmen under the command of Coroticus. When they reached Glevum the army of Arturo was camped outside the south gate and close to the river for the watering of horses while the companies and retinues of the war chiefs lay between the west gate and the river. The tribal chiefs and petty kings were lodged in the city in the old half-timbered, half-masonry quarters of the long-gone legions which Durstan had put to order during the winter. Arturo himself had quarters in the old Basilica. It was here that the full congress of chiefs took place in the ancient long hall while the townspeople crowded the Forum and Basilica colonades to see for themselves the coming and going of lords and princes of the far northwest and northeast; and from Cymru beyond the Sabrina; and from Demetia in the far south of Cymru, the flamboyant figure of Difynwal, young and headstrong and heedless of the distant Saxon threat since his country was still hard pressed by Scotti invasions and settlement.

In those first days at Glevum there was much coming and going and private meetings between all these men both with and without Arturo. In those first days, too, the magic which already cloaked Arturo and his name grew, flourishing fast among the townspeople, then with the young warriors from the north who each in his bold, impatient heart knew himself to be another Arturo and longed for the liberty to escape from tribelands to march and fight and readily to risk any death to snatch at honour and fame. And, in those days, wherever he went Arturo—since Durstan and Lancelo had their own affairs to marshal—took Pasco with him, Pasco the shabby, shuffling priest whose eyes missed no passing shadow of doubt or shrewdness on a man's face and whose memory held every word spoken in store to be brought out against a man's turn of spirit.

Sitting alone late one night, and seeing Arturo lapse into a rare, silent mood of introspection, Pasco smiled and said quietly, "My lord, now comes the moment when you have to draw these little earthy gods of flesh and blood together and gain their favour."

"By the grace of the gods, yes. This is a gathering Count Ambrosius longed to see. Much he did against me but I would for his honour have him living and be in my place at the meeting to come. Aye—though there is the difference between us that he dreamt of seeing himself emperor—whereas I dream only of one thing, to be commander of the armies of the kings of Britain in this war."

For a moment or two it was on the tip of Pasco's tongue to say that a commander of kings must of right then be the greatest of kings but, seeing the dark intensity of feeling show on Arturo's face, he said mildly, "And when the great battle is won, what do you do, what will you have become, my lord?"

Surprising him, Arturo grinned and said lightly, "Why, I shall be my own man again. Free to walk without care through the long summer grasses with my wife, to hold a falcon on my wrist and slip it free to hang high and wait for the flushed wildfowl. . . . Aye, free to travel any road or track in this land without fear, and free to hold close to my wife and kin with the humble joy of any ploughman or woodcutter. Men were not born for battle. They were born for the good business of enjoying the fruits and blessings of this earth with which the gods have dowered them. . . ."

Quietly but boldly Pasco said, "The gods have always this in their power yet withhold it, my lord."

"True—but the gods have their reasons which neither the

eye nor the mind of man can read. But good reasons they must be and we must await their revelation patiently.''

Four days later the meeting of the kings and chiefs was held in the hall of the Basilica. All the men stood and carried their arms and had at their sides a grown son or trusted warrior. Arturo stood at the top of the steps at the end of the hall and four companions in full war gear stood on the lowest step as bodyguard. They were Durstan, Láncelo, Gelliga and Coroticus of the Summerlands. Bareheaded, wearing the long surcoat given to him by the bishop of Noviomagus, sword belted about it, Arturo faced them with Cabal couched at his side. Sunlight coming through the high windows of the hall drew rusty glints in his hair and there was a set to his tall figure into which the waiting men, each according to his temper and his own ambition, read arrogance and pride, the firmness of true authority, or the boldness of courage sustaining a great dream. But there was none that could truly deny the force in the stance of the man and the magic of personality which against all odds had set him where he was that day.

And that day, as he spoke, there was no denial of the gift of tongue which the gods had given him. When he spoke of the Saxons his words were sword-sharp; when he spoke of this country, their Britain, it was now the voice of a lover, now the gentle tones of a son to his mother; when he spoke of the need to hold and further strengthen the long line against the Saxons, to give them no westward freedom, his words were cold, and iron hard and relentless with the logic of a far-seeing Caesar; and when he came to name them all, one and separately, with the call to be made on them for men and provisions and the duties which they would have to accept, he spoke without emotion, as a commander making clear the ordering of the battle lines for the coming clash with the enemy.

When he spoke of the dream of the dead Ambrosius, which was now his dream, he did so with truth, sparing neither fault on the side of Ambrosius nor the arrogance of spirit on his own, and ended with a plea without weakness, saying, ''The like of this day will not come again. The great sea tides of this world march under the gods' design, but the full tide of our country's greatness they will hold back forever while there is one least man amongst us who deceives and plots only to feed his own lust for power and riches. Now is the day when the tide of this great country's glory is at the low. But now is the time, and now rests the power in your hands, if you have the courage and the heart and the wisdom, to give me command and men and arms to make battle to win back what is ours. Tread on the adder and it strikes, the wild boar defends its own . . . aye, put your hand under the breast of the gentle dove to rob its nest and it will draw blood with its blows. Are we then to be less than the beasts and to sit quietly and await the slaughter from the east? Under the gods I say I am not, and under the gods my heart tells me that you are not. You are the kings and lords of this country. Give me the means to bring it back to its true glory.''

As he finished speaking, his hand dropping and touching the rough head of Cabal at his side, there was silence in the hall. From outside came the sound of the sparrows quarrelling along the colonnade roof and the rattle of a cart's wheels over the Forum paving stones.

Looking at the gathered leaders, bearded, weathered of face, and most carrying the scars of war, their cloaks and furs and robes and kilts making a field of colour, Arturo knew the passing of the moments of destiny when all that was needed for his triumph was for one man to stand forward, draw sword or raise spear and cry "Arto!" Either the gods touched these men to follow him or he would turn from them and travel his own path and wear down the years of his life with the same spirit and stubbornness that had wrung from him in new manhood the rash promise of Arto.

Then from the front ranks of the company stepped forward young King Difynwal of Demetia, his long black locks greased so that they shone with the bloom of a raven's wing, a gold torque about his brown neck, his stiff beard cropped short to a hedgehog's bristle, and a great chequered cloak of reds, greens, yellows and white billowing over his shoulders and arms and a short sword hanging from his side. Behind him stood his young son, holding the tall standard from which hung the great round shield of Demetia on which was blazoned the fire-breathing red dragon of their country.

Boldly, his voice echoing in the shadowed roof spaces, Difynwal spoke.

"You call for men and arms to come to your command, great Arto. But what warrior is there who goes to battle with a red heart and an iron hand if he leaves behind him kith and kin in peril? What victory is there when the returning bow- or spearman climbs the crag to mountain home or rides the glen to farm and family—and finds death and fire and rapine have gone before him? You would have us face the east and the Saxons. Have you then forgotten that your mighty Esc and his chiefs are leaguered with the Scotti warriors and shipmen and they raid the coasts of the west from the mouth of the Sabrina River to the headland of Octapitarum in my lands and north to the island of Mona and the straits of Segontium and north again to the Ituna estuary and the shores of the lands of the Noventae? They press us back from our own shores, and when we find strength to press against them they move away in their long curraghs and strike again like a moving swarm of wasps where there are few to make stand against them. We all would cry you duke of war, commander of the armies of the kings of Britain. But no warrior will go east to win glory to come back to the west to find none to share his triumphs, and the nettles and charlock of despair growing through the bones of his loved ones, his hearth cold and open to the sky . . . no joy of wife and sweetheart, no red and yellow cattle in the glen, no proud ram to stand and stamp his foot and marshal the ewes and lambs. Rid me of the men from Erin and you shall have the great part of my men. And know this, I speak not alone for myself."

He half turned to the chiefs behind him, and cried, "Look and see those who know the truth of my words and have felt and still endure the suffering of their people. Aye, the gods are with you, but the Scotti are with us and our swords demand their blood!" He drew his sword and raised it and, as he did so, from more than half of the men behind him came also a raising of swords and spears and a swelling roar like the call of a high sea comber in the moment of breaking on the shore.

When the noise had died and the last sword had been lowered and sheathed, Arto spoke and Pasco, lost in the crowd, listened to him, wondering at the change in his manner of speaking. He spoke now as though from an age far beyond his years, and with a gentle patience, each word well honed, but, when he needed, there came the soft burr in his Dumnonian-touched voice, now a caress and now a sad chiding, and he began:

"The first man I killed . . . aye, and that long before I found a taste for kissing and cuddling the maidens of my tribe . . . was a Scotti. I cut his throat with a dagger on the sands at night. And when I was youth, I stood and fought the night raiders from the sea with the men of my tribe. With the passing of years, and the growing of my hatred for the Saxon men do you think I have forgotten the Scotti? Do you think I would ask you to give me men to go east and have no care for the west? What great command could I claim from you if I were so one-eyed that I could not see double danger and turn to meet it? Know this then, without their long-planked and hide-plated curraghs, the Scotti are as my companions would be without horses. When you press them to the sea they take to their boats. But now the days of their boats are numbered. From far Belerium's Point there sailed a handful of days ago a fleet of warships, greater in number and size than any the Scotti command, and this fleet will take watch and ward and make battle with the Scotti wherever they be met off our western shores. And the man who commands them has no more love for Saxon or Scotti than we have. Though"—he grinned—"he is man enough to want payment for his services and the first part of this has already been found from the Dumnonian treasury of Isca. The rest must be met from the war levies laid on us all . . . gold and silver and stores for his ships and harbouring for them. No land grants such as Vortigern gave to Hengist and Horsa. This man lives by the sea and his men are of all nations with their homes far to the south in the country of the Goths below Gaul. This man is Theodoric and he waits now off the mouth of the Sabrina for the beacons on your hills to be fired to bring him into your waters, to scour them free of the Scotti.''

Arto paused and in the silence that held the assembly of chiefs his eyes found those of Difynwal and held them steadily. Then with slow, deliberate words he went on, ''Great Difynwal, I have answered you. I am no beggar to plead with any man for alms for my country. I am no peddler to haggle over a deal for my country's honour. I seek only the glory which was and must be again hers, and if any in this hall turn his back to me now, he turns his back on his country's gods, on his fellows-in-arms against the Saxons. Living there shall be no honour in him and his women and children shall take no joy in him, and dying there shall be no welcome in the Shades for him. I am Arto and have given you my promise. Now, let those who would go tend cattle, lie warm at nights with wives and sweethearts, let them go. I would sooner have a beardless boy with fire in his belly than a grown man whose spirit is a timid hare to send him running at the distant sound of hounds. I am Arto and, with or without you, shall take no rest, nor know any settled hearth until I have done what the gods have commanded me to do.''

For a moment or two none spoke or moved and all eyes watched the two men who had gathered to themselves the ordering of this moment and knew each that the balancing of the future was weighted evenly between them. Against his side Arturo felt Cabal rise to his feet and the soft muzzle came to his hand, while below him Difynwal stood grim-faced and unmoving. Then with a slow movement Difynwal drew his sword, and there were those who thought for bloody work, and he walked up to Arturo and as he came so that only Arturo saw, he smiled, but needed not the smile for Cabal beneath his hand was without sound or stiffening of muscle. At Arturo's side Difynwal turned, raised his sword and shouted, setting the echoes ringing in the roof, ''Arto! Arto!''

Before the echoes died all men in the hall drew sword or

raised spear and the echoes rang again and again, "Arto! Arto! Arto!"

And Pasco, watching, seeing Arturo and Difynwal embrace, remembered the first days of the beginning at the Villa of the Three Nymphs, remembered the marriage of Arto and Daria, the springtime of their love, and the springtime of Arto's manhood; and he knew that now again the season of Arturo's life had changed and, because he gently questioned all God's movements in the affairs of men, yet had no lack of faith, he could find in himself no true happiness for Arturo. From this day he lived apart from men.

CHAPTER TEN

The Immortal Wound

THERE WERE NO DOUBTS IN GWENNIFER. Arturo was commander of the armies of the British kings. It was a title as clumsy and shambling as the movements of a crippled beast unable to fend for itself. The titled would die. But not Arturo. King he would be and once named it would be forever. Through his sons his glory would live. Borio had failed her, but there were others and now that she was at Glevum and bore herself like a queen to all men, there could be no bar to her desire and no mercy shown to any man, no matter his rank, who should smile out of place or boast with or without truth of her brief and long-spaced favours. Always there was with her Lacus, the groom, to use poison or dagger or the turn of designed but innocent-seeming accident.

But while time and time again she remained barren there were those who knew the truth without sound of words or sight of deed, knew just as rain still a day's coming could be smelled in the wind. All kept their counsel. Arturo stood highest in the land and with the full weight of affairs now on him showed a change under which in a few years the old Arturo was buried to all except a few chosen of his companions. Only when he rode or made camp for night in some small party with a handful of tried friends would he talk of old times for a while.

In public and campaigning affairs he was ruthless with any who failed him, expecting all men to push themselves to the bounds of their strength and faith as he did himself. And for the most part men did this, for the torch which had been fired in the Basilica flared high and bright over the land. For those few whose levies or dues to the war chest fell short there was no mercy. No matter the distance and the days it cost, Arturo would ride with a force of his companions and there was then no withstanding his demands for now—as many of the shrewder chiefs and small kings had seen without fear, for they had no desire in themselves for it—his power had grown from the day they had acclaimed him commander. As the years passed he gained an ease and assurance from the knowledge that the men who now served him in the field and garrisons took pride in him, matching their prowess and dedication with his. They were part of him and apart from all men who were strangers to his service. The young sons of tribal chiefs and kings itched to come of age so that they could join him . . . aye, even if it only meant that they did duty on the Saxon line in idleness during winter, cherishing their memories of the scarce summer days of sword-blooding when some rash Saxon warrior had led a foray against them, fretting against the imprisonment of his own enclave. Youth and young manhood held to Arto and many a chief's son shamed his father from trimming his levy or hoarding his wealth when Arto called.

These were years when there were no great battles; these were the years when the slow turn of fortune in favour of the Britons began. The weight of Theodoric's ships and men slowly began to clear the west coasts of the Scotti threat and found them, losing stomach for fight, moving far north to pillage and settle along the shores of the land of the Picts. These were the years when the garrisoning and patrolling of the Saxon line penned in the warriors of Esc and his chiefs and brought to Esc the truth that, with the dwindling of the Scotti threat in the rear of the Britons, the time must come when he would have to come out in force and drive westward to break the budding might of Arturo forever. And these were the years when many a night Arturo sat late in his chamber at Glevum or Isca or Deva, pondering the reports and messages that came to him from paid or willing placemen amongst his Saxon foes. Dead Ambrosius had strung this network and now Arturo spread it wider, and from his gleanings he knew that it would be many years before the itch in his men for true and full battle would be eased by any great march west by Esc. But, though he knew that the time of Esc's coming lay years ahead, Arto lived and planned and worked to strengthen his armies and secure his garrisons and posts as though time were pressing him hard. The gods might at any time ferment the slow yeast to fast rising.

They had now at Corinium near five hundred Great Horses, manned and equipped and held under the command of Durstan with Gelliga to second him. Lancelo, grown man now, he kept with him as he moved through the country, and it was to Lancelo now, more than Durstan, that he sometimes showed his heart. Toward the end of the year 490 as they rode for Isca with a troop of horse, Arturo, finding the turning of the leaves as the year died moving him to melancholy, felt an unexpected need to ease some of the lone burden he bore. His years were forty now, and with the passing of each year the running out of time seemed to speed ever faster.

Riding well ahead of the troops on the White One, the third now of that name, and a new hound Cabal alongside him for the old Cabal was two years dead, gored to death by a boar at hunting, he spoke to Lancelo without turning to him and said, "'Twas this road from Corinium that you rode with your father, Ansold, and your sister, Daria, to bring them first to the Villa of the Three Nymphs."

"Aye, my lord. A day when the young beard on my chin was as soft as goslings' down."

"You have served well, Lancelo, and have always been true companion, but more—you are my brother through your sister, Daria, my true wife. Have you ever turned the truth from me, Lancelo?"

Puzzled, Lancelo said, "We ride at different gaits, my lord."

"Aye, but side by side."

"There has never been else but truth between us. Am I not your man, your brother?"

"You are—and because you are that, you would give me

no grief or pain. But now I speak plainly and would know a truth and you must answer plainly with no trimming of your words. I walked the rounds at Corinium two nights ago. There was a mist and I heard two guards talking about their fire. That I was there they did not know, that they live still comes from the charity of the gods who stayed my hand. They spoke ill of my lady Gwennifer. Tell me, Lancelo—did they speak the truth?''

Lancelo bit his underlip and was tempted to lie for the sake of their friendship. Then, knowing that a lie from him now would serve no purpose, for truth would come some other road, he said, ''It is the truth, my lord.''

Arturo turned and smiled at him. ''For that I thank you. Look not so glum. I am in good company for many a man from Caesars down to charcoal burners have worn the horns. You should know, Lancelo, that most often when the gods give greatness they season it in a man with a spice of ridicule to curb him from thinking himself more than mortal. Mortal I am and chafe not against it.''

On his first night at Isca as Gwennifer sat at her mirror combing her long hair before retiring, while a southwesterly roared the long length of Dumnonia and shook the closed wooden shutters of the window and the flames of the tall candles swayed in the drafts, Arturo, cradling a glass of wine in his palms, spoke to Gwennifer, his eyes on her and no anger in him.

''It was written by Merlin before my birth that I should throw no seed to flower. Merlin whom I have met a few times is a man whose words should always be marked with care. The truth in them is as hard to tell as the counting of the scales of a salmon or the numbering of bubbles in a beaker of cider.''

Gwennifer turned slowly to him. ''You talk in riddles, my lord.''

''No, I talk frankly and without anger. Seed I have and it is good seed and it grew in the body of Daria—but the gods denied it flowering.'' He smiled. ''Good Merlin is always a little less than exact and a little more teasing than truthful.

The gods have marked me for greatness but for long now I have understood that in their wisdom they will give me no heir in flesh to hold and increase my heritage. Would you know why?''

Firming mind and body now against the unexpectedness of this talk, but grateful for the lack of anger in him, Gwennifer said, ''Yes, my lord, I would. If greatness is your part why should there be none of your blood to inherit and increase it? There is shame in me, but that it was done, this thing I did, then it was done to cheat the gods and glorify your name when you were gone. In that lies all my love for you.''

''Your love for me is clear but ill-designed. That you have not borne a child to foster on the world as mine lies in your own barrenness. My seed is good but at its first shooting the gods would wither it and the womb that held it. You wonder that I am not angry with you and send you from me?''

''Yes, my lord, I do for I have deserved both.''

''No. What you did was out of love for me. But now there must be an end of it for there is no ripeness in you. Wife you are, but never mother. . . .'' He stood up and went to her and she rose from her stool to him. Facing her, he saw the slow start of tears in her blue eyes and his nostrils were full of the perfume of her tall, slender body and the candlelight streaked her hair with soft shadows. He took her in his arms and held her to him and against his cheek he felt hers touched now with the dew of her falling tears and her body shook with the slow rack of her sobs.

Later in the darkness, as they lay abed with the night full still of the great shout of the gale winds, Gwennifer said, ''You would have told me why the gods who give you greatness give you no heir to inherit, my lord.''

''And tell you I will, but you must mark my words as you would those of a Merlin. I am not born in this land for the first time. This country has known me before in its hour of need and I have given it peace and greatness, and shall give it that again during this life and then, dying, shall rest in chaos until I am called again to restore its glory.'' He was silent for a while and then, with a little grunt, went on. ''You think that both a puzzle and a dream? Well, it may seem so, but it is also a truth beyond explaining. Some men there are who are marked by the gods with an immortal wound. They die the death of this earth but not the death of the gods . . . and they sleep awhile until the gods call them from darkness to know the joy again of the rising sun, to hear the neighing and tramp of the waiting war-horses in the meadow, and the cries of misery from their oppressed countrymen whose ills they must set to flight again . . .'' He yawned suddenly and then laughed. ''*Aie* . . . I was long aseeing it—but true it is.''

He put out an arm and drew her to him and kissed her tenderly and then as he felt the tips of her fingers carress his forehead, he went on, ''So take no fear from me. Tomorrow you are born again and we shall ride out on the water meadows into a new world to watch the fall of the red and brown leaf, the flick of the white scuts of the moorfowl in the sedges, see the great oaks wrought black like shaped iron against the rising sun, and I shall be your love and you mine and we shall both be content to live under the will of the gods whose judgment is beyond any man's knowing.''

In the year that followed old Ansold the sword maker died, sitting at a tavern bench in Isca after a heavy day at his smithy. As though the drink had fuddled his head, he bent forward and rested his forehead on his arms. Thinking him sleeping, his friends laughed until one touched his shoulder a little roughly and the old man slid sideways from the bench to the ground. He was buried not far from Borio above the horse grounds and close to his smithy, where the sound of hooves on the ground and hammers shaping the iron for stirrups kept him company. Two months later Lancelo married a young woman from Corinium called Hylda, whom Gwennifer took as a companion, found no envy against her when she was soon pregnant, and had no shame when the child was born five months after the marriage.

In that year as the campaign season opened with the firming of the ground and the dying of floods from the valleys, Adipo, the son of the chief of the Durotriges and the

husband of Arturo's sister, Gerta, came to Corinium with the
levy of warriors from his father. With him came Gerta and
their ten-year-old son, Mordreth, who spent his days with the
troopers on the cavalry grounds of the Sabrina wing, learned
fast all barrack talk and oaths, and loved horses with a
passion untouched by fear. He worshipped his uncle Arturo
and found quickly a way to his heart and favour for he was the
nearest to a son, Arto knew, that he would ever have. He set
him up on the broad back of the White One with a wooden
sword in his hand and let him circle the tanbark ring, shouting
and calling, and when the White One half bucked playfully
from the laughter and the cries of the troopers he fell heavily
only to pick himself up, his small dark face straining to hold
back cry or tear, and demanded to be remounted. Arturo
came to love the boy as near-son—and shrugged off the sharp
talk from Gerta at his indulgence of the boy.

In that year, too, Cerdic of the West Saxon settlements
stirred again and Arturo sent word to the bishop of
Noviomagus and the Chief Citizen of Venta to keep him
supplied with all they could find of Cerdic's thinking and
planning, and was content to wait until that tree was in full
bearing before he should cut it to the ground. He knew, too,
that Cerdic was in full league with Esc and could be watched
as a weather gauge to the coming moves of the Saxon leader.
That the move would not now be long delayed he knew to be
true for in all the Saxon enclaves men were restless and called
for an end to their penning and craved the liberty to move
west to the days of fighting and plunder and the nights of
drunken boasting.

In that year, too, Oleric, the son of Theodoric, married a
daughter of King Difynwal and was given a land grant in
Demetia, and many of Theodoric's men married girls from
the towns and settlements of the seacoast of Cymru so that the
fleet was slowly being bonded to the land with ties stronger
than any stout hempen hawser.

In the summer of that year Baradoc, now near his sixtieth
year, took Tia with him to Aquae Sulis, where he was
working on the defenses of an old hill fort to the east of the

town, and they were lodged in the old villa of her uncle, the long-dead Chief Centurion Truvius. They would eat in the courtyard under the shade of the great sweet chestnut tree, the courtyard in which they had been married. One evening, sitting there, Tia looked across at Baradoc, weathered, stiff-armed, hair now greying fast, and teasingly she said:

"Over the silver stream hunts the four-winged fly.
  Each eye holds a thousand eyes;
  But he sees not your beauty."

Baradoc, spooning up from his bowl wild raspberries laced with sweet wine, smiled. "Prettily said. After a day in the sweat and labour of digging, with one's ears deafened by shouts and hammerings, there is no balm like the music of poetry."

Tia ran the tip of her tongue between her lips to stay her laughter and found more words for him:

"I would have built for you a house with a
  roof of green rushes and a flower-pied floor.
  A thousand seabirds would have greeted the
  golden girl with a brow like a lily, the
  young queen who rode the perilous paths
  without harm or hurt."

Baradoc looked up, his face a little puzzled, and wiped fruit juice from his mouth with the back of his hand. "I praise the man who made the words. I would like to have shaped them myself and spoken them for you . . . *Aie,* there was a time in my youth when I could sweet-talk my love."

Tia hid her smile behind her hand for the words were his and belonged to the days when they had travelled to Aquae Sulis and had stayed in this villa. But they were gone from his memory. Men wooed and spoke love words but when the wooing was done the years took their words from them. The past was a load which could not be carried forever by them, unlike a woman, who hoarded its rare treasures never to lose them. Yet, as the thought ran with her, Baradoc suddenly shook his head, laughing, and he rose and came to her and kissed her on the forehead and said, "Aye, now I remember. The last of the words I wrote here in this yard by moonlight for you . . . on . . . on, yes, the wax of your uncle's old ivory tablet."

The next morning as she lay abed by herself, Baradoc having ridden away to work before dawn, she listened to the screaming of the swifts as they hawked over the river below the terrace slopes and the calm joy on her face moved suddenly to a tightening wince of pain. Her hand went to her right side, pressing against it to ease the sharp bite which with the passing of this last winter had begun to assault her more and more. The gods, she knew, had nearly marked the full tally of her days and she would share the secret with no one.

She died in the autumn while she made visit with Baradoc to his tribal lands on the north coast of Dumnonia, moving to sleep in his arms at night and passing to the Shades before dawn broke. She was buried on the cliff top under a high cairn of boulders in sight of distant Caer Sibli, where she had brought Arturo into the world, buried with the purple bloom of the heather moorland behind her and before her the tall cliffs rising over the gold-and-white sands where the seabirds wheeled and called and the red-legged choughs scavenged and quarrelled along the rock faces. The news came to Arturo a month later as he rode south from Eburacum to winter at Glevum.

That night in camp on the road, Arturo walked through the willows of the riverside grove where they rested, alone except for Cabal, and knew the regret that all men have for the passing of a loved mother, and regret, too, that time and affairs had forced them apart. Daria and his mother he had now lost. Loneliness and loss was the constant lot of all god-touched men for they had a greater family to serve. There was a shame in him, too, that evening as he walked by the riverside, for there was a part of his thoughts which rode free of his grief because with the news of Tia's death had come also news from his spies who served him from the lands

of Esc. With the coming of spring Esc meant to move out
against him, but not with a full force, to test his readiness and
the quickness with which he could marshal and move men
against him. To crush such a move ruthlessly he knew would
defer Esc's full effort for years. The Saxons should be en-
couraged to think that for all his strength he lacked the skill to
manage it quickly.

That winter at Isca the young Prince Cato began to show a
rebellious, imperious nature, resenting the wardship of
Baradoc. He had the courage of his father but not his understanding, and the arrogance of his grandfather but an ambition which was far narrower, seeking only pride and pleasure
and power for himself. Mordreth was brought to Isca to keep
him company and there were few weeks when they were not
in disgrace. They were young hawks eager for the onset of
their moult to adult plumage. For only one person were they
gentle and obedient to hand, and that was Gwennifer, who
saved them many a beating. It was, too, through the unruly
boys that Gwennifer met Merlin for the first time.

She was riding down the river toward the horse enclosure
one afternoon of frost-bright sunshine when she heard cries
coming from ahead. Breaking from a small alder growth on
the riverbank, she saw Mordreth and Cato shouting and
laughing as they danced around a brown-cloaked man with
long black hair and an unkempt beard. They were pelting him
with addled eggs from an ancient and spring-deserted swan's
nest which they had found in the reeds. As soon as the man
rushed at one, striking out with his staff, the other attacked
him from behind, and both the boys were too nimble and alert
to take any harm from him.

Setting her horse to a canter, she bore down on the boys,
who, seeing her coming and recognizing her, ran away up the
hillslope and disappeared over the road toward Isca. As she
pulled up in front of the man he plucked a handful of browned
dead grasses and began to wipe egg mess from the front of his
robe. Looking up at her as he did this, he grimaced wryly and
said, "You came at a good time, my lady Gwennifer. A few
more moments and I would have lost patience with their
antics and cracked their skulls with my stave."

"You would have needed their nimbleness."

"And could have found it. But I was content to mark them and make some study of them."

"Why so?"

"Time will show you why."

"You talk in riddles."

"When I need, my lady." He picked broken eggshell from his beard and wiped his messy fingers on his robe.

"To right the ill done to you, you shall come to Isca and be given fresh clothes and lodgings—and the boys shall be whipped."

Merlin laughed. "I need neither clothes nor lodging. But see the boys whipped. It is time their hides were seasoned. And give my good remembrances to your husband, Great Arto."

"How shall I name you?"

"You know not that already, my lady?"

The truth came slowly to Gwennifer and with it she felt the mantling of blood in her cheeks. "You are the one who wrote, 'His glory an everlasting flower . . . He throws no seed.' "

Merlin smiled. "With a fine-pointed slate in his hand and a bare rock face before him . . . aye, why, then I am the kind of man who itches to fill its smoothness with words. I could have as easily written, 'Fish with a feathered hook in these waters and the gods will give you jade-flanked mackerel.' "

"But you did not."

"All poetry comes from the gods and we must abide their choice of words. Time, too, is a succession of small accidents arranged by the gods."

"And why have they arranged this time and chance to bring us together?"

"Could it be that, no matter the truth of the words on the rock, you would have cheated them?"

Angry, Gwennifer said, "You talk overboldly now, Master Merlin. Men have many gods but a woman has only one—the man she loves."

"Well spoken, and true."

"Against all the gods I say that Arto will be Great King of

this country and should have sons to harvest the fruits of his victories.''

Merlin put a hand up to the muzzle of her horse and gentled it as it stirred restlessly under her. "There are no fruits of victory with the sword. Seasons of quiet, yes. The real conquest comes not from the men who invade a country or the men who defend it. The good earth of the country, shaped by the rains and rivers and the seasons, is always victor.''

"Now you talk in riddles again.''

Merlin shrugged his shoulders: "It is a simple one, my lady—except that you would have to live all the years of your life and a thousand more to know it.''

Impatient now with the man, Gwennifer said sharply, pique strong in her voice, "I think you are no more than a fool who makes idle play with the first words that come into your head. So be it—and now, go tell the gods, who made me barren for their sport, that they have my curses!'' Then, as she wheeled away and was poised to set her mount to a gallop, she called back over her shoulder, "And the boys shall not be beaten!''

Smiling, Merlin watched her disappear down the road to Isca. Then holding his nose to shut out the stink of addled egg, he went to the river to wash, chuckling to himself at the flash of fire there had been in Gwennifer's eyes. No matter her deeds she was true wife to Arturo and the gods would take her curses indulgently.

CHAPTER ELEVEN

The Breaking Of The Saxons

IN THE EARLY SPRING Arturo went north to Glevum, leaving Gelliga in command of very much reduced forces at both Isca and Cam Hill and the other fortified camps. Before he went he spoke alone with Gelliga at Cam Hill, the two of them sitting in the strengthening sunshine outside his quarters where none could overhear them. Gelliga's face grew doleful as he listened.

"They will come this year, and long before summer. Esc's men from the ease, keeping south of the Tamesis, and there will be a joining with them by Aelle and Cerdic from the south. You will call your men together from the forts. But make no great haste in the matter, as though the surprise of their coming has left you in doubt whether you should make full battle with them or wait until you can get help from me from the north."

"That gives me a bitter taste in my mouth even now, my lord."

"Then swallow it. I want Esc to think that these past years of success have turned us too confident and slow to act. Harry them and harass them, but make no stand to block their way. They will only come so far to test us—and I want them to find us surprised and slow to act. By the time I come south they will be on their way back to their own lands, and Esc will think that in a few more years he can come again in full strength and overrun the whole length of the Tamesis valley . . . aye, and press on to Aquae Sulis to split the country in two and so gain the rich southern half for himself. Where the young wolves wanton this season, the whole wolf pack will

come in later years—and we shall then make the full killing.''

Gelliga sighed. ''You live ahead of me, my lord. I am still
in the old days when if the Saxons moved we went to meet
them with the sword and lance.''

Arturo plucked a young grass stalk and chewed on it. ''No
more. In these days if a commander has true cunning the
battle must be won before the first sword is drawn and the
Great Horses put to the gallop. All I say here is between us. If
men speak against me saying I left you ill prepared and came
late to your help . . . well,''—he grinned, sliding the grass
stalk to the side of his mouth—''agree with them and grumble a little with them. There will be much spoken against me
and I want the sound of it to reach Esc.''

Gelliga laughed. ''Arto the bear, men call you. But you
have learned the cunning of a serpent. Aye, I will make hard
words against you, my lord, but only from my mouth, not my
heart.''

There were a few others to whom Arturo spoke as he had
done with Gelliga: Difynwal of Demetia, Loth the father of
Gwennifer who was marshal now of the far northern forces,
Baradoc his father, and the father of his brother-in-law,
Adipo, the chief of the Durotriges who held the country west
of the Vectis sea . . . all men in whom he had trust.

That year the Saxons marched as he had known they
would. They came three hundred strong from Esc and were
joined by two hundred men from the West Saxon shore, and
they spread death and took plunder and slaves along the
Tamesis. Aelle and Cerdic joined Esc's men at Calleva and
rumours and tales of bloody slaughter went winging like
black crows over the country. Among Gelliga's men as they
rode and shadowed the Saxons, harrying and harrassing them
when they could but too weak to oppose them boldly, there
was grumbling at and some scorn for Arturo, who was slow
in coming down the old road from Glevum, through
Corinium and Spinis to Calleva with the Great Horses and his
foot troops. When he arrived, to find the Saxons long on their
way back to their lands, there were even those among the

most faithful of the companions—Lancelo and Durstan and others—who found their loyalty to his good name and leadership hard-pressed. This Arturo suffered for he knew it would pass. It was better to lose a little of their love and faith for a few years than to give them the truth to spill when the drink ran in the halls at night and so find its way to Esc.

With Prince Cato and Mordreth, youths now, there was anger in the one and disappointment in the other. Sunning themselves one afternoon on the Isca fortress parapet walk, Cato said angrily, "He grows lazy and too content with the thought of his coming kingship. Aye, and look how he bears himself here. Am I the Prince of Dumnonia or is he? Dumnonia's money, not his, has paid for Theodoric and for the breeding and manning of the Great Horses."

Mordreth said loyally, "I think you talk too soon—like a cock deceived by a late moonrise. There is more in all this than can be openly read."

"You share his blood and so you stand for him."

Pugnaciously Mordreth answered, "Aye, I do. And if you call him badly without truth—then I will spill yours!" He moved toward Cato, his fists raised ready for fight.

"Then try it—for I tell you blood he will spill in time. And that mine. With me gone he will call himself Prince of Dumnonia, name his blood royal, and so use me as footstool to climb to kingship."

Moving close to Cato, Mordreth, his body taut with anger, said, "You speak so because you itch for your wardship to be ended. So now take back the words, for nobody to my face links Arto's name with murder."

For answer Cato spat in Mordreth's face. They fought, rolling and tumbling on the parapet, their angry shouting sending the jackdaws skyward and eventually bringing a guard and Master Ricat, old now but far from lacking strength and authority, to pull them apart and clout their heads. Of their quarrel Ricat asked nothing for scarcely a week went by without a fight between them or the two of them falling into mischief.

Gwennifer, knowing the murmuring against Arturo, understood his mind without need for telling from him. In some ways she had the mind of a man and could guess the thinking of Arto. That autumn when he came to her at Isca there were times when she woke late at night and knew him to be lying alongside her untouched by sleep. Without need of words she would rest her cheek against his bare shoulder and his arm would go around her, taking the voiceless comfort she offered.

The next year, as though he feared that Esc would strike again, Arturo moved the main part of his forces eastward, splitting it to stand in readiness in the south below Londinium and in the north based on Ratae and Durovigutum. But no move came except for a few small raids and attacks made by wayward and venturesome Saxon parties. The following year he did the same as though to stamp on Esc's mind that he had learned the lesson of unreadiness and would not be caught again. But that winter he set the trap for the taking of the Saxons.

Through the merchants, traders and people of Londinium he started the rumour running that the Picts in the far north were massing to move south with the spring. By packmen and peddlers and paid agents he fed the tale of the coming of the Picts to the Saxon enclaves, and long before the turn of the year he began to send men and horses north to Eburacum, stripping forces south of the Tamesis ruthlessly from the march line which Esc must take to gain a lasting hold on the country. Men and horses went north, but they were raw levies, barely trained. They made a marching show for men to see, and the news of their going ran fast to the Saxons. But at Glevum he held the companions and their Great Horses, over a thousand of them, and Coroticus with his marsh bow- and spear-men numbering near another thousand. They camped south of Glevum, spread down the River Sabrina below the high scarp to the east. At Glevum Arturo sat and waited for the coming of Esc and for the first smoke and flame of the warning beacons that stretched from the heights above Londinium to run from hill and scarp and downland crest westward to the last great beacon of piled brushwood and resin-sapped pines on the lip of the heights south of Glevum. A pillar of smoke by day, or a great finger of flame by night: when the sign came Arturo would know that Esc and all his confederates were on their way to split Britain apart, to butcher it and to flay it like a heifer in a slaughterhouse—only to find that the butchers were to become the butchered.

Six days before the feast of Beltine, Arto was sitting in his room at Glevum, the window shutters open to the mild evening air so that he had sight of the southward-curving river over which swung a long skein of winter geese disturbed from their feeding on the flats by some hunter. The long sharp scarp of the hills was warm-lit by the light of the setting sun when Gwennifer, who had lodged with him that season at Glevum came into the room.

With a shadow of a smile touching the corners of her mouth, she said, "My lord, there are two young warriors who would speak with you."

Looking at her and sensing her half-teasing, near-to-laughter mood, he asked, "And should I see them?"

"I think you should, my lord. They come to ask service with you."

"Then send them down the river to Durstan."

"They ask for you, and I think they have claim to that right."

"And since you ask for them they arc fortunate. I will see them." Before she could move away he stretched out his hand and, taking her by the wrist, gently, he looked into her clear blue eyes, touched now by the finest web of lines in their corners, and he knew that she was one of the rare women whose beauty, though changing with the years, would never diminish. He kissed the palm of her hand and then said, "I think these warriors will be no surprise to me—for I was of their age once and know their feelings."

"Then be good to them for my sake."

She left him and a few moments later Prince Cato and Mordreth came into the room. They had grown from boys now to well-set youths who held themselves with the fast-

coming stance of manhood. They were dressed in tunic and
trews without distinction and belted with short swords and
side daggers and as they stood there Arturo caught from them
the smell of sweat and horse. He said, ''You should both be
at Isca, working in the schooling pens.''

Prince Cato said, ''I have but two years of wardship to go,
but am only a few months short of the right to bear arms. For
the sake of standing on the order of those few months, my
lord, would you have me miss the great battle which
comes?''

Not answering him, Arturo turned to Mordreth and asked,
''And you—who lack even more months?''

Mordreth smiled. ''My lord, I lack any good reasons
except that I would serve with you as groom, servant, or ride
messenger and if call arise draw sword to defend myself.
Hard words have been said against you, my lord, in these past
years, and said by Prince Cato and myself—but now we
know the truth. We would be with you in the day of your
triumph.''

He said, ''Men go to battle but the gods ordain which side
triumph shall bless. . . .'' Then with a grin and a shrug of
his shoulders, he said, ''Let it be so, then. Ride downriver to
Durstan and tell him to give you service fit for your years.''

''Fighting service, my lord?'' asked Cato.

''Can it be avoided if the gods throw it your way?''

A week later, a little before sunset, the beacon high up on
the ridge flared into life, its flames rivalling the glow of the
setting sun, its long tail of resinous smoke rolling westward
across the river in ragged plumes. Then began the long wait
which, although all now knew its reason, set men itching for
the move to come against the Saxons. Soon fast-riding messengers, covering the country in relays, began to arrive at
Glevum and on the great war map long ago painted on the
walls in Ambrosius's council chamber the fine-pointed charcoal sticks marked the slow movement of Esc and his
warriors.

They came westward through the country south of the

Tamesis and when they were at Calleva they were joined from the south by Cerdic and his men. Here, under the deliberately scant forces of Gelliga, they were met. Before their strength Gelliga could do nothing and turned away from them, riding west, drawing the Saxons on and convincing them of the weakness of the forces in the south. When they reached Spinis, and it was clear that they were driving for Aquae Sulis to reach the Sabrina River beyond it at Abonae and so split the country, Arturo moved.

He sent Durstan with five hundred horse and two hundred of Coroticus's men to move down to the headwater lands of the Tamesis and the Abona rivers north of the Cunetio—Aquae Sulis road. With the rest of his army he went south from Glevum down the Sabrina river road to Abonae and then turned back east to Aquae Sulis. Beyond Aquae Sulis he drew off the road to Cunetio into the wooded slopes and waited for the coming of Esc.

In the years to pass, the men who fought in the great battle of Mount Badon which crushed the power of the Saxons each told the story he knew. But there is no man in battle who knows its full shape and the terrors and triumphs of all its movements. Each man fights his own battle, lost in his own small world of violence and death and maiming. To a Coroticus marshman, arrow ready-notched, lying screened by the thickets of the slope above the road, there was nothing at first except the distant cloud dust from the marching, unwary Saxons. The droning of the honeybees working the blooms of gorse and harvesting the pollen from the clumps of purple marjoram and the pink-flushed flowers of the convolvulus rose higher than the distant stir of tramping warriors. When the dust cloud became men—axed and sworded, unkempt from days of marching, sunlight flashing from spear tips and bronze armbands, a great snake of warriors crawling toward him, men without care, victory under their belts, and a greater victory to come—then he picked a man, worked his left-hand fingers firmly on the smooth moleskin grip of his bow and lightly began to flex the drawcord, his eyes never leaving his mark, and waited for the low whistle of command to sing down the line of his hidden comrades. When the signal came and his arrow sped high and curving, flighting now with a hundred others, searing the air with sharp-honed tip and stiff flight feathers, his battle had begun and the gods would give him either the mercy of safe sleep that night or the ease of the gentle voyage to the Isles of the Blessed.

In the trees on the slope above the marshmen, each trooper and companion sat his horse, the great beasts' heads tossing against the summer flies and the quiver of muscles, nerved by the communion with their riders, twitching their smooth hides. The same tremor held the body of each waiting trooper, lance lowered and cloak belted back to free the quick drawing of sword from its scabbard when the lance had done its work. Then was the moment when the Saxons halted under the rain of arrows, and confusion held them briefly and each trooper lost all thought of gods or sweethearts or family and, hearing the high call of the battle horns and trumpets, pushed horse to gallop and went streaming down the hillside, leaving marshmen to lie flat and let them through while ahead went the White One with Arturo and at his side rode Lancelo. Following them to join the marshmen came the foot levies from Cymru and Demetia, from the tribes of the north and the south of the land, a moving hillside, an avalanche of Britons to sweep the Saxons back. Red were the swords that day and swift the horses and fierce the spear and lance thrusts and bright under the sun the coloured surcoat of Arto carrying the figure of the Blessed Mary.

The Saxons stood and fought but when they saw the great crescent of Durstan's horses thundering down the far slope to take them from behind, hope went from them. They scattered like a vast flock of crows disturbed from a new-sown cornfield and, seeking escape from the cavalry, turned south away from the road and climbed the steep scarp of Mount Badon to seek the sanctuary of its ramparts, which still waited final ordering at the hand of Baradoc. But, there on the level land beyond the summit, lay Gelliga and his horse to pen them back or to ride down any that looked for escape. Lucky were those Saxons who broke through to pass back along the road to Cunetio, and luckier still those few who, pony-mounted, rode into brake and woods and found escape, among them Esc and his son and the bastard Briton Cerdic.

Unlucky were those who found the shelter of Mount Badon's ramparts for there was no waterhole or spring to slake their thirst, and the bite of thirst is harsher and speedier felt than that of hunger and soon drives a man to desperation. For three days the sun was brazen in a cloudless but not barren sky for the eagles and kites and the crows and ravens swung in a dark circus above them, waiting in patience for the feasting to come.

At sunset on the third day the Saxons broke in force from the hilltop down the steep scarp and the Britons hunted and harried them on foot and on horse through the long nights and the following days. But when the sun went down that third day the Saxon might and threat was broken and tamed for over a hundred years to come.

During the days and nights of the battle and the siege of Mount Badon and the harassing of the retreating Saxons many things happened the memories of which would either be lost or changed by time. Prince Cato and Mordreth killed their first Saxons and with each telling the count rose a little higher. Mordreth's horse stumbled as he tried to force it up the steep scarp to the hilltop in pursuit of the Saxons, youth and beast fell and Mordreth broke his right leg, which being set badly always afterward marked him with a limp. Prince Cato, riding hard down the Cunetio road, reined in to lance a wounded Saxon lying on the ground and gave chance to a gut-ripped Saxon lying by to throw with his last strength an axe and mark the youth's face with a long scar from the side of his mouth to his ear.

On the evening when the penned Saxons on the hilltop, made bold and desperate by thirst, broke out, Baradoc, fighting on foot on the steep scarp side, wielding his sword in his left hand, was beset by four Saxons and killed three before the fourth ran him through with his scramasax and sent him to the gods to join Tia, granting him the only death which he would have wished. He was buried on the vine slope outside old Truvius's villa at Aquae Sulis, where the four winged dragonflies hovered and darted over the yellow flags and the kingfishers flew low like moving fire over the clear waters.

In those days of battle and siege nine hundred and more of the Saxons died, and two hundred of the companions, troops and marshmen and foot soldiers of Arturo, among them Marcos, who with his long-dead brother, the dumb Timo, Christos men both, had been the first to join Arturo and go with him to the villa of the Three Nymphs. Garwain died when his horse was cut down, and many others long tried by service to Arturo. Among those that buried and mourned their dead were few without wounds to show as small price for the victory which the gods had sent them.

In the first charge down the hillslope to the road Arturo took his own wound, a spear thrust that glanced off his saddle bow and took him above the groin on his left side, a wound ignored until the evening of that first day when Pasco bound it with cloth strips while Arturo made light of it. But men said in the years that followed—though not to Arto's face—that the wound reopened always on the morning of the day of remembrance for Mount Badon and ran blood until sundown.

Three days after the battle Gwennifer came from Glevum to Aquae Sulis to Truvius's villa, where Arturo had made his headquarters and where there came to him still the news of the continuing eastward flight of the Saxons, harried and hounded by the forces under Durstan and Gelliga. Gwennifer dressed his wound and as they sat under the covered way above the courtyard she played her harp for him. Knowing the turmoil in his mind, the lasting heat of victory in him still, and the strengthening of his dreams for the years to come, she sang:

"The Great Horses of Arto have broken the sea-men.
Now he is king of the star-bright kingdom,
A lamp to outshine them, an eagle screaming above the crags.
Over this land now the brown leaves that fall are gold,

The white waves are silver on the shore,
The mist rises from the meadows of red clover,
And the misery of years lifts from the hearts of men.''

Arturo, hearing her words, remembered the first time she
had played for him at Lindum and how, though he had taken
pleasure in her and her music, he had not known then that she
would be wife to him. The gods held the future from men, to
let men dream their own future and labour to create it. At
Mount Badon the work and dreams of years had been brought
to fruiting, and each year had levied its own cruel cost. But
there was with him at this moment a wisdom deeper than any
he had known before. The Saxons were broken. But some
small part of this country they had made their own and he
knew that there could be no pushing them into the sea. They
must sit where they were and slowly the seasons and the slow
shuttle of daily affairs would mould their ways and loyalties
to the great shape of this land. Warriors took victory by the
sword, but the gods guided a slower and secret battle. He was
now in his forty-fifth year and knew that the temper of
freedom in a land called for more than the simple acts of
warfare which brought peace. War had bonded this land
together by the sword. Under the gods he must find the means
to hold it so in peace. If the gods still loved him he would find
a way and already in his heart he knew that it was a way
which he would walk alone. Men needed gods no matter how
they named them, but a land and a nation needed a man to be
seen and to act like a god.

Cold with a sudden loneliness, he put out a hand gently and
stayed Gwennifer's playing by touching her arm. He said,
"My lady Gwennifer, sing me no song of war and kings. In
this courtyard my father and mother were married. She lies
by the sea and he by the river so there is always the blue-water
path of joining between them. Give me a song of small
delights.''

Gwennifer smiled and took his hand and kissed it. "I have
no great gift with words, my lord.''

"Then give me a small gift.''

She sipped her wine for a moment and then took the harp and played:

> "I ask the gods small bounties:
> A secret hut in the wilderness,
> A moss-lined well beside it,
> And a thicket for the singing birds,
> Within a row of tall, bright candles
> And under their light the face of my love,
> Her eyes the twin stars' of constancy,
> Drawing me to the smooth haven of her arms."

As she played the thought came to her that long-dead Borio would have shaped the words with truer pace and sweetness and there was a quick wonder in her that the woman of those days was long dead, too. The gods could be cruel in their brief designs but once the due course was run they could sweeten life with new joys. Arturo would be king, but she was content to know that she had long been his queen.

CHAPTER TWELVE

The Dream And The Dreamer

ARTURO RODE DOWN FROM CAM HILL with six mounted companions behind him. Autumn sunshine was mellow over the land. The White One now and then tossed her head to shake away the teasing flies. Cabal, the last of the great hounds to bear the name, moved at the mare's side, limping a little from the stiffness in his right foreleg from sinews torn by a dog otter's bite in his younger days. From the high branches of a great poplar a red squirrel scolded their passage, and, hearing the sound, Arturo smiled to himself, for the squirrel had been in the dream of this day to come, the dream which the gods had sent him seven nights before. It had possessed him with a living, undeniable truth and there was no flaw in his memory of it, and no turning from it to find escape. The will of the gods would run its course this day and there was a weariness in his body and heart which gave welcome to it.

In the dell on the hilltop the willow herbs flowered between the cairn stones of Daria's grave, and the stones were thick-mossed and almost hidden by the spread of ivy growth. The gods had given him the love of two women to comfort and ease the march of his years. Daria lay beneath the berried thorn and Gwennifer, spared the sharing of this day with him, rested at Eburacum to spend the winter with her aged father. The gods had worked the weaving of her days with kindness to take her from his side on this day of golden fruitfulness which was to die into the long darkness of the rest they decreed for him. There was no flaw in the memory of the

537

dream. The flashing of the white rump of a bullfinch flighting across the path had been there, and the rustle of a grass snake through the new-fallen leaves that carpeted the bottom of the dry ditch at his side.

In the twenty years since Mount Badon he had given himself to this country and had learned the art and cunning of being many men, and finally no fixed man to himself. Emperor he had called and made himself to give no rankle to the country's kings. He smiled to himself, hearing the name coming from Difynwal's tongue in the old language of the tribes . . . *Ameraudur*. In twenty years the Scotti were tamed, the whole of the north recovered. Londinium and other cities flourished, though not fully as they had in the last days of the legions. He had forced formal treaties on the Saxons and they lived like docile cattle in their shrunken enclaves. And he had taken great Camulodunum, the first city of the Romans, to split the North and Middle Saxons from the South. Cerdic and his West Saxons lived on sufferance in their land, and all the provinces of the country had their governors and lawgivers and suffered sharply if they failed him or their duties. To bring peace to a country had been the first part of his lifework; to keep that peace he had had to shape himself anew and found many times when the iron of his pitilessness seared him more sharply than his victims. Men told and sang the stories of his deeds and his wonders and coloured them bright and let truth lie unseen like a mouse in a corner while legend flew high like a red dragon over the land. He let the silvered tongues of bards and singers run free for he knew that, while the gods were always above men, men had need to make of one of their own a god of flesh and blood. He had long ago lost the pathway of true life and rode the shining way of myth. This the gods had decreed for his life, and now they had marked him for a death as unreal as the last great span of his life had been.

They came down the slope to the water meadows of the Cam that ran its crooked way seaward and they rode its bank westward to find the road to Isca. But as he moved to the easy motion of the White One, his tawny beard grizzled with the frosts of the years, the lean face weathered and furrowed, and his body held a little bent to ease the old and constant bite of the wound he had taken at Badon, his eyes were soft with a rare joy. He knew that this day of the coming true of the dream was the one which would take him to the long rest of body and spirit and to the peace at heart which had gone from him on that day on the downs above Cunetio when he had killed his first Saxon. He reached his right hand across and touched the hilt of his scabbarded sword and slipped it a little free to prove its readiness, for many a brave but careless companion had died on hard-weather campaigning from the tight grip of rain-swollen wooden scabbard on the wanted blade at the moment of peril.

On a rise in the ground as they left the river the twin green hills of Ynys-witrin showed jewel-clear through the bright air. Coroticus reigned there now and called himself Melwas after his dead father, and Coroticus had lost three fingers of his right hand at the battle of Celidon Wood in the far north, long after Badon; Coroticus, who had always been true to him and read a fuller understanding of his ways than any other. After this day there would be bitter blood between Coroticus and Prince Cato.

Breasting the rise, Arturo marked ahead the pinewood that stood above the road to Isca. It stood now as it had in his dream, even to a kestrel hovering to one side above the harvest stubble of a corn plot and a tethered goat with three free kids watched by an old woman who sat teasing and spinning wool from her hand spindle. A blue skein of smoke rose from a hollow that hid a settler's hut.

After his death, peace would slowly die like a great tree being eaten away by rot and beetles; after his death, for his honour and glory, the bards would call this day a day of battle for although many emperors had died by poison and assassination the gods would have for him the glory of death in combat.

As Durstan rode silently at his side he was tempted not for the first time since the coming of the dream to turn to him and the other companions and send them away, for their deaths, too, had been marked on it. But there was no power in him to speak the words for he rode under the gods as he had done all his life and was their creature.

He looked ahead at the pines again and saw the kestrel slip sideways down the breeze to hover over the trees and then turn away in rapid flight. He knew that the bird had taken alarm at the men and horses hidden within the wood. Prince Cato would not be there with his envy and malice and fears for the curbing of his gluttony for power. There were others like him in the land and there would be feasting when he was gone. Man's nobility under oppression and peril grew feeble after victory. Those who worshipped him after Mount Badon would now see him gone and the gods for their own reasons would not stay their hands. Mordreth, poisoned from long service and boonship with Cato, would ride with the sword drawn to lead the handful of men behind him; Mordreth, who through his mother Gerta was part of that flesh of Baradoc and Tia which framed and filled his own body in full descent; Mordreth, whom he had banished in perpetuity to the lands of the people of the Enduring Crow for trying to lay hands in drunken lust on the lady Gwennifer at Isca, would come to give him death and to meet his own and so forfeit all reward from Prince Cato.

Durstan at his side looked up and said, "The sky clouds and there is the smell of rain coming from the west."

Arturo nodded and say, "Aye . . . Latis will begin her weeping and the lakes and rivers of the Summerlands will rise and overrun their banks." The rain would fall on him, but not on the living Durstan for there was half a day to go yet before the first heavy storm drops would fall to mark the end of the dream and the onset of the long darkness which waited him.

Mordreth and his men came when they were within a bowshot of the pines, but before they showed he knew their coming for the old woman untethered her goat and led it away with the young kids following, and so earned her handful of coins for making the signal of his arrival. They rode without haste to raise no alarm, ten mounted men with Mordreth at their head and no hand lying ready on sword pommel to

signal ill intent. It was then that Arturo turned to Durstan and
spoke the last words to him which had marked his dream.

"My good Durstan, stay by me this day as you have stayed
by me since the night we rode from Isca into outlawry.
Dumnonia which claimed our beginnings now goes to brand
itself with lasting shame at our ending, but it is an ending
which shall bring you into the everlasting glory and companionship of the gods."

Then as the horsemen coming to them broke into a gallop
and the drawing of swords flashed like the soft play of
lightning, Durstan samiled and said, "I am with you, my
lord, and without sorrow for from this day on there is finer
and truer company to be found in the shaded halls of the gods
than here among mortal men." Then he grinned and spat
and, drawing his sword, went on, "But let us give ourselves
the pleasure, dear Arto, of colouring our blades with the
blood of traitors. . . . Aie, 'tis a far better way to end than
by poisoning or midnight-dark strangulation."

They fought without give or flight, the seven against the
eleven, numbers which men's pride and the warping and
swelling of memory and time would mount twentyfold. They
fought stirrup to stirrup, knee to knee, and their movement
was the dark swirl of a whirlpool encircling violence, sucking to its center men and horses. Hooves trampled the fallen
and dying. Blood ran down the fair quarters of the White
One, shone like dew on the proud neck of Durstan's black
stallion, and was trampled beneath hooves to give a darker
hue to the red earth of the rich western soil.

They fought from the high pitch of their saddles, and when
their horses were cut down or threw them in the rising panic
which took the beasts, they fought on foot and no side
showed mercy and no man sought flight. It was a time of
blood and death under the slow clouding sky and none
marked it to live save the old woman and her husband, who
lay low behind the brushwood fence of their steading and
peered through the dead twigs and wished themselves dead
for they had not known that the riders from the east would be
Arto and his companions.

Durstan died of a sword slash across his throat from behind

for his body to fall and be trampled by the hooves of the horses. The call of a raven, the first of the birds of prey to arrive overhead, gave him farewell. Unmanned horses swirled in the circle until they were spun off like sparks from a grindstone to canter away or stand with their heads lowered in heavy breathing. And when to the raven overhead had gathered the first of the kites and buzzards, there rested living only Mordreth and the last man of his band and Arturo. Then the two rode him down, passing each on either flank of the White One, and as Arturo took the blade of Mordreth's man on his own and swept it aside to free his sword point to drive true into the man's throat to give him death, so Mordreth's sword drove into his left side at the place of his Mount Badon wound. But the pace of his mount, and the sudden swing of the White One's haunches as she bucked free of the fallen man under her rear legs, broke Mordreth's hold on his sword and it fell from Arturo's side to the earth.

Knowing it must happen, the dark-strung moments of the dream sliding by under the casting hands of the gods, Arto pulled the White One round and rode against Mordreth, who had jumped from his mount to take a sword from the side of one of the dead. He rode him down, driving the full weight and run of the White One into him, and as he lay on the ground Arturo turned and rode him down again, the pounding hooves of the White One battering his body and breaking his bones. His screams came wailing back in dying echoes from the tall stand of the close-by pines.

Arturo rode back to Mordreth and dismounted. Standing over the son of his sister, blood of his blood welling from the slack mouth, he took his dagger—for there was no honour in the man to warrant the nobility of the sword—and mercifully slit his throat and gave his slipping spirit easier and faster passage to the darkness of the limbo which waits to meld into nothingness the souls of those whom the gods reject. Then he mounted the White One, scabbarded his sword, kicked her into slow gait and then dropped the reins loose about her neck and let her have her own way.

She moved and turned her head to the north to follow the

path of the dream. As she went Arto took from around his neck his red-and-white scarf of the companions. Wadding it, he thrust it under his tunic and held it tight against his wound to stem the steady flow of blood.

When he came to the edge of the marsh lake, through which the river Cam ran, the light was going from the sky and the rain was drifting over the land in thin, soft veils, shrouding close by Ynys-witrin, and pocking the smooth face of the water with its gentle touch. He dismounted, loosed his sealskin travelling pack from behind his saddle, and sat on it to wait the coming of the man who had saved his life from bleeding away in the Circle of the Gods from his first wounding by a kinsman: Inbar of his own blood, who had lived between good and bad, now lay dead many a long year; and now Mordreth was shapeless flesh and bone to make quarrel among the birds of prey. The man would come but there would be no saving; Merlin who had said long ago . . . *there will come a day when I shall be with you in an hour of your own choosing when the war horns shall blow for neither victory nor defeat, but to set the echoes rolling forevermore over this land to give your name everlasting life while you take the long sleep which the gods have decreed for you.*

From the fringing lake reeds a bittern boomed and through the veiling rain a marsh harrier drifted over the waters like a lost spirit. The White One, unscathed, her smooth hide stained with the running scarlet of his own blood, cropped the sweet turf. There was a slow weariness working over his body that numbed him against all pain. The blood ran slowly over his hand that held the wadding to his side and he knew that as it ran so would run his dream.

Cabal came and sat by him, pushing his muzzle fretfully against the back of his free hand. He teased the hound's ears, thinking of the puppy hound that Gwennifer had ridden from Lindum to present to him. In Eburacum now she was safe. There were many sides to love and no man or woman could claim to know them all.

The soft rain thickened and fell hard now to beat the lake

water into a hissing froth. Through it came a narrow flat-bottomed boat of the kind which the marshmen used for duck hunting and fishing. A man sat in the stern and paddled it gently, a brown-robed man, black-bearded, his head uncovered to the fast-falling rain. The prow of the craft drove through the reeds and grated on the gravelled bank. The man stepped ashore and then sat on the prow with his feet resting on the gleaming stones of the lakeside. He nodded his head to Arturo, smiling gently.

Arturo said wearily, "So here the dream comes to an end. What lies beyond it?"

Merlin rose then and, coming to him, answered, "Latis weeps for you. She is the gentlehearted one among the gods, but seldom knows the full truth of her sorrow. The waters are rising for you to make a moving pathway without beginning or end." He wiped his hand across his beard to free it of rain and fingered his dark eyebrows to clear them of their heavy dewing. "But you will not lack for company. There are others who move on it. The good and the bad. Some long-distant Caesar, a drunken poet with a head full of spring music and words that touch the heart before the mind. Maybe a few priests who have come close to knowing the purity of the God who stands above all other gods, and some great bishops who handled charity as though it were a sword. The gods stock the pens of time with all sorts of human cattle."

"Cattle?" The twist of a smile touched the corners of Arturo's mouth.

"Aye. Men are but cattle of a kind and the gods herd them."

Arturo rose and would have walked toward the boat, but Merlin held up his right hand. "There is no moving out onto the waters until you have done the two last things of the dream."

"My dream ended with your coming."

"But the dream runs on through all time and now you must shape it for yourself. Before you move on the waters you must finish the earth dream from your own fashioning."

Arturo closed his eyes and swayed a little from the weakness in him growing from his wound. Then he turned and walked to the White One. She raised her head and he stroked the velvet of her mouth and he remembered the first White One, her whom he had caught and tamed from the great woods above the Villa of the Three Nymphs. Blood from the tearing of his flesh as he had ridden her through thorn and briers and the thick lattice of brakes and undergrowth had streaked her hide that day. His own blood this day, too, stained this mare's hide with a ragged poppy bloom.

Moving from her with Cabal limping at his heels, the hound whining, sensing strangeness and distrusting it, he walked to the water's edge and drew his sword from its scabbard. Holding the bloodied blade before his face he kissed it and then threw it far out on to the waters. Its great splash disturbed a feeding mallard and the bird took flight through the rain, trailing feet and wingbeats marking a foam-flecked path into the growing darkness.

Behind him Merlin, with laughter in his voice, said, " 'Tis no great loss. Until mankind reaches true manhood there will be no lack of swords in this world." Then, as Arturo turned from the lake and went to his rain-sodden campaigning pack on which he had been sitting while he waited Merlin's coming, the man rose and joined him.

Arturo knelt, swift pain unexpectedly scything across his left side, and unfastening the strapping of the pack took from it the silver chalice which had always travelled with him since the day when golden-haired Gwennifer had used it for her salving ointment. It was tarnished and dull but the falling rain fast pearled and dewed it with clinging drops which broke and ran to puddle thinly within it. He was tempted to cup it in his hands to see if the growing water within would turn to the blood colour he had known at the Circle of the Gods. But Merlin reached out and took it gently from him, saying, "Naught will happen, my lord Arturo. In another age and in another's palms the turning will be seen again." Chalice in hand he went to the boat.

Arturo followed him. Merlin pushed the boat free to rock on the waters, which were now loud with the pulse of the heavy rain. Arturo stepped into the boat and, sitting, took the paddle. Cabal would have jumped in with him but Merlin touched the hound's head and Cabal sat, shivering and whining. Looking at the man, Arturo, eyes half-closed with pain, said, "So the dream goes. But before the waters take me, I ask you one last grace."

Merlin smiled. "There is no need for asking. From here I shall go to Cam Hill and make simple prayer for you and Daria. And when I come to Eburacum I will give comfort to your lady Gwennifer."

"My gratitude. And the gods go with you."

Merlin's face twisted wryly. "Aye, I fear they will. But I would give much for the long sleep into which you now drift."

He put his foot to the prow of the boat, sent it free on the waters, and stood watching in the rain as Arturo with his left hand made stroke or two with the paddle to send it out into the river current that now ran with growing vigour through the lake. Arturo dropped the paddle and sat without movement. He drifted on the surge of the growing current into veils of rain and darkness which slowly enshrouded him and hid him from Merlin's sight.

At his going the White One raised her head high and whinnied loud. Merlin laid his hand gently on the neck of the shivering hound, speaking softly to it as the rain gathered fast in the bowl of the chalice on the ground at his side.

MAP

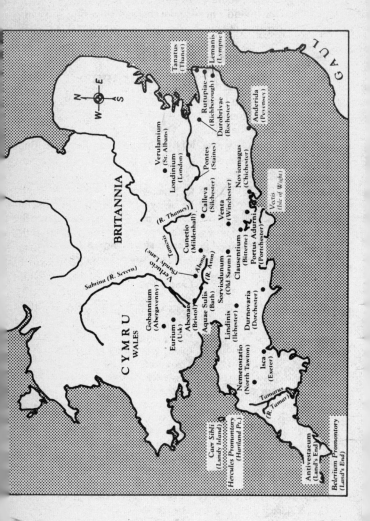

List of Place
and Tribal Names

ANCIENT	MODERN
Abona	R. Avon
Abonae	Bristol
Abus	R. Humber
Anderida	Pevensey
Antivestaeum	Land's End
Aquae Sulis	Bath
Ariconium	Weston-under-Penyard
Atrebates	Middle Thames Valley tribe
Belerium	Land's End
Belgae	West Country tribe
Brigantes	Tribe holding lands north of York from coast to coast
Caer Sibli	Lundy Island
Calcaria	Tradcaster
Calleva	Silchester
Camulodunum	Colchester
Cantawarra	Canterbury
Cantiaci	Kent tribe
Catuvellauni	Essex tribe also holding lands northwest of London
Clausentium	Bitterne
Corinium	Cirencester
Coritani	Lincoln-Leicestershire tribe
Cornovii	Cheshire-Staffordshire tribe
Crococalana	Brough
Cunetio	Mildenhall
Cymru	Wales